THE FOREVER HERO

THE FOREVER HERO

DAWN FOR A DISTANT EARTH
THE SILENT WARRIOR
IN ENDLESS TWILIGHT

L. E. MODESITT, JR.

TOR®

A TOM DOHERTY ASSOCIATES BOOK

NEW YORK

THE FOREVER HERO

This book consists of the novels *Dawn for a Distant Earth,* copyright © 1987 by L. E. Modesitt, Jr., *The Silent Warrior,* copyright © 1987 by L. E. Modesitt, Jr., and *In Endless Twilight,* copyright © 1988 by L. E. Modesitt, Jr.

This book is printed on acid-free paper.

Book design by Victoria Kuskowski

A Tor Book
Published by Tom Doherty Associates, LLC
175 Fifth Avenue
New York, NY 10010

www.tor.com

Tor® is a registered trademark of Tom Doherty Associates, LLC

ISBN 0-312-86838-3

Printed in the United States of America

D 20 19 18 17 16 15 14

CONTENTS

DAWN FOR A DISTANT EARTH

I

In the west wing of the tower of time, abandoned as it is by the keepers of the clock, lies an ancient key. Not an impressive long steel shaft is this key, but a small volume, a compendium of pages enameled against the ravages of the decades and the centuries.

The book has no title, no preface, no table of contents, nor any title embossed on its black spine, nor even printed pages evenly matched and marching end to end.

What is it, you ask?

That question must hold for another. The other question? What is the tower of time? For there are no towers left on Old Earth, only the rambling farms, the sweep of grass, the ramparts of the west mountains, and a few score towns nestled into their restored places in history. There is only a single shuttle field . . . without a tower.

This tower of time rears backward into history, not into the dark starred nights that are so cold to one used to the light-strewn nights on planets that once belonged to the Empire. Backward into history, you say? How far?

Far enough. Back to the time when purple landspouts raged the high plains, back to the time when boulders fell like rain, and when the devilkids were the only beings who dared to run the hillocks outside the shambletowns. . . .

Yes, that far. Back to the days of the captain. . . .

The Myth of the Rebuilding
Alarde D'Lorina
New Augusta, 4539 N.E.C.

II

STEP . . . PAUSE . . . LISTEN. Step . . . pause . . . listen.
The boy crept through the thin bushes and scattered patches of

ground fog toward the shambletown wall. The leathers of his tunic were ripped, and the thonging where the skins were joined was loosening. The rain stung his skin, as the chill wind froze the droplets before they struck.

Overhead, the thick clouds were barely visible in the gloom that passed for twilight.

Most of the torches on the shambletown wall had blown out and would not be relighted until the wind and rain abated. That would not be long. Beneath the west mountains, on the high plains east of the shambletown, the rains seldom lasted. Nor did the purple furies of the landspouts usually penetrate into the hills and gullies.

A single torch by the gate flared back to light, and the boy ducked behind one of the few grubushes left near the walls, just below the outcropping of old brick, powderstone, and purpled clay on which the shambletown had been raised.

In the gloom downhill from the wall, he would not be seen. Even if a sharp-eyed guard did sight the small shadow created by the torches, that darkness would be blamed on a skulking coyote, or even a king rat scuttling for his hole.

The boy's left leg hurt, still stiff from his encounter with the she-coyote. He needed food, better food than he could grub from the plains and the hills, food without the poisons that the wild plants springing from the sickly soil carried.

Most times he could eat the yuccas and needle pears, but the coyote wound and its infection had lowered his body's ability to digest the wild food.

He froze behind a thicker grubush and peered through the scraggly leaves at the wall. Too high—more than twice his height, and even with a healthy leg, beyond his reach.

That meant the Maze. He had known that from the beginning, but had hoped . . . He shivered, but there was no escaping the need for the cleaner food that lay beyond the shambletown wall.

Tightening his grip on the jagged blade he carried in his left hand, he dropped farther down the hillside and edged eastward, bit by bit.

Slide . . . pause . . . listen. Slide . . . pause . . . listen.

The pattern was nearly automatic, his ears straining for the click and scrabble of the rats, or the pad and click of a foraging coyote seeking a shambletowner out alone after dark.

The scattered grubushes grew more thickly as he neared the tangled mass that comprised the Maze. While they never crowded closely enough to provide a thicket or a constant cover, their numbers and sharp leaves and twigs slowed his progress. He checked each before sliding toward it to insure that no rat lay concealed there, no female coyote on the prowl for hungry cubs.

At last, the Maze towered above him.

He stopped, letting his breathing smooth. He sniffed, the thin nostrils in the narrow nose dilating to catch the scents nearby, and those from the Maze.

Crouching by one hole, he edged away as he caught the pungent odor of rat, all too fresh. A second entrance he rejected for the musty smell that indicated neither rat nor the air circulation necessary for an access to the less closely guarded eastern wall of the shambletown.

A third and fourth hole were each rejected.

A fifth was too low and reeked of land poison.

Click, click, scrabble.

The blade flashed. The rat darted—but not quickly enough.

The rat's purpled gray coat was scarred, streaked with silver.

The boy nodded. The rat, half the height to his knee, had been slow. Not sick, but old.

He left the carcass. While the hide might have been useful, only the shambletowners had the ability to turn it into leather. The meat was inedible, even for him.

Checking the hole from which the rat had emerged, he rejected it, and continued his slow movement along the Maze.

Deciding that none of the lower openings were likely to provide the access he needed, he switched his attention to the higher holes.

At last, he located a promising entrance, slightly above his head, but with easy handholds. He climbed to the left side, to avoid appearing in front of the dark opening. He let his nose test the scents, catching the mixture of free-flowing air, overlaid with the scent of shambletowners and their excrement, and the faint hint of omnipresent rat.

Blade in hand, he eased into the Maze, his hawk-eyes dilating farther to adjust to the gloom that was darker than the blackest of the clouded nights.

From behind him, he could hear the wind whistle as it shifted more to the north.

The passage branched, one dark pit stretching below, from where the scent of rat oozed upward, the other darkness twisting leftward, away from the shambletown. With the slump of his shoulders that passed for a sigh, he silently took the left opening, which, as he had hoped, again forked.

From his right came the definite smell of shambletown, although he could detect a gentle incline which bothered him. The last thing he wanted was to pop out high on the Maze wall in clear range of the shambletown guards and their slings.

Two more branches and he squatted just inside an exit overlooking the eastern wall of the shambles. He was higher than he would have liked—more than a body length above the wall and three body lengths above the uneven clay expanse between the Maze and the wall. His exit was to the north of the small eastern gate and the majority of the torches.

He shifted his weight to relieve the nagging ache and the pressure on his left leg and studied the wall. He would have to slip over the wall roughly opposite his vantage point. Unlike the northern wall, which was higher, the eastern wall, behind the bulk and protection of the Maze, also sloped outward as it dropped to its stone base. The slope might be just enough to let him make the climb quickly.

By now, it was as dark as it would get. The frozen rain pelted down in a desultory *click, click, click* that might cover any noise he made climbing down to the clay.

Only a single torch by the gate was lit, and the boy decided that the sooner he moved the better.

With a single fluid motion, he slid out of the hole and let his bare feet search for the outcroppings he knew were there, careful to let the bulk of his weight rest upon his good right leg. That brought him within two body lengths of the hard ground.

Ears, eyes, and nose all alert for rats, coyotes, or shambletown guards, he began easing himself down the Maze's rough surface as quickly as he could.

The animals avoided the freezing rain when they could, as did the shambletown guards, and he reached a position under the wall without an alarm being raised.

Again . . . He stopped and listened, straining to hear, to see if he could sense anyone on the far side of the wall. Had he judged his position correctly, one over the clay bricks he would be opposite a narrow lane leading deeper into the lower shambletown.

No sound came from beyond the wall—just the *click, click, click* of the frozen droplets hitting the hard surface.

Flexing his fingers, toes, he sprang, scrambling quietly to the top, the abrasiveness of the sandpaint giving his extremities just enough purchase to support the effort.

He vaulted over—and down onto a covered clay barrel.

Boom!

Even as the sound of his impact on the empty container rumbled down the cleared area next to the wall toward the guard post, he was dashing for the alley.

"Hear that?"

"Storm, stand?"

"No storm!"

The boy did not stay to hear the debate between the two guards, but slunk down the narrow alleyway deeper into the dark, sniffing and listening.

He sought an empty dwelling. In all those he had passed, he could sense shambletowners mumbling to each other after their evening meal. Either that or sullen silence.

Dark was the shambletown, lit but by a few ratfat torches set behind salvaged glass, and by the dim glow from deep within the clay-bricked homes.

Another alley lane, across a wider street and to the left, beckoned. The boy darted a look, then melted back into the gloom as two figures trudged down the street, not looking to either side. The muted clanking told him they were the replacement guards for the eastern wall, and he shrank farther into the darkness.

Once they disappeared from view, he skittered across the dimly lit thoroughfare, such as it was, and vanished into the darkness again, more like a rat than a boy.

Three dwellings down, he found a likely place. Like all the others, at this time of night the window was sealed with a patched hide cover, but there were no sounds from within, and not even the faintest touch of heat radiating from the hide.

He looked up and down the alleyway, then raised his sharp and jagged blade. One cut . . . two . . . three . . . and the bottom flap of the hide was free.

A glance under the hide and inside told him that no one was within. He needed no further encouragement to scrabble up the flaking sandpainted wall and through the narrow aperture.

The enclosed space was small, just two rooms plus the alcove used for food preparation and cooking, and the flat shelves in the now-covered front window that contained the plant beds.

As he saw the plants, despite the smell of excrement used as fertilizer and the musty smell of unwashed shambletowners, saliva moistened his mouth.

He checked the cooking area and found a small bin with three shriveled and raw potatoes. He took a bite from one, forcing himself to chew it slowly. One swallow of the mealy substance was all he could take, although the taste told him it was free of landpoison.

While he finished chewing, his eyes surveyed the two rooms. In the sleeping room was a single pallet wide enough for a man and a woman, centered on a raised clay platform. In the clay brick alcoves behind the platform where there should have been a few tunics and personal belongings, there were neither.

In the main room were only a table woven from grubush branches and two matching stools.

His eyes darted back to the pallet made of ground cloth, newly pounded into shape, and with no scent of shambletowner to indicate it had been used.

The boy padded over to the largest plant flats, but only sprouts broke the surface. On the far left was a narrow flat with older plants. He sniffed, and could detect no landpoisons. Then he pulled a single leafy stem and attached bulb from the damp soil. Wiping it on his tunic, he studied the rounded white bulb and narrow leaves.

Finally, he nibbled on a leaf. While slightly bitter, the taste was better than yucca. Next, he took a nip from the bulbous part. Nearly tasteless, it was crisp and swallowed easily.

He could have wolfed down the entire plant on the spot, but he knew that that much food that quickly, even poison-free food, could cause his guts to rebel, and he contented himself with a series of small and careful bites.

Leaving the remainder of the bulb by the flat, he retreated to the sleeping quarters and slashed a section off the unused pallet, carefully cutting it to keep one corner of the bottom double-thonged section intact as a bag. After bringing his makeshift bag across the nearly pitch dark room to the slightly lighter area behind the leather hide front window cover, he began to pull out the bulbous vegetables one at a time until he had a small heap.

He shook his head. While he would have liked more, he could carry only so many. If he stayed, he ran the risk that the shambletowners would find and kill him, as they had his parents.

He hoped what he could carry would be enough to get him through the weakness. If not, he would have to come back, and that he scarcely wanted to do.

Every concentrated scent in the shambletown, every odor from the Maze, was an assault, an assault that made it difficult for him to concentrate fully and increased the danger of being discovered.

After loading the bag, he gathered it and tied it shut with a piece of leather cut from the rear window cover. Then he used another loop to hang it around his neck and under his tunic. That left his hands free, although it created a bulging outline—a dead giveaway were he seen. There were no fat people on the high plains . . . anywhere.

A check on the back alley indicated no passersby, and he eased himself out through the narrow window and onto the uneven stone pavement with only a slight scratching and muted thump. He replaced the window cover as well as he could.

Retracing his steps up the back lane, he came again to the single street he had crossed, and, again, he checked both ways, listening carefully, before he slid across into the darkness of the other side.

Whussshh!

Instants before the cudgel struck, he saw it and tried to drop away, away from the flat-faced man who hammered it toward his skull.

Hands grabbed for his thin arms.

Fire burned down the side of his face, but even as his knees buckled his own blade slashed at the four legs around him.

"Fynian! Hold devulkid! Hades! *Eiiiii!*"

The boy whipped the knife from leg level toward the man with the cudgel, his legs recovering and supporting his spring. Though off center, the jagged edge ripped a thin cut in the underside of Fynian's left arm as he brought the cudgel around for another attack.

The fingers grasping him loosened, and the boy broke clear, avoiding the deadly club, and scrambled behind both men, running, regardless of the noise and the growing pain in his left leg, full speed toward the wall.

"Devulkid! Devulkid!"

"Devulkid!"

Still clutching the blade, his bag thudding against his chest, he pounded across the open space before the eastern wall and leaped onto the clay barrel just ahead of the two pursuers and a wall guard. Without slowing, he scrambled up and over the rough bricks to slide to the bottom of the wall with a thump, his left leg buckling under the impact.

His breath hissed from the pain of the fall, but he lurched to his feet and half ran, half scrambled the distance to the Maze, where he began to climb. Halfway up toward the hole, his fingers slipped as an old brick snapped in two under his weight, and he skidded down, the rough-edged rubble abraiding his already injured left leg, which collapsed again as his feet hit the purple clay.

Fssst!

Another wall torch flared into flame. Then a third, and a fourth.

The devilkid ground his teeth against the pain from his leg and scrambled up the Maze toward his escape hole, forcing himself to make sure the handholds were firm before trusting his weight on them.

Crack!

A slingstone plowed into the rubble next to him, shattering a brick. The chips stung his uncovered right shoulder.

He forced himself upward toward the narrow hole that he knew the large shambletowners could not and would not fit into.

Crack!

Another slingstone shattered under his feet.

He could see the hole just above him, could scent the odors he recalled from his entry and squirmed the last body length to it.

Crunch!

"*Ooooo!*" The involuntary exclamation was forced from him, expelled by the force of the slingstone that had hit his side as he had twisted inside the dark passage.

"Got devulkid, Fynian!"

Now it hurt not only to use his left leg, but his left side was bruised.

He slid farther down the winding way and behind an ancient beam to catch his breath.

While an occasional slingstone rattled part way down the hole, he could tell from the outside sounds that the shambletowners were not about to chase him tonight, not with the still-freezing rain, and not into the higher Maze holes. Not his time.

He rested. But before long, he began to pick his way back out of the Maze. He had to be clear of the shambletown, well clear, before the lightness of dawn.

Fynian, the broad man, he would remember.

SCREENS. SCREENS AND their images were what dominated the bridge. Every console on the *Torquina's* bridge had at least three, and each was tied to an accompanying seat that doubled as an accel/decel couch, despite the fact that such usage had never been required.

The main screen displayed the image of a planet, a planet swathed mainly in clouds, except for occasional clear spots over the oceans. The *Torquina* swung in an almost geocentric orbit to allow the sensors and data relays from the exploratory torps maximum analytical time.

Some of the officers and techs watched. Some paid no attention. Some looked periodically.

The data flow centered on a single console with but four screens, in the innermost corner of the bridge. Had the captain wanted, he could have duplicated or monitored the flow. He did not so choose.

The Imperial Interstellar Survey Service officer facing the console continued to juggle the inputs, often manipulating two screens simultaneously.

"What does it look like?" asked the engineering officer who stood behind her.

"Worse than you can imagine. Worse than I'd believe. Some are still alive. Don't see how."

"How can you tell?"

"Patterns. Patterns. Look." She pointed to the top screen in front of her. "See the square here? That's built on top of the ruins. Then there's the background heat. Wouldn't be there if it were deserted."

She shook her head, and her short red hair fluffed out above the silver and black of her watch uniform.

"Background contamination is high."

"How high, Lieutenant Marso?" asked the captain from the command console across the bridge.

"Until we get the sampling data back, Captain, I can't provide figures. There are areas of widespread erosion and a total lack of vegetation in places where by all rights there should be trees, or at least grass, especially by some of the streams and rivers. First class ecological disaster, ser."

"We knew that," commented the engineering officer. "We knew that before we came."

Lieutenant Marso ignored the comment, not even turning her head in his direction.

"Any hopeful signs?" pursued the captain.

"Some. Some areas of habitation. Mainly in the high plains areas and places where there is drainage. Sedimentation areas look the deadest. I can't tell about the oceans, although they should have been affected last and should have been the first to recover."

"Place will never recover. Like Marduk," observed the chief engineer.

"It's not like Marduk. Nothing at all lives there. Here you can see some recovery."

"A few savages, a few thousand square kays where they can eke out a minimal survival. That's recovery?"

The ecologist bit her lip and shifted the image from screen three to screen four, bumped four into memory store, and took the latest torp data on screen three.

As the temperature data began to register, she frowned, then checked the parameters again.

"Trouble, Lieutenant Marso?"

"Not exactly, Captain. But it's cold, a great deal cooler than the old records would indicate. The ice caps are larger, and the high plains temperature, where it should be midsummer local, shows a high of less than ten degrees Celsius. Even taking into account unusual variations, that's more than twenty degrees below either the old records or our modified projections."

"Recovery!" snorted the chief engineer under his breath as he clumped from the bridge back to his own control center. "Recovery indeed."

Lieutenant Marso's fingers continued to flicker over the console controls as the data in her files built, as the ship's torps continued their transmissions, and as the purple landspouts traversed the continent beneath.

The captain waited, and the *Torquina* crept along her surveillance orbit.

FIRST, TO THE south of the small wilds and east of the Maze was the shambletown square, purple-gray clay hard-packed over the jagged rubble of the buried city. Around the square was the shambletown itself, a mass of old stone and clay brick structures threaded with winding ways. Last, around the shambletown were the walls of clay brick painted rough-smooth with sandpaint and backed with walkways for the handful of guards.

East of the shambletown was the Maze, that jumble of toppled buildings of the ancients that crowned the long ridge top, and to the west, below the space cleared by the shambletowners, rising from scattered grubushes, was a marble hulk, once domed, that had been a capitol.

As for the Maze . . .

The boy darted from it, from grubush to grubush beneath the

northern edge of the smooth shambletown wall, until, at last, he could see the cracked and tumbled walls of the old structure.

He rested more weight on his left leg than his right, and when he walked, he limped. The limp was less pronounced when he ran. Even in the dark his blond hair glinted, as if with a light of its own, to match the hawkish brown-flecked yellow of his ever-searing eyes, eyes that also seemed to glow in the darkness.

"Hsssst . . ."

His eyes tracked the sound, his body turning. As he saw the plume of dust rising on the downslope to his right, he checked the wind direction, then relaxed.

The breeze was still blowing toward the mountains and would carry the chokeplume down into the clay-filled rubble that spread across the valley.

The area had been spared the worst of the landspouts and the concentration of landpoisons had kept the scavenging down, but little enough was left of the old city, little enough that few would even have recognized the desolation for what it had been.

The blond boy let his eyes trace the faint outline of what others could not see at all in the night, from the jagged and sand-scoured peaks of the west to the flattened hills to the north and the rolling plains to the east. The ground fog was building in the depressions, gathering its own poisons as they sifted from the poisoned ground, and though the swirls caused by the joining of mountain and plains winds could not be seen, the boy could sense them, as he always had.

"Fssst!"

A new torch flared on the shambletown wall.

"Devulkid!"

"Where devulkid?"

The jumble of voices registered in his ears, echoing and rumbling off the rubble of the Maze, off the rough-smoothed walls of the shambletown. To both the north and the south, the Maze dwindled into low mounds, sometimes little more than humps of clay and sand and brick. From the larger mounds protruded here and there rusted or black metal beams twisted into shapes never designed by their makers.

The thin and golden-haired boy darted a look back over his shoulder, as a gate began to creak open.

The oily smell of torches wafted toward him, ahead of the pursuers who still gathered their courage, but who had waited for him to return.

Taking a last look over his shoulder at the puddle of light outside the shambletown wall, the hawk-eyed youth began to trot to the east toward the diffused and yet-to-appear glow in the sky that would be all that usually represented the sun.

His breath left a ghostly plume that faded into the darkness and into the beginnings of the ground fog.

The leader of the shambletown pack carried a long staff and lumbered to the edge of the downslope just above the point where the last vestiges of the chokeplume trailed away. He looked northward into the darkness and raised his head as if to scent out the interloper.

A second man joined him, carrying both cudgel and torch.

"See devulkid?"

"No. Think went wilds?"

"Too smarmy."

The two turned toward the east. To their right was the higher mass that rose into the Maze, and ahead were the rough hummocks through which their quarry had departed.

"Track out?"

"East, then south," offered a third man.

"South, back to desert," affirmed the man with the cudgel.

"More than desert. Ships."

"No ships! Never ships! Ships brought the death!" The first man laid his staff across the arm of the second. "Never!"

The leader shook his head at the unseen devilkid and pointed his staff back at the gate from which they had emerged.

"Back!"

The wind blew the steam of his breath, like a chokeplume, down the hillside toward the river of ground fog that wound its poisoned way toward the north along the thin trickle that had been a river.

Then he turned and began to retrace his steps toward the shambletown, the oasis of hoarded warmth and frugality that represented the only order left on the high plains.

The second man flexed his sore arm and lifted the cudgel, looking eastward into the darkness.

"Gram saw him. Me. Devulkid." He spat at the ground and made the hope sign in the air.

In turn, he dropped his head, turned, and plodded after the other two as they retreated behind the safety of their wall.

Build with honest iron; build with stone; build with wood. If you cannot build with those, do not build.

For while what you have built may last, while it may tower into the night skies and mirror the sun by day, you cannot afford the cost.

And, in time, your children will grub for their lives in the wilderness, or pay their sustenance to the warlords, if they survive at all.

Jane-Ann D'Kerwin Nitiri
Philosophies of Rebuilding
Scotia, Old Earth, 4011 N.E.C.

THE BOY LOPED across the after-dawn dimness south of the shambletown and north of the windridge toward the hill cave that served as home.

The hide bag he had taken some days earlier from the shambletowners bumped against his chest under the worn, frayed, and ripped tunic that once had been left unattended by a careless owner. Inside the bag, itself held in place by the pressure of the tunic and the loose thonging around his neck, were a handful of the reddish fruits that grew on one scattering of hills south and east of the shambles. The hills were far enough from the shambletown, nearly onto the rolling plains, to discourage casual foraging and open enough to keep the rats from exposing themselves to the coyotes.

The boy had been lucky. Although his battered blade was sharp and his reflexes quick, his leg was not fully healed. But he had not had to test them during the night's trip to the fruit trees.

He feared the foraging parties of the shambletowners far more than the coyotes. The four-footed beasts often traveled alone, almost never in packs, and preferred to avoid him unless they were close to starving.

The towners took whatever they could find from wherever they found it, but avoided foraging at night and generally stayed close to the foothills and the higher ground where the landpoison was less intense.

The boy's eyes never rested, flicking from one hummock to another, from one patch of grass to the next, from one grubush to the one behind, as his untiring and uneven steps covered the ground between him and his cave and the relative safety it offered.

His ears strained for the telltale rustle of a coyote returning to its den, or for the hiss/squeal of a rat, and his eyes periodically checked the clay for the even rarer trace of a firesnake.

WWWHHHeeeeeee!!!

The intensity of the whistling sound jolted him to a stop, and he covered his ears to block the pain. As the intensity dropped, he uncovered them and tried to localize the source. He sensed that it had started above the clouds and had crossed nearly overhead.

He dropped behind the nearest grubush and waited, waited until the whistle dropped to a whispering from the direction of the hills.

A brief glint of sunbright light flashed—again from the west—and was gone.

The silence was deeper than before as he trotted toward the hills and the light and the whispering sound that had died to nothing. The source of the noise and glare was on his way back, and anything that noisy should have frightened off anything likely to bother him.

Though not counting his steps, he had gone beyond what numbers he knew, far beyond, when he saw the silvery arc above the grubushes.

He slowed his trot and began to slip from bush to bush, from bush to hummock, and from hummock to bush as he angled toward the object that had dropped from the sky.

The smoldering grubushes, the charcoal smell mixing with the faint odor of grubush oil, both told him of the heat the object had created. His feet told him of the rumbling in the clay underfoot, and his ears could sense vibrations he could not hear.

As he neared the silvery object that towered higher than a shambletown wall, he slid behind a mound of clay that reeked of old brick and corroded metal. Beyond the mound, the bushes and other cover were too sparse for a safe approach, not to mention the steaming ground heat.

He waited, but the whining and the vibration did not stop.

Finally, the golden-haired boy peered over the mound again at the source of the sounds. After looking at the shining mass of metal, he blinked. Though the whining sound had not changed, a section of the metal wall had peeled back, and a ramp had been extended.

Thud.

He could feel the force with which the ramp settled onto the ground, and flattened himself as well as he could behind the mound, trying to keep himself above the ground fog while not letting the plume of his breath show in the increasing light of dawn.

He shivered, wondering what the metal machine on the desert plain meant. Was it one of the ships that the shambletowners always talked about?

Ships. He shrugged and snorted faintly, ignoring the white plume that trailed behind him. Always there were the ships that would come to save them. Even his parents had wondered. But no ship had come to save them from the shambletowners.

If the metal machine was a ship, or from the ships, would it spend the time to save anyone, devilkids or shambletowners?

The whining sound stopped, and the boy peered back over the top of the mound.

Rrrrrrrrrr.

The sound echoed across the emptiness as a smaller object positioned itself on the top of the ramp and began to move down toward the ground, tracs clanking on the metal of the ramp.

No sooner was the armored tractor clear of the ramp than the whining began again as the ramp lifted and began to retract.

The tractor began to roll directly toward the mound which shielded the boy.

He scuttled sideways to another mound that barely covered him, but he could tell from the sound that the tractor had shifted direction and still headed toward him.

He looked left, then right, for another cover, making a quick dash to the left, scampering as low as he could, even breathing the ground fog that caught in his lungs like fire.

The roaring increased, louder, and he darted a glance from his hiding place.

Once more, the tractor had switched directions and was headed toward him, now less than a hundred body lengths away from him.

He ran, ran as fast as he could, with the practice of years and the spur of fear.

The pitch of the roaring increased, and the armored tractor increased its speed.

Could he make the gully he had passed earlier, the dry one where the poisons and fog were thinner?

He turned directly east and increased his stride.

In turn, the tractor's roar increased.

Although he refused to look back, concentrating on avoiding the grasp of the grubushes while staying ahead of the machine, he knew that the gap was narrowing, bit by bit.

His breath came raggedly, and the cold air he inhaled tore through his throat, burning like fire. His breath plumes trailed him like banners as he felt the ground begin the gradual rise before the drop-off that was the gully ahead.

Thrumm!

He felt a tingling sensation as something sleeted past his left shoulder, but refused to stop, forcing his legs to keep moving. He could see the drop-off just ahead.

Thrummm!

The strange energy barely cleared his head as he ducked just before the sound. Only a handful of steps remained to the gully.

Thrummm!

He tried to duck and twist, but the blackness rolled up around him, and he could feel himself falling even as it did.

CORSON PAUSED OUTSIDE the portal. As the chief engineering officer, he had the absolute right to enter any duty space on the ship, but he still hesitated. Marso had the kind of tongue that could strip flesh from bone.

He frowned, then squared his shoulders and keyed the portal with his own code, the one that overrode all but the captain's locks.

"Nooo!"

Corson saw the streak of blond, bent, and spread his arms.

Thud.

Even at nearly two hundred centimeters and one hundred ten kilos, he was staggered by the impact and set back on his heels. But he refused to let go of the snarling figure that pounded at his midsection and sent kneecaps toward his stomach.

Corson shifted his grip into the patterns he had learned too many years before at the Academy and finally fumbled until he had immobilized the smaller figure.

It had to be the boy that Marso's tractor had stunned down on the surface.

He carried the still-squirming youngster back into the combination sick bay/laboratory.

Marso stood there, leaning on the console with her right hand. The scratches on her left cheek still glistened with the dampness of just-applied quick heal.

Corson did not miss the dark smudge beneath her left eye that would likely become a black eye.

His own eyes widened as he took in the snapped straps on the stretcher that had brought the youngster up from the surface with the shuttle.

"How did . . . ?"

"Damned if I know!" snapped the ecologist. "I came in to check him again, and he jumped me. Then you came blundering along and almost let him get away."

"I . . ." Corson closed his mouth and tightened his grip on the boy, who seemed stronger than most men he had ever dealt with.

"What do you want me to do with him? Your young man here?"

"He's not that far along yet. No sign of puberty, not overtly, and the initial readouts support that."

Marso replaced the quick heal back in the cabinet and reached for a pressure syringe.

"What's that for?"

"Put him under for linguistics. I'd like to be able to talk to him. Then maybe so much force wouldn't be necessary."

"Talk you now," muttered the boy. His accent was odd, but clear and understandable.

"How did he learn Panglais?"

"He didn't. Panglais is a derivative from simplified Anglish. The maps indicate his ancestors spoke Anglish."

"Why ship take me?" asked the boy, still twisting to see if he could escape.

"To see if we could help you."

"Help devulkid? Snort fog!"

Corson raised his eyebrows.

"What does he mean?"

Marso pushed a stray strand of hair back off her forehead. "I suspect it's a rather direct way of saying he doesn't believe us."

"Devulkid believe none."

"He thinks he's a devilkid. What does that mean?"

Marso frowned, but did not look directly at the chief engineer.

"There may be some veracity in that assumption, particularly if the metabolic analyses taken while he was unconscious are fully accurate."

Corson shook his head. Marso had never engaged in scientific doubletalk. Then he nearly smiled. She was trying to clue him without alerting the young savage.

"That much capability for physiological prowess?"

Marso nodded.

"What want devulkid?" interrupted the youth with another squirm that nearly broke Corson's grasp.

"Devilkid needs better talk," offered the engineer.

"Devulkid talk good."

Marso edged nearer the squirming figure, pressure syringe ready.

Corson turned slightly to his right to make Marso's effort easier, carrying the boy with him.

"*Ouggh,*" he muttered with a wince as the devilkid's heels crashed into his leg.

Marso slapped the syringe against bare flesh.

The boy convulsed as if a current had passed through him, and it took all of Corson's strength to hold him.

"Hold him!"

Corson said nothing, but glared at the red-haired officer.

By the time the young savage had collapsed, Corson's arms ached, and his back felt stiff and sore.

"Where do you want him?"

"Back on the stretcher. I'll plug him in there, but that won't hold him for more than a standard hour or two."

"What?"

He'd seen the dosage she'd injected, and it would have laid him out for days.

"Corson. He may be a devilkid indeed. He's not too far from full growth, but the muscular and skeletal development indicates he'll be capable of taking you apart with one hand. If we're wrong, and he's less mature than I think, he could be a physical superman, but I don't think the readouts are that far off."

"What about brains?" the engineer asked dryly.

"Hard to tell. Probably no genius, but bright enough. Be difficult to tell what cultural retardation has done to his innate capabilities, if anything."

Corson stretched the slight frame out on the pallet. Marso used three sets of straps before adjusting the headband and contacts.

"Whew! Could use a little freshening."

"No survival value," snapped the ecologist.

Corson looked over the boy's face. Even unconscious, he did not appear relaxed. A residual tension centered around the closed eyes, and there was a sharpness to the nose uncommon to a mere boy.

"Is that all he is? Just another specimen?"

"Given time, given some education, he might be human. Right now, he's more like the proverbial wolf child, though I'd bet on him rather than on the wolves. I wonder if he really is a child."

Corson frowned and rubbed the middle of his forehead with the thumb side of his clinched fist.

"You just said he was."

Marso continued to work, sitting at the console and adjusting the feed to the headset.

"I said there was no sign of puberty and the associated developments. Those could be delayed because of environmental conditions, diet, who knows what. The other indications are that he may be older than twenty standard years. Brain scan patterns show more than a child's development."

Corson switched his attention from the lieutenant to the child/man/??? and realized that the unconscious figure's lips were moving.

Marso followed his gaze.

"That's a good sign. Shows verbalization ability is present. The sooner we're on the same wave length the better. Once he gets proper medical care and diet, I don't think brute force, other than sheer imprisonment, will keep him anywhere."

The chief engineering officer turned to leave.

"Let me know if you need help, brute force variety. I question whether your specimen believes in sweet reason, particularly on the wave lengths you have in mind."

"We'll see."

He could feel her eyes boring into his back as he thumbed open the portal and continued his inspection of *H.I.M.S. Torquina*, the newest of the Service's survey vessels, and dispatched for that reason alone to begin the preliminary survey of Old Earth, otherwise known as Terra, that would precede the clean-up pledged by the newly crowned Twelfth Emperor.

The first tests of the jumpshift were the drones. They returned unharmed.

The first full-scale test followed with a fusactor-powered in-system inertial driver. It did not return. Nor did the five ships that followed. The small drones continued to function superbly. Their jumpshift was powered with stored energy.

Finally, the UNSRF team theorized that the shift itself might have disoriented the fusactors. In response, they built a ship that was little more than an immense assembly of energy storage cells within a cargo shell. It jumped and returned, with scarcely an erg left.

The next step was another jumpshift, this time including a shut-down fusactor. The ship returned, but the magnetic storage bottle for the hydrogen starter had shrapneled the power room into shredded metal.

Interstellar travel had arrived, but no equipment that relied on the use of electrical or magnetic fields to generate power was able to survive the trip, and the jumpshift did not operate except in the corridors outside the main system gravitational fields.

No independent power generation equipment light enough to carry between the stars has ever been developed, nor was research pushed in that direction after the development of the Cardine molecular energy storage system . . .

Notes on the Jumpshift
Fragmentary text
Old Earth [Date unknown]

IX

HE TURNED IN the straps, testing his strength against them. While the straps were more than adequate to hold him, he could tell from their give that he could squirm free in time.

The headset bothered him, but not so much as the headache it had created. So many words . . . and so many possibilities.

His eyes swam, and he waited, thinking.

". . . so you're awake . . ."

The woman stood on the other side of the room looking at him. "Yeh."

"I'm Lieutenant Marso. I don't know your name. Would you like to tell me?"

"Tell what?"

"I see. Let's start more slowly, and less directly." She frowned and was silent for a moment.

He knew what she wanted, but the words had no reality, no more reality than a shambletowner running the high plains.

The woman began to point at objects, naming each in turn. With each name he found a link in his own mind, and some of the confusion began to sort itself out.

After she had pointed to everything within the compartment, she went to the dispenser and poured herself a drink of water.

He could scent the moisture.

"Would you like some?"

"No. *Yuggg!*"

"This is not like the water on . . . where you live." She drank it. "Try some."

She let him smell the water and dribbled some on his lips. He licked them. The water was nearly tasteless, except for a faint bitter odor and the hint of metal, both far fainter than the landpoisoned water of the plains.

He liked the smell of her better. Clean. Warm, like the flowers of the yucca. Not like the grease of the shambletowners.

"Would you like some?"

"Yeh."

"Yes," she corrected.

"Yes," he mimicked, because she wanted him to, and because there was no reason not to.

She set the cup on the high table beside the bed where he was strapped. After that, she pulled a metal object from a sheath attached to her wide belt.

Thrummm!

He winced at the sound, but watched as the fire from the object struck the floor.

"I am going to let you sit up. If you move toward me, I will use this. Understand?"

"Stand."

He thought he knew what she meant. She was afraid of him, but the blackness thrower would keep him away. He shivered. Still . . . she was a woman. Perhaps . . . later.

Holding the thrower in one hand, she did something underneath the bed with her other, stepping back quickly afterward.

He could feel the straps loosening and began to sit up slowly. Taking the cup in both hands, he sniffed the water again. His nose confirmed that it was safe to drink.

He sipped and waited. After a time he sipped again. The water was clean. Finally, he drained the cup and set it down.

"Are you hungry?"

He looked at her blankly.

"Do you want to eat?"

"Yes."

She tapped her fingers on the surface beside her, not taking her eyes off him, one hand still holding the weapon.

"Lieutenant Marso here. Need some finger food for our guest. I'd keep it bland and as natural as possible."

"Natural?"

His eyes widened at the voice from nowhere, but he said nothing.

"He has a well-developed sense of taste and smell."

"Do what we can, Lieutenant."

"All I can ask. Thank you."

The boy watched. She acted like the headman of the shambletowners. She talked to nothing, and someone answered. He must wait, but he was good at waiting, and listening.

MACGREGOR CORSON FROWNED.

Should he follow through with his impulse? He looked down at the impromptu motor chair he had built. What if he were wrong in his assessment?

He shrugged. Then there would be no problem.

The ecologist had left the devilkid's quarters inside the sick bay, sealed the locks, and headed for the mess.

If she only understood what she would not . . .

He shrugged again and let his long and heavy strides carry him down the passageway to the sealed cabin. Marso was jealous of her prize, and had set the seals herself. But they had been the engineer's first.

No one else had been in the exterior corridor, nor in the sick bay itself, not surprisingly, since the orbiting ship was in stand-down condition while the techs and their monitors gathered the necessary data.

As he reached the sealed portal he pulled the small kit from his belt pouch and touched the analyzer tips to each side of the plate. The first series of pulses was strictly random. The second built on the reactions to the first.

Marso had thought out the combination well, but he still solved the pattern in six sequences. The portal stood ready to be opened, once he touched the access panel.

The analyzer went back into his belt pouch, and he replaced it with a nerve tangler. The weapon ready, he touched the plate, tightened his finger on the firing stud.

His guess had been correct.

As the portal irised he could see the streak of blond, and he triggered the tangler.

The slim form thudded to the decking halfway through the portal. The boy's legs were twitching uncontrollably from the nerve jolt, and his brown-flecked, hawk-yellow eyes threw anger at the big engineer.

Corson did not touch the devilkid, but used his free hand to drop a loop of cord around one ankle. Then, tangler ready, he dragged the boy back into the cabin, sealing the portal behind them.

He leaned against the portal, waiting until the youngster dragged himself into a sitting position.

"All right, devilkid. Let's get a few things straight." He eyed the black bulk of the hand-held tangler. "This is a nerve tangler. If I use it enough, your heart will stop. You die. You understand?"

"Stand. I stop." The tone confirmed the young savage's understanding.

"That's right. Now . . . do you want to go back to where we found you? Or better yet, back to the shambletown? Isn't that what you called it?"

"Not shambletown."

.   Corson studied the boy, realized that in the few weeks aboard the *Torquina* he had changed, more than having gone from a dirty savage to a clean one, or from a scarcely verbal scrabbler for survival to a youngster who could understand most of what the crew said.

Corson nodded to himself. He suspected Marso had been right about diet, and that the ship's food was speeding up, or allowing the return of, physical maturation.

Subtle things, like the look the boy gave Marso when she wasn't paying attention, a bit more heaviness to the jawline, more muscular development across the chest, all were signs of physiological change.

But the devilkid was still a savage, still a danger, mostly because he did not understand the basics of what *any* society was. And Corson was going to have to teach him before it got any later, Marso be damned.

"The shambletown. That's where you'll go if you don't learn." He glared at the youngster. "First . . . keep your hands off Lieutenant Marso."

"Hands off?"

"Devilkid!" snapped the engineer. "You may be the toughest, meanest, strongest animal in the universe, but you hurt *anyone*—anyone!—and I'll tie you in knots with this and leave you in shambletown. You understand?"

There was no response. Corson saw the boy's legs were no longer twitching, and that he was drawing them underneath himself slowly.

Corson fired—twice.

"*Ayiii!*"

The devilkid lost his balance and tumbled onto his side. Slowly, slowly, he righted himself. Outside of the one exclamation, he had uttered no cry.

Corson's palms were perspiring. The shocks he had directed at the youth would have left even an Imperial Marine totally incapacitated for at least a standard hour. All that they had done to the savage was paralyze his legs, which was where the engineer had aimed. The peripheral effects normally left most people stunned or incoherent, not to mention the pain that went with the withdrawal.

"Get this straight, little man," he growled. "You can hurt me. You can hurt the lieutenant. So what? There are one hundred men and women on this ship. One hundred. There are more than one thousand ships where we came from." He lifted the weapon. "And this is a small tangler. That means you don't hurt people."

"Don't hurt people," repeated the youth.

Corson wondered whether he really understood, but decided to go on with his plan. He snapped the tangler in half, separating the butt that contained the power cells from the half that contained the barrel, neural focusing, and trigger. Both halves went back into his belt pouch, since he was bending the regulations to even carry such a weapon within the ship.

Then he palmed the exit stud and reached down, hesitating only momentarily, and lifted the youth.

Corson could feel the devilkid stiffen, but offer no other resistance as Corson carried him through the portal and lowered him into the improvised motor chair.

"Now, we're going to see the ship. All of it. Along the way, I'm going to try to make you understand why you have to behave, why you can't attack people. Force is important, boy. But brute force and strength won't beat a nerve tangler. And it won't beat a ship. It won't beat a thousand ships."

As they came to the main portal from the sick bay, the engineer tapped the access panel and guided the chair through. He wondered if he should have strapped the devilkid in.

"Corson! What are you doing?"

He sighed and turned toward the sharp voice. If only Marso had taken her time at the mess.

"I'm giving him a guided tour of the ship. If you would like to come, you're welcome, provided you don't interrupt—"

"But he's not—"

"Marso . . ." The engineer's normally gruff voice deepened into a tone that would have frozen even the captain.

The lieutenant stiffened.

"We'll be back within two standard hours."

"How did you get him to agree?"

"It took some considerable doing. But I think he understands."

"Devilkid understands," the blond youth affirmed.

"Understands what?" clipped the ecologist.

"Devilkid one. Ships many."

Corson felt his own jaw drop open. He hadn't expected understanding so quickly, and he doubted the boy was sophisticated enough to offer a deliberate lie about an abstract proposition.

"That's right, Mr. Engineer. He's bright. Very bright."

"Then he should enjoy the tour, Lieutenant Ecologist."

"He might at that." The red-headed lieutenant stepped aside as Corson keyed the chair.

Corson watched his charge's eyes follow the ecologist and felt his heart sink.

He was doing his best, but if Marso encouraged the boy (who wasn't likely to stay one much longer), what could he do? He shrugged, though he didn't feel like it.

"Let's start with the bridge, young man."

He could feel her eyes on his back as the two of them headed up the passageway, the whine of the chair scarcely audible above the gentle hiss of the ventilation system.

"WHY START SO high? So far inland?"

"Because it won't do any good to start any lower."

"Run that by me again."

"The chemical contamination is so high that you have to clean the land and the watersheds from the headwaters down. Otherwise—"

"—the rivers and the winds just recontaminate what you've cleaned."

"The rivers. We can't control the winds. Not until we can restore ground cover, get some trees in the high watersheds."

"You're talking centuries."

"Probably longer. We don't have accurate maps of the topography, nor any detailed analyses of the compounds poisoning the land. And Istvenn knows what they did to the ground water."

"What about the oceans?"

"A quick scan indicates they've got some buffering ability, but there's too much in the way of sulfur compounds. Balanced flora/fauna population, but too thin for my liking. But they'll recover long before we can reclaim the land. We'll have to set up a handful of extraction plants for the worst toxic hot spots on the continental shelves. Projections indicate that would do it in the worst cases."

"What about the future?"

"Hard to say, but I'd recommend against any disruption of the soil. Has to be an agricultural economy, if we even get that far, for dozens of centuries."

"You make it sound so cut and dried."

"Hardly. The theory's easy enough. So are the techniques—in theory. But in practice? No. That won't be easy. You can't manufacture anything in this system, and that means a massive resource drain for the Empire. This Emperor may allow it, but this project will need work for the lives of more than a few emperors. Just can't be done in less than centuries and billions of creds worth of equipment... Maybe it can't be done at all."

"YOU NEED A name."

"Have name. Devulkid."

The lieutenant shook her head, short red hair fluffing out with the motion. "That would not be acceptable and could certainly cause problems."

"Problems?"

"Difficulties, hard places."

The blond-haired young man wearing the unmarked tan shipsuit wrinkled his nose, as if at the smell of landpoisons.

"Hard places with name?"

The lieutenant smiled faintly. "It does sound strange when you put it that way. But you need a name, at least two names."

"Two names? One person?"

"Call it the Empire's way of doing things. Like the ships, like the uniforms."

"Two names for one person?" repeated the devilkid.

"Some people have three names," admitted the lieutenant.

"Three names?"

Lieutenant Marso nodded.

"How many names for you?"

"Three. Jillian . . . K'risti . . . Marso."

"The big man has three names?"

"Major Corson? Two, I think. MacGregor Corson."

"Why two names?" asked the blond youth again, as if the lieutenant had yet to answer the question.

"Look. If you want to go to the transitional school, if you want a chance at going to the Academy, you have to have two names. Any two names. You can have three if you want, but you have to have two."

"School needs two names for devilkid?"

"That's right. Both the transitional school and the Academy, if you make it that far, require two names. Two names and a number."

"Number?"

"Don't worry about that. Once you decide on the names, we'll use them to get you your imperial ID number. That won't be a problem at all."

The devilkid frowned as he sat uneasily in the ship swivel across from the lieutenant.

"Devilkid choose names. Empire choose number?"

"Right."

The curly-haired blond pursed his lips, but said nothing.

"Did your parents ever give you a name?"

"No name." His tone was more abrupt than before.

"I could read you some names and see if you like them."

"No."

"All right. But you'll have to choose something."

"Gerswin? Means what?"

"I called you that when you whistled that strange little melody. A gerswin is a music-maker, a wild singer, sort of like a dylanist, but the power is mostly in the music and not in the words."

The devilkid looked back at the Imperial lieutenant blankly.

"Gerswin means music, like your whistling," she repeated.

"MacGregor? That means?"

"Once it meant 'son of Gregor.' Now it has no special meaning."

"Corson means?"

"Son of Cor," the lieutenant answered uneasily.

"The big man, the major? Two fathers?"

Lieutenant Marso laughed. "Some would say he had none. But, no. He has just one father. Sometimes, names are chosen because people like them. They like the way the names sound." She frowned momentarily. "You have several days before you have to choose. Now that you've passed the initial screening tests, the transitional school will give you other tests, tests with more words."

"*More* words?"

"More words," affirmed the woman. "That is, if you want to learn more. If you don't want to go back to the shambletown."

A shadow crossed the young face.

"Learn . . . means not to go back to shambles?"

"Learning means much more than that. The more you learn, the more you can do. If you can make it through the transitional school, they you could go to the Academy—"

"Academy means learn more?"

"If you can."

"Devulkid learn. Learn everything."

IN "WARFARE, BASIC Theories of [4/C, BC W-101]," Gerswin's console was in the third row, second one from the far right aisle.

The instruction hall itself was similar to all the others, with identical consoles with the identical gaps into which unidentical cadets placed their identical bridge modules, incidentally recording their presence while allowing them direct access to their individual data banks.

The thirty fourth-classers stood beside their consoles, waiting at standing rest for Gere Yypres Gonnell, Major, Retired [Disability], I.S.S., who was listed as their professor.

"Ten'stet!" rang the tenor voice of the section adjutant.

Gerswin stiffened with all the others, exactly in key with their motions, although he could have easily beaten them into position.

"At ease," squeaked an amplified voice.

Gerswin watched the instructor's podium and the figure who moved behind it with jerky steps.

"Please be seated, Cadets," the squeaky and raspy voice added.

Gerswin sat, but wondered. He could see the shimmering metal bands around the professor, could see that while the professor's throat moved, his mouth barely opened.

"For those of you who have not met me, and that may well be all of you, I am indeed Major Gonnell, otherwise referred to as 'old-gonna-hell,' 'old metal bones,' or other endearments less flattering. This is the class technically referred to as 'Warfare, Basic Theories of.'"

A raspy sound like tearing patch tape followed.

"Excuse me, but subvocalization is not perfect."

A clanking sound followed.

"All of you are supposed to have read chapter one of the text. Knowing the Academy and the idealism with which you all approach your studies, you all have."

An intake of breath that would have been laughter at any non-military institution punctuated the otherwise silent instruction hall.

"The title of the course is incorrect. A more accurate description might be 'A Few Guesses as to Why Societies Fight.'"

Gerswin tabbed in the new title, noting that few others did.

"A standard hour a day for four months is totally inadequate for those of you who survive the institution to practice the profession, but I hope to make a small dent in your ignorance and to let you know how little you really know, in the hopes that you will at some future time be inspired to actually learn the subject."

The metal figure swiveled as if to survey the hall.

"Cadet Culvra, what does Adtaker mean when . . ."

"Cadet Hytewer, describe the Empire in the terms outlined by Hyrn . . ."

Gerswin noted most of the questions, but few of the answers. From the pace of the inquiries from the professor, he began to understand why the major had gotten the reputation he had.

"Cadet Resia, you have just asserted that wars are caused by scarcities. If that were true, would not all warring between systems be non-existent?"

Cadet Resia did not answer, but kept his square face directly pointed toward the major.

"Come now. We have had wars between systems. I have some personal experience which I doubt is a fiction." At that, he raised a metal-bound arm. "Yet the costs of building jumpships, the energy costs of jumping with stored power, the relative abundance of raw materials in all but the most crowded systems—all these would indicate that scarcity could not be a motive for war except in a limited number of systems, say perhaps a dozen. Those systems, however, lack the knowledge and resources to build a jumpship space force."

"That doesn't prevent others from occupying them," observed a red-haired young woman in the first row.

"While I was prodding Cadet Resia, I will accept that observation, Cadet Karsten. If your interjection is true, then scarcity and weakness prompt others to war over the least desirable systems. Is not that the logical outcome of your observation?"

Gerswin frowned. If what the discussion was leading to actually followed, then war could only be fought for noneconomic reasons.

"Would anyone else care to comment?" asked the major

Gerswin looked down, finally pressing the red stud.

"You have a comment, Cadet Gerswin?"

"A question, ser. If wars aren't fought for material gain, does that mean that there are other logical reasons for war? Or material ones?" he added.

"The original question assumed there was a distinction, if you please, between wars within systems, and wars between systems. Are you questioning that distinction?"

"Yes, ser . . . I mean . . . no, ser . . . I mean . . ." Gerswin closed his mouth.

"Would you like to clarify what you mean, Cadet Gerswin?"

"Yes, ser."

"Please do so."

"Ser, I wasn't going to question the distinction. Not sure now. Text indicates costs of war almost always outweigh the gains. Doesn't say that, but the numbers seem to—"

"What numbers, Cadet Gerswin?"

Gerswin repressed a sigh. "Looked up military budget differentials, reconstruction costs, death benefits . . ."

"I'll accept that for purposes of discussion. Are you saying that the costs to even the victor outweigh the quantifiable benefits?"

"Yes, ser."

"Aha. Cadet Gerswin is suggesting that since the costs of war outweigh the benefits, no wars have a logical basis. A novel approach. Any takers?" Major Gonnell surveyed the hall again, his metal support skeleton swiveling him from side to side. "Any dissenters?"

Another sweep of the room followed.

"I see. Cadet Gerswin's suggestion is so novel none of you have considered it. Very well, your first submission, due in five days, is: 'Wars Have No Logical Basis.'

"The submission must be a proof, although documented anecdotal material may be used, and you must take a definite position. Any submission which fails to support *or* refute the illogicality of war will be failed."

The major surveyed the class once again before concluding in his rasping squeak, "Section dismissed."

"Ten'stet!"

The cadets snapped out of their seats to attention as the major departed.

XIV

"ALL HANDS! ALL hands! Stand by for jump! Stand by for jump!"

Gerswin laid back in his couch, made sure the webbing across his chest was tight, although there was scarcely any chance that it would be needed. As a second class cadet, he had no permanent duty assignment. Consequently, he had no station from which to watch the jump.

Only Tammilan had managed that, and only because the *Fordin*'s number three navigator billet was unfilled. The missing officer had stepped in front of a lift loading a cargo shuttle less than an hour before orbit break. While the emergency releases had stopped the lift in time, not all of the weapon spares had been securely fastened, and the junior navigator was now recovering from multiple fractures in the I.S.S. medical facilities at Standora Base.

Gerswin waited for the blackness that filled the ship during the jump itself, that and the accompanying distortion. Supposedly, the jumps were instantaneous, but the longer the jump, the longer the subjective feeling of blackness and disorientation.

While Gerswin had been on a jumpship before the *Fordin*, this tour was his first trip since learning enough to understand what a jump really was. The upcoming jump was only the third since the cadets had boarded the *Fordin* off Alphane, using the Academy's shuttles to reach the cruiser.

The battlecruiser was headed for quarantine duty in New Smyrna system, along with two other cruisers and two corvettes.

"Jump!"

BRrrinnngggg!!!

The jump alarm seemed to stretch out through the darkness like an organ reverberating in slowtime.

With his third jump, Gerswin could see that the blackness was not uniform, but a swirl of differing blacks, as if each had a different shape and depth.

Just as suddenly as the darkness had dropped over the colored plasteel corridors of the cruiser, it was gone.

Gerswin unstrapped, checked his uniform, and scurried out of the closetlike room he shared with Tammilan. Since he was now assigned to the Gunnery department that was where he headed, down the corridor to the spool and in two layers to the central spoke.

No sooner had he entered the Gunnery operations center, with its spark screens and representation plots, than a voice boomed out.

"Cadet Gerswin!"

"Yes, ser."

"What is the maximum effective range of a Mark II?"

Gerswin braced himself. Lieutenant G'Maine, the junior of the three Gunnery officers, always tried the question on unwary cadets, or so Tammilan had told him.

"There is no effective range for a Mark II, ser, since there is no Mark II, ser."

"A smart cadet. Tell me, Mister Gerswin, the difference between the calibration technology used in the tachead rangers and the EDI detectors."

Gerswin wished the lieutenant would quit booming out questions, but he remained at attention beside the detector console.

"Tacheads have no rangers; calibration is independent and based on mass detection proximity indications. EDI tracks are actually a flow ratio compared against background energy flows."

"A really smart cadet! Can you tell me, Mister Gerswin, the power flow managed by this center at full utilization?"

"No, ser."

"Why not?"

"Because I don't know, ser."

"And why don't you know—"

"Lieutenant, would you spare the cadet for a moment? I have some rather menial and less intellectually demanding tasks for him."

Gerswin was glad someone had rescued him, though he did not recognize the voice. From the corner of his eye he caught a glimpse of the uniform, which seemed to be that of a major. If so, it had to be Major Trillo, the chief Gunner of the *Fordin*.

"Certainly, Major."

Gerswin waited.

"On your way, Mr. Cadet Gerswin."

"Yes, ser."

"And, Lieutenant," added the Major, "I also need a word with you after Cadet Gerswin is dispatched."

The lieutenant nodded, his blocky face bobbing up and down.

"Mr. Gerswin, don't stand there like a statue. We've all got things to do. Get on over here."

"Here" meant to the main console, which was a quarter of a deck high and at one end of the narrow room overlooking the banks of screens.

Gerswin stepped up.

Major Trillo was short, only to Gerswin's shoulder level, square, with shoulders broader than his, deep violet eyes, and short, black curly hair. Her voice was velvet over frozen iron.

One tech stood near her control seat, and the major looked, merely looked, and the tech retreated to the main operating screen level.

Gerswin was impressed. He felt more secure with the Lieutenant G'Maine's of the I.S.S.

"Gerswin, I can't blame you, but it's not smart to make your senior officers look stupid, even when they behave like robomules. You must have known what G'Maine would do. You had the answers down pat. If you'd played a little dumber, G'Maine could have crowed and been delighted to teach you all he knows, which isn't that much.

"Now, I'll have to make him responsible for teaching you more than he knows or he'll make everyone's life miserable. So . . . if you don't learn everything he has to teach you and more, it will go in your record under lack of adaptability. But I don't expect that."

Unexpectedly, the major sighed. "Maybe it's better this way. I have an excuse to force him to learn more. But it takes more of my time, and I have little enough of that anyway. So put it all down to experience, and don't do it again. Do you understand?"

"Yes, ser." Gerswin nodded.

"Understand, Cadet Gerswin, I am not opposed to your knowing more than your superiors, nor to learning anything and everything you can. I am opposed to junior officers flaunting such knowledge when it is totally unnecessary. Do you understand that?"

"Yes, ser."

"Further, young man, if you breathe a word of this conversation to anyone, I will insure that you spend the rest of this cruise on maintenance detail and that there is a half-black on your cruise file."

Gerswin swallowed, swallowed hard. A half-black amounted almost to a bust-out. A half-black with a year to go at the Academy— only two had ever graduated with a half-black, only two in the last century, according to the rumors.

"Yes, ser."

Major Trillo smiled, and the smile was friendly.

"If you understand, you've learned more from this encounter than some officers learn in an entire career."

Her voice hardened slightly. "For the past week, the ES section has been promising to reclaim the contents of the repair and recycle locker and take back the material. Would you please gather it all together—all the junk in bin ER-7 over there—and take it down to the E-section senior tech, Erasmus.

"On the way back, stop by the mess and bring back two cafes, one liftea, and whatever you would like."

"Yes, ser."

"And don't mind Erasmus. He'll grouse."

The major switched her attention from the cadet to the screen, effectively dismissing him.

Gerswin found a snapbag two bins away from the one labeled ER-7 and carefully placed in it all the mysterious pieces of the trans-equips and solicube segments.

He wondered if the major saw through his carefully cultivated facade, if she read the contempt he tried to avoid displaying when he ran across Service types who fancied themselves great warriors. Most wouldn't have lasted a night on the high plains.

His lips quirked as he thought about the major. He had no doubts that she would have survived anywhere.

At the Academy he had avoided cadet rank, had tried to blend into the middle of the class. He had been successful, except in the physical development classes. Even there, he'd minimized his strength by concentrating on skill-oriented combat forms, or on learning and mastering the range of energy weapons.

His reflexes made him number one in unarmed combat. He could usually beat the instructors, when he tried, but he made certain that he never won all the time. Instead he worked on learning new techniques until perfected, at which point he began to learn a new repertoire.

He shook his head and concentrated fully on placing each component within a separate insulated section of the carrying case.

Finding E section was harder than he had anticipated, since it wasn't listed except by spoke and frame number. He had to retrace his steps twice before he knocked and stepped inside.

Grouse wasn't exactly the word Gerswin would have used to express the tech's outburst.

"That malingering she-cat knows I have no use for this despicable pile of misbegotten droppings from the devil's offspring! And she sends an innocent to the slaughter, knowing full well how I feel!"

Gerswin's eyes nearly popped out of his head.

Never had he heard anyone discuss a major in the I.S.S. that way in public, let alone a technician who hadn't even a commission. Even if Erasmus was a senior tech—and Gerswin couldn't tell that because the man's white tech suit, contrary to regulations, had no insignia, not even his name—Erasmus should not have discussed a senior officer so candidly.

Gerswin said nothing, certain he had failed to understand something.

Finally, he spoke. "Will that be all, Senior Technician Erasmus?"

"Will that be all, Senior Technician? Will that be all, Senior Cadet? Is it not enough to have been given sewer sweepings, the remnants of proud equipment, without as much as a by-your-leave? Do you think that good equipment springs full-blown from the heads of gods? Will that be all indeed?"

Gerswin tried to hide the beginnings of a smile.

"And you, would-be officer, smirk upon what you see as the rantings and ravings of a demented technician. Do you also smirk at the equipment upon which your very life rests? Do you?"

The cadet had to take a step backward to avoid the long probe the technician waved in his face.

"Do you?"

"No. Not at all."

Erasmus looked at the carrying case in Gerswin's arms.

"Ah, well. Bring it in. We'll do what we must." The technician shook his head sadly. "But the sheer effrontery, the sheer underhandedness! At least she did not send that bonehead, the one with the skull so thick and so empty that not even a laser would have any effect."

Gerswin repressed another smile. To hear Lieutenant G'Maine so described by someone else was a pleasure.

"And you, Mister Cadet Gerswin by your name plate, what do you think?"

Theoretically, second class cadets outranked even senior technicians, but in practice, Gerswin had known from his devilkid days, things didn't always conform to theory.

So while Gerswin theoretically did not have to respond to Erasmus's questions, he swallowed his smile and did.

"I don't know enough to make an intelligent answer."

"Wish more had the nerve to admit what they didn't know. But you did not answer my first question. Your life rests on technology, on equipment like that." His probe jabbed down at the bag Gerswin had carried in. "Put it on the work bench next to the console."

As Gerswin did, the technician's questions continued.

"That equipment carries your life, and yet you do not understand it, except how to use it? Is that not so?"

"Right now, you're right. I don't."

"Will you ever? Don't answer that. You might answer honestly and disappoint me. Or you might answer honestly and fail to live up to what your answer promises. Or you might lie. Not much chance that you'll ever really understand technology. Not if you become the standard I.S.S. officer."

Erasmus sighed. "That's why you have technicians. To keep you running. Don't forget it, Mr. Gerswin. Don't forget it."

"You make a strong case, Senior Technician."

"Damned right, Cadet. They put up with my 'peculiarities' because I can repair anything in this Emperor's Navy. But I'm right anyway. And don't you forget it."

Gerswin didn't know what else to say. If he used the formal "will that be all?" Erasmus would think he had been merely half listening.

"Would you like me to convey anything else to Major Trillo, generally?"

"Ha! HA! HAAA!" Erasmus laughed, then stopped. "You're cautious, Cadet. But you're learning. She wouldn't take official notice, and no sense putting you on the spot. Besides, we understand each other, she and I do."

Even the chuckling stopped.

"That will be all, Cadet. Keep listening. It's worth all the cubes and lectures at the Academy."

Despite the feeling that he had suffered a mental bombardment, Gerswin found his feet leading him back to the wardroom, where he picked up two cafes and two lifteas, not that he particularly liked liftea, but the tea was far better than the oily taste of the cafe, which reminded him all too strongly of landpoison.

Once back inside the weapons center, he saw Lieutenant G'Maine standing between him and the main console, which seemed vacant except for a single tech.

Gerswin walked straight to G'Maine.

"Lieutenant, did you want cafe or liftea? The major asked me to bring some on my way back, but I don't know which you prefer, ser."

"Appreciate it, Cadet. I prefer cafe. So does Lieutenant Swabo, but the major likes liftea."

G'Maine took a cafe and turned away without another word.

Gerswin searched for the major, located her in the far corner, the missile center, with Lieutenant Swabo.

Once he made his way there he stood, holding the tray, waiting to be noticed, as the two women conferred about something with gestures toward the small plot in the center of Swabo's console.

Without looking up, the major said, "Cafe for the Lieutenant, liftea for me."

Gerswin placed the beverages in the holders on the consoles and retreated to a corner folddown where he sipped his own liftea.

DING! DING! DING!

With the sound of the third bell the captain's face appeared on all the screens on the *Fordin,* and her voice echoed through all the passageway speakers.

Gerswin looked over Lieutenant G'Maine's shoulder to get a view of the skipper. He had met Captain Montora once, when he had been formally introduced by the executive officer after he had reported from the Academy.

She looked as crisp now as she had then, short and bobbed blond hair in perfect place, ice green eyes steady into the screen, square jawed, smooth olive skin. A closer study might have showed the hints of age—the slight shadow and fine lines around the eyes, the sharpened nose, the lines in the otherwise smooth forehead.

"This is the captain. Shortly, we will be changing course and jumping for Newparra. This will be a two-jump trip. Once in-system, we will become the nucleus of the quarantine battle group.

"While a full backgrounder will be available through the ship's infonet, for those of you who have not participated in a quarantine action before, our job is to isolate the system from any outside contact and to keep any system ships from departing until a new government can be recognized by the Emperor.

"We will be joined initially in this action by the *Krushnei,* the *Saladin,* and the *Kemal.* Before system entry, you will be ordered to alert status.

"That is all."

As the screen blanked, Gerswin looked up to the raised deck and to Major Trillo, the Gunnery officer.

"Ten'stet!" The major's voice cut off the rising murmurs of speculation.

"All Gunnery officers and cadets, report to the main console here immediately."

Gerswin tagged along behind Lieutenants G'Maine and Swabo as the three of them trooped between the consoles toward the major.

"Relax." The major gestured vaguely in a circular motion. "I don't believe any of you except Lieutenant Swabo have participated in a quarantine action. When we're done here, you all, and especially you, Cadet Gerswin, need to call up that backgrounder and to review the Imperial articles of quarantine. Study them, if you need to. If what I recall of Newparra is still current, this could be one of the nastier quarantines you will ever see.

"Now . . . we're not organized for full round the clock operations, but you've all seen the combat roster. For the first few days, however, I intend to double the officer count. There will be two officers on duty at all times. For these purposes, Cadet Gerswin will be included on the duty roster as junior Gunnery officer. To balance his inexperience, he will be paired initially with me. Chief Technician Alvera and Sub-Chief Gorta will head the duty techs.

"Senior Lieutenant Swabo will act as Gunnery officer in my absence."

The major waited for the duty pairings to sink in.

Lieutenant G'Maine frowned momentarily, with a puzzled expression following almost immediately.

"You expect some action, ser. When Newparra has been part of the Empire for so long?"

"This is the third quarantine of Newparra, Lieutenant. That may well be a record. The government has been a compromise between radical Christers and Istvennists. By definition, a quarantine is called when no one government controls the entire system. Unfortunately, while the overall level of technology is moderate, the government has maintained nearly twenty jumpships of all classes."

Gerswin kept himself from nodding. While the jumpships were not supposed to be armed, a revolutionary or embattled status government could certainly do so.

"The Empire has always taken a strong stand against revolutionaries being able to export their ideals or wars or to import weapons and other support. That's why we have quarantines. But none of this should be news to any of you. Read the backgrounder. Then I'll answer questions."

Ding!

The screen chime punctuated the major's last sentence.

"All hands! All hands! Ten minutes until jump. Ten minutes until jump."

The major nodded, then concluded, "The first duty tour will be

Lieutenant Swabo and Lieutenant G'Maine. If this lasts as long as it
probably will, in time we'll go to the one in three roster, with Cadet
Gerswin as backup."

Gerswin understood, he thought. Until the major had the chance
to settle G'Maine and him down, she and Swabo would be keeping a
close watch to insure neither went off half-blasted. But the major also
knew that a four on, four off routine was too fatiguing to be effective
beyond a few days.

"Dismissed."

Gerswin hurried back to the closet that doubled as his cabin to
ready for the jump.

Tammilan was not there, probably relishing taking the jump at
the duty station of the absent third navigator.

As Gerswin strapped in, the screen chime rang again.

Ding!

"All hands! All hands! Stand by for jump. Stand by for jump."

The blackness and dislocation seemed longer this time, but his
experience was so limited Gerswin had no idea whether the subjective
feeling meant anything at all.

The second jump was less than ten minutes after the first, and, if
anything, seemed to last longer than the earlier jump.

Gerswin wondered if every jump seemed to take longer than the
previous one, despite the indoctrination materials which had indicated that the objective and subjective time of jump was constant. Not
for him, they didn't seem constant.

After the second jump toward Newparra, he unstrapped and sat
up. There was no reason he couldn't go back to the Gunnery operations center, although he didn't see why he needed to, either. He
wasn't hungry and he'd already missed more sleep than he'd intended on this cruise. All he could do as the *Fordin* headed in-system
was to get in the way.

Yawning, he stood up and undressed, leaving his uniform laid
out. Then he climbed back into the bunk, and, as a precaution,
loosely adjusted the restraining webs.

For a time he stared at the flat underside of Tammilan's bunk before drifting into sleep.

Tammilan tiptoed in several minutes later, as he was about to drift
off. She did not stay, but merely picked up a clean uniform and left.
Gerswin did not look over at her, but wondered why she was so secretive about her actions. The entire ship knew she spent more time with
the number two navigator than in her own quarters, but who cared?

That was her business, and if she hadn't been a cadet, the official cabin arrangements merely would have been changed.

He thought he woke twice with the lurching of a sudden course shift as the gravfield generators compensated for the stress, but with no announcements following in either case, he went back to sleep.

After waking in the still-empty cabin, running himself through the tiny fresher, dressing, and grabbing some fruit and cheese from the open snack table in the Officers' Mess, he made his way back to the Gunnery operations center for his first watch with Major Trillo.

Gerswin slipped behind the console next to the senior tech, Alvera, with only a nod from the departing G'Maine.

Alvera, a small man with jet black hair and eyes and a jerkiness to every movement, jabbed at the screen.

"Cadet. Here's the status. Inbound from exit corridor two." His thin index finger pointed to a green blip on the representational screen. "Here. Comm is running sweep and comm screen analysis. Nav has pulled deep EDI traces. Results came in about ten minutes ago. Solid contact shows in red. Conditional contact in amber. One of ours in green. Understand?"

"I think so."

Alvera pointed to the small screens to the left of the larger representational screen. "Top is punch laser. Energy available. Second shows tachead status and support data. Third is hellburners."

The senior tech looked directly and pointedly into Gerswin's eyes.

"Got that?"

"Yes."

"Fine. Unless something looks wrong, you do nothing. Nothing, understand? My techs make sure these figures are right. You're the backup to the major. You should know every number on these screens, what they mean. You don't. You might learn. I'll try and teach you."

Gerswin did not smile at the man's nervous energy, but instead nodded his head thoughtfully.

"I think I understand. You and your techs provide all the inputs. The major recommends to the bridge. I watch. If something looks strange, unless it's an emergency, I ask you or the senior tech. I keep quiet until I understand what it all means."

"That's right, Cadet." Alvera nodded. "Learn now. Someday you'll be the one making those recommendations, or, maybe, having to act on them. Better know what they mean."

Gerswin nodded once more and began to concentrate on the representational screens, which showed a series of red blips around the fourth planet, Newparra itself, and two red blips circling the third planet, with a lone red blip around the sixth planet, the inner of the system's two gas giants.

The blip closest to the *Fordin* was amber, outside the seventh planet, with a vector indicator showing an outward course that would intersect the *Fordin*'s path in roughly a standard hour. A standard hour?

Gerswin's fingers touched his own comp screen and keys.

The screen confirmed that if the amber blip was a ship, it would intersect the *Fordin*'s path in one point three standard hours.

"Did we shift course for intercept?"

Alvera nodded. "About one stan ago."

Gerswin inclined his head toward the representational plot. "How accurate is that? How many don't show?"

"Good question. Right now, we couldn't pick up anything under corvette size unless it was on full-drive or talking wideband to the universe."

A green light winked in on the top side of the board, across the system from the *Fordin*, then was jumped inward abruptly as the techs made the real time adjustments.

"How many exit corridors does the system have?"

"Not much dust here. Two that are almost particle free. If you don't mind the skewing and the extra energy costs, no absolute need for corridor use."

Gerswin frowned. The only way to control system entrance or exit realistically would seem to be by an orbit patrol of Newparra and the industrial centers on the third planet, and on the two major moons of the sixth planet. But, if the *Fordin*, as the heavy of the quarantine squadron, took station off Newparra, that left two search cruisers and two corvettes to cover the rest of the system.

Glad he didn't have to decide the positioning of the Imperial ships, he returned his full attention to the screens, noting that the amber blip approaching the *Fordin* had become a red blip with a notation symbol beside it.

Rather than ask Alvera what the symbol meant he tried to get an answer from his own screen, but stopped after two unsuccessful tries at asking the system for a coded symbol that neither appeared on the keyboard nor in answer to the standard inquiries.

"Chief . . . how do you interrogate for the symbols beside the blips?"

Alvera chuckled. "Can't get there unless you've already been there. Right?"

Gerswin shrugged.

"Ask for SKS. Stands for 'screen key symbols.' Follow with 'Gun' or you'll get the nav and comm codes as well. The symbols will all display on your work screen, along with the working subscript. That's what you use for your inquiries. Simple enough."

Gerswin dutifully followed the instructions and discovered that the approaching blip was listed as a "system heavy patrol" with class two armament—tacheads and punch lasers. That brought up another question.

"Why the puzzled look, Cadet?"

"System patrols don't carry jumpdrives. Non-Imperial jumpships don't carry weapons. No one knew when we were coming. That means that patroller was on a jump exit course *before* he knew we were inbound. Either that or he has jumpdrives."

"He knew *someone* was coming. Manual for quarantine actions are no secret. Imperial force has to get to main system planets at max speed. Means clearest corridors. Delay means more to clean up."

"They'd try a direct attack against a battlecruiser?"

"No. They know that some incomers are cruisers. That's an even match. If they can blow a cruiser or the corvettes, then that buys them time before we can fully cover the system, until our torps reach the fleet commander. We lose ships, that means the captain will have to take more drastic action."

Gerswin let Alvera's comment pass. What drastic action could the captain take, besides destroying the patrollers and whatever other craft the isolated and embattled system government had managed to arm and retain?

By now his ears were beginning to sort out the verbal messages coming from the comm link of the console, words mixed with static and garbled transmissions.

". . . stand off between Satanists and Brotherhood on Demetros . . ."

". . . Gabriel to Archangel Michael . . . successful, divert Gyros . . . Satanists hold Gyros and Janus . . ."

". . . *norstada cin trahit . . . Gyros stadit* . . ."

". . . negative diversion this time . . . negative . . ."

". . . have no lucifer for Demetros . . ."

". . . *fiela cor Gyros, cor Janus* . . ."

". . . EDI standing wave . . . heavy battlecruiser . . . Imperial . . . presume Imperial presence . . ."

". . . Gabriel . . . negative diversion . . . understand battlecruiser . . ."

". . . unleash Cherubim on north coast. . . . North coast . . ."

Another green blip pinged into existence in the jump corridor out-system behind the *Fordin.* That made three out of the four comprising the Imperial quarantine squadron.

Gerswin studied the representational screen, then the three green dots upon it. Three ships. Just three ships? Where were the corvettes?

He checked the closure on the Newparran patroller and found that the closure time had dropped to less than thirty minutes.

"Cadet Gerswin, Chief Alvera, give me a weapons spread proposal for target one." There was no mistaking the voice of the major.

Gerswin turned to Alvera and raised his eyebrows. He'd done proposals at the Academy, but was the major serious?

"Like this, Cadet. Patroller characteristics under subscript . . . here . . . armor, screens, power max. Then factor the profile, closure rate, and acceleration . . ."

"Acceleration?"

"Acceleration. Don't teach that at the Academy. Acceleration takes power. Less power for screens. Too much acceleration and you can't shift from gravfield to screens without losing control. Some ships have limited shunt capability. Bigger the ship, less shunt capacity. That's why the battlecruiser is the biggest effective single action ship."

Alvera's fingers danced across his controls, and then touched a stud.

"Hit accept, Cadet."

Gerswin touched the stud, and a duplicate of Alvera's proposal lined up on his work screen.

Gerswin studied the recommendation for a moment. Alvera had suggested using six tacheads spaced in a bowl-like pattern, whose detonation would be preceded by a series of quick-spaced bursts from the punch laser. No hellburners, obviously.

The cadet pulled his lips together as he tried to follow the tech's reasoning. The actual energy that could be diverted to the laser would scarcely dent a corvette's screens, let alone the heavier ones carried by a patroller.

"Understand the tacheads, Chief. Why the laser? Energy level wouldn't break his screens."

"Not the purpose. With his profile against ours, no laser could make a physical impact. The laser bursts are powerful enough to blind him for six–seven seconds. That forces him to move, but he'll

have to move blind, and the tacheads are spaced on the most probable computed evasion tracks.

"Odds are that no local system government would be able to pull
together a complete crew experienced enough to handle the course
changes. They'll have to trust their AI, and that's what the tacheads
are programmed against."

Alvera touched the stud to transmit the recommendation.

"Cadet Gerswin, do you concur with the chief's recommendation?"

"That is affirmative, Major."

"Chief, what delay factor did you compute for reaction time to
the first laser?"

"One point five standard seconds."

"Too quick for a crew that will be shorthanded or inexperienced.
Run it at two point five for the inner spread and angle it back to four
point five for the outer."

Alvera nodded.

"Will do, Major."

Gerswin watched as the chief made his corrections.

"Looks good, Chief. Set the spread for execution from the command console."

"Stet, Major. In the green."

The noise level in the already quiet Gunnery operations center
dropped further, and the silence, unbroken except for a faint humming, stretched on and on.

"Ten until contact. Program running."

Gerswin looked down, was surprised to find his fists were
clenched, and forced himself to relax them. The shipboard version of
a fight was so dispassionate, so far removed from the jagged blade and
the threat of a king rat or a she-coyote on the prowl. Here, his fate was
in the hands of so many others. . . .

The background scent of fear, faint enough not to reach the
awareness of the others, acrid, lingering, began to fill the center. To
Gerswin, even the ventilation system seemed to stop, while the air
hung heavy over the screens and consoles.

Cling.

"Laser punch on. Burst one."

The lights in the center dimmed momentarily, flickered, then remained at the lower level.

"Burst two."

On the representational screen, the green blip that was the *Fordin*

spouted a yellow lance that crept toward the Newparran patroller
only slightly faster than the *Fordin* did.

Gerswin detected the gentlest of shudders in the battle cruiser's
frame.

"Burst four."

"Tachead spread one away."

"Burst five."

"Spread two away."

"Burst six."

"Three away."

Ding! Ding! Ding!

"All hands! All hands! Evasive maneuvers! Evasive maneuvers! Remain at stations! Remain at stations!"

Gerswin glanced over at Alvera, discovered the tech was studying
the screen, his hands resting on the edge of the console, unmoving.

"... *fiela Gyros ... cor Janus* ..."

"... Imperial target ... heads away ..."

The whispers from the comm monitors took on an added loud-
ness in the comparative silence of the center.

"... *fiela Janus ... nir nulla trahit* ..."

"Imperial EDIs out-system ..."

"... releasing and commencing beta ... evasion ..."

"... diversion when appropriate ... when appropriate ..."

The lighting level dropped further, to emergency levels, and the
gravfield dropped toward the null point before surging momentarily
to almost two gees, then dropping to a stable one gravity.

Through it all, Gerswin kept his eyes on the representational
screen, watching as the simulated punch laser impacted the Newparran patroller's screen image, and as the images of the tachead bursts
began to blossom on the screen, and as the course line of the *Fordin*
veered left, then angled back.

The red blip that had represented the Newparran patroller flared
brightly, then vanished.

"Target termination complete," announced the major as the
Gunnery lights returned to normal.

As the former devilkid watched the silent kill of who knew how
many men and women, he shook himself, almost like a wet coyote,
but he continued to watch the screen. The *Fordin*'s course line again
shifted, this time toward the sixth planet, presumably for the two
satellites rather than for the gas giant itself. Better the sixth than the
seventh, which was a third of the way around its orbit from the Imperial battlecruiser, reflected Gerswin.

Since there were no blips, hostile or otherwise, he wondered about the reason for the course switch.

In the meantime he noted that the fourth green blip, the *Krushnei*, had appeared on the system farside, out-system from where another Newparran patroller raced toward the *Saladin*. The *Kemal* remained out from the *Fordin* and remained on a more direct in-system course.

Less than two standard hours since he had come on duty, and the *Fordin* had been attacked and had destroyed the attacker. After thinking a moment, he corrected himself. The *Fordin* had simply attacked and destroyed the unnamed Newparran patroller which had tried, unsuccessfully, to stop the Imperial quarantine.

He pulled at his chin. Even before contact, the two ships had been poised to destroy each other.

As he wrestled with the implications, he continued to watch the representational screens, to listen to the comm bands and to wait as the *Fordin* began to slow in her approach to the nearer satellite.

"*Pleutfiere, Empire sur transit Gyros . . .*"

"New Jerusalem, Faust has struck. Michael has been cast down. EDI tracks indicate course shift . . ."

"*Trahison! Couvrey des plaques! Comprennez? Des plaques de Janus et de Gyros . . .*"

". . . *norstada nil . . . premiere . . . Gyros . . .*"

"Cadet Gerswin, Chief Alvera. Specs for maximum surface damage on Gyros, centered on the landing traps and the linear accelerator."

"Stet," answered Alvera.

Gerswin said nothing. He looked sideways at the tech, whose movements were slower now, not quick or jerky.

"Hellburner?"

"Not much else. Not enough sealing power in a tachead. Probably take an above surface burst, about five kays. Maybe two. Depends on terrain and separation."

Gerswin opened his mouth to ask why, but remembered his earlier conversation with the major and shut his mouth without saying a word.

"Good thought, Cadet," murmured Alvera in a voice low enough not to be heard beyond their consoles. "Good thought."

Gerswin sighed silently and began to run the problem off on his own console. As he finished, he saw Alvera was waiting.

"Let's compare."

Gerswin shrugged and studied Alvera's solution. Both had recommended two mid-class burners with a five kay separation and a three kay burst height.

"Looks about the same," he commented to Alvera.

"About identical." Alvera raised his head and touched the transmit stud.

"Cadet Gerswin, do you concur?"

"My solution is identical to the chief's, Major."

"Do you concur?" There was an edge to the velvet voice.

"Yes, ser."

Gerswin and Alvera sat side by side, neither looking at the other nor talking, but silently viewing the screens and the symbols as they changed.

Gerswin listened to the intermittent transmissions whispering from the comm link, like ghosts about to flee at morning light.

The *Fordin* shuddered faintly, once, twice.

"Burners away."

This time the representational screen showed nothing, nothing except the number two followed by a single symbol, both next to the disc labeled "Gyros."

Gerswin shifted his weight, beginning to feel stiff after nearly three hours hunched before a single console.

"Cadet Gerswin, prepare the specs for a similar interdiction pattern for Janus. Key seven for background. Chief Alvera will verify before you transmit."

"Yes, ser."

Another set of hellburners? For what? Another dome and burrow mining and heavy industry settlement on an isolated satellite? For perhaps five thousand, ten thousand people?

Despite his deliberate pace, the equations were easy. Three hellburners—there were two lines of steep hills separating the landing traps, the accelerator, and the comm complex—at a height of one point five kays.

Alvera nodded.

Gerswin transmitted.

"Do you concur, Chief Alvera?"

"Yes, ser."

Gerswin listened as he waited for the *Fordin* to complete her creeping approach to Janus, or for his watch to end. But the comm bands were less active now, only a distant garbled whisper or so.

"...got...Michael...out Gyros..."

"...*fiela*...*trahit*...*Demetros*..."

The blinking of a green blip caught his attention, and he concentrated on the representational screen. The blinking green was the *Saladin*. Had been the *Saladin*, Gerswin realized as the light flared red and white and vanished, to be replaced with a subscripted line at the bottom of the screen.

"Major said this one would be nasty," muttered Alvera.

Gerswin did not even shake his head. He didn't pretend to understand. If the Christers had control of most of the ships and the government, why were they attacking Imperial quarantine vessels? And why was the captain searing the launch and port facilities on Janus and Gyros when they belonged to the Istvennists, who weren't attacking the Empire?

The *Fordin* shivered three times, so slightly that Gerswin doubted whether anyone else noticed, wrapped as they were in their own concerns and the interest in the fate of the *Saladin*.

"Burners away."

He checked the time. Not too long before Lieutenant G'Maine was due to relieve him.

The course line on the screen changed again, showing the *Fordin* returning toward the original in-system destination.

Gerswin noted that the red dot that had totaled the *Saladin* was still headed out the system jump corridor toward the incoming *Krushnei*.

Given the lag times, they might not know the results of that confrontation until he was back on watch. He shook his head. In-system maneuvering time took so much longer than the between-system jumps.

"Cadet Gerswin, ready for relief?"

G'Maine's hearty voice startled Gerswin. He hadn't expected so burly an individual could move so quietly, or, perhaps, he had not been so aware as he should have been. Perhaps his skills were slipping in the confined ship environment. He'd have to work on that.

"Ready for relief, ser."

Gerswin stood and vacated the console.

"You stand relieved, Cadet." G'Maine smiled. "From what I've heard, you had quite an indoctrination."

"Yes, ser." Gerswin nodded. "Also told me how much I don't know."

"Good healthy attitude. See you in four." G'Maine swiveled into position to study the console and the screens.

"Cadet Gerswin?" The voice was the major's.

"Yes, ser."

"Would you join me? I'm on my way to the Mess. No seating arrangements during alerts, and I'd like to go over your performance."

Gerswin wondered what he'd done that merited evaluation. Some of his skepticism must have been communicated to the major.

"Mister Gerswin," she commented in the antique form of address, "you did well, much better than anyone would have expected. Mathematically, your last solution was better than mine or the chief's." Her eyes raked over him, and despite the fact that he was a shade taller than she was, he felt momentarily as though she were looking down at him.

"Let's go. I'm starved."

Gerswin matched her quick, short steps.

The mess, predictably, was half full. The major piled her tray high and launched herself toward an empty square table at one side of the narrow dining area. She left the other side for him.

"Sit down. You like the fruits and vegetables, I see."

Gerswin nodded and pulled his chair into place.

The major took three large mouthfuls of a mixed cheese and meat dish that looked like synthleather covered with glue. Gerswin had avoided it for his fruits, vegetables, and a thin slice of meat that hadn't seemed to smell too artificial.

He sipped at a glass of water, ignoring the metallic tang that was unnoticeable to anyone else.

Tammilan walked in, smiling, between two junior navigators, both lieutenants, saw Gerswin, and grinned. Both eyebrows went up, and she shook her head in mock-disapproval.

In spite of his glumness, Gerswin returned the smile.

"Friend?"

"Roommate. In name only."

"You seem down."

"Private thoughts?" asked Gerswin.

"All right. Provided it's nothing illegal, or that I would be forced to enter on your record."

"Nothing like that." Gerswin shook his head. "No. I just don't understand. From all the backgrounders, the comm freqs, everything I can pick up, the Newparran Christers control the ships, or most of them, and most of the government. But they're the ones sending patrollers to blast the quarantine squadron. Then we sear off two moons to seal off the Istvennists, who haven't threatened us. There must be a reason, but I can't figure what."

The major packed in another three mouthfuls before answering. While she was solid, she didn't seem overweight, and he couldn't believe how she kept that way with her food intake.

"Gerswin, what do you know about the Christers? Or the Istvennists? Or Newparra?"

"Not much beyond the background and the comparative religions course at the Academy. Christers are fundamentalist believers in a single god. Istvennists believe in their own god above all others, but within a context of total personal religious freedom."

"Carry those trends to their logical extreme, and think about it. That would explain the way the Empire has had to act." She drained half a glass of a purple punch in a single gulp. "Christers believe they are the only true believers of the only true God. They are fanatical achievers in anything and everything, and they usually end up in disproportionate numbers in government and business. Both their government and their businesses are honest, but cruelly so, and without much compassion. Less than twenty percent of Newparra is Christer, but they control the government. They passed a law to require religious prayers in all institutions of learning and another law to forbid voluntary euthanasia—in which the Istvennists deeply believe as a matter of personal choice. Then they blocked genetic improvements as unnatural, despite the fact that the majority of Istvennists come from a weak genetic background.

"I won't go into a more detailed blow by blow, because I don't know all the details, but the upshot was that the Istvennists called for elections to throw the Christers out of government, and the Christers refused to leave and seized the government and control of the major weapons systems of the small military. The Christers saw it coming and managed to smuggle in some high tech equipment before the Empire quarantined the system, and Christers from all over the galaxy are dying to get help to their brethren here.

"The Christers can't win over the long run without outside help because the numbers are against them. The Istvennists claim they should have outside aid to shorten the inevitable result and reduce the loss of life, and, besides, the Christers cheated on the quarantine.

"Imperial policy is simple. This is a local system matter and will stay that way. You have a revolt, and the locals have to settle it themselves. Our job is to make sure no one leaves the system, and no one enters, except on an Imperial warship. Period. When a government emerges that has total local control, we leave."

"That why the captain sealed off the moons?"

"She didn't have much choice, especially once the Christers blew the *Saladin*. Not enough ships to cover the system, and it would take too long to get back and forth between the outer and inner planets."

"But what happens if they fight forever?"

"Has happened before," mumbled the major as she finished another huge mouthful. "Will happen again. But local problems have to stay local, and local killings have to stay localized. If the people of a system can't get along together, then why should we let them spread the disagreements?"

"What about refugees? People unjustly oppressed?"

"Two problems. First, half the so-called refugees are people who don't get along in the system and don't have the guts to change it. Either that or they lost out because they couldn't change and they want to run out with their creds and try somewhere else. The other half are various bad apples."

"What about real victims?"

The major snorted. "Victims? Real victims don't have access to a jumpship or to the money to pay passage out-system. They get hurt no matter what happens. But if you force a system to deal with its problems, over time, in most cases, the average person gets hurt less. Not always true, but you don't make policy on exceptions."

Gerswin took a bite from the rubbery yellow fruit. It tasted better than ripe yucca, but not much. He chewed slowly.

The major stood and headed for the serving table and seconds. Gerswin studied the food before him, mostly still uneaten. She made it sound so simple, as if the hellburners were just another tool, as if the ten thousand people trapped under the molten rock and airless surface of Gyros and Janus had personally created the rebellion.

Had they?

He shook his head. So much he needed to learn. So much.

He tried a bite of the bland meat as the major plowed back to the table with another full tray.

M. C. Gerswin, Cadet 1/C
Section Beta Two
The Academy
Kystra, Alphane

This is printing off the main engineering screens, devilkid, because I was never much for the fancy cubes you talk and put your smiling face to.

Still black-jumps me to see you as a namesake of sorts. That's why the initials, but congratulations. We all got the invitation, and you deserve it. You earned it. Can't say I thought you'd make it, not because you lacked brains or talent, but it takes a lot of patience to put up with it all. You've surprised us more civilized types more than once, and probably will a few times more.

Hard to picture you as a fresh-scrubbed I.S.S. officer, but I'll get used to that. Marso—she cubed me—can't get over it either. She's gone straight line, the exec on the *Martel,* scheduled for promotion to commander in the next circular.

Guess I ought to offer some advice. It's free and worth that, but even an old engineer who's a broken-down commander has something worth passing along. People—they're important. I know it, but I could never put it into practice. That's the single most important thing. Don't you forget it.

Second thing is machines. You've studied the histories by now, how Old Earth went down despite its machines and how the colonies barely survived. That's history. But we didn't learn enough from it. I know, why should an old machine wrestler like me worry about machines? I do. Machines are tools. Every time you use a machine, you make a decision. When you build a new machine, you decide that machine and the resources it takes are more important than something else. That's fine if you know what you want.

A machine can cut a tree and turn it into lumber. A machine can pull ore from an asteroid and turn it into hull plates. The machine didn't make the asteroid, and it can't grow like a tree. All Old Earth's machinery didn't save it from the collapse. The Federation learned something, and the Empire learned from the Federation. We're careful about what machines we use, and more careful about where we build them and use them. We try to put them in deep space or on unusable planets or moons. We manufacture the dangerous stuff away from the planets we live on. But we manufacture, and we build ships.

We still deal with the Devil; we got better terms. That's something to remember. What it means, I don't pretend to know. Call it all the ramblings of a has-been engineer.

Anyway . . . congratulations again, and good luck, lieutenant!

MacGregor Corson
Commander, I.S.S.
COMM/ENG STAFF
Vladstok, MANQCH

THE BLACK AND silver of the I.S.S. officer's uniform merged with the long shadows and the lingering twilight of New Colora, even on the lower terrace of the Officers' Club.

A single officer sat at a small table in the walled corner farthest from the circular stone staircase that led to the upper level, a table that seemed to draw the shadows around it like a blanket.

Gerswin leaned back in the padded plasteel chair and let his shoulders rest against the stone wall behind him, let his eyes range out over the sloping lawn beyond the waist-high sitting wall on the far side of the circular table for two.

Now that his flitter and shuttle training was over, all he had to do was wait for the *Churchill,* due in less than two standard weeks.

He began to whistle, creating another tune as the double notes whispered out onto the vacant terrace and drifted downhill toward the training fields out beyond the manicured greenery of the club grounds.

The club was nearly empty, as it had been for the last half month, when the previous training cycle had been completed. Since half of the flitter pilots were techs, and weren't commissioned, and the latest officer class had yet to arrive, and the assault squadron normally based on New Colora, the Fifteenth, had just left for deployment with the Third Fleet, only a handful of officers were left to rattle around the club.

Within days, the Twelfth would be arriving for refresher training and regrouping. The next Academy class's pilot trainees would soon follow.

For now the club was empty, except for the cadre, the high-ranking staff officers, and a few transients, and special assignees, like Gerswin.

Gerswin broke off his soft whistling as the waiter approached.

"Another, ser?" The orderly's neutral tone nonetheless expressed concern about Gerswin's less than formal position, but he did not lean forward.

"No. Thank you. Not now."

He stared across the nonreflecting polished surface of the table, out over the stone sitting wall, and toward the low purple of the distant hills. In full daylight they were red-purple, not surprisingly, since most of the native growth had at least a trace of red in it. Only the mutated home grass had green or blue in it.

Gerswin laughed, a short bark, soft for all its harshness.

His home had been the original source of the blue green grass, but Old Earth looked more like New Colora than it did like the histapes showed or than New Augusta, supposedly the most Old Earth-like of the colonized planets that had become, first, the Federated Worlds, and then, the Empire.

"That will change. Right? You're going to make it change. Right, Gerswin? Right, devilkid going home?"

He stared at the empty beaker and set it precisely in the center of the table.

Once more, he leaned back in the chair, aware how his posture irritated the always proper orderlies of the club. He began another song, with the off-multitoned whistle that no one else had ever seemed able to imitate.

This one—he'd composed the basic melody years ago, not long after he'd been picked up by the *Torquina.* While he'd elaborated it

over the years, the sense of loss, the lack of identity, were more refined, a shade understated, but still the same basic theme. His theme,
and it always would be.

Waiting to go home, he wondered if he ever could, as the notes
spilled from his lips and whispered their clear wistfulness into the
darkening twilight:

As he finished, he leaned forward and let the front legs of his
chair touch the smoothed stone of the terrace. By now, the drier cool
of the true evening was arriving on the hill breeze, with the scent of
raisha. The long shadows had merged with the forerunner of night.

"Beautiful," a soft voice said.

He started, and looked to his left.

Sitting on the stone wall, her skirted legs hanging over the outside edge and over the grass a meter beneath her feet, the woman was
half-turned and looking at him.

With an athletic motion she lifted her legs and turned so that she
was still sitting on the wall, but facing him directly.

"You must be Lieutenant Gerswin."

With the terrace lights not on, and the last glimmer of twilight
fading behind her, it took a moment for Gerswin to focus on the dimness of her face.

He stood.

"Would you care to join me?" He gestured to the empty chair, but
did not move.

"I'm comfortable right here, and that might be best."

Her voice was young, but husky, and he judged from her profile,
as she turned her head toward the staircase that led to the upper terrace, that she was little more than a girl.

In his loneliness, he had hoped for a woman. But she had heard
the melody.

"As you wish," he answered, inhaling slightly as he reseated himself, not moving toward her. Her scent indicated she was a woman,
but, as he had guessed from her profile, young. Obviously, the daughter of an officer, a very senior one. Few officers pulled accompanied
tours anywhere.

"Would you please do another?"

Gerswin surveyed the terrace. Even the orderlies were gone. The
girl had a pleasant voice, and the request was neither patronizing nor
wheedling.

"Anything special?"

"Whatever pleases you."

He began to whistle softly, so low that no one more than a few meters away could have heard him, a greatly amended version of an old ballad he had learned at the prep school.

He recalled some of the words, and they flitted through his mind, though he could not, nor did he wish, to sing them.

> . . . and I met my love, and I learned her worth,
> on a faraway planet, a faraway planet called earth . . .

When he halted at the end, there was silence. For an instant, he thought she had gone.

"Are your songs always so sad?"

"No. Feeling down tonight. I just whistle what I feel. Not sophisticated enough to lie in my songs." He frowned. "How did you know who I was?"

"You whistle, and you're from Old Earth. There's only one pilot with that combination, isn't there?"

Gerswin laughed, a bark again, but softer yet, and forgiving. He had his night-sight now that the twilight was gone and the terrace lights remained out. He studied the girl.

Short dark hair, cut just below her ears, large eyes, broad forehead, small ears, and a jaw that stopped just short of being square. Smallish, more handsome than pretty, but she smelled good and had a lovely voice, Gerswin decided, both qualities as important, to him, as mere looks.

Too bad she was the young dependent of some flight commander or marshal. Touch her, and he'd end up on some isolated station, or suicide assignment, if not planted under a shambletown.

"Your name?"

"Oh . . . I'm . . . Caroljoy."

"Carol Joy."

"No . . . Caroljoy." She firmly made the name one word.

"Sorry."

He looked away from her and into the western darkness.

"Lieutenant? Are you really from Old Home?"

Gerswin did not look away from the silhouette of the distant hills, where no light marred the blackness.

"I suppose so. That's what they tell me."

She let the silence be, and waited.

At last, he spoke.

"I am from Old Earth. That is what those who picked me up have told me. The place I knew does not resemble the Terra of the old tapes and stories. You cannot see into the sky beyond the clouds. The grass is purpled, what grass there is, and the trees are few, and only in the sheltered hills. There are some ruins, but most have been leveled. The people ... some still remain, mostly in the shambletowns. And the others, the devilkids, hold the high plains, and, in turn, are hunted by the shambletowners. When I was not dodging the landspouts, or the ice rains, or the rivers of death, I was dodging the shambletowners and their slings.

"Sometimes that is a dream, only a dream, and sometimes this is."

From the stillness, her voice came back, husky soft now. "Do you want to go back?"

"Sometimes ... but there I have to go, first, to become what I am. ... To do what must be done. ..."

"To remain a dreamer after all you have seen ..." Her voice trailed off.

He laughed, a chuckle that was not.

"You sound older when you laugh."

"Perhaps I am."

"I must be going."

"Good night, Caroljoy."

"Good night, Lieutenant."

Gerswin watched her slip off the stone wall and onto the grass. His eyes followed her as she circled the pines and took the sheltered path that would lead her back to the side entrance to the club.

He knew the ladies' lounge was off that entrance, and wondered if her father or mother, whoever the senior officer she belonged to was, had suspected where she was.

Caroljoy—a pretty name. He had enjoyed her presence, and her voice.

He glanced down at the empty beaker once again. Should he wait for the orderly? Should he go back to the main bar for a refill? Was he really that thirsty?

There were sure to be the few regulars there, and all would fall silent once he walked in, except for a few conversations in secluded booths. Not one of the handful of junior officers would ever meet his eyes. Few enough had even through the Academy years.

He shook his head and eased himself out of the chair, leaving the beaker on the table.

As he did, as if the slight scraping of his movements had been a signal, the terrace lights went on, destroying the welcome shadow of the night.

Gerswin had to blink hard, squinting his eyes tightly against what seemed glaring floodlights, although he knew that the lighting would have been regarded as dim by most. His eyes were still unaccustomed to abrupt shifts in light intensity.

He held himself erect, refusing to stagger and admit any weakness, as his eyes adjusted and as he continued across the terrace toward the walk away from the club and toward his temporary quarters. He had already tabbed the drinks, the simple juices he had drunk.

For the time, and until he embarked on the *Churchill*, he was billeted in the farthest of the transient officers' quarters from the club, and he was the only one in his entire wing. While he enjoyed the isolation, he doubted that his room assignment was for his personal convenience.

The stone walks were dimly and indirectly lit, for which his eyes were grateful, and he saw no one as he walked the two hundred meters plus toward his billet. On his left were empty rooms, windows blanked and reflecting the glow of the walk lights, and on his right, sloping downhill, was the Terran grass that was no longer native to Old Earth.

From his own quarters a small glow lamp beckoned, and the old style door creaked as he opened it.

The room was empty, as always.

After slipping out of the still-unfamiliar officer's uniform, he stood in the small fresher unit to wash up. Then he pulled a robe around himself and turned to the standard planetside officer's bed. Back came the uniform coverlet, and he piled up two pillows before turning off the lights and stretching out in the darkness.

He had rearranged the furniture in order to be able to view the greens of the valley below from the bed, since the two straight-backed chairs were less than comfortable for any extended period.

Downslope, as his eyes adjusted, he could pick out the faintly luminescent shapes of the glowbirds as they began to dive for the emerging nightworms.

Every so often he could hear the hum of an electrobike making its way up or down the gentle slope that led up to the officers' quarters from the skitter fields and the training areas. The trainee barracks were shielded by an artificial berm, but he could pick out the glow above the darkness of the man-made hills that concealed them.

New Colora was a quiet planet, not that Gerswin minded that, but the stillness grated on some. There was always background music in the club, sometimes loud enough to be heard from his room.

Gerswin's eyes narrowed. Something, someone, had slipped across the corner of his vision. He sat up and put his feet on the floor, more puzzled than alarmed, as he checked the time. Almost local midnight.

He hadn't realized so much time had passed since he'd gotten back to his small billet.

Tap. Tap.

Gerswin sniffed the air automatically and stood, his bare feet welcoming the chill of the floor tiles.

Tap. Tap.

He had seen someone, and that someone was at his door. The tap was gentle, almost delicate, but he did not know any woman, not since Marcella had left with the rest of the Fifteenth. And she'd been a friend, not a lover.

He stood beside the door, ready for anything, he hoped, and opened it.

His mouth dropped.

"Not a word, Lieutenant."

She slipped past him and into the darkened room. When he did not move, she turned, took the edge of the door from his hand and closed it quietly.

A rustling sound followed, and he found her hands unloosening his robe, circling him, and drawing him to her.

"Why . . . ?"

"Don't ask . . . my choice. . . ." And her mouth left no room for words.

He stood, locked against her, returning the warmth of the kiss she had given, his ears pricked for the sound of footsteps, for an outraged parent, a marshal's duty officer. But only silence filled the air outside, silence and the distant murmuring of the birds hunting nightworms.

As that lingering kiss ended, as the outward silence stretched out and outward, he bent and gently, oh, so gently laid her upon the narrow bed, and folded himself into her scent, her warmth, and the huskiness of her murmurings.

He could not have spoken, had he wished to do so, nor would the woman have let him, for while her hands were gentle they were insistent, in the timelessness that is forever between two souls.

Later, much later, when she had gone as silently as she had come, Gerswin stared into the darkness, listening, unable to sleep, unable to dream.

Caroljoy Kerwin. The marshal's daughter. An innocent, he was sure, innocent no longer.

Why him? Why now? Why such intensity?

He was awake as the gray grass turned blue-green with the dawn, his questions still unanswered.

That key from the tower of time? Yes, that one, the one whose pages can unlock the mysteries of the myths? Could any words be that immortal in spanning the gulf between the days of chaos and the quiet order prevailing on Old Earth today?

Not words . . . not exactly, for the key is a small volume of coded entries, the order book of the operations center of Imperial Reclamation Corps base one [Old Earth].

What does it say? The words might be dry, but the stories told between their lines must be grander than the myths that surround them, if we could but decipher those order codes and sterile words.

The Myth of the Rebuilding
Alarde D'Lorina
New Augusta, 4539 N.E.C.

XIX

"FIVE RIGHT," SUGGESTED the voice from the console.

Gerswin eased the stick right.

"Ten right," insisted the distant voice.

Gerswin ignored the latest suggestion as he felt the flitter rock, automatically leveling it while studying the vortex that loomed off the nose and above the ground fog that shrouded the prairie.

"Tall mother . . . ," he muttered, not caring whether the relay was open.

"Scan indicated probable effective height of twenty kilometers."

"Spread?"

"Less than a kay at the spout, maximum before altitude dispersion is eighty kays."

"Range?"

"Twenty kays."

Gerswin wanted to wipe his forehead with the back of his gloved right hand, but did not. Both hands stayed in position, the left on the stick and the right on the thrusters.

Beep!

He glanced at the trim warning and bled enough from the starboard fan to correct the incipient yaw.

"What's the closure?"

"Half kilo a minute."

The pilot shook his head. He was headed east at damned near two hundred kays. The spout was tearing across the high prairie south and westward at more than one fifty.

"We got the data in the cube?"

"Need another five on this heading, Lieutenant." That comment was from the Ops duty officer at Prime Base, although Prime was the only base so far.

"That's cutting it close."

"Your choice. If we don't get another five, then we'll have to scrub and rerun tomorrow."

"What's Met say about tomorrow?"

"Could be worse than today. The jetstream's dropping and dipping south, and the ground level temperature will be higher."

"Hades! We'll do it!"

Beep! Beep!

Gerswin used both the fan bleed and the hydraulic boosted rudders to straighten the yaw while leveling the flitter again.

The purple black of the landspout now filled nearly half of the flitter's windscreen.

"Grit intake at ten percent," announced the console's warning system.

Gerswin could feel the dampness on his forehead.

"Three minutes to go, Lieutenant. Sure you can hold it?"

The voice belonged to Major Sofaer, coming in from Prime.

"Fourth time on the same flamed line. No landspout . . . going to back me out."

"Port thruster in the yellow. Running time three point five."

THUD! THUD!

"Impact on rear port stub. Impact on forward port stub."

"Flame!"

Ding! Ding! Ding!

"Starboard thruster in the yellow. Running time three point five. Port thruster in the yellow. Running time three point zero. Closed system reserve two point four."

THUD! THUD! THUD!

The flitter slewed left, the nose jerking up, then from left to right.

"Multiple impacts, main fuselage."

Twisting full turns into both thrusters, Gerswin stamped nearly full right rudder and leveled the nose again. Then he dropped the power back to eighty percent.

"Prime outrider. Prime outrider. Data's in the cube. In the cube."

"Stet. In the cube. Flaming clear. Flaming clear."

THUD!

Ding! Ding! Ding!

"Starboard thruster in the yellow. Running time two point five. Port thruster in the yellow. Running time two point zero."

Gerswin blinked, blinked again, from the sting of the salty sweat running into the corners of his eyes, even as he completed the left hand bank away from the towering purple vortex of the landspout.

THUD!

Beep! Beep! Beep!

"Grit level at fifteen percent. Five percent power loss on port thruster."

THUD!

"Unidentified impact on forward port stub."

"Flame. Flame. Flame," grunted the pilot.

Gerswin eased the flitter back level and twisted up the power on both thrusters with a half turn more to the left. The sweat kept dripping into the corners of his eyes, but he left both hands in place, gave his head a quick downward snap to drop the helmet's impact visor.

The purple of the spout dominated almost the entire armaglass windscreen.

Gerswin flicked his eyes to the lower right corner of the bubble toward a spot where the ground fog had thinned momentarily.

Had he seen some sort of structure?

He caught himself before he shook his head, resuming his normal scan of the instruments.

THUD!

Beep! Beep!

"Impact on upper starboard stub."

"Grit level approaching twenty percent."

"You've got one minute, Lieutenant. Just one."

"Stet, Prime. Stet."

Ding! Ding! Ding!

"Impact on the rear port stub."

"Grit level at fifteen percent and dropping."

"Prime outrider. Wind sheer at ten kilos, two nine five and closing."

Gerswin glanced at the homer. Fifty-six kays to Prime.

"Interrogative closure rate."

"Three point five per minute."

"Interrogative course line of the sheer front. Interrogative sheer angle."

"Sheer angle unknown. Course line estimated at one zero five."

"Stet. One zero five."

The pilot edged his own course to two eight five, lifted the flitter's nose, and twisted in full turns.

"Grit level at twelve percent and dropping."

With the flitter stable for a moment, Gerswin snapped his head to retract the helmet's impact visor, and with his left hand wiped the sweat away from his eyes, and off his forehead.

That done, he snapped the clear impact visor back in place.

"Should have opted for arcdozers," he muttered.

"Where would the glory be, Lieutenant?"

"Thanks, York. Thanks, loads."

"Grit level at ten percent and stable. Permanent power loss at ten percent."

Gerswin frowned. The fans in both thrusters would have to be repolished and retuned. Either that, or replaced with another set, if there was one to be had.

"Prime outrider. Less than one minute to sheer impact."

The pilot's eyes flickered from the thrust indicators to the balance lines, to the speed readouts, to the radalt, and down to the VSI, which still indicated a constant rate of climb.

He took a deep breath, exhaled slowly, and squared himself in the padded shell seat.

"Stand by for impact."

Even as he glanced through the armaglass of the canopy at the indistinctness of the western hills, blurred as they were from the clouds and the fog, the flitter lurched, throwing him against the broad harness straps.

Not only his stomach, but the instrument balance lines showed the flitter nearly ninety degrees nose down. The VSI pegged momentarily, then dropped back to a descent rate of two hundred fifty meters per second.

Gerswin twisted the thruster throttles around the detente into overload while bringing the stick back into his lap.

"Ground impact in fifteen seconds!" screeched the console.

A thousand kilos piled onto Gerswin's muscles and slender frame, and his vision blurred around the edges.

"Ground impact in thirty seconds!" screeched the console mindlessly.

Whhheeeeeeee!

"Prime outrider. Interrogative status. Interrogative status!"

"Stuff your status," he grunted without keying his transmitter. Instead, he eased the stick forward and to the left to bring the flitter level and back on course for Prime Base. Next came the down-throttling of the thrusters.

"Prime outrider. Interrogative status. Interrogative status."

Gerswin sighed.

"Status summary. Flying strike. Flying strike. Fusilage overstressed. Fans set for repolishing. Assorted external damage. Flitter down. I say again. Flitter down."

"Interrogative ETA."

"Estimate arrival in fifteen plus."

"Understand fifteen plus. Interrogative special procedures."

"Prime Base, that is negative this time."

Gerswin sighed again and checked the homer. Forty kays to go, and the screens showed clear skies between him and the foothills base.

Clear skies between him and base, but not overhead, where the high clouds still brooded. Clear sky, except for the ground fog.

He readjusted the thrusters and returned to his normal scanning pattern.

Another few minutes and he would begin the landing check list.

GERSWIN TOOK ANOTHER step toward the Maze.

Did he want to go through the twisting and turning tunnels, where anything might wait in the upper reaches? Or where rats the size of Imperial cats lurked in the darkness for their next chance at dinner?

He laughed. There was no reason to face the Maze, not while wearing an Imperial uniform and stunner, but the old instincts died hard.

Overhead, the clouds rolled eastward in banks of darkened gray, but the air was dry and cold.

He circled more to the north, along the outcroppings that felt like rock, but were, instead, massed metal and bricks and compressed purple-red clay. Between the upthrust chunks grew an occasional patch of the purple grass or a small grubush, with its thin branches and straggly leaves.

Eventually he had worked his way north and west far enough to get around the pile of rubble from which the Maze rose southward and stood in the cleared area beneath the northern wall of the shambletown. He stood looking southward and uphill to the roughly four meter height of the shambletown wall, running as it did slightly more than half a kay from the eastern end of the Maze to the western corner.

The shambletowners kept the area immediately downslope of the wall clear of debris, grubushes, and skinned carcasses. The debris and bushes offered too much concealment for both rats and coyotes, while carcasses, those too poisonous to eat, would have attracted the rats.

His nose twitched. In the confines of the more fastidious Imperial society, the odors were muted. Machine oil and deodorants, while strong, were blandly dulling as well. The mix of unwashed shambletowners, excrement, assorted garbage, and the underlying bitter stench of omnipresent rat all reached him, although he was well outside the walls and a good three hundred meters east of the gate.

The lone wall sentry had marked the Imperial uniform and passed the word, so well that by the time he had reached the gate, several others awaited him.

One—older by years than the last time they had crossed paths— he recognized immediately. Fynian, still squat and hulking, stood behind the conslor. Gerswin had not met the conslor, not this one or any of his predecessors, and he was amused by the indrawn breath as the man looked into his eyes.

While the conslor said nothing, Gerswin could hear Fynian's muttered "devulkid."

"Lieutenant Gerswin, Imperial Service," he announced.

"Conslor Weddin. What you want?" answered the other in clipped shambletalk.

"Want see shamble," Gerswin replied in kind, even getting the lilts in the right places.

"Devulkid," repeated Fynian under his breath, loudly enough for Gerswin to hear clearly.

"All right, stand? No kill, stand? No woman, stand?"

Loosely translated, "You're welcome, but keep your hands off everyone, and don't try to make off with anyone's woman or all bets are off."

"No kill. No woman, stand," repeated the pilot. "You no kill, no fun, stand?"

Conslor Weddin frowned. That a visitor should place reciprocal conditions on a shambletowner was unheard of.

As the conslor debated, Gerswin discarded the idea of displaying the stunner and its powers. Using it would only induce some idiot to try to take it. He wished he had developed a few other weapons skills besides stunners, lasers, and hand-to-hand. None were exactly suited to his situation. The Imperial policy stated clearly that advanced and lethal weapons were prohibited for use against any civilians. And hand-to-hand combat was chancy merely as a display of force.

At last the conslor, presumably after meditating on the flitters and skitters that crossed the cloud-covered skies, nodded.

"Stand."

Gerswin bared his teeth in response, and to signify his agreement.

Weddin and his party stood aside, but Gerswin motioned for them to precede him, which, after a moment's delay, they did.

Inside the gate, a cobbled-together mass of twisted metal and woven grubush that screeched as it was dragged back into place, the stench was as high as Gerswin had remembered. He swallowed hard to keep the contents of his stomach in place and thanked himself for his foresight in eating only a light meal before setting out.

The one-, two-, and occasional three-story clay brick buildings were crammed together, with narrow streets, narrower alleyways. Unlike the plains clay, the building clay was reddish-brown, without the purple tint that usually signified some degree of landpoison.

The pilot nodded. He had seen the outside clayworks often enough, had even stolen a food basket or two from the clayworkers as they turned the clay into a slurry and let it settle, then repeated the process time after time.

The "finished" clay was lightly fired in grubush-fueled ovens. Once the bricks were mortared in place, the walls were covered with a sandpaint mixture that hardened the bricks further and gave both interior and exterior walls a dingy white appearance. The few times the sun did shine, the walls sparkled, and that sparkle gave the shambletown a glitter totally unwarranted by its interior occupants, human and otherwise.

All the houses in the upper shamble, the newer section, had porches, not for people, but for the continual plant flats, designed to allow in light but not the continual rain or ice rain. The precipitation was collected off the inclined roofs and funneled to either the clay collecting barrels or the main settling ponds.

Outside of the stink of unwashed bodies, the people appeared relatively healthy, though uniformly thin. The men all had beards, usually straggly. An occasional limp or twisted arm showed a broken bone that had not set properly.

From the open space inside the gate, Gerswin strolled down the narrow street toward the square, watching to see if Conslor Weddin continued to keep an eye upon him.

The square, an oblong paved with rough stone fragments and measuring no more than forty by sixty meters, contained only a single platform, used for a variety of purposes, surmised Gerswin. It was vacant except for a few passersby, and for Gerswin and Fynian, who had apparently been instructed to follow the Imperial officer.

The muted sounds of children drew Gerswin to a freestanding porch off the southwest corner of the square, where close to a dozen toddlers were gathered. Gerswin stood by the brick wall enclosing the space under the roof and watched.

Two children, dressed solely in rough stained leather tunics, used miniature clay bricks to build a wall. Behind them, an even smaller child sat on the smooth brick flooring and sucked on the end of a wooden rattle. None of the children's hair appeared more than roughly cut, nor did any wear more than a loin cloth and sleeveless, patched-together leather over-tunics, despite the brisk breeze. The chill from the morning's frost had yet to leave the air.

A somewhat older child sat on the bricks at the feet of a shriveled and gray-haired woman and used a battered wooden pipe to produce a series of shrill squeaks, some of which resembled musical notes.

A toddler barely able to walk caught sight of the gray Imperial tunic and the touches of silver-embroidered insignia on his collars and pointed at the clean-shaven pilot.

"Ummm! Ummm!"

Gerswin looked at the wide gray eyes, and finally grinned.

She frowned and closed her mouth. Finally, she repeated the phrase again. "Ummmm!"

The wind shifted, and a new stench wrenched at Gerswin's gut, an acidic odor burning into his nostrils from the lower section of the shambletown.

He took a last look at the toddler, waved, and turned toward the half dozen steps that stretched the three meter width of the street that led southward to the older part of the shambles.

"Ummmm! Ummmm!" Was there a plaintive ring to those words?

Gerswin nearly stumbled on the first step, but caught himself and continued downward.

The street remained level for another fifty meters, flanked on both sides by the relatively newer and larger dwellings of the upper section, before narrowing at the top of another set of steps.

The officer could hear the uneven sound of Fynian's dragging limp as they continued downward.

Beyond the second set of steps, the narrow grid pattern of the upper shambletown dissolved into the twisting lanes of the lower town. The houses were no longer uniformly sand-painted, since in places the old facade had crumbled or been washed away.

More plant flats appeared in sheltered and glassless windows or on rooftops under patched old leather tenting, rather than in the relatively ordered porticos of the upper town. But the relative silence prevailed—a few whispers, a word here and there among the handful of people passing in the lanes, and few shambletowners at all.

Gerswin nodded. The old patterns had not changed, not yet, and perhaps never.

He turned down a lane he thought he remembered, glancing over his shoulder to see if Fynian still followed. The old guard trailed ten meters back, mumbling under his breath.

From a crossing lane appeared a woman, carrying an empty pottery crock half as tall as she was.

Gerswin stepped back barely in time to avoid colliding with her, intent as he had been on watching Fynian and trying to recall the path he had taken the single other time he had traversed the shambletown.

Like the others, the woman wore the sleeveless patchwork tunic that reached halfway between waist and knee, with a braided leather neckring to signify she had a mate.

She stumbled as well, and her eyes involuntarily made a momentary contact with Gerswin's.

As she recovered her jar and her balance, she froze, as if afraid to move either toward or away from Gerswin.

Gerswin stepped back another pace, until his back brushed the wall behind him, then walked around her, and continued on his way as if nothing had happened.

"Devulkid," explained Fynian in a rasping whisper, as he in turn passed her in his shadow trail of the Imperial pilot.

In the quiet broken only by murmurs and whispers, her indrawn breath whistled in the still morning air.

Gerswin shook his head and followed the lane through another series of turns, glancing upward at a familiar window only in passing, as he moved into totally unfamiliar regions of the lower area. He glimpsed a gray head through one window and a shadowy figure through another, but did not stop or increase his pace.

In the dimness of the lower shamble his breath formed a thin white cloud, like his own personal ground fog.

At the next turn, the reek of the leatherworks jarred him to a halt with the solidity of a wall.

He smiled, ruefully, and turned to the left. The last thing he needed was an in-depth look at or smell of the facility that converted rat and coyote and other skins into the leather that was one of the few materials resistant to the acidity of the rain.

The eastern end of the lower shamble ended abruptly in a three meter wide cleared space, followed by a two meter high wall. Beyond and above the wall, he could see the twisted beams and heaped bricks, stone, and clay where the Maze towered.

The single eastern gate, barred and manned by a single sentry, was to his right. He did not approach it, but turned back toward the upper town, seeking another route to avoid retracing a path close to the tannery.

Fynian followed, still mumbling and muttering, every third word some pejorative elaboration on "devulkid."

Three twists later, Gerswin halted at the small open area surrounding the covered settling ponds that ran like steps from the upper side of the shambletown into the lower section.

The woman he had upset earlier was at the lowest pond, along with a boy and an old woman. All three had brought large crockery vessels and were skimming water from the open section of the pond and pouring it into their own crocks.

Without retracing his steps or passing the three, he did not see any way to return to the upper square and the northern gate. So he waited in the gloom, his breath still a thin fog in the chill that seldom left the narrow lanes until late in the summer afternoons.

The older woman was the first to leave, staggering under the burden of the water.

The boy, who bore a smaller crock, was next.

Finally, the brown-haired woman finished dipping into the pond and stepped away, gracefully, Gerswin noted. She tugged and eased the heavy pottery vessel into a harness. Despite the lack of light, he could see the cleanness of her profile clearly.

For reasons he would not try to understand, for an instant he was reminded of another moment in darkness, another silence in time, another woman in another place barely familiar to him.

He shook his head to clear the image.

Caroljoy? To see her again? Not likely. Not at all likely, and even less likely that he would be successful if he made such an attempt.

A cough, and the whispered "devulkid," distracted Gerswin, called him back to the present, all at once. He glanced over his shoulder to see Fynian, still four meters behind him, like a tracking coyote, eyes bright.

When Gerswin looked back at the settling pools, the woman was gone. He shrugged and started for the steps that rose beside them to the level of the upper shambletown.

Behind him the shuffle of uneven steps reminded him that Fynian followed, stalking the devilkid through the shambletown.

Gerswin regained the square, this time from the northeastern corner and glanced over at the covered portico where the children had earlier played. They still played, from the sounds and motions, but he started for the northern gate from the far side of the square, avoiding the children, and the toddler who had cried out, "Ummm!"

The walls and the narrow streets felt more like a prison with each passing step, and he wanted out.

Forcing himself to maintain an ambling walk, he continued toward the gate, ears alert for any change in Fynian's conduct or pace.

The gate was closed, but the two guards leaped to push open the massive patchwork as if they were all too ready for the Imperial stranger to depart.

Gerswin could hear from the sounds behind him that Fynian was moving closer, but he was surprised that the older man followed him outside the shambletown and onto the flat beneath the wall.

Gerswin faced the shambletowner and watched Fynian pull a stone from his pouch as the gate squealed shut.

"No kill, stand?" Gerswin snapped sarcastically, as Fynian straightened the sling straps.

"Devulkid out shamble."

Gerswin pulled the stunner.

Thrummmm!

The sling and stone dropped on the hard clay, followed by the inert form of the shambletowner.

Both guards peered over the wall from their posts beside the gate.

"Guard. No kill, stand? Fynian try kill. Dreamtime, stand?"

Gerswin kept the stunner in full view until he was certain both guards understood that the shambletowner was only stunned. He retreated downhill, pace by pace, facing the wall as the gate squealed ajar and a single guard ventured out and began to drag the unconscious Fynian within, by his foot.

Gerswin glanced toward the discarded sling and stone, then at the closed gate and blank wall. Blank, as it had always been.

He turned and walked down the long slope through the scattered bushes and to the north.

THE PILOT PEERED into the work area.

"Still down?"

"Yes. It's still down," answered the gray-clad technician. "Some of the fans looked like fuel strainers, and we have one gilder/polisher. That was meant for touch-up work, not for rebuilding an entire fan structure. That's just the beginning.

"There's the frame. Not a single millimeter that doesn't need restressing. Got to be more than a half-million creds of damage."

Gerswin frowned, then let his face clear.

"How long?"

The tech put down her analyzer probe and turned to face the pilot.

"Lieutenant Gerswin, we do our very best. So do you, in your own way. But our ancestors, Istvenn take their souls, left a forsaken mess. No one ever designed atmospheric crafts to fly through stone rains and acid winds and come out intact." She looked down at the already stained permatile flooring.

"Is it our home, anymore? If they didn't tell us so, I'd never have guessed. Purple-shaded grass, where it grows, and ground fog that can eat your lungs." Her eyes came up to meet his. "How you ever got this back, I couldn't guess. And how long it will take to rebuild it would be a bigger guess."

"Thanks," Gerswin said softly, before turning away from the tech and the battered flitter. "Thanks."

He could feel her dark eyes on his back as he walked from the temporary hangar-bunker that served more as a mechanical infirmary than as a maintenance facility.

"Four flitters, and not a one fit to fly."

His steps echoed as he entered the underground tunnel back to the administrative building, buried, like all the others, in the clay and native stone.

Even though the portal to the ecological laboratory was open, he rapped on the wall, as if he were knocking at another officer's private quarters.

No answer. He rapped the metal bulkhead harder.

Finally, he stepped inside.

As it often happened, he found the two consoles humming, but unattended, and the swivels all empty. He scanned the telltales on the airlock control chambers, but the indicators on five were amber. Number three blinked both green and amber.

That was where Mahmood had to be.

He slumped into one of the swivels opposite a busily humming console to wait, tapping his fingers lightly on the console and whistling a slow dirge.

Gerswin ignored the cycling of the lock and kept whistling without looking up, even as the ecologist finished unsuiting and racking his labsuit in one of the dozen wall lockers.

"That's cheerful . . . about as uplifting as the subsonics on a hell-burner." Mahmood Dalgati clicked the locker shut and straightened his impeccable whites before settling himself in the armless swivel behind the farther console, tapping out a series of inquiries on the screen.

"That's the way I feel."

"I take it that the flitters are all down?"

"Right. You know that. They've been down for days."

Senior Lieutenant Dalgati did not immediately reply, but pursed his lips as an entry scripted itself upon his screen.

Gerswin resumed his dirgelike whistling.

"Greg."

Gerswin stopped the whistling.

"You and your whistling can depress anyone. I'd suggest another theme, but whatever it was, it would probably get on my nerves. I take it you want to talk."

"No."

"Oh . . . you want to fly, to feel productive."

Gerswin shrugged.

"You can't. Not unless you can figure out how to repair the flitters better and faster than the techs. So why don't you put that overtrained, but undereducated and underused mind of yours to work instead of haunting the poor techs?"

Gerswin did not resume his whistling, but kept tapping his fingers on the edge of the console.

"Now you're feeling sorry for yourself, that you're just a poor barbarian from Old Earth, that no one understands you."

"Mahmood. . . ."

The ecologist laughed, gently. "Please don't bother with your dangerous voice. I'm well aware that, as a relatively untrained Service officer, your reflexes make you about twice as deadly as the average Corpus Corps officer."

"You exaggerate, Mahmood." Gerswin returned the laugh, his initial bark subsiding to a chuckle, although he did not sound amused. "Are you suggesting something?"

"I suggest nothing, my underactive friend. All things come to those who wait, particularly if they understand what they're waiting for."

"Ridiculous."

"No. Realistic. One's expectations color the surrounding world, and yours more than most. You have yet to learn what to expect, or what you want to expect.

"Have you ever studied the tapes of the Old Earth master painters? Or read the old Anglish poets in the original? Studied the old and outdated terrain maps? Tried to understand the ecology before it collapsed?

"Do you want your planet restored? Or do you want to badger the techs?"

Gerswin straightened up in the swivel.

"So I have to know what I want, is that it? What difference does it make?"

"I wouldn't put it quite that way. Permit me to digress momentarily, my friend."

"You always do." Gerswin leaned forward in the swivel, then tilted himself farther backward.

Mahmood pursed his lips and looked down at his screen. He touched the keyboard in several places until he was satisfied. Finally, he stood. Circling to his left, he looked at Gerswin, halting behind his console. The effect was undeniably that of a professor behind his podium.

"Right now, Greg, you're little more than a step above those barbarians you call shambletowners."

Another short bark issued from the pilot. "That's probably more than some would grant me."

"You are marvelously trained in techniques, and better trained than that in some weapons, but your mind has never considered the reasons for such training."

"Mahmood, spare me the rationalizations and the philosophy. If a flitter is up, it's up. If it's down, it's down. If it can be fixed, then you fix it."

"And if it can't be fixed, you give up?"

"You don't fly."

"Do you need to fly? Isn't there more than one route to a destination? Do you always have to rely on the biggest or the fastest or the latest piece of machinery?"

"Don't ask such stupid questions. You're humoring me, and I'm not in the mood for being humored." Gerswin was out of his seat, circling the other side of the office. "I'm flying through trash because no one else seems to be able to get even one damned data run. Because no one can program the dozers without terrain data. Because we're going to run out of time . . ."

The blond man with the eyes of a hawk turned on the professor and jabbed a finger. "You can sit and lecture. Or stand and lecture. Puzzle the riddles of the universe. Take forever to find the perfect solution. Right now, good old Terra is a curiosity. Oh, yes, the wonderful Empire will fix her up good. Now. What about tomorrow? Is it going to last? How long? How many flitters? How many dozers? How many young techs and pilots will they let good old Mother Earth murder before the great, grand, and glorious Empire gives up?"

"There's nothing of worth left. No cheap metals. No radioactives. Nothing grows."

Gerswin picked up a swivel one-handed, holding it at arm's length.

"Look, Mahmood! Look! Now, how long can I hold this thing? Twice, three times as long as you can? Ten times? After some time I have to put it down. So . . . old Terra has an emotional hold on the Empire. For now. But what happens when the next Emperor has to let go? What happens if they put us down before the ecology is fixed?"

His voice softened to a whisper as he replaced the swivel on the tiles.

"Nobody thinks I think, just that I react."

He stared across the office at the ecologist, who had involuntarily retreated until his back had touched the row of wall lockers.

"Maybe I will read some of the old poets . . . and look at the old master painters. Maybe I will . . . and maybe I'll learn more weapons and the philosophy behind them. It just might make me angrier. But I'll take your advice, Mahmood, until everything is trained. And I'll read everything I haven't read. And then we'll see."

His voice sounded more like the call of the hawk he resembled as he concluded, "Then we'll see."

The ecologist wiped his damp forehead in the silence of the laboratory where he stood alone.

XXII

GERSWIN TOUCHED THE inner portal stud and stepped through the endurasteel arch as the door irised open. The inner and outer portal arrangement that led outside reminded him of an airlock.

He laughed once, aware of the sharp echo from the composite blue walls of the small chamber, and touched the second stud.

As the exterior portal opened, he marched through the center, out into the chill of the twilight, the wind ripping through his uncovered hair, the fine dust gritting against his skin like a continual abrasive.

Once outside, he kept walking eastward over the hard and uncovered clay, the reddish purple like solidified blood in the dim light that signified the sun's descent behind the shadows of the mountains to the west.

He stumbled as his right boot caught in a depression concealed by the heavier dust that took nearly a landspout to lift. He lurched, but regained his balance without slowing his pace.

Each meter forward took him that much farther away from the sheltering bulk of the artificial ridge under which the administration complex was housed.

Looking to the south, he could see the general outlines of the next artificial ridge, the one that contained the hangar bunkers.

When the ground dipped toward a dust-filled ravine, he stopped. No telling how deep the gully was under the heavy dust.

With the adjustment of his eyes to the darkness and his hearing to relative stillness, Gerswin turned back to face northeast, where remained the shambletown, the Maze, and what was left of the ruins. The Denv ruins were one of the few clusters left on the Noram continent, protected from the worst of the landspouts by the natural depression in which the old city had been built, and by the closeness of the foothills and the mountains behind.

His breath left a trail. The freezing temperature would have chilled most Imperials, but Gerswin was more than comfortable in his light jacket and flight suit, free of the continual pressure of people and walls.

Strange how he never noticed the crowding until he took the time to step away from it.

He began to walk north, lengthening his strides until the ground seemed to melt away under the quick steps, until the bulk of the artificial hills dwindled away behind him and he was exposed to the full bite of the wind cutting in from the plains.

A rustle in the bushes to his right signaled a rat scurrying away, dropping into a hole leading beneath the surface and into what Gerswin imagined was an intertwining of rubble, animal tunnels, and undamaged foundations long since covered and forgotten beneath the hilly terrain above.

A low series of isolated bulges appeared to his left. Gerswin slowed, then stopped, and studied the evenness of the spacing.

He stepped toward the uprisings, each waist-high, each circular and perhaps a meter across. Bending down, he squinted, then ran his fingers over the powdered smoothness. The pressure caused more of the white powder to flake off.

Gerswin studied the low pillars. The sides toward the mountains were relatively straight, but the eastern sides sloped outward as they neared the ground, the weathering clearly directional in nature.

He began to walk westward, then turned north again, his eyes piercing the dark and running over each pillar he passed. After completing a quick circuit of the area, Gerswin pursed his lips. The thick pillars covered an area nearly a half a kilometer square.

He didn't know whether to be more impressed by the size of the structure they had supported, or by the fact that nothing but what appeared to be the foundation remained.

Shaking his head, he turned his steps back to the north and the ridge ahead, from which, if he remembered correctly, he could survey the territory he had once foraged.

Under his light steps, as the temperature dropped, the ground began to squeak. The wind's whisper rose to a thin whine to match the cutting edge it turned upon the rolling hills and the man who walked them toward a ridge top.

Gerswin ignored the sound of his footsteps and the familiar song of the night wind as he trotted up the increasing incline toward the lookout, toward the ledge he remembered, where, in the darkness, a careful devilkid could watch the coyotes slink out of the hills toward the edges of the shambletown in their efforts to drag down an unsuspecting towner, or watch the movements of the ratpacks from the hidden tunnels that were all that had remained of the city that had stretched for kays along the front of the hills.

He patted the pair of stunners tucked inside his jacket. While neither should be necessary, to be prepared for the unnecessary was how he had survived outside the walls of the shambletown for so long, away from the guards, the walls, and the fires, and away from the scrawny plants that grew in carefully purified soil beds.

A two-toned whistle added a mournful air to the song of the wind, to the darkness of the starless night, as the man who had been a devilkid slipped up the trail to a view of his past.

"RED THREE! RED three! Lieutenant Gerswin to the Ops center. Lieutenant Gerswin to the Ops center. Red three!"

Gerswin yanked on his boots and palmed the exit panel stud, ignoring the chimes from his own console. He could learn more once he was in Operations.

Moving through the portal at double time, he twisted and flipped himself to the side to avoid the other man in the corridor.

"Excuse me, Commander." The pilot snapped off a quick salute.

"Don't mind me, Mister Gerswin. Just get to Ops."

"Yes, ser," Gerswin said over his shoulder.

He could see Commander Lancolnia's reflection in the metallic joints between the building sections. The commander was still shaking his head as Gerswin turned the corner toward the tunnel from his quarters to the Ops center.

While Operations was protected by a double portal, only a single guard was stationed at the entry console, not surprisingly, since the entire complex was secured, built to take the worst the weather and the locals—what few ventured from the shambletown—could dish out.

"Lieutenant Gerswin."

He offered his pass and slammed his palm onto the console screen.

"Captain Matsuko said for you to meet him at G.C., ser."

"Thank you."

"Yes, ser."

Gerswin went through the portals on a double bounce, feet scarcely touching the tiles.

Ground control was fifty meters down the operations corridor, directly beneath the low control tower that crouched over the bunker. The tower monitored both the flitter approaches, as well as the infrequent shuttles from the few I.S.S. ships to visit Old Earth.

Captain Matsuko was waiting, standing behind the three consoles monitoring the flitters and the field traffic.

"Interrogative power status, Outrider three. Interrogative power status."

"Port thruster in the yellow. Point seven zero. Starboard in the red. Point five zero and falling."

Matsuko drew Gerswin aside.

"Zeigler took three out, with Frantz as copilot. Topographic profiles, shot at an angle, for the ecologists. Zeigler hit a sheer line wrong, forgot to lock his harness, hit the overhead. Out cold."

"You need me to get her back? Talk her in?"

"Stet."

Gerswin pulled a seat up to the center console and scanned the screens, trying to assimilate the position of the disabled flitter and the meteorological data.

Without thinking, his head was shaking.

"Outrider three, Gerswin here. Interrogative full power on starboard thruster."

"Point five at the detente."

"Interrogative altitude and airspeed."

"Altitude is one thousand minus. Airspeed is one fifty. Rate of descent is one hundred per minute on full power. Estimated time on starboard thruster is two to five minutes."

Gerswin looked at Matsuko, blanking the comm link.

"She's over the rock piles. Take her more than six minutes to clear."

His eyes took in the displays, measuring, trying to calculate a vector to the flatlands or even the plains hills that would not force her to cross the sheer line again.

The line that had crippled the pilot and the flitter was nearly stationary, due east of Outrider three.

"Turn one six five."

"Turning one six five. Power on starboard thruster is point four and falling. Power on port is point six. Altitude above ground nine hundred minus."

Gerswin watched as the blip, representing the flitter edged more southward toward the flattest terrain possible.

"Outrider three. Lag factor on that radalt is fifty meters. Lag factor is fifty meters."

"Stet. Lag factor is fifty."

"Interrogative status on tail compensator. Status on compensator."

"Tail compensator—what . . . ?"

"Status of tail compensator." Gerswin's fingers curled around the console keyboard's edge, digging in, but his voice remained level.

"Compensator has no reading. Crew visual indicates no compensator."

"Stet. No compensator. Begin blade deployment sequence. I say again. Begin blade deployment sequence."

"Stet. Beginning blade deployment sequence."

"Outrider three. When the blades lock, hit the power disconnect. As soon as the blades lock, hit the power disconnect, and dump the thrusters. Do you understand?"

"Blades locked, hit the disconnect . . . dump thrusters."

"That's affirmative. No power descent. Pick out the levelest spot you can dead ahead. Keep your nose down. Radalt hits one fifty, you flare. Flare at one fifty. At one hundred, pull full-blade angle. One hundred, full-blade angle."

"Stet. Power flare at one fifty, full-blade angle at one hundred."

"That's affirmative."

Matsuko's hand blanked the comm link.

"What are you doing?"

Gerswin did not take his eyes off the console.

"No power for a turn, not without hitting the sheer line. Not enough power or time to cross the rock ridge ahead. No compensator for a powered blade descent. Flat rock auto is the best I can do."

He brushed Matsuko's hands from the console.

"Interrogative altitude, airspeed."

"Passing four hundred at one hundred." The woman's voice was low, but clear and steady.

"Nose up. Nose up, three. Airspeed at sixty to seventy as you pass two hundred."

"Stet. Nose up. Passing two fifty, airspeed, eighty."

"Nose down a shade."

"Stet. Nose down. Speed seventy."

"Flare at one fifty. Flare at one fifty."

"Flaring—"

The transmission ended as if cut by a knife.

Gerswin stood so abruptly the swivel slammed and clattered into the console behind.

"Was that a transmission loss?" asked a new voice.

Gerswin shook his head, slowly, forcing himself to unclench his tightened fists. He looked at the two console screens, then at the floor.

Matsuko looked at Gerswin's face, then snapped. "Is two ready to lift?"

"Yes, ser."

"Launch and vector to three's last position. Medic on board?"

"That's affirmative, ser."

"Launch."

"Two. Outrider two, this is Opswatch. Cleared to lift. Vector to target is three four five. Three four five."

"Opswatch, Outrider two, lifting. Will be turning three four five."

Gerswin looked at the met screen, then at Matsuko.

"Captain, that vector's wrong. They'll cross the sheer line."

The tech on the end console began computing.

"He's right."

"Outrider two. Course correction. Course correction. Sheer line at three five zero. Turn two seven zero. Two seven zero."

"Thanks, Opswatch. Turning two seven zero. How long this course?"

"Outrider two. Estimate five minutes, then a vector of zero zero five."

"Stet. Turning two seven zero. Climbing to one thousand. Climbing to one thousand."

"Understand climbing to one thousand."

Gerswin took his eyes away from the screens and stepped farther back, still shaking his head slowly, as if unable to believe that the flitter had crashed into the rocky flats northwest of the Imperial base.

". . . killer planet . . . Istvenn take it. . . ."

". . . the lieutenant couldn't . . . no one could have . . ."

Gerswin's steps took him to the backless couch outside Matsuko's office, and he sat down, staring at nothing, trying not to think about how Miri Frantz must have felt as the flitter mashed into the rocky up-thrusts with both forward speed and a descent rate approaching a thousand meters a minute.

But what else could he have suggested? Leaving her on thrusters would have plowed her into solid rock at nearly two hundred kays. If only he'd tried to get a better reading on the actual terrain slope. . . . But there had been so little time.

If he'd been there. . . . But he wouldn't have flown through a sheer line unprepared.

". . . have the target in sight . . ."

Gerswin's ears caught the transmission from Outrider two, and he jerked himself erect, walking back to the control area, standing quietly behind the swivel where Captain Matsuko sat.

"Understand you have the target in sight?"

"That's affirmative. Deploying blades now."

"Stet. Understand blade deployment."

The console was silent, with only a single amber blip, motionless, as the flitter began its descent.

"Interrogative target status."

"Opswatch. Target has sustained maximum structural damage. Maximum structural damage."

Matsuko winced. Gerswin and the other pilots understood the implications of the shorthand expression.

Maximum structural damage to the flitter meant maximum struc-tural damage to the crew.

A hush dropped over the operations area, as the surrounding techs and officers waited.

"Opswatch. Hovering over target. Lowering medic. Preliminary indication is that target crew totally immobile. Totally immobile. Will report later."

"Stet, two. Standing by for later report."

Gerswin took a last glance at the screens and moved away until he was in the silent and open corridor between the comm consoles and the now-vacant administrative section of Operations.

He knew the results, but hoped against hope that someone, somehow, had survived the crash, even though flitters did not carry the same crash capsules as shuttles.

The muted sound of murmurs in the control section died away enough that Gerswin could hear the last of Outrider two's transmis-sion.

". . . say again, no survivors . . ."

The I.S.S. lieutenant took a deep breath, squared his shoulders, and started toward the exit portal. He needed to be alone.

Ignoring the sound of steps behind him, he reached the portal before Matsuko touched his arm.

Gerswin stopped.

Matsuko gestured, as if to pull him aside, and the lieutenant followed.

"Greg. You did the best you could, the best anyone could have."

Gerswin swallowed.

"I made a mistake. Wouldn't have if I'd been in the cockpit, but so hard to do through comm link."

"Mistake?"

"Radalt has vertical and horizontal lag. Makes a difference in rugged terrain. She wasn't experienced enough to look beyond the heads-up to gauge terrain. Can't do that over remote."

He shook his head again.

Matsuko shook his head slowly in reply. "I liked Zeigler, and . . . Miri . . . you know . . . but, you . . . Can't you not . . ."

Gerswin looked at the polished tiles of the floor, knowing Matsuko had broken off his response and was studying his face.

"Look, Greg. Nobody else could have given her half a chance."

"Half wasn't enough."

"No. But unless you can find another dozen like you, it's better than she would have gotten otherwise. Zeigler bent orbit, not you. You even had enough sense to keep the recovery bird from doing the same thing. Don't forget that."

Gerswin said nothing.

Matsuko patted him on the shoulder.

"You try too hard to be perfect. Do the best you can, but don't expect perfection on everything, all the time, even when lives are at stake. That's a bigger trap. Think about it."

Matsuko stepped back to let Gerswin leave.

Gerswin could feel the deputy ops boss's eyes on his back long after the portal had closed between them, long after he had retreated to his quarters.

"TELL ME, GREG. Does the flitter do what you want? Or do you make it do what you want?"

Mahmood scarcely looked up from his console as he asked the question.

"What does that mean? Another theoretical question?" snapped Gerswin, still wearing his flight gear.

"Not so theoretical as you think. Presumably, you have a goal in mind. You seem to assume that the goal is independent of the means."

"No. Even a dumb devilkid knows that the means will influence the end." The pilot took four steps away from the console, turned, and paced back toward the biologist.

"Then why don't you apply that knowledge to your flight techniques? Without looking at the maintenance records, I'd be willing to bet that while you have the best record of accomplishment, you also have the record of most damage to equipment."

"Mahmood, have you ever tried to fly gently through the fringes of a landspout? Or to gather data through stone rains and acid winds?"

"Have you?"

"I've flown through everything."

"Gently?"

"You don't understand."

"Greg. I'm not fighting you. You are fighting yourself."

"Fighting myself?" Gerswin paced toward the blank inner wall, and turned before reaching it, pacing back toward the man and the console.

"There are at least two ways to do anything. Usually, the best way requires both the most understanding and the most direct application of that understanding. Very few people are capable of that. Mostly frustrated athletes."

Gerswin frowned. Again, the philosophical biologist refused to get to the point. He didn't know why he ended up coming back to listen all the time. Except . . . he brushed the thought aside.

"Frustrated athletes? Would you stop to explain that?"

"No. Not unless you will consider stopping to listen, and begin by stopping that continuous pacing. Sit down."

Gerswin sighed. Loudly, and partly for effect. He let himself thud into the low couch, turn, and let one leg dangle over the arm as he faced the other.

The biologist straightened behind the console, and, for the first time, concentrated directly on the pilot.

"Greg, think about it this way. Our military culture tends to separate people into those who can build or repair things and those who use them. You are a pilot and an officer, trained to understand enough about technology and people to use both. Your techs understand how to repair things, but not really enough about their missions for you to be able to use their products to the fullest degree possible."

Mahmood waited.

Finally, Gerswin answered.

"So you think I'm just a user? That it's bad to be just a user?"

"I never said that. Nor did I say that you were. I merely made an observation on the training imparted by our system. Would you say that what you do with a flitter requires as much as you can get from the machine?"

"Sometimes more."

"Have you really ever studied the flitter? From each single composite plate up? From a series of stress vectors? Have you ever tried to rebuild one with the technicians?"

"Of course not. I'm not a tech."

Again, Mahmood waited.

"Where are you going? What are you asking? You telling me that I ought to be a tech?"

"Not exactly. Let me ask the question more directly. How can you get the most out of your flitter if you have no feel beyond the superficial?" Mahmood waved aside the objection the pilot was beginning to voice. "Yes, I know. You have your spec charts, and your performance envelopes, or whatever all the facts are that you learn. You are taught all the maneuvers that a flitter will take, and the associated stresses. But who designed those maneuvers? Who set those limits? And how? By trial and error? Or did someone really dig into what a flitter is and what a pilot can do and put the two together?"

"Test pilot."

"Are you a test pilot?"

"No."

"Do you want to be one? Or better than one?"

"Of course."

"Then how do you propose doing it? By going out and doing the same thing day after day? Destroying flitter after flitter, and maybe yourself in the process, by going beyond the established numbers without understanding the machine?"

"You make it sound so simple. Just go out and be a tech. Learn the flitter. Be an instant expert!"

"No. I never said that. You said that. I never said it would be easy. I never said it wouldn't take time. I only said that it was the best way, and the hardest."

Gerswin bounced to his feet.

"I don't know why I listen to you."

Mahmood did not respond, just let his dark eyes meet the hawk-yellow glare of the young pilot's.

Finally, the hawk-eyed one looked away.

"Thanks, Mahmood. I think."

And he was gone, quick steps echoing in the long corridor outside.

FLUORESCENT LINES ON the clay marked the landing area.

Gerswin lined up the cargo skitter, sluggish with the weight of the technical team stuffed into the passenger section and with the effect of the higher altitude, on the rough square between the hills and below the target mountain.

As the nose came up, he began twisting more and more power to the thrusters, bleeding off airspeed as the skitter wallowed downward. Theoretically, the skitter had more than enough power, but the currents swirling around the hills to the north and south of the landing site had left him the choice of an approach into the wind—with the mountain blocking any wave-off—or with the downwind approach with a steeper descent angle, but room for error. Gerswin had chosen the downwind approach. At least that way he could break it off without plowing into the mountains.

He didn't expect any ground cushion, and there wasn't any as the skitter mushed down and thumped onto the ever-present purpled clay well within the landing box that had been outlined by the advance team.

"Perdry!" he called. "Too much gusting here. Make them sit tight until I fold the blades and shut down."

The pilot knew the major would complain, at least to himself, but the last thing Gerswin wanted was some eager beaver tech, running out after the greatest find of the old technology, getting himself bisected by a rotor caught in the uneven gusts.

His fingers moved through the retraction sequence quickly but evenly.

"Blade retraction complete," he announced. "Clear to disembark."

As Perdry let down the ramp, Gerswin methodically continued through the shutdown checklist, matching his actions against the lightlist on the console.

By the time he had secured the cockpit, the entire technical team had disappeared over the rise, and he and Perdry were left with the skitter. The cargo, except for a few light cases, also remained, untouched.

Gerswin frowned. Was there any reason why he couldn't see what all the enthusiasm was about?

"Perdry?"

"Yes, Lieutenant?"

"I'm going to walk up there and take a look. When I come back, you can. Think one of us ought to stay with the bird."

"Fine with me, Lieutenant. They're going to be here awhile. A long while. Besides, I saw it."

"Why do you think they'll be here awhile?"

"They left all their gear just to take a look. And what they're looking at isn't an easy orbit break."

Gerswin inclined his head quizzically.

"Big doors, like huge portals into the mountainside. They're carving away the lock with the lasers, but so far nothing touches the metal. Never will, I'll bet."

Gerswin closed the canopy, swung himself down from the high steps in the fusilage, and jumped the last meter to the hard clay.

"See you later, Lieutenant," called Perdry. His long legs dangled from the side of the ramp where he sat staring up at the few patches of grass between the rocks, mostly on the higher parts of the hillside that was mainly red sandstone.

Gerswin took the pathway toward the ridgetop nearly at a trot, absently noting the lack of grubushes and the signs of coyotes or rats, and wondering why. Grubushes and rats existed in the worst of areas. But he did not smell a high level of landpoisons.

At the top of the ridge, he stopped and looked. Scarcely fifty meters below, the technical team was gathered around a portable screen. Fifty meters beyond them—

Massive! That was the first word for the metal portals that hulked above the chunks of fused stone that had already been carved away from the black metal. With the darkness of the metal that reflected no light, they could have been the proverbial Gates to Hades, looming as they did out of the mountainside that rose another thousand meters above them.

As he began down the gentle slope, a number of incongruities stood out.

For one, the stone chunks that had been carved away by the Imperial tech team's lasers were the same glassy texture all the way through. Second, the last thirty meters before the gates were not clay, but the same blackish and glossy stone that had been carved from the area surrounding the gates. Third, the gates were sealed, not merely closed. Two half-meter wide black metal beams, seamless, crossed the entire front of the gates, including the thin line that marked the break between the two.

Gerswin moved silently downward until he could hear the discussion, but not so closely that he seemed to be eavesdropping. Only the first set of Imperial physicians had noted, right after his initial capture, his exceptional hearing and actual reflex speed, and he had done his best since to insure that both were overlooked. Recent examinations indicated only very good physical abilities.

". . . . some sort of nuclear bonding. Anything that could break the bond would probably destroy most of this mountain range."

"Why not bring in an accelerator?"

"Darden, do you happen to have one stashed in orbit? Or do you have the fifty million creds it would take to get one here and assemble it?"

"So a frontal approach can't work."

"Why don't we bore parallel until there isn't any shielding and come in from the side?"

"Do you have any guarantee that they didn't surround the entire complex with that black metal shielding?"

"Look at it. It had to be added later. Along with the beams. It's just plated over everything, even over the joint between the two doors. There's no break at all. Besides, if they could have shielded the whole thing with a nuclear bond, why build it under a mountain?"

"Any other ideas?"

The conversation lapsed for a moment, except for a few mumbles Gerswin could not hear clearly enough to understand.

"Then we'll try Peelsley's idea. Take the number one laser bore and probe the sides. Take the most promising, and see if we can find a weak spot."

Gerswin watched as the cart was wheeled up to the rock next to the right-hand door and connected to the pulse accumulators, which were, in turn, connected to the portable generator.

The pilot shrugged and walked back to the skitter.

Perdry was still propped against the frame of the open ramp door, legs dangling down. He was eating from a ration pack.

"Got another pack here, Lieutenant. Want some?"

"Wouldn't mind at all. Techs have their own."

The crewman leaned back to reach behind himself and brought forward the square pack. Field issue, cold but edible, and about half protein, half carbohydrate.

Gerswin found himself wolfing the ration, metallic overtaste and all.

"Lieutenant?"

"Ummmm." Gerswin had to swallow before he could answer.

"What are those things?"

"Don't know. Look like the Gates to Hades. Expect there's a lot hidden here on Old Earth, if you knew where to look."

"Is it true that they could do things that the Empire still hasn't figured out?"

"Could be," the pilot mumbled while gulping down the last of the cakebread. "There's a sphere in the weapons museum at the Academy that hasn't been broken with any weapon or tool short of a tachead.

"Maybe not that. Nobody's tried. Say it was pre-Federation, Old Earth make, just before the collapse. About the size of a ball." He sketched a circle in the air with his right hand. "Weighs nearly as much as a corvette. Mass? Who knows? Doesn't seem to follow the laws we know. Takes special supports."

"Old Earth built it?"

"Who knows?" Gerswin shrugged. "It was found on an Old Earth installation, somewhere . . ."

Perdry tucked his legs up and braced them on the ramp edge.

"Could we build doors like those in the mountain?"

"Doors wouldn't be a problem," he answered deliberately, recalling the conversation he had overheard, "but the black metal they sealed them with . . . I don't think so."

"If they could do that, why did they let everything fall apart?"

Good question, thought Gerswin the devilkid. "Have to feed people, and something went wrong. Not enough food, not enough power, not enough time. Riots, fighting, starvation . . ."

"So we really don't know?"

"Not really."

Gerswin crumpled the recyclable container and put it into the bin built into the cargo door. Ducking back out, he stepped onto the ramp and stretched.

"Think I'll go back and see how they're doing. Unless you want to."

"No thanks, Lieutenant. Those big portals freeze me cold. Take your time."

Gerswin dropped off the cargo ramp and began the trek back up the hillside.

By the time Gerswin reached the technical team, the laser had disappeared into the deepening bore. Still visible were the two techs in self-contained suits.

A light rain of vaporized rock was dropping onto the clay/rock apron outside the tunnel, while the other techs and officers clustered around the portable screen.

Gerswin caught a motion out of the corner of his eye and drop-turned, but recovered when he realized it was one of the three sentries on the surrounding ridgetops.

A single tech, hands on hips, stood several paces away from the group that monopolized the planning screen. Gerswin forced himself to amble up slowly.

"How does it look?"

"It may take a while longer, Lieutenant. They slapped that black stuff and the beams over the whole thing. Then they covered it with rock and fused the rock solid. It looks like they did it to guard a tunnel into the mountain. They had to have done it in a hurry. The laser should get past the shielding before long. I'll bet it's less then five meters back."

Gerswin nodded, then asked, "Have you ever seen anything like this before?"

"No. I don't think anyone else has, either, if you can believe how excited the commander was. He sent off a message torp as soon as we got a good cube of the exterior. I'll bet he shows up as soon as we can get inside."

The pilot shook his head slowly, hoping the commander and commandant did not arrive with another complete entourage.

"You're right, Lieutenant. You're right."

While Gerswin wasn't exactly sure what he was right about, he decided to stay close to the tech, since the commander, assuming that distinguished officer did arrive, might not question anyone presumed with the technical party, but might well instruct Gerswin to stay with the skitter if he went back to the landing area.

The tech shivered in the rising chill of the afternoon wind, drawing his jacket tighter as the light dimmed.

Overhead the swirling gray clouds seemed a shade darker than usual, but Gerswin had already checked the meteorological situation. There were no landspouts in the area. Even had there been, few if any went beyond the first line of hills, and the gates were well beyond the first foothills.

The area seemed strangely quiet, and Gerswin and the tech looked up. The rain of recongealed stone had stopped, as had the hissing of the laser.

The pilot and the technician watched as the laser and the accumulator cart slowly backed from the tunnel bore, guided by the two suited techs.

The shorter suited figure, whose gray shiny suit did nothing to conceal her physical endowments, raised a clenched fist overhead and shook it.

"I guess the commander will miss the opening of the show, Lieutenant. Why don't you come along?"

The man grinned.

Gerswin repressed his own grin.

"I'd like to, thank you."

"It will be a bit, until the tunnel cools and we're sure there's decent air inside. They'll have to check for background radiation inside as well."

"Background radiation?"

"You couldn't prove it by me, but the only way I know to get the front of a mountain turned into solid glass is with a nuclear device."

"But there's no radiation outside, is there?"

"No. That just means they used a clean burst."

Gerswin took the time surveying the hillside, the clouds, and the massive gates themselves, still standing there in unshining black, as if

Old Earth's ancients had been led to Hades and the gates barred behind them.

The gray of the clouds lightened and the wind dropped to a mere breeze.

Another equipment cart was trundled into the laser bore, where it remained for a time before being withdrawn. Another data bloc was taken from the cart and inserted into the portable screen console.

Whatever the results, they appeared satisfactory, from what Gerswin could see from all the heads nodding.

Major Hylton, the tall officer directing the operation, led the first group into the laser bore, less than two meters high.

The technician nodded at Gerswin, and the two trooped with the second group, just a few meters behind the major. Nearly half the party had to stoop.

After roughly eight meters, the tunnel veered to the left and broke into a dimly lit space. One by one, the officers and technicians, and, finally, the former devilkid, stepped through the ragged opening into a larger passage ten meters wide and more than five meters high.

Twin strips of glowing panels built flush into the ceiling lit the unadorned passage, unless the light blue, fist-sized, square tiles which walled the sides of the corridor could be considered decoration.

Looking to the left, Gerswin could see only a set of three meter high doors, black metal finished and also apparently welded shut. There was no indication of the giant gates which stood on the far side.

He turned back and looked at the corridor before the party.

The passage sloped downward gradually for another fifty meters to end in still another set of doors. The massive endurasteel doors, each three meters high and two meters wide, hung open, sitting intact on twin hinges each longer than Gerswin's arm.

The pilot sniffed. The air had but the slightest tinge of age to it, and Gerswin could feel the hint of a breeze coming from the open doors.

"Why didn't they lock those as well?" asked Major Hylton.

"Maybe they figured anyone who could break the exterior bonds could break these as well."

"No time," muttered Gerswin, but the corridor was so silent that his low words carried to the major, who turned to identify the speaker.

"That might be, Lieutenant. That might be."

The major glanced back at the sealed doors behind them and at the ragged breach through the tiled wall.

"Darden, you and N'Bolgia stay here. Just in case," ordered the major.

In case of what, wondered Gerswin. Two people won't be able to stop those doors if they're powered.

Despite his misgivings, he followed the major and the others through the opening and into a square hallway, from which branched three other corridors.

The major took the right-hand one, the one which had a red arrow pointing again downward. That corridor ended abruptly less than a hundred meters farther when it expanded into an archway which led to a semicircular hall. The hall was filled with low, wide consoles arranged in arcs facing the circular section of wall. On the wall stretched a map of the Earth, continent by continent.

Gerswin frowned at the arbitrary markings within the continents, then relaxed as he realized they represented not only the topography, but some sort of political boundaries.

He searched and found the Noram boundaries and tried to compare them mentally with what his current charts showed. The wall display was different. To what degree he was uncertain, although some of the differences were obvious. While the coastal areas seemed the same, off the western Noram coasts, where the display showed ocean, there were also a series of lines enclosing "political" boundaries, as if to indicate that the continent had extended farther once than it now did.

Several moments passed as the group surveyed the room.

"Look!"

Gerswin studied the map again, trying to figure out what he was to look for, when he saw the blinking red dot slowly traversing from the lower left toward the upper right.

He pulled at his chin. Something else about the wall map bothered him, not just the moving dot, although he wondered about it as well.

His mouth dropped as it hit him all at once, and he wanted to pound his own head for his slowness in understanding. The display was neither painted nor embossed, not a static display, but a composite projection.

The display showed the actual terrain as it existed right at the moment. The lines represented some sort of governmental or political boundaries dating back to the time the projection had been developed. That was why the lines on the western Noram coast were projected out over the ocean.

But what were the occasional lights on the map? Some seemed

stationary while others moved. Gerswin could see three red ones, two pale blue ones, and a green. .

One of the red ones—stationary—seemed to match the position of orbit control.

"That's it!" he whispered, but his voice carried in the quiet.

"That's what, Lieutenant?" asked Major Hylton.

"Just a guess, Major. Red lights represent strange orbiting bodies. Blue and green are known, probably what remains of their network."

"Are you suggesting that this equipment is operational?"

"Has to be. One red light moves."

"After more than a thousand years, Lieutenant?"

Gerswin shrugged, wished he had kept his exclamation to himself. "Check it out. One red light should have orbit control position. Others may be captured satellites, hulks, objects in orbit. Wouldn't be surprised if the green or blue lights are satellites in orbit, maybe beaming information here . . . somewhere, somehow."

"That center light is about right for orbit control," offered one of the techs.

"If you're right, Lieutenant, this could be the find of the century. Think of it. Actual operating pre-Federation equipment."

Gerswin refrained from shaking his head. While they would have discovered what he had speculated, sooner or later, the discovery only left a sour taste in his mouth. Why, he could not have described, but the bitterness was hard to swallow.

He edged back toward the archway while the technicians' speculations continued.

"What sort of power . . ."

"Can you believe the clarity of that display? Must have a resolution . . ."

"Consoles sealed shut . . ."

Quietly, he ducked out and headed back up the passageway to where the three corridors had branched. Since the two guards were on the outside of the portals, chatting to each other, where neither could see the junction, he was able to follow the green arrow without being challenged.

Despite the passage of who knew how many years, there was no dust on the smooth and seamless floor.

Gerswin shook his head. Could the Empire build something to last more than a dozen centuries, without any outside direction, and still have it function? He doubted it, and that bothered him as well.

What else lay under the scoured rolling hills and the rock of the mountains?

The green arrow led him to a series of five doors, plain ordinary hinged doors, doors that stood open.

Gerswin peered inside the first door.

Another narrow corridor beckoned, lined with doors at three meter intervals. The pilot walked down the passageway to the first door and stuck his head within.

His suspicions were correct. The small rooms were quarters, each with an alcove for a bunk, though none remained; a built-in desk with an oblong console, now covered with a flat metal plate; and two built-in lockers. Besides the gray metal of the built-ins and the console, nothing had been left.

A quick survey of the next few rooms showed only a similar pattern.

Gerswin retreated to the larger corridor and checked the second of the five doors. Same pattern. That was true of the third and fourth doors as well.

The fifth door led him down a wider corridor to a set of double doors, closed, but not locked. He glanced back the thirty meters to the open door before opening the double doors and stepping through. A vacant room, roughly thirty meters on a side, greeted him. On the far side, two sets of double doors, spaced equidistantly along the wall, stood closed.

Gerswin suspected he would find another room behind them, empty except for plated-over spots in the wall and flooring, but he crossed the room he would have described as a dining hall in quick steps and pushed back one of the swinging doors. It moved silently at his touch, and he looked into a narrower room with plated-over spots on walls and floors that had once been a kitchen. A sealed archway was the only other sign of an exit.

Gerswin nodded as he recrossed the ancient dining hall and retraced his steps back to the original junction. The two guards did not hear him as they discussed the merits of freefall dancing.

He slipped past the open portals and began to follow the black arrow. As he turned the first corner and walked toward another set of open portals, similar in size and construction to the pair he had just passed, he could hear the murmur of voices behind him.

Once he was through the still-shining portals, he stood at the top of a sharply descending ramp that made a right angle turn roughly every twenty meters. He started down.

The overhead lighting was still furnished by the twin panel strips built in flush with the overhead, still with the same constant intensity.

After what Gerswin judged to have been a descent of nearly fifty meters and four complete circuits, the corridor ended abruptly. Facing the pilot was a wall-to-wall, floor-to-ceiling sheet of the black metal that had sealed the main exterior gates. Unlike the outside, this time the metal was featureless, merely a smooth finish across the corridor.

In the middle, at eye-level, were a series of symbols. One was a red hand held up in the human halt signal. The second was comprised of three luminescent green triangles within a shining yellow circle. A single word was beneath, which Gerswin could not read. The third symbol was a skull and crossbones.

Gerswin smiled grimly in spite of himself. The message was clear.

After a last look to make sure the way was completely sealed, he turned and trudged back up the ramp.

He slowed as he heard the sound of approaching footsteps.

"Gerswin here!" he called.

"Lieutenant?"

"The same."

He waited as one of the techs peered around the corner, laser in hand.

"It's him, ser."

"What are you doing here? Why didn't you wait?" Leading the crew was Major Hylton.

"Just wanted to take a look around, ser. Didn't want to get in your way."

"Lieutenant, in the future, please refrain from exploring on your own. We could have failed to recognize you, and we do need some transportation back to Prime Base."

Gerswin smiled.

"Sorry, ser. I'll be more careful."

"What's down below?"

"Hades only knows. Sealed with that black metal about two turns down."

"Sealed?"

"Yes, ser. Three clear danger signals posted."

"Should see that . . . ," muttered one of the techs standing next to the major.

"Yes, we should see that," repeated the senior officer.

Gerswin stepped to one side. "Probably more your orbit than mine, Major."

"Well . . . We should have at least an overall idea of what's here for our report."

Gerswin stood next to the wall as the dozen technicians followed the major on his downward travels.

Then he turned and climbed back up to the portals and the two guards, who were still swapping stories.

"Gerswin here," he announced. "I'm returning to the skitter to get ready for the return trip."

"Fine, Lieutenant."

"Hey, what's down there?"

"Something they'll wish they hadn't found. My guess, anyway."

At the inquisitive, nearly hurt look on Darden's face, Gerswin expanded his cryptic remark. "A current geographic projection still operating from satellite transmitters, a bunch of empty quarters, and a sealed tunnel they'll never open, marked with universal danger symbols. The projection seems to be updated moment by moment."

"Still operational?"

"Absolutely. The major doesn't know whether to be in ecstasy or worried as Hades."

"Worried is what he ought to be," opined N'Bolgia.

"You serious about that projection, Lieutenant?"

"Dead serious. Shows the mountains, the oceans. Think it even shows I.S.S. orbit control."

"Anything else?"

"That's enough. Sealed consoles, empty rooms. Place was closed down permanently for a reason. Don't understand why the projection was left operational."

"Doesn't make much sense."

"No. Not now." Gerswin shook his head. "Anyway, that's all."

"That's enough," offered N'Bolgia.

"Might be," returned Gerswin as he turned away from the two and headed up the corridor toward the exit tunnel and the skitter.

Outside the clouds had lightened, and another group was making its way down the hillside from the ridge.

In the middle of the group, mostly officers, Gerswin could make out the slightly rounded figure of the commandant, Senior Commander Mestaffa.

Gerswin sighed and waited, standing beside the laser-bored tunnel until the others reached it.

"Lieutenant, have you seen Major Hylton?"

"Yes, ser. He is checking out the installation."

"Installation?"

"Yes, ser. I am sure the major will be able to brief you. It begins about eight meters back into this tunnel. That's the entrance to the old structure. Fully lit."

Gerswin did not smile at the thought of acting more like a tour guide than a pilot.

"Thank you, Lieutenant."

"Yes, ser."

Gerswin started to head back toward his skitter when Captain Carfoos snapped, "Where are you going?"

"Back to my skitter, Captain. Make sure it's ready for the return. Can't leave it here overnight. So I either take it back empty or full. Need to get it preflighted and ready."

"All right, Lieutenant." Carfoos tapped a Marine near the rear of those waiting in line to follow the commandant. "Kyler, you take the lieutenant's position here."

"Yes, ser."

Gerswin snapped a salute at the captain and took a long first stride toward the skitter. Trust some career types to post a guard long after the real need had passed.

The wind swept through his hair as he reached the ridgetop and looked down. Four skitters were lined up across the flat space below.

He started down.

Perdry was checking the tail section when Gerswin reached the cargo ramp. The tech dropped to the clay and took several steps toward the pilot.

"Interesting, Lieutenant?"

"One way of describing it."

In short sentences, Gerswin recounted his tour of the ancient installation, concluding with his encounter with the commandant and his entourage.

"Sounds like them," observed Perdry, pointing in the general direction of the other three skitters. "Took three to bring in what we brought with one."

Gerswin nodded slightly.

"Lieutenant? That place bad news?"

"I think so, Perdry. Think so. But not for the reasons they think. Has secrets they won't be able to understand. Drive them crazy with worry. Wonder what else is hidden here."

"Bad news," affirmed the tech. "Definite bad news." But he returned to his checks.

Gerswin started on the other side of the skitter, letting the mystery of the gates drop into his subconscious, for the moment.

Not that he could do anything at all. Not now, perhaps not ever.

XXVI

"PUT ON YOUR gloves first, Lieutenant," suggested Markin.

"Gloves?"

"The plasthins. You can still feel what you're working with."

Gerswin frowned. "Why the gloves?"

"The turbine blades are polished as smooth as we can get them. The tolerances are in thousandths of millimeters. You touch that blade edge with your fingertip—there's a touch of dampness and acid there. Also, it's sharp enough to cut your finger. Then we have to worry about blood and water and acid. Sooner or later, that could unbalance the blade or weaken it." Markin laughed.

Gerswin did not bother to hide his puzzled expression.

"That's the official line. But most times, especially here, one of you hotshots will beat the blades to frags before they have a chance to weaken."

Gerswin finished pulling on the ultrathin tech gloves.

"So why the gloves?

"A couple of reasons. It gets the techs in the habit of being careful around delicate machinery. Also keeps you from carrying in contaminants that really could scratch things up."

Markin stood by the thruster access panel.

"Move over here, Lieutenant."

Gerswin stood to the left, but as close as he could to see what Markin was doing.

"Here's the standard access, the one you use for a preflight. Now . . . see here? Through the tech access panels? Don't open this in the open hangar bays or out in the field except in an emergency. It will change the temperature too quickly and let in contaminants at the ring level."

Gerswin edged forward.

Markin pointed.

"This is what I wanted to show you. You can see the joint here, the whole series."

The tech touched the base of one of the individual blades with his gloved fingertips and gently worked it free. The entire curved blade was soon in his hand, nearly half a meter long and perhaps ten

centimeters wide, the curve so slight as to be forgotten, so smooth it
was mirrorlike in finish despite the darkness of the alloy.

"See how easy it comes out?"

Gerswin nodded.

"Don't you wonder why it stays in when you're flying?"

"Never thought about it."

"All right. You saw how I took it out. You try another one."

Gingerly, gingerly, the lieutenant touched a blade. He could feel
the wobble, though he could not see the motion, as he eased it out of
the mounting ring.

"Now put it back in."

Gerswin did, with the same exaggerated care, oblivious to whatever Markin was doing.

"Now take mine and replace it."

Gerswin took the proferred blade. It felt faintly warm to the
touch even through the plasthin gloves, which were supposed to be
thermally insulated.

He eased it into the slot, but for some reason, the blade jammed
when it was halfway into place.

"Seems jammed."

"Leave it there. Don't push it. Don't force it. Just support it."

The pilot frowned, but did as he was told.

"Does it feel cooler now?"

"Yes."

"Try again. With just a tiny bit of pressure. Just a bit."

The blade eased most of the way in, but an edge remained, not
visible, but Gerswin could tell.

"There's an edge stuck out."

"Is there?"

"I'm sure."

Markin lifted a scopelike instrument from the kit at his feet and
stood beside Gerswin, who stepped back to let the tech look at the
mounting ring.

"Where?"

"There."

"You're right." Markin put down the instrument. "We'll wait a
moment, till it cools down enough to get out easily."

"Cool down? You mean the blades are that heat sensitive?"

"I played a bit of a trick on you, Lieutenant. I gave you full therm-
thins there, for hot engine work. When you're done, I'd like them
back."

Gerswin shook his head.

"Not sure I understand, Markin."

"Simple, ser. The thruster blades and the mounts are heat sensitive. Cold now . . . they are. That's why the blades are loose. If you shook the engine without the seal ring in place, every one would fall out.

"While you were taking out the second blade, I switched blades and used a lasertorch on the one I gave you to heat it up. That's what happens when you light off. As the thruster speed builds, the heat increases, blades tighten.

"Now, before we forget, would you pull the one you put in?"

Gerswin was tempted to pull the wrong one out of perversity, until he remembered he might be the one flying with the flawed blade. He handed the substitute, which had cooled enough to slide out easily, to Markin, who examined it with the scopelike instrument.

"Stet. Right one, or should I say wrong one," grunted the tech. "Here's the right one. Want to put it in?"

"If you don't mind."

"Go ahead. You're the pilot who'll fly it."

Gerswin tried to insure that the blade was seated correctly and identically to the others.

He felt relieved when Markin inspected his work with the instrument and rechecked the retaining seal. As he waited while Markin reclosed the tech access panel and then the preflight panel, he let his eyes run over the smooth finish of the flitter, admiring the way in which the techs had managed to return it to flying condition time after time.

"Lieutenant, the question is: Did you get the point?"

"Markin, I'm just a dumb pilot. Can see the reason for care. If something got inside the housing once the thruster heated up, you would get increased stress on both blade and housing. Enough to cause a fracture?"

"Lieutenant, I'll give you half. You might make a better tech than a pilot. That's the tech answer."

Gerswin shook his head. What was the pilot answer?

Markin smiled.

"Lieutenant, what happens if you're in a hurry and feed full power to that thruster before the blades have heated up?"

Gerswin almost pulled at his chin with the gloves still on his hands, then jerked his left hand away, realizing that his skin was damp and not wanting to contaminate the gloves.

"Oh . . . sorry, Markin. Not thinking clearly. If the blades aren't tight, they'd vibrate. Could that vibration snap them at the base?"

"They're probably stronger than that," answered the tech, "but if

you had some that had already been stressed by too many full power
cold starts, you could throw at least one. And if it let loose at the
wrong angle, you'd lose the whole thruster."

Gerswin shivered.

"Would it go through the housing?"

"Never seen that. The composite is tough. A loose blade could
bounce back into the fuel line sprays."

This time Gerswin nodded slowly.

"Guess I've got a lot to learn, Markin."

"You're young, Lieutenant. You got time. Especially here, you
have time."

Gerswin nodded again, slowly pulling the thin thermal gloves off
from the wrist backward, careful not to touch the outside surfaces.

"See you tomorrow, Lieutenant."

"Tomorrow, Markin," agreed the pilot.

Tomorrow, and tomorrow.

XXVII

GERSWIN RECOGNIZED CAPTAIN Carfoos. The last time he had seen
the rail-thin officer with the limp brown hair had been outside the
Gates of Hades, when both the commandant and Carfoos had assumed that Gerswin was a sentry.

At the recollection, Gerswin repressed a snort.

"Major Hylton is waiting. Go on in, Lieutenant."

Gerswin wondered at the tone of the captain's voice, if it mirrored indifference or resignation. Gerswin seldom saw Carfoos, and
could not tell what the flat inflections meant.

"Yes, ser."

The major was alone.

"Sit down, Lieutenant."

Gerswin took the armchair across the console from the major.

"We have a problem, Lieutenant. Not a major one, but one of
which the commandant and I felt you should be apprised, since you
were in at the beginning."

"Something to do with the black gates into the mountain?"

The major nodded. "The Gates to Hades, as they are popularly called around the base." He cleared his throat. "We had hoped to find some material, some artifacts, which might give us an insight into pre-Federation high technology, particularly into the composition of that nuclear bonding metal.

"We were successful, in a way. We did get an insight."

Major Hylton motioned to the junior officer.

"Come over here, Lieutenant, where you can see the screen."

The major moved his swivel to one side. Gerswin stood and moved around the console to the major's left.

"Watch. We found one operating console, but it was locked—except to provide the following message. After we copied the message—you'll see and hear it in a minute—we tried to analyze both the console and the message, but when we opened the console, which took a stepped-up cutting laser, it triggered some sort of destruct circuitry that none of our scans had even revealed. The whole thing melted down."

The major frowned and looked back at his screen. "So did everything else. The lighting, the screen wall projection are gone. So far, at least, the orbital controllers have had no luck in locating the feeder satellites."

Gerswin kept from shaking his head and waited.

Major Hylton touched a stud on the console.

A text was displayed on the screen, slowly scrolling upward, with the top line fading as it moved off the top as another replaced it at the bottom of the screen. Gerswin could pick out some of the words, but many were totally unfamiliar, and the thrust of the message eluded him.

This time, he did shake his head.

"I thought that with your background you might have a better understanding than any of us did the first time through."

"No, ser. Got some words, but that's it, and most of them are Imperial. Remember, there is really no written language left on Old Earth, especially for a devilkid."

"Devilkid?"

"Types like me. Running around outside the shambletowns."

"I see."

The major cleared his throat again. "In addition, there was an audio tape." He touched another stud.

Ding!

The single clear tone echoed through the office before the words began to roll from the console speakers.

This time Gerswin caught some of the phrases, recognizing that the intonation was closer to shambletown than Imperial. The ancient voice tolled like bells from the oldest cathedrals of New Colora, and Gerswin shivered at some of the phrases.

"What do you think, Lieutenant?"

"Warning, with the sound of a dirge."

"Did you understand what was said?"

"Not all of it, but enough to know that unless we understand a lot more than they did, we'd better not play with their tools."

Hylton frowned. "You understood more than I did, more than I still do when I hear it." He pointed vaguely toward the screen. "Here's the translation into modern Imperial, at least according to the scholar from New Avalon. Both text and verbal messages match, of course."

The written version was not as long as it had sounded. Gerswin watched the words march up the screen, each one pounding against him like a laser against his personal screens.

> To our future, should there be one:
>
> This was once a military installation before we put aside weapons based on our planet. Would that we had put aside the other dangers.
>
> The outside gates were designed to bar anyone with less than advanced technology; the interior precautions are designed to stop all but the most enlightened.
>
> The satellite map was left to show the product of a somewhat advanced technology and to provide a record should a great time have passed.
>
> You may be beyond us, and our secrets may be both insignificant or incomprehensibly simplistic. In those cases, this message is irrelevant.
>
> If you are puzzled by the black metal bonding and cannot conceive of any way to breach it, do not try. Beyond the metal lies only those radioactive wastes from the most hellish weapons and systems ever conceived by the mind of man. The wastes are buried in solid granite far beneath the installation, and surrounding the granite, itself enhanced in density, is a shield of impermite, the black metal.
>
> Why do we leave such a heritage? It is possible that a future society may need those resources. While we cannot conceive of such a need, we have secured them. Even we could not reclaim them, had we the time. Anyone who has the abil-

ity to recover them should be aware of their legacy. A complete listing of the materials follows this message.

Today, our vaunted technology is beginning to take its revenge upon our planet.

The ocean levels are rising and the mean global temperature is increasing. The winds are steadily wreaking more destruction, and the earth can no longer sustain the billions who must eat.

We have reached the stars, but the stars cannot reach us. We have tried to rebuild our sister planets to sustain life, but cannot complete that effort, for those resources have been diverted to produce food now that our arable land is vanishing.

We had attained an uneasy global peace, based on sufficient food for all. But the food is no longer sufficient, and the riots have begun.

Nothing is certain, nor whether this message will survive. No monument upon the tortured face of the Earth is assured of survival, for already the winds throw boulders across the high plains. Nor will the warrens beneath the surface long survive, not when so many organic toxics permeate the very soils and rocks of the continents.

This is not the original message of this monument. The installation was converted once from its military purpose to a memorial for that peace which we felt would be permanent, and as a monument to the success of our technology. We have converted it once more.

Call it a mausoleum, and learn from what you see, and from what you do not.

Gerswin looked up.

The major said nothing, waiting for Gerswin's reaction.

"So that *was* what happened."

"You speak as if it were nothing new."

"Close enough to the shambletown legends."

"Shambletown?"

"That's where the people live now. The descendants of most of the survivors. In the shambletowns."

"Oh, that's what they're called."

Gerswin just nodded, puzzled at the major's apparent indifference to the scope of what he had just reviewed, even if the senior officer had seen it a dozen times.

"Anyway, Lieutenant, I wanted you to hear the cube and see the translation, since you were there. I wanted to make sure that you understand the situation."

Gerswin shifted his weight.

The major looked up at him, seemingly unaware that Gerswin had been standing the entire time, but said nothing.

"What comes next, ser?"

"We've referred it to High Command and resealed the tunnel for the time being. The scientists tell me that not even a tachead would dent that material. There's some low-level background radiation around the outside gates. It would seem that someone tried a hell-burner, unsuccessfully, against them. A long time ago. All it did was melt rock over and around them."

This time Gerswin did not comment.

The major shrugged. "What else can I do? No equipment to do more is available. No one seems interested."

Gerswin repressed a nod.

"Could be discouraging if the knowledge became widespread," he volunteered.

"It could be," affirmed the major, "but it wouldn't change anything. I doubt that the Emperor would broadcast that Old Earth had a pre-Collapse technology which we still cannot match."

"I understand, ser."

"I believe you do, Lieutenant. I believe you do, but not for the same reasons." He sighed. "But that's not the issue." The major stood. "Do you have any more questions?"

"No, ser. Appreciate your sharing this."

"Just my duty, Lieutenant. Just my duty." He gestured toward the portal. "Have a good tour."

"Thank you, ser."

Outside in the staff office, Captain Carfoos glanced up and fixed a glare on Gerswin. "You done, Lieutenant?"

"Yes, ser."

"Then we'll see you at mess some time."

"Yes, ser."

Gerswin turned and walked out, not for the Officers' Mess, but for his own quarters.

He wished Mahmood were still on Old Earth, but the senior ecologist had left nearly a standard year earlier on the *Casimir*, which had carried in the new ratings and officers and carried out those going on to new and generally better opportunities.

Not that Mahmood had continued in the Service. The former

ecological officer was doubtlessly now fully ensconced in his new position as the Chairman of Ecology at the University of Medina.

"But why?" Gerswin had asked. "Why?"

"My studies and recommendations here are complete, Greg. There isn't much more I can do. I'm a scholar, just a scholar. All I can do is to get people to think."

The memory of that statement still churned Gerswin's stomach if he thought too much about it.

So much knowledge . . . unused . . . lost . . . ignored . . . as if no one cared, as if no one remembered the tired planet that had destroyed itself to give men the stars.

He tightened his lips without breaking step.

THE LIEUTENANT SHOWED the sketch and specifications to the technician.

"Can it be done, Markin? With the balances like that?"

"Strange-looking knife, if you ask me, Lieutenant."

"Need weight, penetrating power."

"I don't see how it could be effective much beyond five, six meters."

"Computer says it will do what I want up to six meters all the time. Beyond that . . ." The lieutenant shrugged.

"The weight specifications make it heavy. I'd sure rely on a stunner. Could you even throw this thing?" The technician lifted the sheet as if to somehow better picture the weapon.

"Can't throw it until I have one in hand. Like at least three, but probably need five or six, if we could manage it."

"We?"

"I'd like to help. Want to understand how. They may have to last me a long time, and the next time you'll be in some other forsaken system."

Markin chuckled.

"Lieutenant, any time you want to use your hands is fine with me. We'll use one of the out-of-the-way bays, where the commander doesn't see one of his officers, Istvenn forbid, dirtying his hands and learning metalwork."

XXIX

GERSWIN CHECKED THE time. 1752. Too early to enter the mess.

He passed the mess portal and entered the next one, the one to the junior officers' lounge. Lieutenant Hermer sat in the recliner nearest the door, her tall figure buried in her own thoughts, hair as dark as the black finish of the chair in which she sat. The small room, less than six meters on a side, was otherwise empty.

Gerswin saw a faxtab, obviously a recent reproduction of one from the latest supply ship, which meant the news inside was three to four weeks old. He picked up the flimsy sheets and began to read as he circled the table, unwilling to sit down in either the other recliner next to Lieutenant Hermer or in the too-soft bench couch.

Usually he ignored the faxtabs for the technical publications which he took off the screen in his quarters at night. The Service kept its bases up-to-date on technical information through the torp network, but items such as soft news, the latest updates on the Emperor and his Court, came through personal torp messages or the straight news bulletins fed into the commnet.

Faxtabs were a mixture of everything. Gerswin noted that Newparra was still under quarantine, and the *Okelley* was listed as returning from there, mainly because the son of a prominent baron was on the commodore's staff. Gerswin knew the replacement ship was the *Sandhurst,* a fact ignored in the once-over of the faxtab.

Absently, he turned to the second flimsy page. A name caught his eye, and he stopped.

His mouth dropped open as he read the small item:

His Grace, Merrel, son of the Duke of Triandna, and Caroljoy Montgrave Kerwin, daughter of Honore Balza Dirien Kerwin, Admiral of the Fleet and Marshall of the Marines, were married under the Old Rite ceremonies at the Triandna Estates recently. The ceremony and reception were private, but the Emperor is reported to have attended, according to informed sources. No comment was available from either the Imperial Court or His Grace the Duke.

Gerswin put the faxtab down on the table.

Could he have expected anything else?

Five years, and he had sent nothing, said nothing, written nothing. Nor had she. Not that he had not thought about her. But what could he have sent to someone he was not even supposed to know?

He glanced over at Lieutenant Hermer, who was still buried in the old-fashioned text, then at the table. He checked the time. 1755. Still too early, and right now, he didn't want to stand at the edge of the table waiting for Captain Matsuko, who would arrive promptly at 1801.

Gerswin looked back down at the faxtab and its slightly scattered pages, then away, as if it burned his eyes.

"Forget it!" he muttered, louder than he intended.

"Forget what?" Lieutenant Hermer's head popped up from her text like a turtle's from its shell.

"Nothing, Faith. Nothing. Forgot anyone was here."

He turned away, shaking his head.

Hard it was, sometimes, for him to remember that he was just a devilkid from Old Earth, and one lucky enough to have gotten an I.S.S. commission.

"Are you all right, Greg?"

Faith Hermer had not gone back to her book, but had marked her place and closed it. She was standing by her swivel.

"I'm fine. Surprised, that's all."

He refrained from glancing back at the faxtab, not wanting to call her attention to it, but wishing he had not left it folded to the page on which Caroljoy's marriage announcement appeared.

Marriage, of course. No mention of anything else, but the union announced as if it were a matter of state or of commerce. Probably it had been a bit of both, if the Emperor himself had attended.

"Are you sure you're all right?"

He jumped and turned at the sudden touch on his shoulder.

"Hades!" He bit off the exclamation as soon as he had said it. After sighing and taking a deep breath, he looked up into the woman's pale green eyes. He had to. Faith Hermer was nearly two meters high and stood taller than any other officer on Old Earth.

"Faith. Sorry I jumped. Surprised and thinking about it. You caught me off-guard."

She chuckled, deep-throated, and the sound relaxed him even before she spoke again. "You must have been surprised. No one has ever caught you off-guard. Not to my knowledge."

He nodded and checked the time. 1800.

"Late if we don't blast."

"All right. You don't want to talk about it now. I'll be around if you do." She smiled and pointed to the exit portal. "Blast, Greg. That is, unless you want to sit at the foot of the table opposite Matsuko."

He was already moving toward the mess before she finished the sentence.

Caroljoy—married, of course. So why did it surprise him?

GERSWIN HEFTED THE double-ended knife, cradled it, and flipped it from hand to hand. Not at all like the jagged blade he had carried as a devilkid, or the sterile, straight survival knife in his flight boot sheath.

He looked up from the knife to the target—a plastic square set at man height on a hummock of clay five meters away. The plastic presented roughly the same resistance as an unarmored man.

"Here goes," he muttered to himself.

The first cast missed the square entirely.

The second knife wobbled, but hit the plastic and dropped onto the clay beneath the target.

The third hit the plastic square at an angle and skittered off.

Gerswin sighed and marched forward to reclaim the three knives, casting a sideways look at the clouds gathering over the plains. The afternoon's pale sunlight had been the first in days, and, as usual, had not lasted more than a few hours.

He leaned down to get the first knife.

From what he had studied of the meteorological data, the only places where there was more sunlight than cloud cover was over open ocean. No one could explain to him the reason for the phenomenon, at least not in terms simple enough to be sure it wasn't scientific doubletalk.

He put the first two knives in the hidden belt sheath and picked up the third.

The wind began to whine. Soon, if the darkness roaring in from the east were any sign, it would begin to whistle as the temperature again dropped toward freezing.

With the one knife in hand, he retreated to the one spot he had measured out and scratched in the bare clay.

Feel the knife; sense the balance; and . . . release!

And miss.

"Hades!"

Gerswin took the second knife and let it fly with full force.

The twinge in his left hand brought him up short. He realized he had gripped the double-edged blade far too tightly. A slash ran across the base of his thumb, scarcely more than skin deep, but blood welled out.

He squeezed the edge closed with the fingers of the same hand, then let the cut bleed as he threw the third knife with his right hand.

All three had struck the target, but none had stuck.

Gerswin studied the target before starting after the knives.

The gathering clouds choked off the last scattered beams from the sun, and the first gust of wind ruffled his tight-curled blond hair. Absently, he started to push the hair off his forehead before he realized that it was too short to get in the way, as it had been for nearly ten years.

He reclaimed the three knives once more and straightened the target with his right hand. He walked back to his mark, juggling the unsheathed knife in his right hand. He intended to be equally proficient with either hand.

"Right now, it's equally inaccurate," he mumbled.

His next cast bounced off the plastic, but the second did not. Gerswin tried to reclaim the feeling of the second with the third. He did, and two heavy knives remained solidly within the plastic as he walked up to reclaim all three.

Four steps to the target in the whine of the wind. Reclaim the blades and straighten the target. Four steps back to the mark.

Three more throws.

Reclaim the knives.

Throw again.

Reclaim.

Throw.

Reclaim.

Throw.

He kept up the pattern until it was automatic.

When he finally quit, not because of darkness, though most would have had to, two out of three casts were sticking within the target, either right- or left-handed. He quit because the increasing wind gusts kept knocking over the target, not because the ice rain bothered him, light tunic or not, nor because of the nagging twinge in his thumb.

The bleeding had stopped, but streaks of rain-diluted blood decorated his trousers as he headed first to stow the knives in his quarters and then to the medical section. He did not intend to wear the knives until he was one hundred percent accurate with them within their range.

. With practice every day, within weeks he would have that skill. After that . . . another weapon. But first, the knives, for they could be used anywhere.

Anywhere in the Empire and on Old Earth.

XXXI

THE FLITTER DROPPED from the clouded sky toward the plateau and its grasses and grubushes. Gerswin watched the readouts in the heads-up display as he eased the flitter down into the clearing nearest the site he hoped was there.

From the topography maps, he had narrowed the search to six plateaus corresponding to his memories. This was the fifth he had actually investigated. His searches of the first four had failed to disclose any indication of the brick stairwell, the garden plots, and the hidden trail he remembered.

The computer and the maps had been better in some ways than his memories. The pilot smiled wryly at the thought. In two of the first four sites he had discovered evidence of recent habitation. In the future he would look into recruiting possibilities, assuming those whom his descent had frightened away were indeed devilkid types.

As the flitter settled, Gerswin let more and more weight drop onto the skids, leaving power on the rotors until he was certain that the flitter was solidly grounded on the mesa top. Next came the blade retraction and storage. Before shutting down the fans, he checked both the EDI and heat scanners. Both showed negative.

He shook his head. A devilkid could be waiting in a below-grade gully, or a buried and fully charged laser pack could have been sitting right in front of the flitter, and neither detector would have shown a thing. They weren't designed for terrain work.

Much of the Service's equipment wasn't designed for Old Earth usage.

After half-vaulting, half-climbing from the cockpit, he touched the closure plates and tapped in a lock combination. While it wouldn't stop a trooper with a laser, the flitter was secure against anything less, and Gerswin didn't expect to meet the equivalent of an Imperial Marine marching through the grubushes in the chill and steady wind of the gray fall morning.

He sighted against the hills to the west, checking his orientation. If he were right, then the hidden stairs he hoped to find were nearly a kay to the west, just above a sharp drop-off to the more sheltered valley beneath.

Light as his steps were, each one crisped slightly on the heavy sand that surrounded the flitter. His breath, slow and even, formed a trailing plume behind him as he slipped toward the shoulder-high grubushes a hundred meters westward.

He sniffed the air gently, trying to detect a scent that might have been there once, a faint odor part soap, part perfume. All he could smell was the bitter-clean odor of the grubushes, nearly uncontaminated this far above the plains and near the mountains. Only a single line of foothills remained between the mesa and the granite peaks that divided the continent.

The air was cold and, outside of the grubushes and the faintest scent of landpoison carried from the plains by the east wind, clean. No rat scent, nor the lingering odor of coyote or kill—the smell was right.

His right hand brushed his waistband, under which was the double-ended sheath with the twin throwing knives, and touched the butt of the stunner. While he had practiced with the knives to the point where his accuracy was nearly one hundred percent on stationary targets, targets were only targets, and the stunner might be more reliable. For now, anyway.

Glancing at the sky, he gauged from the thinning of the clouds whether there might be some sunlight later in the morning. He shook his head, although he could sense some warmth on his back. The thin jacket he wore over his flight clothes was enough to break the wind, and that was all he really needed. Imperial officers born on New Augusta or other warmer planets avoided the outside whenever possible, wearing the double-layered winter uniforms and parkas whenever they were exposed to the cutting winds of Old Earth.

As Gerswin neared the area he intended to search more closely he stopped to check the grubushes, looking at the waxy berries and branches for some sign of harvesting. He found none, not even any sign of the mountain mice that lived on little besides the berries, or so he recalled.

He straightened and surveyed the western end of the mesa that lay before him, checking the hills to firm up his bearings. Turning more toward the north, he headed for the unseen drop-off he knew lay ahead.

Suddenly he stopped, cocked his head, and looked at the all-too-even notch between the two hills to the west and at the dark wedge of gloom behind the notch. He compared that gray to the indistinct gray of the clouds and the line of gray leading to the notch.

"The road of the old ones . . ." he murmured, not sure where he had heard the phrase, but knowing that he had, somewhere, sometime.

His eyes traveled the small open sand and clay space around him, checking the bushes, trying to find a pattern, any pattern at all. Finally, he settled on a slightly wider spacing between two grubushes. He eased through what seemed almost a lane toward the western edge of the mesa, a path that became increasingly rocky as his steps closed the gap between himself and the nothingness that waited as the surrounding bushes became shorter and less closely spaced.

Again, he stopped, not for a conscious reason, but because he felt he should, and studied the area around him.

To his right, his eyes settled on an irregular heap of stones, seemingly random, but too regular and too high to have been an accident of geology.

He took one step and paused, sniffed the air. He found nothing but the eastern plains odor of landpoison and the cleaner and nearer scent of grubush.

He took another step, another pause, another sniff.

Finally, he took a deep breath and a quick dozen steps until he stood before the tumbling wall fragment that failed to reach his waist.

It had been higher, he recalled, but, then, he had been shorter, and it had been years earlier. How many he never knew, for time had no meaning to a devilkid on the run, forced from the only home he knew by shambletowners with torches, running and hiding, burying himself beneath grubushes in the pouring rain that had hidden the killers' approach.

He bit his lower lip and studied the rough wall of hewn red rock. At last, he looked over the edge and down the steps—to find them half-covered with drifting sand.

The wooden cover he remembered was gone, and only the nitches in one line of stones supported that memory.

With a sigh, he stepped over the stones, tapped them to insure they were solid. None moved with the taps, nor even with a push, and he eased himself down into the dimness.

After twenty rock-hewn steps and a half-turn west, he was past the drifted sand and in the tunnel where he could stand, just barely. A faint hint of grubush oil tickled the edge of his senses. Memory, or a residue of what had been?

Another fifteen steps and another turn, this time to the south, took him into the main room.

The embrasured and now-uncovered window slits filled the space with more than enough light. Two piles of leather fragments and dust sat across from each other in the southwest corner, the dust spilling across the corner of the permanent clay brick table whose surface was covered with glazed tiles. Each handmade tile had a slightly different design, but all bore a sun/cloud motif.

Gerswin swallowed and turned to the other outside corner, where a second waist-high clay brick counter topped with the crude fired tiles stood. Beside it was what could only have been a ceramic oven, equipped with a chimney and handmade clay piping. One section of the pipe, where it entered the brick wall, had broken apart, and the fragments were scattered across the golden brown floor tiles.

Outside of the centimeters-thick dust and the two piles of leather fragments, nothing perishable remained in the room.

He looked up at the ceiling—a good half-meter above his head. Faint grease-smoke lines traced themselves across the smooth surface, smoke lines he did not remember.

His feet took him to the room that opened northward off the main room, but with one glance he turned away.

The drifted dust outlines of two skeletons on a thicker pallet of dust were all that inhabited the room.

He did not enter the small room next to his parents' room, but did dart a look at the dusty outline that had been his pallet.

The one remaining space was the south room, the one which had looked out over the canyon. Gerswin found himself standing there.

The single window gaped open, the hide covering long since gone, above the flat tile-topped brick expanse where his father had done so many strange things.

Gerswin nodded, more to reassure himself than anything else.

He turned his palms up, looked at his hands, a young man's hands, then at the dust on the floor, and finally at the alcove in the narrow corner behind the archway, the alcove that contained the air duct that a small boy had crawled up so many years earlier.

How many years earlier? How many?

For a time he studied his hands, then stared out the unglazed window at nothing.

He looked once more at the dust on the floor tiles, sniffed again the total emptiness, and turned back toward the tunnel to the mesa top. He did not need to take the other stairway, the one that had led down to the spring, the one through which the shambletowners had poured one distant night, slings and spears in hand, with their rat grease torches flaring.

As he entered the tunnel leading upward, he looked at his hands still yet again. He shook his head to clear his vision.

Later, at the top step, he paused, but turned away and did not look back, and stared instead at the clouds overhead, which reminded him of night, not morning.

The clouds were thicker than when he had brought the flitter down, as if they had decided against allowing the sunshine to break through. And the wind was stronger, the chill more pronounced, as the click of ice droplets began to pelt his jacket and burn his face.

XXXII

GERSWIN GLANCED UP from the Operations oversight console. Captain Altura, the Imperial auditor, was leaving Major Matsuko's office. She did not appear particularly pleased.

Her lips were set even more tightly than when Gerswin had met her at the hangar-bunker right after the shuttle had dropped her three days earlier. The captain's fists were half-clenched as she marched out toward the tunnel to the number one hangar-bunker.

"Opswatch, this is Outrider three. Interrogative permission to lift."

Ferinya, the duty controller, looked at Gerswin. His eyebrows raised questioningly. "Permission to lift?"

"Why not? Met status is clear now. Squall line coming in."

"Outrider three. Cleared to lift. Interrogative destination and fuel status."

"Artifact survey run. Plan on file. Estimate air time at two plus stans. Fuel status is plus four."

"Stet. Understand survey run for plus two. Fuel status four."

"Stet. Outrider three lifting."

Ferinya turned to Gerswin. "Do you know what that was all about, Lieutenant? She already had clearance."

Gerswin shrugged. "No. No passengers or cargo on the schedule."

"What was what all about?"

Lers Kardias stood by the console, his stubby fingers tapping on the hard console top.

"Lieutenant Starkadny requested clearance to lift twice. No explanation," explained Gerswin.

"Oh . . . That is funny." Junior Lieutenant Kardias shook his head. "You ready to be relieved, ser?"

"More than ready."

"You stand relieved."

"I stand relieved, and you have it."

Gerswin picked up the light pen from the console and slipped it into the arm pocket of his flight suit. "Good luck, Lers. There's a squall line coming in."

"Thanks."

"Which of you was responsible for sending that flitter off without me?" The chill voice of the Imperial auditor stopped Gerswin in his tracks.

He turned back to face both the console and Captain Altura. Lieutenant Kardias had swiveled in the chair, but had not stood.

"I was, Captain," answered Gerswin.

"Could you explain why?"

"First, no passengers listed. No cargo either. Second, pilot requested clearance. Third, no one notified Opswatch that you were to be included."

The sandy-haired captain said nothing, but clamped her lips together until they were nearly white.

Gerswin waited a moment, then asked, "Is there anything I could do, Captain?"

He caught the "now what have you said?" look from Lers Kardias as Captain Altura glared at him.

"Mister Senior Lieutenant, you have done quite enough for the moment. Anything else would only compound that."

Gerswin laughed—a single harsh bark.

"Ms. Captain, I followed the order book. I would have gladly delayed the flitter if anyone had asked me."

"I told the pilot."

"On every Imperial base, schedules and clearances are controlled by Operations. Bases are not ships, Captain." He paused. "Would you like a tour of the maintenance facilities?"

"I've seen them. The conditions and status are better on Charon."

"Charon's an easier planet."

"Than Old Earth?"

Gerswin nodded. "I'll show you. Come on with me."

"Show me what?"

"Not what. Why."

"Why what?"

Gerswin had already turned away, as if to lead the captain, his quick steps heading toward the southwest base exit.

The captain looked at Lieutenant Kardias, then at Gerswin's back, before, with a shrug, she followed the senior lieutenant.

At the inner portal of the exit he turned to wait for her.

"Your home system?"

She clamped her lips shut tightly, then released them.

"New Augusta."

He nodded and stabbed the portal release. Once in the small room between the inner and outer portals, he walked over to the line of lockers. He checked one, then another, rummaging through several until he located a double-lined jacket with thermal gloves.

"You'll need this."

"It's summer."

"You'll need it. Ice rain."

"Hail, you mean?"

Gerswin shook his head in disagreement and offered the jacket to the captain, who donned it but stuffed the gloves into the side pockets and did not seal them.

As the outer portal opened and the two stepped through, a gust of wind from the east, sweeping along the edge of the berm, caught the captain unaware, knocking her into the lieutenant.

Gerswin steadied the woman with his left hand, submerged a grin, and continued toward the point where the ridgeline began to slope away toward the south.

"Watch the clouds."

Captain Altura said nothing, looked at the bare clay interspersed with grassy humps. Finally, she took his advice and raised her eyes to the roiling and speeding mass of varied gray that hurtled toward the mountains in the distance to her right.

Gerswin watched her, not the clouds, as the winds quickly turned her pale cheeks reddish with the cold, and fluttered her short and sandy hair with each gust above the steady chill breeze that whipped around them.

The darker cloud that presaged ice rain was nearly overhead before the droplets began to sound against their clothing and the hard clay.

Click! Click! Click, click, click!

The captain held one in her bare right hand. So cold was the droplet that it did not begin to melt for several moments.

"Why don't you put on the gloves?"

"I might, thank you."

As she struggled with the two gloves too large for her long-fingered but narrow hands, Gerswin glanced at the clouds. Not quite dark enough for a landspout, but the wind velocity would continue to rise and the temperature to drop.

As she finished donning the gloves and looked back at the darkening clouds, Gerswin whistled the first three notes of a tune, the one he thought of as a lament for Old Earth.

The melody had come to him after he'd seen the black Gates to Hades. With the auditor's impatience, the chill, and his own wondering what he was even doing trying to explain Old Earth to a number-cruncher, the first three notes had slipped out before he cut off the melody.

"What sort of instrument was that?"

"What?"

"That you were playing." Captain Altura was still adjusting the too-large gloves, trying to make them fit and to keep them from falling off her hands.

"No instrument. Sometimes I whistle." Gerswin gestured, as if to change the subject. "Warm day. Wind is still lighter than normal, only about twenty kays here."

"What's normal?"

"Here? Around thirty. Hundred's not uncommon. Had two hundred a couple of times. Once or twice we lost the measuring tubes. Spout threw a two-ton chunk of rock through the number four hangar-bunker door one time."

"I don't believe that."

Gerswin shrugged. Why bother? "Check the logs. About two years ago."

He gazed out to the southeast, still lighter than due east, then back to his left, toward the main body of the ice storm.

"Lieutenant?"

"Yes, Captain."

"Why is everyone so prickly here? I ask Matsuko to justify some costs, and he throws a databloc listing of logs and damage reports at me and tells me to search out anything that would contradict the official reports. He practically dared me to question him."

Gerswin frowned, glanced down at the damp clay, and said nothing.

"Lieutenant?"

Gerswin shrugged again. "What can I say? Doesn't sound like him. He's punctual, proper. Polite."

It was the captain's turn to look down at the clay underfoot, to scuff at a tuft of purpled grass.

"I overstated the case. He was proper, very proper. I questioned, and he politely referred me to the databloc containing every single listing that supported every single item."

Gerswin looked at her oval face and strong nose, at the scattered freckles that seemed blanched in the gloom, and raised his eyebrows.

"Don't you understand? He didn't explain. He didn't even take the time to show me an ice storm. In effect, he said, 'Waste your own time. Don't waste mine.'"

"He's like that."

"But everyone is like that here. At least, that's how it seems. Even when you want to explain, you don't. You just say 'Follow me' and head off into a storm. A few sentences about how cold it is, and you think that explains something."

Gerswin sighed, scuffed the clay with his right foot.

"I'll try to put it in perspective. Old Earth is something you experience. You don't explain it. How could you? People think that it's just like the his-tapes, except nothing will grow, and some fertilizer and a little technology sprinkled over the clay will do it.

"How can you explain landspouts that rip the tops off hills, that turn all-weather flitters into crushed metal in microseconds? You try, and someone says that it's just a tornado. But it's not. There were ten million people within three hundred kays of here right before the collapse. Maybe three hundred shambletowners and a couple dozen devilkids left. Not a single building or a ruin more than a meter high left standing. Place flattened by the spouts, except in one or two valleys.

"You try to tell someone, and they say that it was just the collapse. You stand here, and you don't believe me when I say it's summer. Winter here . . . You think it's cold on the poles of Charon? Winter ice rain will sand off three mills of metal from a flitter in a single flight on the exposed side, and that's just on ground or stationary time."

Gerswin looked over at the captain, who did not raise her eyes from the ground.

"Right now, more than twenty percent of the pilots sent here are casualties. Those who make it through become the best in the Service, and you can check their records if you doubt it. That's the young ones. Older pilots avoid flying around here. Better for them and us.

"Get a good dozen cases of toxic shock every year, just from the hot spots no one has found. But it's not glamorous, like scout duty or combat.

"The rain's so acidic that outside uniforms don't last a tour, and you should know what replacement costs mean to a junior officer.

"But that's the story no one tells. How could anyone on New Augusta believe that Man's home planet is dangerous to Man's existence?"

Gerswin laughed once, and the bitterness echoed against the whistle of the rising wind.

"Why are you here?" Her voice was nearly lost in the wind, so softly had she spoken.

"Another question. Most people here believe there's something to save. Something that should be saved."

"I think that's what you believe. This is nowhere. Oh, yes, it's Old Earth, and the home of Man. But everyone here is either local, a problem child, or on a preretirement tour.

"Can't you see it, Lieutenant? The great crusade to save the home planet was over before it began."

"Is it? Just got three arcdozers on the ship that brought you. Decon teams have cleaned up most of the toxic hot spots around the headwaters of the two nearest rivers on this side of the continental divide. Starting on the big one now. Years before the results come in, but it's a start."

"Nobody on New Augusta really cares. The new Emperor . . ."

"Long as they keep funding, we'll keep plodding."

"You're just like Major Matsuko."

Gerswin shook his head, then noticed the whiteness at the tip of her ears.

"Time to go in. Frostbite."

"We haven't been out that long. And you only wore your uniform."

"That's me. Not you. Face a bit numb? Ears?"

"Yes, but—"

"Inside." He took her left arm and firmly guided her back to the portal.

Once inside, he helped her take off the heavy, ice-encrusted jacket and placed the jacket and gloves in the heated equipment locker.

The Imperial auditor half-shivered, half-shook herself. "Is there any place to sit down and relax, get a cup of cafe or liftea?"

"J.O.'s lounge, off the mess."

"That sounds fine. Is it warm?"

"Same as anywhere else."

He tapped the inner portal release, and they stepped through, Gerswin leading the way up the tunnel until it intersected the outer perimeter corridor. Gerswin turned right, quick steps clicking on the smooth floor.

Neither said a word until Gerswin stopped at the lounge portal and touched the access plate.

"After you, Captain."

"Dara, please."

Instead of replying, he inclined his head momentarily as if posing himself a question. He did not answer the unthought question, but followed her through.

He went straight to the sideboard.

"Cafe?"

"Liftea."

He poured two and set both mugs on the narrow table where Dara sat. He seated himself across from her.

"You're from where?"

"Here. Local. First, last, and only, so far. Except for some of the kids from the civilian techs on the farm."

"The farm?"

"That's what they call the research center south of here."

She put a forefinger to her chin, then dropped it as a furrow appeared momentarily in her forehead.

"Wasn't there a report—"

"—about the training and education of an Old Earth native. Yes. There was. I was. *Education Review,* New Augusta, Volume 87, number three, if you want to look it up. End of subject."

The auditor closed her mouth and studied his face. Gerswin looked at the sideboard and the two steaming pots—one for cafe, one for liftea.

"Oh . . . I think I understand. Do you talk about your impressions of the Empire?"

"Sometimes."

"What about Old Earth? Not what's happened in the Service, but your own feelings."

"Home. Like to see her restored. Don't know if it can be done. Like to see it."

The captain took another sip of the tea, holding the old-fashioned mess mug in two hands and letting the steam drift up and around her face, so near her chin was the mug.

Gerswin took a sip and placed his own mug back on the dark gray plastic of the table.

"How did you end up an I.S.S. officer?"

"Why not? Good reflexes and enough brains to scrape through the Academy. Besides, didn't know enough Imperial culture to do it any other way. Devilkids don't know all the graces. The Academy assumes nothing."

"Do you regret it?"

"The Academy? The Service? No."

"You paid a high price, Greg."

He stiffened fractionally at the use of his first name, but said nothing, and nodded for her to continue.

"You've been commissioned what, ten years, and you're a Senior Lieutenant? I was commissioned eight years ago, and not from the Academy."

"And you're a captain. You're an auditor."

"You're a pilot. Direct line. I'll bet most of your contemporaries are captains."

"You may be right."

He took another sip of the liftea before adding, "But it always takes longer in non-Fleet commands."

"I hope you're right." She pursed her lips, wet them with her tongue, and pursed them again. Then she looked at the sideboard, before glancing down at the table. Finally, she met his eyes. "How can you whistle like that, like you did outside?"

Gerswin wondered if he had made a mistake. Captain Altura was nice enough, outside of her role as Imperial nitpicker and auditor, and attractive in a stiffly friendly way. But she was no Caroljoy, nor even a Faith Hermer, who was always warm and friendly even when she disagreed violently on specific issues.

Gerswin looked at the tabletop.

"Can you whistle like that again?"

"Captain—"

"Dara, please."

"I don't often. Personal. Escaped me outside. Was watching the clouds and wasn't thinking."

She reached across the narrow table and laid her hand on his. Her fingers were cool.

"Would you whistle or sing, whatever you like, just one song?"

Gerswin wet his lips, half-closed his eyes, and began. The first notes were shaky, but he let them come, hoping that no one else would walk into the lounge while he did.

As he finished a shortened version of the lament, he realized that both her hands grasped his right hand.

"That was beautiful."

He tried to withdraw his hand, but her fingers tightened fractionally, and he did not want to seem as though he were yanking his hand loose.

"I'd like to change. I'm still cold. Would you come with me?" Dara Altura stood slowly, her grayish-green eyes fixed on his, as her fingers lingered on his hand before slowly sliding off as she rose.

Gerswin stood also, but let his hand slide away from hers.

"You're too kind, Dara. But I appreciate it."

Her eyes hardened slightly.

"Not you. Me. Long story, and I'd rather not go into it. Not for a while. I'll see you at the mess, if you like. And I enjoyed talking with you."

"You sure?"

Gerswin smiled, trying to convey the mixture of sadness and confusion he felt.

"Unfortunately."

"Friends, at least?"

"Friends."

She laughed, with a gentleness he had not heard before.

"You're probably right." Then she shivered. "I am cold, and I will see you later."

Gerswin stood there watching the portal as she left, then shook his head after she had disappeared. The last thing he needed was getting entangled with someone who mistook his songs for him, or someone who thought they understood and didn't.

"Understand what?" he asked aloud, breaking off his conversation with himself as the portal opened again.

Faith Hermer marched in.

"See you're at it again, lover boy." While the words were sarcastic, her voice was soft.

"Don't understand," he said to her, not exactly caring if she understood, but knowing that she did.

"You understand. You just don't want to, Greg."

"Suppose you're right."

"Do you want someone to talk to?"

"No. Not now. Appreciate the thought, though." He looked into her clear gray eyes, ignoring her twenty centimeter height advantage. "Really do."

"I know."

He turned to go, since he felt grubby and wanted to clean up before 1800. Captain J'rome carried on the punctuality established for the Junior Officers' Mess by her predecessor, Major Matsuko.

His steps were a shade slower than normal as he marched up the corridor.

Why the blatant invitation by Dara Altura? Why had he turned her away? She was attractive, bright, not unsympathetic. He had no attachments, certainly not now.

Or did he?

It wasn't as though he were celibate.

He shook his head again, and it seemed like he was always shaking his head. He wondered about Faith's arrival, Faith Hermer, who had never pushed, but never pushed him away, though he had kept her at arm's length and then some.

He kept walking toward his functional quarters and the console with the texts on circuit design and security. Circuit design and security.

He kept walking.

XXXIII

THE BLOND-HAIRED captain pulled the functional armless swivel up to the console. After bending over and touching the rear power stud, he sat down and squared his frame before the pale screen.

"Access code?" the machine scripted.

He looked around the dimly lit office. At the far right end of the Operations bay he could see the island of full light where the duty tech waited and watched.

"Access code?" The query blinked twice.

"BlindX, Beta-G." The letters did not show on the screen, and the officer hoped his finger placement had been accurate.

"Login at 14:18:33 N.A.E.M.T. VM/TSTAT NOT AVAIL. Request subset/matrix."

The captain frowned, then finally tapped in his request.

"Beta Jumpsched."

"**invalid entry**"

He gnawed at his upper lip, tried again.

"Beta sched jumpship."

"Please enter type of matrix and parameter dates."

"Array."

The single word blinked on the screen for a moment before the console scripted the system's reply.

MATRIX ARRAYS:
1. By inbound date
2. By j/s type
3. By dptg sys
4. By ult dest sys
5. By comb array; enter in pref ord.

The captain gnawed at his upper lip once more. Slowly, he touched the keyboard studs before him.

"Array 1/2// after 1/1/3025."

"35 data elements found. Do you wish all included?"

"Yes."

"Wait. Display follows."

The captain shook his head. Thirty-five jumpships. Just thirty-five since the rediscovery. He sat and waited for the matrix display to print out on the pale screen.

He leaned around the console to check the main Ops area, but the duty tech had not moved, nor had anyone else entered the bay.

As the matrix printed across the screen, he quickly scanned some of the names. The *Torquina* was there, not the first, but the second, and that made sense. The scout would have had to have been first. He just hadn't thought about it.

The *Churchill* was there as well, near the middle of the matrix. He ran over the totals—three scouts, two research ships, four corvettes, three destroyers, two cruisers, and twenty-one transports. Roughly two transports annually for the past five years, less than that before.

He tapped the reset.

"Subset."

"Gamma sched jumpship."

"Authorization codes."

The captain frowned again. There had been no request for the code for historical data. He shifted his weight in the armless swivel, worried his upper lip with his teeth, and finally tapped out a random-appearing mixture of numbers and letters. He lifted his fingers and waited.

"Request subset matrix."

He let his breath out slowly and lowered his fingers back to the keyboard.

"Array 1/2."

Only two ship names printed on the screen, the *Aacheron* and the *Khanne*, both transports, the first scheduled for Old Earth arrival in three months, the second in ten.

He tapped two more studs.

"Subset."

"Pers/File/Ops."

"**invalid entry**"

"File/Pers/Ops."

"**invalid entry**"

"Personnel/Operations/File Alpha."

"Authorization code."

He tapped in another set of numbers and letters.

"Operator not authorized. Do not repeat."

He frowned before hitting the reset.

"Subset."

"Personnel/Operations/File Alpha."

"Authorization code."

The captain tried another code he had picked up.

"Operator not authorized. This station not authorized. Do not repeat."

"Istvenn!" The exclamation was low and followed by a headshake, then by another keyboard entry.

"Subset."

"Clear."

"Sysoff."

The screen blanked.

The captain leaned forward and reached around the console to cut its power. Then he eased the swivel back and stood, stretching and looking toward the still-quiet duty section of the Operations bay.

"Need to know more before you try again," he said to himself, as he turned to leave the dimly lit row of consoles.

He shook his head once more, then squared his shoulders and was gone into the shadows of the off-duty hours.

XXXIV

GERSWIN SHIFTED HIS weight slowly, soundlessly, as his eyes continued to adjust to the darkening night. He lay stretched behind a hummock topped by a single scraggly yucca.

The evening breeze, light for a change, carried the faint and
chilled bitterness of grubush, reclaimed soil from the fields ten kays
to the east, and the even fainter scent of landpoison. Here, in the
lower foothills and under the scattered table mesas, the already faint
smell of landpoison was lessening with each passing year.

Gerswin stiffened as his ears picked up the faintest hint of a
padding step, a scraping sound of leather against bush. He thought
he felt the faintest of vibrations in the packed clay under his elbow,
but dismissed it as imaginary.

The breeze picked up, and with the moving air came the unmis-
takable musk/spice scent of a devilkid—male, young. With that scent
came the more rancid odor of shambletown leathers.

The sounds, faint as they had been, dropped away as the devilkid
froze to listen.

Gerswin smiled, but did not move a muscle otherwise. The wind
favored him this time.

A faint scrape rustled through the night.

Gerswin brought up the starlighter camera, checking to see that
the light intensifiers were operating. He waited, breathing lightly as
the spice scent grew stronger.

He hoped he was far enough from the coyote track to the hidden
spring, and that his own route to his stalking spot had been circuitous
enough that no trace of his own scent would be carried to the approaching devilkid.

Brown hair, shining somehow with nothing but the darkness of
black clouds overhead—that was what Gerswin caught sight of first.
Brown hair bound with a single twist of thong and hacked off ten to
fifteen centimeters below the leather.

The I.S.S. officer waited, unmoving, starlight camera focused, for
a clear shot. One would be all he would get.

The devilkid slipped out from the opening between two
grubushes five meters in front of Gerswin. He pressed the stud.

Click.

Swish! Thud!

Rolling to the left and cradling the camera, Gerswin came to his feet even as the sling stone buried itself in the clay where he had been lying.

The even, pad-pounding of quick feet indicated that the retreating devilkid had opted for speed rather than silence.

Gerswin grinned wryly. Noise was relative. He doubted that any Impies more than a few meters away would have heard any of the encounter except for the thud of the sling stone. He looked over at the gouge in the clay.

Had they been watching from where he had waited, they might have heard nothing. The gouged path showed the stone had passed through the spot where his head had been.

He scowled, then focused the starlighter lens on the gouge and the position where he had waited. He could use the lab equipment to add an outline once he was ready to present the pictures to Matsuko.

By themselves, the pictures might not be enough, but then again, they might be.

Hoping the first picture had turned out as clearly as he had seen the devilkid, Gerswin straightened and began to whistle as he trotted back toward the base. He had a ways to go, since Matsuko had forbidden him to take a flitter. Getting the Ops officer to allow the camera work had been hard enough, even with Mahmood's backing.

While Gerswin could have borrowed it without the Ops officer being the wiser, the problem was that he needed the pictures to make his case. Trying to explain how he had obtained them would have been sticky, to say the least.

He shrugged. The pictures were the first step, just the first of many.

GERSWIN CAUGHT HIS breath, forcing himself to inhale and exhale slowly. He waited behind the crumbling, sheered-off pillars that no longer supported anything but air, each now a two meter high pedestal nearly a meter across.

He sniffed lightly, aware that he was still downwind of his quarry, hoping that the wind direction did not change before the devilkid arrived at the spring.

Pursing his lips, he studied the ground, the hill rising on the far side of the thin trickle of water that passed for a stream. What water there was soaked itself into the clay less than a kay down the valley—less than a kay from the clean spring to a poisoned sinkhole.

The deadness of the lower part of the hill valley was more evident than in the worst of the high plains locales, and the odor of the land-poisons stronger, and even more bitter. The flattened quagmires to the east, the flats running to the sea, contained little besides black-ened and poisoned water seeping seaward.

The shambletown to the north was smaller than Denv, and poorer, and the lack of any healthy flora or fauna besides rats, a scrag-gly variety of ground oak, scattered coyotes, and an occasional grubush underscored the reasons why the Imperial ecologists, Mah-mood and his predecessors, had chosen to begin with the high plains and work seaward.

So far the dozers and the techs and the farmers had managed to push the habitable line a hundred kays east of the main base and roughly fifty kays north and south.

At that rate, Gerswin estimated as he waited, it would take nearly ten centuries just to reclaim a sizable chunk of the eastern side of the Noram continent. The techs claimed the work was getting easier as they developed their techniques, but how much better could it get?

He shrugged and gave up the mental estimation process as he concentrated on listening for the sounds he knew had to come.

Shhhhhppppp.

His devilkid quarry was easing along the far side of the small val-ley, dancing from one concealed position to another, still well beyond the range of the stunner Gerswin carried.

From his prone position Gerswin did not strain to see the other, but watched, relaxed, as the other moved closer.

The wind began to die. The I.S.S. captain checked the swirl of clouds overhead to see if the wind patterns were about to change, if they might leave him upwind with a sudden shift.

He frowned, easing his head back to focus on the devilkid, who had slowed unexpectedly as he sensed something was not quite right.

A pebble buried in the clay on which Gerswin rested chose that moment to begin digging through his camouflage suit and jabbing at his thigh muscles. Knowing the devilkid was studying the approach to the spring, the part where the water was nearly pure, Gerswin ignored the sharp ache, and waited unmoving.

Finally, the devilkid darted from behind a low heap of blackened stone and across ten meters of open ground before ducking behind one of the truncated pillars that matched the one sheltering Gerswin.

Gerswin gauged the distance. It was still too far for a clear or a clean shot. He let his eyes ease toward the clouds overhead, which seemed motionless in the gray stillness, to recheck the possible wind patterns.

The eastern hills were warmer than the high plains. This showed in subtle ways—the more rounded terrain, the damper nature of the clay, and the lack of organic rubble of any sort.

The devilkid moved again, and Gerswin refocused on the quarry as the other slipped from pillar to pillar until he was directly opposite Gerswin, less than twenty meters away across the thin ribbon of water.

Once the devilkid moved, Gerswin would have a clear shot. He waited, putting aside the growing discomfort from the clay and the imbedded pebbles that dug into his legs and thighs.

The wind ruffled his hair from behind.

From behind?

Gerswin uncoiled like an attacking coyote, legs driving him straight across the soggy clay banks of the stream, lifting him over the thin trickle with one long bound.

The devilkid had begun to streak back toward cover nearly as quickly as Gerswin had moved, weaving between the pillar stumps, back toward a narrow crevice in the valley wall from which Gerswin suspected he had come.

Thrummm!

The running devilkid dodged to the right.

Thrumm!

Crack!

A nut-sized stone struck the pillar Gerswin was passing, but he plowed on.

Thrumm!

Crack!

Thrummm!

Crump.

The devilkid collapsed as his last stone rebounded off a pillar into Gerswin's ribs. Gerswin ignored the bruised feeling and approached the limp body carefully. While he could tell the youth was unconscious, he had to wonder if there was another devilkid nearby.

The boy could have easily beaten Gerswin to the nearly hidden split in the rocks at the edge of the valley had he not changed directions.

Gerswin threw himself sideways.

Crack!

The second devilkid also had a sling, and knew how to use it. The stone had passed through the spot where Gerswin had been standing instants before, and only a faint whir had tipped him off, a sound so soft he doubted that anyone but a devilkid could have heard it.

Crack!

Gerswin dropped behind a pillar.

Nodding to himself, he calculated the newest devilkid's position, right behind a stone heap beside the split in the twenty meter high stone wall from which both had come.

He uncoiled himself across the distance to another and shorter pillar, skidding behind it as his boots nearly lost all purchase on the clay-covered pavement underfoot. The next pillar stood five meters uphill, a distance he would have to cover mostly in the open, but that position would give him the altitude to get a shot behind the stones.

Glancing back, he could see the first devilkid still lying unconscious and face down on the dark clay between the truncated pillars.

Gerswin knelt and pried loose a rock, or rather what looked to be a section of an antique brick of some sort. He hefted it in his right hand, still holding the stunner in his left. Lofting it toward the stone pile shielding the devilkid, he timed his departure for the next pillar as the stone clattered down.

Skidding behind the pillar, Gerswin watched as the devilkid ran downhill toward the stream, well out of range before Gerswin could bring the stunner to bear.

The I.S.S. officer bounded back downhill, sprinting full speed for a moment, then settling into a ground-covering lope.

Gerswin's smile was fixed on his face, grimly fixed. There was no cover below the pillared area where the spring rose for at least two kays, just scoured and smooth clay, which meant that the devilkid had every expectation of being able to outrun him.

Gerswin stepped up his pace slightly, and immediately saw he was beginning to close on the tattered tunic of the other. The devilkid had cleverly maneuvered him into a position where he couldn't use the stunner until the devilkid was well on the run.

By now the ground was flatter, and the edges of the valley were beginning to melt into the rolling terrain of the lower plains. Gerswin kept his legs moving evenly and his stride in rhythm, even as the devilkid tried to increase the pace.

Gerswin did not break stride as he watched the other gain ten meters. Slowly, his longer and more even stride began to narrow the distance between them once again.

Still, by the time he was within thirty meters, he could feel his own heart thudding, and he slowly brought the stunner into position.

Thrumm!

The devilkid's right leg spasmed. He tumbled into a heap, but still tried to crawl before fumbling with a set of leather straps.

Thrumm!

Thrumm!

It took Gerswin two shots to get the devilkid, in his haste to avoid taking another hit from the deadly sling.

As he closed on the stunned devilkid, he noted the red hair, the too-thin face, the concealed curves, and realized that his second quarry had been a girl.

He bent to scoop up the sling, suppressing the wince he would have liked to express as his ribs protested. While he doubted that the rebounding stone had cracked them, the muscles were certainly bruised.

He shook his head, gingerly. The computer analyses had given him more than enough locations to check out, and he still had another ten of the most likely to do, with less than two weeks remaining on his leave.

Matsuko had been firm. Firm, but fair. If Gerswin spent his own time corraling devilkids, and if they could be reindoctrinated with some basics, and if they could pass the intelligence and aptitude tests, then, and only then, would he recommend training.

Gerswin shouldered the girl's limp and all-too-light body and began the uphill march back to the first devilkid, trying to make his steps as quick as possible.

He disliked leaving anyone unconscious in such terrain, but neither the rats nor the coyotes liked daytime, and there had been no shambletowners near when he had taken off after the girl.

He broke into a trot, slipped another power cell into the stunner, awkwardly, since he was moving and balancing the girl. Then, as he holstered the stunner, he picked up the pace.

As he passed the blackened sinkhole where the stream disappeared into the clay, the hint of a familiar and rancid odor drifted to him on the wind.

He sighed, and tried to step up his trot, hoping he could get back to the pillar area before the shambletowners took out their frustrations and long-time hates on the unconscious devilkid.

Scrpppp.

The sound had come from the rocks on the left side of the valley, and the scent of shambletowners strengthened.

Gerswin glanced over at the rocky area in time to see a figure diving for cover.

He was on the right side of the stream, exposed to view, but too far from any of the sheltered spots on the left for a slingstone to have too damaging an impact, if indeed any of the shambletowners had the nerve to try.

Except for a quick survey of the area, there had been little contact with the Birmha shambletown, and no reason to maintain such contact when the base resources were already spread so thinly and when the shambletowners themselves seemed to resent any intrusion.

Plick! Plick!

Large, isolated raindrops began to fall from the darkening clouds as Gerswin topped the last rise where the ground leveled out onto the narrow valley floor.

A slinking figure darted toward the clearing where the devilkid presumably still lay.

Thrumm!

Plick! Plick, plick.

The stunner bolt passed over the pillar behind which the shambletowner had dived. The scene was silent, except for the rain and the pad-pound of Gerswin's feet.

He slid to a stop at the edge of the clearing, nearly losing his hold on the girl. The boy was still crumpled where Gerswin had dropped him. Gerswin lowered the girl next to a pillar and crossed to the boy, studying the surrounding area and listening.

Whrrr!

Crack!

Gerswin rolled forward, wincing as his bruised muscles protested the sudden movement.

The two shambletowners were neither as sure nor as quick as the devilkids had been. He located them instantly, still not in cover.

Thrummm!

One pitched forward. The other ran.

Thrumm!

The second shambletowner dropped in midstride.

The Imperial officer waited, studying the valley, breathing deeply, and listening.

After the silence had continued and when he had restored his own oxygen balance, he bent and checked the condition of the dark-haired boy.

The youngster had moved slightly, and his breathing was returning to a pattern more like a deep sleep. Gerswin shook his head. Either the Impies or the shambletowners would have been under full stun for at least another hour.

Slowly, he shouldered the boy's form, nearly as light as the girl's, then walked the several meters to recover her.

With the double load, and with the fine drops of rain pelting on his head, his face, and shoulders, he concentrated on putting one foot in front of the other as he headed down the valley to his pick-up spot. His feet left deep marks in the clay, marks that were being erased by the light rain within minutes of his passing.

He never looked back at the unmoving forms of the shambletowners. The coyotes might get them, and so might the rats. And they might not.

His even steps brought him back down toward the rolling plain that eventually, kilometers eastward, would turn into a black quagmire, back toward the pick-up spot where his equipment was sealed into a stun-protected pack, and from where he would signal for a flitter.

He sighed.

A grim smile then flitted across his damp face, as the rainwind swirled about him and plastered down the tight blond curls of his hair.

The two he had picked up would make it, Matsuko be damned. He suspected the others would as well, if he could keep them from destroying each other and the Impies who would have to guard them at first.

If . . . If . . . If . . .

He sighed again, but did not slow as he slogged downward through the wind and the rain.

XXXVI

GERSWIN SCANNED THE screen, studying the eight figures, all stretched on the flextile flooring. The cots were empty.

Five young men, three women—the results of six months of preparation and two weeks of leave—waited like the caged animals they resembled.

"Eight, Captain? Just eight who meet the minimums?"

"That's an estimate, Harl. Just an estimate."

Eight, thought Gerswin. Were eight all there were, or all he and

Imperial technology could find and drag from the ruins of the planet?

He took a deep breath.

"Hold these, Harl."

He handed the weapons belt to the technician and palmed the portal release.

"Ser! Clerris and N'gere are still recovering."

"I know. That's why this is my job."

He eased inside the portal, waiting until it was securely closed behind him before moving farther into the converted dormitory.

Quiet as he had been, the two figures closest to the portal rolled out of sleep and into a crouch.

The first one to his feet was dark-eyed, with the shining depth of cat-eyes, dark-haired, and wore the tattered, raw, and uneven leathers and fur of the plains coyote. He was bareheaded and barefoot.

The second slid to her feet with more grace, but just as swiftly. Instead of leathers, she wore the discarded sack trousers and jacket of a shambletowner. Green eyes burned under the short-hacked thatch of black hair.

Gerswin stood there, barehanded, balanced, waiting for the attack he knew would come.

The boy launched himself—a dark streak half invisible in the darkened room.

With even greater speed, Gerswin stepped aside, letting his arms strike so swiftly that they never seemed to have moved from their half-raised position in front of him.

Thud.

The fall of the crumpled figure that had been Gerswin's attacker shook the flextile floor.

The girl pretended to look down and turn away, scuffed one bare foot on the smooth surface underfoot, then the other. A third scuff, and a fourth, followed, each one narrowing the distance between her and the I.S.S. officer, each one alerting the six others in the dormitory.

Gerswin smiled, flicked his eyes to the still-slumped figure in the corner and back to the girl.

"You lose, devilkid," he observed.

"No!"

Again . . . Gerswin faced a dark streak, so quick that the men watching through the screens could not see what happened, only that the results were the same.

Two figures lay beside each other in the corner to Gerswin's left, both breathing, both stunned.

The six others attacked—roughly together. Seven bodies merged and blurred, the motions so fast that the Service observers and outside sentries did not move, uncertain what to do next.

Before they could decide, the chaos sorted itself out, with bodies falling and being thrown aside, until a single figure stood alone.

Gerswin shuddered, took a deep breath, and wiped the blood off his forehead with the back of his right hand. His ribs ached again, and crisscrossing his forearms were a net of gouges. The blood continued to ooze from his forehead.

He took three steps to his left and yanked the boy, his first attacker, into the air.

The youngster's eyes blazed, but he did not strike.

"Devilkid you. Devilkid me." Gerswin pinned the boy with his eyes as he spoke, although his attention was also on the seven others. "I talk. You follow. Stand? Stand clear?"

He set the boy on his feet and turned away, toward the girl, listening for the possible signs of another attack.

The whisper of a foot was enough.

Like lightning, Gerswin whirled and struck, ducking under the streak of the other, planting a stiffened palm under the youth's sternum, followed by an elbow across the jaw, and a sweep kick to leave an even more crumpled heap of devilkid.

"Devilkids you. All devilkids. Head devilkid—me! I talk. You follow. Stand? Stand clear?"

He grabbed the girl who had attacked second.

"You stand?"

"Stand."

Less than five standard minutes later, he stood in front of the eight—all eight—his back again to the portal, the blood still dripping from his forehead.

"Teach you talk good. Teach you clean good. Teach you learn good. Stand?"

"Teach us fight good?"

"Learn good first. Then fight. Stand?"

"Stand."

Gerswin went down the line, repeating the process with each one, forcing a commitment and a personal loyalty, which was all that could bind them now.

"Be back. You wait. No fight."

Not one moved as he turned his back and walked out through the portal. Once he was gone, the eight approached each other warily.

Outside, the two techs, the two sentries, and the sergeant of the guard stepped back as Gerswin moved away from the portal.

"Long flight ahead, Harl." There was a twist to his lips as he said it. "Long flight."

"Yes, ser."

"I'll be at the flight surgeon's, then over with Major Matsuko and the commander."

"Yes, ser."

"Don't go in there. Not one of you. You wouldn't last a minute."

"Yes, ser."

His quick steps echoed on the tile, then faded as he entered the tunnel.

Finally, Harl cleared his throat.

"Eight of them . . . like him?"

"He's better."

"Fine. Eight of them half as good as him?"

The guard sergeant shook his head slowly. "They kept saying he was as good as a Corpus killer. They were wrong. He's better, lots better. Lots better."

Harl looked at the corridor down which the captain had disappeared. "Who would believe it?"

"That's a weapon, too."

Harl screwed up his face as he wrestled with another question.

"Why does he want them?"

"Why did the commander let him round them up?"

Harl frowned, then relaxed.

"He has a reason for everything. He always does."

XXXVII

About that tower of time on Old Earth where no towers exist? A metaphor, no doubt, but D'Lorina never makes that clear.

A tower in the traditional sense would rear to the skies, but in the days of her mythical captain, for whom she presents a rather convincing case, by the way, nothing reared into the skies

of Old Earth, and even the mountain tops were scoured lower by
the stone rains and the landspouts.

The only tower that she could refer to is the single building
dating from that period, and it is less than a tower—far less. That
building, and I use the term loosely, is the administration and operations bunker of the original Imperial Interstellar Survey Service. It is now preserved as a monument. A fortress of time would
have been a far better metaphor, but precision in imagery was not
the principal purpose of D'Lorina's scholarship.

She makes a convincing case that *a* captain, more likely a series of strong captains, existed, but it is doubtful that such a case
could ever be completely verified or disproved, or that anyone living today could ever understand the darkness of that period, or
unravel the darker secrets, or, if sane, would want to do so.

> *Critiques of the Mythmakers*
> Ereth A'Kirod
> New Avalon, 4541 N.E.C.

XXXVIII

THE FLITTER TOUCHED down on the flat expanse of sand protruding
from the purple-gray waters. The whine of the thrusters faded and
was followed by a *click* as the canopy slid back.

Two figures in coveralls emerged and dropped to the grayish
sand, their knees and black flight boots vanishing in the mist that
drifted above the waters and over the sandspit.

With the dampness and the chill, with the gray mist and purpled
water rippling solely from the tidal pressures beyond the delta, came
the odor of death. Not the hot odor of death in the arena, nor the
odor of hot metal and oiled death, nor the decay of swamps, nor even
the moldiness of an ill-tended graveyard, but the metallic residue of
death so long embalmed that only the inorganic heavy metals remain,
those and the faintest whiff of past life.

Gerswin turned to his left, toward a black shimmering stump with
a single limb that rose three meters from the purple waters.

"Maps say this was a heavily forested delta two thousand years
back. Another century and it will be gone."

"Just kill-water," answered the other. "Why show me? Kill-water is kill-water."

Gerswin shook his head, jabbed his left hand at the stump.

"Didn't have to be. Doesn't have to be. We can change it. You can change it."

"Kill-water is kill-water."

The pilot snapped his head up in a single fluid motion to let both visors retract into the helmet housing. His hawk-yellow eyes caught the youth, slightly built like Gerswin himself, but with a fringe of dark hair showing beneath the back of his helmet.

"I'm the captain, Lerwin. Captain. Life-water is what we need, and you're going to New Augusta and Alphane and New Colora. You're going, and you're coming back. Life-water. That's the reason. You forget, and I'll chase you to the corners of the universe. Stand?"

"Stand."

Gerswin did not contest the sullenness of the response, instead motioned to the flitter.

The two figures climbed the recessed hand- and toeholds of the military craft and settled back into the cockpit. Within moments, the whine of the thrusters broke the stillness of mist and silent water, and the *click* of the closing canopy was lost in the power of the engines.

The gray mist swirled away in the small tornado of lifeless sand and hot air that spurted behind the lifting flitter. No sooner had it lifted into the overlying haze than the gray mist oozed back over the sandspit, concealing it from all but the most careful, or well-instrumented, observer.

In the flitter itself, Gerswin touched the course plate, let the course line and map come up on the screen in front of the other.

"You heard of Washton, Lerwin? Washton, stand?"

"Stand."

"Watch."

Gerswin triggered the recorded sequence, the tapes and visions he had screened from the Archives, from the old records, scanning the course readouts as he did.

"Opswatch, Prime Outrider. Interrogative met status. Interrogative met status."

"Prime Outrider, landspout at three four five, thirty kays. Negative on sheer lines. Interrogative fuel status."

"Ten plus. Ten plus."

"Understand ten plus. Your course is green."

"Stet. Prime on course line."

Lerwin did not comment on the transmission, engrossed as he was in the visions of sweeping green velvet lawns, white structures, and antique vehicles traversing pavements of black and white. And everywhere was sunlight, the glittering golden sunlight no devilkid on Old Earth saw.

Gerswin glanced from the instruments at Lerwin, then back at the course line and through the armaglass of the canopy at the ground fog and the swamp beneath it.

Lerwin did not look up from the glitter and the brilliance of the old records until his small screen blanked.

"Real? Here? People?"

"Not here. Where we're headed. Washton."

"Prime Outrider," the commnet interrupted, "Opswatch. Landspout at three four five. Twenty kays and closing."

Gerswin switched his attention back to the long view screen, then nodded.

"Opswatch. Interrogative course change."

"That's affirmative. Affirmative. Suggest change to zero eight zero for point five. Say again zero eight zero for point five."

"Changing to zero eight zero for point five."

"Understand course of zero eight zero for point five."

"Stet, Opswatch."

Gerswin leveled the flitter on the more eastern course and checked the projected fuel consumption of the new course line and timing. The change would cost him fuel, but the extra consumption was well within the reserve.

He hoped that convincing Lerwin would do the job. Since Lerwin was the most stubborn of the bunch, if Lerwin could be persuaded to understand the problem, he could reinforce the urgency Gerswin was attempting to instill in the remainder of the devilkids.

Gerswin sighed, and his shoulders slumped momentarily as his eyes flicked across the board before him.

The studied simplicity of the controls and indicators reflected all too well the Imperial design and expenditure, an expenditure level that could and would not be continued once the uniqueness of the great home planet cleanup campaign gave way to some other quixotic quest, once the Imperial Court decided that Old Earth would take forever to fix up.

The contrast between the devilkids and the Imperials . . . the devilkids were brighter and already had the potential to be far better of-

ficers and pilots than all but the very best of the I.S.S. Not that ability
meant much in any large organization, but it would take ability to
solve the environmental problems of Old Earth, not politics.

Despite the landspouts and sheerwinds, most of the first-stage
land mapping of Noram was completed. In real terms, the handful of
reclamation dozers had just begun the sifting of soil, gram by gram,
to remove and destroy the landpoisons, and the reclamation crops
had been harvested twice. Ten thousand square kays so far—it
sounded so impressive and was so small.

The task was big, so big, sometimes he wondered about the possibility of anyone ever completing it.

"Dark glooms got you?" asked Lerwin.

"Hell of a contrast," responded Gerswin, ignoring the thrust of
Lerwin's question. "Old Washton and landdead here. No!"

"Different," grunted Lerwin. "Old Washton like that? Real like
that?"

"Real. Outplanets like that now. You'll see. Old Earth was greener
than all. What we need. What we'll get."

Even though he hadn't looked at the screening Lerwin had just
seen since he had canned it weeks earlier, Gerswin could still remember the emerald grass, and the sun, the golden sun that had
shone down on everything, on the white marble buildings, the towers,
the water that had seemed so blue.

He'd managed to compare some of the vistas in the tapes to the
rubble, enough to convince himself that the ruins identified on the
maps were indeed the sites on the ancient tapes. For the others, after
Lerwin had a chance to spread the word, he had planned a set of comparison tapes, side by sides of the ancient tapes and the present ruins.

"Prime Outrider, this is Opswatch. Cleared to resume direct approach to target."

"Opswatch, Prime Outrider, steering zero five zero."

"Understand zero five zero. Zero five zero is green. ETA point
eight."

"ETA at point eight on zero five zero."

"What did you say?" Lerwin asked after listening to the transmissions and cocking his head in puzzlement.

"You'll learn. Like a new language. Takes time. Takes practice.
Just practice."

If Lerwin was anything like he'd been, speech was so much slower
than thought, particularly when the devilkids had so little use for anything beyond the rudimentary trade talk.

Gerswin kept up his continual scan of the board before him, the screens, and the gray vistas spread out toward the unseen horizon. Gray was the color of the clouds above, the intermittent ground fog beneath, and darker gray the barren hills themselves, with occasional patches of purpled grass, bushes, and an infrequent bent tree.

Contrasting with these omnipresent grays were the bare brown shades of short rocky hilltops or small mountains.

"Deadland," observed Lerwin.

"Deader here than on the high plains. Landpoison collects on the lower grounds."

A green dart lit on the homing panel.

Gerswin edged the stick and the flitter leftward and locked in the course change, centered on the beacon he had placed on his surveillance runs.

"Clear look, Lerwin. Clear look. Stand?"

The younger man shifted his weight in the copilot's seat.

"Clear look, stand," he agreed, but the tone of his response and his restlessness indicated what Gerswin was afraid might be a lack of comprehension.

The gray-brown hills beneath became less pronounced, but even with the gentler terrain, the deadland grass remained sparse and harder to pick out as the ground fog patches became more frequent.

Every so often, the flitter passed over a darker and shinier gray, with mist rising above it, that denoted water—a slow-flowing river, a dead lake.

"Prime Outrider, this is Opswatch. Interrogative status."

"Opswatch, Prime Outrider. Status green. Locked on target locator."

"Understand locked on locator."

"Affirmative. Affirmative. Will report arrival."

The pilot shifted his attention from the communications back to the terrain. The first visible signs of what once had been a capitol city were becoming more evident—the white line of cracked and fragmented shards that had been a highway, the all-too-regular mounded humps, and, here and there, the actual stump of brick and steel that remained after the twisting and grinding power of the centuries of landspouts.

The green beacon dart began to pulse on the console.

Gerswin noted the dark steel gray band below the eastern visual horizon. That was the river, and the speckled dark gray and white beyond was the swamp that had been a capitol.

"All those humps—houses. Places to live. Stand?" Gerswin gestured with his right hand briefly, before dropping it back to the thruster controls.

Lerwin followed the motion with his eyes.

"People, all?"

"Millions."

"Deadland now," concluded Lerwin.

Gerswin gave a small nod of agreement and recentered the course line for the beacon and the white stump of stone where he had placed it. He began to throttle back on the thrusters before deploying the rotors for the slow overflight circles he had planned.

As soon as the airspeed dropped below two hundred kays, he began the deployment sequence. Shortly, the high-pitched whine of the thrusters dropped into a lower key and was supplemented by the *thwop-thwop* of the blades as the flitter began a slow circle of one island in the swamp.

"Opswatch, this is Prime Outrider. On target. Status green. Estimate time on station at point five. Point five on station."

"Prime Outrider, understand arrival on station. Time on station point five. Request you report departure. Report departure."

"Stet. Will report departure."

To the west was the flat, near-glassy expanse of the river, and to the east, a series of islands of varying sizes, each surmounted with white marble block, some conveying structure, others merely a jumble. Gerswin continued to circle the island closest to the point where the swamp merged with the river, letting Lerwin see it clearly.

From the center of the island the flitter circled, rose the square stump of white marble perhaps sixty meters long. At the sixty meter point the former spire ended, not with a clean cut, but along jagged edges, as if a giant had broken off the top with a single blow. To the northwest, midway between the island and the higher ground that led out of the swamp, was a line of shattered marble, lying barely exposed above the swamp water like a stone quarrel pointing the way to an unknown destination.

Gerswin tapped a stud on the panel.

"Lerwin. Watch the screen. Check the island, then the screen. Stand?"

"What?"

"Watch the screen. Watch outside."

A scene from the ancient tapes flashed onto the screen in front of the copilot's seat. On the screen stood a marble obelisk, stretching from emerald grass and stone walks into a clear blue and cloudless sky. The view changed to show the spire from the air, as well as the lower marble buildings at the edge of the rectangular expanse of grass that surrounded the marble spire.

Lerwin's eyes flitted from the stone stump on the island to the screen and back to the island, and back to the screen.

"No. No . . . Yes?"

Gerswin banked the flitter out of the circle and headed slowly eastward to the hilltop less than two kays from the ancient monument.

Again, he put the flitter into a circle. The building or buildings beneath had also been white marble. All that remained were white stones streaked with rust and coated with a grayish film. Under the stone jumble, this time Gerswin thought he could detect a squarish pattern of sorts, although when he had first surveyed Washton, he had found it difficult to match the tapes with the devastation that time and the landspouts had wrought.

He tapped the screen controls again, this time to bring another view of the ancient capitol before Lerwin.

"Washton, Lerwin. What was. Now what is. Stand?"

"Was . . . is? All landdead, swampdead. This was that?"

Gerswin nodded enough for the motion to be clear, still concentrating on trying to keep the flitter close enough to the right angle and altitude for the comparisons to be clear to Lerwin, and to take his own shots of the ruins with the small tapecubes mounted on the port forward stub. The views he had taken this time and the time before would have to do for the others, since trying to convince the commander and Matsuko to allow him such a cross-country jaunt for each of the devilkids wasn't even an off-nova possibility. Two flights—the recon run and this one—had been justified for research purposes this year. And he couldn't wait another year.

As he circled, while the devilkid Lerwin looked from screen to ruins to screen, Gerswin scanned from board to horizon to screen to Lerwin to board, trying to gauge the impact on Lerwin.

Lerwin said nothing.

Finally, Gerswin broke off the circle and headed for the religious shrine on the top of one of the higher hills.

There, again, he repeated the process, and through the screen shots and the comparisons, Lerwin said nothing.

"Prime Outrider, this is Opswatch. Recommend departure no later than point two. No later than point two."

"Opswatch, this is Prime Outrider. Understand departure in point two. Interrogative met status."

"That's affirmative. Landspout line developing to the northeast."

"Interrogative closure."

"Projected at one five zero kays. One five zero."

"Stet, Opswatch. Will notify of departure."

Gerswin scanned his own small weather screen, saw nothing, and switched his attention back to Lerwin.

"Time for one more, Lerwin, before we sprint back home."

The flitter eased out of the bank and toward the scrubby hills to the southeast of the pile of darkened stones that the map had indicated was once a cathedral.

"Another shrine."

Gerswin jabbed the screen tapes control to bring up the second shrine. While it had not been so impressive to begin with, the destruction was more clear-cut. The landspouts had scoured everything clean except the foundation outlines and dumped the stone and iron into a twisted heap at the eastern end of the unnaturally flattened hilltop.

Lerwin shook his head through the entire three circuits by the flitter.

"Could show you more, but most places are gone, covered with swamp. Some I couldn't identify. Sides, don't want to end up scrapped by the landspouts," observed the pilot as he began the rotor retraction sequence.

"Opswatch, this is Prime Outrider. Departing target this time. Course two seven five. Two seven five."

"Prime Outrider, understand two seven five."

"That's affirmative."

The moments in the cockpit dragged on as the whine of the thrusters built along with the airspeed.

Gerswin wondered why he was depressed. He had apparently succeeded in getting his point across to Lerwin. He had been able to get some solid shots of the ruins, which would please Matsuko.

"Prime Outrider, this is Opswatch. Suggest two eight five. Suggest two eight five."

"Two eight five. Coming to two eight five. Steady on two eight five."

The flitter rocked, and Gerswin checked the thrusters. Steady and in the green. Course two eight five and five standard hours to go before touchdown.

Another standard hour passed before Lerwin spoke.

"Why?"

Gerswin didn't answer immediately. What could he say?

How could a people reach the stars, how could they build systems that could still map continents, shelter them under a mountain, and have them operate fifteen to twenty centuries later? How could they build materials that Imperial technology could not understand or duplicate and not stop the devastation of their own planet? How could they forge materials impervious to hellburners and indecipherable to Imperial engineers and have been so unable to stop the collapse?

"Why?" asked Lerwin again.

"Don't know." What else could he say? What could anyone have said?

KIEDRA STUDIED HER reflection in the mirror one last time before glancing down at the single packed kit bag by the bunk. She still wasn't used to a bunk. Even with the hard panel of composite she'd found to put under the mattress, the Imperial bedding felt too soft.

The plain gray tunic was adequate, certainly better than patched leathers stolen from shambletowners, and although the cloth was soft, it resisted everything but the rain. Nothing resisted the rain. Best were the boots, supple enough to run, but hard enough to shield feet from the shards . . .

She frowned. Hard to forget that there wouldn't be any shards where she was headed. No shards, no landpoisons, no king rats or she-coyotes—just machines and people.

Gerswin had emphasized the people, and the piling of scent upon scent, all muted, as if the people were locked behind windows.

She looked back into the mirror, green cat-eyes facing green cat-eyes, tight-curled black hair facing tight-curled black hair. Gerswin had told her, when she had asked, that she was attractive. But he'd never raised a hand to her, and the other devilkids—the males—were more interested in the Imperial women. The Imperial men . . . the techs eyed her appreciatively, that she could tell from their breathing and the conversations they thought she had not overheard, but they shied away from her.

The officers were another matter. All were taller than she was, but while they were polite and would help her learn anything, not one ventured even a casual touch.

"Devil-woman . . ." Kiedra had heard that enough.

She bit her lip. Just because she had objected to being pawed that one time.

Gerswin had not been exactly kind to her when he had arrived on the scene after that incident, although he had certainly been cool enough to Lieutenant Kardias and not at all sympathetic about his broken arm. But then Gerswin had glared at her when no one was looking.

She shivered. There was the real devilkid, with the cold fire in his soul and the weight of the night on his heart.

She sighed, squared her shoulders, and left the kit bag by the bunk. She had more than a standard hour before she had to be at the hangar-bunker for the shuttle to the *Churchill.*

As she marched toward the captain's quarters, her quick strides made up for any shortness of leg she might have had.

While the faint trace in the fainter dust outside his portal indicated he was gone, she buzzed anyway. Waited. Buzzed again. And again.

Then she checked the time. Still enough for her to look outside and make it to the shuttle.

Her steps took her to the south lock portals, and she went through the inner and outer ports as quickly as she could. The whistling wind flapped the lower edges of her tunic and tugged at the flat waistband, but the absence of machine oil and musty human stink was a relief. She took a deep breath of the ice cold air, exhaled slowly, and turned her head to search the ridgeline and hillside, while her ears strained.

Crack!

The sound of a slingstone hitting something came from the left, and Kiedra hurried toward the sound, unconsciously adopting the quick sliding run of a devilkid on the hunt, hugging the side of the earth-covered administration building until she crossed the highest point of the ridge.

On the other side, as she had hoped, was Gerswin, practicing with a shambletown sling.

She stopped and watched as he effortlessly fired off three stones in a row.

Crack! Crack! Crack!

The last split a head-sized rock, placed above the man-shaped target, in two.

Gerswin walked over to the target, reclaimed the stones, replaced the "head" with another rock, and stalked back to another position, with a different angle and distance.

Thwick!

Kiedra blinked. She had not seen the blade, but there it was, buried so deep in the target that only a sliver of metal showed.

Gerswin turned and started to walk farther from the target, then turned and dropped, letting go with a single sling cast, all in one fluid motion.

Crack!

The stone bounced off the "chest" of the battered plastic target.

The captain looked uphill, and even at that distance, she felt the yellow of his eyes chilling her. He motioned her toward him with a single curt gesture.

Within moments, it seemed, she had covered the distance between them.

"Should be on your way to the shuttle."

"Should. Will be. Came . . . to say good-bye."

"You'll be back. Not too long."

"Too long." She shook her head, violently. "Why aren't you there to see us go?"

"Don't like good-byes."

"We do?"

He looked at the clay.

Slowly, as if she were moving it a great distance against heavy grav, she extended her left hand until her fingers wrapped around his. She squeezed gently.

"Kiedra. You'll be fine. Learn everything you can."

She said nothing. Their eyes met, hers drinking in the cold, brown-flecked yellow of his, and the darkness behind the yellow and the chill they radiated.

"Late for the shuttle," he reminded her.

"I'll make it." She did not let go of his hand, squeezed his fingers more tightly.

Finally, he smiled faintly, and leaned forward to brush her cheek with his lips.

A fatherly kiss, she felt, though she had never known one.

"Do what you want and what you must, but come back, Kiedra. We need you. All of us."

She withdrew her hand and stepped back, wanting to dash away, to run for cover, any cover. Instead, she inclined her head.

"I will be back, Captain. We all will."

She sensed Gerswin did not move as she turned and marched back toward the portal, back toward her single kit bag and the shuttle to the Empire, and the training that awaited her and seven others.

She let the single tear on her cheek dry untouched as she hurried through the portals toward her bag and the shuttle.

Gerswin relaxed slightly, but his position scarcely changed, not that it had been Marine-straight to begin with.

"Sit down. I know it's not in your nature, Greg, but sit down anyway." The major gestured to the chair across the blank table from him. Matsuko was one of the few officers on Old Earth Base who ignored consoles and the access to the central data banks they represented.

Gerswin sat.

"I have orders, orders to New Augusta."

Gerswin did not look directly at the olive-dark face of the Operations officer, nor down at the shining surface of the table from behind which Matsuko presided. Rather, his glance appeared disinterested. If he looked too intently at anyone, the automatic intensity of his gaze made the subject of his observation uncomfortable.

"Congratulations, Major. Know it's what you wanted. Hope the duty assignment is also what you requested."

"I'm being assigned to the War Plan Staff—Admiral Ligerto—after three months home leave."

"That's not why I asked you here, however." Matsuko held up a set of six fax flimsies. "I recommended you as my successor and your promotion to major, since Captain J'rome has also been transferred, as you know."

Gerswin did not breathe a sigh of relief at Captain J'rome's transfer, but most of the techs would.

Matsuko laughed, but the sound was forced. "I suppose one and two halves out of four isn't bad."

Gerswin frowned. "One and two halves."

"You know the one. The remaining two halves out of three? You get a temporary promotion to major, contingent on continued performance, and permanent no later than five years if not remanded or made permanent before, and you are assigned as Deputy Operations officer."

"That's what I've been doing, in fact."

"But not in name, and this makes it official."

"The new Operations officer?"

Matsuko nodded. "Reiner D'Gere Vlerio."

Gerswin raised his eyebrows. The impressive-sounding name meant exactly nothing to him.

"You might be one of the few who doesn't know him, or his family, I should say. He's the youngest son of one of the more powerful Barons of Commerce in the Empire, Baron Fredrich Reiner Vlerio. His house controls the databloc licenses."

Gerswin nodded in response. He could understand the money and power involved there.

"You don't seemed impressed, Major."

Gerswin appreciated the immediate promotion, but shrugged. What could he say?

"Some skepticism might be healthy. Major Vlerio was the lead scout pilot on the Analex Reconnaissance, and he was the only pilot from his section to return. We'll leave it at that. That's what is in the official records. Since then he has been attached to assignments at headquarters."

Gerswin was seeing a picture he didn't appreciate.

Matsuko laughed the short laugh that was not a laugh.

"He brought his orders with him, as well as yours and mine. Your promotion is effective today, but you do not take over as Deputy Ops boss until tomorrow, when Reiner takes charge."

Gerswin understood. How he understood. Major Reiner Vlerio needed a good fleet or out-systems tour, and the fleet wouldn't have him after the Analex screwup. No one trusted him not to foul up. Gerswin was appointed official custodian. If one Major Gerswin failed, there was no great loss to the Service, and if he succeeded, his status and promotion were assured, although only a few would know the special circumstances.

"I see."

"I think you do. I think you do, but not as much as you need."

"Would you care to explain, ser?"

"Major Vlerio is wasting no time. He has already requested a flitter to survey a landspout and tasked Lieutenant Deran as his copilot. While I could overrule him, since he doesn't take over until tomorrow, I won't."

"I understand, Major." And he did. Vlerio had had assignments at headquarters and certainly had friends left. Or acquaintances who would bow to the family's power.

"I'll take care of it. When does he lift off?"

"One stan."

"Then you'll excuse me."

"Good luck, Greg."

Gerswin merely nodded. He left the office and headed for Jeri Deran's quarters, hoping she was still there.

She was.

Petite, black-haired, black-eyed, dark-skinned, and with a hard and brassy voice that had more than once stunned male officers expecting a soft-spoken lady.

"To what do I owe this visit, Captain?" Jeri Deran had not stood up, but had remained seated on the edge of her bunk, pulling on her second flight boot.

"Your health, Lieutenant."

"My health. Healthy as a damned scampig! What's this health crap?"

"What do you know about Major Vlerio?"

"That he's Matsuko's successor. That he'll make the officer evaluations, and that he's the only ticket out of here. That's all I need to know right now."

"Wrong, Jeri. Need to know that most officers who fly with him don't survive. Also need to know that Matsuko is still Ops boss, and that I'm now Deputy Ops boss."

"Crap, Captain! Sheer unadulterated crap! You're trying to blow the one chance I've got to get out of here."

She had yanked on her second boot and stood, glaring at Gerswin.

"You run around like a tin god, and all the techs bow as you pass. So do half the pilots, and damned if I can see why. So . . . no one else can make a flitter do what you can? So what? You can do your own repairs? So what? You've been here ever since you got out of training, what, fifteen years ago? You're still a captain—"

"Major, now," Gerswin corrected quietly. A faint smile played around the corner of his lips.

"Pardon me, Major. So you're a major, so recently you don't even have the insignia. After fifteen years you finally made it, and you'll have to spend another five here to pay it off, until you're so specialized you'll never get off this stinking ball of poisoned mud. I beg your pardon, you are from here. I forgot. If you wanted to, you could never leave our revered ancestral home. But I want out, and not after fifteen or twenty years of 'Yes, ser, anything you please, ser.'"

"Going through a landspout will get you out quicker, and in a silver urn." Gerswin's eyes flared, and even Jeri Deran took two steps back away from him, though he had not moved, until her back was against the bulkhead. "You want to fly with Vlerio?" he pressed. "Fine. I'll see that you do, until you're sick of it and sick of him. But not today. For other reasons, I've got to see that the . . . major . . . survives in spite of his . . . impetuosity."

"You talk a good line . . . Major . . . but no orbit break."

"Do you want the next long-distance spout study? Solo?"

Gerswin looked at the lieutenant, whose glanced dropped.

"Do you want to be permanent shuttle liaison?"

He waited.

Only the hiss of the ventilators broke the silence of the small quarters.

"What do you want, Major?"

"Call in sick in about fifteen minutes. Call me. I'll be there. That's all."

"All right . . . Major. But if you—"

"Understood, Jeri, understood. I don't break any promises." Gerswin started to leave, then turned back. "Understand this, too. You say a word, one single word, and the whole base will know how you want to use Vlerio, both on and off duty! That I can insure."

"You are without a doubt the meanest bastard left on this mud-ball and I hope you end up the last."

"Do you understand?"

"Yes, I understand. Now would you please get the Hades out of here so that I can get sick, recently promoted Major Gerswin, not that you haven't given me every possible incentive?"

Gerswin left, at a walk approaching double-time, for the Operations center to rearrange the schedule, and to insure that Markin was the tech on the flight.

He'd already made sure that the equipment crew would take as much time as possible in issuing Vlerio his gear.

He shook his head. A flight to see a landspout, for Hades' sake. There were much easier ways to commit suicide, but the last thing he needed was Vlerio's death under any circumstances, much less under those that could be construed as suspicious.

Gerswin stepped up the pace. Vlerio might not be pleased, but the major wouldn't complain publicly . . . not until he took over as Operations officer.

In the meantime, all Gerswin had to do was to get him through the flight in one piece, if he could.

Getting Vlerio to the flight line would be the easy part. Getting him through the flight and getting him to accept what he needed to know would be the hard part.

Gerswin sighed as he turned into the Operations center, only half-aware of the way the other officers and techs backed away from him. He had a lot of arranging to do before he and Vlerio took off. A lot.

He gnawed at his lower lip as he dropped in front of the console. The flight time would be pressing before he knew it.

Three faxcalls and fifteen minutes later he was heading for the tunnel toward the hangar-bunker, hoping Markin had already gotten there.

He could see as he approached the flitter that Vlerio had already arrived, and that the major had brought his own gear, tailor-made from a shiny black fabric.

Gerswin refrained from shaking his head. The material would be worse than useless if Vlerio were ever forced down away from base.

"Captain! I had requested Lieutenant Deran for this flight."

"Sorry, ser. She called in sick. Nausea. Might be toxic shock. No one else was ready, and I thought you wanted to leave on schedule."

Vlerio looked as if he had not decided whether to frown or glare.

"All right, Captain. We'll do the best we can."

He slapped the fusilage of the flitter next to the thruster intakes. *Thud.*

"Disgraceful, Captain. This hull is a patchwork, absolute patchwork. Hope the thrusters aren't in the same sorry condition."

The major moved toward the inspection panel, but Gerswin was there first, easing the fitting and holding the panel open for the major's inspection.

"They've had some care, at least." Vlerio frowned as he checked the seal dates. "Why such a short time between overhauls? So many frequent rebuildings are expensive, Captain, extremely expensive. Hard to justify on a budget these days, you know."

"Yes, ser. Airborne debris level is much higher than standard here. Requires replating sooner."

"Ah, yes. The Service had that problem on New Colora part of the year. Stormy seasons, you recall. But we solved that one with the installation of particle screens. You should have looked into that, Captain."

"We did, Major. The density altitude and power requirements would have required the installation of HG 50s, and it's cheaper to replate than to re-engine and re-engine."

"When we get back and when I'm settled in, I'd like to review that data, Captain. We might be able to find a way around that particular problem."

"Yes, ser." Gerswin closed the access panel and trailed the major as Vlerio checked the skids and completed the rest of the preflight with noncommittal grunts.

Vlerio took the left-hand seat, the pilot's position, as Gerswin strapped himself into the right-hand seat.

"Checklist?"

"Up and ready," answered Gerswin.

"Aux power?"

"Green."

Vlerio continued through the checklist and through the start-up completely enough.

"Ready to lift."

"Opswatch, Outrider two, ready to lift, request met status and bunker clearance."

"Bunker clearance?" asked Vlerio without putting the question on the comment.

"Sometimes the wind sheers outside the hangar-bunker can hit eighty kays. Need a reading before we lift and clear the doors."

"Eighty kays?"

Gerswin ignored the question to listen to the clearance.

"Outrider two. Met status is green. Winds less than twenty kays. Cleared to lift and depart. Interrogative fuel status."

"Opswatch, fuel status is four point five."

"Understand four point five."

"Stet."

Gerswin nodded at Vlerio, who was gripping both stick and thrusters too tightly.

He waited a moment before clearing his throat. "Major, we're cleared to lift. The wind will gust from the right as you clear the bunker."

"Oh . . . Stand by, Captain."

"Outrider two, lifting."

"Stet, two. Have a good flight. Watch those purple beauties for us."

"That was an unauthorized transmission, Captain."

"Yes, ser."

"Find out who made it."

"Yes, ser. I'll check the log when we get back. The wind is from the starboard."

The flitter lurched forward on ground cushion and through the hangar bay portals.

Gerswin kept his hands near the controls, afraid that Vlerio would fail to compensate for the loss of ground cushion if an unexpected gust swept the flitter, or that he wouldn't get the aircraft pointed into the wind quickly enough.

While the flitter rocked and the skids nearly scraped the tarmac outside, Vlerio slowly maneuvered it into the wind and tilted it forward into a liftoff run, quickly feeding turns to the thrusters.

Once airborne, as the major studied the heads-up display, Gerswin surreptitiously wiped his forehead with the back of his sleeve, then dropped the helmet's impact visor back in place. His mirthless smile, as he watched Markin do the same from the corner of his eye, was hidden behind the tinted impact visor.

"What's the vector to that storm, Captain?"

"Zero four five, Major. Approximate range is six five kays."

"Estimated time to closure?"

"On thrusters or with blades deployed?"

"Thrusters," answered Vlerio as he began the blade retraction sequence.

"Ten standard minutes, give or take two."

"Stet. Blade retraction complete."

"Outrider two, this is Opswatch. Suggest course change to zero seven zero. Probable windsheer one zero kays before the leading edge of the landspout."

"Understand recommended course change to zero seven zero," answered Gerswin, since Vlerio showed no inclination to handle the communications with base.

"Negative course change," said Vlerio on the intercom.

"Opswatch, this is Outrider two. Negative on course change. Maintaining zero four five this time."

"Outrider two. Understand maintaining zero four five. Advise that probable windsheer differential is plus one five zero. Plus one five zero kays. Running three three zero slash one five zero. Strongly recommend course change."

Gerswin studied the horizon and the purpled mass rising above the gray of the lower-lying clouds that obscured the ground.

"Opswatch, this is Outrider two," answered Gerswin. "Understand recommendation for course change. Interrogative met status behind sheer line."

"Outrider two. Met status behind sheer line estimated at plus seven."

"Understand plus seven."

Gerswin cut in the intercom.

"Recommend immediate course change, Major. You have two minutes to sheer line impact."

"Captain, the air is clear for another seven kays, and we're at three thousand, no tac-running."

"Major, I recommend a course change to zero nine zero."

Gerswin watched the faint line as it appeared on his met screen, so close that it was about to kiss the screen point that represented the flitter, and put his hands on the controls, waiting for what he knew would happen, sensing Markin tightening his harness behind him.

"Captain, I've been through—"

Thud! Thud!

"EMERGENCY!!"

BRRIINNNGGG!!!

"Ground impact in less than two minutes!"

The scream of the emergency warnings rang through the intercom as the flitter pitched nearly ninety degrees nose down and to the left.

Gerswin glanced at the EGTs running into the red, and at the airspeed, which was climbing back from a reading of next to nothing. He overrode the major's frantic attempts to yank the stick back into his lap, only letting the nose ride up slightly.

"HELL!! Damned nose won't come up!" grunted the major.

Gerswin felt the perspiration pop out on his forehead as he watched the instruments and fought the major's actions, waiting before pulling out. He kept the nose down.

"Ground impact in thirty seconds! Impact in thirty seconds!"

Thud!

The flitter shuddered at the impact on the port side, and Gerswin again leveled it, his strength overriding the major's easily.

Lurching to the right as the left thruster dropped to half power, the flitter continued to fall as the airspeed climbed back across the two hundred kay mark.

Just as the speed reached two hundred, Gerswin smoothly brought the stick back into his lap.

"Ground impact in thirty seconds!"

"Ground impact in sixty seconds!"

As the airspeed bled off in the climb, Gerswin began to lower the nose, keeping the thrusters at full power, studying the EGTs and the vertical speed indicator.

Slowly, he eased off the power on the right thruster, aware that the major had finally released his hold on the controls. Gerswin did not look at Vlerio as he began a turn to starboard.

"Outrider two, this is Opswatch. Interrogative status. Interrogative status."

"Opswatch, status is green. Port thruster is amber. Say again. Port thruster is amber. Overall status green this time. Course is one zero zero. Altitude is point eight, climbing to three."

"Recommend course of zero eight five."

"Changing to zero eight five."

With the purpled mass of the landspout to the west blocking the direct rays of the afternoon sun, the light level in the cockpit was scarcely greater than on the ground below the clouds.

Gerswin could see that while Vlerio had clenched both fists, they were unclenching slowly as he watched the purple fury passing the flitter kays to the west.

Clunk! Clunk! Clunk!

The flitter rocked slightly at the three rapid-fire impacts.

"Ice, Captain?" asked Markin.

"Think so. Could get hit with a few more."

Gerswin eased the stick more to the right to get a greater separation from the trailing and more diffused end of the spout.

The EGT on the port thruster refused to drop from the amber to the green, and the power loss was approaching fifty-five percent.

"Major, we're going to have to cut this short. We've got about twenty minutes max left on the port thruster."

As he spoke, Gerswin began a climbing right turn designed to gain altitude for a return to base behind the landspout. The altitude would be helpful in case the thruster quit altogether.

"Go straight back in, Captain."

Gerswin sighed.

"We can't, Major. Wouldn't have enough time to set down, much less clear the hangar-bunker before the spout hit, and we'd have to use a high power approach."

"You have it, Captain. Do what you think best." Vlerio's words sounded like they had come from between clenched teeth.

"Stet, Major."

"Opswatch, this is Outrider two. On a return curve for touchdown behind the spout."

"Outrider two, understand returning to base."

"That's affirmative. Returning to base. Turning three three five for ten."

"Outrider two, recommend three five zero for twelve, then one nine five for approach."

"Stet. Turning three five zero, and leveling off at four point zero."

The cockpit flared with the return of the sun as the flitter cleared the shadow of the landspout. Gerswin squinted until he tossed his head to drop the dark helmet visor in place. The brightness of direct sunlight still bothered his eyes.

Backing off power to both thrusters, Gerswin reduced the right to fifty percent and the left to thirty. But the EGT on the left continued to inch through the yellow toward the red.

"Outrider two, this is Opswatch. Landspout shifting to course of one seven zero. Spout will pass east and south of main base. Estimate CPA in one minute. If necessary, you can commence approach on heading one nine zero."

"Stet. Heading one nine zero."

"Landing checklist . . . up and green."

Gerswin did the checklist himself, rather than ask Vlerio to do so, forcing himself to go through each item methodically.

"Outrider two, cleared for approach and touchdown."

"Stet. Interrogative met status and damage."

"Damage estimate not available. No reports of structural failure. Strips clear. Grids clear. Standing wave antenna down. Landspout now three kays at one six five."

Gerswin nodded. The spout was following the normal pattern of steering back to the southeast once it neared the foothills. Most didn't make it to the base itself.

"Opswatch, Outrider two commencing descent."

"Understand commencing descent. Interrogative power status."

"Port thruster is in the red. Three zero percent power. Will use low power, high angle descent to full touchdown."

"Interrogative emergency status."

"That's negative. Will require ground tow. Will require ground tow."

Gerswin eased the nose up as he triggered the blade extension sequence.

Once the rotors were fully operational, he eased back the power on the left thruster, with most of the power to the blades coming from the right engine.

Thwop, thwop, thwop, thwop. . . .

The sound of the rotors always reassured Gerswin. If necessary, he could always bring the flitter down on blades alone, with no thrusters, but he'd rather not have to do an autorotation with Major Vlerio sitting in the pilot's seat.

"Opswatch, this is Outrider two. Have base in sight. Commencing final."

"Stet, Outrider two. Tow crew standing by."

"Have crew in sight. On line to grids."

"Harness tight?" he asked over the intercom.

To the left, even across Vlerio's immaculate flight suit, he could see the half kilo wide swath of raw clay where the landspout had plowed through a hilltop east of the base.

"Little damage over to the left, Major," Gerswin remarked as he brought the nose up another increment before the final flare to the spot on the grid outside the bunker.

He thought he heard a cough from Vlerio, but he was concentrating on the EGTs, the power, and the touchdown itself.

He smiled behind the tinted visors as he got the flitter on the grid without even a jar.

"Commencing blade retraction, Markin."

"Stet, ser."

Markin had the crew door open, watching the retraction and folding sequence.

"Opswatch, Outrider two on the deck. On the deck and shutting down."

"Stet, Outrider two. Interrogative damage status?"

"Port thruster down. Probable replacement. Fusilage impacts."

"Stet, two. Cleared to shut down."

"Blade retraction complete," Gerswin announced, and Markin vaulted from the crew door to the tarmac to take charge of the tow hook-up.

Gerswin began the shutdown sequence, starting with the exterior lights and the fusilage heating.

"Ah . . . humm," coughed Major Vlerio.

"Yes, Major?"

Gerswin turned in the seat to face the senior officer.

"All right, Captain. I am neither stupid, nor unnecessarily vindictive. But I do not like being treated like an idiot, and before we leave this flitter, I think we need to get some things straight."

"I understand, Major."

As he spoke, Gerswin completed the thruster shutdown. He could finish the rest once the flitter was towed, if necessary.

"Starting tomorrow, I am the Ops boss. Period. You are my

deputy. Deputy, not puppet master, not the power behind the Ops boss, but deputy. Do you understand?"

"Major, I understand completely. You are the Ops boss, and you can't afford to make mistakes. If you don't succeed, then neither do I."

Vlerio snapped his head, and both sun and impact visors retracted. His forehead was damp.

"Then why did you go out of your way to make a fool out of me in front of the senior tech?"

Gerswin snapped his own visors up and let his hawk-yellow eyes bore into the major's. "Because you insisted on this damned flight. Major Matsuko wouldn't tell you no, and no one else could."

Gerswin jabbed his hand at the raw clay gouge on the hillside nearly a kay behind the major. "No one who hasn't spent some time here ever seems to understand how dangerous the spouts are. I could have let you go out and kill yourself. I didn't have to step in. You would have. Lost a flitter and crew. For what?"

The major was beginning to tremble with what Gerswin feared was out-and-out rage.

"Markin wants to go home. He's got half a tour left before he can retire. He'll say nothing. Nor will I. Everyone knows you saw a spout up close, and maybe it was a damn-fool thing to do, but you did it and you're back. No problem. May be an asset because the pilots will all know you've been through it. I take the responsibility for the damage, and you become Ops boss."

"You're clever, Captain. Too clever."

Gerswin sighed, grabbed the edge of the seat. The flitter rocked as the crew turned it for the tow back into the bunker.

"Major, think about it. Did I do anything against your interests? Anything? If I had wanted you out of the way, I could have stayed in the Ops center and vectored you right into the sheer line. With Jeri Deran as copilot, we wouldn't have found as much as a kilo of scrap metal."

Gerswin waited, wondering if the apparently hotheaded major would stop to understand.

"I guess you're right, Captain. At least, I see what you tried to do. But I still don't like being treated like an idiot."

"Major, I'm sure there was a better way to handle it. But I didn't have much time. You have a great deal more managing experience. That's why you're the Ops boss. I understand all the local problems. That's why you need me as deputy. I'll tell you the problems, and you make the decisions, and if we do it in private, you get all the credit."

"And the blame?"

"Major," and Gerswin forced a laugh, "Headquarters will *always* blame the boss. That's why you need all the credit you can get."

Vlerio nodded, slowly.

"All right, Captain . . . or Major, I should say. We'll try it. But don't ever, *EVER*, pull a stunt like this one again!"

"Yes, ser."

Gerswin waited until the flitter came to a halt inside the hangar-bunker. Then he finished the last three items on the shutdown check-list.

By the time he looked up from his work, Vlerio was gone.

XLI

THE TAP ON the portal was gentle, yet a dull and hollow sound rang through the metal—so much metal for a planet which had so little that had not been oxidized, fragmented, or scattered in dozens of differing and unique ways.

Although he had been sleeping, his bare feet touched the cool tiles before the first echo from the tap had died away.

"Yes?"

"Greg?"

He touched the entry stud, and the panel irised open.

Faith Hermer stepped through the half-open portal, not waiting until it was fully open, her head a scant few centimeters under the top of the frame.

She touched the closure and locking studs in quick succession, and sat down on the foot of his bunk, automatically ducking her head to avoid the non-existent upper bunk.

Gerswin remained standing, leaning against the wall next to the built-in console. He could sense all the conflicting emotions she radiated—impatience, excitement, fear, and . . .

He shook his head.

"It might be that bad," she said lightly, "but you'll survive. You always will."

He frowned. "Not what I meant."

Amazingly, she returned his gruffness with her shy smile. After all the years he had watched her, he had come to appreciate that shyness, the gentle warmth it conveyed without invading or demanding anything.

His frown easing, he asked, "You're in a hurry?"

"In some ways. The shuttle brought my orders, mine and Lieutenant Glyner's. They're on a tight turnaround. After they unload, they'll take us to the *Andromeda.*"

"Orders?"

"I told you. I asked for reassignment to a combat position."

He had asked the same, and he nodded slowly. For all her size, Faith had quicker reflexes than all of the other Impies, and a better sense of judgment.

"The Dismorph thing?"

She nodded in return.

"What about me?"

"The only orders I know about were mine and Glyner's." Her eyes met the hawk-yellow of his. Then she looked at the smooth and faded gray of the Service quilt on which she sat. "Greg, they'll never let you go. Once Vlerio is retired, they'll just send another. You've given them enough native-borns to begin running this place in a few years—but only if you're here to control them. They'll never release you, even if you are the best combat pilot in the Service. Once Vlerio is retired . . . Don't you see?"

"See? See what?"

"You're all that holds this place together."

"Me, and an Ops officer, an exec, a commandant, and another two hundred assorted military and civilian types."

"Greg." Her voice was low, in the quiet, no-nonsense tone he had come to recognize.

"Appreciate the flattery, Faith, but it's hard to believe."

She sighed, and the slight wash of air carried her scent toward him, the odor of excitement muted, and the sense of sadness deeper now.

Shifting his weight slightly, he wiggled his toes against the cool tiles, abstractly glad that he did not have to pull on his boots just yet.

"I could have said it better. What I meant was that you will be the only one who can hold things together in the future, when things really get tough."

He barked a two-note laugh.

"When they really strip us for combat support? Aren't we where they put people to keep them out of trouble? To keep them from fouling up the great and glorious combat arm?"

She did not answer his questions, her eyes dropping.

Her hand strayed toward the top fastening on her tunic, but tugged at her shoulder, straightening the fabric where it did not need straightening.

She patted the bunk.

"Please sit down, Greg."

He slid onto the quilt next to her, but she did not look at him, instead letting her hand touch the top fastening of her tunic, then dropping it.

She turned to him, and he could see the liquidness of her wide eyes. At the same time, he was more aware than ever of how she towered over him and wondered if that was why he had always avoided getting involved with her, despite the attraction she held.

"Greg?"

"Yes?"

"I don't have much time. Not here, perhaps not ever, and . . . and . . ."

"Sssshhh."

He touched her lips with his forefinger, understanding finally, with a cold certainty, that she did not want to ask, had never wanted to ask, and had waited year after year for him, while he had waited for her.

This time, his fingers touched the top fastening on her tunic, and the second, his eyes widening as he realized that she had worn nothing under either tunic or trousers. He closed his eyes as his lips touched hers, and her hands found him.

Despite the heat building between them, between skin and skin, the sense of time dropping forever through an hourglass that would never be turned, each touch tingled, and lasted, lasted and tingled, as they moved together, clothes falling apart, as if in slow motion and freefall.

When the last shudders had died away and her hands traced his body as if to store him within her memory, within her fingertips, he traced her cheekbones with the forefinger of his left hand.

She sighed, regretfully, once, twice.

"It's better this way."

"Better?"

"You're still afraid of women, you know. Yet your whole body breathes desire. Half the women in this base would give anything to have what I've just had. And you don't see it. Maybe you can't, or won't."

"Better?" He repeated his question.

"I'm not sure I could have left if this had become a habit. You're addictive, you know." She laughed lightly, but with an emptiness behind the teasing tone.

"Why not? Most of the men here feel that way about you. Give them a chance—"

"Greg."

The quiet stretched between them, as he ran his forefinger along the line of her collarbone and downward across her satin skin.

"Not—" But she broke off the protest, and drew him to her, her fingers digging into his shoulders as her lips covered his.

Some time later, as they lay side by side, shoulder to shoulder and thigh to thigh on the narrow bunk, she repeated her earlier statement.

"It's better this way." But the sadness was stronger.

This time, he waited.

"You belong to no one, not even yourself. Or maybe you belong to Old Earth. You can give without giving everything, and that's not enough for me. Not in a lifetime. But I'd stay, hoping that you would, and you wouldn't. You couldn't."

Again he said nothing, but held her closer and stopped her words, and let her tears bathe them both.

Presently, she leaned away and took a deep breath.

"Time to go. I nearly waited too long to come. The shuttle lifts in less than two hours."

He wondered how he would have felt if she had not come, but only watched as she stood, slipping her uniform back on with quick gestures.

"One last thing. Greg?"

"Yes?"

He met her eyes, but she did not flinch from his level hawk gaze. "Don't see me off."

He dropped his glance, not that he had to, but because he understood, though he wanted not to understand, and because all he could do was look as she walked away.

As she tightened the waistbands on her trousers, he stood and slipped over to her, aware and not caring how much taller she was.

He lifted his head, and she bent hers, but only their lips touched, sharing salt and sadness.

"Good-bye, Greg."

"Good-bye."

He watched as the portal closed, then slowly began to pull on his uniform, single piece by single piece.

The boots came last, always last.

XLII

COMMANDER BYYKR LEANED back in the swivel. With his considerable additional bulk on the joints, it creaked.

Gerswin stood at attention.

"Sit down, Major. Or stand, whatever you want, whatever's comfortable. I know you're not the sitting type. Strange officer you are, young man and old man, patient and impatient."

The green eyes that peered from the rounded frame of the base executive officer were the man's sole sharp feature, the only hint of intensity.

His soft voice continued, as Gerswin relaxed slightly and settled into the straight-backed chair opposite the corner of the commander's console.

"This is the second year in a row you've requested assignment to a combat position, and I'm going to recommend that your request be denied. Before I do, I'm going to tell you why, and I hope you will understand. My decision, of course, is not final, but the commanding officer usually takes my recommendation, and the recommendations of commanding officers are rarely overturned."

Gerswin nodded without speaking.

"Do you have anything to say at this point?"

"No, ser. Like to hear your reasons."

"You don't seem terribly surprised, and I'm not surprised that you aren't. I wouldn't even be surprised if you had put in this request merely for the purposes of declaring your loyalty. I won't put that to the test, nor will I attempt to find out if your request is a bluff. For your sake, I almost hope it is, because the stakes are far higher than I suspect you understand. You belong here, not in combat, unlike Captain Hermer, who is now a major, by the way, and who was kept here far longer than she should have been."

Gerswin shifted his weight slightly, but did not turn his eyes from the commander.

Byykr coughed twice and leaned forward in the swivel, which creaked as he moved, and turned in his seat to look at the mural to his left, and to Gerswin's right. The often reproduced holoview was that of the Academy Spire, mirrored in Crystal Lake.

Byykr's sharp green eyes came back to rest on the younger major.

"In some ways, Major, you would have been better as a chief tech, but you're too aggressive and quick for that. I'm not being critical, but you have the kind of understanding and technical competence that is usually provided to the Service by its technicians. I'm told by those who should know that you can probably rebuild a flitter from the deck up, and that you know biologics better than all but the best of the ecologists.

"I wouldn't know how much farther your abilities go, but I do know they go farther than any other officer on this base today. That kind of knowledge in a line officer will make you invaluable as some-one's executive officer someday, but, combined with your skill as a pilot, it makes you extraordinarily dangerous to the standard political-type officer. And outside of the field bases, like Old Earth here, most commanding officers are usually political types. Why do you think that mortality is so high in combat? No—don't try to answer that. It wasn't meant for an answer."

Byykr cleared his throat and continued. "I hope you can under-stand the point I'm making."

"It would seem that my career is at a dead end. The more I learn, the more dangerous I become, and the less likely I am to ever leave."

"That's possible. But it doesn't mean that your career is ended. You'll doubtless become the operations officer, probably as soon as Vlerio leaves next year, both of which I've already recommended. After a tour or a little more in that slot, if you don't retire, and I'd cer-tainly recommend against that for you, you'll become the base exec-utive officer, and probably, by that time, the odds-on favorite for base commandant."

"But I'll never leave Old Earth on a Service tour, is that it? Why not?"

"Simple. You know too much, and you're far too good a pilot, and a good leader, even if you are a loner. You get assigned to combat, and with your record, any combat coordinator would give at least his right arm to have you as a heavy corvette or destroyer commander. The problem is that you'd get assigned the suicide missions. You're good enough to survive most of them.

"That means they'd start dumping you with missions they'd like to have done, but couldn't delude themselves into believing anyone could pull off. From the point of view of the Service, that would be a disaster."

"Disaster?"

"Absolutely." Byyker coughed once. "Every young hotblood would be trying to beat your record, and all of them would die, along with a lot of innocent crews. If you survived yourself, the Service might never recover from your example, and even if you didn't, they'd have to award you the Emperor's Cross posthumously, which would inspire too many others to emulate you.

"So any good, experienced, political officer would immediately assign you a dirty quiet job guaranteed to kill you and your ship. Without any gain to the Empire and without any publicity. That's too much of a waste of talent, even for an old cynic like me.

"Besides, you're doing a good job here. Things get done. People are happy, for the most part, when by all rights they ought to be miserable. We old goats can complete a tour here and retire with a pat on the back. So you stay."

Gerswin smiled a wry smile. "You aren't totally encouraging."

"That comes later. What I'm trying to make clear is that the combat service represents a form of suicide for you, at least in a conflict environment like the present."

"And it doesn't for Major Hermer?"

"Not as much. For reasons embedded in the psychology of the race, most commanders don't regard women as a personal and physical threat, unless the commander is female. Then, there are still few enough top women commanders that they need to nurture every possible ally for their own future.

"My hopes for the major are that by the time she's recognized for her abilities either this war is over, and that should be soon from the spacio-political outlines I've seen, or she will have been promoted or otherwise protected by a political officer type with enough brains to see what an asset she can be.

"You, on the other hand, are not a team player, even though you build better teams than any officer I've ever had the privilege of supervising. You are goal-oriented, and nothing seems to stop you, except death, and one gets the feeling you've already bought him off."

The commander swiveled to look at Gerswin directly. He cleared his throat and coughed, louder this time, blocking the cough with his clenched and pudgy fist.

"I know, Major, you've got nearly twenty-five years in service, but these days careers of fifty aren't uncommon, and there's no mandatory retirement age. All you have to do is pass the stress physical every year. I won't, according to my private med source. But you, you've got plenty of time, and who knows? I could be wrong. Maybe you can convince my successor, if you want.

"By then, in any case, this Dismorph thing will be over, and at least it will be harder for a political type to use you as an expendable."

Gerswin nodded for what seemed the tenth time in the largely one-sided conversation.

"Understand your points, Commander."

"Now," continued the executive officer, "you can appeal, which will leave a record in the files, or you can wait until next year, and resubmit without prejudice in the annual career plan order request submissions."

"I'll have to think about next year when the times comes. No appeal now."

"Do you have any other questions, Major?"

"None you haven't already answered, ser."

The swivel creaked as the hulking, white-haired officer eased himself to his feet and offered his hand to Gerswin.

Gerswin snapped to his own feet and took the proffered handshake.

"It's been a pleasure to watch what you can do, Major, and I hope to be able to continue watching for a while."

"Thank you, Commander. Based on your advice and observations, I expect I'll be doing the same type of job for a time to come."

"I hope so, Major. I hope so."

Gerswin stiffened into full attention.

"That's all, Major."

As Gerswin left, behind him he heard the creak of the overtaxed swivel as the commander replaced himself in it.

H.M.S. *Black Prince*

MacGregor C. Gerswin, Major, I.S.S.
Old Earth Base
I.S.D.C. 1212
New Augusta, Sector III

Dear Greg,

I thought about sending you a cube, but this is quicker and more certain. In my vanity, I thought you might have heard about the difficulties we had to surmount here last week. If not, you should get the whole story some time, but not, for the reasons of official censorship, from me.

Enough to say that we came through all right, although a measure of that is that I was among the more junior COs (that's right, commanding officer of my very own Imperial corvette) of the squadron, and now am the senior commander of a rather less impressive squadron, led by the *Black Prince.* What you taught me helped a lot, and so did the skipper of the *Graystone.* (Rumor has it that he was the only Academy graduate not from Old Earth ever to come close to your record in piloting at New Colora.) His family will probably receive the Imperial Cross. Never have I seen such incredible coverage from such a small ship. They say it was a corvette, but looked more like an armed scout to me.

I wish I could tell you what's likely to happen next, but now that everyone understands the situation, I expect our operations will become more measured and deal from our strength. In a way, I feel sorry for the Dismorphs, but not sorry enough. Without the *Graystone,* and, I admit to some degree, the little we were able to accomplish, we might not be here to talk about the next offensive.

Enough said about it. We could have used you, but had you been where you really could have been used, none of this might have happened. I know that's cryptic, but let's leave it at that.

Surprisingly, I miss Old Earth. Not just you, although I can't delude myself into believing that isn't a big factor, but the planet itself, for all the grayness, the winds, the ice rains, and the cold, cold, and cold. It was home to our ancestors for a long, long time. Out here, or should I say, in here, where the stars spray together like clouds in the night skies, Earth seems so far away, and yet important that it should be reclaimed for what it was. I once thought that it ought to remain as it stands as a memorial to human stupidity, but that will always be with us. . . .

The console is blinking red in three points, and I'll close because who knows when I'll be able to steal another few minutes, and I do want to get this off to you. I regret nothing, except that I didn't have the nerve to come to you earlier, but you have made a light where there was none, and the path ahead is brighter for it.

> My love,
> Faith

XLIV

THE MAJOR GLANCED toward the open doorway, then stood, brushing back the swivel, and leaving the torp fax flimsy on the flat working surface of the console.

Thud!

The old-fashioned door shuddered in its frame with the force he had imparted.

The flimsy fluttered off the console in a back-and-forth sideways flight before diving to the floor behind the swivel.

The major retrieved the message before it had finally settled, holding it firmly in his left hand.

He read it again, knowing he had not overlooked anything, centering his attention on the last paragraph.

". . . In addition to next-of-kin, Major Hermer's Form DN-12 requested you be notified under clause 3(b), principal-at-interest . . ."

His eyes skipped upward toward the beginning.

". . . in the most honorable tradition of the Empire . . . Major Faith X. Hermer . . . awarded the Emperor's Star (posthumously) . . . action beyond the call of duty . . ."

The words spilled through his mind like the spring run-off of the Great West River, roaring past him without meaning. He placed the single flimsy back on the console.

His feet carried him in a tight circle in front of the console. Two, three circuits, and he reversed direction automatically, feet moving him back around the circle, though he could hear the whispers from outside the closed door.

Twenty minutes ago, he had been reviewing a recon pattern for the southeast basin when a junior tech had tiptoed in and placed the flimsy on his console, bowing and scraping the whole three meters from door to console and the whole three meters back from console to door.

The major stopped his circling and took a single deep breath, then another, clenching and unclenching his fists, tightening the muscles in his forearms, loosening them. The inside of his left forearm brushed his waistband and the hardness behind it.

Without volition, the throwing knife was in his left hand.

Thunk!

Heavy and impenetrable as the plastic of the door was, it could not resist the knife buried there to half its depth.

He walked to the door, slowly eased out the heavy blade and replaced it in the waist sheath.

He opened the door deliberately, not looking back at the flimsy on the console and stepped outside his small office into the general Operations area.

Two of the techs at the end of the nearest row of consoles failed to look away quickly enough, but the major ignored them as he marched toward the duty console.

Frylar, Technician First Class, said nothing, waiting.

"Tell Vlerio . . . be back later. Sick leave . . . if necessary. Need air. Be outside."

He stepped away, conscious of the faint click of his boots in the envelope of silence that seemed to surround him as he hurried toward the southwest lock doors.

Mechanically, his hands touched the correct studs, and he passed through the inner door, and, in turn, through the outer portal, and into the rain.

Rain sleeted from the low clouds, not cold enough to fall in ice droplets, instantaneously soaking the thin gray indoor tunic.

The man ignored the chill, and the cold passed from his awareness as if it had never been. His long strides carried him toward the practice yard.

He held throwing knives in each hand, advancing on the rain-swept targets as if they were the enemy.

Thunk!

Thunk!

He recovered his weapons and stepped back, three steps, four, five, six, turning, hefting them as if to drive them through the plastic coated foam of the target heads.

Thunk!

Thunk!

The thin wail of the wind inched toward a shriek as the storm center neared the Imperial bunkers crouched under their cover of stone and heavy clay.

Thunk!

Thunk!

The rain sheets became waterfalls pouring from gray oceans overhead.

Thunk!

Thunk!

The wind shrieked like a corvette with its screens wrenched apart, and the waterfalls became solid walls of water from which the major emerged, still hefting the knives that seemed to cut through the storm itself, ignoring the calf-high torrents that pulled at him.

Thunk!

Thunk!

"YOU'VE BEEN AVOIDING me."

The I.S.S. lieutenant had green hawk-eyes and tight curled black hair. Her eyes were level with the major who stood by the battered console.

Outside of the panoramic pictures of the western peaks spread on the wall behind the console, the small office was bare of decoration. The flat top surface of the console and the working surface to the right of the screen were also bare, except for the small pile of hard copy reports in the left-hand corner, and for the thin and tattered publication lying next to the console screen.

The lieutenant's eyes darted to the publication and drank in the title—*Program Key Locks—Patterns and Uses*—before returning her eyes to the hawk-yellow stare of the major.

"Have I?"

"Yes," she answered.

Each waited a moment, then another.

At last, the major's lips quirked slightly. "Guess I have." He shrugged.

"I said I'd be back. I know you didn't promise anything. But you're cold. Like the ice rain. And you're not."

Inclining his head, he returned her statement with a puzzled frown.

"Cold like the ice rain, but I'm not?"

"You know what I mean. Under your ice . . ." She broke off her own statement with a half-shrug, half-headshake.

"Suppose so." He cleared his throat, looked down at the smooth flooring, then back at her. "Didn't mean to hurt you. Or to string you along. Hoped you'd understand."

He looked away from the directness in her eyes.

"Techs say you lost the woman you loved. That you won't let yourself care again. That you throw your knives like hate."

She glanced over his shoulder at the half-holo view on the far right, the needle spire of Centerpeak.

He did not look up.

"Lost . . . one way of putting it. Lost both." His head came up abruptly, and his eyes locked hers, both unwavering. He said nothing.

This time she looked away, her eyes seeking the thin volume on the console, noting the irregular print of the title, the yellowed tinge to the pages. *Program Key Locks* had all the hallmarks of an underground datapick manual. She wondered where the major, the devilkid dedicated to the Service and to the reclamation of Old Earth, had discovered it, and why.

Realizing that she was letting her thoughts avoid dwelling on his isolation, she forced herself to raise her eyes back to his.

"You make it hard to talk," she said.

"True. Hard for all of us devilkids. Harder for me, I suspect. Maybe not."

He took a half-step away from the console toward her.

"Kiedra . . . not the one for you."

She did not move, standing perfectly still as if encased in solid ice rain.

He took another step, lifting each of her hands into his. Gently.

"Not now. Not ever."

He could see the glistening sheen building in her eyes, refused to let himself be moved, refused to let the ice that surrounded him crack, and stood, hands holding hers.

"Not ever?" She tilted her head fractionally to the side and back, moistened her lips.

Gerswin resisted the urge to brush her lips with his, instead leaned forward and let them brush her forehead. He stepped back, but did not release her hands.

Kiedra blinked twice, though no tears fell from the corners of her eyes, and swallowed.

"Still not easy," her voice husked, almost dry.

The major shook his head gently, squinting once as if the soft light in the small office were more like the glare above the clouds or on the peaks represented behind him on the wall.

"No. It's not."

"Can you tell me why?"

"Not now. When I can, you won't need me to."

"Should I understand?"

Gerswin shrugged.

"Depends on what you remember. Depends on what you value, and on what I value. Right now, we have to value different things."

He released her hands. His own tingled from the contact with the strong coolness of her fingers.

"Greg . . ."

She did not finish the statement she began, but looked down, to the console, to the floor, then back to the yellow hardness of piercing hawk-eyes.

Finally, she began again. "Can't be Greg, can it? Has to be Captain. Or Major. Or Commander. You have too much to do, too much to let yourself go right now."

He did not answer, but met her eyes. Again, she looked away.

"So strong . . . and so hurt . . ." She lifted her head, her chin, and gave a little shake. "So few will look past the hawk."

His lips quirked once more.

"Hawk? I think not."

"Hawk," she affirmed. "A hawk with a heart too big for hunting, and a purpose too vast not to."

He shrugged. "Hawk or not, poetic words or not, some have stood by you . . . and will when I cannot. Will be for you alone, when I cannot."

"There is that."

"Then do not disregard it."

"I do as I please."

"Do as you please, Kiedra. Do as you please."

"Do I sound that awful?"

Gerswin had to grin at the mock-plaintive note in her question.

"Not quite."

The lieutenant studied his grin and the forced twinkle in his eyes. After a moment, she returned his expression with a smile.

"Should I laugh or cry?"

"Should I?"

"Both!"

The lieutenant followed her exclamation by throwing both arms around the major, kissed him hard upon the lips, and dropped away as quickly as she had struck.

"That's for what you've missed, and for treating me fairly. Not sure I wanted to be treated fairly, and I reserve the right to reopen the question."

With that, she turned.

The major did not move as he watched her cross the last few meters and leave the office, an office that felt barer than before.

He swallowed, then took a deep breath. His chest felt strangely tight, and he inhaled deeply again, shaking his shoulders and trying to relax. His eyes felt hot, not quite burning, but he blinked back the feeling, finally looking down at *Program Key Locks*.

"Hope Lerwin appreciates her . . ."

His words sounded empty in the office, echoed coldly against the flat walls.

He sat and stared for a long time at the console screen.

Long after the echoes had died, long after the lieutenant had vanished, long after, the index finger of his left hand touched the console keyboard.

He sighed once more, then resumed the work he had started what seemed ages ago, before an early spring had come and gone in the space of a few afternoon moments.

THE RED-HEADED lieutenant waved.

"Come on, Captain."

Gerswin smiled. The devilkids, as they trickled back to Old Earth, uniformly referred to him as "Captain," for all that he wore the single gold triangle of an I.S.S. major on his tunic collars or his flight suits.

The lieutenant waved again from the open hatchway of the dozer's armored cockpit. "Come on."

Gerswin broke into a quickstep for the remaining fifty meters across the tarmac.

"Getting slower there, Captain."

Gerswin shook his head to dispute the fact, but grinned and said nothing as he swung into the cockpit and closed the hatch behind him.

Lieutenant Glynnis MacCorson closed her own hatch and strapped in.

"Damned cargo run," she grumped.

"You still like it."

"You're right. Since they didn't want any more flitter pilots, had to find something else to run. Didn't matter if it was big and ugly."

She turned to the controls before her, controls more like a spacecraft than a flitter.

"Everyone's aboard, Lieutenant." The tech peered into the cockpit through the hatchway from the small passenger/cargo/living section of the arcdozer.

"Stet, Nylen. Commencing power-up."

Gerswin watched, unspeaking, as she ran through the checklist which centered on the fusactor powering the behemoth that could have swallowed an I.S.S. corvette for breakfast and converted it into constituent elements.

"GroundOps, Dragon Two, departing for town. Estimate time en route one point one."

"Understand time en route one point one. Cleared for departure."

"Stet, Dragon Two on the run."

Gerswin shook his head. Speed, the dozers weren't made for. The new town, as yet unnamed by the transplanted shambletowners, the few retired techs, the married Service techs, and the handful of immigrants, was less than ten kays away, down a wide and hard-packed causeway with no turns. What would have taken a minute or three by flitter was a major undertaking by dozer. But then, dozers weren't normally used for transport, except on their way to and from major refits at the base.

Before too long, Gerswin reflected, it might be worth the expense to set up a forward maintenance facility, particularly as the dozer operations moved eastward.

Dragon Two was carrying the back-up fusactor for the town. While it could have been airlifted in sections by flitter, assembly was easier at the base, and the arcdozer's slow and even speed made the transport practical.

Once the power source was deposited on its foundation, the structure and distribution system would be completed around it.

Glynnis smiled happily as she checked the monitors, and as the dozer tracks rumbled across the hard packed clay, compacting it still further.

Gerswin shifted his weight in the seat normally used by the senior tech and let his eyes slide over the blanked out bank of controls that would normally monitor intake, processing, and treatment of the tons of dirt, clay, and organic matter that a dozer processed hour by hour, day after day.

A movement caught his eye, and he glanced up.

At the top of a low embankment ahead of the dozer and to the right of the causeway stood a group of shambletowners, old shambletowners dressed in tattered coyote leathers. They stood, blank-faced, and watched as the dozer rumbled toward them.

Their eyes were slits, their faces hard in the bright light of a morning that was only partly cloudy, with a few traces of a cold blue sky above the mottled white and gray clouds.

"Not exactly friendly," observed Glynnis.

"No. We've changed a few things."

"And they don't care for the changes. Can't say I have much sympathy. Did so well under the old way, didn't we?"

Gerswin saw the leathers of the sling and repressed the urge to jump as the missile hurled toward the dozer.

Crack!

The stone slapped against the cockpit armaglass, leaving only a streak of dust.

A figure on the end of the line of shambletowners was reloading his sling with another smooth stone.

Fynian, Gerswin thought, although the man was looking down and not directly at the major.

Crack!

Glynnis shook her head.

"Really are out after us."

"Devilkids and Impies one and the same to them."

"We know different, Captain."

Gerswin smiled faintly. "For them, it's all the same." He looked back over his right shoulder at the shambletowners, still standing in a line on the embankment. "If we succeed, Glynnis, won't be the same for us, either."

"Take longer than I've got, Captain."

Gerswin nodded slowly and settled back to watch the lieutenant as the causeway rolled slowly by. He drank in the tall plains grass that was beginning to fill in the spots where nothing had grown, and glanced from checkerboard field to checkerboard field where the organic sponge grains grew and would be harvested again and again until the soil was ready for grass or food crops for people or livestock—not that there would be much livestock for a long time to come if he and the ecologists had much to say about it.

How long before the land was ready? He shrugged. Mahmood's prediction had been ten years after the first sponge grains and outcropping. So far, for the few lands that had completed the process, Mahmood had been right.

He missed the idealistic ecologist, but who could blame him for retiring to take the ecology chair at the college on Medina?

Time passed people by, slowly, ponderously, just as the dozer had passed the shambletowners, but with the same kind of unstoppable force.

"You know your records will stand, Captain?"

Glynnis's words broke his reverie.

"Records?"

"The ones you set for the Academy Ironman. Lerwin came within five minutes. No one else has come within twenty, and they never will."

"Someday, someone will. Time passes."

The cockpit lit as the clouds let the sun break through, and Gerswin absorbed the warmth momentarily before tapping the vent to bring in more cool air from outside. Too much light and heat still bothered him.

"They say ice water runs in your veins."

"Anti-ice, maybe."

Gerswin knew he was being distant, but he hoped she would understand.

Whether Glynnis did or not, the lieutenant said nothing else as the dozer rumbled over the highest point on the trip and began the equally gentle descent toward the town.

Gerswin relaxed as much as he could, and tried to enjoy the slow pace of the trip, away from the base, from the constant flow of communications that cluttered the Ops screens, all of which had to be monitored and evaluated before Vlerio had a chance to see it, much less act on it. With Vlerio off with the base commander for the three days ahead, Gerswin could leave Lerwin to watch the screens and the day-to-day activities.

Anything really serious and Lerwin could reach him in seconds.

Gerswin watched as the town wall appeared ahead on the right. Before he knew it the dozer was slowing, gradually, heavily, but certainly.

"GroundOps, Dragon Two at destination. Beginning cargo drop this time."

"Stet. Understand cargo drop. Report when drop complete and proceeding to station."

"Stet. Will report when proceeding to station."

Gerswin eased himself out of the operator's seat. He stood in the space behind the two front seats as Glynnis and Nylen began to maneuver the dozer around to place the materials drop section, where the fusactor sat, as close as possible to the reinforced ferroplast slab.

"Twenty reverse on the right rear."

"Twenty right rear."

"Bring up the left a touch."

"Stet."

"Stress load on the ramp is point nine five and steady."

"Lieutenant, we've got it on the downslope and clear of the joints. Hold the tracs."

"Locked and holding . . ."

". . . three more on the left . . ."

". . . right corner sticking . . . liquid slick it . . ."

". . . clearing top section . . ."

". . . load factor on the ramp at point eight three and dropping . . ."

". . . clear of the ramp, and in position."

"Understand clear of the ramp."

"That's affirmative, Lieutenant. You're clear to move forward."

Gerswin watched as Glynnis wiped her forehead with the back of her jumpsuit sleeve.

"On the roll."

Hands flicking across the console, Glynnis eased the dozer away from the uncompleted section of the town wall and back down the incline onto the causeway, bringing the dozer to a stop.

"That's done, Captain."

"Nicely," he commented with a smile.

"No . . . But we got it done. Sloppy on the trac balancing."

She pushed several stray red hairs off her forehead and squared herself in the seat.

"You leaving now?"

"Don't want to go out on station while you plow up my favorite purple clay and change it into old-fashioned dirt. Not now, anyway."

"Sure about what?"

"I'm sure."

"Have it your way, Captain." She flashed a smile. "See you in a week or so."

He nodded, then ducked down the passageway and out through the crew exit.

The other tech, Krysten, snapped a salute at him as he slipped outside and landed lightly on the packed red clay.

After returning the salute, he walked back toward the uncompleted section of the wall, paralleling the half-meter deep prints the dozer had left in the work ramp.

As he reached the spot where the fused clay wall had been left untouched, he waved again at the dozer. Glynnis had already begun to inch Dragon Two forward and toward the golden plains beyond, toward a destination out beyond the golden green of the sponge grains, out over the horizon where the line of dozers methodically extended the borders of arable land.

Even seventy meters away, Dragon Two still towered over the wall and Gerswin, seemingly taller than either as it crept eastward.

In time, Gerswin turned and walked through the opening in the wall and past the ferroplast foundation where techs were already beginning to erect the remainder of the back-up power station around the fusactor. His feet took him toward the central square of the town that had no name.

At first glance, the new town could have passed for an updated and cleaner version of the old shambletown, with white glazed finishes over thick walls of fired bricks. But the streets, rather than narrow canyons, opened to the sky, boulevards radiating from the square. The houses, neither individual nor wall-to-wall, clustered in groups, standing in the midst of more open space than any shambletowner would have ever dreamed, although none were taller than two stories, and all possessed the thick walls. Instead of hide covers the windows had double-paned armaglass for their still small apertures.

The streets were paved with gray stone slabs cut with lasers, and stone flower boxes appeared at irregular intervals, filled with blue ice flowers and a yellow flower Gerswin did not recognize.

He passed an expanse of green turf, a park with several skeletal structures on which two children clambered. The grassy space was surrounded on three sides by clustered housing, and by the boulevard on the fourth.

One child wore a jumpsuit, the other a leather tunic over cloth trousers.

The major nodded at the mix of shambletown and Empire, but kept walking toward the central square.

The sunlight dimmed as the clouds above darkened and cut off the direct rays, and as the wind rose again. So much for the hint of a real summer.

He sniffed the air, drawing in the hint of the rain which would likely fall, rain since it was midsummer. Only in the warmest of the supposed summer months was there little or no chance of ice rain, not that the ice rain bothered him much.

"Good morning, Major."

"Good morning."

Gerswin returned the greeting although he did not recognize the man who had passed him. From his dress, the man was a retired tech, one of the few who had elected to remain once their obligations had expired, despite the landspouts and the cold.

Like the shambletown, at midmorning the central square was mostly deserted, except for the handful of older men of Imperial origin, and three younger women, all noticeably pregnant.

Gerswin surveyed the buildings, all white glazed brick except for the community hall, which boasted a stone columned front and a short bell tower that reached roughly fifteen meters above the square.

The square itself consisted of a boulevard running in a rectangle around a central park two hundred meters on a side. Despite the grass, the bushes, a few flowers, and the pathways, something was missing.

He looked again.

Trees! Only a handful of dwarf trees were scattered amid the statues, the pathways, and the hedge maze on the right side where two boys and three girls shrieked as they tore down the dead-end and hidden corridors.

He nodded in understanding. With the high winds, the town couldn't afford the damage of a substantial tree thrown into a building.

After sniffing at the air, and discovering nothing but the smells of newness—new brick, new stone, new plastics—he glanced around the square again before beginning his walk to the right and toward the street that would lead to the landing field at the western side of the town.

His steps slowed as he passed two women who sat at opposite ends of a stone bench rising out of the too-green grass imported from New Colora, grass originally from Old Earth.

". . . that's him . . . one they call the captain . . ."

Gerswin ignored the whispers and kept walking.

"Captain of what? He's a major."

"Some say he's the devil's captain . . . Was a devilkid. . . ."

". . . good-looking in his own way. . . ."

Gerswin kept walking and let the voices fade into the background as his steps brought him opposite the community hall.

His eyes passed over the closed endurasteel doors. Automatic portals would have taken too much energy—particularly for civilians, the Service had noted. Gerswin had agreed with the decision, but not for that reason.

He turned right, down toward the main gate and the short landing strip beyond.

A patch of green before the wall and the gate appeared as he approached—another park. The tops of the mountains behind the foothills were barely visible under the whitish gray of the higher than normal clouds. The lower stratus layers that raced westward above the town had not reached the foothills yet, nor had the rain begun to fall, although it would.

Gerswin caught the glint of a flitter, the one coming to pick him up and increased his already quick steps.

While the town represented the future, he felt ill at ease on the wide streets between the low buildings. He understood why the older shambletowners had not taken the offer to move from their crowded lanes, even though the confinement of the shambletown was not for him and never had been.

Would he always feel uncomfortable in the future he was helping to build? Would the reclaimed lands seem strange after the desolate high plains of purple clay, purpled grass, coyotes, and ice rain?

He paced onward, his face set in an expression showing neither joy nor sadness.

XLVII

GERSWIN JUGGLED THE heavy, double-ended and double-bladed knife in his left hand, then balanced it on his fingertip, finally flipping it end over end into the air, where he snatched it right-handed at its midpoint.

He glanced at the targets, ignoring the figure who waited behind the wall at his back, the wall that surrounded the makeshift practice range. The last glimpse he had caught indicated that Major Vlerio was still waiting, although it had only been minutes since he arrived.

Vlerio's approach had been diffident, almost hesitant. When Gerswin had stopped to walk over, the other had motioned him back, saying, "Finish up. However long it takes. I'll wait."

Gerswin raised his eyebrows in puzzlement, but turned from the target and began to walk away.

Abruptly, he dived to the left, twisted in midair, releasing the knife, and tucked. He came out of the roll on the balls of his feet, the second knife in his left hand momentarily—before it too sped toward the target.

Dusting his hands on the legs of the old flight suit, he trotted forward to retrieve the knives. As he covered the nearly ten meters between him and the target he had chosen, he checked his accuracy.

Both knives would have penetrated the heart, had the target been a man, although the first had not gone through the plastic-shielded and stiffened foam as much as he would have liked.

He frowned as he stepped up to the target, listening, but there was no sound of movement from Vlerio. He eased the first knife from the target and replaced it in the waistband sheath. The second followed.

Glancing upward at the clouds, he could see the light gray darkening in the north, a sign that the ice rain would be returning.

He sniffed, but the air remained dry, with little hint of moisture.

Reiner Vlerio still sat quietly on the far side of the back stone wall, waiting patiently, although Gerswin knew he was ready to leave Old Earth for his promotion to commander and his transfer back to New Augusta in whatever obscure screen-shoving assignments detail his orders had brought.

Gerswin took a deep breath and walked to the far left end of the unofficial practice yard. Once, he had been the only one who used it, but most of the other devilkids had taken up his example and practiced with their own versions of unpowered weapons. The sling was one of the few that they all used. As if by unspoken custom, none practiced together, and anyone who might be using the range left whenever Gerswin appeared.

Improvements had appeared from time to time. While Gerswin had built the wall behind the targets and the target stands, Lerwin had added the side walls and the swinging target. Lostwin had added the rear wall and the stone bench, the one on which Vlerio waited. Glynnis had provided the sandy pit and the high target.

Gerswin smiled and broke into a sprint for the right side of the yard.

Crack! Crack!

As he fired the second stone, he dove into a roll, discarding the sling and coming up with the knife, right-handed this time.

Thunk!

He surveyed the three targets. Had they been human, two would have been dead. One he had only struck in the "shoulder." That had been the second sling stone.

Retrieving the two slingstones, the slingleathers, and the knife, he replaced all three in their hidden sheaths and trotted to the rear stone wall, only meters from Vlerio, whom he ignored by failing to acknowledge the other's presence.

He turned to face the targets, his back nearly touching the stone wall, then began a zig-zag sprint toward the swinging target to the left of the three "standing" targets.

Crack! Crack!

He flung himself into a dive that would land him in the sand pit, bringing out the knife with his left hand and releasing it before he plowed into the heavy sand.

Thud!

After picking himself out of the sand and dusting off the cold and damply clinging grains, he shook his head.

The sling shots had been on target, but the first had merely been to get the target moving. The knife had not been accurate; it had bounced off the middle standing target.

He retrieved the sling stones, the sling, and the knife. This time, when he picked up the second stone and pressed his fingers against the rounded smoothness, the stone split, as stones often did after hard and repeated use.

He tossed the fragments over the wall behind the targets, ignoring the twin *clicks* as they struck the rocky clay of the slope.

Vlerio was still sitting on the stone bench.

Gerswin pursed his lips, exhaled deeply, and replaced the weapons. The major wasn't known for his patience.

Rather than vault the chest-high irregular wall, Gerswin walked around it.

Vlerio looked up as he approached.

"Rather impressive, Gerswin."

"Like to keep in shape."

"It must help your coordination, although I doubt you need much help there. Such primitive weapons might not be much good in combat, not against lasers or stunners, but you'd probably be safe in any back alley in the Empire."

"Possibly," Gerswin answered noncommittally. He smiled as he seated himself on a section of the wall where he generally faced Vlerio, who, in turn, twisted toward Gerswin.

"Not primitive," added the junior major. "Unpowered. Difference there. Knife and sling are much better in-close weapons than lasers."

"I didn't come to debate weapons, but I would be interested in a less cryptic explanation of why you think so."

Gerswin shrugged.

"Close in, lasers aren't that selective. Hit innocents as well as targets. If you intend to destroy whole companies of troops, why bother with hand weapons at all? Use tacheads or particle beams and boil off the whole area. Hand weapons are designed for individuals. Otherwise, just dangerous toys to make people feel good. You can run out of charges for a laser or a stunner. Damned difficult to run out of stones, and you can use a knife over and over."

"What if you want to occupy territory or seize a specific objective?"

"You can't take it with unpowered weapons, have to question why you want to take it at all. A laser or beam firefight won't leave much behind. So why bother with losing troops? Vaporize it with a beam or tachead. Costs less in money and personnel."

This time Vlerio was the one to shake his head.

"You're still a barbarian, Gerswin. Dangerously direct."

"Never said I wasn't. Just don't believe in wars unless it's for survival. Or freedom. Anything else is an excuse," Gerswin paused. "But you didn't come to talk about philosophies of conflict."

"No. I'm leaving tomorrow, and I wanted to talk to you before I left. Alone."

Gerswin automatically scanned the slope before nodding. Not certain what he could say, he waited for Vlerio to go on.

"I don't like you. Not that I dislike you, because I don't. Not that I don't admire you, because I do. But I don't like you. You can be as direct as a knife, and as sharp. One way or another, if you want it done, it gets done."

Vlerio gestured toward the practice yard. "Like your training. I've watched the Corpus Corps practice. You want more perfection than they do. You don't know all the techniques, but if I had to bet on the outcome of a contest between you and any one of them, I'd bet on you. When you and Lerwin practice on the mats, people watch, and they swallow. Like watching carnacats.

"You're a modern barbarian warlord, Gerswin. One who knows all the technology, but who's kept touch with the need for personal example and the inspiration of personal combat.

"I don't like you, but my success as Operations officer is because of you. Because of you, I'm going to get a promotion I thought I'd lost when I was assigned here. You know that, and I know that, and Commander Manders knows that. Now, my last tour will still be a nothing, but it's a nothing with the diamonds on the collars, and that's important to me."

Vlerio stood, and Gerswin slipped off the wall.

"I didn't like you when I came, Major, and that hasn't changed. But whether you're a barbarian or not, whether I like you or not, you do a damned good job, too good to be wasted. So you're my successor, and I'm told that your promotion to major has been made permanent."

The older officer smiled a tight smile. "I wish I could be more positive personally, Gerswin, but that's the way it is."

Gerswin met the other's eyes, trying not to be too direct in his glance. "Appreciate your honesty, ser."

"Don't worry about that. Just prove I was right." Vlerio nodded curtly, and turned, his heavy steps carrying him eastward toward the portals back into the base complex.

Gerswin swallowed, knowing that what Vlerio had said had cost the man. Maybe he'd been too harsh in his private judgments of the major.

He looked down at the hard-packed clay, then at the empty bench.

Click! Click! Click!

The ice rain splattered against the stones of the walls and against the slabs of the bench as the wind picked up, and as the whispers of the air built into a thin wail that announced the oncoming storm.

CRUNCH. CRUNCH. CRUNCH.

Each step echoed, ringing off the dingy white walls between which the man walked. His deliberate steps left a track in the centimeters of ice crystals that formed a layer of pavement above the stone and clay that served as the foundation of both streets and alleys.

He crossed the main street, scarcely wider than the back way he tracked. Both were empty in the late winter afternoon.

A quick glance to his left, up toward the old square, revealed no

one, nor any tracks down toward the older section of the shambletown where his steps had taken him, as they always did on his infrequent visits to the past.

So cold were the ice flakes that his feet scarcely slipped as he completed crossing the larger lane. Once past the crossing and back between two walls of the narrowing lane, he stopped, listening.

... *crunch* ...

The single step stopped.

He nodded, waiting, but his distant shadow moved not at all.

Click! Click! Click, click, click!

The ice crystals continued their faint clatter as they struck both
the walls and the smoothness of the Imperial all-weather jacket.

His eyes flickered up toward the nearest window, vacant, with
only a small remnant of thonging wrapped around the lashing post to
show where the vanished hide covering had once been secured.

Most of the crowded-together structures on the old lane were vacant, for they had been the ones given to the younger couples, or
those without status in the shambletown—those who had been the
first to move to the new town.

He took another step, silently until his boot touched the crystals,
and the *crunch* reverberated back up the lane behind him. The echoing step-*crunch* from his unseen shadow whispered back down the
slanted lane to him.

... *crunch* ...

A tight smile creased the slender man's face, framed loosely by
the jacket's unlined hood, as he resumed his journey down the crystalline lane and away from the larger cross street. With his gray
trousers and the silver gray of the jacket and his light steps, had there
been no sound of ice, his presence would have been silent. Then the
one who followed could truly have believed that a graying ghost again
stalked the old shambletown.

Whhhrrr.

The man in silver and gray sprinted the three steps around the
curve.

Crack!

Powdered white wall plaster puffed out from the impact of the
sling stone and drifted downward to join the white crystals that had
already covered the clay and stone of the shambletown pavement.

Crunch. Crunch. Crunch.

This time, the man in silver timed his steps to match those of his
hidden pursuer as the two seemed to float through the ice fall toward

the wall of the abandoned tannery where the lane dead-ended into an even narrower cross lane.

Whhhrrrr.

Crack!

Another stone powdered the flaking white and time-dimmed wall plaster, striking less than a meter from the hooded man and breaking off enough of the plaster to show a brown circle of crumbling brick beneath.

The silvered man dropped his deliberate stride and sprinted the last few meters down the remaining and steepest section of the lane, darting around the corner to the left.

Crack!

Crunch. Crunch, crunch, crunch.

The shadowy figure of the follower edged down the lane, a bent figure, dark in tattered tunic and leathers, with a gnarled right hand on which there were white hairs above the scars, twirling the sling with a killer stone within the straps. His head turned slowly from side to side, as if he listened for the faintest of sounds.

He neared the dead-end corner and paused.

. . . crunch . . .

The sound was light, but not immediately on the far side of the blind corner.

The dark and bent man studied the crystals and the widely-spaced footprints held therein. The distance between prints stated that the man in silver had continued his head-long flight around the corner, possibly into the distance toward the wall and the Maze beyond.

The bent man lifted his head slightly, as if sniffing at the steady wind that brought the ice crystals down in their steady beat against walls, leathers, and faces, and piled those icy fragments on flat roofs, empty clay, and stones.

Finally, he eased around the corner, still bent, then straightened as he whipped the sling up and around toward the slim man in silver who stood ten meters away twirling his own sling.

Crump!

Crack!

The bent and gnarled man swayed, then bent farther over, as, at first, his fingers let slip the leathers of the sling, and as his heavy legs refused to hold him erect any longer.

The man in silver folded his leathers into a flat package, returning them to their hidden pouch, and strode forward into the crystal rain toward the fallen figure.

At last, he stood over the man in leathers and pushed the thin silver hood back off his short and curled blond hair.

His yellow hawk eyes glittered in the gloom of the approaching dusk as he saw that the fallen one still continued to breathe, though he lay face down in the heaped ice droplets.

Gently, as if the older man were a friend, the silver and blond man turned the wounded man over until he rested on his back.

"Devulkid . . . yaaa . . . devul . . ."

His eyes opened wide as he gasped the last word, but no longer did they see.

The man in the all-weather silver shook his head, then stooped and lifted the body in his arms, ignoring the sour odor, the grease, and the blood from the old man's caved-in temple.

Surprisingly, the body was light, and the more-than-once pursued man in gray and silver carried it lightly as he retraced his steps back toward the upper town and the bare stone slab where he would leave the few remaining shambletowners another legacy from their past.

Click. Click. Click.

The ice rain continued to fall on the all-weather finish of the Imperial jacket.

Crunch. Crunch. Crunch.

Each step, each sound, carried the survivor farther into the past and the future simultaneously, aging and rejuvenating him at the same instants, until he found it increasingly difficult to focus on the narrow lane before him.

A deep breath, then another, and he resumed his journey with a body that weighed heavier with each step upward.

With steps more and more deliberate on the slippery footing, he at last entered the square. A single line of footprints, nearly obscured by the ice rain that had fallen, appeared at right angles to his path. He wondered who else had stalked the old ghosts of the shambletown, before realizing that the other prints were also his.

He placed the already-stiffening figure on the white stone of the single upright bench and turned, plodding out toward the gate that was frozen ajar only slightly wider than a body width.

This time, he did not turn back. In time, had there been anyone out in the ice storm, they would have seen a silver-gray ghost with glittering yellow eyes and hair like yellow flame vanishing into the storm from whence he had come. But no one was abroad, and he vanished as silently as he arrived.

Click. Click. Click.

GERSWIN SLAMMED THE console stud.

A single flitter and the spares for one dozer. *One* dozer. Period.

He shook his head and called up the justification that had arrived with the inadequate spare parts.

"Req. 1(b) three(3) class delta flitters, mod. B(4).

"Sup. One(1) class delta flitter, mod. B(3), per ConsComp Reg. D-11(b), as modified Alstats 11-yr."

While as Operations officer Gerswin did not know the exact content of the Alstats message referenced, he had a good idea of how it had been applied to Old Earth, and the fact that all Old Earth Base requisitions had been cut by two thirds did not surprise him. Virtually everything but trace element foodstuffs had been cut back over the last three years, and from what he could tell from the few supply ships, all the out-bases were being shorted, some worse than Old Earth.

Right now, though, the base needed equipment. There wasn't any metal, nor any native power source to speak of, except the wind, and maybe, near the coasts, some sort of tidal power. The sun shone a fraction more, according to the records, than it had thirty years earlier, the first time detailed records had been entered, but until the ecology could be returned to its pre-collapse state or some approximation thereof, and the particulate-based cloud cover reduced, solar power was out as any sort of reliable alternative.

Gerswin sighed. Everything wound together in a web.

He needed more dozers to reclaim the land and re-establish a usable ground cover and a solid agriculture base. Each dozer required support equipment, personnel, spare parts, and the power to maintain them. Imperial deployed technology was based on fusactors, handy unitized fusion reactors easily produced by any technologically advanced system and impossible to produce anywhere else. Most important, fusactors were expensive to transport. Since an arcdozer was essentially a moving fusactor, the Empire disliked shipping them to distant points. Finally, since fusactors were unitized, once assembled, they were almost impossible to repair and were designed to melt into an impermeable bloc within their own shielding in cases of malfunction.

Without dozers, he couldn't reclaim. Without reclamation, the base couldn't support itself, except slightly above subsistence level, because Imperial technology was all geared to either fusion power or high-energy synthetics.

Without local metals, which no longer existed except in deep deposits or in-system asteroids unreachable without high energy technology, the locals had no way to develop substitutes with which to rebuild their planet and their society.

Gerswin didn't have enough dozers to continue full-scale reclamation more than a tour or so into the future, and that was assuming rather optimistic projections. And so far, the base had just begun to make a dent in reverting the ecology.

"So you worry . . ."

He hadn't realized he had spoken aloud until he heard the echo of his words in the small office.

He frowned.

The Empire wouldn't close down Old Earth Base yet, but with the resource commitment it required, he could see the supply lines getting tighter and tighter, year after year.

"What can you do? Order more equipment they won't send you? Exaggerate the requirements along with everyone else? Then they'll cut everyone back farther."

He flicked off the screen and stood, stretching, looking at the lighter gray square where Vlerio's holoview of his wife's estate house had covered half the wall opposite the console.

His steps circled the console.

The old exec, Byykr, had understood some of the problem. But Byykr was gone, and Commander LeTrille was merely going through the motions. Commander Manders understood, but was too tired to start a fight with the Imperial bureaucracy, although, Gerswin admitted to himself, Manders usually took his recommendations.

What good was a recommendation when you couldn't get what you needed and didn't know what else to recommend?

What did Old Earth need?

Metal, power, and arable land.

The arable land might be possible before too long. Acreage had increased to the point where at subsistence level it would support most of the scattered Noram population, assuming the produce could even be distributed. But the land still required a sponge grain scavenge crop every third year.

The power was barely adequate and completely dependent upon the Empire. One possibility existed—coming up with an oilseed plant that could be refined to approximate synthetic fuels—but that re-

quired more land, reduced food crop yields, and demanded a refining technology which would require metals and power.

He shook his head.

"Face it, Gerswin. You don't know enough. You can't figure your
way out of this one."

As for the metal—unless they could literally mine something . . .

His eyes glinted, and he sat down at the console, flicking it back
on and beginning to punch in the numbers, the requests for data.

Finally, when all the requests had been routed, he sat back in the
swivel.

Then he laughed.

"It works, or it doesn't."

With that, he stood and walked over to the small wall locker, from
which he removed his set of practice knives and sling, plus the quarterstaff.

He whistled three double notes, then stopped before touching
the exit stud and stepping out.

"Marliss, I'm going to get some exercise. Should be back in less
than an hour."

"Yes, ser."

The major refrained from frowning. The man, a former shambletown youth, was fresh from recruit training and nearly cowered
every time Gerswin looked at him.

The idea just might appeal to someone, and the scale was modest
enough. A mere two fusactors to power a river reclamation plant.

He remembered what Mahmood had said about drainage. If all
those metals were still being leached into the waters, then they'd have
to end up in the major drainage rivers.

Now . . . If the ecologists and the engineers could figure out how
to make it work and package it, and if Manders bought the idea . . .

He shrugged. If not, he'd try something else.

He straightened the leathers of the sling and whirled it experi-
mentally as he touched the southeast interior exit portal, easing himself and the staff through. He needed more work with the quarterstaff,
but Zyleria was on leave, and she was the only one with real training
in handling it as a weapon.

He stepped through the outer portal and into the chill outside air.

Plick. Plick. Plick.

The scattered rain droplets hit his flight suit, the last from the
passing dark shower under the overclouds, and were gone with a gust
of wind.

Gerswin turned west, toward the area he used for his practice with what both Vlerio and Matsuko had called "primitive" weapons.

The key was hope. If he could convince the Empire that certain investments would reduce the long-term costs, and that the improvements would begin fairly soon, he had a chance. No Emperor really wanted to be the one to abandon Old Earth, but it would be harder and harder to get more than a token commitment in the years ahead.

He glanced at the lower hills to the west where the first generation pines had been planted. Trees—they would help. Then some oilseeds; a source of metals—not much, but enough to keep things going for a while, and time.

Crack!

The first stone smacked into the center target head.

Crack!

Crack!

GERSWIN BLINKED AND studied the figures on the console again.

Old Earth Base was getting shorted again. Transport costs were attributed by the mass-cube ratio multiplied by the energy cost. The farther a destination drop, the higher the imputed cost. Although the out-base runs were supposed to be rotated so that every base was assigned the first, second, third, or fourth drop in roughly equivalent numbers, Gerswin could find no record of Old Earth ever having been assigned first or second drop order. The effect was to increase the energy costs. Yet Old Earth was not listed on the "hardship" destination drop port list, which would have allowed a greater cost ratio.

While the I.S.S. picked up all the costs from its overall transport budget, and not from each base's budget, the political implications bothered Gerswin. If it had only been the mass-cube energy cost assignments, he would not have been so concerned, but the same sort of calculations had been employed in determining costs for foodstuff supplies, personnel transfers, spare and replacement parts, and even for dietary trace elements. The composite gave a picture of Old Earth Base as either inefficient or exceedingly expensive to operate or both.

Gerswin pursed his lips.

Added to that were the actual personnel assignment policies, which tended to order either low performers or troublemakers to Old Earth. Although he doubted that anyone was trying to close down the base, or that someone was benefitting from the current allocation practices, there was no doubt in his mind that no one in the I.S.S. hierarchy was able or willing to stand up for Old Earth, even to suggest simple fairness in an allocation system that failed to account for any of the special problems the reclamation effort faced.

Cling!

"Gerswin."

"Major, five minutes before your meeting with the commandant."

"Thanks."

Gerswin tapped the console and stood, straightening his tunic, shrugging his shoulders to relieve the tightness caused by too many hours in front of the screen. With a last shrug, he left his own space and covered the short length of corridor that separated him from the commandant's slightly more elaborate office.

Manders was standing beside his console, which was switched off, as Gerswin swept in.

"Good afternoon, Greg."

"Afternoon, ser."

"What landspout did you tangle with now? You have that look, the one that spells trouble."

"That obvious?"

"With you? Yes." The senior commander sighed, then gestured toward the swivel across the console from him. The older man sank into his own chair.

"Now . . . Can I do anything about your problem?"

"Don't know. Thought I'd ask." Gerswin frowned. "Just finished an analysis of the outship cost-formulas. Do you know why we're always last drop, or next to last drop, but why they don't classify us as hardship or special circumstance?"

"Commander Byykr brought that up once, shortly before he retired. I do not recall the reasons, but I do know that he looked into it rather thoroughly. I'll have it checked on and get back to you. No sense in your doing anything more until you see what, if anything, he did."

Manders cleared his throat. "Not sure it makes any difference in any case, since the shipping costs aren't tabbed against our account."

"Not in the budgetary sense, Commander. Presents a one-sided holo. Shows Old Earth as a conventional base with twice the operating/transport costs of other comparable bases."

"Are you suggesting that is deliberate, Greg?"

"No, ser. More likely that there's no champion at headquarters.

It's not that anything's *wrong*. More that Old Earth deserves a special category and hasn't gotten it."

Manders looked over at the wall holo of the Academy Spire, mirrored in Crystal Lake.

Gerswin did not follow his glance. He knew the holo well enough. If it were not a duplicate of the one which had hung on Commander Byykr's wall, it was close enough that the differences were insignificant.

"I've had some of this conversation before, Greg, with Commander Byykr, and there's a bit more to this than meets the eye. I just can't remember why at the moment." He turned back toward Gerswin. "Now. There's something rather more personally important you should know."

"Something I should know?"

The senior commander turned in his swivel. "I'm sure you've heard the rumors." He paused. "About the *Hildebard*?"

"Know she didn't arrive as scheduled," responded the major, still standing.

"Sit down."

Gerswin eased into the swivel.

"Do you know the implications?" The base commander leaned back in the padded swivel. His office was the only one in the entire base with comfortable chairs for visitors.

"Equipment shortages . . . especially turbine fans. Hardest to get around. Morale problems for Imperials due for transfer . . . general feeling of being abandoned."

"There are a few other difficulties, Greg." The commander paused theatrically.

Gerswin frowned. Commander Manders had used his first name twice in minutes. The familiarity was unusual. It was also a message, and the ramifications were even more unexpected.

"The new executive officer?"

Old Earth Base had already gone without an official and permanent executive officer for more than six months, and not a few of the duties had fallen in Gerswin's lap, in addition to his own responsibilities as Operations officer.

"That's the second most important."

Forcing himself to avoid frowning, Gerswin tried to figure out what Manders was hinting at. Usually, the commander was direct, sometimes sarcastically so in private, and the guessing game implied that it was important for Gerswin to come up with the answer.

"All right," began the major. "Assuming the *Hildebard* is a casualty, another three months is the minimum before we get another transport. If High Command can juggle the schedules. Nine months is double the time for critical replacements. Means a rush courier, breaking regulations, or promotion from base cadre."

He shook his head as the implication hit. "Only one officer here meets minimum standards, ser."

The commander nodded in return. "That's right. The message torp that arrived today confirmed that. There's more, Commander."

Gerswin swallowed at the cavalier announcement of his promotion. Promotions to commander were nearly impossible for non-Imperials to get these days, with the cutbacks in ships, and the reliance on smaller and smaller craft and their lower operating costs.

"More?" He knew the statement sounded stupid as he said it and tried to follow on. "That sounds like it means unpleasant news of some sort."

Manders snorted. "And for what are executive officers being groomed, Commander? Think a bit, Greg."

The combination of sarcasm and the gentler use of his name momentarily stopped Gerswin from saying anything.

"Base command. They need you somewhere else?"

"I wish that were true. My stress profile is edging up into the red. That's the real problem."

Gerswin nodded. If Manders was being pushed off the edge, which his generally low key approach, his willingness to delegate, the pressures must be more than Gerswin realized. Either that, or the senior officer pool was thinner than the Empire let on.

"You're nodding. Would you care to share your thoughts?"

"Just a guess, really. But XO and CO are high stress positions here. Require tech knowledge, quick decisions. Weather makes it combat environment without combat. Project is long term. Requires engineering no one has ever tried, and no quick way to verify results. Material failures are high. Few officers interested or qualified."

This time, the base commander nodded.

"You're right. The new exec was one of only two out-base commanders or majors within the qual envelope." Manders grinned wryly. "That leaves one major, or should I say, commander, Greg, who fits."

"In the entire Service?"

Manders shook his head.

"Not necessarily, but among those who can be reassigned. What good does it do to move a qualified officer from one spot to another if the replacement officer needs the same qualifications?"

"I see. There were others, but you'd have to replace them."

"Right. you could be transferred to Bolduc, losing the advantage of your local experience, and the exec there promoted to exec here, and the Service would lose two experienced people . . . not to mention the transfer costs, and the ships . . ."

Gerswin pursed his lips. It made a certain sad sense, especially if the Empire really didn't want to plow too much into Old Earth.

"What about you?"

Manders laughed a laugh that was half-sardonic, half-chuckle. "In simple terms, they told me to dump everything I could on you in the next year, and to keep my stress levels down. In other words: Manders, survive until your executive officer knows enough to take over, because there isn't anyone else, and we don't have the ships and people to pull you out."

The new commander looked down at the tiles and the worn carpet.

"Stupid to project ahead, but doesn't that imply that every base commander will have to be either Old Earth born or trained here? Or someplace equally tough?"

"Not stupid. Unfortunately true, as far as I can see. My own records indicate there may be as many as five or six who could succeed you."

"The devilkids?"

Manders nodded. "And perhaps the two pilots from The Hebrides."

"Understand their home environment's as rough as anything around here, and just as cold."

The base commandant stood and turned to the console. He picked up a hard-copy flimsy and handed it to Gerswin.

"That's the text."

Gerswin scanned it, observing that he was indeed promoted to commander, permanently, and effective immediately, in order to take over duties as executive officer, Old Earth Base. Evaluations on his performance would be submitted via torp quarterly, vice-annually. The expected transfer/retirement date of the current base commander was hereby extended six months.

"Get your stuff up here immediately."

"Ops?"

"Have to detail Hassedie for the next six months. Next Ops boss will be incompetent, or worse, but Lerwin's too junior, even in our circumstances, and no one else has a prayer."

"Rule of thumb is no incompetents above the Ops boss level?"

"Usually, Greg. Usually. But don't count on it."

Gerswin quirked his lips. "Understood."

"And . . . ?"

"And?"

"I've got some spare insignia. You'll need them for your swearing in tomorrow."

What was, was. The past defines itself. Historians refuse to accept that definition and instead superimpose their analysis of the past through the eyes of the present. Thus, history becomes a pale reflection of the present, while the true past is lost behind the reflected image presented by historians who would have us see what they believe, rather than what was.

> *Politics in the Age of Power*
> Exton Land
> Old Earth, 2031 O.E.C.

THE COMMANDER FROWNED as he read the report again.

"In black and white, no less . . ."

Commander Byykr had been thorough, exceedingly thorough, exploring avenues Gerswin would not have considered, but the avenues made no difference in the conclusion.

"The ideal world is described as 'earth-type prime,' or ETP, based on the original biosphere of Old Earth. Those worlds classified as unique or with special hardships are measured in terms of their deviation from ETP parameters. . . .

". . . any attempt to classify Old Earth as a hardship station or as severely deviant from existing standards would (1) cast doubt upon those standards; (2) cast doubt upon the original standards-setting process, which could lead to pressure for reconsideration for a number of bases and systems; (3) require an unpleasant explanation of the circumstances leading to the collapse of Old Earth, which, in turn, would cast some doubt upon the Empire and its traditions; (4) would require a recomputation of all mass-cube ratios and other costs for all out-systems . . .

". . . under such conditions, the ETP model could then be attacked as a mere statistical standard, and one with no basis in reality . . ."

There was more, phrased in a scholarly manner, but what was left unsaid by the scholarly phrases of the former executive officer was even more interesting.

While Gerswin did not have Byykr's or Manders's background in Service politics, he understood enough. The politics of the situation meant that any attempt to change Old Earth's status would undermine the tacit consent on which all Imperial hardship and transport formulas were based.

Hidden more deeply in the report was that cost ratios and transport formulas were skewed to make a profit for suppliers of energy systems, particularly for those who had backed the Old Earth reclamation effort. While Gerswin couldn't be absolutely certain, Byykr's report seemed to point clearly in those directions.

The commander shook his head. If he attempted to improve the cost ratios, then Old Earth would lose supporters immediately if he succeeded. If he did not, over the long run current Service support would erode, as more and more members of the headquarters staff saw what they regarded as a disproportionate amount of funding going into a planet with no military significance, funding that could go for ships and equipment in short supply.

Gerswin reread the entire report again, looking for other possibilities. Then he stored a copy in his own personal files.

Manders had been right. There wasn't much that could be done—not now, at least.

With a sigh, he flicked his console from the Byykr report to the day's stacked messages, and to the long vertical row of amber lights on the right side of the screen.

GERSWIN LOOKED AT the empty office, the walls freshly cleaned and resealed, the old furniture recoated with yet another layer of flexcoating, enough to erase all but the deepest scratches.

"Commander?"

He turned in the portal to face his orderly/gatekeeper, Senior Technician Nitiri.

"Captain Geron needs to speak with you, ser."

Gerswin shook his head. Manders had barely lifted planet-clear and the calls were already coming.

He fingered the linked diamonds on the dress grays. Senior commander yet, if only because they couldn't find anyone else remotely qualified that wasn't more urgently needed elsewhere. Or was it because, if they had to scuttle the base, they could blame it on a native-born?

Wondering how long he really had, Gerswin sat down before the antique but perfectly functional console.

"Gerswin."

"Yes, Commander. Captain Geron at the river separation plant. We have a difficulty here."

Gerswin frowned. "Thought you were only at pilot stage."

"We are, but we still have a problem."

The new base commander nodded at the image in the screen to continue.

"Do you remember the initial bioassays, which showed a small fish population with high heavy metal and toxic concentrations in their tissues?"

"Recall the problem, but not the specifics. Go ahead."

"Apparently, that shows more than bioaccumulation. It may signify actual biological adaptation."

Gerswin winced, realizing as he did that commanding officers were supposed to be impassive in the face of the unexpected.

"It looks like you understand before I finish the explanation."

"Let me guess. Those fish that swim through the cleaner water you discharge are showing signs of distress. Is that it? One species, or across the board?"

"It's preliminary. Only one species so far, but it could be some sort of benchmark."

"How much of the total flow are you diverting and processing?"

"Istvenn, this is only a pilot. Less than twenty percent at the lowest possible flow levels. Have to estimate as little as two percent at flood stage flows."

"Dilute it."

"What?"

"Dilute it," repeated Gerswin. "Pump some of the untouched river flow and mix the two streams before discharge back into the river.

"Dilution isn't a solution."

"I know. But it will give both us and the fish time to adapt. Hate to think we stopped trying to figure out ways to clean up the water because cleaner water proved toxic to one kind of fish. If they adapted one way, there's always the chance they can revert to the original stand, or that we'll end up with two varieties—one that likes arsenic or lead or whatever, and one that doesn't."

"Commander, that assumption is not fully grounded in any science."

"Probably not. But we need cleaner river water for the other organisms we'll have to reseed, and we need the metals as well. What's the iron concentration?"

"Low. Lower than the estimates so far. Lead is higher. So is cadmium. Arsenic is about as we suspected. Organics are higher, but they're relatively easy to shunt and reduce."

"How much iron are you getting?"

"Peak is less than a half kilo an hour in present operations."

"All right. Go ahead and figure out a dilution mechanism to use until you have a chance to figure out a better solution."

"Yes, ser."

The captain's cool tone told Gerswin that the scientist was not pleased. Neither was Gerswin. Some forms of carp could, and had, adapted to anything. That didn't mean the water should stay dirty. Besides, the pilot operation was just the first step. If the mechanism worked, Gerswin intended to duplicate what could be duplicated and see if he could wrangle the spares necessary to open another station, the second one powered by natural sources, like the tidal bore in the Scotia area.

If all the remaining metals on Old Earth were dissolved, then they'd have to be undissolved.

At least *that* problem could be defined and resolved.

After viewing the remnants of Old Earth a century following the Collapse, the theologian Mardian was moved to say, "There are no saints in Hell, nor dawn on Earth. For neither Hell nor Earth permits hope or light."

While this view of the ecological condition of Old Earth may have been exaggerated, there are enough accounts of the damage verified by Federation records, and later by Imperial records, that it would be difficult to ignore the extent of the devastation.

Yet all of recent history within this sector of the galaxy has been affected at least indirectly by the scars of the fall of mankind's first home, and by the later struggles to reclaim that once-shining symbol. . . .

The Empire—The Later Years
Pietra D'Kerwin J'rome
New Avalon, 5133 N.E.C.

Lᗡ

GERSWIN STUDIED THE text on the console, frowning as he did so. The ambiguities troubled him, but any good regulation should have some just to allow for local flexibility.

Still . . . B.P.R. 20012(b) was specific. ". . . all officers and technicians, as well as any detailed or civilian personnel under contract, shall be housed within the base perimeter in all but Class II(b) installations . . ."

Old Earth Base was not a Class II(b) installation. Period.

Gerswin leaned back in the swivel he had inherited from Manders and pursed his lips.

Sitting forward after a period of reflection, he tapped another inquiry into the console.

As the response began to appear, he smiled.

"Had to be there, somewhere . . ."

The intercom buzzed.

"Gerswin."

"Commander, the executive officer is here."

"I'll be ready in a minute."

"Yes, ser."

He scanned the lines on the console, picking out the key phrases.

". . . as defined by either (a) the Standing Order of that Base's establishment . . . or (b) a current survey of the boundaries as entered in the Base Operating Procedures and as maintained by the Service . . ."

Gerswin put the regulation on hold, blanked the screen, stood up, and headed for the portal.

"Come in." He nodded at Commander Glyncho, who wore dress grays, as he usually did.

Gerswin had on a new flight suit, the only concession to rank being the linked diamonds of a senior commander on his collar. He turned, knowing Glyncho would follow him back into the office.

Gerswin motioned to the swivel at the corner of the console.

"Seat?"

"Thank you. I do appreciate your courtesy in seeing me, especially given your busy schedule, and the heavy demands on your time."

Gerswin inclined his head and raised his eyebrows in inquiry.

"I have been thinking about this awhile. As you know, my family has remained on New Augusta, what with the close family ties that exist there. I'm sure you understand. While I was hoping that I could make a unique contribution to the reclamation of Old Earth, sometimes things seen from New Augusta take on a different perspective when experienced in person. I'm sure you also appreciate that."

Gerswin nodded. "New Augusta does have a unique perspective."

"My talents, as you have pointed out, are mainly administrative in nature. Frankly, on a base which has become more and more involved in actual hands-on reclamation, my special expertise just isn't fully applicable and can't be utilized to the degree I had originally hoped for when I was assigned here as executive officer."

Gerswin nodded again. "Afraid this has become a highly tech operation, not at all a normal Service base, Glyn."

"That's just it. The mission is important, but it's not the typical I.S.S. mission. And I don't have the specialized technical knowledge to be much more than a supervisor of the clerical staff and a high-powered screen monitor."

Glyncho swallowed. "Now—"

BUZZZ!

"Excuse me, Glyn."

Gerswin turned and jabbed the stud.

"Gerswin here."

Captain Lerwin's face filled the screen.

"Captain, emergency report from the Scotia station. Class I spout caught their research sampler on the water."

"Damage?"

"The sampler's fusactor cracked. They shut it down, abandoned it, and it's sunk in twenty meters of water."

"That in the tidal bore?"

"No. Offshore."

"Stet. If you can reclaim it, lift the team out there and do it. If you can't, send the techs with that silicon fusing gel and encapsulate it. Then we can lift it out safely."

"Cost?"

"Blast the cost. Need the fusactor if we can save it. If not, we'll let the mass cool and reclaim what we can later." Gerswin paused. "Lerwin?"

"Yes, Captain?"

"Find out why that sampler wasn't secured with a Class I spout incoming."

"Yes, ser."

Gerswin broke the connection and turned back to Glyncho.

"You were saying, Glyn?"

"Nothing, really."

"Take it you're thinking about transfer, or retirement?"

"You saw the response to my transfer request."

Gerswin nodded.

"That doesn't leave me much choice. I can either stay and route screens, or retire. Since my family can't come here—"

Gerswin did not bother to correct Glyncho. Any family that wanted to could come, provided the sponsor opted for a double tour. What the executive officer was saying was that his wife was not about to leave New Augusta for more than ten years on Old Earth.

"... you would rather retire and spend some time with them," Gerswin finished the sentence.

"That's right."

Gerswin smiled his official pleasant and warm smile.

"I can't say I blame you under the circumstances, and if you want, I'll be happy to endorse your request with an observation that I recommend speedy approval in view of your past service, and for humanitarian reasons."

"That would be most appreciated."

"No problem. Look right to it."

Gerswin stood.

"Like to talk further, but you heard the problem that just surfaced."

Glyncho stood in turn.

"I understand. I just wish I'd been able to take more of the load off you."

"I know. I know."

Even before the portal had fully closed behind Glyncho, Gerswin was back at the console, checking the status of the fusactors assigned to the base, to see if there were any spares left.

No spares remained in inventory. The virtual freeze on high tech shipments to all but the highest priority bases was beginning to tell in more ways than one.

The old dozers were getting harder and harder to repair, and simpler and simpler to operate as Glynnis and her technicians eliminated and cannibalized to keep them running. While the town was starting to sprout some local technology, there was neither the technical nor the personnel background for sufficiency, and there wouldn't be for years to come.

Besides that, there was the bigger resource problem. The Empire's military and its machines were equipped with metallic support systems or those based on complicated and high tech synthetics. Old Earth had no metal deposits left, not to speak of anywhere near the surface. That meant no local metal to replace plates worn by years of struggling against unyielding clay and the corrosiveness of the land-poisons. No metal with which to convey power beyond the single new town outside the base. No metal for trinkets such as jewelry. No metal—except through the Empire, or from Imperial mining of the system's few remaining metallic asteroids. Both sources were expensive.

The only local source were the few kilograms produced from the Scotia and river reclamation works. While those small stocks were insignificant, over the years they could help.

But even the reclamation metals required energy. And the cost of either transport or reclamation energy was dear, Gerswin knew, so dear that every piece of equipment sent to Old Earth cost as much, if not more, to ship than to build, and required the commensurate paperwork and elaborate justifications.

He bit his lip. For a time, he had hoped that Glyncho could have helped in circumventing the Imperial bureaucracy, but the man had simply no real understanding of technology, or ecology. Without either he had been unable to comprehend the needs, the rationales, or the sheer magnitude of the task.

More than rock-bottom basic sufficiency in nonrecycled food and wood replacement for synthetics was a decade away.

"Decade?" he muttered as his fingers closed out the arcdozer inventory check.

Glyncho, he reflected, unable to dismiss the commander from his mind, had been nice enough, just incapable of dealing with the situation.

Gerswin sighed. Who knew what sort of replacement the Service would throw at him?

Already, the base had far too much deadwood. Lerwin ran Ops, rather than Major Trelinn, who was no improvement on Major Limirio, who had resigned after one year of her tour. Trelinn still had three years left on a tour that unfortunately might well be extended.

Major Hassedie, who was nominally in charge of Administration and Facilities, was smart enough to give most of the real work to either Glynnis or Kiedra. But the native personnel gap was still a problem. The devilkids were one generation, but there weren't any more coming along, not more than two or three since Gerswin had drafted the first batch. Devilkids were good, but scarce, and the oldest of the children from the new town were a good ten years away from an Imperial education, those that could qualify. That was assuming the Empire would even continue the policy of educating the brightest of the outworld youngsters with the continuing cutbacks.

Personnel, metals, energy—his head pounded with the concepts and numbers he juggled.

The amber light on the console reminded him of the housing question, the one he had laid aside earlier, before the Scotia problem and Commander Glyncho.

Lerwin—Lerwin and Kiedra—if they wanted to live in the town, as opposed to the cramped base quarters, that was all to the good if he could find a way to do it, and a way that represented an advantage to Old Earth, the Service, and the base. A cursory look at the regulations only exempted agricultural and research personnel, and they were certainly neither.

Buzz!

"Gerswin."

Lerwin's face appeared on the screen.

"The exec gave the number one and three research techs on the sampler R&R back at base. Number two broke her arm when a sampler sling snapped. She was flitted back here for regeneration therapy. Number four was left with two warm bodies and asked for replacements, but the exec never got around to handling it."

Gerswin sighed again.

"Glyn has requested retirement, and I have concurred. Need me to work on the techs?"

"No need. No sampler. Have to encapsulate."

For a moment, the two exchanged looks through the screen.

Finally, Gerswin laughed. "Still think this is a better place than your hills, devilkid?"

Lerwin snorted.

"Better you than me there, Captain. Encapsulation team on the way. No spouts expected for another forty hours in Scotia. Should be enough." The captain and former devilkid paused, then licked his lips. "About our request, Captain?"

"Think I may have a way to do what the regs say I can't. Let you know."

"Thanks."

Gerswin tapped the stud, stared at the blank screen, then touched the intercom stud.

"Yes, Commander?"

"Would you tell Major Hassedie that I need to talk to him about a base survey, in order to update the Base Operating Procedures? Later this afternoon, if possible."

"You're scheduled clear at 1445."

"That would be fine."

As the screen returned to dark gray, Gerswin looked at the line of blinking lights on the console and shook his head.

First things first, like resurveying the base perimeter to include the new town. He might even get more equipment that way. If not, at least the native borns wouldn't have to stay cooped up in the burrows of the old base, and that would help morale.

He touched the first light on the console.

"COMMANDER, THIS IS most irregular."

Gerswin raised his eyebrows at the image of the dapper major.

"Most irregular. Captain Lerwin is not the most senior of the captains in Operations. As a matter of fact, he is near the middle of seniority, yet the records show he was a temporary captain, over the heads of a number of officers senior to him."

"Linn," Gerswin sighed, "you've known that for two years. Why are you bringing it up now?"

"Because of this." Trelinn raised a white square of paper. "How can you justify recommending him for major? There are men and women here who have spent a decade more in the Service than Captain Lerwin."

"Are you questioning Captain Lerwin's ability? Are you ready to put any complaint in fax?"

"Commander, Captain Lerwin is a most capable officer. That I do not dispute, but his range of experience is rather limited."

"I happen to prefer excellence in a limited area than mediocrity in many. Commander Manders was satisfied with his performance when he made Lerwin the deputy. I have been satisfied, and you have given him good solid ratings."

"But what about the impact on morale of passing over more senior captains?"

"Haven't noticed a problem. Everyone knows that the people who work for me are judged on ability, not seniority. Sometimes seniority and ability go together. More often, they don't."

"I see," answer Trelinn slowly.

"No, you don't, Linn. You use that phrase whenever you disagree and don't want to say so."

Trelinn's mouth opened to protest, but he stopped short of saying anything as he saw how Gerswin watched him, the intensity obvious even through the antique console screen.

"Linn," continued Gerswin implacably, "four kinds of personnel end up here—troublemakers, incompetents, dead-enders, and natives. The incompetents are almost always senior to everyone else. This is not a forgiving planet. Check the record, in case you've forgotten. Ability is what's needed, not seniority. Ability is what I reward. What I encourage."

He cleared his throat for emphasis before continuing. "And what I expect you to encourage."

PAD, PAD, PAD, *pad* . . .

His breath coming easily, Gerswin continued to put one foot in front of the other, step after step, as he narrowed the distance between the base administration/operations complex and the new town.

Lerwin had taken a fresh uniform and underwear for Gerswin when the junior officer had left earlier. He had only smiled when Gerswin told him he wanted to make the trip on foot.

Gerswin hadn't bothered to point out that he ran at least five or

six kays every day. The new town was only about seven, certainly not
any more difficult for him along the clear expanse of the causeway
than his normal forays through the hills, the young trees, and the old
grubushes.

Pad, pad, pad . . .

He kept his breath patterns even, step after step, as he reached
the top of the low rise that marked the rough midpoint between the
two complexes.

Ahead, against the overhead clouds that darkened the twilight,
he could see the glow of the town, as well as the nearer light beams
of the official base shuttle as it headed back from the town to the base
center.

His steps were heavier than they often were, not because of
weight, but because he ran with military issue boots rather than barefoot. At least twice a week, to keep his feet tough, he ran barefoot.
Only once in all the years since he had returned to Old Earth had he
cut his feet, and that had been near the base itself.

His barefoot runs usually carried him through the more deserted
country, away from the park used by the non-native Impie personnel,
and away from the bunkers and landing grids.

Pad, pad, pad . . .

The ground shuttle was less than a kilometer away. Gerswin could
hear the whine of the electrics as it neared him.

Realizing he was beginning to shorten his steps, he consciously
made the effort to stretch each stride slightly, still keeping his rhythm
as even as possible.

The lights of the shuttle swept over him as the squat bus eased
over a rise and the whining let up. The driver raised a hand, and,
without breaking stride, Gerswin returned the gesture. He resisted
the urge to grin as well. How often did the driver and his passengers
see the base commander running down the causeway, complete with
frayed flight suit and boots?

He suspected the whole base knew of his obsession with exercise
and hand weapons, but to know and to see the boss trotting down the
causeway were two separate matters.

Thinking about the weapons, his hand dropped to his belt to insure that knives and sling leathers and stones were still there. While
there were fewer predators around the base, both the coyotes and the
shambletowners continued to roam the area, and neither were terribly friendly.

Gerswin smiled wryly, a substitute for a shrug as he kept his legs
moving.

As he came through the last hillside cut, the new town and its few scattered lights blinked into place, and he began the gentle descent toward the northern gates, still open in the gathering dusk.

The former devilkid doubted that the gates would ever need to be closed again, but had left that decision with the elected town council.

With the leveling of the causeway tarmac for the last half kilometer, Gerswin stretched out his stride and picked up the pace. He slowed only when he reached the gates.

Once inside and past the single guard who had saluted in surprise, he began to walk to cool down before reaching Lerwin and Kiedra's new quarters—home, he mentally corrected himself.

Inside the town walls and directly behind the guard post was the shuttle station, used by both the military shuttle, which had passed him on his run, and the town's shuttle, which stood waiting and empty except for the driver.

Gerswin nodded approvingly as he passed the town shuttle, which used an alcohol-powered external combustion engine system. The brains, talent, and initiative for rebuilding were beginning to appear—just not the raw materials, at least not yet. That was his job.

Beyond the station was a small park, two hundred meters on a side, with low trees, supposedly Old Earth stock, and cold-resistant grass. On one side stood a brick and earthen composite, partly pyramid, partly tunnels, and partly labyrinth walks.

Gerswin could hear the shrieks and murmurings of children at play, but paused, since he could not see any. To his right, out of a grass hummock, popped a curly blond head, which disappeared so quickly Gerswin might have doubted he had seen it in the deepening dusk.

The base commander smiled and resumed his walk along the boulevard toward the central dwelling section.

Shortly, he turned left onto a stone walk. A hundred meters later, he stopped.

The Commander checked the dwelling, a single-story, white-walled structure with two doors, one for each of the two families. All of the quarters buildings in the new town were multi-family, ranging from the relatively smaller ones such as the one before which he stood to larger structures that accommodated three to five family groups.

Even the smallest were more spacious, and certainly more comfortable, than the old shambletown dwellings or the stark base quarters and their bunkered recirculated air.

Lerwin and Kiedra's new home was like all the others, with an old-fashioned hinged door. The door itself was a syntheplast, and the only distinguishing touch on the exterior was a square plaque set into the whitened exterior plaster on the right side of the sheltered entryway. Gerswin studied the design on the plaque and chuckled.

A single slender pine tee appeared above a pair of crossed weapons, the weapons being a double-ended throwing knife and a standard issue hand laser.

Just before he stepped up to the door, it swung inward. Lerwin stood there, grinning.

"Sooner than I thought, Captain, but not much." He stepped back. "Welcome to our home."

"Glad to be here, Lerwin. Glad to be here." He forced himself to keep from mumbling the words, wondering why he suddenly felt so tongue-tied when he had known them both for so long.

Lerwin wore a pair of rough-woven brown trousers and a shinier Imperial-made tunic. While Gerswin could hear footsteps farther inside, he did not see Kiedra.

"The curtain to the right is the guest quarters, for now, at least," announced Lerwin. "Your clothes are there. If you want to, there's an old-fashioned shower down the hall, and the water is . . . well . . . warm."

Gerswin nodded and stepped into the small room—bare except for a single bed, a red-and-black woven rug, and a small table next to the head of the bed. All the furniture appeared handmade.

His undress grays, without insignia, his dress black boots, and a set of clean underwear were neatly laid out on the bed.

A curtain covered what he presumed was a closet. He walked over to the curtain and pulled it back. The clothes shelves were empty, as were the hooks and hangers. The inside of the closet and the walls were all plastered in a light tan finish. The floor was a silver-shot synthetic black stone, made locally with some Service help, Gerswin recalled.

Gerswin noted the towel beside his clothes, scooped it up, and peered out into the empty hall before he walked to the room that contained the shower, a built-in bath, and sink. Toilet facilities were connected, but behind another wall. The only doors in the house appeared to be the front door and the door to the bath and toilet, not unexpectedly, since doors required either Imperial synthetics, imported substitutes, or high-energy local products.

Within another ten years, some locally grown timber would start to become available, but the major timber supplies were closer to twenty years away. The real problem would be to keep down demand and native cutting until the newly replanted and re-established forests had succeeded in stabilizing the ecology.

Gerswin shook his head as he undressed. One complication always led to another.

A clink and a clatter from the kitchen area reminded him to hurry, and he finished stripping off his damp flight suit.

The shower was an enclosed tile stall, curtainless and doorless, but with a baffle-staggered wall design to minimize spray. The tiles were reddish glazed squares set in mortar.

Lerwin had been right. The water was warm. Not hot, not cold, but warm. His shower was quick.

After shutting off the water—there was a single, long-handled faucet lever—he toweled himself dry, rubbing his hair with the thin towel which resembled worn-out Imperial issue.

A glance out the door showed an empty hallway, and, towel wrapped around his waist, he carried his exercise clothes back to the guest room where he dressed. Once presentable, he folded the exercise clothes and put them on the table, then straightened the bed, and headed for the front room.

The living room, a boxy space roughly four meters on a side, was vacant, although the small table at one end was set for three. Closer to him, and to the entryway where he stood, with the front door to his left and the sleeping rooms behind him, were a low couch and two tables, one low and square, the other to the right of the couch, and two fabric sling seats. The dimness of the room was only partly lifted by the single lamp on the table to the right of the couch.

"Now you look the part, Captain." Lerwin marched through the archway by the dinner table with a covered bowl, which he set down there.

"Part of what?"

"Visiting dignitary."

"Visiting, yes. Dignitary, no."

Lerwin grinned. "Ha! Almost got you to act like an Impie."

Gerswin couldn't resist giving him a grin in return. "Almost. Not that far gone. Yet."

"Sit down, Captain. Ki says dinner won't be ready for a while. Deputy Ops boss's requests kept her working too late."

"You didn't?"

"Afraid I did."

Gerswin eased himself into the left-hand sling chair. Lerwin took the right.

"Where did you get these?"

"Lostwin makes them."

"Makes them?"

"Scrap. Whatever he can get."

Gerswin frowned. Supposedly, the Imperial scrap went to the converters, both for power purposes and for security reasons.

"Just the common things. Broken seats, furniture, panels. He has to replace it with equal mass conversions. Perfectly legal."

Gerswin ran his hand along the frame of the chair in which he sat, recognizing it was a section of flitter bracing that had been cut and molded into its new function.

"Nice work. What about the shambletowners?"

Lerwin understood the answer. "Not much into furniture yet. Lostwin can make about enough for those who are interested. Has a waiting list already."

The base commander nodded. He needed to push up the schedule for tree planting. Resource needs were growing faster than food requirements. Without Imperial synthetics, and without wood, the incipient recovery would turn into a sickening crash.

"Need more trees."

Lerwin nodded.

Gerswin stood as Kiedra walked in.

"How do you like it, Captain?"

"Much nicer than quarters. Much . . . warmer."

"You made it possible—everything possible."

"Just helped. Just helped." Gerswin gestured toward the couch, a movement as much a question as an invitation.

"Dinner won't be ready for a few minutes." Kiedra sat on the low couch, tucking one bare foot under her as she settled down.

The quiet stretched out.

"Haven't seen anything like the couch. Lostwin's work?"

Kiedra laughed, three soft musical notes in a row. "Not exactly. He made the frame. Ler, here, made the cushions."

Lerwin looked at the black synthetic stone floor.

Gerswin shook his head in an exaggerated motion. "The talents I never found out about."

Kiedra bolted upright. "I forgot the liftea!"

Returning moments later with three mugs on a tray, she offered the first to Gerswin. He took the mug, but waited until she had reseated herself.

"To you, and to your home, and future happiness."

"To your own success, Captain."

"To your future, Captain."

The three sipped the hot tea with the orange spice aftertaste.

Gerswin cupped the smooth pottery mug in his hands, letting the steam from the tea drift into his nostrils, and studied the dark and slender black-haired woman opposite him.

Happy enough, she seemed. More than happy—more alive than he ever recalled.

She and Lerwin were good for each other, he decided, while repressing a sigh at the memory of a devilkid who had not wanted to leave him, though he had never touched her. His lips quirked momentarily.

Better the way it had turned out, much better for everyone. They had been the ones who had pushed for the changes that had let Imperials, devilkids and all, live in either the town or base quarters. They would provide the nucleus for rebuilding—if he could keep enough Imperial support coming.

"You look rather serious, Captain."

"Reflective."

"You're always reflective."

Gerswin laughed, a single bark. "Point. Point." He took another sip of the hot tea, letting the heat relax him as the liquid warmed his throat.

"Long time from Birmha to here, that what you thought?" asked Lerwin.

"Something like that," admitted Gerswin.

"And that you've got a long way to go?" added Kiedra.

"Ki!"

"He does. A lot farther than we do. A lot farther."

Gerswin's eyebrows went up. "What do you mean?"

"You were a captain when you gathered us together. Now you're base commander. Have you looked at your official holos? Or your physicals and stress tests?"

"Of course."

"Notice any changes?"

Gerswin frowned, not wanting to follow the conversation in the direction it was heading. "Not really. A few lines, perhaps."

"Not even that. In more than ten years, you haven't aged. We may look a bit older, but haven't you seen that devilkids don't age as rapidly as the Impies? The Impies notice. I can tell you that. And they sure notice that about you."

"That's absurd."

"Is it, Captain?" Lerwin's voice was low, but gentle. "Is it really? I remember more than I should, that is, if I'm only as old as the medics tell me I am. Hard to say, when day follows day in the hills with the coyotes and the king rats."

"Time will tell." Gerswin shrugged, and forced a soft laugh. "Time will tell."

He wanted to ignore the quick look between Lerwin and Kiedra, and the look of resignation and agreement, but decided against it.

"You two. You think I know something special. Or am something different. I could die tomorrow, and I suppose I could live a long time. I don't know, and all I can do is keep trying to do my best."

Kiedra lifted her mug.

"To your best, Captain. To your best for a long, long time." She sipped the tea before putting the mug down and standing. "If you will excuse me, it's time to see if dinner worked out. Next time, Ler can do it."

Lerwin shifted his weight and turned toward Gerswin. "You think we're crazy?"

"No. Don't like to think about it. Too much to do, and too little time even if you do have five score years. And if you have more . . . have to ask how human you are, especially . . ."

"Especially if you're a devilkid," finished Lerwin.

Gerswin nodded.

The two officers sat in the sling chairs, silently, watching as the deputy administrative officer placed two low serving dishes on the narrow dining table.

"That's it, for what it is," she announced.

The scent was spicy, but clean, and carried a strong scent of vegetables, but fresh vegetables, not the few dehydrated types carried in on the supply ships or the standardized varieties grown in the base tanks.

The two stood, and Gerswin pulled the straight-back chair from the corner to the place indicated by Lerwin.

"Smells good."

"Should. All fresh."

"Fresh?"

"Local gardens beginning to produce," explained Lerwin.

Gerswin took a mouthful. The taste was vaguely familiar, although he could not remember ever tasting anything like the dish. The meat was chicken, easily enough explained by the embryos he had ordered and received right after he'd become base commander. But the meat was wrapped in a thin coarse flour shell and covered with a reddish hot sauce.

"Tastes good."

"Recipe from the archives, from that cache of old books they dug up and stored in the library. Had to modify it some because we didn't have everything, but the second or third time it turned out pretty well."

"Second or third time?" Gerswin swallowed, suddenly realizing another facet of common town life he'd overlooked—food preparation.

As a devilkid, he'd eaten whatever he could get, fresh, raw, or occasionally cooked over open coals. As a career unmarried officer, he'd eaten aboard ship or station, or rarely, in private homes.

Now, Lerwin and Kiedra had to figure in food preparation, at least for off-duty periods, and who knew what other additional things, into their routine.

He shook his head.

"Something wrong?"

"No," he mumbled after swallowing. "Just a few things I hadn't fully considered." He took another mouthful, savoring the taste and trying to recall where he had tasted it before. . . .

on a clay plate . . . flickering lamp . . .

The already dim lighting of the room seemed to dim more, and Gerswin stared at the table, at two tables—one smooth and plastfinished and narrow, the other heavy, covered with dark tiles. One with matched crockery, the other with cruder and darker pottery.

Gerswin blinked, squeezed his eyes, uncertain whether he was trying to call up the image or push it away. His eyes burned.

"Are you all right, Captain?"

Lerwin's voice sounded ages and kilometers away.

"Captain!"

Gerswin opened his eyes and took a deep breath. The boxlike room swam back into focus.

"What happened? You all right?"

"Was it the dinner?"

He shook his head, strongly, then wiped the dampness from his cheeks. "Just realized where . . . why the food was familiar . . . that's all."

Lerwin's frown was half-puzzled, half-concerned.

Kiedra's mouth dropped open. She shut it, then asked, "Serious?"

Gerswin shrugged. "Don't know why I'd remember something so far back. Don't know if it really happened. Couldn't have been very old. Table seemed so big."

"Do you remember your parents?"

"Just glimpses. Think my mother had the blond hair. Father was heavier. Maybe not. All men look big to children."

Gerswin reached for the heavy tumbler—local manufacture—and took a long swig of the water, still a trace metallic, but far better than the best once available.

"Speaking of children, Captain," Lerwin asked softly, "what do you think?"

"Think about what?" Again, Gerswin caught the shared warmth between the two, and felt himself on the outside looking in at something he could not share.

"It's like this . . . ," added Kiedra.

"Ki . . . we agreed . . ."

Gerswin swiveled his head from one to the other. Children? Children. Children!

Lerwin's increasing protectiveness toward Kiedra, their pushing for their own quarters, the room for guests, for now, as Lerwin had put it—all of the indicators were there.

"Congratulations," Gerswin said softly, catching Kiedra's eyes and holding them. He turned to face Lerwin. "Won't be easy, but I wish you the best."

"You don't object?"

"To what? You love each other."

"But . . ."

Gerswin barked a laugh. "Look. Why are we reclaiming our planet? To make it into a pastoral museum? Has to be for people. People and their children."

Gerswin could sense the relief in Kiedra, feel her tension ebb. But Lerwin still sat on the edge of his chair.

"You mean that?" asked the other man.

Gerswin did.

"Yes." He did not explain, but the absolute assurance in his voice seemed to satisfy Lerwin.

"Obviously," added the commander, "I made the wrong toast, but time enough to rectify that." He looked back at Kiedra. "When?"

"Seven months, if all goes well."

Gerswin shook his head and laughed quietly. "You'll make an old man out of me yet."

"Never!"

"Never."

Kiedra's affirmation of his relative youth held a note of sadness, almost pity, that Gerswin pushed away with another mouthful of the dinner.

Lerwin followed suit, but Kiedra stood.

"I'm full. Be back in a minute."

Gerswin frowned. He'd never seen a devilkid full. Not hungry, but never full.

"Pregnancy," Lerwin answered the unspoken question. "Medics say that's normal."

Neither said anything while finishing what remained.

Lerwin stood and took both his plate and Gerswin's.

"No. Be right back. Kitchen's too small for everyone."

True to his word, Lerwin reappeared with three steaming mugs, disappeared again, only to return with three tiny squat glasses.

"Not brandy and cafe, but liqueur and liftea."

Behind him followed Kiedra, her face a shade paler. Lerwin helped her into her seat, and she immediately took a small sip of the liftea, and smiled faintly.

"Some aspects of motherhood I can do without. They'll pass, I am told." She took another sip, and Gerswin could see the color begin to return to her face.

Lerwin eased his chair up to the table, and inhaled from the glass without drinking.

Gerswin followed his example, trying to place the scent, half bitter grubush, half spice. "Another local product?"

Lerwin nodded.

Gerswin sipped carefully, expecting the liqueur to burn. He was not disappointed.

Kiedra left the liqueur alone, but continued to sip from the liftea, saying nothing.

"How much leave do you intend to take?"

"Do I have to decide now?"

"No. Just wondered who I'd get to do the job, and for how long." He grimaced. "Shouldn't get into shop talk, but too many Imperials are just putting in their time."

Gerswin took a swallow of the liftea to clear away the residual flame from the grubush liqueur, then stood.

"Enjoyed the dinner. Enjoyed the company, and especially your news. Won't mention it. That's your joy to spread."

"You aren't going? So soon?"

The base commander forced a grin at Kiedra. "Duty calls. Lucky my locator didn't already summon me." He raised his right arm and let the sleeve slide back to reveal the wrist circlet. "Besides, you need the rest, and don't tell me otherwise."

He stepped back from the table. "You've done a lot here, more than I could have expected. I appreciate your including me. Means a great deal."

Lerwin did not move to stop the commander, but eased toward the front entryway.

Gerswin smiled at Kiedra. "Take care. See you."

He reclaimed his exercise clothes, and boots before making his way to the front door.

"Good night, Lerwin. Wish you both the best. You deserve it."

"We owe it all to you, Captain."

Gerswin shook his head. "No. A bit perhaps, but we all owe a bit to someone."

Lerwin stood at the open door, waiting.

Gerswin gave him a last smile and went down the walk in quick steps. A hundred meters down the walk, he glanced back over his shoulder. Lerwin still was outlined in the entryway. Gerswin did not look back again as he headed for the shuttle station.

He looked up, instead, and toward the north. He could see a scattering of stars through a break in the clouds which closed even as he watched.

His boot steps echo-whispered in the stillness, matched only by the faint swish of the southerly wind.

His lips tightened as he thought of Lerwin, Kiedra, the two of them. Lerwin, with his arms around her, despite the whipcord steel that underlay her being.

The single barked laugh that exploded from him cracked across the sleeping new town like thunder from a departing storm.

He speeded up his steps toward the waiting shuttle, feeling one step ahead of the ice rain, and two ahead of the landspouts.

The linked diamonds he had not worn to dinner weighed on his empty collars and on his thoughts.

"Someday . . . someday . . ."

The words sounded empty, and he could see the shuttle and the driver waiting, waiting, waiting to take the base commander back to command central.

THOWP, THOWP, THOWP. *Thowp, thowp, thowp . . .*

Gerswin ignored the regular sound of the flitter's deployed rotors as he surveyed the irregular patch of felled pines and the scattering figures of the shambletowners.

"Not just a tree or two," he observed, a wry smile invisible beneath the helmet's impact visor.

"Lower, Captain?" asked Lostwin from the pilot's seat.

"Barbarians," a third voice murmured.

Gerswin glanced up to see Glynnis leaning forward between the pilot's and copilot's positions, trying to get a better view of the damage to the trees, trees that she and her crew, or other crews, had laboriously tanked from seeds, then planted in the hillside they had treated earlier.

"Anything else to see?"

"Not for me," answered Gerswin. "Glynnis, anything you need?"

"No. Not here. Need mulchweed, and we'll have to do it by hand. Slope's too steep to leave uncovered, but we'd do too much damage with heavy equipment. Need the weed until the trees we replant take, and that's another couple of years."

"Back to base?"

"Back to base," Gerswin affirmed, taking a last look over his shoulder as the flitter banked southward into a nearly one hundred eighty degree turn.

As he suspected, even as the flitter turned, the industrious shambletowners were creeping back from cover with their ax-knives to worry down another batch of trees.

"They're at it again!" protested Glynnis.

"Lostwin can't run cover for the trees forever, Glynnis. Whenever we leave, they'll be back. The wood, young as it is, is better than grubush on scrub. They'll use it, now they have the habit."

"Just let me get my hands on them."

"My sympathies," offered Gerswin sardonically.

"Don't you care?"

Gerswin ignored the question. He cared, but his options were limited.

Lostwin said nothing, leveling the flitter on a direct descent toward the base landing grids.

Click, click, click.

A swirl of ice rain slapped at the fusilage, ceasing as suddenly as it had pelted from the dark gray clouds overhead.

"Been a cold year," reflected Gerswin, leaning back in the copilot's seat. "Not as much grubush since we reforested."

"We left a five kay patch around the shambletown. How many of them are left there, anyway?"

"Enough to need more fuel. Maybe saving their grubush and using our pine."

"Are you defending them?"

"No. Speculating."

"Do you know what you're going to do to stop them, Captain?"

"Not yet. Some things to consider."

"Opswatch, Outrider Two turning final. Commencing descent."

"Outrider Two, Opswatch. Field is clear. Ground crew waiting."

"Stet."

Gerswin checked his harness and straightened himself in his seat. Automatically scanning the gauges and finding no fault, he watched Lostwin as the younger man's sure touch brought the flitter to a hover outside the number two hangar-bunker.

As soon as the flitter was down inside the hangar, blades folded and shut down, Gerswin vaulted out, helmet under his arm, to head for his office.

Glynnis was right, in one respect. The problem wasn't about to go away.

His quick steps covered the distance across the hangar, through the tunnels, and to his outer office.

Nitiri looked up as Gerswin marched through.

"Anything major?" the base commander asked the senior technician.

"No, Commander. Two buzzes and a fax of some sort from Major Trelinn. Major Geron left word that he's got most of the equipment he needs for the Scotia refining plant, all except one part. It's all on your console."

"Thanks, Nitiri. Hold anything except an emergency."

"The tree thing?"

Gerswin nodded. "More ways to botch it than to solve it."

He locked the portal behind him and set the helmet in the small locker.

While he could have consulted the files through the console for exact citations, he did not. He knew the Imperial law that applied and that governed, since Old Earth had neither laws nor governing bodies larger than the individual shambletowns.

Imperial law was simple. If the locals did not injure Imperials, the most that any base commander could do was to remove the locals from the area to avoid damage to Imperial property and citizenry—provided that did not conflict with existing treaties, local laws, or special provisions. None of the latter existed.

The minute he issued a relocation order, Trelinn and who knew who else would be protesting, both on general principles and because they would have an issue with which to assault the commander. On the other hand, if he didn't, the devilkids, the civilian Imperials, and the people of the new town would be upset at his failure to protect the forest.

Gerswin glanced at the I.S.S. banner on the wall, smiled a hawkish smile, and touched the console keyboard.

"Get Major Trelinn and have him up here as soon as possible."

"Yes, ser."

Trelinn arrived as if he had been on call.

"Commander, I'm so glad you've found time in your crowded schedule. I was hoping we could discuss a number of things which have come up."

"Sit down, Linn. First thing is the tree problem."

"The tree problem?" Trelinn frowned. "The tree problem? You mean that bit of vandalism by the locals. Shocking, but minor. What else could you expect? No, I was hoping we could review your review of the annual performance standards—"

"Linn. Performance standards can wait. The tree problem is more urgent. Now why did you say it was expected?"

"There's been no attempt at education, no ethnocultural field work, merely a strong-arm attempt to recreate a vanished ecology, rather than a thought-out and studied effort to build on the existent flora and fauna."

"How would you define a studied attempt?"

Trelinn paused, giving Gerswin a long look, before continuing. "I would think that the first step should have been a study by a well-respected expert, backed by a full team data-gathering effort, plus, at a bare minimum, the in-depth study and analysis of at least one member of the culture."

"Would the ecology chair at a major Empire university qualify as such an expert? Say, from Medina, Saskan, New Augusta, or Hecate?"

"What are you leading to, Commander?"

Gerswin smiled. "Just trying to see where you stand, Linn. Now, would someone like that fit your definition?"

The dapper major shrugged. "How could they not?"

"The name Mahmood Dagati chime?"

"The one who wrote *Principles of Planetary Ecology*?"

"The ecology chair at the University of Medina?"

"He's the one," confirmed Trelinn.

"Is indeed, Linn. Conducted the field studies here. Took him nearly seven years. Give you the console keys to his work."

"That does not mean his recommendations were followed."

"After we're through, I'd suggest you read them yourself and make that determination. Fair enough?"

Trelinn nodded cautiously. "I would say that would be a fair procedure, so fair that I'll probably do little more than skim them, because your willingness to share them indicates to me that the Service has followed Dagati's recommendations." He paused. "What about the evaluation of the culture?"

"Cultures," corrected Gerswin quietly. "Or perhaps survivors and culture."

"Rather a curious description, Commander."

"As you suggested, Linn, the studies were done. Give you those keys as well. Have to access them through a security console."

"What?"

"Rule 5, Section 3, of I.S.S. Procedures—'data prejudicial or containing a judgment prejudicial to a native culture . . . shall not be disclosed to that culture . . . nor made available in any form where it can be disseminated.' The so-called prejudice rule."

"Would you summarize what you recall of the cultural reports?"

Gerswin shrugged. "Simple enough. Two cultures, if you can call them that. Shambletowners and devilkids. Term devilkid coined by the shambletowners. Shambletowners exhibit strains of a genetic predilection toward cultural and personal paranoia in the extreme, manifest high degree of xenophobia, rigid customs, low level of innovation, low birth rate. In this climate, traits that maximize group survival."

"And the devilkids?"

"Survivors. Adaptable, intelligent, quick reflexes, open-minded to the point of amorality. Egocentric, loners, avoid society. Largest social unit the family. Might tend toward a clan structure if numerous enough."

Major Trelinn shook his head for the first time. "Neither sounds terribly appetizing. One cooperates without intelligence; the other has intelligence without cooperation."

"Shows why field work or preaching won't work. The shambletowners won't trust a word you say. The devilkids are impossible to find, and respect only force, or their own conclusions. We don't have the resources to deal with either, except on a few case-by-case instances."

"But there are some shambletowners in the new town?"

"A few. Mainly because they had no hope in the old town. Too far down the social ladder, or too ambitious. Probably lose some of their children, or the children will adopt the new town as the basis for their paranoia. Culture's insane, but so are some of the individuals, in or outside that culture."

"So what are you going to do about the tree problem?" asked the major.

Gerswin repressed a sigh, glad that Trelinn had finally gotten around to asking the question.

"What would you do if you were in my position?" countered the commander.

Trelinn pulled at his chin. "The shambletowners won't believe you, and you can't force them to leave the trees alone. What about some sort of barrier?"

"Possibly the best ideal solution, but we don't have the power or the equipment to cover all the area they can and will damage."

The dapper major frowned. "How much damage can they really do?"

"If they could, they would heat with wood all the time. They need it for their pottery, tiles, and cooking. One reason we got some younger shambletowners was that they were cold.

"Shambletowners could take out a whole watershed in the next two years. Trees are too young and the undersoil isn't stabilized yet."

"That much damage from so few?"

"Linn, those are only five- to ten-year-old trees. There's not much undergrowth yet, either. Another twenty years and there'd be no real problem. But not now. Check what deforestation did to Old Earth to begin with."

Gerswin kept from shaking his head and waited.

"You only have two choices, don't you? You can accept the damage, or you can relocate them. Is there anywhere they can go?"

Gerswin nodded, as much in relief as in agreement.

"That's one reason for the whole reclamation effort. Only a few of the shambletowns had stable or positive population projections. Some few areas they can go to until the land here will support them in higher standard."

"But not so desirable?"

"Very little difference for the next century. After that, shouldn't matter."

"I don't know." Trelinn pulled at his chin again. "Difficult procedural problem you face, Commander."

Gerswin stood. He'd gotten the best that he could.

"Well, I appreciate having your thoughts, Linn. Think about it, and if you have any other ideas, let me know. Here are the access keys I promised, if you still want to check them."

The commander handed a small square of paper to the major, on which he had noted the pertinent key words and numbers.

"There were a few others matters . . ."

Gerswin managed to repress yet another sigh.

"I understand. Until I get this resolved, afraid I can't focus on other things as clearly as I would like."

The commander moved toward the portal, toward Trelinn.

The major took the hint and stood, inclining his head.

"I appreciate your involving me in this, Commander, and look forward to continuing our discussions later."

Gerswin said nothing, but inclined his own head in return.

The major left, not a hair on his head out of place, his uniform still creased and immaculate, and without a sound.

Once the portal had closed behind Trelinn, Gerswin permitted himself the luxury of a deep breath. The man was so obsessed with procedure that thinking came last, if at all.

He reseated himself at the console and drafted the order he wanted. Then he buzzed Nitiri.

"Look this over. Fix it, if you think it needs fixing, and then fax it to Admin Legal. About half an hour after it hits the legal console, expect a buzz from Trelinn and whoever else is on the side of the benighted shambletowners."

"Yes, ser."

Gerswin stood, stretched, and paced around the office. Finally, he sat back down to address the blinking lights on the console.

THE FLASH OF the double red lights at the edge of the console caught Gerswin's attention before the sharpness of the sound.

Buzzz! Buzzz!

"Gerswin."

The image on the other end was Lerwin's.

"Problem, Captain. Lostwin was bringing in the fourth load of those Denv shambletowners, landing them outside Birmha."

Gerswin nodded.

"Finished off-loading, and one of the Birmha types unloads a sling on the Denv group."

"And it went downhill from there?"

"Worse. Trelinn orders them to stop. They didn't. He scrambled out of the cockpit and starts using his stunner. The Denv types know better, but not the Birmha types."

"How badly was he hurt?"

"Cracked ribs, medics think. Gash across the face. Still en route back to base."

"That the last flitter load for now?"

"Yes."

"Tell the medical staff. I'll take care of the rest."

Lerwin nodded, and Gerswin jabbed at the console, waiting for Nitiri's face to show.

"Yes, Commander?"

"Anyone out there?"

"Haskil."

"Come on in, then."

Gerswin turned and walked toward the portal. He did not feel much like sitting in any case, and the office seemed smaller and more enclosed than ever.

"Yes, ser?" repeated Nitiri as the portal closed behind him.

"Need to convene a Board of Inquiry on Major Trelinn's actions this afternoon. As soon as possible, and within the next few days. Done strictly. Make sure the board is totally impartial. Rather have officers sympathetic to Trelinn than openly hostile."

Nitiri's head moved frantically, as if in disapproval.

"You disapprove, Nitiri?"

"No, ser."

"I do, but that's not the question. Imperial law is rather strict about firing on civilians except in self-defense."

Gerswin glanced at the blank wall across from his console, the spot where he had never hung any holos or honors, unlike Manders and his predecessors.

"Is that all, ser?"

"That's all, Nitiri. That's all."

THE DAPPER MAN with the pencil-thin mustache stepped through the portal, followed by two armed technicians. He wore a plain gray tunic and matching trousers.

"You can go." The commandant motioned the techs back through the portal.

"But . . . ser . . ."

"Where can he go?"

"Yes, ser."

They left, and the portal closed behind them.

"Have a seat, Linn."

"No, thank you, Commander. What I have to say will not take long. While I appreciate your kindness in seeing me before I leave, and while you know I am less than perfectly happy with the way in which the Service has considered my years of devotion, those are not the reasons for my request."

The commander nodded, remained standing.

The dapper man, stockier but no taller than the commander, coughed, then cleared his throat and looked from one side of the office to the other.

"I suppose it doesn't matter," he continued, "but as a matter of principle alone I wanted you to know that I understand exactly what you are doing and why. Although I can applaud the technical skill with which you have managed to accomplish your goals well within the laws of the Empire and the regulations of the Service, I find your ultimate objective of eliminating the shambletowners nothing less than genocidal."

The stockier man paused, as if waiting for a reaction.

"Linn, unlike you, I did not attempt to stun down an entire population."

"That misses the point, as you well know!" The dark-haired former major's voice began to rise, in both pitch and volume.

"Who knows you are a former devilkid? Who knows the shambletowners killed your parents? Who knows your drive for reclamation is merely a tool to destroy the shambletowners and their culture?"

"Linn." The hawk-yellow eyes of the commander caught the other, who fell silent, stepping back a pace in the face of the glance.

"First," responded Gerswin, "the I.S.S. and everyone else knows I'm a devilkid. Never hid it. Second, parents' deaths are a matter of record for everyone. You found it. Third, shambletowners are doomed whether I do anything or not. Mahmood Dagati proved that. Fourth, you are incompetent and refuse to face it. Fifth, you'd rather have a dead Earth man abandon your precious belief in procedures or do anything remotely resembling work."

The commander stopped as he watched the other's bright eyes and realized that Trelinn was not listening, but merely waiting to finish his statements.

"You still want to destroy the shambletowners, and they know it.

They fear you like the devil. They cringe when you appear. They frighten their children with stories about you."

The commandant took a step forward. Trelinn backed away.

"Fear. You project terror and fear. You use it to cow everyone. But I'm not afraid of you, and I know what you are."

Gerswin shook his head.

"Sorry you feel that way, Linn. Won't be easy for you. Anything else?"

"No, Commander. Just remember that *I* know what you are, and I'm not totally without friends on New Augusta."

"Suppose you're not." Gerswin smiled as he finished the observation, and the former major stiffened as if repressing a shiver.

"Is there anything you want to confess?" asked the officer who had resigned.

"Confess? Hardly!" laughed the commander, with a single hard bark. "Stand by what I've done, and what has to be done. Still a job to be done here, a real job. Will be a lot to do long after you're dust, Linn. Has nothing to do with shambletowners." He paused before concluding, "Have a good trip home."

The commander leaned back and tapped the intercom. The portal opened, and the two techs came bursting through.

"Mister Trelinn says he's through."

The ex-major said nothing as he was escorted from the commander's office.

EXECUTIVE SUMMARY

WRIT OF APPEAL
IN RE
Gillis Marjinn Trelinn
Major
Interstellar Survey Service

Charge: Use of deadly weapon against non-Imperial citizens (I.J.C. 40(b))

Finding: Guilty, with mitigating circumstances

Charge: Endangering I.S.S. Personnel through violation of
            Imperial Judicial Codes (I.S.S. Regulation, Part C.3)
Finding: Guilty, with mitigating circumstances

SUMMARY OF DEFENSE:

1. The defendant claimed that a standard issue stunner was not a
    deadly weapon within the meaning of the Code; that the conduct
    of the non-Imperial citizenry constituted a threat to I.S.S. per-
    sonnel; that the local commandant's decision to relocate a por-
    tion of that citizenry incited the non-Imperial citizenry against
    which the weapon was used; and that the use of nonlethal force
    was solely to protect Imperial citizenry.

2. Defense further contended that the non-Imperial citizenry was
    incited by the local commandant's relocation decision; that the
    defendant's use of force was necessary to prevent injury to Impe-
    rial personnel; and that since the stunner could not inflict lethal
    injuries the defendant did not violate the Imperial Judicial Code
    for the reason that his actions did not constitute the use of a
    deadly weapon and were designed to protect rather than endan-
    ger Imperial personnel.

COURT OF INQUIRY FINDINGS OF FACT:

1. Historical, practical, and legal considerations all define a military
    issue stunner as a deadly weapon.

2. No actual violence nor injury occurred to Imperial personnel
    until after the defendant attacked non-Imperial citizenry with
    the stunner.

3. The defendant and three other Imperial personnel suffered in-
    juries of various degrees requiring extended medical treat-
    ment.

4. In the outbreak of violence that followed the discharge of the
    stunner by the defendant, between five and fifteen non-Imperial
    citizens were injured.

SUMMARY OF APPEAL OF VERDICT:

With regard to both counts, the defendant claimed that procedures were irregular in Court of Inquiry findings of fact; that pro-

cedures were irregular in the assignment of personnel to the Court Martial; that the disregard of seniority in base assignments and duties deprived the defendant of due process; that the standard definition of a deadly weapon should not be applied to unique and primitive circumstances; and that the behavioral pattern of the particular non-Imperial citizenry is uniquely prone to violence, thereby requiring an earlier reaction than in the case of normal self-defense tests.

SUMMARY OF APPEAL TRIBUNAL FINDINGS:

1. The verdict on both counts is upheld; the appeals are denied.
2. The local commandant acted within the scope of both the Imperial Judicial Code and the Regulations of the Interstellar Survey Service.
3. The finding of mitigation and suspension of sentence upon receipt of the defendant's resignation from the I.S.S. is within the scope of the code and the service regulations.
4. No further appeals need be heard.

THE GREENISH-BLUE tint of the wall imparted a restfulness to the small room with the empty console and the two standard padded chairs. Three tattered faxtab flimsies lay upon the single table. The flextile floors were the standard dark gray of Imperial outposts everywhere. The portal to the main corridor was open, but the interior archway to the rooms behind was closed.

Three lights on the console blinked, then shifted from green to amber as the messages were recorded and stacked for replay.

After a time, a thin-faced technician wearing a pale blue coverall and the insignia of the Medical Corps walked through the open portal from the corridor and took the small swivel chair behind the console. She shook her hands as if to relieve the stiffness in her fingers and forearms and pulled herself up before the twin screens.

Carelessly pushing a wisp of short black hair back over her right ear, she touched the studs on the keyboard and began to scan the incoming messages that had been held for review.

She did not look up at the hum of voices that approached as the archway opened from the consulting rooms in the rear.

Through the archway stepped a short and stocky, though not heavy, woman with strawberry blonde hair, blue eyes, and a peaches and cream freckled complexion. Her coverall was the dark brown of the reclamation technical support staff. On her shoulder patch were the twisted spears of fire and water, above the twin linked spheres of barren wasteland and green forests—the insignia of the landbuilders, whose dozers systematically scoured the poisons from the land and prepared the way for the replantings and reforestings.

The second woman, of medium height with natural silver hair marking her as from Scandia, wore not only the coverall of the Medical Corps, but the linked gold bars of an officer on one collar and the twined serpents and staff on the other.

"You're sure?" asked the blonde in a tone that indicated she was repeating a question in hopes of getting another answer.

"That's what all the tests show."

The blonde woman, her eyes still bright with tears unshed, looked down at the dark gray of the floor tiles, then at the blank wall to her right. "I don't know. I just don't know."

"Decanting wouldn't hurt you, not at all," pressed the doctor.

"Can I let you know tomorrow? I need to think."

"Take as much time as you need. Don't push it. If you're sure tomorrow, that's fine. Another few days wouldn't matter one way or another. But make sure you think it through." The doctor's voice dropped a note as she saw the technician at the screens.

"Thank you." The support tech squared her shoulders, turned, and walked out through the still-open portal.

The medical tech at the console looked up at the doctor to catch her eye. Then she waited until the footsteps had faded down the corridor outside.

"Another one, Captain Lysendra?"

"Oh . . . Madrigel, I'm sorry. What did you ask?"

"Another one?"

"Yes. Another one. I just don't understand it. They don't want to carry the children, and yet somehow none of them can remember taking the contraceptive antidotes."

"And the problem?"

"They don't want to carry the children, but they want them to live."

"I wondered why you mentioned decanting. Can we actually do that here on base?"

"If it doesn't turn into an epidemic. Of course, the children will have to be fostered or sent to the Academy home. Under the regs, if they chose a Service career, they'll owe two tours here."

"Will she," and the technician gestured at the open portal, "opt for decanting?"

"So far, four have. One decided to carry the child to term."

"Five? Out of how many?"

"Five."

"That's a lot for this base."

"Or not enough, depending on your viewpoint," mused the doctor, as she turned and headed back to her small private cubicle to think.

"Not enough?" wondered the technician.

Her fingers traversed the keyboard. A series of items appeared on the left-hand screen.

With a coding she was not supposed to know, the woman entered an authentication and another inquiry. The response to that second inquiry replaced the other material on the screen.

Her mouth formed a slight "O," and her eyes widened as she read the lines as they formed on the screen. So the would-be fathers were from the captain's reclamation finds, the devilkid pilots and dozer drivers that tackled the hotspots and fought the landspouts.

"I wonder . . ."

She tried another inquiry, but the screen only printed:

"Unauthorized information. Restricted by regulation R/C 230(b) and standing order I.S.S. 435."

Two lights on the incoming lines blinked green, and the technician erased the left-hand screen, while taking the first call on the right.

"Medical Services, Technician Hru-Sien. May I help you?"

Standing Order 435? There was no Standing Order 435.

She could not shake her head, not while routing the call, but smiled instead, mechanically, and she directed the call to Dr. Lysendra.

Standing Order 435 indeed.

LXIII

THE COMMANDER GLANCED down at the plastone tiles of the corridor flooring, absently noting the swirled smoothness of the surface. One way to tell the older or more heavily traveled sections of the Administration bunker was by the flooring. The clear sections were new or total replacements. The swirled sections were those that had been remelted and refinished, the colors washed together in abstract but regular patterns.

His boots clicked faintly on the opaque swirls as he approached the open Operations portal.

The corridor lights were at half-intensity, their normal off-duty setting, but the lack of full interior light was artificial dimness, not the honest gloom of twilight or dawn.

Without thinking, he adjusted the linked diamonds on his right collar before stepping through the portal.

"Who's . . . oh, Commander . . . Anything I can do for you, ser?" The duty tech stiffened behind the console as he recognized the base commander.

"No, thank you, Derla. Just checking. Carry on."

He walked to the left, around the console toward the small cubicles that served as offices for the senior ops tech, the deputy ops boss, and the Operations officer. The last office was the one he had used, after Vlerio, and the one Trelinn had used before he'd been replaced by Lerwin.

From behind him, the lights of the duty section cast his shadow, a hazy outline, over the plastone floor blocks before him. The shadow was clearer near his feet and grew increasingly indistinct as it stretched away toward the unlighted sections of Operations in front of him. To his right, the two rows of consoles hunched in the darkness, vague outlines at the edge of reality.

He stopped at the first cubicle on his left, that of the senior tech, and looked through the old-fashioned open doorway. Not even the Operations officer himself rated a full portal. The technician's cubicle was dark, though Gerswin could easily make out the console, the two straight chairs that faced it, and the swivel that was neatly drawn up before the blank screen.

The neatness of the arrangement reflected the organized mind-set of Versario, the current Operations senior technician. Gerswin nodded before continuing to the next doorway.

The second darkened room also contained a console, a swivel, and straight chairs, but none were aligned neatly, but almost randomly, with the swivel pushed back from the console, as if Captain Harwits had shoved it back on his way out of the office. On the wall facing the console was the holo view favored by most Imperial-born graduates of the Academy, the Academy Spire. This one outlined the tower against the setting sun, rather than showing the reflection in Crystal Lake. A pair of solideo cubes rested on the console, glowing faintly, though brightly enough for Gerswin to see that they represented two different young women.

The corners of his lips twisted upward momentarily, and he nodded before resuming his tour.

The office in the left rear corner of the Operations section belonged to the Operations officer. On this night, as on every other night when the Ops boss was not on duty, merely on call, the door was open, but the lighting off.

Gerswin stepped into the office, the faint click of his boots dying out as he crossed onto the thin local carpet that Lerwin had brought in. Other than the carpet, three solideo cubes, and a wall hanging of an intricate corded design that screamed the name of its creator to Gerswin, the office was as bleakly Imperial as it had been ten, fifteen, twenty, or fifty years earlier, the personalities of the men and women who had inhabited it erased by the sheer functionality of the standard equipment and layout.

The commander turned to face the diamond-shaped wall hanging, the starkness of the black and white cording a symbol in itself, studying the straight lines that seemed to curve, and the knots linking black and white, black and white. Kiedra's work, and impressive, he thought, although he had never considered himself as any judge of art.

After a time he backed away and stepped toward the console and the three solideo cubes. The one on the left corner was the closest. He leaned over to study the image of mother and son. He judged that the image was less than a year old from the fact that Corwin's chubbiness of cheek had nearly disappeared. The boy sat on his mother's knee, held gently with her right arm and hand, and the cleanness of the devilkid profile was already emerging from the chubbiness of infancy.

The commander stared at the cube. Last week, he'd watched as the boy had walked in with Kiedra to meet his father as both parents went off-duty. The steps had been fiercely independent.

Would Corwin have the strength of his parents?

The cube offered no answer, and the commander shifted his concentration to the second solideo, the one of Kiedra standing alone in the doorway of their home, in full dress uniform and with captain's bars glinting. Shortly, Gerswin knew, her promotion to major would come through to match Lerwin's, but her decision to go into facilities planning, while a great help to Gerswin, had put her on a slower advancement track.

The third cube showed all three—father, mother, and son—standing in the sunlight that was still infrequent, in the square of Denv Newtown.

The commander's eyes locked onto the image of the child again, scarcely more than knee-high to his parents, but with his jaw squared as if to declare to the world that he was ready to stand on his own.

"Wonder what it would be like . . ."

The inadvertent words escaping startled him, and he broke off the vocalized musings with a shake of his head.

With what he was, and with what he had to do, better Kiedra and Lerwin than he.

A child . . . What would he do with a son? Or a daughter?

Had Faith survived . . . or had Caroljoy . . . he pushed his past out of his mind. Those had been different days, and, besides, he was what he was, and the job was not done. As if it ever would be, the thought crept back into his mind. He pushed that away as well.

Resisting the urge to look back at the cubes and the wall hanging, he walked toward the door, heels clicking softly as he crossed from the patterned weave of the rug to the milky refinished swirls of the floor tiles.

Once outside Lerwin's office he paused, but did not turn, before continuing back toward the duty tech.

"Everything in order, Commander?"

"Everything . . . as it should be, Derla. As it should be."

"Good night, Commander."

"Good night, Derla."

His boots echoed more sharply as he picked up his steps on the return trip to his quarters, and sleep. Sleep that would be dreamless, he hoped.

He fingered the linked diamonds on his collar absently, then dropped his hand as he turned into the proper radial for the commander's quarters.

LXIV

"TAKE HER STRAIGHT up," stated the commander calmly. "Ten thousand meters above the base."

"Straight up?"

"Circle if the power consumption worries you."

The flitter's liftoff was shaky. Adequate, but shaky, as the lieutenant twisted power into the thrusters, and as the flitter, older than the pilot by far, shuddered out of ground effect and into flight.

"Opswatch, Outrider Five. Departing prime base at zero nine four zero. Estimated return at one one zero zero."

"Outrider Five. Understand return at one one zero zero. Interrogative fuel status."

"Fuel status is two plus five. Two plus five."

"Understand two point five," corrected the voice from the console. "Cleared to depart."

The commander stared straight ahead from the copilot's seat through the armaglass canopy while the pilot completed departure procedures, and the flitter circled into the morning sky.

Inside the cockpit, the faint odor of machine oil and ozone dissipated with the slow but steady influx of colder air as the flitter circled upward.

"Do you know why you were assigned here, Lieutenant?"

"That was the requirement of my contract, ser."

The commander could have added the unspoken sentences and resentments to the technically correct answer, but chose to ignore them. Instead he asked another question.

"I take it that you would rather have had a first assignment with the fleet, then?"

"I'm grateful for the education and training that the Empire provided, Commander—"

"But you question the value of I.S.S. officers being assigned to Old Earth when they didn't chose their parentage."

The commander's thin smile was hidden behind his impact visor.

The young officer said nothing.

"What would you do, Lieutenant, if you lost all power—like this."

As he spoke, the commander twisted all power off both thrusters and yanked the stick back into his lap.

Whheeeee!

Pitching up and to the right, the flitter bucked once again, and the port stub wing dropped sharply.

The pilot pushed the stick forward, leveled the flitter and dropped the nose, at the same time swinging the port thruster throttle back around the detente and manually feeding fuel to the engine.

Two coughs and the flitter was back under power.

Without hesitating the lieutenant completed the airstart on the starboard thruster and matched both thrusters at the three quarter power level, leaving them there until the exhaust temperatures dropped into the green and until the flitter was reestablished in a gentle climb.

"Just now, Lieutenant, your actions answered one question."

The pilot refused to look toward his senior officer, instead kept his attention on the controls and indicators, still scanning the exterior view as well.

"Would you explain, ser?"

"An airstart is difficult in one of these old birds. Most Service pilots come close to crashing or bring them in with cold rotors. Blood will tell, Lieutenant, like it or not."

The commander cleared his throat and continued. "Take her back up, and I'll show you what's been done before we put it in context."

The flitter leveled off at ten thousand meters, with the slight hiss on the background which indicated the efforts of the pressurization system to keep up with the inevitable leaks.

"Keep heading zero nine zero."

"Yes, ser."

To the east, near the horizon, was a patchwork of gray-brown and purple-gray. Closer to the nose of the flitter, at roughly a thirty degree angle below the horizon, an irregular swath of darkish brown marked the division between the wastelands and the green and gold that stretched from beneath the flitter out toward the purples and browns. The commander gestured.

"See that line? What we've reclaimed. Basically three hundred kays from the mountains, runs five-six hundred kays north–south."

"Yes, ser."

The commander turned in his seat to study the lieutenant.

The junior officer shifted his weight, but kept his eyes running through the continual scan patterns embedded by his training.

Only the hiss of the pressurization system and the whine of the thrusters murmured through the cockpit.

"Remember the landspouts? Or were you too young when you left?"

"I remember one. It killed my mother, Commander."

"Now that we've reclaimed this sector this far out, we've reduced the annual numbers at the base and the new town to less than ten anywhere nearby. Climatologists tell me we'll never eliminate them, but we will be able to reduce their intensity to normal tornadoes." He paused. "There were a hundred my first year. They still have a hundred or so on the Scotia coast. One reason why our latest push is there."

The flitter crossed the demarcation line between the reclaimed land and the ecological wilderness to the east, bucking several times to the hiss of the pressurizers.

Farther to the east began to appear dark gray clouds, thicker and more threatening than the scattered gray and white puffs above the flitter.

"Bring her about to two seven five, then due north along the border line."

"Yes, ser. Coming to two seven five."

"To bring back a planet's a big job, Lieutenant, and I need the best people possible, no matter how I have to get them."

The commander scanned the board himself, but refrained from pointing out the slight imbalance between the port and starboard thrusters.

"You wonder if I mean that. Whether it's just words. But I do. Just how much you'll find out."

The tightening of the pilot's muscles was apparent to the commander, who shrugged. That was the first reaction they all had, all of them who came home from the comforts of the Empire and the excitement of the Academy and the advanced training.

"Turn north, and steady on zero zero five."

"Yes, ser."

"Wild outside the northern perimeter, and you need to see it all before you understand."

"Yes, ser."

The commander smiled again behind his impact visor, and the flitter, pressurizers hissing in the background, steadied on zero zero five.

BALLAD OF THE CAPTAIN

I flew home one night, as skagged as I could be,
and found an Eye Corps Impie
a-waiting there for me.
I asked the Ops boss, and my dear O.D.,
what's this Impie doing,
a-waiting here for me?

The Ops boss, my dear O.D.,
here's what he said to me.
You devilkid, you dumb kid,
can't you plainly see,
it's nothing but a rubbish dump
that Eye Corps sent to me.

Oh . . . I've cleaned this wide world,
a million kays or more,
but a rubbish dump in uniform
I hain't never seen before.

I flew home the next night, as skagged as I could be,
and found an Eye Corps cruiser
a-blasting out at me.
I asked the Ops boss, and my dear O.D.,
what's this Impie doing,
a-blasting out at me?

The Ops boss, my dear O.D.,
here's what he said to me.
You devilkid, you dumb kid,
can't you plainly see,
it's nothing but a landspout,
a-heading out to sea.

Oh . . . I've cleaned this wide world,
a million kays or more,
but a landspout with a laser
I hain't never seen before.

I flew home the last night, as skagged as I could be,
and found an Eye Corps fleet,
a-boiling up the sea.
I asked the Ops boss, and my dear O.D.,
what's this Impie doing,
a-boiling up the sea?

The Ops boss, my dear O.D.,
here's what he said to me.
You devilkid, you dumb kid,
can't you plainly see,
it's nothing but your captain
a-coming home for tea.

Now . . . I've cleaned this wide world,
a million kays or more,
but the captain drinking tea,
I hain't never seen before.
But the captain drinking tea,
I hain't never seen before.

Anonymous Ballad
Reclamation Period
Old Earth

"WHAT'S THE BARE minimum?" asked the hawk-eyed officer. His gray flight suit bore the worn embroidered silver diamonds of an I.S.S. commander.

The woman behind the console looked up from the screen.

"A full cohort?"

"That many?"

"Commander . . . you are asking that about the most ambitious project anyone ever tried?"

"But one hundred plus arcdozers? Are there that many in the entire Empire? We've got thirty—not much better than scrap. Each year, there's less in the way of supplies."

"You've been here a long time, Commander. It's sometimes easy to forget the size of the Empire." She paused, as if amazed that she had dared to correct him, then completed in an even softer tone. "Think of it this way. If each system only needed ten, the total number in the Empire would still exceed 5,000. New Glasgow probably builds or refits close to a thousand annually."

The commander nodded. "You're right. Too parochial. Problem isn't the total resources of the Empire, but the diminishing surplus available for out-bases and lower priority activities."

The gray-suited commander pursed his lips tightly, frowned. Only after the silence had dragged out for several minutes did he smile. As he smiled, the commander could see the technician trying not to shiver at his expression, and, not certain why, he barked a laugh, either at her or to distract her, or both.

"Since there are so many, then we'll just request them." His smile faded, and he stepped back from the console. "Put in a request for two full cohorts, to be delivered six standard months from now. Code it priority red."

"But . . . Commander. No one here has the authority for a priority red."

"Fine. Code it as a 'recommended priority red.' I can certainly recommend, can't I?"

"The form doesn't allow it."

"Put in priority red where the level code is. Note that it's a recommendation in the remarks section."

"Yes, Commander."

He could smell the scent of fear, could almost feel the questioning in the mind of the black-haired petite technician.

"Wondering whether the old man has gone jump-struck? Thinking I'm sealing my fate? Could be. But only fifteen of thirty dozers are operable, and half of those are cripples. There's a freeze on parts and fusactors, and the only things with enough power to do the job are dozers. So we need them, and we'll get them."

The technician glanced back at the screen, but did not move her hands from her lap.

"Go ahead, Evyn. Recommended priority red, with copies to everyone you can think of."

"Copies?"

He nodded.

"That way, they won't be surprised when the Emperor gives them to us."

Her eyes widened farther, if possible.

For no reason that Gerswin could fathom, the look in her eyes reminded the commander of the look in Lerwin's eyes, the look when the medical diagnosis on little Jurrell had come in. How many years ago had that been? How many years? Corwin had been four then, and Jurrell had barely been walking, a little over a year old. Gerswin could still recall, could still sometimes see, the darkness behind Kiedra's eyes, although Ellia's birth had helped.

Gerswin kept from shaking his head.

"Not crazy, Evyn," he temporized. "Just planning."

He smiled a hard smile again, in spite of himself. This time he saw her shiver.

Still, she lifted her hands and began to code in his request.

The request was the first step, the sole easy part. Getting the dozers would be harder. But with all the cutbacks in the fleet ships, not impossible. No, not impossible.

He smiled again, and turned, heading back toward his own office.

LXVII

FOR THE FIFTH time in as many minutes, the man in the undress black uniform of a senior commander in the Imperial Interstellar Survey Service glanced over at the blank screen of the single room's faxset. Then he stared out the narrow window.

Not that the view was wonderful. On any other planet besides New Augusta, a visiting commander would have rated at least a small suite in senior officers' quarters. On New Augusta, it was rumored there were more admirals than battlecruisers in the I.S.S.

The rumors were true, particularly if they included the Imperial "retired reserves," those members of the Imperial and high court families who had served a single tour of active duty and then been "retired" to the Emperor's Reserve Corps. The I.R.C. had a small squadron of its own, permanently based in Gamma sector, in which the titled and untitled members of New Augustan society served their reserve time.

Gerswin laughed out loud, thinking about a corvette captained by a reserve fleet admiral, with a full admiral as an exec, and where senior commanders served as seconds in comm or drive billets.

With the laugh, he looked again at the blank screen, then at the narrow window, and stood, stretching, in his blacks.

He eased toward the thin pane of armaglass through which he could view the courtyard. While the window did not open, he could almost imagine the scents from the garden that ran down the center of the quadrangle. From his second floor vista, he could estimate what the view of the rows and rows of silverflowers spilling out over green leaves might be from the higher floors, particularly from the suites with the balcony terraces.

His room was dim, partly because he had damped the polarization to cut the glare from the midafternoon sun, and partly because, with the interior lights off and a single window not much wider than a man, there wasn't that much light to begin with. Add to that a color scheme based on dark green, highlighted with thin silver slivers, said to be the favorite of His Highness J'riordan D'Brien N'Gaio, and the room made Gerswin think of evening, even at dawn.

"Will you, someday, go forth in green evenings, Commander?" he asked himself sardonically, before turning from the garden view back toward the screen.

Three days he'd been waiting so far, just for her to return. While he had quietly inquired about her schedule when he had left Old Earth, she had been scheduled to be on New Augusta. Now the days mounted up, and it would be harder and harder to justify additional days in a duty status, as opposed to leave. More important was the return jump-ship schedule. Three days, that was how long she had overstayed her planned return date, and no one could say when she would be returning.

Cling!

The screen chimed but once before the commander had crossed the room and punched the acknowledgment stud. Hawk-yellow eyes peered at Nitiri's image on the screen.

"Yes? No?"

"Too easy," returned the senior rating, who wore the technicians' counterpart of the I.S.S. undress blacks. "Her social secretary deferred. I insisted she ask the Duchess herself. The Duchess took the call personally."

"And . . . ?"

"Senior Commander Gerswin? From Old Earth, I presume? I would be more than happy to receive the commander personally late this afternoon. At six, Mister Nitiri."

Gerswin frowned.

"That's what she said?"

"Word for word."

Gerswin pursed his lips.

"I've arranged for a flitter to the estate. At the officers' gate, 1725. Satisfactory, Commander?"

"Yes. More than satisfactory. Thank you. See you then."

"No, ser. Protocol."

"Alone?"

"She said personally. Means you." Nitiri looked levelly through the screen at his commanding officer.

"All right." Gerswin paused. "Thanks . . . again."

"My pleasure, Commander. And good luck, ser."

"Need it, I think . . . ," Gerswin mumbled as he concluded the transmission and edged toward the window once more.

For some time he surveyed the green and silver garden, motionless at the armaglass.

At last, he turned and sat down on the couch that doubled as a bed. After easing off his boots, he stretched out on the cushions, narrow as the space was configured as a sofa.

Three hours to go. What would she say? What could he say?

He regarded the ceiling, blinking occasionally, letting his eyes traverse the sooth translucency that gave the impression of ivory depths.

For a time he regarded nothing, letting his thoughts drift.

For an even shorter time, he dozed.

Finally, he sat up and began to strip off his clean uniform to shower and to don an immaculate set of blacks.

At 1720, senior Commander Gerswin arrived at the visiting officers' transportation gate.

"Commander Gerswin?"

"Yes?"

"Ser, I hope you don't mind . . ."

"But?" asked Gerswin.

"The Duke of Triandna has sent his own personal flitter for your transportation, and I took the liberty of rescheduling the Service flitter you had requested."

"Fine."

"It's the lavender one, straight ahead."

The flitter the technician pointed out shimmered in a cream and lavender finish that could only have been obtained with lustral plating.

Rather than the military steps into a cockpit, or handholds to a canopy, the passenger flitter offered a side portal opening into a small salon, furnished with a settee and two chairs, lavender hangings and a low table. Behind the hangings, Gerswin glimpsed a single pilot, uniformed, unsurprisingly, in lavender and cream.

"Commander," announced the pilot, standing and stepping around the hangings, "please make yourself at home. I know you'd be more comfortable up here, but in the interest of space, this was configured without a copilot's station."

"Appreciate the thought," answered Gerswin, as he settled into the chair that gave him the best view of the small cockpit.

The pilot resumed his position.

Shortly the aircraft lifted smoothly, without a shudder, but, reflected the passenger, a trace heavily.

At 1755, the flitter touched down, and the passenger portal swung open.

"End of the line, Commander. I'll be waiting whenever you're ready to return."

"Appreciate that. You have any military background? Nice handling there."

"A bit. I did a tour with Blewtinkir. That left me mustered out, fit just for domestic transport, but it's not a bad job. Duke and Duchess are better than most here on New Augusta." There was a faint pause. "See you later."

Gerswin took the hint and exited.

At the far side of the landing stage stood another functionary, female, young, black-haired, and nearly as tall as he was, also garbed in the apparent ducal colors of lavender and cream.

"Senior Commander Gerswin?" Her voice held a tone of uncertainty.

"The same. Were you expecting someone else?"

"No, but . . ."

"I suppose I don't look my age."

"The Duchess is expecting you, ser. If you would follow me." She turned as if she expected he would fall in line.

Gerswin smiled, but said nothing further to the woman, who either had a far different picture of what to expect of Commander Gerswin, or who did not believe he was himself.

The exterior gray glowstone walk led to a gentle ramp of what appeared to be glowstone tiles, but the ramp, which ended at an open and arched doorway, seemed to grab at his boots and legs.

"There's a restrainer field here. The faster you try to move, the more it slows you. If you came through the portal running, it would be like hitting a bulkhead."

Gerswin nodded but said nothing, noting the military phrasing of her veiled warning.

Inside the portal, the gray glowstones continued as the floor of an open-walled corridor running through the center of the villa, room after room opening away from the cream columns of the hallway. Gerswin dropped his eyes momentarily, wondering how the glowstones could be so gray and yet add illumination.

His eyes came up in time to stop him in front of a painting done in some sort of old-fashioned oils. The canvas was a good three meters wide and taller than he was.

He ignored the incongruity of an oil painting depicting a space battle and, instead, read the golden plate at the bottom of the severe but gilded frame.

"Death of H.M.S. *Graystone*, Battle of Firien's Star, Dismorph Conflict, 3121 N.E.C."

Gerswin stepped back a pace and studied the painting again, ignoring his guide.

The style was as restrained as the medium. At first glance it merely showed an I.S.S. scout in space, several energy beams focused on her screens, with a starry background. One star, with a distinctly green tinge, was brighter than the others without seeming larger. The scout's screens glimmered with the unhealthy orange tint that preceded total screen collapse.

Gerswin noted another oddity. The canvas was unsigned, and though he was not expert, the obvious quality of artistry of the work evoked an intense sense of impending doom. At least, it did to him.

He shook his head.

"Well, you are an I.S.S. officer, it seems."

Gerswin frowned at his escort, who stood waiting.

"Every one of you, the good ones, sees the pictures and stops. Some of them sigh. Others, like you did, shake their heads sort of sadly."

Gerswin looked at the oil again.

That battle had taken place nearly fifty years earlier, about twenty-

five years after he'd finished his training on New Colora and gone to
Old Earth. Firien had been one of the few Dismorph successes, before they'd been ground down by the sheer might of the Empire.
He'd read the analyses and couldn't fault the Dismorph tactics. The
Imperial tactics could be and had been faulted by virtually every independent military analyst within and without the Empire. That particular battle had cost a number of senior admirals their careers, not
to mention the loss of lives and ships. Follow-ups had not been without losses, either, Gerswin recalled ... one very personal ... He
pushed the thoughts of Faith back, but his eyes remained on the canvas, though unfocused, for a time.

Gerswin brought himself back to the present and regarded his
guide.

"The picture is a mystery to everyone now in service here, except
the Duchess, and, of course, one presumes, His Grace. She commissioned it, but from whom and for what reason no one else knows."
The guide looked down the corridor before continuing. "She hoped
you would see it." Again, the guide glanced around, before continuing even more softly, "And it's said that the only open argument between Her and His Grace was over the placement of the canvas. That
was before my time."

Gerswin took a third long look at the scene.

The junior lieutenant who had commanded the scout had received the Emperor's Cross, he recalled—posthumously.

The senior commander resisted the urge to shiver, although the
corridor was not at all cool.

"Her receiving chambers are to the right."

"You're not coming?"

"No. You're expected alone. Her Grace can summon anyone instantly, of course."

Gerswin nodded. He would have expected no less.

"Thank you."

He turned and walked toward the indicated portal, the open one
framed in cream hangings.

The room inside was not the immense chamber he had anticipated from viewing the rooms through which he had already passed.
Rather it was more like a rustic summer study, with white plaster-
swirled walls, dark wooden floors covered with rich wine-patterned
carpet. The wall farthest from the portal was entirely of armaglass and
overlooked the sweeping west lawn and the shadows of the late, late
afternoon.

The lady stood behind a carved but simple bleached wooden desk with flowing lines.

Her hair was white, but her face was unlined, and her figure as slender as it had been the one night he had known her nearly eighty standard years earlier.

Gerswin inclined his head, willingly, as he had done to no one from the day he had left the Academy.

"My lady."

"Caroljoy, Commander. Caroljoy."

"You know I did not know. Not then."

"I didn't want you to. Nor do I regret it now."

She moved around the desk, gently, gracefully, but with the deliberate grace of an older woman who understood her fragility, and settled herself on the loveseat.

"Sit down, please." Her eyes were still clear. Still bright.

Gerswin sat, shifting his weight on the firm cream silk cushions to face her.

"Your face is a little sharper, I think, and there's a bit more muscle to your upper body, but you haven't changed much at all."

"Nor have you."

"Spare me the polite necessities, Commander dear. For all the capabilities of Imperial medical technology, I know what I am. And that's an old woman. Perhaps a lovely old woman, but an old one."

Gerswin opened his mouth, and she held up her hand.

"Oh, I know. I'll be around for years yet. I'm not in the grave. Not even close, but I'm old. You . . . you're still young, and you may be for centuries yet to come, from the look of you.

"I don't know which is worse, dear Commander, but now I'm content."

He did not attempt to answer, or to question, but sat, waiting in the deep afternoon light filtered by the tinted armaglass, watching, and studying the still-fine features he had only seen before etched in the darkness, etched in his memories as if it had been yesterday.

His vision blurred momentarily, and he blinked, shook his head.

"You do remember. I'm not surprised. Not surprised, but gratified." She paused.

Gerswin swallowed, and waited for her to go on.

"What did you think of the painting?"

Gerswin could feel the chill in his spine.

"Impressive . . . sad . . . Almost a memorial, I would think."

"That's important, particularly for you. Though you wouldn't know why."

Gerswin shook his head again. So much was unsaid, so much implied.

"I've sent for some tea, and I would appreciate it if you would join me."

"Pleased to."

"You're still the quiet one. Can you still whistle that odd and two-toned singing?"

He nodded, feeling as shy as he had so many years earlier.

"Don't give it up."

"I don't whistle much now, not in company."

"Would you mind terribly?"

The commander smiled, a tentative smile, a smile as if more than eighty years had been wiped away for a moment. He cleared his throat, made two gentle sounds, and began the melody she had been the first to hear, the only one to hear completely.

He wondered if she had dimmed the light to the study, as, for a moment, the light-strewn study dimmed to call up an evening parsecs and generations away. He did not look up, but concentrated on the intertwining of the two themes, the strength of a weary Old Earth and the fire of love won and lost.

As he let the last paired notes trail off, his eyes came to rest on the Duchess. Her cheeks were wet, and the dampness showed him that after all the years, she still needed no cosmetics for that perfect pale complexion.

Gerswin swallowed again, hard, and looked away. Looked out into the afternoon that was shading into twilight, looked for the shadows he felt gathering in the back of his mind. Looked and waited.

After watching the sun touch the distant trees, he turned back to Caroljoy, who met his eyes.

Without smiling, he extended his right hand and took her left, squeezing it gently.

She returned the pressure, holding his hand as he held hers. After a time, she lifted her long fingers from his.

"I believe the tea is ready."

Her Grace, the Duchess of Triandna, nee Caroljoy Montgrave D'Lir Kerwin, touched the inset controls on the arm of the loveseat. A younger woman entered instantly, also wearing the Duke's colors, and guided a slide table toward them.

On the table were two lustral teapots and a pair of Djring cups in their saucers, the porcelain already glowing as the light level in the study dropped.

A faint clink echoed through the silent room. Gerswin glanced at the woman serving the tea, catching sight for the first time of the pallor beneath her already pale face, and the tightness of the muscles in her arms which had nearly snagged the table on the chair across from the loveseat.

The younger woman had also wiped tears from her cheeks, as Gerswin could see from the smear beneath her left eye. Unlike Caroljoy, she relied on cosmetics.

"Almost," said the Duchess. "Almost I could reach back."

There was another clink as the server placed the porcelain cup and saucer on the elbow height table that had appeared beside Gerswin. A second clink followed as another cup was placed next to Her Grace.

"That will be all, Drewnique."

Gerswin took a sip of the liftea.

"Liftea is both simple and complex, and has a clean taste," she said quietly. "Martin didn't like flavor mixtures, and I assumed that preference came from you. But he did like liftea, and I thought you might."

Gerswin frowned. Martin? From him?

The sense of chill returned to his bones.

He looked into the Duchess's eyes, Caroljoy's eyes. This time, he dropped his glance, feeling a hint of tears that never came.

"Martin?" he asked, his voice barely above a whisper.

"Martin MacGregor D'Gerswin Kerwin."

"Why didn't you let me know?"

"Because I wasn't brave enough to leave New Augusta. Because I did not want to continue bouncing from Service planet to Service planet. Because I came to love Merrel and because it was important to my father that we marry."

She stopped and took a sip from the Djring cup.

Gerswin stared out through the armaglass at the shadowed lawn and took a breath deeper than normal, mentally cataloguing the scents in the room as he tried to gather himself together.

Caroljoy . . . the spice of her was richer, fuller, but had not quite peaked to the cloying of age.

The liftea . . . the pungency similar to cinnamon, but without the dustiness and with the orangeness and mint.

Trilia . . . the background fragrance that hinted of flowers that were not present.

"He didn't object?"

"How could he?" The statement was simple, the implications of strength profound.

Gerswin did not pursue. He darted a look at the glowstones before taking another sip of the liftea from the Djring cup that weighed less than a trilia blossom in his fingers.

"Martin . . . looked much like you, with the hawk-eyes, except his were green, and with the fantastic reflexes. Of course, he became a pilot, after he graduated with honors, and then went from the corvette to commander of his own scout. He was so proud, and even Merrel was proud of him."

Weight, with the inexorable chill and mass of a glacier, settled on and around Gerswin.

"Firien's Star?"

"He could have escaped, but he covered the *Sinta Mare* . . . and the others. The Emperor's Cross . . . upstairs with my jewels." She shrugged, as if trying to lift a burden off her shoulders and not quite succeeding. "Now, once in a while, I can look at it."

Again, silence cupped the room in its unseen hands.

What could he say? He caught himself before he started to shake his head.

"Lieutenant . . . I mean, Commander, we all have our chains to the past. I am not asking you to share mine, nor would I trade anything that has been, and that includes you. At times, I have wondered, but I would not. Martin's childhood was one of the most wonderful times of my life, but that time had passed already when he died, and I had not understood that. All parents die a little when their children become real."

She smiled, and while the smile was faint, the warmth brought a benediction to Gerswin.

"Young Jane made up for it, later, some, but neither Analise nor Jerzey were comfortable here. Jane liked to visit, and who could deny her? She had Martin's eyes, and saw everything. She still cubes me, but they come in batches, now that she's on the Rim expedition."

Gerswin felt more lost at each word, and concentrated on trying not to shake his head at all the implications that tumbled from her words. If Analise had been Martin's wife or the woman who had his child, who was Jerzey?

"Jane? Jerzey?"

"Jerzey was Analise's husband. I've lived with it all for so long it's really quite clear. Lieutenant . . . pardon me, but, you know, dear Commander, I still think of you as that dashing young lieutenant."

She cleared her throat, softly, and took another sip of the liftea. "Like his father, Martin fascinated the ladies, but he never even knew he had a daughter. Neither did we. I found that was a possibility several years later, well after Firien, from his friend Torvye, who brought it up to console me."

She held up her hand. "No need for details, but Analise was adopted out, and by the time I found her, had married Jerzey, a decent sort, if a rather mundane barrister on Herkimer. Jane found it too mundane as well."

"So she joined the Service?"

"A familial weakness, I would guess," suggested Her Grace, her mouth upturned slightly at the corners. "She also took her grandfather's name, but, enough of the history. You do well to humor an aging lady."

"Not humoring," he protested. "Not at all."

Martin a grandfather? What did that make him? Or Caroljoy?

"You've been most kind," he began hesitatingly, "particularly in view . . . of everything . . ." This time, he did shake his head. There were no words to express the conflicting feelings ricocheting back and forth under the black undress armor he wore.

"No," she answered with a smile best described as sad, "I am not kind. I had always wondered, but never had the will to search you out, to learn whether you had survived the deserts of Old Earth and intricacies of the I.S.S. I'm the type who always wants to know how the story ends, even my own story, but not at too great a cost. . . . You should understand . . . those of us who are weak, dear Commander."

Weak? While he could understand, weak was not a word he would have applied to the woman beside whom he sat. He touched her hand again, grasped it gently.

He could not ask the favor for which he had come, not for Old Earth, but, most of all, not for himself.

Instead, he glanced at the glowstone floor tile once more, then around the study, finally settling his eyes on the small flower bed visible straight through the armaglass and centered in the lawn ten meters out from where the two of them sat.

"You hold your keepsakes in your thoughts, don't you?" he asked.

Gerswin suspected that from the villa itself, from a hundred little signs, from the lack of solideo cubes on display, from the simplistic lack of ornateness that surrounded him. Only the oil painting in the main hall that would someday be acclaimed a masterpiece was an exception to that pattern, and even the deep feelings behind the painting were cloaked in simplicity.

What else could he say? Except his good-byes, and he was not ready for those. Not quite yet, not when he had just discovered he had lost two precious things he had never known he had had.

Instead, he picked up the Djring cup and sipped the single cold drop of liftea left in the bottom. That single drop was no more pungent than the first, but held a hint of bitterness that he welcomed.

"That is where they mean the most. Most keepsakes, I have found, are displayed for the impact on others. For memorials, that is suitable, but not for one's self."

"The painting?"

"Martin deserved that, and more. Every spacer who sees it will never forget it, and what else is a memorial for? The sorrow is mine, and, now, perhaps a small bit of it will be yours."

The senior commander nodded to the Duchess, Her Grace, as if to acknowledge a pleasantry, and put his hand to his cup. He did not drink, belatedly remembering he had finished the last bitter droplet already. He centered the cup and saucer on the table by his elbow.

"Getting late," he observed, his eyes flickering toward the western panorama. His right hand covered hers gently.

"Yes. It is. Night falls sooner for some."

He shifted his weight, edging slightly closer to her, but without turning to look at her. A faint breeze brushed his cheek, as if the conditioners had come on, but noiselessly.

Gerswin worried his upper lip with his teeth, then decided.

The senior commander eased his hand from hers and stood, bowing to Her Grace.

"Again . . . you've been most kind."

"Commander dear, is that all you have to say?"

Gerswin felt the sigh go through him, stiffened his shoulders against a slump, and forced a slight smile.

"No . . . Caroljoy . . . Not all that I would say, not all I can say. . . . Never good with words . . . Not from the heart. Guess I came to them too late. Time has passed differently for us. For all your sorrows, you have your loves, your joys, a past, a clear conscience, and memories you can treasure." He stopped, swallowed, and looked directly into her still-clear dark eyes. "I have your memory . . . your warmth . . . some hope for the future. One of the ancients said it. Miles to go before I sleep. It's a long way home. If I get there, then you or . . . Jane . . . or others from your blood will have a home . . . and I will not." His lips quirked. "Sounds too dramatic. Overdone—"

"You've never given up your dreams. That is why you will always be my lieutenant, Commander dear, why you will be loved, why you will be followed, and why you will never rest. Because you cannot surrender."

Caroljoy, his lover and Her Grace, one and the same, young and old, stood. She took a step toward him, and a second, until her hands reached for his. Her fingers were cold within his already cool hands.

"You came to ask for something, and you will not. You cannot."

He nodded, unable to deny the truth as she looked into his eyes, unflinching.

"You are too direct, still, to deceive those whom you love. That is why you love so seldom, my Lieutenant. Because you care, you will not use me, though I used you." She laughed, gently. The sound echoed sadly in the study lit only by the glimmer of the glowstones and the dimness of the twilight. "And I, the more fool, for all the same reasons, will ask you to tell me."

Gerswin told her. Told her about the need for the arcdozers, about the only way he could find to get them for Old Earth, and how both the Duchess and the Duke could help without personally being involved.

"All you want is the opportunity to borrow one of Merrel's yachts on its way for a refit?"

"Steal," corrected Gerswin, smiling wryly. "And it seems like a great deal to me."

"I suppose it would, but for the stakes for which you play, and the price you have already paid, how could I refuse?"

Gerswin looked down, but squeezed her hands in his, feeling how cool and smooth, how strong, even after all the years, they seemed in his.

"A foolish old lady. But more fortunate than you know. Far more fortunate, and someday, when the stars have dimmed, and you look into your own twilight, you may see why. I have loved, and been loved, three times, and that was almost too much, even though I treasure each of you."

He looked up to see her smile.

"You will have the yacht, of course, but the Duke will offer it to transport you and your man back to your duty station. Would that suffice?"

Gerswin nodded, unwilling to speak. The lump in his throat made it difficult even to swallow.

"Consider the arrangements made, Lieutenant. Consider them made." She tightened her fingers around his.

His arms slipped around her, and his lips brushed hers, and, cheek to cheek, two sets of tears mingled while the twilight flowed into night, and while a younger woman watched the embrace on a screen while her own tears streamed unchecked, unknown to the two who had loved only once, yet always.

LXVIII

CRIMRA, COMMUNICATIONS TECHNICIAN Second, frowned and studied the comm board again. Had there been a flicker on the lavender band?

He peered at the register plate below the indicator light, but no signal strength was registering, even if there had been a flash a moment before.

The *Sanducar* was loaded, except for the small priority and security items that would come aboard when the captain returned. The old lady was planetside, along with the third section, and wasn't scheduled back for another twenty standard hours.

Crimra glared at the offending light that refused to glow lavender, but it remained dark.

"Lots of luck, Crimra," he muttered aloud. "No Imperial comms for your watch."

Tomorrow, after the captain came back and delivered her usual rivet-scouring inspection, Crimra and the *Sanducar* would push away from New Glascow to cart their load of combat decon dozers off to New Hades, where the Imperial engineers would use them to train the latest crew of planet busters and clean-up troops.

The comm tech shook his head. He was not totally thrilled with the thought of all those deactivated fusactors in the holds. If even one was operating . . . Crimra didn't want to think about that, not that it would matter one millisecond after the *Sanducar* began to jump-shift. The return trip would be more dangerous, since they would doubtless be carrying busted dozers for rebuilding, and Crimra wondered if the field engineers were as scrupulous as the factory types. There wasn't much of an option, since New Hades was not exactly conducive to large scale on-planet repairs.

Crimra leaned forward in the standard ship swivel and looked at the seamless gray deck beneath his feet.

From the corner of his eye, he thought he saw the same lavender flicker, but when he stared at the board and the register, there was no indication on any transmission.

He licked his lips and scanned the entire board, indicator by indicator. Next he checked the cube board, to insure the fields were holding for all the E-mail the *Sanducar* was carrying.

Everything was as it should be.

Slowly, slowly, he leaned back into the swivel and waited.

Cling! Cling!

As the communicator chimed twice, both the green and lavender lights above the blank main screen lit.

Crimra pursed his lips.

Cling! Cling!

Finally, he leaned forward and tapped the acknowledgment stud.

"*H.M.S. Sanducar,* Communications, Comm Tech Crimra."

The officer in the screen wore a uniform similar to the standard Service undress blouse, but in lavender, with cream piping and no rank insignia.

"Tech Crimra, this is the *Sindelar,* ducal flag of His Grace, the Duke of Triandna. I am Commander Carlesir, commanding for the Duke. His Grace would like to make a courtesy call, if that would be possible. After that, His Grace would be pleased to have the captain and the senior officers as his guests."

"Yes, ser, Commander. Would you hold while I patch in the exec? Captain Cortalina is planetside."

The sharp-eyed yacht-master nodded.

Crimra's fingers danced across the panel.

"Sindra, there's a Duke's yacht out there. Came in on the lavender. Can you locate and verify?"

Another flicker of fingers.

"Niter. Crimra here. Yacht out there that claims it's a Duke's boat. Sindara's trying to find it. Want to put a turret on the tracer?"

"Crimra, take it easy. If it's small enough and far enough out not to trigger the screens, it can't be a danger yet. Besides, who'd dare to impersonate a ducal boat, and who'd have the equipment to come in on a reserved Imperial band?"

Crimra's eyes glanced from one screen to another, from the frozen image of the yachtmaster to Sindra in navigation, to Niter in gunnery, to the fourth screen where he was calling the executive officer's rating.

"Fores, Crimra here. Yacht blasted in on the lavender. Duke of Triandna, or so the yachtmaster claims, would like to pay a courtesy call, then return the favor by having the exec and senior officers over for grub."

"Gerro will love that. I'll get him ready. Not really started on this run, dozers yet, and he's grumbling about the mess."

Ping!

The navigation screen indicator lights blinked.

"Get back to you with the details, Fores."

"Yes, Sindra? What's the gather?"

"According to every single code, outline, and verification, you have indeed the *Sindelar*, number two yacht of the Duke of Triandna, and she's statted one and a half screens out, precisely, just like protocol says. No heavy weapons or energy concentrations."

The Gunnery screen indicators blinked, and Crimra switched to Niter.

"Yes?"

"We've put number two on the yacht, but it wouldn't matter."

"Wouldn't matter?"

"Crimra, yachts can't carry weapons. Emperor's edict. So they got screens like battlecruisers. Accel/decel like corvettes. We're a big fat freighter. She'd be gone before we could even put a load on her screens. Anyway, her screens are the genuine article. Codes and all in the energy warp."

"Thanks."

Crimra paused and wiped his suddenly damp forehead with the back of his left hand before switching back to the executive officer's screen.

"Fores, we've checked and comm, nav, and guns all say it's the genuine article, one certified Duke's yacht. So Gerro can play gracious host and get a decent meal in afterward . . ."

He paused and wiped his forehead.

"Still . . ."

"Still what?"

"What's a Duke's yacht doing here off New Glascow?"

"Blast it, Crimra. Those boys go anywhere. Sometimes just on a bet. And remember, half of them hold reserve I.S.S. commissions as commodores or admirals. Anyhow, even if it weren't a Duke, who'd want a couple hundred dozers? For anything?"

"Admirals?"

"Right. They never really get to command except in practice games out in Gamma sector once a year. So they run around in their own little boats. Who knows, maybe this Duke will punch old Gerro's ticket."

"He wouldn't!"

"Never know what can happen, Crimra. You never know." The exec's screen blanked.

The comm tech cleared the board, except for the still-frozen image of the yachtmaster, waiting in his lavender uniform for the response from the *Sanducar*.

Somehow, the cramped comm center seemed to constrict around Crimra. He shook his head, wiped his forehead again with the back of his hand, and tapped the panels in front of him.

LXIX

"SHUTTLE'S HEADING BACK," Crimra observed, simultaneously notifying the gunnery section so they could drop the screens.

"Got it. Screens down. If five isn't enough, Sindra, let me know." Crimra monitored the exchange between guns and nav.

"Five's plenty, Niter. The little boy's almost clear now."

Crimra checked the board. The homer was clear, the green light showing the near-empty shuttle was locked on.

He checked the board again. All clear. With a sigh, he leaned back in the anchored swivel so that the air flow from the vent could dry the remaining dampness from his forehead.

From the outside, the *Sanducar* was huge, but the habitable space was not much more than in the ducal yacht. Most of the *Sanducar*'s space was devoted to drives or cargo, and the ship could have been handled easily by a third of its thirty crew members, as was routinely the case with the handful of commercial freighters equivalent to the *Sanducar*.

Crimra stretched his legs and watched as the screen light indicators blinked amber twice, then settled into the green to show the screens were back in place.

The faintest of clinks and a nearly infinitesimal shiver occurred as the shuttle entered the receiving locks and clicked into place.

The homer signal beeped once, and the light switched from green to the amber of standby.

The comm tech relaxed further now that the shuttle had returned. Stand-down watches weren't half bad, with one section gone. Now, with the exec and his two tagalongs over playing with the Duke, all he had to worry about were any incomings, not that there were likely to be that many.

He straightened in the swivel and brushed a strand of hair back off his forehead.

Then he shook his head. He'd only seen pictures of the Duke before, but, in person, he seemed thinner, more military than the faxers had shown him. The Duke and the yachtmaster had really looked at the *Sanducar.* They'd been quick, but they'd asked questions, almost like an inspection.

Crimra didn't see Gerro getting his ticket punched by that Duke. He acted like he knew more than the exec, not that that was any great surprise to any of the *Sanducar*'s crew.

Crimra yawned. He shouldn't feel sleepy.

He stretched again, trying to stifle another yawn, aware that the breeze from the vent was stronger, with a faint scent of . . . something. He shrugged.

And yawned again. Blast! He shouldn't feel that sleepy.

The comm tech concentrated on putting his feet in exactly the correct position in front of the swivel. Next, he grasped the arms and concentrated on lifting himself out of the seat.

His arms wouldn't lift him, and he was yawning again, his mouth so far open that his jaw ached.

From somewhere, the blackness came up and hit him.

GERSWIN BENT HIS forefinger in the odd configuration required to seal his suit, and the face plate slid closed.

He hoped none of the onboard crew of the *Sanducar* had been suited, not that there would have been any reason for them to have been, not while in orbit and on stand-down.

He raised his hand. The shuttle was sealed into the hold, both locks opened. Gerswin and his crew of ten were outside the shuttle itself, hidden behind the more than man-tall driver shields from the vid scanners and from the direct vision of the tech who was in charge of the hangar and lock operations.

Gerswin was betting that there would be a single tech on duty, two at most.

If not, he was prepared to employ more direct means.

Nitiri, wearing the shipsuit of the shuttle's pilot, went through the power-down procedures, locked the shutting onto the mesh, and exited from the forward shuttle hatch. He stepped out, turned to look over the shuttle as if to give it a cursory inspection from outside, then turned back and took careful steps toward the interior lock.

The single on-duty tech looked up as Nitiri appeared, suit still sealed.

"Hey! You—"

Thrumm!

The tech crumpled across the table. Nitiri lifted him off the board. Carefully, because he was wearing the heavy suit gauntlets, he made a number of changes to the status board, the last of which unlocked the interior lock for Gerswin and the nine others.

Gerswin clumped in last and manually sealed the battle locks to prevent anyone from surprising them in turn. By the time he had finished cranking the heavy bolts into their jackets and entered the hangar lock control room, Nitiri was stretching out the unconscious tech in the only vacant corner. The others had split into three different parties, each group with a small gas canister.

The commander traced a question mark in the air, unwilling to use the suit radio, since most suit frequencies would trigger the automatic defense alarms of Imperial ships unless accompanied by the ship's own carrier code.

Nitiri stood, straightened, and shrugged, both gray gauntlets held palm up.

Gerswin motioned to the nine to go ahead, then took a thin cable from his suit pouch, along with the tool pack, and began to work. With three movements and the use of two tools, he was plugged into the console.

The odds were against their completing the changes to the ship's air systems before someone stumbled across the intruders, and Gerswin wanted to know when it happened.

He switched from frequency to frequency, from console station to console station, but picked up nothing on the first sweep.

Ideally, he would have preferred the comm center, but that was obviously impractical. Any alarm would show on the common channels within seconds, in any case.

In the interim Nitiri placed himself, stunner still drawn, to cover the now-closed portal from the main access corridor into the cargo control lock center where they waited. The room was so small that anyone who entered would see them at once.

Gerswin plugged to the lit stations on the comm panel.

"Sindra, Niter here. Do you know if Weryon is pushing dust again?"

"Negative, Sindra. Could be. Fores said that the exec's cabin was getting air that smelled oily. Thought they'd fixed it."

"Just thought I heard some noise below in the vent system. . . . Oh . . . ohhh . . . Wish Peres would get here."

"Why? You said she doesn't like you."

"Doesn't. Sleepy, and she's my relief."

"Got a while. It must be the waiting. Feel the same way."

"Dorfstuff! Hurry up and wait. Exec's off. Captain's gone. We're here. Who's in charge?"

"The senior lieutenant . . ."

Another light blinked, and Gerswin shifted frequencies.

"Fores! Fores! Get the O.D."

BRING! BRINGG! BRINGGG!

The piercing ringing of the general quarters alarm shook Gerswin even through his suit's armor.

He tabbed his own transmitter.

"Blue team. Blue team. Interrogative status."

"Blue team to Captain Black. Status is green and sealed."

"Commence cleanup. Commence cleanup."

"Affirmative. Commencing."

Gerswin tabbed his transmitter the second time.

"Green team. Interrogative status."

"Green team to Captain Black. Status is three plus until green."

"Split. Plan beta. Plan beta."

"Stet. Affirmative plan beta for green team."

Gerswin hit the button, then dropped behind the console as he saw the disruptor preceding the big tech barreling into the lock control room.

Crack!

Thrummm!

The intruder dropped under the stunner, but not before his disruptor left what had been the right corner of the lock control board as a molten chunk of metal and plastics.

Gerswin stayed low behind the console.

"Red team. Interrogative status."

"Red team to Captain Black. Shunts complete. Communications blanked. One plus to green on seals."

"Red team. Commence plan beta."

"Stet. Commencing beta. Good luck, Captain Black."

Gerswin looked across the small room to Nitiri, who by now had shifted the stunner into his left gauntlet. He held the disruptor he had recovered in his right.

Gerswin returned to monitoring channels. While several lights continued to blink, indicating keyed or open channels, no actual communications were on-going. Either the crew had succumbed to the sleep gas or stunners, or there was a fight going on somewhere, and the Imperial freighter's crew was not talking because they knew their communications were being monitored.

Gerswin glanced across at Nitiri, but could only see his own reflection in the other's face plate.

Belatedly, he unholstered his own stunner and leveled it in the direction of the portal to the main corridor.

"Captain Black, red team leader. Area is now secure. Area three now totally secure. No casualties. I say again. No casualties."

"Captain Black, blue team leader. Area one is secure. No casualties."

"Captain Black, green team leader. Area two secure with one exception. No casualties, but one exception. Armored and at location level three, frames 192 and 193."

"Green team leader, Captain Black. Interrogative weapons status of exception."

"Captain Black, exception has not standard weapons, but has officer's sword."

"Green team leader, Captain Black is on the way. On the way."

Gerswin unplugged from the console and handed the jack to Nitiri.

"Watch the inboard freqs from below."

Nitiri nodded.

Level three, frame 193, was the space armor locker.

Only Lostwin waited for Gerswin. The rest of the team continued to work.

"Every one of those suits has a disruptor, Captain."

"I know. I know." Gerswin surveyed the area. "Is this place saturated under full atmosphere?"

"Yes, ser."

"Have a medic standing by. Hope I can do this without too much danger, but . . ."

"What—"

Gerswin cut off the exchange with a downward chop of his hand. If the Imperial officer were any kind of fighter, he'd be on Gerswin's frequencies already.

"Blue team leader, this is Captain Black. In one point zero from mark, pull your board for one point zero. Do you understand?"

"Captain Black, blue team leader. Pulling my entire board for one point zero. That is one point zero from your mark."

"Stet. *Mark!*"

"We have mark."

Gerswin gestured to Lostwin, pointing to the space armor locker portal and to the controls box.

Lostwin got the idea and nodded, using hand signals to move his team out of any possible line of fire, then moved to the controls. He began to operate the manual overrides of the internal locks. As the portal began to iris open, a beam of red energy flared against the inside of the portal once, then again.

Gerswin smiled. The officer inside was trying to fuse the portal shut.

He moved closer, waiting.

The grav generators went off, and he launched himself to the overhead. In three quick mincesteps he was by the edge of the portal, crouching low, and throwing the knives.

One!

Two!

A silent flare of red energy died with the second knife.

Captain Black was through the half-open portal like a streak, plowing into the Imperial officer from above and knocking the disruptor away.

As the other dropped to the deck more easily than Gerswin expected, he had a sickening suspicion.

"Lock guard, get medic here on straight line full accel/decel. Casualty may need immediate medical attention."

"Affirmative, Captain. Affirmative."

Gerswin didn't see any blood, but both knives had hit the holdout officer, one in the right shoulder, and the other in the left thigh.

"How could he throw it through armor cloth?"

That came through the suit intercom. Gerswin didn't recognize the speaker's voice.

"Ever seen his knives? Ever seen him throw?"

"Yeah, every year or so he takes up a new weapon. Keeps him alert."

Gerswin ignored the background chatter, and hoisted the faintly struggling figure over his shoulder and headed for Nitiri and the lock control center. The last thing someone who was bleeding needed was a full dose of sleepgas, and until he could unsuit, there wasn't a thing he or anyone else could do.

As he reached the hangar locks he felt the vibrations of the *Sindelar*'s boat locking in with Winsters.

The young officer was limp by the time Winsters and Gerswin had her unsuited in the yacht boat, the single place aboard the *Sanducar* not permeated with the gas.

Winsters began working, and without glancing at his commander, observed, "She should be all right. While you pinned the one in the thigh pretty deep, you missed about everything you could miss. Shoulder wound's mostly muscle. She'll be laid up for a while, but it doesn't look like any permanent damage."

Gerswin sighed, followed it with a frown. One casualty wasn't bad, but why did it have to be a female officer? On some planets that wouldn't set well at all, if it ever got out.

"Remember, Winsters, no names, and no treatment once she's conscious without privacy gear and an armed guard."

The former shambletown kid nodded with a grim smile. "Understand, Commander. Understand."

"You take her back with you. We'll go on as planned. Have Dewart bring back the officers when you get the signal."

"Need more support?"

"We're set, unless something changes. We're securing the crew, and we've got the supplies for the jump. If they have any spare torps, I'll send them back when you send over the exec. Best we break before someone sends out a corvette."

Gerswin sealed his suit and headed back into the *Sanducar* and the command bridge, leaving Nitiri to outlock the *Sindelar*'s boat and lockseal the outer doors as well.

On the bridge, he began the checks.

"Interrogative drives."

"In the green. Power up sequence at minus fifteen to touch point."

"Navigation, interrogative screens."

"Up and in the green. Course feed input on schedule. Will have break point computations adapted in twelve plus or minus two."

"Gunnery?"

"Captain, for our purposes, no guns. Permission to divert to screens."

"Go ahead, if you can reshunt without leaving traces after arrival and downloading."

"No problem."

Gerswin wondered how small that division problem really was, but extra power to the screens certainly wouldn't hurt.

"Drives, interrogative governor status."

"Plan to reset at plus point two. Enough to throw off the Impie computers, but not enough to hurt our passengers."

"Navigation, interrogative visitors."

"Captain Black, no visitors in sight. None anticipated."

So now all he had to do was wait . . .

He needed one quarter of a standard Imperial hour, one quarter hour before His Imperial Majesty's freighter *Sanducar* could vanish from orbit for an unknown destination.

At that point, the *Sindelar* would also vanish to deliver a few messages, and to send out a raft of messages torps, before being returned to its rather surprised refit crew.

Then—Gerswin shook his head, violently, and refocused his attention on the screen before him. One thing at a time.

First, his teams needed to finish securing the crew. Second, they had to bring the freighter from stand-down to full operation. Third, they had to recover the exec and two officers and leave orbit without discovery and attack by Imperial vessels.

"Captain, incoming from yacht."

"Stet. Lock in and recover."

"Captain Black? Incoming on standard comm net. Interrogative response."

"Respond without screen. Explain you're doing last minute maintenance. Ask to feed back in three to five."

"Affirmative. Will do."

Gerswin checked the readouts. Minus ten until full power-up sequence was complete. He hoped the *Sindelar*'s boat was clear by then. He jabbed the engineering stud.

"Interrogative drive status."

"Minus nine until green."

"Report when ready."

"Yes, ser."

"Navigation, interrogative status."

"Minus seven until course feed complete."

Gerswin sat watching the screens, looking at the flow of information on the status of the ship, watching the green panels light, watching the red shift to amber, and then to green.

Another thought crossed his mind, and he tapped the tight beam back to the *Sindelar.*

"Landspout, this is Captain Black. Interrogative status of messengers."

"Captain Black, messengers ready to depart within one plus of your completion."

"Affirm one plus."

"Stet."

He turned back to the unfamiliar bridge board.

"Captain." This time the voice did not come from a distant channel, but from the suited figure to his right, from the opening portal where Lostwin stood.

"Crew totally secured and unconscious. Ship will be flushed and clean within twenty."

Gerswin nodded, part of the tightness in his gut subsiding.

Lostwin settled himself into the O.D.'s swivel, trying to match what he'd studied and the board of the freighter against the small ships he had piloted.

"Captain, red team leader. Estimate thirty plus for unsuit time. Nav indicates after first jump point."

"Stet."

"Navigation to bridge. All systems green. Course feed complete."

"Stet."

"Engineering to bridge. All systems green."

"Stet."

"Hangar deck to bridge. Transfer complete, and visitors clear."

"Screens dropped for departure?"

"That's affirmative."

"Guns to Captain Black, diversion complete and green."

"Stet."

Gerswin took a deep breath within the confines of the suit, exhaled, and began to move his gauntleted fingers across the board.

At last, he touched the pulsing green stud that would mesh the inputs and boost the *Sanducar* from orbit to the first jump point.

"Landspout, this is Captain Black. We are green and departing. Green and departing."

"Stet. See you later."

Gerswin watched the screens, the course line display that represented where the *Sanducar* was headed, and the real-time monitor that showed the blackness outside, punctuated with unwinking stars. He watched the screens, the familiar displays in unfamiliar positions, his face blank, expressionless behind the suitshield.

As the outward velocity of the *Sanducar* mounted, he saw a spark break from the small circle captioned "New Glascow" on the representational screen.

"Comm, any interrogatories?"

"Standard inquiries from planetary ops and from the geosynch high ops, but we're farside. Not much they can do. We're maintaining full-band silence."

"What's the breakaway?"

"Breakaway is high speed shuttle. Has the *Sanducar*'s C.O. Guess he's afraid of being left."

"Any combat ships?"

"No other energy concentrations."

"Navigation, interrogative closest approach of shuttle."

"He's already past CPA. We're clear to jump point."

"Stet."

Clear to jump point meant clear to Old Earth, and clear to unload nearly two cohorts of dozers, and get them operating before they could be easily reclaimed. But Old Earth would be exactly where his real troubles began, Gerswin reflected.

Lerwin had protested being excluded, but there had to be someone officially innocent should things go wrong, someone who could pick up the pieces.

Gerswin shook his head, still watching the screens, still waiting to insure that no untoward Impie combatant appeared from nowhere, waiting until the real battles began.

LXXI

"COMMANDER GERSWIN TO the Ops center. Commander Gerswin to the Ops center."

The senior commander under summons swung his feet off the narrow bunk and sat upright, pulling his boots onto his feet.

Buzzz! Buzzzz!

He ignored the harsh noise from his console. He had no doubt about the reason for the summons, none whatsoever.

He smiled and took a deep breath. After all the years, the room—and he had never put in for a suite, which he rated—still smelled like a mixture of wilted trilia and machine oil. It always would, he supposed, not that it was likely he would be the one worrying about it for much longer.

As he finished fastening the undress black tunic, he was through the portal and into the main corridor. It was empty, unsurprisingly, since it was just before dawn local Old Earth time. Then, the Imperial Interstellar Survey Service had never operated on anything other than New Augustan Imperial District time, and by that clock, it was mid-morning.

Lerwin, wearing his new linked diamonds of commander, met him at the Operations portal.

"They're here, Captain. Upset, too."

"Did they announce it?" asked Gerswin with the same disinterested smile.

"In their own way. Arrived with five corvettes, two destroyers, and a battlecruiser. That's a full battle group."

"Lunar pick-up?"

"Right. No comm link yet."

"Open a link with them. Welcome them and ask innocently what we can do for them."

"What?"

"No sense in acting guilty, is there? Or giving them an excuse to use all that firepower?"

Lerwin nodded slowly.

"And . . . Lerwin . . . ," the senior commander added slowly, "hope those dozers are well dispersed and very actively reclaiming the land."

"We already did that. They can't get them without destroying everything we've reclaimed, and then some."

The dark-haired executive officer with the eyes like an eagle smiled. Both his smile and that of the commandant were like sun over the northern ice, like the moon above winter tundra.

The two turned together wordlessly and strode through the portal and into the Operations section.

"Captain, there's an admiral out there!"

"They wouldn't send less, would they?" Gerswin cleared his throat. "I'll speak to him. Put him on the main screen. That way everyone in the base can see. Make sure you catch a cube of it. We might find it helpful . . . later."

The image on the central screen in front of Gerswin flickered blue once, then focused on an officer with iron gray hair, a man wearing the drab gray of ship battle dress, distinguished only by the silver stars and joining bar on his collars.

"Welcome, Admiral," offered the senior commander, his vagueness deliberate since he hadn't the faintest idea which of the Empire's several dozen admirals he was addressing.

"I appreciate the courtesy," returned the I.S.S. functionary, "and would appreciate the opportunity to speak with Senior Commander Gerswin."

"Speaking."

"So you're Gerswin . . . I could believe that." The admiral stiffened his already stiff bearing and lifted a single sheet of permafax into view. "Senior Commander Gerswin, by virtue of the authority vested in me by His Imperial Majesty, I hereby relieve you of your command. That command is temporarily transferred to the authority of Battle Group Delta Seven, pending outcome of the forthcoming Board of Inquiry proceedings.

"You are requested to make yourself available for interview, and for possible trial under the articles of the Service. Pending the outcome of the inquiry, Senior Commander Beloit will be acting as Commandant, I.S.S. Reclamation Base, Old Earth."

Gerswin raised his hand. "One question, Admiral. Or two. Who are you? And with what have I been charged, if anything?"

The chill in the admiral's eyes was clear, even through the screen transmission. "Senior Commander, right now, you are charged with nothing. Any possible charges will await the outcome of all phases of the investigation of the irregular transfer of two cohorts of Imperial arcdozers from the Marine Engineering Command to the Reclamation Base, Old Earth. Under the Emperor's orders, I am conducting phase one of the inquiry."

Gerswin, while remaining at attention, smiled slightly. "You have yet to identify either yourself or the orders under which you are operating. Without such verification, I am not empowered to surrender my command, even in the face of the superior force which you have mustered."

Gerswin heard several hisses of indrawn breath around the Operations center. Even Lerwin had taken a step away from him at the last statement.

"Please be so kind, Senior Commander, as to activate your authentication system."

Gerswin nodded twice at the technician across the center. Three half-hearted jabs later, the panel blinked amber twice and settled onto the green.

"Authentication on."

The admiral placed his own verifax sheet into a similar device, and waited, still ramrod stiff in the screen.

"Admiral Ferrin," whispered Lerwin, out of range of the screen focused on Gerswin.

The authenticator blinked green twice.

"Apparently your orders are genuine," admitted the senior commander. "What would you like me to do, Admiral Ferrin?"

"A shuttle will be arriving with the first members of the investigation team. They will interview every I.S.S. member in your command with two exceptions. I will interview you and your executive officer, Commander Lerwin, after all other interviews are complete.

"Senior Commander Beloit will also be arriving to take temporary command. I would appreciate it if you would remain in the general vicinity of the main base while the investigation is being conducted."

"Yes, ser. Will that be all?"

"For now, Senior Commander Gerswin. For now."

"Yes, ser."

The admiral nodded briskly, and the screen blanked.

"They're out to get you, Captain."

"Blasting inquiry!"

"Why so harsh?"

"They'll try him and never let him go."

"How many bodies do they want?"

"All of us?"

"All of us."

Gerswin stood silent until the comments died away. Waited until all those who had seen the Imperial transmission had gathered around him.

"Think," he began quietly. "Do they really want to admit to the Empire, to the whole Galaxy, that their old battered and tattered home planet had to steal dozers to reclaim itself? Do they really want to create that kind of image? Do they want to make a martyr out of me or anyone else?"

He shook his head, as if to emphasize his points.

"They can't do anything about the dozers. But they'll come down like tacheads on anyone who is defiant, insubordinate, or whom they find guilty of any easily documented transgression.

"Be polite. Be helpful. Tell the truth, always the truth, but volunteer nothing. Since it's allowed, insist on copies of your statements for your own records. That's allowed. Then send copies to Service HQ for the official hearing files. That's also allowed."

He could see the frowns, the puzzled expressions.

"Two people can sometimes keep a secret, but three never can, not about something this big."

He paused, then decided to reemphasize a point.

"Remember, if you don't know about something from your own

firsthand knowledge, don't discuss it. That can only get you into trouble. If you do know, limit your discussion to the facts. The facts are our allies."

He surveyed the room again.

"Don't . . . get . . . them . . . angry," he concluded, spacing each word for emphasis. "Don't give them the slightest excuse."

He smiled, and his expression was colder than the moon's dark side.

"It's time to get ready for the temporary commandant."

LXXII

The mathematics of purely mechanical ecological reconstruction would have been stupendous. The largest single water purifying or recycling unit ever developed processed five hundred cubic meters of water per standard minute. Had one million of these units been employed and had they been required to purify every drop of water on the planet, and had no drop ever been processed more than once, the process would have taken more than 50,000 years.

Beyond that, the resource drain on the Empire would have been astronomical. For a self-contained unit to be effective, an incorporated fusion power plant was required, with all contaminants processed either reduced to basic elements or elemental hydrogen.

While nature's natural processes, given time, are also effective with the most critical areas of land and water pollution, neither nature nor the puny mechanical aids of man could have been totally effective in reclaiming Old Earth, not in the time scale in which reclamation was actually accomplished.

Viewpoints
Accardo Avero
New Avalon, 5132 N.E.C.

LXXIII

THE ADMIRAL PICKED up the executive summary, waved it once, and dropped it on the long green table.

"You know what this is worth? That's what it's worth."

None of the other Service officers around the table spoke. No one opened his or her mouth.

"I take it that you all agree?"

Vice Admiral Boedekkr nodded her head slowly up and down.

"Admiral Boedekkr. Your thoughts?"

"The same as yours, Admiral. We know the *Sanducar* was diverted. We even have solid evidence in some cases. We could probably prove it in a court martial. But what would we gain? We would prove to most of mankind that we care nothing about Old Earth. It isn't true, but that is what such a trial would indicate. We could make the Emperor look foolish by denying all the press reports of his good will and largess toward our parent planet. And, also to be considered is how foolish the Service would look."

"Foolish?" questioned a white-haired admiral.

"Foolish," repeated Admiral Boedekkr. "First, the ease with which a heavy Imperial freighter was diverted would have to come out. Second, we would look like we were trying to punish some idealistic officers for making us look foolish and for doing what most people think was right. And last, to the Imperial Senate, we would look as if we were trying to weaken the Emperor's position.

"Then, too, by issuing denials of the press releases that were circulated to the major media in who knows how many systems, we would end up making the media look as silly as we would. All in all, prosecution seems unwise."

"Why?" demanded a commodore from the end of the table, as if he had ignored her entire argument.

"Because, Commodore," and her flint eyes bored into the man, "in addition to the entire argument you have apparently ignored, I would not wish to put the Emperor in the position of denying reclamation efforts on Old Earth. Nor am I terribly anxious to admit that a handful of Service personnel managed to divert a major amount of Imperial resources and a freighter without our even knowing about it until the ship disappeared for an unknown destination. Furthermore, we could not even follow up until they kindly returned both our ship and a ducal yacht with the crews unharmed."

"Almost unharmed," corrected the commodore.

"Thank you, Admiral," nodded the senior admiral at the head of the review board. "Most important, it would be difficult to prove other than circumstantially exactly who was responsible for what. Not one of the ship's crew saw any of the pirates. Nor can the Duke's personnel identify whether or not their passengers were associated with those who took over the yacht. We have conflicting reports of someone impersonating the Duke, and the Duke, of course, is most reluctant to press that charge unless we can prove it beyond any doubt whatsoever.

"All we have are two cohorts of arcdozers which are busily reclaiming sections of Old Earth, and demonstrating to the Empire that Emperors keep their commitments."

"So we're going to hold a court martial to prove it's all a hoax and return those dozers to a training hellhole in Gamma sector?" he asked rhetorically.

"Wrong," he answered himself quietly. "But we won't let the guilty get away with it, either. The Service takes care of its own, one way or another."

"How?" asked the vice admiral to his left, the vice chairman of the review board.

"Thank you, Virl, for asking the question on schedule."

The two grinned at each other.

"We have a solution. One that will give the Emperor great credit for taking an important step toward reclaiming Old Earth. One that will remove the financial burden of Old Earth from the Service and return it to the Senate and the Court, and one that will send a clear message to everyone in the Service who knows without alerting anyone else."

His voice became matter-of-fact. "Obviously, you must approve the solution, but, if approved, the whole incident becomes a lesson learned relatively cheaply. We got the ship back. The Emperor will get the credit, and our budget will benefit. And we have a chance to change shipboard procedures so this cannot happen again."

"Might I ask you to outline the solution?" That was Vice Admiral Boedekkr.

"Shortly, the Emperor will announce that Old Earth needs a special effort. He will declare the formation of the Imperial Reclamation and Reconstruction Corps—Recorps, for short. Recorps personnel will be recruited locally from Old Earth and from volunteers throughout the Empire. Any officers and technicians now at Old Earth Base may transfer without prejudice, and with good recommendations to Recorps in order to take advantage of their experience and dedication."

"In effect, it becomes a lifetime tour on Old Earth?"

"Assume those who don't elect to transfer will face some 'prejudice,' if you want to put it that way."

"Will it work?"

The admiral waited, then cleared his throat.

"Those who choose not to volunteer, in order for the Service to avoid 'conflicts of interest,' must elect another home of record and will sign a release acknowledging that they will never be stationed in that quadrant again. Further, because of various Service-related difficulties, they will have to accept a marginally satisfactory rating for their last Old Earth tour. If they remain in Service, unless they truly accomplish a heroic deed, they will probably never be considered for promotion beyond captain or their present rank, if they are already above the rank of captain."

"Clever."

"Very neat."

"Marvelous."

Vice Admiral Boedekkr did not join in the comments. She alone smiled faintly, and leaned back in her swivel.

Admiral Roeder observed her silence and made a mental note to follow up. He wanted to know what her reservations were. In the meantime, he tapped the gavel.

"Follow-up briefings will begin after lunch."

The flag officers filed out on each side of the long green table, most with their shoulders high, as if an enormous weight had been lifted from them.

Roeder refrained from shaking his head. Most still didn't understand how they had been maneuvered, and he didn't know whether he was glad they didn't, or appalled at their density.

He twisted his lips in a thin smile before he set down the gavel and left to follow the others.

LXXIV

"THE DOZERS ARE only a symbol, as are the promises of pumps and purifiers."

The senior commander frowned at the screen a last time before blanking his calculations. What would they say, those for whom he had made the choice? Those who would be forever grounded or forever exiled?

He took a deep breath and exhaled it slowly, letting it out with the sigh of a hot flitter touch-down.

He could only hope that the few young and Imperial-born officers who had reelected to remain in the Service would be quietly re-reviewed once they left Old Earth, since he had made sure that the record showed they had had no part in whatever had occurred.

If the Service was inflexible enough not to . . . he shook his head.

None of the choices were easy, and even the best of dreams sometimes faded.

He stood and took a step toward the portal, his eyes flicking from one corner of the commandant's small quarters to the other, from the pale gray of the right, with its built-in locker, closet, and console, to the pale gray of the left, with bunk and flat walls.

His own decision had been made before it had been offered, for he had no other choice. Already he had stayed too long, and it was time for change. He could not come home until it was no longer home for him, but for all men and women.

If he stayed, the Service and Imperial hatred would focus on Recorps. At least, it might, and that he could not risk.

"Hope is so fragile, and for now, the dozers will help . . ."

He picked up both packets off the console, then slashed a line across one, the one with the new symbol at the top, and placed his signature across the bottom of the second.

Two kit bags—all that he intended to take—stood by the portal.

His fingers found their way to the console, which lit and focused on nothing as he tapped out the codes he wanted.

The commander's face snapped into view.

"Captain."

"Just Commander Gerswin, Lerwin." He paused. "It's all yours. Your command will take effect immediately, and you'll have to work out the reorganization plan to get the best out of what you have. You know who they are."

The other nodded, his hawk-green eyes never leaving Gerswin's.

"Don't say I understand, but if that's it, that's it."

"Someday, it will become more clear. Lived with it so long I never bothered to explain. Little late now."

Neither said anything as the moments stretched out.

"You're the captain now. Make sure you are."

"And you?"

"Just say that I had no choice. They know whose idea it was. For me to stay would cost everyone too much. So I have no choice. Besides, my work's not done."

"No choice. That's the best way to put it. Keep them on edge against the Empire, and they'll need that to begin with."

The senior commander agreed, but did not nod this time.

"You're the captain," he repeated. "Whatever you think best."

"Now?" asked the new captain.

Even through the screen, Gerswin could see the incipient signs of age, the faint lines around the eyes, the heavier muscles. Lerwin would outlive the Imperials, had already outlived some before showing any age, but he would not see the rebirth for which he worked. Even Corwin might not see that, assuming Corwin followed in his parent's footsteps.

Corwin . . . Gerswin scarcely knew the child, and had seldom even seen his sister Ellia. With the growth of the children, while she did her job well, Kiedra had turned her personal side inward to Lerwin and Corwin and Ellia. Like all devilkids, reflected Gerswin sadly.

"Now?" asked Lerwin again.

"Shortly. I leave on the next shuttle." Gerswin frowned. "Afraid I left you in the lurch. My file keys are on the commandant's console. Everything's there. Try and do a better job for your successor, Lerwin."

"You did fine, Captain."

"Thanks, but we know better. I'll be down in ten plus."

Gerswin tapped the console once, and the image of the commander who would be listed as the first Commandant of Recorps faded from the screen.

Gerswin was ready to go, but he stood shifting his weight from one foot to the other, waiting. Lerwin needed the time to round up the remaining devilkids. They all needed to see him enter the shuttle, needed to see the departure, to understand that he could no longer stand behind them.

Lerwin needed the visual image of his departure also. While there was no ritual such as a change of command, because the old Command had been abolished, and the new one was not in place, they all needed some sort of ceremony to mark the end of the old era and the beginning of the new.

The senior commander, his short and curly blond hair untouched with silver, his hawk-yellow eyes as fierce as ever, his face unlined, smiled at the blank wall. The sole imprint of the years had been the slight sharpening of his features—that, and the hint of blackness that lingered behind his eyes like a reminder of the eternity itself.

He picked up the kit bags himself, though he could have had them carried to the shuttle, and tabbed the portal. As it irised open, he stepped through into the main corridor and the omnipresent but faint scent of ozone.

He half-shook his head. Someday, sometime, the closed buildings would not be necessary. Nor the fortresslike or half-buried construction. Already, the new town construction was halfway there, though the residents were far hardier stock than the average Imperial. The landspouts were less frequent in the reclaimed areas around the base. Elsewhere, they raged scarcely abated, and those "elsewhere lands" comprised the majority of the globe.

Gerswin's steps did not resemble those of a senior commander with more than eighty years' service. Quick and light, his feet, even at a walk, scarcely seemed to touch the pale and milky gray of the plastone floor tiles.

He slowed as he approached the last turn in the corridor before the Operations center.

Had Lerwin had enough time?

He shrugged. If necessary, he could prolong good-byes and remarks until they all straggled in.

The portal stood open. Inside the center, the entry console was vacant. Only a single technician manned the duty console, and the corridor leading down to the departure portals was also vacant. So was the tunnel to the hangar-bunker that served the shuttle.

The shuttle from the *Relyea* was grounded in beta two, and Gerswin picked up his pace as he entered the sloping tunnel. After about fifty meters the tunnel slope flattened before beginning the gradual ascent toward the hangar-bunker.

As he stepped through the last portal into the hangar, he straightened.

"Ten'stet!"

Crack! Crack! Crack!

The ceremonial volley of the ancient long guns caught him off guard as it continued.

All eight of the remaining devilkids, four on a side, in full-dress Service uniform, stood at attention. They formed an honor guard between him and the open port of the waiting shuttle.

Behind them, also in full dress, was Lerwin, and it had been Lerwin's voice that had given the commands.

Gerswin stood, waiting.

"Captain," began the new commandant, "there will be a commandant of Recorps here on Old Earth who will succeed you. And he will have a successor, as will his or her successor. But there is only one Captain, and there will be only one Captain from Old Earth. Either here, or out among the Imperial stars."

"Ten'stet!" another voice barked.

Crack! Crack! Crack!

"Any words, Captain?"

Gerswin swallowed. Hard. Waited.

Finally, he cleared his throat.

"You all understand. Remember what we did. More important, remember why. Time will make it easy to forget. I'll be back, one way or another, but it may be a long cold trip. It's all in your hands, and you have a big job. The biggest ever tackled." He paused. "We know it can be done. I did what I could, but the biggest part is up to you, and I know you're up to it. You can do it. You just have to forget the past and get on with it."

He turned to Lerwin and saluted.

"Your command, Commander. Your command. Permission to depart?"

"Your command, Captain. Always your command. We may hold it for you, but it will always be yours. Good luck . . . from all of us . . . for all of us."

Lerwin returned the salute.

Crack! Crack! Crack!

Gerswin waited until the last volley died away before bending to retrieve the two kit bags. He lifted them and marched through the eight devilkids and across the plastarmac toward the shuttle.

Once inside the lock, he set down the bags, turned, and gave a last salute before the shuttle ports closed.

A long trip so far . . . and a longer one that was just beginning.

THE SILENT WARRIOR

TECHNICALLY, THE ROOM was not supposed to exist, for it appeared neither on the official floor plans of the Admiralty, nor in any of the references, nor even in the classified briefing materials provided to the Admiral of the Fleets.

The Admiral of the Fleets knew of the room with its unique equipment, as did the man called Eye. That they did was obvious from their presence within.

The interior walls were not walls, but an arrangement of polygons upon which other equipment remained focused. The soft flooring was designed as well to resist echoes and any duplication or recording of the proceedings.

The admiral wore dress blacks, as he often did. The three others around the table were garbed in black full-fade cloaks with privacy hoods. The man called Eye was distinguished only by the seat he had taken at the head of the five-sided table.

"You called the meeting, Admiral." The scratchy tone of the voice indicated that Eye employed a voice distorter.

"I did. I have a commission. The file is there." He pointed to the blank cover of the folder on the table in front of Eye.

No one said a word as the Intelligence chief read the material, then passed it to the figure on the right, who in turn scanned the contents before passing it back to the last Intelligence controller.

"We have some questions," began Eye. The hooded heads of the other two nodded in agreement.

"Questions yet?"

Eye said nothing, and with the face lost in the shadows of the hooded cloak, the admiral wondered if he had pushed too far.

Finally, Eye cleared his throat, and his distorted voice, low and even, responded.

"We probably know more about the subject than you do. We considered him as a candidate for Corpus. We chose not to pursue the matter, and based on your material, I would agree that choice was probably wise.

"For many of the same reasons, we are concerned about reopening any possible involvement here, and question the advantage to the Service of doing so."

"Would you feel free to explain?" the admiral asked, not pleading, but with his tone making the other aware that he was asking so far, not demanding.

"His personality is stable, except under extreme stress. Under such stress, he will lose all sense of restraint, common morality, and go for the jugular. His level of stress is higher than anyone ever tested, however, which offers us all protection. His reflexes are naturally better than any single agent, possibly by a factor of two or three, and he has spent at least the last fifty stans teaching himself virtually every single personal weapon known.

"He is adept at circuit design, is probably a good journeyman systems breaker, and is one of the best pilots in Service history. We checked the drives of the *Sanducar* after she was returned. Although they tested normally, indications were that the grav governors had been reset to a higher tolerance, then returned to normal. Given any amount of time, he could do the same to any ship. We do not know what level of acceleration he could tolerate and still function at peak efficiency, but it is high enough to give him an insurmountable edge over any ship fast enough to pursue . . ."

The admiral nodded, not quite impatiently.

". . . also has contacts within the Court able to gain him an open portal to any installation. With his skills, only access would be necessary."

"But the man sleeps, doesn't he?"

"He may. Remember there are at least eight other so-called devilkids fully trained, most of whom have similar skills, who remain within Recorps. All are fanatically loyal to him, and he has charged them with carrying out the reclamation effort on Old Earth. That means that they are effectively neutralized at this time."

Eye's hood lifted, and although the admiral could not see the man's eyes, he felt a chill in spite of himself.

"Don't you see, Admiral," asked the Intelligence head, "where this all leads? Do you understand why I am reluctant to take on a commission that could lead to eight totally unrestrained fanatics declaring war on us? It could take a full battle group to catch and subdue each. And for what? Because your subject made you look silly? His actions are centered on one planet. Those actions are considered idealistic by the majority of the Imperial citizenry, by the majority of the Court, and probably by the majority of the I.S.S. officer corps. Further, he has removed himself from the scene in order to prevent any reprisals at him from affecting the reclamation effort. With all that, you ask that we stir up the mess by trying to remove him?"

"Yes. No individual should be bigger than the Empire. No individual should be able to manipulate public sentiment to break Imperial laws with impunity."

"He didn't, Admiral," added Eye, his voice even softer. "He renounced any claim to return to his planet, even in death. For someone that dedicated, that is punishment. Perhaps not what you wish, but punishment nonetheless. More important, it is regarded as punishment by the majority of the older devilkids. Some of the more recently commissioned officers, as you know, still opted for the Service, and I seriously hope you rereview their records and expunge the Board of Inquiry findings."

The last sentence was nearly a command, and the admiral stiffened. "Are you telling me what to do?"

Eye shook his hooded head. "No. Just hoping you would understand all the factors Intelligence must consider. The man wants to restore his planet. He used force only when necessary and went to elaborate lengths to avoid injury to Imperial personnel. He willingly gave all the credit to the Emperor, and I might add that such news was worth a plus ten week rate for nearly a month. The Emperor knows that and appreciates it."

"But he stood the Service on end."

"That I doubt. He did upset the High Command. The Service is alive and well." Eye cleared his throat. "Do you want us to deal with the problem?"

"Yes."

Eye turned to the figure on his left.

"Clause five," suggested the cloaked figure, and even with the voice distorter, the softness of tone suggested that the speaker was a woman.

Eye returned his attention to the admiral, whose fingers drummed on the table with scarcely concealed impatience.

"We will solve the problem in our own way, subject to clause five of our charter."

"That means . . . ?"

"We undertake to solve the problem, either within or without the solution suggested, subject to the Emperor's personal review."

"Which means?" asked the admiral again.

"It means, Admiral, that I will not undertake an ill-advised removal action surely geared to cause severe casualties to both Eye section and the Service, as well as public relations and public opinion reversals of the first order, just to soothe the wounded pride of the High Command. Because you feel so strongly, however, I will take action to insure that the Emperor is protected. If my decision is incorrect, I will be removed. Removed, not replaced."

Eye nodded to the figures who flanked him.

The admiral's eyes widened, trying to focus on all three figures simultaneously, on the way the two at Eye's sides lifted their robed hands, with the strange devices.

"No—"

The admiral could feel the sudden constriction in his chest, feel the alternative waves of red and black washing up over him.

"Get him back to his office, and call a medical tech. I believe the admiral is suffering a massive heart seizure, poor man."

Clause five. That was the admiral's last thought.

Clause five.

There was in those times a prophet, and when the people asked his name, he answered not, saying instead, what I do should be remembered, for in deeds there is truth, and that truth should be remembered and live, even as men die.

A man from Denv asked the prophet this question.

If a mountain is called a mountain, men call that a fact, for the mountain is, and they can see it is. Likewise a wilderness. Likewise the stars. But when a man calls his deeds truth, are they?

When he calls a mountain the ocean, all can tell he is mistaken. But when he calls himself a prophet, or allows others to call him a prophet, no man can prove or disprove his naming.

Should the prophet walk on water and heal the sick and raise the dead, no one can say whether he is prophet or no, whether he is sent by the angels or the devils, or whether he is master or slave.

Goodness may be done by the evil to ensnare the unwary, and evil by the good to test the worthiness of the people. So by what measure can any person weigh the truth of another's deeds?

The Book of Deeds
Authorized Version (First Revision)
Old Earth, 3788 N.E.C.

III

GRIM—THAT WAS the appearance of the gardens in the central court-yard of the senior officers quarters, reflected Gerswin.

Heavy gray clouds poured out of the eastern hills and down over New Augusta, scudding across the sky so swiftly that their motion was apparent with even a single glance through the narrow windows of his room.

No rain dropped from the mass of gray, and the air beneath was preternaturally clear, as if the sky held its breath.

The senior commander turned and glanced toward the vid-screen.

"Seems like you've done this before," he said quietly, but neither the screen nor the room answered him.

High Command had not expected him to choose the Service over the newly created Recorps, and now the admirals didn't know what to do with him.

Gerswin could understand their dilemma. A desk job in New Augusta might give him access to influence or to make more trouble. At the same time, his rank would guarantee him a job with access to people and resources at any out-base. At the moment, there were no handy combat or high risk assignments for commanders where he could be placed with the hope of his not returning.

Although Corpus Corps involvement in shortening his life span was a possibility, Gerswin hoped that no one in their right mind would seriously consider assassination or removal. The subsequent inquiry would prove too unsettling and would expose too many weaknesses in both the Empire and the Service, not to mention the possibility that the devilkids might feel compelled to take on the Empire because they would regard the Empire's commitments as worthless.

But ego was a touchy subject, and Gerswin would not trust rationality to prevail, not for a time at least. For that reason were the throwing knives concealed behind his artificially stiffened waistband, the sling leathers in place. He also was devoting increased attention to his surroundings, especially when he went out.

In the interim, while the admirals decided, he reported to the detail section every morning, was updated on how no new assignments were yet available, and asked to check back the next morning. Three days earlier, he'd spent the day taking a battery of tests, and the first thing after he'd arrived had been a three-day physical.

The fact that they were still looking for somewhere to put him told him that he was disgustingly healthy, and as sane as anyone could test out.

He paced back from the portal toward the window and stopped, staring out at the grayness. Still holding back rain, the heavy clouds continued their race across the central city.

Buzz!

Making an effort not to charge the screen, he took three slow steps and acknowledged the call.

An unfamiliar face filled the screen—a tech of some indeterminate rank.

"Senior Commander Gerswin?"

"Yes?"

"This is Curvilis at the orderly's console. There is a messenger here for you."

"Yes?"

"Ser. This is very unusual. It is from the Duke of Triandna, and his person insists upon handing it directly to you."

Gerswin shook his head, then stopped as he realized that meant exactly the opposite of what the orderly expected.

"I'll be right down."

Was it Caroljoy or the Corpus Corps?

He tapped off the screen image before checking his knives. Then he palmed a miniature stunner and slipped it into the special pocket in his left sleeve.

As he departed he pulled the privacy cloak from the locker and swirled it around him. He didn't need the privacy, but the material was supposedly designed to block low energy projectiles and lasers. He let the hood fall back on his shoulders.

The corridor was empty, but rather than taking the passenger drop shaft, he turned left and headed for the freight shaft.

In quick and quiet steps from the back of the exit on the main floor, he slipped toward the main entry and the orderly's console. From the archway that separated the triangular entry hall from the back corridor where he stood in the shadows, Gerswin could see the "messenger" from the Duke, or most probably from the Duchess.

The messenger was none other than the retired I.S.S. pilot who had taken him to the Duke's estate the last time he had been in New Augusta.

No one else entered the area, nor was anyone else in evidence besides the pilot and the orderly.

"Commander?" Gerswin offered as he stepped out boldly toward the lavender-clad pilot.

"Senior Commander Gerswin, a pleasure to see you again, ser." The older man bowed slightly from the waist and straightened, handing the I.S.S. officer a sealed package that weighed close to a kilo. "Those are the papers the Duchess wanted you to have."

Gerswin covered his confusion by bowing in return. What papers?

"My thanks, Commander," Gerswin responded. "Her Grace . . . ?"

"Perhaps you should read them before . . ."

The pilot did not meet Gerswin's eyes.

"Appreciate your bringing them."

"No problem at all."

With that, the Duke's pilot was gone, leaving Gerswin holding the sealed package.

This time Gerswin took the passenger lift to his third floor room. The corridors were deserted, unsurprisingly, since most of the senior officers billeted there were undergoing full-day briefings at the Octagon, or were stationed there.

Once inside his quarters, he used some makeshift extender tools to open the package, still unwilling to stand over it and unseal the tape.

His fears proved groundless, though he put a small slit in the cover of the loose-leaf book which had been enclosed within the wrappings. A small sealed envelope, with only the notation "Lieutenant Gerswin" on it, was tucked inside the black leather covers, just in front of the title page, which stated simply: "OER FOUNDATION."

He opened the letter, setting the book on the top of the console.

Dear Lieutenant (please pardon my remembering you this way),

I think it is fair to say that I understand you a little, and have helped you in the ways that Merrel and I can. The book represents, in its own way, my only lasting gift of a material nature. Jane, of course, is another gift, but it is rather unlikely you will cross paths.

You are trying to light a light in darkness, and may this help. Other than this note, which for my own selfish reasons I cannot resist, there is no connection between the Foundation and us, nor would His Grace wish it otherwise. The Foundation is yours, and you are the Foundation. While it is modest by Imperial standards, it need not remain so, and used properly may provide you the lever you need to reclaim your heritage, and Martin's.

You have a long future, or, as the ancients put it, "many miles to go before you sleep." My rest will come soon, sooner than I had thought.

To that I am reconciled, my lieutenant, and with you go my thoughts, my memories, and what we have shared, and might have shared.

Farewell.

                                                                         CJ

The scent of the note, like the clean scent of her, burned through him with the words as he stood staring, his eyes looking through the narrow window at the courtyard garden he did not see, his left hand clutching the note, his right the envelope.

Sooner than she thought?

OER Foundation?

Miles to go before you sleep?

Reconciled to what?

The questions swirled through his thoughts like the fringes of a landspout, ripping at his composure, tearing at his guts, until the tightness in his stomach matched the stabbing behind his unfocused eyes.

Darkness, the darkness of youth, and the touch of lips under his, with the cool warmth of New Colora outside the louvered windows of a junior officer's room. Darkness, and the cooling silence of rest after fire. Darkness, after the first time he had ever whistled his song of Old Earth for anyone.

Darkness . . . darkness . . . always the darkness.

A flash of light across the rain-damped gloom of the courtyard outside finally broke through the ebbing flow of his memories, and he looked up from the chair he found himself sitting in.

1534. That was what the readout on the screen indicated. Three hours . . . more than three standard hours he had wrestled with the past, a past he had not even known meant so much until he found himself losing it, piece by piece.

He stood, squinting, shrugging his shoulders to loosen the stiffness, and trying to repress the shivers that threatened.

He looked down. The envelope was on the flat section of the wall console, but the note itself was still clutched in his left hand.

Caroljoy. I never knew . . .

"Didn't you?" he asked aloud. "Didn't you?"

There was no answer from the dark green walls, nor from the blank screen, or from its flashing red light that indicated messages stored in the system.

He ignored the messages and turned to the book—only because the pilot had suggested he read it before reacting. Carefully refolding the note, he placed it in the pocket inside the front cover, though he would remove it shortly, as she had implied he should.

"OER FOUNDATION"—that was stamped in silver letters on the spine of the book and on the otherwise blank front cover.

He leafed through the pages, skimming the contents, still standing before the console.

The shakiness in his knees reminded him that he had some physical limits, and, flicking the room's light level higher, he sat down in the single gray swivel.

After racing through the first ten pages, he shut the cover. The rest could wait until he could devote the right attitude to study and learn the contents.

Caroljoy had been right. He was the OER Foundation. Of course, she was right. She had designed it. While the Halsie-Vyr Group controlled the base assets, all income from the trust went to OER, to an account blind to Halsie-Vyr, and from which only one Senior Commander MacGregor Corson Gerswin could draw.

He shook his head. The details were overwhelming. In essence, the book was a personalized how-to manual for him . . . how to set up a double blind operation to protect himself . . . how to comply with the Imperial Tax Code—

"No!"

Caroljoy had been so thorough. She had personally picked out the offices—through an intermediary—and included a floor plan. So thorough, as if everything had to be done completely right the first time, as if there were no tomorrow. As if . . .

"Farewell?"

This time he could not stop the shivers. So he sat and trembled until they passed.

After a time he stood and went to the screen, tapping out the combination he had never used.

A woman's face appeared in the screen—hair snow-starred in the latest pattern, but slightly askew, composed, but with the smudged circles of tiredness under her eyes, eyes from which radiated the fine lines of a middle-aged woman under stress.

"Commander Gerswin, I believe."

"How did you know?" He could tell his voice was ragged.

"The Duchess left a solideo cube. She thought you would call. I think she hoped you would not accept a mere farewell note."

"Could . . . I'd like to talk to her. Come and see her if at all possible."

"It's not possible, Commander, though we all wish it were. She has some pride, and forbade it."

"I don't understand."

"She left for H'Liero yesterday, for the Mern'tang Health Center."

"Oh . . ." Another chill passed through him. The famous center accepted only cases diagnosed as terminal, and only patients who could afford the astronomical costs.

"Her mother and grandmother both died of Byclero's Syndrome. His Grace had hoped that continual treatment would lessen the chances . . ." The woman's voice died off.

Gerswin shook his head again, and again, his eyes unable to focus on the screen.

He reached out to break the connection.

"Commander." Her level tone reached him.

He stopped, blinked back the tears he did not know he had shed, wiped his eyes with the back of his sleeve, and cleared his throat.

"Yes."

"I wish she could have seen you, but you know the final stages of the disease break down most of the body's cartilage. She refused to have either you or His Grace accompany her. His Grace would have had you go in his place, even. He did not want her alone—" The woman's voice broke this time, and Gerswin waited, swallowing hard. "You know how strong-willed she was . . . she is.

"She insisted I wait for your call. She did not want to upset His Grace, but she *knew* her lieutenant would call, and someone had to tell you . . . she knew her lieutenant would call . . ."

The woman with the snow-starred hair looked down, saying nothing. Gerswin could see her fists clenched, feeling his own knotted at his sides.

"She knew you would call . . . ," repeated the woman helplessly.

"She knew," repeated the senior commander. "She knew so much." The silence fell on both screens. "What can I do?"

"You have done all that you can . . . more than . . . many . . ." The woman visibly pulled herself together. "I asked her what I could say to you—if, when, you called. She said you would know, but that if I had to say anything, that she would see you at the end of time. That hers was the shorter journey, and the easier."

He said nothing, but nodded twice. Then he cleared his throat again. "Let me know. Let me know." He could say no more, and his hand lashed out at the screen controls. The image faded into gray.

Forcing himself to unclinch his fists, he took four steps to the narrow oblong window and peered at the smudged lights above the rain-damped garden.

"Hers was the shorter journey . . . Caroljoy . . . I never knew . . . never knew . . . But you did . . . You always did."

As he stood before the rain and storm, the darkness solidified within.

THE FOREVER HERO

Call him hero after all heroes had died.
Call him champion when none else had tried.
Call him saviour of a land left burned.
Call him a destroyer of shambles unlearned.

Call him a name, a title, a force.
Call him devil, or the land's source.
Call him soldier, pilot, or priest.
Call him the greatest, or term him beast.

But remember he stood, and stretched tall,
Where others crawled, or stood not at all.
Remember the captain, and call him Lord.
Remember the sheath is not the sword.

Anonymous
Quoted in *Ballads of the Captain*
Edwina de Vlerio
New Augusta, 5133 N.E.C.

THE CAPTAIN OF the *Fleurdilis* frowned as he studied the hard copy of the schematic. He supposed he could have used the screen, rather than having gone to the trouble of having the pages printed, but he liked to be able to wander around the cabin with the diagrams, to be able to make notes at odd times without having to code up the file, to puzzle through the codes and routings.

He still didn't understand all the details represented in the diagrams, but he knew enough to understand that the ship whose command he had just assumed was not configured according to her own specifications, or that the ship's own databanks did not register the differences.

Admittedly, the majority of discrepancies were minor, where conduit blocs had been shifted less than a meter, in one case, to accommodate modifications to the forward launch tubes. But some were scarcely minor. The *Fleurdilis* no longer carried the installed equipment for its own emergency field recharging, nor did it carry the original energy capacitators, nor the original drive field equipment.

The newer equipment was not only smaller, but, compared to the original specifications, far less powerful.

In short, he was saddled with command of a nominal cruiser, but one with less real power than an old-style corvette. The lower power capability reduced range, screen defenses, and survivability.

He touched the console, without looking at the image that formed on the screen.

"Yes, Commander?"

"Send up Senior Technician Relyea, if she's available."

"Yes, ser."

The senior commander straightened his blacks, set down the schematics, and paced in a narrow circle in the small stateroom as he waited.

"Technician Relyea, Commander."

The woman was petite, scarcely even to his shoulder, with brown hair knotted into a neat bun, black eyes, and new senior tech insignia on her collars.

"Sit down." He pointed to the single guest chair.

She sat.

"Have you studied the basic schematics?" He pointed at the diagrams on the console.

She peered at them momentarily. "Not in detail. Those are really not much good."

"Figured that out. Why weren't they updated? Means that the information in the databanks isn't reliable."

The senior tech pursed her lips. "Not exactly, Commander. The data entries are not all they should be, but the correct information is there. Provided you know the keys . . ."

The Commander, still standing, turned and looked down at her. "Go ahead."

"When the downsizing orders came through, as each ship went through refit, new specs were added to the databanks. The originals were left." She lifted her shoulders. "Just in case, I suppose."

"Downsizing orders?"

"The CommFleet Order . . . about five years ago . . . the one that was to reduce fleet energy consumption by thirty percent, except for the First and Fifth fleets, and, of course, the scouts."

"Did the rest of the galaxy downsize as well?" the commander snapped. "Forget that," he added abruptly. "Planetside at the time." He paused before continuing. "Was there any official explanation?"

Relyea cocked her head to one side. "Then I was number two on the *Bolivar*, chief tech ops, not on admin, but I recall the official reason was that an analysis of the Fleet had shown that in ninety-eight percent of all operations no more than fifty percent of the available power levels was ever required. Don't hold me to the exact numbers, but that was the general idea."

"Too much peacetime." He frowned. "About the specifications?"

"Yes. The new ones are under 'Ship Specifications—downsized.' As you'd expect . . ."

"If one knew," added the Commander.

"If one knew."

The five-by-five cabin seemed to shrink, though it was more than twice the size of most cabins on the cruiser.

"If I might ask . . . Captain," ventured the technician.

"Ask."

"How did you end up with the *Fleurdilis*?"

The commander smiled. The senior technician, for her more than thirty years of service, shrank from the expression.

"Because someone wants to file me away, preferably to make a mess of it as well, Relyea, and I don't intend to." The hawk-yellow eyes bored into her. "Now. What other technical changes and booby traps are buried in this obsolescent excuse for a fighting ship?"

"That would be hard to say, Captain."

"Don't care how hard or how long. You either know, or you don't. If you know, start telling me. If you don't, tell me, and go and find out. If I find out before you, we'll discuss your request for a transfer."

"You aren't serious . . ."

"Relyea, I am very serious. We have orders to break orbit for my first patrol in two standard weeks. I intend to know the personnel background on every crew member cold before we break. Same for technical specs. Same for the teamwork that exists or doesn't."

"Captain, I doubt that any line officer has requested or learned the technical details of his command."

"I did, and I will here. As for the others, I wouldn't be surprised. Precedent is irrelevant. By the way, can you install a power diverter from the screens and grav fields to the drives?"

"Could be done, I suppose."

"Good. Let me see your proposal by, say, 1800, tomorrow."

"What do you have in mind?"

"Without full screen power, at least ought to be able to get to hell and gone out of trouble."

Relyea nodded slowly.

"Anything else I should know?" asked the captain.

The senior technician frowned, looked at the deck, then into the hawk-yellow eyes. She looked back at the deck. Finally she stared at the wall.

The captain waited, knowing this time he could not afford to push.

The technician cleared her throat, once, twice.

The senior Commander slowly folded the older schematics, until they were small enough to fit into the single drawer under the console.

"Personnel . . . have you studied any . . . ?"

"Taken a quick scan through the entire crew."

"Your initial reaction?" The brisk voice was now tentative.

"Take some work to shape up."

Relyea nodded once.

Again the captain smiled the smile that flared like a predator's before he spoke.

"Noticed a few other things, Relyea. Not one senior rating with time in grade left. Not one outstanding performance score. Forty percent of the crew transferred in within the last three standard months. The scheduled refit postponed until *after* our first two patrols. Are those the sorts of things you're suggesting?"

The senior technician frowned, "Outside of the specs, you seem to have found out a great deal in the three days you've been aboard."

"One thing I haven't found out, Relyea. Most important of all."

"And that is, ser?"

"Who I can trust. Who is responsible."

The senior technician swallowed. Swallowed again. "Captain . . . you give us orders. We'll get them done."

The senior commander nodded. "Understand." His voice was surprisingly soft. "I understand, Chief Technician. And I'll make it clear, quite clear, that *you* are the senior technician."

"Thank you, Captain." Relyea's voice picked up. "Do you want a quick rundown on what the other spec changes are and the difficulties? Now? Or later?"

"Can you run it into the system, under 'Captain's Specs,' for me to study later tonight?"

"Give me two or three hours."

The captain nodded. "Tomorrow," he added, "right at 1400, Relyea, you'll take me on a tech walk-through. Want to meet every one of your techs. Every last one. Let them see me, see that line and tech work together."

He turned directly to the thin-faced and older-looking woman. "I will work through my senior tech, and the senior tech will work for the captain and for the good of the ship."

Relyea shivered at the intensity in the yellow eyes.

"I understand, Captain."

His face smoothed out into a calmer expression, somehow, although none of his features had changed. "Looking forward to seeing your analysis. Very much. Anything else?"

"No, ser. No, ser."

"Until 1400 tomorrow, then."

She stood, saluted, and left.

The captain slowly shook his head. He hoped he could pull the *Fleurdilis* together . . . somehow.

"TORP AWAY, CAPTAIN."

"Stet."

Gerswin returned his full attention to the ranked screens before his control couch, but did not tighten the accerleration harness.

"Determined their frequencies, Comm?"

"That's affirmative, Captain. But they're using a nonscanned transmission. Burst-blast."

"Complete new image with each burst, rather than a continuous scan?"

"Stet."

"Can we convert?"

"Negative. Not within orbit time."

"Guns, do we have a better screen analysis?" Gerswin's eyes flickered over the third screen.

"Negative."

Take one outmoded cruiser, underpowered, out on the Imperial fringes, and order the captain to investigate strange transmissions, without any backup. Then have the ship find a new alien space-going civilization, and leave the decisions in the hands of the captain. That was what he faced.

No time to torp back for instructions, instructions that would probably amount to "Use your own judgement."

"Captain?"

Gerswin snapped his head up at the voice of the Executive Officer.

"Yes, Major Strackna?"

"Do you intend to continue toward orbit around the home planet?"

"Yes."

"Might I ask why?"

"Because our orders indicate that if initial survey indicates the culture is less advanced, we are to initiate contact."

"There are four large ships there, waiting, and the emissions beyond their screens indicate they are all carrying fusactors, or the local product." Strackna's thin lips pressed together tightly after she finished.

Gerswin nodded. "That would seem to indicate no jumpshift technology."

"Captain, Comm here. How soon before the next out-torp?"

"Hold on that until we have something new to report."

"Stet."

"That gives them more than eight times the power reserves we possess," persisted Strackna.

"Without anywhere near the screens we have, Major."

"This could be suicide."

"I'll do my best to avoid that, Major. Suggest you return to your station. May need all the screens and power I can get."

Gerswin refrained from shaking his head. Of the entire crew, the Executive Officer remained the biggest headache he had inherited. The only possible reason for her rank was her family connections. Once Gerswin had thought the I.S.S. above that. While he knew better, it didn't make solving the problem any easier.

The *Fleurdilis* was edging toward the alien's geocentric orbit station, right above the largest broadcast power source on the planet. Gerswin would have bet that the station was close to directly above the planetary capitol or what passed for it.

The ship shivered slightly as the antique antigravs failed to compensate evenly for the deceleration. Gerswin frowned as he scanned the screens, but he did not move to take over from Senior Lieutenant Harsna as the lieutenant continued the approach to the orbit station.

A tight smile played around the captain's face.

He knew all too well the gambit the *Fleurdilis* represented. An obsolete ship, crewed by a group of misfits, would be no loss to the Empire. Since the Dismorph Conflict, and the years that had passed since without event, more and more systems had come to question the value of the Empire and the resource taxes necessary to support it. Another alien adventure would be just the thing to drum up enthusiasm.

The Imperial strategists couldn't lose. If the *Fleurdilis* succeeded, then the newshawks would be told how a single obsolete ship, which was all that could be spared, overcame incredible odds continually one step from disaster. And if the *Fleurdilis* failed . . . what could one expect without greater support from the allied systems?

Besides, if the failure led to another war, then the Empire could use the war as an excuse to rebuild and strengthen its holds on territory and resources and to discredit the peacemonger critics.

Gerswin glanced across the command bridge at Major Strackna, who scanned the power screens, all of them, not just the summaries represented on his console. Her jaw was tightly clinched, he could see.

He doubted she would ever understand just how expendable the Empire thought she was.

"Stationary in orbit, Captain."

"Thank you, Harsna."

"The four alien ships are spreading."

"Stet." Gerswin could see that himself. He stabbed a glowing stud. "Captain here. Any guesses on the magnitude of their screens?"

"Nothing definite, but from the background radiation, which seems to be residual secondary associated with fusactors, I'd have to say that their screens are not designed to block energy weapons or even high-speed torps."

Gerswin pursed his lips. If so . . . the aliens had one or two obvious options.

If they were xenophobic, they would have already tried to destroy the *Fleurdilis* before it settled in orbit. That they hadn't meant that either they didn't think they could or didn't want to.

If they couldn't—

"Multiple launchings."

"Permission to destroy attackers, Captain!" demanded Strackna.

"Permission denied," snapped Gerswin, touching another stud. "Estimated ETA at *Fleurdilis?*"

"Twelve plus, Captain."

"Strackna, draw our screens back to hull plus one."

"Retreat screens, Captain? Hull plus one?"

"Screens at hull plus one. Screens at hull plus one."

"But—"

"That's a boarding party, Major. They're not about to fry their own, which means they either don't have penetrating lasers or particle beams or tacheads, or that they don't want to use them. Blast their boarding party and Istvenn knows what they'll do."

"Batteries on full. Stand by to fire!" ordered Strackna.

Gerswin could see Lieutenant Harsna's mouth drop open, and the look of disbelief in Relyea's face.

Gerswin stabbed his own overrides.

"This is the captain. Negative the last. All batteries stand down. All batteries stand down."

No sooner had he finished the statement than he dove off the command couch like a hawk toward the Exec's station.

"Stand by! Stand by—!"

Thud!

Gerswin's shoulder knocked the Executive Officer away from her console. His hands flashed twice.

Then he stood up abruptly and touched the vacated console.

"All batteries stand down. I say again. All batteries stand down."

"Standing down. Standing down."

"Lieutenant Harsna!"

"Yes, ser."

"As of this instant, you are acting Exec. Have Major Strackna confined to quarters and a guard posted. She is relieved until further notice."

Gerswin ignored the collective sigh that crossed the bridge and checked the figure lying on the deck. Strackna, unconscious, was breathing evenly, and had no obvious injuries.

"Estimate plus eight for arrival of alien boarding party."

"Get my suit ready, Riid. My suit and a scooter."

"Captain . . . do you think that is wise?" That was Relyea, the senior tech.

"If I'm wrong, and if the aliens blast me, or if I don't return within a standard week, then you can release Major Strackna with my posthumous apologies. Until then, Lieutenant Harsna will be acting Captain."

"You're not leaving the ship?"

"You must have a reason, Captain," said Harsna slowly.

"I do, Harsna. I do. Too many people lost their lives unnecessarily in the last great Imperial adventure. Some were close to me. These aliens aren't a threat now, and they may never be one.

"If I'm right . . . well . . . you'll see. Guns! Have a spare tachead?"

"Not spare, Captain. But we have one."

"What's the closest point at which a detonation is safe for those aliens? Assume our metabolism and no suit shields."

"I wouldn't recommend any closer than a thousand kays, and that's probably too close."

"All right, set one for two to two point five straight out. Ninety from the orbit station. Launch when ready."

"Plus one from launch, Captain."

"Five plus for alien arrival."

Gerswin nodded.

"Suit ready, Riid?"

"Ready, Captain."

"As soon as we get a burst on the tachead, I'll be down. Have the scooter ready."

"Yes, ser."

"You think the tachead will awe them?" asked Harsna.

"No, but their techs will note torp speed and burst size. Shortly it might dawn on them that we possess the power to pulverize their system. That won't awe them at all, I suspect, but it should make them cautious."

"Tachead away! Tachead away!"

For the miniature jumpshift of the torp, two thousand kays amounted to an instantaneous burst.

For an instant, a second sun flared far behind the *Fleurdilis.*

Gerswin did not wait for the light to fade, but headed for the main lock, and the suit that waited for him.

"Plus three to alien arrival."

Now all he had to do was survive and return before an entire week passed.

"Confident, aren't you?" he muttered as he swung into the armorer's bay.

"Suit's here, Captain," Riid said quietly.

Gerswin repressed a smile.

Riid had ignored the letter of his order, instead had readied one of the five Imperial Marine Marauder suits, obviously previously tailored for Gerswin without his knowledge.

"Feedback circuits might be rough, Captain, but you're not going without the best I can do."

"Appreciate it, Riid. Appreciate it."

He reached across to the console. "Bridge, Captain here. Harsna, bulge the screens a little, and push them back gently for a couple of minutes. Soon as I'm clear of the lock, drop the screens and reform them right on the hull itself. Understand?"

"Stet. You need the time, and we'll reform behind you. Major Strackna's under restraint. No problem."

"Thanks."

Gerswin devoted his energies to getting installed inside the armor.

It could be a damned-fool idea, but he owed something to Martin, and to Faith, and to the poor, unsuspecting aliens. And this was the best he could come up with on short notice, the best possible with an obsolete cruiser that the Empire would have preferred as a martyr to Imperial expansion.

Not that any devilkid, even one who now wore the insignia of an Imperial Senior Commander, intended to submit to martyrdom, inadvertent or otherwise.

He grinned behind the suit's face screen. All the years of practice in esoteric and often theoretically obsolete weapons just might prove useful in the official line of duty. Official line of duty—wonderful phrase.

Absently he wondered if Martin had felt the same inane relief at the thought of action and the ability to use long-sharpened skills. Had his son felt the same way on that day so many years earlier? He could feel the sweat beading on his forehead. Martin certainly hadn't wanted to be hero or martyr, any more than his father now did.

"Are you subconsciously out to avoid the duty Caroljoy laid on you?" The words were low, addressed only to himself.

"What's that, Captain?"

"Muttering to myself, Riid."

He wanted to wipe his damp forehead with the back of his hand. He settled for rubbing it against the suit's sweat pad.

Besides, Caroljoy hadn't forced him to do anything. Just made it possible to follow his own expressed dream.

Dream?

He pushed away the question, refocused his eyes on the suit's internal indicators, and steeled his thoughts on the encounter ahead.

THE WAILING FROM the four-piece group reminded Gerswin of a landspout when it struck a fast-flowing river—screeches, gurgles, and dull thuds. Despite the strange assortment of sounds, behind the surface chaos was a clearly identifiable theme—harmony.

Only the silence of those listening around the arena kept Gerswin from snorting aloud, but he maintained his attentive and superficially reverent position while studying the guards around him, and beyond them the red stone arena. He had mentally dubbed the aliens Ursans, for want of a better term, and because they resembled bears more than any other of the animals he had run across.

One of the Ursan officers, or clan leaders, or whatever their class of leaders were called, stepped a pace closer, but did not look directly at the I.S.S. officer.

While Gerswin didn't understand the language, he had a fair idea why he had been escorted to the arena near what he thought was the capitol. He hoped he was right.

Although he had misgivings about leaving the *Fleurdilis* in Lieutenant Harsna's hands, with Major Strackna unstable and under restraint, there hadn't been any real alternative. Strackna was not only Imperialistic, but xenophobic to boot. While she was a competent Service officer in peacetime or in all-out war, she was precisely the wrong person for any sort of alien contact. Strackna would have no compunctions about unleashing all of the *Fleurdilis'* tacheads at the Ursan capitol, without even understanding the implications.

Gerswin repressed a sigh as the strange musical wheezings continued. While the Empire might benefit from another repeat of the Dismorph Conflict, that was the last thing he needed, the last thing needed by the majority of the people of the Empire, and certainly the last thing needed by the Ursans, whether they understood or not.

Gerswin brought his mind and thoughts back to the present and the red stone arena. To forestall Strackna and the rest of the hawks, he would need every bit of skill he had developed over the last half century. He wondered if it had really been that long.

The captain of the obsolete cruiser that orbited directly overhead, albeit nearly thirty-five thousand kays above his head, hoped he had guessed correctly about the aliens, and about their culture.

He shrugged to himself. If not, it was already too late, but the signs were there that he had not.

He took a deep breath and almost choked. The Ursans smelled like a cross between wet coydog and rancid fish.

They resembled the pictures of bears he had seen in the archives, but their pelts were red—eye-searing red. Their heads rose directly from broad shoulders, with no necks as such. Their respective heights varied only slightly, but most stood ten to fifteen centimeters shorter than Gerswin. Their squarish bodies massed more; how much would have been a guess.

Like bears, they had claws, but thinner claws and fully retractable. Their fingers were more like claw sheaths, and the lack of flexibility was offset by two opposing thumbs on each hand, which did not contain claws.

He studied the Ursan closest to him, watching the slight chest movements in an effort to analyze the breathing patterns. From what he could tell, both chest and back expanded. He speculated on whether the lungs were based more on a bellows concept and jointed cartilage separating two stiff rib plates.

The anthem, if that was what it had been, screeched to a close, and the honor guard shambled forward, their motion designed either to force Gerswin to come along, or to start a fight under the arched gate to the arena.

From the opposite gate he could see another guard group, although the individual being escorted was an Ursan of some rank.

That, again, was a guess, but the guards around Gerswin wore only plain purple leather harnesses, on which hung servicable long knives and short swords. The dignitary around whom the other guards clustered wore a silvered harness with clearly more refined weapons.

Gerswin carried no weapons, none except for the throwing knives concealed in his waistband.

Despite the lack of technology in their personal weaponry, the Ursans were not primitives. The four spacecrafts that had met the *Fleurdilis* had been nuclear powered and carried defensive energy screens against meteors. They had to have chosen the boarding party technique for cultural reasons, not for lack of more sophisticated weapons.

Gerswin almost shook his head in retrospect. With a handful of devilkids, he could have disarmed the Ursan boarding parties on the spot.

With Lerwin and Lostwin and Kiedra, or Glynnis . . . but the devilkids were on Old Earth, busy trying to reclaim their poor poisoned planet, busy buying time for Gerswin, busy and secure in their belief that their efforts mattered.

They did, but not in the way the left-behind devilkids thought.

Still, a handful of trained devilkids could have prevented the situation in which he found himself. When the Ursans had launched four shuttles filled with warriors, Gerswin had faced the choice of incinerating the shuttles and possibly starting another system war, which meant the destruction or immediate subjection of the Ursans, or ignoring the shuttles, leaving the *Fleurdilis* safe behind unbreachable screens. The passive use of screens could only have encouraged the Ursans in the belief that the Imperials were personal cowards, and such a belief would lead to contempt . . . and to eventual rebellion and war.

That had left Gerswin with the need to outface the Ursans personally, meeting them alone outside the *Fleurdilis*, in the hope of instilling respect for the Empire without the cost of destroying the Ursan culture and society. Not that some Imperials wouldn't have relished that destruction.

Strackna had tried to blast them out of existence—until Gerswin had her locked up. And Harsna thought he was crazy. Maybe he was.

So . . . here he was, standing in the middle of an arena, basing his future on the possibility that he was facing a warlord-personal-honor-type mentality.

The guards backed away abruptly and left Gerswin in the center of a hollow square of Ursans. The silver-harnessed Ursan stood on the other side.

Gerswin saw the scars, the slight discoloration of the bright red pelt hairs, and spit on the hard-packed clay in the direction of the other.

A hiss ran around the arena. Gerswin couldn't tell what it meant for certain, but it was the first reaction of any sort, and he couldn't tell what the following grunts and clicks signified.

Two of the guards lifted their knives. Gerswin stepped toward the guards and motioned them back. They looked at each other and halted.

"Look. I didn't say I wouldn't fight. I said I wouldn't fight him or her, or whatever. No status."

He elaborately raised his hands and frowned, dropped his arms to his sides, half-turning from the Ursan champion.

A series of sounds, more screeches and gurgles, issued from the four Ursan instrumentalists, and the square of guards opened. From the far side of the arena a series of steps was extended, and another Ursan appeared sedately strolling down to the hard-packed clay.

Gerswin turned back to study his potential adversary. The second Ursan was not scarred, not obviously, though the reddish pelt could conceal most anything, and it moved with greater assurance than the first.

Gerswin repeated his charade.

This time the entire squad of guards reached for their knives.

"Only once?"

Gerswin motioned them back and turned to face full on the recent arrival, noting that the first "dignitary" had retired to the side of the arena.

His current opponent motioned to a guard, who stepped forward carrying a short sword or long knife, and a longer sword, apparently a match to what the Ursan wore strapped to his or her harness.

The commander took the knife first, testing its balance and construction. It was designed as a thrusting instrument.

The sword was more of a heavy cutting blade. Both fit with what Gerswin suspected about the Ursan physiology. He hoped he could give the aliens a lesson in psychology as well.

Smiling wryly, he took the heavy blade, after thrusting the knife into his waistband.

Talk about ethnocentrism! The Ursans obviously believed that any culture would follow patterns similar to their own. Most I.S.S. Commanders would have blasted all four boarding parties and proceeded from there.

Gerswin was gambling, gambling that his reflexes and abilities would enable him to come out on top, gambling that his observations were accurate enough for him to do what he wanted.

Each of the score of Ursan guards stepped back several more paces and the square expanded again.

The Ursan champion faced the I.S.S. Commander and touched his sword to the clay before him.

Gerswin raised his sword, then touched it to the arena clay, whipping it up and dancing aside just in time to avoid the pounding rush of the Ursan.

No polite fencing here! Gerswin avoided three back to back cuts from the other's heavy blade with footwork, using his own more as a shield than as a weapon.

The alien's slashes, seemingly awkward, whistled by Gerswin's legs or arms.

Gerswin leaned in, back, forward, occasionally deflecting the other's slashes, but carefully avoided taking the full brunt of the other's attack.

Almost as suddenly as the rushes had begun, the Ursan circled backward and began a circling stalk, as if to get behind Gerswin.

The Ursan's breathing deepened into an odd wheezing sound.

Gerswin moved toward the Ursan, bringing the heavy blade around.

The Ursan countered, trying to catch Gerswin's blade edge on. Gerswin twisted the borrowed blade, letting it slide off, and ducking inside the other's sweep, tapped the alien on the chest with the dullish point. There was no penetration of the solid bone plate under the reddish fur and muscles.

"*Wheeze!*"

Rolling hard left, Gerswin could feel the other's sword crossing where he had just been.

Once more, the Ursan began a furious attack of crisscrossing sword sweeps that would have been awkward were it not for the speed of the blade.

"All right, friend. Play for keeps."

Again, after the mad and sustained fury of the attack, the Ursan backed off and wheezed; almost as if pumping up his system with oxygen.

The Ursan tactics were becoming painfully obvious. Whichever fighter could last longer in the high effort attacks, whichever fighter needed less of a recharge would inexorably force the other into an ever-increasing oxygen debt—unless the less conditioned fighter was far better with the pair of blades.

Already Gerswin's arms were feeling the strain, and he'd been careful not to take any blows directly. So much for conditioning.

Thud! Thud! Hiss! Hiss!

The Ursan was back at it, throwing quick stroke after quick stroke at the I.S.S. Commander.

Gerswin continued to duck or deflect the other's blows, watching the pattern of cuts.

This time the Ursan kept at it nearly twice as long, as if he sensed the human's tiredness, before retreating to the circling and defensive stalk.

As soon as the Ursan dropped beyond quick thrust range, Gerswin switched the long blade into his right hand and the short thrusting blade into his left hand.

With a flowing motion, he threw the thrusting blade, rifling it straight at the right-side junction between the Ursan's shoulder and head.

The sharp-edged blade went half its length into the heavy muscles and stopped with a clunk. Maroon fountained darkly down the Ursan's chest for an instant before the alien dropped both knife and long sword and collapsed in a heap, still clawing at the embedded weapon.

"Hsssssssss!"

The disapproval of the crowd was deafening, but Gerswin marched forward and extracted the short knife, picked up the deceased dignitary's weapons, and marched through the square of Ursans toward the black-rimmed box from where he hoped the powers-that-be had watched.

He located an Ursan wearing a black-rimmed silver harness, bowed, and placed all four weapons on the clay between him and the senior Ursan.

"All right, fellows or ladies, I'd like to go home."

The Ursan looked undecided. At least, he did nothing.

Gerswin took a deep breath and pulled one of the throwing knives from his belt, displayed it, then let it rest on his palm. He studied the crowd, looking for a suitable target. The arena was plain, with a straight metal railing and no statues. Gerswin shrugged.

Finally, he took his foot and scratched an *X* in the clay, then turned and walked five, six, seven, eight paces, then whirled, throwing the knife as he turned.

The heavy blade buried itself to the hilt at the crossed lines of the *X*.

Another *"Hssssss"* roared from the crowd.

Gerswin continued his steps and stooped, pulled the knife from the clay, wiped it clean on his tunic, and replaced it in his belt.

Then he walked the last steps to the laid-out weapons, picked up the Ursan knife he had used, raised it as a salute, and plunged it into the clay so it stood like a cross between him and the Ursan leader.

The Ursan stood, and in turn raised his arms, claws extended, then lowered them, retracting the claws and turning his hands upward, so that they remained empty and weaponless.

Gerswin repeated the gesture, minus claws, since he had none. *"Ummmmmmhhhhh."*

Gerswin could sympathize with the disappointment of having to acknowledge the loss of the local hero, but when they learned the real score, he suspected the Ursans would be much happier that the local hero had lost to the outlander who had cheated by, stars forbid, throwing a short sword.

Already the guards who had escorted him were reforming, but this time he noticed with a scarcely concealed grin, the leader was offering, by gesture, the place of honor.

He followed the guards back to one of the Ursan shuttles for the ride up to the *Fleurdilis* and a sure-to-be-disappointed Major Strackna.

FOR THE FOURTH time the Commodore frowned at the senior commander across the wardroom table that had been covered temporarily with the red felt that signified a Board of Inquiry.

"Let me get this clear. You felt that accepting a single combat challenge would make life *easier* for the Empire? By setting a precedent where every time the Ursans feel like it, they could challenge an Imperial ship on a man-to-man basis?"

The senior commander shook his head. "No, Commodore. The point was much simpler. They lost on their own terms, on their own territory, with their own weapons, to an outlander who had no experience in their rituals. The next step is to demonstrate that they are so outmatched in weapons and technology that they have to join the Empire on our terms."

"What about the risk? How did you know you could win?"

"I didn't. Good guess. Based on several factors. Had to be a unified planetary culture. Also had to be based on individual combat."

The commodore waved vaguely at the sheet before him. "I know it's in the staff report, and the ethnologists have supplied sheet after sheet of ethnology equations that support your guesses. But how could you subject the Empire to that kind of risk through mere guesses?"

"Commodore, ser. Considerable risk for me. None for the Empire. Also considerable risk for the Ursans."

The commodore motioned for the senior commander to continue.

Gerswin cleared his throat. "If I had been defeated, then the Empire still could have blasted chunks out of Ursa IV, and with even greater justification. Done what most commanders would have done in the first place. Ursans have no heavy screens, only for debris, and have avoided developing long range weapons. That's why they have to have developed a workable planetary culture."

"How does that follow?" The commodore's puzzled expression indicated his lack of understanding.

"Nationalism always puts the culture above the individual. Culture based on individual prowess almost always loses to one based on nationalism. In the crunch, nationalist cultures use whatever they have to, no matter what the consequences. What nearly destroyed Old Earth the first time.

"In an individualist culture, some things you will not do. If you do, the culture will destroy you. So . . . Ursans couldn't have space travel, advanced technology, *and* individual prowess tests unless they had unified planetary culture."

The commander was still shaking his head. He could not understand, and Gerswin understood why.

Finally the commodore asked another question. "Why did you say there was considerable risk to the Ursans?"

"Simple. If I lost, the Empire would have blasted the planet, or at least the space-going ships. Would have claimed that the Ursans were barbarians who demanded that their leaders solve disputes through personal combat. Incompatible with civilization and decency."

"Barbarians indeed," confirmed the commodore. "One last question, Commander. Why didn't you just ignore their boarding parties?"

"Thought about that. Problem was that it would take years to undo the image. If we didn't at least meet them face to face, then the Empire would be regarded as bullies and cowards rolled into one. Ursans might knuckle under to brute force, but would begin relation with the Empire from a basis of contempt. Leads to unrest, maybe revolution. So we'd be back on a conflict basis within a decade. This way, we bought some time."

"How much?"

"A good century, my guess, if you get a couple of good Corpus Corps types to act as champions every once in a while."

The commodore nodded, then tapped the stud on the control box by his right hand.

"Now, Commander," growled the commodore, "the question is what to do with you."

"Nothing," suggested Gerswin.

"Commander—"

"I'm not being flippant, Commodore, ser. Your experts have begun the real work with the Ursans. I made the entry easier. Take credit for the peaceful contact. If I had failed, you would have taken the blame."

The commodore reflected, pursing his lips. "And what about Major Strackna? Your Executive Officer? She recommends your court-martial."

"That's because she wanted to blast the Ursans out of existence. Wouldn't let her. Her specialty was alien relations. She had an attack of acute xenophobia and tried to blow the Ursan boarding parties into dust, after I ordered her not to. Not for her distrust of my decision that I recommended her court-martial and dismissal. Because she disobeyed a direct order when the ship was not in danger."

"Wasn't your report rather harsh?"

"Don't think so, Commodore," answered Gerswin, ignoring the implied suggestion that he change his recommendation that Strackna be cashiered from the Service. "Major Strackna did not act to override me from a well reasoned difference of opinion or knowledge, nor to save the ship. Just because she hated aliens she hadn't seen. Aliens couldn't hurt the *Fleurdilis*.

"Preliminary evidence showed they had no projective weapons, no screens to stop our weapons. She kept trying to destroy them against evidence, against orders." Gerswin shook his head. "No captain should ever have to tolerate that, and no subordinate should have his or her life risked by such an attitude."

"How should we handle you?" The commodore's glance was direct.

"Don't. Ships survive because they act as a team. Think you should give the entire ship a letter of commendation, outlining the contribution the whole crew made."

"Commending them for what?"

"For handling a delicate situation with the care that reflects favorably upon the Service and the Empire. The Ursans are learning who's boss, and it only cost one tachead and not one casualty for us. Only cost them one casualty."

The commodore worried his thin lips, darted a look at the closed portal before speaking again.

"Assuming your analysis is correct, and the experts seem to feel it is, *you* deserve the commendation, not the ship."

"Commodore, the crew deserves the commendation for not going off half-blasted and trying to pull their C.O. out of a mess. I blasted it. Nearly failed. Didn't because the Ursans have some common sense, and because their leader's sharp."

The commodore sighed. "Everything is more complicated than it seems. Would you mind explaining, since I don't seem to understand the logic here?"

"Ursans don't fight to kill. Probably only have a few flesh wounds. We're not built like them. I had to kill him—her—because I couldn't figure out the rituals. That's why the Ursan crowd was so upset. Don't like unnecessary killing."

A wintry smile crossed the commodore's leathery face.

"The implications are obvious, and far-reaching, Commander." He looked down, then at the red felt covering the table, picked up the sheet before him, and looked up. "Your talents are underestimated, and I wish we could afford to promote you to the General Staff. In any case, I'm taking your recommendation, with a slight upgrading. The *Fleurdilis* will be recommended for a distinguished service medal for all crew, and you will receive a polite letter of personal commendation. Enough to make it clear that you did a good job and that the letter is *not* a formality."

"Thank you, Commodore. The crew will appreciate the honor, and they do deserve it." The senior commander waited, eyes meeting the commodore's.

"That will be all, Commander Gerswin."

Gerswin rose. "Yes, ser. By your leave, ser?"

The commodore nodded. "I'll have the announcement made shortly." He gestured toward the portal.

Gerswin saluted, then turned and left.

Wars are fought because someone can generate the impression of loss, or the impression of gain. Take away that impression, and you make it that much harder to generate support for war.

Wars can only be fought with popular support or with centralized government control. Centralized and strong governments arise because of the perception of unmet needs. They maintain power because they generate new perceptions of needs which are unmet or by fueling the impressions which lead to war—or both.

Take away the perception of unmet needs, and strong governments find it increasingly difficult to maintain power without becoming ever more tyrannical.

> *Politics in the Age of Power*
> Exton Land
> 2031 O.E.C.

THE YOUNG WOMAN arrived at the suite portal, which did not open automatically at her approach. With a frown, she stepped aside and tapped the contract button beneath the small screen set into the left portal support panel.

The light under the screen flashed amber and settled into the green, but the screen remained blank.

"Yes?" The disembodied voice was a male, youthful sounding baritone, with a slight edge.

"I am Lyr D'Meryon. I had an appointment for 1430."

"Your pardon, Ms. D'Meryon, but a previous interview has not been completed. If you would be so kind as to wait for just a moment. When the light flashes again, please enter."

With that, the green light went out.

"What . . . what are you getting yourself into?" she asked herself. Then she shrugged and stepped back.

Should she walk to the other end of the corridor? Or stand and wait? What if the light flashed while she was turned in another direction?

If only the specs for the position hadn't been so intriguing . . . but the independence that had been spelled out between the lines was rare for any foundation, much less for the smaller ones of the type who would consider relatively junior administrators.

She glanced down at the reddish glimmers of the corridor glow tiles, then back at the screen. The light remained dark.

Next she hitched up her portfolio under her left arm and walked to the other side of the portal. The panels on the right were featureless, and she looked back at the screen on the left side. Still dark.

She bit her lower lip.

Even before the interview, she'd put hours of effort into filling out the application, which had arrived after she had expressed an interest in the position.

The original display had been simple. She recalled that clearly enough.

FOUNDATION ADMINISTRATOR

Small and independent foundation seeks full-time administrator and research coordinator. Must have background in hard and bio sciences and interest in environmental pursuits. For further information and application, contact . . .

Both hard and biological sciences, that had been the interesting point. Most foundations headquartered on New Augusta were either involved in the arts or with very specific pursuits.

Her musing almost distracted her from the flashes of the portal screen.

She hoisted the portfolio under her arm and approached the portal. This time it irised open as she walked toward it.

Once inside, she understood the reason for her wait. The small area was but a single room, served by two portals at opposite ends, presumably on different corridors. The narrow office contained two consoles, three severe straight-backed chairs, one console recliner, and a small loveseat.

Standing by the console recliner was a slender figure garbed in a black privacy cloak with a peaked hood and a black mask.

"You'll pardon the privacy, Ms. D'Meryon, but the need for a continued confidentiality is one of the reasons for our search and one of the principal reasons for specifying the qualifications we need."

Gesturing vaguely toward the arrangement of chairs and the loveseat, the man sat down.

Lyr was convinced that the man, although soft-spoken, had some sort of military background from the alertness of his carriage. She seated herself in one of the straight-backed chairs.

"While the foundation has a worthy purpose, it would not be appropriate for some of the anonymous backers to become known. Others do not wish public recognition of any sort."

"Might I ask the goals of the foundation? And its name?"

"The foundation's title is the OER Foundation, and the founders have never seen fit to disclose what the initials represent. The goals are modest, basically to endow research in certain biologic and ecologic fields. Center primarily on development of self-perpetuating reclamation, biological stabilization processes."

The black-cloaked man's masked face remained shadowed as he cleared his throat softly and continued. "Why were you interested in this particular position?"

"For a number of reasons . . ."

The standard questions about her background, her qualifications, her interest in science, all took nearly a standard hour.

Every question was politely phrased by the inquiring figure, and while the light was soft, by the time that first hour had passed, Lyr felt as though the interview was approaching an inquisition.

Finally, too late, she suspected, she interrupted.

"What does that have to do with the job? You have obviously verified all my qualifications, my references, and my background. Is this intensive reexamination merely to verify my interest or my ability to endure? What is there about this foundation that requires such painstaking evaluation of its possible administrator?"

"Are you sure you want to know that?"

"That's an odd response. My first reaction is that you're up to something illegal or exceedingly unpopular. Are you?"

"No. Popular reaction right now would probably be boredom. Intellectual reaction would probably be positive. But we're an odd foundation. Not interested in publicity. Not interested in glory, or space in the faxnews. Don't want an administrator who is. Need someone who shares our goals, someone who will pursue them and who doesn't need public acclaim to be happy on the job."

"Can you assure me that what you are pursuing is legal?"

"I can assure you that it is legal on New Augusta and throughout the Empire. Wouldn't want to speculate about other legal codes or mores."

"Fair enough." She paused, then hurried on before the man in black could speak. "The publicity angle is strange. I'll admit, because most foundations want publicity either to gain contributions or to reflect favorably on the founder. But it's not strange enough for all this secrecy. As for the goals, other than some very general guidelines, which would be impossible to follow without more detailed information, you haven't really stated a single concrete objective that an administrator would find usable. So what do you want? What are you really pushing for?"

"Before I answer that, and I will, what do you want from this job? Not the polite phrases. We're beyond that. What do you really want?"

Lyr took a deep breath.

"In one word—meaning. In two words—responsibility. And if I get three—money."

"We can deliver all three, in greater quantities than you expect. But there is a price, a high price. Perhaps higher than you would pay."

"My life?" She pursed her lips. "You can't be that melodramatic."

The interviewer laughed once, a short harsh sound. "Scarcely. Not in the sense you meant. The position could easily be a lifetime position. That's one reason for the in-depth nature of the application, the interview, and the reference checks. We also have done a background check."

Lyr's mouth opened in a small "o."

The interviewer continued, politely ignoring her surprise. "The administrator will have sole operating authority. That authority may not be delegated, although you may hire administrative assistance and other services as necessary and financially responsible."

"You are asking for a bond slave, not an administrator."

"The starting salary is sixty thousand Imperial credits annually, plus expenses and living quarters."

Lyr didn't bother to keep her mouth from dropping open.

"What unpaid other 'services' do you want? Is this offer open only to attractive young women?"

"The sarcasm doesn't become you." The gentleness of the reproach disarmed her angry cynicism.

"I don't understand. That's more than the administrators of the Emperor's Trust get paid, and they don't get quarters."

"You'll have a bigger job, and one without the overt acclaim and prestige. It may be more important in the long run."

"How big?"

"Big enough that if we go beyond this point in the conversation, and you decline, you will not walk out of here with any memory of what was discussed."

"You couldn't! You wouldn't!"

"Said it was a big job, job that requires a big person. Stakes are as idealistic as you are. More so, perhaps. Less risk from a memory blanking than from disclosure. Besides, who would you complain about? This isn't the foundation office, but rented for the interviews."

Lyr moistened her lips with her tongue.

"My head says to walk out. My heart wants to hear your offer."

"What do you know about ecologic reclamation? About the impact of organic chemical poisonings?"

"The problems with Old Earth, Marduk, and even with New Glascow. That's why the really dangerous manufacturing processes are in deep space or on hell-planets."

"How do you clean them up?"

"You don't. You'd have to scrub the soil, filter all of the groundwater, probably any oceans as well."

"So you go along with the tacit Imperial policy of avoiding the questions?"

"Take Old Earth," Lyr countered. "The government has devoted close to fifty billion creds over the last fifty years . . . maybe more. What do they have? A few thousand square kays of marginal land and a river or two that won't poison you on touching." She paused. "What does this have to do with the job? Directly?"

"Everything. The sponsors feel that real cleanup is possible with biologic agents. Agree with your assessment so far as mechanical reclamation goes. Ancient records say biological reclamation was started once, even begun to terraform totally hostile planets, but it stopped with the Great Collapse. Old Earth and Marduk were avoided since there were better places to live. Federation, and then the Empire, tried to avoid the problem by avoiding organics on inhabited planets, manufacturing in space or on waste planets for materials they couldn't do without."

The man in black stood up, his shadowed eyes looking at a point somewhere behind Lyr. "Now, the inhabited systems are growing, as well as the demand for more and more consumer goods. The Collapse is long past, and the commercial barons base their power on production. The trend is not obvious yet, but it is there."

Lyr felt, for an instant, an impression of age coming from the young-looking figure who moved with such quickness and grace that he had to be her own contemporary.

"And the foundation is worried about that?"

"By the time anyone else is worried, just as happened on Old Earth, it will be too late to do anything." The man laughed. "Even if we're wrong, biological cleanup methods will make those consumer goods cheaper."

"Istvenn . . . ," she murmured. "You really do care. . . ."

"Some of the people who created the foundation do. They wanted to encourage the discovery, the development, and the use of biological processes to reclaim chemical wasted lands, self-perpetuating and benign biological systems to maintain the ecology under the worst of stresses, and to make these processes widely available once they have been developed and field tested.

"Your job will center on the first phase, since none of these processes are known. They may be out there in the Empire, but if so, they are buried and unrecognized. As you pointed out, no one can reclaim a wasted planet like Old Earth, not even with the resources of the Empire. And already, reports of space-based contamination drifting in-system are being reported. A number of the nastier organic by-products can withstand reentry heat, particularly if they're in dust form.

"More important, with the energy costs of space transport, virtually every industrialized system has some organic production somewhere, and as demand keeps increasing, so will possible sources of contamination."

Lyr coughed to break the other's gloomy monologue. "You paint a depressing picture."

"Don't all fanatics?" He laughed again, but the laugh was without humor, except in the self-deprecation.

"What sort of operation now exists?"

"Are you interested?"

"Yes. I couldn't say why. But I am."

"Fine. The foundation has offices, plus financial resources, and an approved charter. You will not need to raise funds, but you will need to create the entire mechanism for reviewing and screening grant and research proposals, the procedures for follow-up and field testing."

"You're not serious?"

"Quite serious."

"Handing this over to someone you scarcely know?"

"Do you want the job?"

Lyr paused.

The man in black said nothing, just waited.

"Yes."

"Fine. You have it."

"I do?" Lyr looked at the other blankly.

"You do." He stretched and withdrew a card from his cloak, along with a small databloc. "The card has the foundation address. In those quarters are the basic information and equipment you will need, as well as access to the consoles. Currently, the master console is locked to your retinal prints. You can change that if you wish, but it was the safest way to begin."

"My retinal prints? But . . . how . . ."

"From this point on, you control the day-to-day operations of the Foundation, its assets, investments, and its grants."

"How did you know I would accept?"

"Didn't. But it was likely. I said we did a thorough background check on the most likely candidates. We did. Thorough. Even to the time you told your family you were going to Eltar for the summer, when instead you used the summer to raise your tuition for the university by entering that bond-contract with Farid El-Noursi. You used the name Noreen Al-Fatid. . . . Should I go on?"

Lyr could feel herself turning crimson on the exterior, and the fury building on the inside.

"Take your filthy job—"

"No."

The single, quiet word, for some reason, deflated her anger.

"Purpose wasn't to embarrass or to push. But to let you know how thoroughly we screened you. What you do with your private life is for you. But you are trustworthy, totally trustworthy, whether you will admit it publicly or not."

"If I weren't?"

"You wouldn't be here."

"What if your administrator changed? If . . . they . . . he . . . she . . . cheated you?"

"I will let you in on one thing."

"What?"

"One of the founders is a graduate of the Corpus Corps."

Despite herself, Lyr shivered.

The man gestured toward the portal, the one she had not used.

"Once you get settled, I'll be in touch to fill in the details. But remember you are the OER Foundation. Without you, it is merely an assembly of assets. For your own peace of mind, I'd suggest you tell your friends and acquaintances that you were lucky enough to land the spendthrift trust of a well-connected Imperial fuctionary.

"By the way, there is an emergency call function in the console. It cannot be tracked. No good if someone is standing by you and has a stunner to your head, but the normal security systems should prevent that. Emergency function is more for substantial policy questions where you would like guidance or to talk over the *thrust* of future decisions. Not for nuts and bolts questions . . ."

The portal opened.

"But . . . I don't understand. . . ."

"You will . . . once you look it all over. . . . You will. . . ."

Lyr stood alone in the empty corridor, shaking her head, wondering. She looked down to find her portfolio, still unopened, under her left arm, and in her right hand, the small square databloc and the foundation card.

After locking the databloc into her beltpak, she studied the address on the card.

"Hegemony Towers . . ."

She shook her head, nearly forgetting the address. How had he found out about El Lido and Farid? She had forgotten that summer as quickly as possible, even though the contract had been the only way she could have finished the university after her father's death and mother's suicide. She still shuddered at the thought . . . and the thankfully infrequent nightmares.

"Hegemony Towers . . ." She repeated the address, as if to drive away the memories.

Certainly a modest but respectable address in one of the business parks north of the capitol.

She shrugged, as if lifting a weight from her shoulders.

"Off to Hegemony Towers . . ." And to find out what she had volunteered for.

Not understanding why, she hummed happily with each step toward the drop shaft at the end of the long corridor.

"HE'S REQUESTED THAT his orders be changed to maintenance, out-base station."

The Vice Admiral for Logistics and Administration looked up from the hidden console screen, pushed back a short and straggly gray hair, one of the few he retained for impressions, and nodded. "Did he say why?"

"Standard language. For the good of the Service and for a broader exposure."

"Where's the most out-of-the-way place where there's an opening?"

"Standora. Base Commandant."

"Could he mess things up much there?"

"Admiral, that's not the problem," replied the commodore, who stood across the console. "We've checked his profile. He can run anything, probably better than ninety percent of the Service's senior officers."

"So why is his folder red-lined? Political problems with the Court?"

"Not exactly. Remember New Glascow? Where the official explanation was that the Emperor suddenly decided to dedicate more resources to rebuilding Old Earth and when he created Recorps and diverted two cohorts of combat decon dozers for effect?"

"Where the Duke of Triandna's yacht spread the word?"

"That was the official line. . . ."

"And the unofficial one?"

The commodore looked over his shoulder before realizing the portal was closed behind him.

"Commander Gerswin hijacked the *Sanducar,* borrowed the yacht without asking, and delivered the arcdozers in person, claiming that the Emperor had donated them to Old Earth. The message torps and all the publicity were touches he orchestrated . . . but no one could ever totally prove it. . . ."

"Not prove it?"

The commodore nodded slowly.

"That good. . . . I see. And how do you know?"

"My cousin was the navigator on the *Sanducar.* None of the officers ever made another rank, except one. She was wounded fighting them off."

"Your cousin?"

"Unfortunately . . . no. He's a cernadine narcie on Duerte."

"So you think Gerswin's up to no good?"

"I don't know. But he's the type that always has a purpose."

"How long has he been on the fringes?"

"Fifteen standard."

"Maybe he's tired. Even someone like him has to be running down. Send him to Standora. Five year tour. Or double tour. Surely we'll close the place by then."

The commodore kept his face expressionless. He did not argue. When the vice admiral decided, the decision was final.

"Yes, ser."

The vice admiral smiled. "I know you don't agree, Medoro, but the C.O. of an out-of-the-way, nearly unused naval refit yard isn't going to upset the Empire. How could he? The place is nearly obsolete. It only handles scouts these days, and it wouldn't be there except to funnel currency to the locals under the terms of the Sector agreement."

The Commodore nodded in return and stepped back off the Furstan carpet, his heels clicking as they touched the tiles.

Then he turned.

"If it makes you feel better," added the vice admiral, "you can code a memo to the file on your misgivings. I'll even review it."

"I just might, Admiral."

"Always the cautious one, Medoro. Remember, caution saves worlds, but it doesn't make them."

THE SCREEN LIT as Lyr acknowledged, and the cloaked face of her interviewer appeared.

"Have you had a chance to study the accounts in detail?"

"Yes." Her voice was cold. She had been waiting to question him.

"Questions?"

"Who is empowered to draw on the Special Operations Account? For what? Then there's the Reserve Fund, and the way the system is set up I can only tell what goes into it, not what it's for, and the charter doesn't specifically mention it."

He raised a cloaked arm and gloved hand.

"Answers? Or do you want to resign?"

"Resign? Who said anything about resigning? I'm administrator of the Foundation, and I don't know where more than thirty percent of the funds could go, or why."

"Very well."

"Very well, what?"

"Let me explain. You are the administrator. You are not the trustee. The trustee is empowered to draw from the Special Operations Fund. Everything he draws will be reported, and the system will give you an itemization. That will allow you to comply with the Imperial record-keeping requirements."

"I cannot draw on that fund?"

"That is correct, not unless you have a special need and ask the trustee to transfer funds to your accounts. Remember, you alone control the disposition of seventy percent of the Foundation's income and more than half its assets."

Lyr frowned. "Only half the assets? The trustee controls the other half?"

"No. Thirty percent of the assets are in the Forward Fund, with half their income being returned in addition to current income."

"I know that."

"—and the other half being invested in Forward Fund assets, which are currently a mixture of first line Imperial Money Houses."

"That's not the best investment policy."

"If you have a better one, present it, and have the system put it forward for the trustee to evaluate."

Lyr worried at her bottom lip with her teeth.

"Let's get back to the unanswered questions. Why the Special Operations Fund? Why the Forward Fund?"

The man in black's shoulders slumped, as though he were sighing, although no sound was conveyed by the screen.

"The Special Operations Fund was set up by the founders to allow sufficient funds for the trustee to carry out the aims of the foundation. If you will reread the bylaws, those funds can be spent on anything which is legal under the law, including, if necessary, the living expenses and transportation of the trustee."

As he looked straight into the screen, Lyr shivered as she saw the hawk-yellow of his eyes. She would know the man by them, should they ever meet when he was not in privacy clothing, and she had to ask herself why he chose a disguise that did not conceal his most prominent feature.

"The Forward Fund is set at thirty percent of assets for one simple reason. That is the maximum allowed under current Imperial law. At some point in the future it is anticipated that large capital grants will be required. To expend those funds requires a proposal by the trustee *and* the approval of the administrator."

"*Capital* grants?" asked Lyr with the horror of the financial professional who avoided use of capital whenever possible.

"The goals of the foundation are to pursue biological technology. What if extensive laboratory or production capability could not be obtained without actually building it?" He waved a cloaked arm. "Premature at the moment. Job now is research. Later, the capabilities."

Lyr kept worrying her lower lip. The answers made sense. And she certainly couldn't object to the trustee, anonymous as he might be, who was also her superior, having access to less than a third of the fund income when he reported to her what was spent.

That left one unanswered question.

"What about the Reserve Fund? That's nearly twenty percent of the assets, and I have no control there at all."

"Reserves may be converted by the trustee without your approval, but only for the purchase or acquisition of buildings, facilities, permanent transportation equipment, or property."

"Does that give me any control?"

"Only indirectly. The more the trustee spends, the less he has. The more he spends, the more you control. Call it a balance of power."

"Sort of. But he could replace me at any time."

"He could. And the founders could replace him. Or the Empire, if he ever should break Imperial law."

Lyr stopped worrying her lower lip. She still didn't have the satisfaction she wanted, but she had some answers, and some implications that were even more far-reaching. The assets of the foundation were far greater, far greater, than she had been led to believe when the unknown hawk-eyed man had interviewed her and given her the job. And the emphasis on long-range contingency planning for capital grants and expenditures indicated a more action-oriented mentality behind the foundation than was usually the case.

She looked at the screen. Was the man in black a founder? Or the trustee? Who were they? Imperial family? Court? Commercial? Or an Ethics Conscience Fund set up by a manufacturing consortium?

"Any other questions?"

She realized she had said nothing, caught as she had been in her own thoughts.

"Uhhhh . . ." The nonsense syllable escaped her, and she clamped her lips shut. What else could she ask?

"Nothing. Not yet."

"Check with you later."

The screen blanked, without even a good-bye.

Lyr frowned, almost biting her lower lip. Was she being co-opted? *What* was she managing? Or more precisely, for what end was she managing the foundation?

"You worry," she said, wanting to express her feelings aloud, "but you don't have a thing to point to. Except that the people who set this up don't want to be publicly identified. Have you been asked to do anything shady? Haven't they been overly concerned about insuring that all the legal formalities are complied with?"

She looked at the blank screen, then at the blank walls. In the operating plan for the year was an amount reserved for decorating the office, however she wanted. An amount large enough to do it quite nicely, even extravagantly, although she could certainly reduce that if she wanted. Altering the plan was well within her discretion, but she suspected it had been a polite way of letting her know that she was welcome to decorate as she pleased.

"You already have more control over your job than many of your contemporaries will have in their whole careers."

She stopped the monologue, ran her upper teeth side-to-side over her lower lip.

She knew one other thing. Without a better reason, a great deal better reason, she wouldn't walk away from the money, the title, and the mystery. Not now, maybe not ever.

But she worried at her lower lip as her hands dropped to the console keyboard and the financial projections.

HIRO'S FEET WERE beginning to hurt. The new C.O. had insisted on walking through every single hangar and viewing every single stasis dock. Every single one, including some Urbek Hiro himself had never seen in his ten years at Standora.

Hiro had tried to steer the senior commander around the Delta complex entirely, which shouldn't have been all that difficult since the only ground level entry was through the back of the last hangar in the flitter repair section.

Senior Commander MacGregor Gerswin had just pointed to the portal and said, "To Delta complex."

It had not been a question, and Captain Urbek Hiro had just nodded.

Unlike most new commandants, Commander Gerswin had either committed the entire plan of the base to memory or was personally familiar with it. Neither possibility appealed to Hiro.

Three steps behind the senior commander, the captain shook his head.

The senior commander frowned, and for the moment appeared nearly as old as a senior commander should. His hand jabbed at the pile of assorted metal parts in the corner of the dusty hangar.

"And that?"

"Sort of an unofficial spare parts inventory, Commander." Hiro repressed a sigh. He had hoped the new chief would be as easygoing as the last. According to the records, and to his HQ sources, senior commander Gerswin had close to a century in Service, and was *the* senior commander of the I.S.S. With that sort of record, Hiro had expected a silver-haired, lightly wrinkled man ready to enjoy a graveyard tour.

Commander Gerswin looked more like a thirty-five-year-old, fast track deep selectee, but one of the medical techs had informed Hiro, off the record as usual, that the senior commander was indeed the senior commander.

"Captain Hiro. Correct me if I'm wrong, but some of these parts belong to Beta class scouts. The I.S.S. hasn't had a Beta class scout in service since before I joined."

"Yes, ser. I'll have them removed."

The commander patted Hiro on the shoulder. The captain couldn't stop the quiver.

"No. Don't remove them. Might find them useful. But not in a heap. Have them sorted and categorized, those that are serviceable."

"What . . . I beg your pardon, ser?"

"Captain Hiro. I don't like messes. Not terribly fond of people who try to cover up. But Standora is nearly a junkyard. You know it, and I know it. Rather have a museum than a junkyard. Least that's good for something."

Hiro shook his head again, so imperceptibly it was scarcely visible. The senior commander made no sense at all. He avoided thinking about it by lifting his eyes from the discolored plastone floor to the open hangar end. Outside, the sun had disappeared behind the thick gray clouds that usually formed by midafternoon of every day.

The new commandant's laugh—like a series of short barks—shook Hiro's disintegrating composure further.

Across the hangar one of the idle techs had lifted her head from the unused console where she had been dozing. As she saw the silver triangles, she came to her feet and began to wipe off the console with brisk strokes. The fact that it had no screen did not deter her sudden enthusiasm.

"Look at that, Hiro," added the commander in a softer voice. "People need something constructive to do."

Hiro didn't like the idea of something constructive to do at all. Not at all. But he smiled, as he had learned to do so many years earlier.

"I also don't like being humored, Captain."

Hiro could feel the sweat beginning to trickle down his back. What in the Emperor's mangy name had they sent him? And why?

"I understand, ser. I understand."

The senior commander did not respond, instead stepped up his pace through the hangar, heading for the empty stasis docks outside.

GERSWIN CHECKED THE time. 2303 standard Imperial.

Easily, almost lazily, he moved to the locker and began pulling on the black uniform stored in the back of the bottom drawer.

When he was finished, he studied his image in the mirrored back of the locker door, aware that even his own eyes wanted to avoid the indistinctness of the full-fade black uniform. Only his eyes were uncovered.

After palming the light stud, he eased into the narrow space between the portal frame and the wall, letting his eyes adjust to the darkness, and waited.

Shortly he could hear the muffled feet of the four, slow step by slow step, as they approached his temporary quarters.

He grinned in the darkness.

Click. Click.

The portal irised open, and a dim sliver of light pierced the room, followed by a searing yellow glare.

Thrummm! Thrumm! Thrumm!

Three stunner bolts, wide angle, blanketed the small room.

"Mange!"

"Gone!"

Rather than leaving, as professionals would have, the four crowded in through the portal.

Gerswin noted the heavier bulk of Hiro as the last inside.

Striking with the silence of unseen black lightning, Gerswin garroted Hiro with his forearm, while knocking the captain's knees and legs from under him. The quick, brute-strength maneuver left the heavy captain unconscious in seconds.

Gerswin dropped the maintenance tertiary and dispatched the pair next before him with alternate hands.

"What—"

The cry of the fourth man died as Gerswin's elbow crushed his throat.

The senior commander, still scarcely breathing heavily, tapped the portal shut, relocked it, and tapped the light plate.

The three dead men—Morin, Zorenski, and Vlaed—all had stood close to a head taller than Gerswin. The hawk-eyed commander nodded, rearranged two of the bodies. Next, Gerswin pulled the unconscious form of Hiro around so that the maintenance captain was propped against the side of Gerswin's bunk.

"Uhhh . . ."

Last, Gerswin picked up the stunner, already set to the setting that was lethal at short range. Lifting Vlaed's body, he stood, supporting the dead man in front of him, and waited for Hiro to react.

Hiro's eyes opened, and he grabbed at the side of the bunk. He looked, wide-eyed, at the dead man, who with open eyes had a stunner leveled at him, then scrambled toward the weapon.

Thrummm! Thrumm!

Gerswin changed a few patterns in the floor scuffs, avoiding all four bodies, and removed the black uniform, easing himself into a robe, and wiped the butt of the stunner he had used on Hiro clean before he finally unlocked the portal.

Brinnng!

He leaned down and picked up a second stunner and stood against the wall waiting for the response to the alarm.

"Ser?"

The security rating decided against touching his weapon as he measured the C.O. leaning against the wall and looking at the carnage on the deck.

"Captain Hiro came charging in here to warn me about an attack. Before he could make me understand what was happening, those three"—and Gerswin gestured toward the three bodies beyond Hiro—"charged in. Hiro took them all on, but they got him."

"Yes, ser. If you say so, ser."

"Not only do I say so, D'Ner," Gerswin said, picking the rating's name off his tunic, "but that's exactly what the retinal images will show, and what all the evidence will indicate."

Not only that, reflected Gerswin silently, but the disclosure that the commandant had discovered the illegal diversion of funds from the Imprest Fund and the selling of unused maintenance spares would certainly bolster the fact that the three were guilty of attempted murder, or would have been, had not the courageous Captain Hiro stopped them.

Hiro, of course, had been careful to keep himself above the illegalities.

D'Ner saluted. "Yes, ser."

Gerswin looked down at the four, then back at D'Ner.

"Let's get this taken care of, D'Ner. We've got a base to run, and one that's supposed to repair ships."

"Yes, ser."

D'Ner's shiver was not lost on the commandant, who smiled at the security tech.

"Think about it, D'Ner. For what earthly decent purpose would three like those be dressed in dark clothes and sneaking into any quarters? And why would they be carrying stunners?"

D'Ner bit his lower lip, then looked up. "When you put it that way . . ."

Gerswin shook his head slowly. "Tell me, D'Ner . . . how long has Technician Morin been holding off the completion of the repairs and improvements to the regular commandant's quarters?"

D'Ner frowned. "I don't understand, ser."

"Not up to you, D'Ner. Up to the Board of Inquiry. But you deserve to know. Put it in question form. Could this kind of attack take place if the commandant's regular quarters had been ready? With all the security checks?"

"No . . . no, ser."

"Why weren't they ready? Did it have anything to do with the fact that Morin was in charge of the day-to-day work?"

It did. Hiro had put Morin in charge, which had been one of the things that had alerted Gerswin in the first place.

"Never thought about it. . . ."

"Well . . . damage done already. Lost a good officer . . . and I owe the captain a great deal. Hope the Board of Inquiry can get to the bottom of the whole thing." He let his voice turn cold as he finished.

D'Ner shivered, glanced at the cold eyes of the commandant, as if to say he was not sure whether he would rather face the commander or the Board of Inquiry, then glanced out the portal as he heard the steps of the security reserves.

"In here . . ." The security technician's voice was faint, but firm. "In here."

Gerswin handed the stunner to D'Ner. His face was impassive.

Who are the men who own the skies?
A tall man, a thin man, a mean one.
A man who has no heart, and one who has no eyes.
A man who laughs, and one who never dies.

Do no women own the skies?
A tall one, a thin one, a mean one?
A woman who has no heart, one who has no eyes?
A laughing woman, or one who never cries . . .

. . . you cannot own the skies and stars.
You cannot prison them with bars . . .

And yet, a steel-crossed heart,
with ports that never part,
with daggers from his eyes,
has let the captain hold the skies.

And who will melt the steel away?
Who will steal the daggers' day?

> Who will split the clouds in two,
> and with her heart the stars pursue?

Fragments from *The Ballad of
the Captain* (full text lost)
Songs of the Mythmakers
Edwina de Vlerio
New Augusta, 5133 N.E.C.

THE LIEUTENANT WALKED quickly, as if he were trying to outdistance Gerswin.

"Just ahead, Commander. Just ahead."

Torn between a sigh of exasperation and a smile of amusement at the young supply officer's nervousness, Gerswin kept his face impassive.

"All the security systems in place, Hursen?"

"Yes, ser. Checked them this morning." The dark-haired man did not look back as he followed the walkway through a right angle turn and toward the massive open stone archway.

Through and over the archway, the wide sweep of the rejuvenated but antique commandant's quarters dominated the crest of the low hill.

The hill itself had been raised at the "suggestion" of Standora Base's first commanding officer, in order to allow him to view the entire base from his quarters.

The two men halted before the archway, an archway that concealed the low level personnel screen that ringed the entire grounds, gardens and all.

"You have to go through first, Commander. The screen is keyed to you."

"Just me?"

"For now. You could add anyone you wanted. Did you have anyone in mind?"

Even as the words escaped the lieutenant's mouth, Gerswin could see the young man swallow hard, as if he wished to take the words back.

Gerswin could not quite hide his grin, nor the smile in his voice.

"Don't worry, Hursen. There isn't anyone like that."

The smile left his face as he considered the import of the words. No one like that—no, there wasn't. Not now.

Caroljoy was dead. Dead, for all the memories, and so was their son, the one he had not even known. Three memories of her—once scarcely out of girlhood, for all her warmth and wanting. Once as a Duchess, aging, but still warm and vital. And once as a dying woman, not even in person, but captured in cold print and foundation incorporation charters.

He shook his head. Twice. Only twice had they been together in a century. And twice had not been enough.

He had spent more time with some casual lovers. And those casual affairs had sometimes been too much, far too much.

He shook his head and looked up at the all too imposing quarters he would occupy, quarters that were obviously left from the days of earlier Imperial expansion, days when the energy had been abundant and cheap, and when every base had been another attempt to recreate the glory of the Empire's rising sun.

Like the day itself, Gerswin reflected with a wry twist to his lips, the Empire had moved into its afternoon.

"Commander?"

"A moment, Lieutenant. A moment."

When he stepped through the archway, he did not immediately key the release to allow his supply officer through, but paused and surveyed the formal garden to his right, and the clipped green velvet of the lawn as it sloped down and away from the pathway that hugged the artificial ridgeline, as it led to the wide stone steps that waited to greet the commander.

On the other side of the quarters, he recalled, was the truly imposing main entrance, designed to accept groundcars of size and splendor. Even if none had been seen at Standora Base in more than half a century.

The formality recalled Triandna to him, clear as the single time he had been there, clear as that day he had seen Caroljoy the second time and learned he had lost the son he had never known.

"The Emperor's Cross . . . for this? For what it stands for?" The senior commander remained unmoving in the sunlight of the early afternoon.

"Commander?"

The plaintive sound in Hursen's voice jerked him back to the present, where he stood in a pleasant garden before a large, but not ducal, military home.

"Sorry, Hursen. Just . . . remembering . . ."

He took several steps back to the stone archway and coded the momentary release that dropped the screens for the younger officer.

"Come on in."

"Than you, ser." Hursen cleared his throat, once, twice, then finally spoke again. "You were here before, ser?"

"No. Just reminded me of something that happened a long time ago. A long ways from here."

"I imagine you've seen a great deal, ser."

"Hardly, Hursen. Hardly. Sometimes it amazes me to find out how little I've seen."

He turned and began to walk slowly down the stone walkway toward the small but well-restored formal garden, with the dark green of its low hedges, and the intermittent splashes of small flowers.

Had Caroljoy known he might have rated such quarters, would she have considered contacting him after she discovered she would have his child?

He shook his head once more, slowly and with a faint smile.

The Lieutenant Gerswin he had been could not have competed in the same universe as the Duke of Triandna. In life, they had inhabited separate worlds, and not even death, whenever it might come, would change that.

Death? Hardly yet, he thought with another quirk to his lips.

His steps picked up as he marched toward the house. So much time for self-pity and reflection, and no more. Neither sadness or self-pity would help reclaim Old Earth . . . or Standora Base.

"Come on, Lieutenant. Let's get on with it."

He did not smile as he sensed the puzzled expression on the young supply officer's face. Instead he took the stone steps two at a time.

"THE SMALL HANGAR at the end? Those are the museum pieces, ser."

The I.S.S. pilot laughed. "Museum pieces? You have to be joking."

"No, ser," answered the technician. "When the commander got

here, he said that since we were only fit to work on museum pieces, we should at least make them the best there were. Was before I came. Each year, we restore another old one from the scrapyard. Make it fully operational. Off-duty time, but it gets to you."

The pilot—young, female, blonde, square-jawed—stared at the technician. "You're serious?"

"Ser . . . why don't you take a look? The hangar's open to the public, too. Got headquarters to classify it as a public exhibition. Must get a couple hundred visitors a day."

"All right. Nothing else to do."

As the young officer strolled down the plastarmac, she could feel the technician grinning behind her back. She wondered if the man told the same tall tale to all the transients at Standora.

Still . . . the hangar was less than half a kilo, and she had little enough to do until the emergency repairs on the *Dybyykk* were completed.

"Standora . . . for Hades' sake." She shook her head. The place should have been closed down years ago.

That was what the Operations officer had said.

She glanced at the arrayed hangars, all clean, and the clear tarmac that stretched to the "museum" ahead. While the base appeared less busy than many, it did not appear deserted or run-down, nor did its personnel conduct themselves as if they had been consigned to a dying installation.

She glanced inside the hangar to her right, then glanced again. The grids positively glittered, and the hull inside seemed the focus of a full crew.

This is the junkyard of the fleet, supposedly? What other ships had been sent here recently? From the Fleet Dispatch log, she couldn't remember any.

Her steps brought her to the hangar at the end closest to the main gate toward the local community.

A sign a meter square caught her eye.

IMPERIAL SMALLCRAFT—HISTORICAL DISPLAY

None of the craft displayed here are currently in Imperial Service. For historical and academic research purposes, all displays are fully functional and in complete working order.

She read the caption twice before entering the hangar.
Once inside she had to blink, for she had been expecting the

hushed, dimly lit recesses of a museum. Instead, the lights were those of a first class repair installation, clear illumination from both direct and indirect sources.

The plastone underfoot was the clear blue of a newly constructed hangar, and outside of the faint hint of metal and ozone, the air was fresh.

From where she stood inside the hangar entryway, she could see eight smallcraft, the largest of which was an ancient corvette.

Another look around the hangar revealed details she had missed. Both entrances, the one from the base and the one from the other side, open to the locals, were guarded by I.S.S. techs. Not by Imperial Marines, but by armed technicians who wore regulation side arms and whose uniforms matched almost any marine's for sharpness.

Beside each craft was a small stand with a vidcube display to explain the background of the particular boat or ship. And at the far north end of the hangar, suspended from the overhead, were the crossed banners of the Empire and the I.S.S.

Each of the displays appeared as ready for liftoff as the outside caption had claimed.

The pilot headed for the one she recognized from the tapes, a Delta class flitter, which had been retired less than a decade earlier, and which seemed to be the most modern of the craft displayed.

She grimaced as she approached, realizing that the canopy was seal-locked, as it should be if the flitter was indeed operational. She climbed the steps to the platform to view the controls. At least she could get some idea whether the flitter was indeed functional.

"Lieutenant?" A voice intruded upon her observations.

She turned to see a senior technician at her elbow.

"Would you like to try the controls?" He did not wait for her answer, but turned to the seal and made some adjustments. The canopy recessed, and the climbsteps extended from the hull.

"Why—"

"Commander likes to have pilots see what ships used to be like. Can't open them to everyone because they're all hot. He does most of the test flights. Makes sense. Only one checked out in most of them."

"Checked out . . . all of them hot? Even—"

"Even the old black scout, even the Federation Epsilon corvette. If it doesn't work, then it's not on display. We've got some in the work area below. May take years to get in shape. Big project is the *Ryttel.*"

The lieutenant dropped suddenly into the padded accel/decel control shell.

"The *Ryttel*?"

"No one could bear to scrap her. Been out in the 'serveshells for two cees."

Her hands touched the controls, controls that felt new, as recent as the shuttles and flitters of the *Dybyykk*.

"These don't feel old."

"They're not. They work. Commander insists they all work. Every one is absolutely stet with the original specs, except in cases where the original specs were changed in Service to improve operations."

She touched the power readout plates. Ninety-eight percent power. Again she shook her head for what she felt was the hundredth time.

"I don't believe it."

"Not many do. Commander says it shows what we can do." The tech paused. "Just close the seal when you're done. Set to relock."

The pilot shifted her weight to get the feel of the shell, and of the flitter, letting her fingers run over the controls, trying to set up a scan pattern with the different positions of the board instruments.

Even without the power assists on, without the full panel lit, or the heads-up display projected, the flitter felt new, felt ready to lift clear of the hangar.

At last she took her hands from the stick and thruster controls, unfastened the webbing, and eased out of the cockpit. With a final look at the interior, she touched the closure panel and stepped back onto the platform as the canopy slid into place with a muffled *clunk*.

Straightening her tunic, she turned and took the steps back down to the hangar floor.

She wanted to see if the old Federation Epsilon class corvette felt as new as the Delta flitter had, knowing in her heart that it would.

Before she reached the wide steps to the viewing platform, she could tell her assumption had been correct. Not a single scratch marred any individual plate, leaving the full-fade finish more perfect than any she had yet seen. Her eyes wanted to twist away from the corvette, to forget it was there.

Licking her dry lips once, she glanced around the rest of the hangar, surveying the six crafts she had not yet approached.

What could he do if he had a real ship to work with? she wondered.

Then she laughed. The commander, the mysterious commander both techs had mentioned almost reverently, did have a real ship to work with. He had the *Dybyykk*.

If his crews were half as good with the cruiser as with the antique wrecks they had reconstructed, the captain wouldn't need to go on to New Glascow.

The lieutenant turned back to the corvette, concentrating on the details such as the placement and finish of the heat drops, to avoid having her vision twisted.

From the corner of her eye she could see the same senior tech moving toward the stand.

She knew she would have to check out the controls of the corvette, and perhaps the Alpha shuttle . . . if not the scout in the far corner.

FROM:	C.O.
	H.I.M.S. *DYBYYKK*
TO:	12 FLT HQ
	LOG/SUPP (CODE 3B)
SUBJ:	REFIT STATUS

1. *DYBYYKK* ARRIVED STANDORA
   DEC/12/2100/76.
   STATUS: DELTA ARO BTTL ACT
2. SPECIFICS   DRIVES: OMEGA WITHIN 10 W/O REPAIR
   SCREENS: OMEGA
   SYSTEM INTEGRITY: DELTA
3. REPAIRS/REFIT COMPLETE SEC/07/0900/77.
4. *DYBYYKK* DEPARTED STANDORA
   SEC/08/2100/77.
5. SYS/CHK/STATUS: ALPHA   DRIVES: ALPHA PLUS
   SCREENS: ALPHA SYSTEM
   INTREGRITY: ALPHA
6. OTHER: (A)   REFIT UNNECESSARY THIS TIME
   (B)   *STRONGLY* RECOMMEND
   GREATER UTILIZATION
   STANDORA RP
   (C)   REQUEST REPLACEMENT LT
   A.L. INGMARR/I.S.S./PLO/2:
   MEDICAL LWP(MAT/DET
   DUTY STANDORA)

XIX

THE NEWBORN HAD only cried once, enough to clear his lungs, and, placed on his mother's stomach, had immediately tried to go to her breast.

Both the mother and the nursing tech pushed him gently into position, somewhat awkwardly because neither had much experience in the matter.

The I.S.S. surgeon completed her work, focused on the sterilizers, and gave the mother a quick jolt from the regen/stim tube, all according to the tapes she had studied and studied for the past week.

The infant resisted when the surgeon lifted him away from his mother for the prescribed checks, reflexes—respiratory and neural—but did not cry, though his eyes were wide.

His look bothered the surgeon, but she completed the checks as surely as she could, and returned him to his mother's breast. Then she entered the results on the health chart, a standard Service chart suitably modified for the newborn, whose reflexes had topped the scale, and who plussed the green for neural potential.

Dr. Kristera repressed a sigh. Standora wasn't the best place for a newborn, not with the background contaminants from the facility, and not with the lack of dependent care facilities.

The mother, stretched out on the light-grav stretcher, cradled the tiny boy at her breast with her right arm.

The doctor could see the sucking movements, and both the gratitude and tiredness on the mother's face.

"Why?" murmured the surgeon to herself. To have had the child could not have been a spur of the moment decision, not when having a child had to have been a positive choice before the fact. And the interruption in the young lieutenant's career as an I.S.S. pilot wouldn't help her promotion opportunities, since it would be more than a year before she could leave detached duty for accel/decel related duties—*if* she chose to stay in Service and if she chose to leave the child.

The I.S.S. surgeon looked again. Carefully, she approached the mother and child. "How do you feel?"

"Tired. Tired." Her smile was wan. "But glad."

"How's your friend?"

"Hungry."

The surgeon bent down, trying to get a better look at the boy's eyes, which opened for a moment, as if the newborn had sensed her approach.

The baby's eyes were not blue, but yellow-flecked green, a strong color intensified by the short blond fuzz that would become hair. Dr. Kristera had to stop herself from pulling away from the intensity of the newborn's look.

"He's . . . strong . . . ," she temporized to the mother.

The pilot nodded, closing her eyes.

The surgeon straightened and took the mother's pulse. Strong. The pilot was in excellent condition, had kept in shape, obviously, even though the birth had cost her more than any single high gee maneuver in the operations manual.

The surgeon stepped back as the nursing tech returned.

Maintenance stations were not equipped for childbirth, and for some reason the mother had rejected adamantly the local civilian health care. The C.O. had granted her request to use base facilities.

The surgeon wondered if his permission were yet another part of his efforts at upgrading Standora. Already, the load on the docks was increasing, after decades of neglect.

"You can go now, doctor," suggested the nursing tech, a stocky mid-aged woman.

The I.S.S. surgeon nodded and turned, worrying at her upper lip with her lower.

What was it about the child?

The blond hair was uncommon at birth, but certainly not rare. But the eyes . . . it had to be the eyes.

She wished she had more background for O.B. work, but who expected much in the Service, particularly away from the main staging and training centers?

All babies had blue eyes at birth. Or dark ones. Didn't they?

Who had eyes like that? Like a hawk?

She sucked in her breath.

"It couldn't be . . . it couldn't . . ."

She remembered who had eyes like a hawk, eyes that missed nothing. How could she have forgotten? How could she have possibly forgotten? Was that why he had given his permission?

Mechanically, Dr. Kristera began to peel off her gloves. She shook her head.

Who ever would have thought it?

Shaking her head slowly, she began to remove the rest of her operating room clothing.

XX

SCREEE . . . THUD!

The mass of metal that had once been a pre-Federation scout came to rest in the makeshift cradle in the middle of the small hangar.

The man in the gray technician's suit, a repair suit without decoration or insignia, watched as the salvage trac eased back out into the gray morning. His hawk-yellow eyes scanned the black plates and fifty meter plus length of obsolete aerodynamic lines.

The pre-Federation scouts had been a good thirty percent longer and more massive than present scouts, with the attendant power consumption, but they had one impressive advantage from his point of view. They had been true scouts, able to set down and lift from virtually any world within thirty percent of T-type parameters.

Not that the jumble of metal, broken electronics, and missing equipment before him was really a scout. But it had been, and would be again.

"You MacGregor?" asked the trac operator, who had returned with the clipack after stopping the salvage trac outside on the tarmac. The shuttle port outside the hangar door served the few commercial interests of Standora and the small amount of native travel.

"Same."

"Need some authentication."

"Stet." The man in the technician's repair suit produced an oblong card.

The trac operator inserted the card in her clipack, which blinked amber, then green.

"That's it." The salvage operator glanced over at the long black shape and shook her head. "What you going to do, break it down for higher value scrap?"

"Client wants her restored."

"Restored? That'd take years, thousands of creds."

"You're right."

"Why? No resale. Black hole for power use. Wrong construction for a yacht."

"Prospecting."

"If you say so."

The salvage operator was still shaking her head as she left the hangar for her cab.

The technician, who was not exactly a technician, cranked down the hangar door. At one time, when Standora had been on more heavily traveled Imperial trade corridors, before the increasing power consumption of the newly colonized planets had pushed jumptravel for commercial purposes into fewer and fewer ships and trips, all the hangars had possessed luxuries such as individual conditioning units and powered doors. As the commercial travel had dropped, so had the amenities.

The long-term lease on the hangar barely covered the taxes and expenses to the owner, but the lease terms provided that any upgrades in the facility would revert to the owner at the end of the twenty year contract.

According to the logs that had accompanied the mass of metal that had once been a scout, the official name of the craft had been the *Farflung*.

While the hull contained the fragments of drives, generators for screens and gravfields, all the communications gear and the minimal weaponry associated with scouts had been removed before the auction. That was fine with him, since weaponry mounted for use was illegal and since he intended to use the equivalent of equipment associated with more impressive craft.

He laughed once as he turned back toward the graving cradle. The power consumption from what he planned for the main drives and screens would really have stunned the salvage operator.

As she said, it would take time.

But time . . . that he still had.

Time—while the devilkids struggled half a sector away at the mechanically impossible task of restoring Old Earth. Time—while Eye and Service headquarters watched him and wondered how soon he would begin to age and die. Time—while the ghosts of Caroljoy and Martin nibbled at the warmth provided by Allison and Corson.

Yes. He had time. For now.

XXI

HIS STEPS WERE measured as he came through the stone archway. His black boots, not quite polished to the sheen expected of the Imperial Marine he was not, barely sounded on the stone steps of the rear entrance to the quarters.

"Good evening, Commander." Ramieres nodded at the senior officer respectfully, but did not leave the cooktop.

Gerswin sniffed lightly, appreciating the delicate odor of the scampig. "Evening, Ramieres. Smells good. As usual."

"Thank you, Commander. I do my best."

The commander smiled. The rating was the best Service cook he had run across in his entire career, and better than a score of the so-called chefs whose dishes he had sampled over the years.

He knew he would miss Ramieres when the younger man finished his tour in less than three months.

"How long before dinner's ready?"

"For the best results, I'd rather not hold it more than another thirty minutes, ser."

"Try to make it before that. See how the upstairs crew is doing."

Ramieres did not comment, instead merely nodded before returning his full attention to the range of dishes and ingredients before him.

Gerswin swung out of the huge kitchen through the formal pantry and took the wide steps of the grand staircase two at a time.

From the faint scent of perfume to the additional humidity in the upstairs hall, he could tell that Allison had just gotten out of the antique fresher that resembled a shower more than a cleaner.

She was sitting in the rocking chair—another antique that he had found and refinished for her—with Corson at her breast. His son's eyes widened at the sound of the door and his footsteps, but the three month old did not stop his suckling.

Allison wore a soft purple robe that complimented her fair complexion and blonde hair.

"Interrupted your dressing?"

She nodded with a faint smile. "I always dress for dinner like this."

Grinning back at her, he sat on the side of the bed next to the chair.

"Are you going to stay home tonight? Or go out and play with your new toy?" Her voice was gentle.

He forced the grin to stay in place. "Thought I'd spend the time with you and Corson."

"That would be nice. He's had a late nap, and I think that he will have to have dinner with us."

"He about done?"

"In a minute. He's like you. There's not much in between. When he's hungry, he's hungry. And when he's not, he's ready to tackle the world." Allison brushed a strand of long hair back over her left ear.

Since she was no longer on high-acceleration duty, she had let her hair grow far longer than when they had met, during the refit of the *Dybyykk*.

He watched as her eyes studied the greedy man-child as he fed. "Hungry?"

"I am. He eats so much that I can eat just about anything."

"Corson?" he asked quietly.

She laughed a soft laugh. "Why ask? You know he's always hungry, the greedy little pig." She paused. "Like his father."

Gerswin quirked his lips.

Abruptly the baby's mouth left his mother's nipple. He turned his head and eyes toward Gerswin.

"See? When he's done, he's done."

The mother, who had been and remained an I.S.S. pilot, swung her son onto her shoulder and began to pat his back gently.

"I'll do that. You get dressed."

"You don't want me dining in my finery here?"

"You'd shock Ramieres."

"I doubt that. The fact that you might let me appear in anything this revealing might shock him."

Gerswin leaned forward and extended his arms.

In turn, edging forward from the rocking chair, Allison eased Corson into his father's arms.

The commander stood and inched the boy baby farther up onto his left shoulder, holding him in place with his left hand and patting his back with his right hand.

A gentle *"brrrp"* rewarded his efforts.

"You do that so easily. It amazes me that he's your first."

Gerswin did not make the correction. He had never held Martin, had never even known Martin had existed until well after his first son's death. And perhaps he had had other sons or daughters—that was not impossible, although he did not know of any.

His lips tightened, and he was glad he was looking out the window, facing away from Allison.

How would he know? Much as he attracted women, he also drove them away. How would Allison feel two months, two years from now?

Gerswin repressed a shiver. She had already picked up that he had intended to work on the old scout after dinner. Now . . . how could he?

She had obviously come back to the quarters after a full day in the operations office, determined to look good for him and to spend the time with both Corson and him. So how could he leave?

He forced his face to relax as he turned toward the dressing area where Allison was pulling on a long and decidedly nonuniform low-cut gown.

He could feel Corson's fingers digging into his shoulder, could feel the small body's heat against his, and the smoothness of his son's skin as he bent his head to let his cheek rest against Corson's.

Gerswin let the sigh come out gently, silently enough that Allison would not hear.

"How do I look?"

"Exquisite."

She frowned. "You make me sound like a piece of rare porcelain."

"Not what I had in mind." He grinned, not having to force the expression as much as he feared.

"I know what you had in mind. But I'm hungry, and Corson won't be sleepy until after dinner. *Well* after dinner."

"Then we shouldn't keep Ramieres waiting."

"No. Not tonight, at least."

Gerswin ignored the hint of bitterness and reached out to brush his fingertips across Allison's cheek.

She grasped them, pressed them to her lips, and smiled her soft smile.

"Shall we go, Commander dear?"

He nodded, and the three of them made their way down the grand staircase toward the dining room, which would dwarf them.

XXII

LYR TABBED THE portal. Halfway into the foundation office, she realized that someone was sitting before her console.

Without breaking stride, she grabbed the pocket stunner and raised it with her right hand, coming to a halt as she squeezed the firing stud.

Thrummm!

Thud.

The console recliner spun into the console as the intruder flashed to the left before she could readjust her aim.

Thrummm!

Crack!

The stunner flew out of her hand as the intruder, clad in some sort of black that twisted her eyes away from him, swung her around and caught her in a grip that felt unbreakable. She tried to catch a glimpse of his eyes, but he kept her firmly turned away from him.

She attempted to shift her weight, to stamp his feet, to get her elbows into play . . . anything. But none of her self-defense tactics seemed to work. Screaming was useless within the total soundproofing of the office.

Thrummm!

This time the stunner bolt hit her legs, and she felt them collapse under her, although the intruder continued to support her weight. She decided to stop the pointless struggle and see what developed as her assailant, who scarcely seemed any taller than she was, bound her hands behind her and set her on the single settee.

"Stop being ridiculous." The light baritone voice sent a chill through her. She had met him before. The question was when, or where.

"Ridiculous? When there's an intruder using my console?"

She tried to twist her body to catch sight of his face, but he had kept one hand on her shoulder, and without any control of her legs she could not override his light grip.

"Exactly. Are you the only one empowered to use the console? Do you shoot and then ask questions?"

"Only the trustee has the right to use this equipment. And he's never—"

"Ah, Lyr. I interviewed you, give you instructions, and you don't even recognize my voice. Even if it has been a few years, I expected better."

She shivered. Had he been the interviewer? And had the interviewer actually been the anonymous trustee?

"You never said you were the trustee. Am I supposed to ask every common thief, 'Oh, pardon me, are you supposed to be here?' "

She tried to squirm around to face him, but he had not let go of her shoulder.

"Ha!" The single harsh bark resembled a laugh. "Point. Point for you."

"I would like a bit more than points."

"Who else could have given you the access codes?" His voice softened. "And how could anyone have gotten through your defenses without a trace unless they knew the system?"

She was silent for a moment. Finally she responded. "You honestly expected me to think about that when I saw an intruder?"

"Perhaps that was expecting too much."

His tone made her feel guilty, and then angry as she rejected the guilt for being human in her reactions.

"I quit! Right now!"

"If you wish . . . but I won't accept your resignation until we're through talking."

"I told you. I quit."

"Fine. But we're still going to talk. You're not going anywhere under your own power for a few minutes, at least."

Lyr said nothing.

"While your financial management has been excellent, outstanding in fact, I have not been as pleased with your grant policy. Came to suggest some changes."

"I followed the guidelines, exactly as outlined."

"Lyr," answered the soft voice with the hint of iron behind it, "what is past is past. No time to argue. Only to change."

"I'm not arguing." She worried her lower lip. "What were you doing here?"

"My job. I have access here whenever I want. Access built into the system. If you changed that, which would be most difficult, your own employment would have been automatically terminated."

The hard sound of his last sentence gave her the impression that more than her employment would have been terminated.

She could smell him, like the faint scent of wild grass, although only his hand rested lightly on her shoulder. She ignored the scent, pleasant though she found it.

"You never did say what you were doing here."

Instead of answering, he picked her up from behind as if she weighed no more than a small child and carried her the half a dozen steps across the antique carpet to the swivel chair. He placed her in the seat in front of the console. His arm reached across her and tapped the keyboard, his fingers even faster than hers would have been.

"Revised Grant Guidelines"—that was the title that lit up on the screen.

"If you hadn't decided to work in the middle of the night—"

"It was only 2110."

"—you would have found them waiting for you in the morning. As you have on a few other occasions."

"That was you?"

"None other."

"Why all the secrecy? Who are you? Why don't you want anyone to know who you are?"

By now Lyr was not angry, but furious. She'd nearly stunned her real employer because he'd believed in sneaking around with cloak and stunner, and she could have risked her job and life if she'd toyed around with the wrong parameters in the foundation's information and control network. To top it off, he had handled her—her!—as if she were a child, mentally and physically.

"You're angry."

"I am angry. You're right. This time you understand. I am very angry." She forced herself to space out the words, to keep her voice low and even.

"I owe you an apology."

"You owe me nothing except back pay. I quit. Remember?"

"Didn't accept your resignation. Yet." He paused. "Offered an apology. What else will it take to get you to listen with an open mind? To remember that the foundation is not your private fiefdom?" He laughed softly. "You've already reminded me that it's not mine."

"How about some honesty? I know. You've never lied. But there's too much hiding, especially now. Anonymous calls over the screen I can take, but not anonymous intruders sneaking around my office. I'll think, *think*, about reconsidering once you've shown me who and what you are."

"Still better you don't know. For you. For the foundation."

"I'm beyond someone else deciding what's better."

"You're sure?"

"Sure enough to quit on the spot."

"You're right about one thing. I haven't been totally fair."

"No. You haven't. You expect me to guess what you want or what the founders of the foundation want, then you change the rules without even telling me why." She sighed, once, twice. "But you're right in a way, too. You know I don't want to quit. But I will."

"Unless?"

"First, untie me. Then we'll talk. Then I'll decide."

He said nothing, but she could feel him bending over her, and his hands touched hers. His were warm against the coldness of hers, with their impaired circulation. The bonds fell away.

She gripped the arms of the swivel and straightened herself. She did not turn around.

"I would like to see you, face to face, but I don't want to jeopardize my life or my future by doing so."

"Let's talk first. I'll try to answer your questions, and leave the decision in your hands when we're done."

"In my hands?"

"After I've answered your questions, you decide. Fair?"

"Fair enough."

"Your first question. Why the secrecy?" He paused, as if to gather his thoughts. "Most important. The fewer people know the foundation exists and what it does, the better the chances for its success without interference. Two people is about the maximum for keeping a secret. You and me. Second, in my own obscure way I am extremely controversial. So controversial I believe considered as possible Corpus Corps target. Third, what you do not know, you cannot reveal. More important, cannot be hurt for it."

Again he paused. "There are other reasons. Those are the most important."

"Secrecy implies that there is opposition. That indicates there is a purpose behind the avowed goals. What is it?"

Lyr could sense him behind her, but kept her eyes in front of her.

"The purpose behind the goals? I may have one, but that's not the same as the foundation. The foundation is set up to do exactly what it is doing. To try to develop biological techniques for improving or reclaiming the environment. Low cost ones. Not that the research has to be low cost, just the eventual techniques."

"You're convinced about that?"

"I know that. I wrote the goals."

"What about you? You said your goals weren't the same as the foundation's. What are they?"

"My goals? Not sure they affect what you do." He sighed. "But you'll claim that they do. And the foundation needs you. So . . ."

The silence drew out.

"I appreciate the vote of confidence, but you were right. I am interested in your goals for the foundation."

"In a nutshell, I have a strong personal and vested interest in the successful application of the foundation's techniques. Call it, if you will, the only way I can reclaim my heritage."

"Sounds rather dramatic."

"No. Just truthful."

"What else?"

"That's it. The foundation has to be successful. That, or some other entity, or me personally. Need bio reclamation techniques. Believe me or not, that's it."

Lyr could sense the exasperation behind the words, an exasperation that indicated truth, if not the whole truth.

"Did you set up the foundation?"

"No. I know . . . knew . . . one of the founders."

"Would you tell me who?"

"No. Condition of being trustee. Not to tell anyone."

"Where does the incoming funding in our blind account come from?"

"It's an account which channels dividends, interest, from a large portfolio. Totally legitimate."

"How would I know?"

"The firm handling the account is Halsie-Vyr."

"The Halsie-Vyr?"

"Yes. Think about it. The Imperial Treasury verifies our receipt of funding by matching our blind account number against the one to which Halsie-Vyr deposits. Treasury insures that to make certain taxes are paid. Information stays confidential."

"How could it?"

He laughed. "What I asked. Star in the sky principle. Last time there was a public report, five years ago, Treasury reported 100,000 blind trusts with assets over ten million credits. Safety in numbers. Who could match? Depository bank only knows that Halsie-Vyr deposits and that deposits are posted to another account number in another bank. Treasury doesn't care, so long as they get their cut."

"Cynical, aren't you?"

"No. Creating the foundation wasn't my idea. Presented to me as sort of legacy. Came unasked and unanticipated."

"You have another occupation, then." Her statement was more seeking verification than inquiring.

"Yes. That's why the foundation needs an administrator of independence and nerve."

She almost turned to catch a look at him, but stopped herself, looking instead at the knotted Targan wall hanging in the right corner, just beyond the portal. Its curves seemed to fade into oblivion, yet twisted back upon each other with abrupt changes in the thread colors.

"What was wrong with my grant policy?"

"Too conservative. Need to take changes. We'll lose credits. Know that, but best chances lie with the researchers and professors outside the clear mainstream. Someone not tied to orthodoxy. The kind others say, 'He's brilliant . . . strange . . . never know where he's going.' That sort of thing."

"How do I tell who's unorthodox and who's fractured?"

"Design a questionnaire, as a condition of grant application. Make it simple. 'How do you propose to solve your problem, Honored Scientist?' 'What science or evidence do you have to support your theorem?' If you make it too complicated, too orthodox, the really creative types won't play, and you'll get lots of second-raters who are first-rate at filling out forms."

"I think I get the idea. How do I know, with a limited scientific background, what's good?"

"After you've read several hundred, you'll know."

"Are you willing to waste all those creds while I learn?"

"Won't be wasted. Not if you learn. Some things can't be done any other way."

"The foundation . . . you really are looking for a pure research solution, aren't you?"

"No. Looking to support research that will lead to practical solutions. Simple ones."

"How simple?"

"Spores that break down chlorinated organics. Plants that reclaim poisoned land. Biological solutions that primitive or resource-poor cultures could use."

"Primitive cultures haven't poisoned their lands," Lyr objected.

"Not yet. Not in the Empire. Foundation has to look forward and back. Could use Marduk, if we could reclaim it."

"Don't tell me—"

"No. No one knows how long ago that was."

Lyr rested her head in her hands. Her legs were shaking as the muscles contracted involuntarily, trying to rid themselves of the paralysis imposed by the stunner.

"Nothing makes any sense. You don't make sense. I can't even ask questions that make sense. You won't answer the ones that would help me understand."

"Such as?"

"Who are you?"

"How about starting with what I am?"

"That's a start."

"Mid-grade officer in Imperial Service. Technically, I can serve as a trustee of an Imperial chartered foundation, but cannot permanently administer a trust."

"How can you keep who you are a secret?"

"I don't. Same star in the sky principle. My name is on the foundation charter. Charter lists are not subject to public search. The bureaucrats who monitor foundations and trusts are not the same bureaucrats who monitor officers of Imperial Service."

Lyr wanted to turn and grab him, shake him, or stamp her foot . . . or something. The more he answered, the less she knew.

"So why shouldn't I see who you are?"

"Decision is in your hands. Finished asking all your questions?"

"What questions have I missed?"

"Is there a danger to you from knowing who I am? Do you really want to know, or are you angry that you've been kept in the dark?"

"I am, but that won't be why I decide. Is there a danger to me?"

"Thought there was. Not so sure now. Probably more danger to me than you."

"Why?"

The trustee did not answer. Finally she could hear him take a deep breath.

"Because I'm out to change the galaxy."

"You sound too sensible to be that crazy."

"Wish I were. If the foundation is successful, could change popular perception enough to upset the Empire's economy, perceptions, and power base. Might not, but it could."

"How? Even if we publicized grants, who would care about reclaiming a poisoned spot here and there with plants instead of machines? That's assuming we get these grants to a workable state."

"Look beyond the near orbit. Techniques that let you clean up chemicals are the same techniques that can be used to make them.

Bio techniques, when they work, are usually cheaper, less energy intensive. Right now, less efficient. But we could change that."

Lyr frowned. He seemed to be assuming that the foundation would be successful, as if there were no doubt at all.

"You're assuming a great deal."

"Could be." He laughed. "Maybe the fact that the foundation is the only one supporting biological technology means we're the only crazy ones. Maybe I'm just paranoid."

Lyr frowned again, but said nothing.

"Any other questions?"

"I'm sure I have dozens. I just can't think of them." Her leg twitched involuntarily and threw her off balance.

His hand touched her shoulder as if to keep her from pitching sideways.

"Thank you."

"Any last questions?"

"No." Her lips were dry, and she licked them once, then again. "I'm probably wrong, but I just don't think I could stay here, not unless I have some better idea of who and what you are, what you look like."

"All right. Will you consider staying, then?"

"I'll consider it."

His hand squeezed her shoulder gently, and he stepped around the swivel and stood before her, next to the screen.

She looked up.

The familiar hawk-yellow eyes caught her attention first, that and the hint of darkness behind them, a darkness that hinted at a man far older than the one who faced her. She studied his face, the sharpish nose, the unlined and smooth skin, thin lips, and the short and blond curly hair cut military-style. He had neither beard nor mustache.

While his chin was not pointed, it narrowed in a way that almost gave him an elfin look, had it not been for the penetrating power of his eyes and the strength of his nose.

Once more, she tried to focus on his body, but the black of the formfitting singlesuit he wore kept pushing her eyes away from his form and toward the floor or his face.

He noted her confusion. "It's a full-fade combat suit."

"You aren't . . ."

"No. Just something useful."

She licked her lips again. His face, even with the hawk-eyes, looked familiar, but she could not say why. She had never met him,

outside of the interview years ago, that and the scattered screen contacts. That she knew; yet he seemed familiar.

"No horns. No black cloud." He smiled.

"No recognition, either," she countered.

"Didn't say you'd recognize me. Said the ability to recognize me
might be dangerous."

Lyr cocked her head to one side. For all the clipped sentences,
the shortened words, his speech pattern had a touch of a lilt, an odd
tone that she had never heard before. She wondered why she had not
picked it up earlier, even though there was no doubt now that he was
the man who had interviewed her. The unique hawk-eyes were enough
to confirm that. Perhaps the screen speakers did not reproduce the
lilt, underlying his speech as it did.

"Shall we dive for the event horizon?" she asked.

He raised his eyebrows in inquiry, but said nothing.

"Who are you?"

He shrugged. "If you insist . . . MacGregor Gerswin, at your service."

"I don't recognize the name, either."

"Never said I was famous. Glad to know I'm not." He took a step
to the side. "How are your legs?"

Lyr tried to lift her right foot, could feel the effort, but the leg did
not move. "Better, but I still can't move them."

"Shouldn't be too long." He spread his hands. "Now that you've
unmasked me . . . what next?"

"I don't know."

"Still want to quit?"

"Common sense screams that I should, but I wouldn't want to
force anyone else to go through one of your employee searches, Ser
Gerswin."

"What can I say?"

"Don't. Just be thankful I'm as crazy as you are. But," and her
voice hardened, "don't sneak in again and change the files without at
least warning me that you might be in the area. And fax me directly
without that damned hood and mask."

He laughed. "I'll do both, unless I can't reach you. Promise me
you'll look before pulling your stunner."

"I promise."

A frown crossed his face. "I should have left some time ago."

"Another woman. I knew it."

He shook his head. "Duty, so to speak. I have . . . other obligations. I will stay in touch. How is your leg?"

"The feeling's back."

"Good." He nodded, bent, and picked up a small case from beside the base of the console, a case she had never seen, for all the time it had apparently lain there.

With a salute, he turned and was gone.

So quickly had he departed that Lyr shook her head to make sure he had indeed gone. What else had she missed? Besides everything?

MacGregor Gerswin? Was he in any of the lists?

She bent over the console, nearly losing her balance again as her legs twitched. Feeling had returned to both, along with the faint sensation of needles jabbing at her skin.

"Might as well search while you wait," she said softly to herself. She did not trust her legs to bear her weight yet.

No MacGregor Gerswin appeared in any of the New Augustan Imperial Government directories, not even an M. Gerswin.

Imperial Service? Which one?

She tried the Marine Directory.

Nothing.

Aeorspace Defense?

Nothing.

Retirees?

No such listing.

Interstellar Survey Service?

"Individual names and assignments are not available for security reasons. An alphabetical listing of names is available with rank and communications locator code. Do you wish to continue search?"

She tapped in "Yes."

"Gerswin, MacGregor Corson, Senior Commander, 455 NC 466/OS."

That was all.

Lyr shook her head tiredly, conscious of the fatigue in her legs as the stunner wore off. It had been a long day before the evening's events.

"Just a senior commander. Not even a commodore?

"But he never claimed anything," she answered her own question.

She tapped the screen and erased the inquiries. She'd have the time. Cursing and damning herself for a fool, she knew she would have the time.

XXIII

What forecast the fall of the Empire?

Was it the increasing development and resource require-ments of the associated systems, pushing inevitably as they did for use of those resources for more local needs? Was it merely a turn-ing away from the Imperialist nature of the Empire? Was it a re-pudiation of the growing corruption manifested in New Augusta?

Was it the development of the totally impartial Galactic Com-munications Network by the fanatically honest Ydrisians, whose peaceful intentions were never doubted and with whose fairness the biases of the Empire contrasted so unfavorably?

Was it the growing awareness of social change, manifested Empire-wide in such movements as the Ateys, the Droblocs, the Aghomers? Or was the Empire merely one of those accidents of history that lasted so long as it did because it took fifteen cen-turies for its peoples to discover that it had really never lived?

The Last Great Empire
Ptior Petral, IV
New Avalon, 5467 N.E.C.

##

LYR D'MERYON STEPPED out of the electrocab and into the warm-lights of the entry tunnel.

To her right was a towering figure—a doorman—whose weight and bulk might have qualified him for the Imperial Marines' Front Force.

She hesitated, then began a series of quick steps toward the por-tal, where she presented the card that Commander Gerswin had left for her. Was he the trustee or the commander to her?

She didn't know, but apparently the invitation was his apology. At least she hoped that was all it was.

The portal accepted the card, but did not return it as it opened for her.

Inside, the lighting was brighter, though fractionally, and the tiles were replaced with carpeting. She looked again as her eyes took in the decor. The foyer where she stood was about the same size as her private office and was floored in dark wood, over which laid an individual carpet with a central design, in turn bordered by a more geometrical design, both woven in a harmonious blend of blue and maroons.

"Administrator D'Meryon?"

The voice came from a short, gray-haired man who stood by the tall wooden table flanking the exit from the foyer into the next room.

"Yes?"

"Your patron has arrived already and is expecting you. If you would follow me?"

Lyr inclined her head in assent and followed the man through the archway into a dining area, dimly lit, with the tables arranged in a circular pattern, each in its own paneled recess to create a sense of full privacy without closeness.

The dark and heavy carpeting, the wood paneling, and the crisp white linen all gave the impressions of a time from history, of a place removed from the here and now.

Commander Gerswin, in a formal gray tunic and trousers that resembled a uniform, stood as she neared.

She almost smiled, more in embarrassment than in pleasure, as his eyes came to rest on her. She wondered if he saw through people the way he seemed to when he looked at them.

"Lyr. Pleasure to see you."

"I appreciate your asking me, Commander." Her tone was as cool as she could politely make it.

He nodded in response, but said nothing until she was seated in the comfortable armchair opposite him at the square table.

"Would you like something to drink?"

"Squierre and flame."

Lyr did not see the waiter until the commander looked up over her head and repeated the order.

"Straight fizz," he added.

She surveyed the room as well as she could from her chair without turning around, and waited.

He waited.

And the waiter returned with both drinks, set them down in the appropriate places, and departed without saying a word.

"Owe you an apology. Perhaps more. Start by saying I apologize."

The directness of his words took her breath away. She took a sip of the squierre before answering.

"It's not that simple, Commander. You don't ask me to an obviously expensive private club, say, 'I apologize,' and assume that everything is forgotten and forgiven."

"No. I know that. So do you." He paused. "Have to start somewhere. Foundation needs you. I need you."

"Fine. I'll accept that. But it means more trust on your part. Why don't you start by telling me who you really are?"

He shrugged. "You know a lot already. Broken-down and passed-over I.S.S. Commander. Pressed into public service in my off-duty time. One reason why I need you." After sipping the nondrug, nonalcohlic drink, he waited for her response.

"That doesn't compute. Broken-down commanders don't end up as sole trustees of powerful foundations, unless they're related to Court families or the Imperial family."

"I'm not. I'm originally from an impoverished and forgotten outer system. Used the Service to improve myself, but, as ambitious officers will do, ran into difficulties with High Command. Finis to promotions."

"It couldn't have been too bad or you would have been cashiered or had to resign."

"Delicate orbit. Some pushed for that. Public opinion ran my way, and High Command backed off."

Lyr smiled wryly. "And you're just a poor, broken-down commander? If they backed off because of the publicity, you must have had an extremely high profile."

"Wasn't like that at all. Would have been inconvenient for the Service to deal with me."

"The more you say, the more mysterious it gets. But you offer no substance. No glorious battles from years in the I.S.S. It sounds more like a series of screen-pushing assignments in headquarters."

"Ha!"

The single barked laugh startled Lyr, and she set down her goblet too hard, hard enough for the liquid to splash and dribble down the outside of the crystal. She dabbed at it with the napkin.

"I take it you have done more than screen pushing."

"A bit. Rated skitter and flitter pilot. Had command of a cruiser for two tours."

"Which one?"

"*Fleurdilis.*"

"The *Fleurdilis*? The one that discovered the bearlike aliens? The . . . Ursans?"

"Same one. Yes."

"Yes?" Lyr's face screwed up into an inquiry. "Yes to what?"

"Was the C.O. at the time."

"Oh . . ." A slow smile crossed her face. "I suppose I owe you a bit of an apology, Commander."

"No."

"Yes, I do. I've been thinking of you as more of an administrative officer, a man who postures more than acts."

"All men posture," snorted the commander.

"Some have reason. And I can see why High Command left you well enough alone for whatever else you did."

The commander nodded with an odd expression on his face, one which Lyr could not place.

"Did you actually engage in hand-to-hand combat with an alien, the way the faxers showed?"

"Combat, one on one, but not so romantic as the newsies recreated. Pretty grubby. Should have been able to avoid killing him, her, it. Wasn't good enough for that. Turned out all right in the end. Better than the Dismorph first contact."

Lyr took a sip from the goblet.

"What about you?" the commander asked.

"Me?"

"Know your background, and you're a good administrator. Can tell that from what you've done with the assets, new investments, even the protection of the few early research returns. Why do you do it? What do you want? More money? More time off? Or more knowledge about . . . anything in particular . . ."

She set down the goblet and frowned, then worried her lower lip.

"Think about it. We'll come back to that. Time to pick out your dinner."

"As your guest, Commander, I'll defer to your taste. I'm not terribly fond of red meat. Other than that, anything is fine. Whatever you think best."

The commander looked at the silent waiter, whom Lyr had not heard approach this time either, then cocked his head to the side momentarily, as if trying to remember something.

"The lady will have the flamed spicetails, the bourdin cheeses, the house salad, and the d'crem. I will have the scampig, the cheeses, the salad, and lechoclat."

The waiter vanished.

"You eat here often?"

"When I'm in New Augusta. Not all that often. Car—one of the founders proposed the membership, I suspect. Took it. It's helpful."

"Helpful? That's an odd way of describing it."

He shrugged, then picked up his glass for another sip.

She emulated his example, but set the goblet down as the waiter reappeared with the two salads.

She glanced up from the salad to find him studying her face.

"Lyr? If you could do something entirely different, what would it be? Where would you go? What are your dreams?"

The laugh bubbled up in her throat even as she tried to swallow the remaining drops of squierre in her mouth.

"Phhhwwwww . . . uuouugh . . . ucoughhh . . ."

He stood, but she waved him away, dabbed her chin with the cloth napkin, coughed twice more to clear her throat. Finally she managed to swallow.

"Dreams yet, Commander. Please . . ."

This time she held up her hand before he could interrupt.

"Dreams? Commander, you must be joking."

"No joke." He laughed once, the hard bark that chilled her, that reminded her that for all his directness, the directness that bordered on uncouthness, he would be a dangerous adversary. For anyone.

"I'm sorry," she added in a softer voice. "But the question was unexpected. You really don't know, do you?"

"Unexpected? Why?"

Lyr frowned. Should she tell him? Subtlety wasn't likely to work, one way or another.

She sighed. "It's like this. You said once that there were more than a hundred foundations with greater possible endowments than OER. It's more like fifty—"

"That's now. Because of your efforts."

"—and they have one thing in common. That's a lack of initiative. My job isn't good. It's the best in my field. That's why I'll stay unless you force me out. You handed me something that no one ever expects, much less at my age, and said, in effect, and despite all the mystery, go and do your best. And you didn't second-guess every investment and every fund transfer. So I've done my best."

"Very well," added the commander.

She stopped and worried her lip. "So you see why I have to laugh at your asking about dreams. I'm worried about your forcing me to leave a dream, and you're asking me about a dream beyond a dream. You don't want me to leave, do you?"

"No. Your work is just beginning, now." His voice softened on the last word.

She saw his eyes lose their intensity momentarily as he repeated quietly one of her phrases.

"A dream beyond a dream . . ." Then his eyes were back on her, boring into her. "Humor me. Give me a dream beyond a dream."

Lyr looked away, damning herself for revealing too much, feeling like she had worn nothing to the table.

"Do you have dreams beyond your dreams?" she countered quietly.

"Sometimes. Sometimes I dream of rolling hills covered with grass, and streams, sparkling from mountain rocks." He looked up. "Land . . . so . . . poor . . . where I grew up . . . no green grass." He looked away and took the last gulp of his fizz. "What about your dream, Lyr?"

She did not answer, but took a sip, a small sip, of the squierre, ignoring the salad before her, and stared at the white of the linen on the table as she let the warmth trickle down her throat.

"If I couldn't do this . . . I'd have to get away. Some place like Vers D'Mont . . . with mountains but culture. I haven't been there, not even on my salary, but you asked me to dream. People, but with privacy. I—" She stopped, watching him nod as she spoke.

"A small cottage?"

"A chalet, on a hill, not a sharp peak, but one where you could see the high mountains, and the valley below, with a lake. A chalet that had balconies on all sides."

The commander continued to nod as if her fancy were as possible as sitting across the table.

"But that's impossible!" she burst out, then lowered her voice. "Why encourage an impossible dream?"

"No dream is impossible. Wasn't encouraging, but inquiring."

"But why?"

"Dreams are important." He said nothing to amplify that, but took a last bite of his salad, then sat back as the waiter placed the scampig before him.

Lyr nodded at the man to take her unfinished salad.

"What are they?" She studied the question-marklike objects on the porcelain plate.

"Spicetails. Seafood delicacy. My second favorite dish, but should I tell you that?"

She smiled in response to the commander's gentle self-deprecation.

"I'll try them anyway."

The longer the meal went on, the more confused she became as to the commander's motivations. His attitude was not apology, exactly, nor seduction, nor exactly interest, though he continued to ask gentle questions.

"Do you have other interests . . . hobbies . . . besides numbers? . . . Would you travel widely? . . . Your family? Were you close? . . . Whom of the public figures do you admire the most?"

Those questions she could not avoid, she answered, gently and as briefly as possible, not forgetting to enjoy the dinner.

The cost of the meal had to have been astronomical. The setting, the cutlery, which was worked sterling silver, the antique porcelain, the linen, the use of well-trained help—they all pointed to an establishment for the extraordinarily affluent.

And yet, the man across from her, while born a leader, had obviously not been born to wealth. For all his Service training and accomplishments, he was only a commander.

Or was he?

Even when she had left the Aurelian Club, headed back to her own more than comfortable apartment, the hundredth floor of the Hegemony Towers, she could not decide.

He was more than a Service commander, she knew. But what?

SCF-EC-4 (Sector Red, CW-3)

SCF-EC is a spectral type G-2, population 3 anomaly. Seven planet system, four inner hard core/crust. Planets three and four within T-compatible life zone. Planets five and six are gas giants. Planet seven is captured comet accretion satellite with irregular orbit . . .

Planet three possible for future intelligent NH life. Wide spectrum, classification range O/N, WAL, LP/MP, FSR . . .

Planet four limited organic classifications N/N, SMS/MS. CrB. Site of nonidentified intact Class I artifact (See Aswan, legends section, and SCF-EC-4—Engineering/Structures) . . .

Chartbook, Sector Three
Commonality of Worlds
5573 N.E.C.

XXVI

BOTH CIRCUIT BLOCS remained black.

With a sigh, the man in the working tech's jumpsuit set them aside and stood up.

Each aspect of rebuilding the courier took more time, more credits, and more equipment than even he had anticipated. He reset the test probes, and reattached the cube blocs. His fingers played across the tester's console.

This time, the circuit bloc on the right turned crimson. But the one on the left remained black.

He sighed again and stood up, glancing across the hangar at the incomplete structure in the graving cradle, the structure that he hoped would someday be the ship he needed.

His eyes strayed to his wrist and the comp-timer there.

2230—far too late already. Allison would be asleep, assuming that Corson was not giving her trouble. But Corson seldom did, despite his intense interest in the world around him and his already too active efforts at crawling.

Corson and Allison—there was never enough time for them, not with the demands of being Standora Base Commander and the invisible deadlines for completing the courier that crept up toward him.

How could he tell Allison that he had to finish the ship before his last tour at Standora? She thought he had all the time in the universe.

Caroljoy had thought that, too.

Perhaps they were right, but he could be killed as easily as any other man, and would be, once the Empire discovered his plans. On that basis, he had little enough time, and no one in whom he could confide.

Allison, wrapped up in her moments of joy, and in Corson, could not understand the desperate need of a distant and antique planet forgotten by all but the myth tellers, the historians, and one Imperial senior commander.

Caroljoy, who had understood, had also opted for her moments of joy in her son. But she had left him the means and, indirectly, yet another pressure, to pursue his obsession.

"Obsession?" he asked himself wryly.

"Obsession," he conceded as he placed another circuit bloc into the tester, ignoring the tightening in his guts as he felt the night inch toward morning, as he could sense the loneliness radiating from a large house on a high hill.

The third circuit bloc flared crimson, and he smiled, using his lips only, as he placed it inside the screen relay he was reconstructing.

"Only five more," he muttered as he selected yet another bloc from the case of scrapped components he had obtained through the Ydrisian free market.

He shifted his weight as he began once more to work the testing console, probing the minute circuits before him to insure their integrity and functions.

Taking a deep breath, he settled back into the routine. Select, set up the test patterns, scan, and test. Select, set up, scan, and test.

He hoped Corson was sleeping well.

And Allison. And Allison.

XXVII

"CONGRATULATIONS, ADMIRAL. CONGRATULATIONS."

"Appreciate it, Medoro." The newly sworn Admiral of the Fleet surveyed the palatial office, the wide armaglass windows that overlooked New Augusta from the hillside that the I.S.S. had claimed generations earlier, and the small group of Imperial courtiers, functionaries, and subordinates who waited at the far end of the high-ceilinged room.

He repressed a smile as he glanced back at Medoro. The senior commodore, who had served as Chief of Staff for the last two Fleet Admirals, obviously would lose no time in pressing his own agenda. The admiral nodded at his Chief of Staff. "It's time to play politics, I gather."

"It's always time to play politics, Admiral."

The admiral let the smile come to his lips. "Always and forever, from now on. Right, Medoro?"

"If you want a long and healthy tenure, ser."

Medoro's tone was light, but the admiral caught the bitterness of underlying truth. The most senior officer of the Service took a step toward the white linens of the over-laden table where the official "informal" celebration of his swearing-in would commence.

"Any space for truth?" he asked the commodore, almost as if the question were an afterthought.

"Only if you are careful, ser . . . and now is not the time to begin . . . Admiral Keraganis is the one on the far right . . . next to him is Admiral Fleiter, head of logistics and personnel . . . and behind him is Rear Admiral Thurson, Information Services—"

"That's basically the Service rep to the Eye Council, right?"

"He does sit as liaison to the council, currently."

The admiral refocused his attention on the officers approaching as he moved up to the table area.

"Congratulations, Admiral Horwitz," boomed out the man Medoro had identified as Keraganis. "Look forward to working with you. Heard a lot about you, especially the way you handled the original Ursan contact. Brilliant strategy."

Horwitz inclined his head. "Thank you. Just fortunate to have the right people in the right places. I look forward to having the benefit of your unique experience, and your distinguished advice will certainly be welcome."

"Glad to see you again, J'rome," broke in another admiral, a silver-haired and thin man who stood a half head above the others.

"Marsta! Didn't expect to see you. When did you get here?" The Fleet Admiral sidestepped Keraganis, favoring him with a pat on the shoulder that he hoped would get the point across that Keraganis was not working with him, but for him, and around the end of the laden table.

He stopped before reaching his friend.

"All of you, it's a happy occasion. Please enjoy the food and the company. Dig in."

Immediately several junior commodores and a senior commander, appearing rather out of place among the senior officers of the I.S.S., took refuge in the food.

"J'rome. Didn't expect to make it, but we wound up the Rim maneuvers almost a week ahead of schedule. For once, everything worked. Smart idea that Alexandro had, insisting on premaneuver checks at Standora."

"Alexandro? Standora?"

"C.O. of the *Dybyykk*. He had some emergency work done there a year ago. Better than any Service yard yet, he insisted, and since no one else out that way could fit the squadron in, I agreed. Took a week more than we thought, but it cut the down time on station by twice that. So I'm here."

Horwitz frowned. "Standora? Why is that so familiar?"

The rear admiral laughed. "How could you forget? Gerswin? He's the commandant at Standora."

"Gerswin is still around? He was ancient at the time of the Ursan contact."

"Doesn't look it, but I understand he's on his last or next-to-last tour—"

"Congratulations, Admiral Horwitz," broke in another voice. "Marc Fleiter, here. Logistics and personnel. I just wanted to meet you informally before we get together officially, and I wanted to let you know how much I look forward to working for you."

Horwitz repressed another smile. Fleiter was sharp, and had seen Horwitz's reaction to Keraganis's attempt to put the Fleet Admiral down.

"Good to meet you, Admiral Fleiter. I'm sure we will do well together, and I appreciate your interest."

"Not at all, Admiral. Just wanted to say hello, and I apologize if I intruded."

"No problem . . . no problem."

As Fleiter stepped back and away, and as Horwitz and Marsta were left alone momentarily, Marsta smiled a brief and rueful smile.

"What out for that one, J'rome."

"Sharp, isn't he?" Horwitz responded. "And dangerous, I suspect," he added in a lower voice. "But not the most dangerous one."

"Who's that?"

"I think it was Gerswin. Too bad he got mixed up in that Old Earth mess. Or maybe it's a good thing he did."

"Admiral Horwitz . . ."

The new Fleet Admiral turned to greet the next in the stream of well-wishers.

Admiral Marsta nodded and turned toward the fruit.

XXVIII

THE EMPTINESS STRUCK the commander as soon as he stepped through the portal into the foyer, with its real slate tiles that had been left from the days when the base had boasted a commodore in residence.

Boots clicking, the slender officer in working grays glanced into the salon, into the living room, into the formal dining room, and into the kitchen that was twice the size necessary even for the entertainment needs of the base commandant it served.

Empty—the main floor rooms were empty.

A dozen quick steps carried him up the wide formal staircase to the second floor, opposite the room she had used as a nursery. The standard crib, which had been presented to them by a local acquaintance, stood empty; the handmade quilt the boy loved, gone with him and his mother.

The I.S.S. senior officer crossed the small room and checked the closet. No clothes remained.

With a sigh, he surveyed the room once more.

Another deep breath, and he left, heading for the master suite, knowing she would be gone, and that the room they had shared, briefly it seemed, would be immaculate, and vacant.

In the wide hall outside the old-fashioned doorway, he paused, not wanting to burst in, nor wishing to find what he knew he would discover.

His eyes traced the perfectly squared panels of the wood. Finally he reached and touched the handle. The door swung inward at his touch.

For a moment, an instant, everything seemed normal. The crimson trimmed gray quilt still covered the outsized bed. A solideo cube still graced the bedside table on the side where he slept. Late afternoon sun still poured through the western windows of the sunroom and spilled through the archway into the bedroom itself.

His fears were confirmed by the other absences—the bare tabletop on the right side of the bed, the empty space on the wall where the portrait of the three of them had hung, the missing daccanwood box where she had kept her uniform insignia.

With slow steps he reached the closet, opened it, and saw his own uniforms on the right, and the emptiness on the left.

He turned, paced back and forth three times along the foot of the bed, almost as if she were still there, always back before him, her long legs curled under her, Corson at her breast, listening to him tell her about the day.

His eyes flickered to where she usually sat, then back to the floor before he realized that a white square lay across her pillow.

The commander pounced upon it, so quickly an onlooker would not have believed the speed with which he moved, and studied the script, the nearly childish lines with the large loops and clear and precise letters.

My dear Commander—

It is time to go. My resignation has been accepted. While it will hurt, it would hurt so much more later, when Corson and I would become a wall between you and destiny.

Already, you pace the floor at the foot of the bed at night. A thousand projects are on your mind, and you are torn between us and what you must do. I can see the fury building, though you have never been other than gentle.

The Service owes me a last trip home, and that is where we will head. I do not expect you to follow. This is *not* a hidden plea to show how much you care. I know nothing could stand in your way if you chose to find us, and I have hidden nothing. All that can stop you is your own good sense.

Please do not come after me. I would rather have eighteen months of wonderful memories than a lifetime of resentment. I bear you only love. Both you and having Corson were my choices. Most would say I was foolish. Now, perhaps, I should admit that I was. That is past. I have Corson, and to keep him, in any real sense, I must resign. I have, because he is too wonderful to leave.

For his sake as well, we must leave. No matter how brilliant and talented he grows up to be, he would always stand in your shadow. Because he is you, and your son, he will need his own light.

In time, I will lose him as well. Already he resembles you. That is why time is precious, and why I will give him what you never had. He may not be the great man you are and will be, but I trust he will find the universe a more loving place.

It is strange, how you inspire love. You do not want to accept it. As you accept it, you become outwardly more gentle. But the furies inside you build. Istvenn help the universe should you ever unleash them.

I can say no more. I love you, but I love Corson more, and, for now, he needs that love. If you love him, if you have ever cared for me, let us be, Commander dear.

The formal notecard in hand, he straightened and let his steps take him into the sunroom. From the wide windows, he looked downhill toward the empty shuttle field.

She and Corson had taken the *Graham* back toward the Arm, back toward Scandia and its tall conifers and rocky islands.

Scandia . . . the name even sounded like her.

He shook his head and turned away from the vista.

She had liked the view from the commandant's quarters. How many times had she sat in the swing chair in the late afternoon, after she had gotten home, Corson cradled in her left arm, just looking out?

"Destiny . . ." The single word seemed to cast a shadow on the sunlit carpet.

Was he that driven? Was it so obvious that those who loved him turned away? Or did they really love him at all? Were they just drawn to him for some other reason?

He laid the notecard on the arm of the swing chair before he left the sunroom, before he looked through the rest of the quarters for the two he would not find, for any trace of the pilot, woman, and officer who had loved him, and of his son, whom he had known so briefly.

The sunbeams played across the weave of the Scandian carpet he had bought for her, illuminating the soft golds and browns in the silence.

XXIX

SENIOR WEAPONS TECHNICIAN Heimar scanned the list on the screen again. Shipment four—standard heavy cruiser replacement pack—was listed as having been picked up by the *Bernadotte*'s tender.

Heimar checked the orbit schedule and frowned. According to New Glascow orbit control, the *Bernadotte* had closed orbit less than four standard hours ago. The pick up time had been more than ten hours earlier.

The technician compared the screen list to the hard copy receipt. Then he called up the code section. The authentications were identical.

Finally he turned to the impatient major.

"Your shipment is listed as already having been picked up. It's not here, either. That rules out screen error."

"How could it have been picked up?"

"That's what we'd like to know."

Heimar tried not to show the shaking he felt inside. A standard weapons pack for a heavy cruiser consisted of a dozen tacheads and four hellburners.

One pack was apparently missing, properly logged out, apparently properly picked up by a cruiser tender with the right identifications, the right codes, and loaded by Heimar's own crews.

The only problem was that the tender couldn't have belonged to the *Bernadotte*.

Would the commander be upset? Would he? Heimar shuddered. Although it had not happened in his watch, his men had obviously been the ones suckered, and Heimar did not want to be the one to notify the commander.

He reached out and slapped the red stud on the console. Then he waited, but only for a few seconds.

"Commander, this is Heimar, at off-load. The weapons officer of the *Bernadotte* has some information that you should know."

Heimar stepped back and motioned the major to the screen.

He stared at the dome above, thinking about the murky atmosphere outside, the nearly unbreathable air, wishing he were anywhere, even there, besides on-duty and in reach of the commander. It had never happened before, not that he knew. Sixteen nuclear warheads gone—disappearing from a tightly guarded Imperial system, disappearing without even an alarm being raised or anyone being the wiser.

Heimar had heard the rumors about the great dozer theft of a half century earlier, or whenever it had been, but that had happened in orbit, not planetside.

But twelve tacheads, and four hellburners? He bit his lips. It wouldn't be as bad for him as it would be for the commander, but that wouldn't make it any easier.

"HEIMAR!"

He stepped back to the screen to explain what he had discovered.

THE MAN STEPPED inside the building's foyer. Although the wind whipped snow with the force of needles along the broad expanse that would be a boulevard in the short summer, he wore but a light gray jacket and black, calf-high boots. Hatless, he showed blond hair, like the majority of Scandians. Unlike theirs, his was short and tight-curled to his skull.

Once inside, he shook himself, and the light dusting of snow fell onto the wide entry mat. Three steps took him to the directory block, where he confirmed a suite number before taking the low stairs behind it two at a time to the second story of the three-floored building.

The office he wanted was at the rear northern side, and, as he walked through the open archway he could immediately see a panorama of the lake at the base of the hill on which the building stood. Below swirled drifts, and frozen white covered the lake. The wind-sculpted drifts ran from the stone wharves and the docks of the town on the right, and from the treed slopes of the park on the left out into the indistinctness of the white north.

"May we help you?"

The young man who spoke was black-haired—the single dark one of the five in the office—and clean-shaven.

Before answering, the visitor studied the other four, two men and two women. All five wore collarless tunics, trousers, and slippers. He glanced to the rack at the side, where parkas and heavy trousers hung above thick boots.

"Looking for Mark Ingmarr."

"That's me," laughed the darker man, who stood more than a head taller than the slender visitor. "You are—?"

"Corson . . . MacGregor Corson."

"You mean Gerswin?"

"Said Corson. Meant Corson."

The two women exchanged glances, but said nothing.

"If that's the way you want it . . ."

"That's the way I want it."

"You called earlier." The tall man's tone was flat.

"That's correct. You are an advocate . . . an attorney?"

"I told you that."

"Satisfactory. Need your professional ability."

"What if I don't want to give it?"

The visitor looked up at the heavily muscled young advocate. "You don't have to. Find someone else. You would be better."

Ingmarr stared down at the other, found his eyes caught by the hawk-yellow intensity of the smaller man's stare. For an instant, it seemed as though he were trapped in blackness. He dropped his eyes, breaking the contact.

"I'll talk about it," the attorney conceded.

He pointed to a console and two chairs in the far corner, half concealed behind a bank of indoor plants.

The man in gray took the right-hand chair, the one farther from the console.

"What do you want?" asked the advocate.

"A modest trust. Designed to receive funds from a blind account in the Scandian Bank. Should include certain provisions for education, an alternate to the trustee, and a termination and succession clause."

"That's rather general."

"The beneficiary is about seven standard years old. I'm acting for his father's family. His mother felt that his father was not the most stable of individuals. Mother left with son when the boy was less than a year old. Father couldn't do much. Family feels son should be provided for, particularly education. Half the trust would be his ten standard years after he reaches statutory majority. The other half goes to his mother, ten years after he reaches majority, or after he would have. Should he not reach majority, his half would be used to endow scholarships in his name at the university."

"What if the boy's mother doesn't want the money?"

"We can't prevent her from not using it, but the funds would be his at some point regardless."

"You seem rather determined."

"It is both the least and the most that can and should be done under the circumstances."

"Rather a strange way to put it."

The shorter man shrugged. "Strange situation."

"Why didn't you have the bank set it up? You wouldn't even have had to make a long trip. They could, you know."

"Some things require a personal touch." He handed Ingmarr a sheet. "This contains the securities that will compose the trust, as well as the specified asset composition for incoming cash flows."

"I'd have to advise against too much inflexibility."

"Only the investment parameters are inflexible. The categories, not specific choices."

"You said a modest trust . . . this looks to be more than that."

"In addition to the listed securities, the initial credit transfer will be fifty thousand credits. Annual payments will be in the neighborhood of about five thousand credits for roughly the next ten years. After that, the trust will be expected to be self-sustaining."

Ingmarr looked at the list and touched his console, his eyes darting back and forth between the information he called up and the securities listed.

The man who called himself Corson watched in silence.

"For Scandia, this is much more than a modest trust, much more, ser . . . Corson. This would set . . . the boy . . . up comfortably for life."

"Not wise without conditions. Mentioned those earlier. First, may not collect even any of the interest unless he finishes primary studies. Second, not more than half the interest until he finishes graduate level. Third, he may not *ever* acquire control of the principal capital until he is commissioned as an I.S.S. officer *or* completes the full Nord Afriq survival course."

"But if he cannot collect without the schooling—"   .

"Sorry. Should have made that clear. Trust pays school expenses directly, as necessary. Any excess income is reinvested, unless he needs it for living expenses, but he or his mother must submit records, like an expense account, to the trustee."

"I think I understand your interest and reasoning, ser . . . Corson."

"One final stipulation. He is not to be informed of the trust until he completes primary studies, or until ten years after majority, whichever comes first."

"At that time, do you want him to know the source of the trust?"

"I would leave that to the trustee and his mother. She could also tell him that the money was left for him by a distant relative. An eccentric old Imperial officer. That might be best, but that would be her choice."

Ingmarr frowned. "Any other conditions?"

"Not unless you think there should be."

"All right. Let me get started on this, if you don't mind. We'd all feel better if it were completed and you could get on with . . . could get on with . . . whatever . . ."

"I understand."

The outsider leaned back in the chair and transferred his sharp glance to the snow-drifted lake and the gray-clouded skies and the fine sheeting snow that appeared more like fog.

He could tell the taller of the two women kept looking at him, although he did not need to turn to check, and his keen hearing could pick out some of the phrases.

"... same eyes, same curly hair ..."

"... but her brother?"

"... scary ... when you think how old ..."

"... fascinating though ..."

Ingmarr continued to work with the legal terminology on the console, apparently oblivious to either his client or the rest of the office.

After a time, the stranger straightened in his seat and removed a thin folder from inside his light jacket, which he had opened but not removed. He checked the contents, then left it in his lap and returned his attention to a line of skiers moving smoothly across the lake toward the town with practiced strides.

"Ser Corson ... if you would like to check this out ... and fill in the necessary names and details."

"Fine."

The outsider slipped into the seat in front of the console, eyes running over the displayed text.

Ingmarr noted the ease with which he operated the equipment, changing pages, cross-indexing, checking references.

"No problem ... except here. Think you should add something about 'with the approval of the mother, Allison Ingmarr.'"

The man in gray stood back from the console, still holding the folder that he had brought.

"All right." Ingmarr sat back down and made the changes, scanning through the text to insure that his client had supplied all the necessary information.

The smaller man stepped up as Ingmarr looked up from the screen.

"You'll need these."

"Which are?"

"The portfolio securities. In Corson's name."

Ingmarr took the folder without opening it.

"Let me run out the copies of this for authentication and registration."

The stranger nodded and half-turned toward the winter scene outside.

As Ingmarr touched the last stud on the console, he stood, laying the folder on the flat top of the equipment. He moved away from the console. Looming over the stranger, he cleared his throat and flexed his shoulders as if to assure himself that his muscles were loose.

"Who are you, anyway? As if I didn't know."

"I told you, MacGregor Corson."

"I don't believe that for an instant." The Scandian reached out for the smaller man with a huge right hand and grabbed him by the shoulder.

"Let go." The words were quiet.

"Who are you? Why are you here?"

Thud.

Ingmarr stared up from the carpeted floor into a yellow, hawk-eyed glare. He appeared stunned.

"Doing my best to hold to her wishes. Without disinheriting him. No more questions."

Each word, though whispered, seared. Ingmarr stiffened, but did not get off the floor.

"You! . . . never believed . . ."

"Get the trust finished. Sooner the better." The stranger's light baritone voice was calm.

"Agreed," conceded Ingmarr, rubbing his hand and then his shoulder. The smaller man had handled him as if he were a doll, and for the first time, he was beginning to understand his sister, her tears, and her fears. And her reasons for having to trust the man.

Ingmarr stood up slowly and repeated himself. "Agreed."

Both men ignored the whispers from the other side of the open office as they moved toward the printing station in the middle of the office.

". . . like a child . . ."

". . . so fast . . ."

". . . has to be *him* . . ."

Outside, the wind picked up, and the snow fog thickened until the gray light resembled twilight rather than midafternoon.

Inside, two women shivered in thin tunics while a tall man continued to massage a sore shoulder, and a shorter blond man began to authenticate a legal document.

XXXI

GERSWIN LOOKED OVER at the innocuous set of plasteel shipping containers that filled the small aft hold of the *Caroljoy*. Twelve bore labels indicating they were high-speed message torps, and four bore labels indicating long range torps.

Not that the labels were totally inaccurate, mused the commander. Someday they might have to be used to send a message of sorts, but he had obtained them now, when it was still possible, without too much difficulty.

The maiden voyage of the refurbished former scout had gone well, well indeed, although it would have proved difficult, if not impossible, to have traced the supposed private yacht through three separate identities, two military, and four systems, not including Scandia. That diversion, on the return trip, had been for other reasons, later than he would have wished, but accomplished nonetheless.

His eyes lost their sharp focus for a minute as he recalled the snow-covered firs of Scandia, and, more distantly, a pair of eyes as clear as a cloudless winter morning. He shook his head to bring himself back to the small hold.

Gerswin checked the hold locks once again before extricating himself from the hold and climbing back into the former crew room. Loading the shipping crates from outside through the exterior cargo lock, an armed tender lock converted for his purposes, had been far easier than inspecting them from inside the ship. Small as the aft hold was, the forward hold was even smaller, containing only emergency stores and an emergency generator and solar array.

There was less crew space under Gerswin's internal redesign than in the ship's original configuration. As a scout, the former *Farflung* had carried a four man crew under tight living conditions. Gerswin had reconfigured the newly and officially registered *Caroljoy* (IPS-452) as a single pilot ship, with emergency capacity for two passengers on short hauls.

The drives were not those of a scout, but of a small corvette, with total power cross-bleed between the corvette screens and gravitics. The extra power and range had come at the cost of habitability and because Gerswin had installed higher quality control and communi-

cations systems—the lower weight and improved reliability offset by
the considerably higher price.

The commander sealed the hatch beneath him, which resembled
another tiled floor square of the cabinlike section of the ship, which
contained the fresher, wall-galley, and bunk. He stood, surveying the
trim and efficient interior.

"Stand down mode, full alert," he ordered.

"Stand down mode, full alert." A voice, feminine, but impersonal,
answered the commander.

He sealed the locks behind him, and stepped out into the hangar,
which, as he had rebuilt the *Caroljoy* from scratch, he had turned into
a maintenance facility capable of handling all but the largest of private yachts. The equipment within the hangar could also have served
virtually all Imperial scouts and corvettes, although that capability remained the secret of the commander.

He had not kept secret from his subordinates that, after Allison's
departure, his sole vice was his "hobby"—building a private yacht
from surplus scrap for his eventual retirement.

Some of his officers had even visited the hangar and the *Caroljoy*—
at suitably arranged times when the disarray was maximized—and
while all were impressed by the commandant's personal expertise,
they shook their heads sadly behind his back at his tales of spending
all his savings on his project.

None knew that the *Caroljoy* was already spaceworthy. He had not
registered her until after he had returned from the maiden voyage.
While the fact that his ship was spaceworthy would leak out sooner or
later, both the registration date and his officers' memories would reflect a much later first launch than the reality.

Gerswin smiled wryly at the recollection of some of the looks as
they had seen the scout in the graving cradle, looking as if it would be
forever before she lifted.

His steps carried him across the hangar toward the outside lock
and the groundcar that would carry him back to Standora Base, back
to the empty quarters of the commandant. Back to a short night's
sleep before another day of shuffling priorities, fleet repairs, and the
fragile egos of ship captains who had heard that Standora Base could
perform miracles and who all wanted to be first in line.

The commander shook his head as he thought of the sixteen
slender missiles sealed in the *Caroljoy*'s aft hold. Just as he hoped he
would not need them, he knew he would, although he could not say
for what. Not yet. But that time would come, had to come, as the Em-

pire began to crumble and the commercial barons began to grab for more and more.

Not yet did he need them. But to reclaim Old Earth, he had no doubt he would need them, and that he would have little or no time to obtain them by the time he needed such power. By then, too, the source of the weapons might have been forgotten.

As he slipped from the hangar, he automatically scanned the area, but the private shuttle port was quiet, as usual.

He guided the official groundcar across the plastarmac and toward the south gate of Standora Base more than twenty kays away.

THE SENIOR OFFICER accessed the private personal line, fed in the privacy links, and scrambled.

The screen colors swirled, then settled into the even lines of text provided by the agency.

"Quarterly Report—Corson Ingmarr."

The title was scarcely larger than the text that followed, but the commodore devoured each word, line by line, of the ten pages that had been transmitted by torp, each page costing as much as a set of undress blacks.

At last he keyed the report into his own personal files, though he doubted he would reread it, not for years, since he could remember the last reports verbatim.

Finally, he shut down the small console, the single piece of furniture or equipment in the rambling quarters that he could truly say was his own, along with the private comm relay he had leased with it.

Most of his creds had gone into the *Caroljoy*, along with the discretionary funds allowed him under the foundation bylaws, although his personal investments were still considerable, since he had attempted to fund the restoration out of income, rather than capital. The fact that his assets were more than comfortable was not surprising, not considering his years in Service, and his few personal needs.

He stood, blond, slender, despite the loose-fitting flight suit he wore, and walked around the console and out of the paneled room that bore the archaic term of "library," though there were neither books nor tapes within or upon the wooden shelves.

The room echoed with his steps, and light-footed as he was, their echo recalled the tapping of other steps. She had never liked the library, and Corson, of course, had not been walking when she had taken him.

"Why do you do it?"

The words did not echo as he left the room. The issue carpeting in the front foyer insured that, and his steps were silent as he climbed the wide steps to the second floor. Only the commandant's quarters had two stories, with the wide staircase, but then the quarters had been designed with entertaining in mind, back in the expanding days of the Empire, when energy had been more abundant, and before the rights of the occupied and colonized peoples had been taken quite so seriously.

Most nights, the commodore did not mind the quiet and the isolation.

Most nights . . . except for those when he thought about a curly-haired blond youth skiing across frozen lakes parsecs away.

Most nights . . . except for those when he dreamed about another curly-haired blond boy scuttling in terror from flaring torches through a tunnel, toward a night filled with king rats and landpoisons.

He shook his head as he entered the bedroom, not glancing at the overlarge bed he had never replaced when she had left.

Not that he always slept alone . . . but none had ever asked or hinted to spend another night. Not that he was ever other than gentle . . .

ALREADY THE VISITORS' stands were filled to overflowing, though the seats had been designed to hold more than five times the base complement. Civilians from Stenden were continuing to pour through the main gate.

The woman who would be the next commandant stood behind the reviewing stand and surveyed the ad hoc parade ground, the rows and rows of I.S.S. technicians wearing silver and black dress uniforms creased to perfection, the thousands of Standoran civilians wearing their best brikneas, the crisp white and green dominating the stands.

She wanted to stamp her foot, to stand on the podium when her turn came, and to bellow that she could do more than anything Commodore Gerswin could ever have done. She knew it was childish, that it might not even be true, but seeing the wistful look in the technicians' eyes, she still wanted to. Instead, she looked down at the spotless gray-blue plastarmac and took a deep breath.

Despite the base's reconstitution as one of the busiest and most efficient refit yards in the Empire, the light breeze bore only the faintest tinge of ozone, and none of metal and oil. Underlying it all was the scent of trilia from the formal gardens planted around both the tech and officer quarters, and from the hedgerows that flanked the small squared sector for accompanied personnel.

A cough at her elbow brought her head up.

A young captain, wearing the crossed ships of a pilot on her breast pocket, stood at the commander's shoulder.

"Commander H'Lieu?"

"Yes, Captain?"

"I believe the ceremony is about to begin."

The senior commander turned away from the crowds that flanked the reviewing stand, with a smile that could have been described as wry, straightened, and looked toward the steps of the reviewing stand itself.

She would sit on the left side of the podium, on the left of the crossed banners, for the review. Then the commodore would say a few words before turning over his sword. She would take the podium to say a few words, then return his sword, and then change places with him to review the departure parade as the new commandant.

All in all, a civilized and ritualized turnover of administrative authority. The only problem was that Headquarters had never told her that the man she was replacing had made himself into a living legend, both to the personnel he commanded and to the locals.

She had reviewed the base procedures, seen the audit reports, and interviewed a few key people—quietly, of course. All gave the impression of a competent and dedicated Commanding Officer, fair, impartial, and knowledgeable. But the records and procedures still did not show how he had turned the base around, nor did anyone seem to be able to tell her.

Yes, the man worked hard. Yes, he had improved operating procedures. Yes, he had instituted outreach programs with the locals. Yes, he insisted on absolute accuracy and perfection. Yes, he insisted on discipline and order.

She pursed her lips and dismissed her misgivings. Putting her hand on the railing of the temporary stairs, she glanced over at the visitors' stands. She could not recall a local community ever showing up for such a mundane affair as a change of command, even for a C.O. who had spent an unprecedented three five-year tours as the commodore had.

"Impressive, isn't it?" asked the captain. "Even the locals practically worship the ground he walks on."

The senior commander snapped her head back without commenting and stepped up to the landing.

The commodore was already there to greet her. She remembered the piercing eyes from a meeting on New Augusta years earlier.

"Welcome, Commander H'Lieu. Good to see you again."

"A pleasure to be here, Commodore." From the landing she could survey the entire area, and she let her eyes do that. "You obviously command a great deal more than Standora Base."

He chuckled, a self-deprecating sound, and then met her eyes. Both their brilliance and intensity were too much, and she eyed the raised stage with the two empty chairs, the podium, and the backdrop with the crossed banners of the Empire and the Service.

"I pleaded with the exec for something simple, but, as you can see, lost."

Face to face, she realized that she stood taller than he did, but that wasn't the way she felt.

"Commodore . . . Commander . . ." The captain's voice moved them apart and toward their seats.

As the commodore stood before the crowd, the rustlings stopped, as did the background conversation, until there was a hush.

The sound of the ancient trumpet calls echoed back from the hangars at the bugler below. As the notes died away three squads of technicians snapped into motion.

The tech drill team's silent performance was marred by neither mistakes nor by excessive length.

Commander H'Lieu glanced at her timestrap and realized that the performance had taken well less than ten standard minutes.

As the drill team returned to position, the ranks of arrayed techs began to move, marching by units before the commodore, who still stood at attention, perfectly straight and yet perfectly relaxed, while giving the impression of total alertness.

The commander stopped herself from shaking her head. The

man looked less than forty stans, yet he'd been at Standora for fifteen, and, if the rumors and records were correct, had more than a century in Service, which was possible, certainly, but totally unheard of.

The continued hush bothered her. In her own thirty plus years of Service, never had she heard such sustained quiet, almost as if it were a funeral or memorial rather than a mere change of command.

Her eyes swept the parade ground, the crowd of support personnel, and the visitors. No frowns, no laughs, no signs of fear, but no signs of celebration.

When the last detachment had stepped past the stand and back into position, then and only then did the commodore move, in quick steps, to the podium.

He offered no salutations, no jokes.

"All things must end, and all things must begin.

"My time here must end, and the time of Commander H'Lieu must begin. Standora Base is respected, appreciated, and, I believe, a worthwhile place to be. That it is all of these things is not because of a commandant, and not because it merely exists, but because the whole is greater than the sum of the parts. Because together we can do what none can do separately.

"No man, no woman, no child . . . stands alone. Nor have we. Together we have accomplished much. In this, I must include those who were stationed here and who have since departed, as well as those of you who have remained. Times and people have changed, but Standora Base remains. Change is a necessity for excellence, and excellence has been your greatest achievement.

"With Commander H'Lieu, I expect you to build upon that excellence, for much as we have accomplished, much remains to be done. We have forged strong working ties within the Service, within the Empire, and with Stenden, its people, and have begun to work well with the Standoran government. But that work must continue.

"Never forget that your success is built upon more than machines, on more than discipline. It is built upon the spirit. In the end, that spirit can move and change planets. That spirit alone can achieve excellence, and understand its price and responsibilities. And for that spirit, which you have demonstrated year in and year out, must all of you be commended.

"In my leaving, my departure, you lose a commandant, and you gain a new one. But your spirit you keep. May it always be so."

The commodore bowed his head momentarily in the silence that held, if possible, deeper than before.

"And now"—and he lifted his sword—"I offer my command and sword to Commander H'Lieu." He turned. "Commander H'Lieu?"

The commander stepped forward to the podium, marveling yet at the understated eloquence of the commodore and beginning to ask herself, for the first time seriously, how she could follow the example he had set.

She stood opposite him, accepting the sword he had offered, then laying sword and scabbard on the half-table on her side of the podium.

What could she say, knowing that her lengthy remarks, at least by comparison, would have been totally inappropriate?

"Thank you." Her words came slowly. "Unlike you, I have not had the privilege of working with Commodore Gerswin. The example he has set is one to which anyone could and should aspire.

"I am not Commodore Gerswin. We are different people; we have different backgrounds. However, I share his striving for excellence and his belief that such excellence can happen only when we work together.

"Beyond that, the commodore has said what must be said, and I wish him well. I look forward to continuing his tradition and working with and for you all."

She stopped, deciding against any flowery conclusion, and bent to pick up the plain sword and black scabbard.

"Commodore, while I accept the responsibility you have passed to me, your sword is yours. May it always be so."

The commodore stepped forward to take back the sword. Then they exchanged places, and both faced the command and the crowd.

Still . . . silence lingered across the upturned faces.

After a long moment, nine notes sounded from the trumpet, in three groups of three, and the reverse parade began as the two senior officers presided over the retreat.

This time as each squad passed the reviewing stand the commodore received a salute from each. The squads did not reform on the parade area, but continued down the plastarmac to the nearest hangar, into which they disappeared.

When the parade area was at last empty of military personnel, except for the corner sentries, nine more notes sounded from the antique trumpet.

The commodore broke the spell by twisting toward the new commandant.

"Nice touch with your acceptance. They'll like it, and you'll come to believe it, if you give them the fairness, the discipline, and the hearing they deserve."

She inclined her head toward him stiffly.

"It is rather difficult to follow a living legend." She pointed toward the civilians who were now filing out toward the main gate. Even from the reviewing stand she could see that several were wiping their eyes.

"Hasn't always been so. Won't be." He patted her shoulder. "You'll make it, probably a lot farther than I did."

"Did?"

"Resigning. I have a few things left to do, and I need the time to do them." He paused. "Shall we go? Captain Ihira is waiting to show you to your office and quarters."

"You're out?"

"Out and packed. With the ceremony, my resignation is fully effective."

"Just like that?"

He shrugged. "Traveled light for a long time. Still do. Seems to work that way whether I decide to or not."

"What . . . where . . . will you go?"

"Intend to travel. Check on some research."

"If I'm not too bold . . . Commodores are well paid, but not for extensive travel."

"Been careful. A small bequest. Position with a group . . . and there's the *Caroljoy*."

She could not have missed the accent on the name.

"The *Caroljoy*? A ship?"

"Patchwork of sorts, but certified and speedy. Keeps me more than busy."

"*Caroljoy* . . . unusual name . . . understand your—" She broke off the sentence.

"No . . . wouldn't have been right to name it after someone still living. She made it all possible, and a great deal more that I never knew." His eyes seemed to mist over for a few seconds, and he stopped speaking.

"Who was she?" asked Commander H'Lieu softly. "She must have been rather special."

"Special?" laughed the commodore, and there was an underbite to the self-mocking expression. "Like saying Old Earth was special. Or that devilkids are unusual. She was a—" He stopped again. "Getting old, I guess, because I'm tempted to talk too much. Leave it at that. She was special."

"I'm sorry," apologized the commander. "I didn't mean to pry."

"You didn't. You asked, and I did not have to answer." He grinned. "But I'm just a relic on the way out, with time on my hands."

Commander H'Lieu could not help grinning back at him. "You're scarcely a relic, and I doubt seriously that you will ever have time on your hands."

"Perhaps not, but I won't have my hands full the way you will. Especially if High Command finds out how good your people really are. Then some senior commodore, a *real* commodore, not a preretirement commodore like me, may decide to take over Standora Base."

"You think so?"

"Unless you make commodore first." His tone was light, and the shadows that had crossed his features minutes before were gone, gone as if they had never been.

Captain Ihira was waiting at the base of the now nearly empty reviewing stand for them.

The commodore returned the captain's salute, crisply. He turned and was gone.

Commander H'Lieu swallowed twice before speaking.

"Lead on, Captain. Lead on."

G. Kyra J'gerald, Bio. D.
Department of Environmental Biologics
University of Suharta
Faith, New Hope Code FNH-Red-Sec 3 - RT
DL

Dear Dr. J'gerald:

The foundation has reviewed your proposal for the development through genetic substitution and accelerated environmental stress of "fuel globes" suitable for use in vehicles as a nonpolluting fuel source.

Your proposal has been approved for a Class II grant, for a maximum of seven Imperial years, as you proposed. Class II grants are reviewed annually, and funds are disbursed for the following year upon successful completion of the annual review. If the final specimens meet the criteria outlined in your prospectus, and function as you have outlined, an additional sum will be paid, equivalent to the total amount of the seven-year grant, either in a single payment or annually for ten Imperial years.

The attached contract contains all details. If you agree to the proposal, please authenticate and return three of the copies. On receipt, the foundation will disburse to the account you have specified the first year's funding.

Failure to make specific annual or semiannual reports will constitute breach of contract. Failure to undertake the work, for reasons other than illness, will be taken under advisement and treated under both local and Imperial law.

We wish you the best.

Sincerely,

Lyr D'Meryon
Administrator

Narla Div Kneblock, Bot. D.
Drop D-100
Full City, Urbana Code FCU-Blue-Sec 2 - RT
BG
Dear Dr. Kneblock:

Thank you for your proposal to create structural and building materials through the accelerated genetic selection and cultivation of deciduous T-type flora (trees).

Unfortunately, this work has largely been perfected, and the foundation is not in a position to expend funds for incremental improvements at this time. Since we may not have fully understood all the implications of your proposal, if you have amplifying material, of course, we would be more than pleased to review that in light of any updated submission you choose to resubmit.

Again . . . thank you for your proposal, and for your interest in improved biologics.

Sincerely,

Lyr D'Meryon
Administrator

Restra Ver Dien
Professor of Sanitary Engineering
University of San Diabla
Ghila, New Arizona Code GNA-Green-Sec 1 - RT
                                                    HY

Dear Professor Ver Dien:

Thank you for the update in your annual report on your progress
in modifying water sylphweed to provide the dual function of
water purification on a commercial scale and to precipitate toxic
and nontoxic contaminants in a reusable mineral form.

In view of your success with water purification, the foundation is
pleased to extend your grant another two Imperial years to allow
you the additional time necessary to develop the precipitation capabilities in selected sylphweed strains.

An addendum to your contract is attached. Please authenticate
all copies and return three to the foundation immediately. Upon
receipt of the copies, the foundation will disburse the first of the
four additional payments provided for in the addendum.

                                          Looking to your success,

                                                    Lyr D'Meryon
                                                    Administrator

All planets have life. Somewhere . . . somehow . . . there is life. It
may be in hibernation forever, created when there was heat,
sleeping until moments before a final conflagration. It may be
buried in sheltered ravines, or float in high clouds over burned-
out lands, but there is life. With one exception.
    That exception is Marduk.
    Picture a T-type world, with an old red sun still close enough
to maintain life, half-covered with oceans, and circled by three
small moons.

The seas are crystal violet, and when the waves crash on the rocks, the droplets coating the stone sparkle with the shimmer of blood red diamonds in the sun.

The clouds are white, towering, with a hint of purple.

The sands are purpled silver, and bare, as bare as the dark brown-purple of the mud flats that stretch where there should be marshes.

Where there should be forests stretch only kilometers of purpled clay. Where there should be grass roll on kilometers of purpled bare hills that slowly ooze toward the depressions where rivers should run and do not.

No spires grace continental divides, but aimless heaps of weathered crimson and maroon stone, some buttressed from the bedrock, some lying loose.

The planet promised life, and there was none.

All the explorers found was death.

N'Doro—dying in his shuttle. Crenshaw—screaming for death for days in the Service wards at Bredick. The crew of the *Copernick*—found dead to the last soul in orbit. The list is long, longer than it should be because the planet should, by all rights, have supported life.

The deaths bolstered the argument that there *had* to be life, for what else besides unknown viruses or alien organisms could kill so many so terribly?

The answer, when it came, was disappointing. Chemicals—just chemicals. Every virulent chemical known to intelligence existed in the oceans and lands of Marduk. Every stable synthetic concocted by the late masters of Old Earth had been concocted earlier by the departed masters of Marduk. Concocted and left for the universe to find.

If it is violently mutagenic, teratogenic, carcinogenic, oncogenic, or toxic, Marduk has it.

And for some, Marduk held a certain promise . . .

ANNALS
Peitral H'Litre
Bredick, 6178 N.E.C.

XXXVI

THE OER FOUNDATION administrator checked the itemization from the Special Operations Account again.

"Unique power source (obsolete) for nontech planet—C/r 1.5 million. Special equipment transport (one time charge)—C/r 4.5 million."

No explanation on the official accounts, just the figures. The commander, and she thought of him as the commander despite his preretirement promotion to commodore, had spent more than a third of his annual operations budget on just two items. If they were audited by the Imperial Revenue Service, she'd better know what they represented.

On the off-chance that he had had an explanation, but didn't know how to code it, or wanted to leave that to her, she checked the "notes" section, which was sealed except to her personal key.

Wonder of wonders, she thought. There was an explanation.

"The unique power source is an obsolete atmospheric pulse tap. Couldn't buy an equivalent source for less than ten times this, but gadget is good only on a planet with an atmosphere and without intelligent life with a metal based technology. Somewhat limited, but fine for my outspace operations. Even have a place to put it. Will reduce the power costs for the ship. Could be as much as eighty percent less."

Lyr nodded. It sounded crazy, but if he was right, and about equipment he had always been right, the cost would be absorbed in less then a standard month. His energy bills ran nearly C/r 10 million annually, and that was what he drew from the foundation. From his private sources, who knew what he was paying?

"The one-time transport charge is what it cost for a one-way disposable jump hull to carry that and some other equipment to base. Didn't want to charter a freighter, though it would have cost half as much, for obvious reasons. Hope you can figure out a way to explain this."

She worried at her lower lip once more.

Some things he was so secretive about, as if the Empire really cared about the doings of a foundation promoting biologics research and use. The secrecy, she was sometimes convinced, might cause more problems than the mission.

She frowned, but finally settled on the standard classification of equipment freight charges, with a few codes and supporting figures that should get her through all but the most thorough of audits, if one were even requested.

In more than twenty years, she had been requested to appear before the Imperial Revenue Service twice. Once had been for a grant to Sadukis University, which had been diverted to support the candidacy of the University Chancellor for delegate—unknown to the OER Foundation.

The second time had been because the receipts to and assets of the Forward Fund had exceeded, for a two month period, the thirty percent maximum requirement. That had been her fault, because of a rather spectacular increase in the value of some Torinian bonds that the banking community had written off as worthless.

Still worrying at her lower lip, which was always chapped despite the moisture shield cream she used religiously every night, she began to input the information.

If the commander, in his capacity as trustee, were not so obviously committed to the foundation and its aims, she would have been more worried. At times, his single-minded pursuit of improved biologics scared her, and now that he was pushing the implementation of the basic research and research into actual applications . . .

She shook her head. If she knew more, she would only worry more, and there was more than enough to worry about with the research grants and the accounting legalities.

XXXVII

"THE ASSIGNMENT IS a standard one—the father and the son. The baron, if one could call him that, and the heir. That means the timing must coincide."

"Explain."

"The father has his own yacht, and can pilot it himself. He is surmised to have a hidden base, probably in an uninhabited system. The son lives with the mother and her clan, separated from the father. But he remains the only heir."

"Then there is a preferred order."

"Exactly. Father, then son. The client did not specify the order,

but preliminary investigations indicate that the father is the more for-
midable of the two, and would be even more so if alerted by—"

"The action against the son."

The woman nodded. "You understand."

"If the man travels so freely, how can one predict where he will
be?"

"That takes patience. He does have a philanthropic connection
in New Augusta and must travel there occasionally. That is the sole
predictable factor in an extremely irregular and unpredictable schedule. He has never made less than a trip a year, often two or three. We
have taps on the torp center and on the clearance sector in Imperial
control. Those should give us advance notice, but you will have to
take up residence in New Augusta.

"From there, it should be routine. Routine, but not easy."

"On New Augusta?"

The woman lifted her shoulders. "It cannot be avoided. The commission was large, and not to be turned down."

"How much of a bonus?"

"Double your normal."

"I assume the rules for actions on New Augusta have not been
changed by the Guild."

"They have not."

"Then energy and projectile weapons remain forbidden?"

"Correct."

The heavyset man glanced at the floor. "You are sure this is the
best way to accomplish this contract."

"Are you questioning the Secretariat?"

"No. But a man who could be called a baron and is not, who pilots his own space yacht, and all that implies, who is strong enough to
have captivated, even for a time, a Scandian woman, that sort of man
will be alert to such things as accidents, poisons. That means—"

"I know what that means. That is why you were assigned."

The heavyset man's hands moved toward the long knife concealed in his trousers.

"He is said to have some familiarity with hand weapons, including
knives."

The man smiled. "Some familiarity with knives. How interesting."

"The details are in the envelope."

The man picked it up, but did not break the seal, knowing that
exposure to air would destroy the material within minutes, as intended.

"Once you have begun, send the signal. The second upon completion."

"Understood." He nodded and turned to go.

As he stepped through the portal from the small office into the main corridor of the commerce clearing house, his face was composed into the look of boredom common to many small businessmen, a look perfectly within character, since eighty percent of the time he was in fact a small businessman specializing in the brokering of odd lots of obscure jellies. The twenty percent of his time devoted to the Guild, however, demanded one hundred percent loyalty and provided eighty percent of his not insubstantial income.

For all his bulk and blankness of expression, his boots scarcely sounded as they touched the corridor tiles and as he moved toward the central exchange.

XXXVIII

GERSWIN SIPPED THE liftea slowly as his eyes traveled from one side of the small dining area to the other. While he did not fully appreciate the intricacies of all the varieties of teas, perhaps because to him all their tastes were strong, he found liftea the most pleasant, and far more enjoyable after a meal than the alternatives, particularly cafe.

After all the years since the *Torquina*, he still failed to appreciate cafe, and he knew he never would.

He shook his head wryly, thinking about it. Cafe had to have been invented by a failed chef, one who wanted all remembrance of food seared out of memory by its bitterness.

With the hour as late as it was, only the smallest dining area of the Aurelian Club was in use, but the staff was as helpful, as quick, and as alert as if the Duke of Burglan were in attendance.

Gerswin did not know what influence Caroljoy had employed— or had it been the Duke himself—to procure his membership in the club. Realistically, he assumed that it had been their influence, although that had never been confirmed one way or another.

He had just received the simple card, stating that he had been proposed for membership, and that, after consideration, his name had been accepted.

The rules were even stranger than the acceptance.

No member could ever invite more than three guests at once, and there were no bills or charges. Restraint in use of the dining facilities was expected, but no such restraints were necessary for the use of the library or the moderate exercise facilities. Extravagant use of the facilities constituted grounds for revocation of membership.

Members were expected to propose one or two qualified individuals for membership at some time, and such proposals were to be accompanied by the entire membership sponsor fee. If the individual proposed was found unsuitable, the club retained the fee, which would be applied to the first suitable individual recommended by the member. The sponsor fee was 250,000 credits.

As he took another sip of the liftea, Gerswin wondered how many people were willing to spend that for a friend or worthy citizen. At some point he probably would, but currently he had no candidate he thought suitable—except Lyr, and he shied away from the idea of proposing her for membership in his sole club. He might anyway, but not for a while.

Two other tables were occupied, the one directly across the open central parquet flooring from him and one two tables to his left. At the opposing table sat a woman, alone, in a severe dark purple tunic.

While he did not know her, she was either wealthy or powerful in her own right, since guests were not permitted without members, and spouses were considered guests.

At the table to his left were three individuals, two men and a woman. Their conversation was politely modulated, with neither whispers nor low jovialities, suggesting that the subject was whatever commercial interest they shared.

After more than twenty years of membership, Gerswin knew less than two dozen other members by sight, and he doubted that many knew him.

"More tea, ser?"

"Yes, thank you."

He had asked Lyr if she wanted to accompany him after they had gone over the annual reports he was required to authenticate, but, despite the wistful look on her face, she had declined.

"Damon has been pressing me for months to go with him to the free fall ballet, and I agreed. Next time, do give me more notice, Commander. Please."

Gerswin shook his head. For all his long range plans for the foundation and his own enterprises, his management of his own personal schedule and life had been less than exemplary.

Two sons, one dead long before he had even known he had a son, and the other as lost to him as if he scarcely existed.

His lips tightened as he pushed away the thoughts of Corson, of the boy no longer a boy, who had inherited, as indicated in the cubes he received and reviewed quietly, his mother's height and father's strength.

Was he right to have let Allison raise him alone?

"And what would you have done? Carted him all over the galaxy? Settled on Scandia?"

He took another sip of tea.

Just because he had answers to all the questions did not mean he could lay either questions or answers to rest.

The woman in purple had entered shortly after he had, but had sampled a salad of some type, two mugs of cafe, and now stood to leave. Her face was familiar, and the former commodore suspected she was a government minister of some portfolio, just from her carriage.

The conversation to his right continued, with a trace more intensity and a fractionally reduced volume, as if the trio was getting to a critical point in negotiations.

Gerswin sat back, decided that he might as well return to the shuttle port for the trip to the orbital station. New Augusta was one of the handful of systems prohibiting deep-space ships or, for that matter, any non-Imperial shuttles from entering the planetary envelope.

The *Caroljoy* was docked in a magnetolocked position off station three beta.

Gerswin frowned. At some point, he suspected, it was going to be far too dangerous to travel to New Augusta in person. The time was coming when he and Lyr would have to work out other arrangements. Either that or he was going to have to develop a series of alternative personas with enough depth to pass all Imperial screening.

When it became more obvious who he was and what he was doing, if he continued as successfully as recently, he would doubtless develop both government and commercial opponents. He hoped that point was years or decades away.

He almost laughed, but repressed it, knowing how mocking it would sound in the dignified confines of the aristocratic Aurelian Club.

Instead, he eased himself out of the comfortable chair and around the table, nodding to the waiter.

"Very good, Commodore. Hope we will see you more often."

Surprisingly to him, the term "commodore" was not used with the condescension he had heard in the voices of even the staff of more than a few commercial barons.

"Never can tell, but thank you."

He took a last look around the circular room of less than ten tables, and at the group of three at the single occupied one remaining. Neither the woman nor the two men looked up from their discussion.

"Would you like transportation, Commodore?" asked the submanager at the front desk.

"Yes. That would be fine."

He might as well be heading back to the shuttle port.

While he waited for the electrocab, he studied the main foyer, pacing quietly from one side to the other.

Unlike many clubs, the Aurelian Club had no pictures of individuals anywhere, nor any listing of officers, nor any posting of rules. Gerswin wrinkled his forehead in concentration. Thinking about it, he could not recall any written captions anywhere within the club, except for the signatures on some of the paintings, a few of which he recognized as originals for which any number of collectors would have bid small fortunes.

"Transportation, Commodore."

"Thank you."

Gerswin went through the double portals quickly.

The electrocab was a shocking silver, radiating a light of its own bright enough to make Gerswin shake his head.

The outside doorman saw the gesture and smiled.

"Not exactly tasteful, ser, but at this time of evening, they're mostly out for the nighters. This is conservative for that crowd."

Gerswin raised his eyebrows, but said nothing as he stepped into the backseat.

"Destination?" The inquiry was mechanical.

Gerswin tapped the code for Shuttle Port Beta into the small screen.

"Thank you. Please authorize the sum of ten Imperial credits."

Gerswin used the foundation card for the fare, since the purpose of the entire trip had been strictly for OERF reasons.

The electrocab hummed from the club portal and after less than a hundred meters dropped into the high speed tunnel that slashed diagonally under the city and toward the shuttle port.

He closed his eyes as he leaned back in the seat, but his thoughts did not come to a similar rest.

Should he continue his detailed tracing of the grants issued by the foundation? Was commercialization the only way to produce the products he needed on a wide enough scale? If so, how soon should he start trying to implement such projects?

What about Corson? Was there a way to channel some of his considerable income from his own investments over the years to his son? Was it wise, given the trust fund already created? Would too much money without a purpose leave the boy, the young man really, adrift? Or make him a target of the unscrupulous?

What about Lyr? Was he being fair to her in piling more and more upon her? Were additional salary and appreciation sufficient?

"Destination approaching." The mechanical voice of the electro-cab was almost a relief. Why was it that New Augusta triggered so many questions? Was it the memory of Caroljoy? Or was it that New Augusta symbolized what he must oppose and had not?

He sat up, eyes flicking toward the window to take in the increasing illumination as the vehicle slowed and completed the climb to the beta concourse.

As he stepped out into the even flow of bodies heading to or from the various shuttle gates, Gerswin wished he could have worn full-fade blacks. The sheer numbers handled by the Imperial shuttle ports always made him uneasy. Numbers could conceal so much.

His hands flicked to his belt, where the knives and sling leathers were still in place. He began to scan the crowd while his steps carried him toward the less crowded section of the port that served private ships and travelers.

Most of the crowd were commercial or in-system travelers, which was the case at most ports throughout the Empire. Few indeed could afford the high cost of either a private ship or interstellar passage.

The majority of travelers were human. He caught sight of a single Ursan, flanked by an Imperial Marine honor guard, and two Edelians, looking more like walking sunflowers than the sentient beings they were.

While he should have faxed ahead, he had not, assuming that the shuttle to station three beta would lift on a recurring and regular schedule. The departure portal was closed, with the message board flashing.

"Next shuttle to beta three in fifty-five standard minutes. Please insert your access card for your shuttle seat. Ten seats remain."

Gerswin took his permanent squarish pass from his pouch and inserted it.

The message board changed to fifty-three minutes and nine seats remaining.

Satisfied that he could do no more for the moment, he turned to head back to the main terminal lounge for a place to sit down. His steps clicked on the hard tiles, the sound echoing through the pre-dawn lull of the nearly deserted section of the port terminal.

A scraping sound, barely a whisper, rustled ahead of him, as if someone had brushed the archway to the public fresher three meters ahead of him on his right. The clarity of the faint sound bothered Gerswin, and he edged his steps toward the far left-hand side of the five-meter-wide corridor.

As he drew abreast of the fresher entrance, he saw the shadow of a man, presumably about to leave, but the shadow did not move as the retired commodore continued onward.

Gerswin glanced over his shoulder as he entered the main lounge area, with its circles of padded seats mostly vacant. Behind him walked a heavyset businessman carrying a black sample case, his expression blank, as if his thoughts were systems away.

Gerswin sat down in the middle of a three-seat row, facing the direction from which the businessman had come. In turn, the heavy, brown-haired man slumped into a seat perhaps three meters away and to Gerswin's right. He did not look at Gerswin, but opened the case in his lap and pulled a folder from it.

A smile quirked the devilkid's lips.

For whatever reason, the man was looking for Gerswin. His build ruled him out as a Corpus Corps type, which meant he was either an intelligence operative for some out-system government, for an out-of-the-way Imperial bureaucracy, or a private operative contracted to find Gerswin.

Gerswin dismissed government intelligences immediately. Out-system governments would not send operatives into New Augusta, particularly after obscure and retired commodores, and all the Imperials had to do was to monitor his reservation on the shuttle and wait for him at the lock to his ship.

Since the man had required a clear look at Gerswin and a comparison of facial profiles, that further supported the fact that he was representing a nongovernment source. And since the operative was on New Augusta, whoever hired him had money.

Gerswin pursed his lips.

The Guild?

That meant trouble he had not anticipated this early.

The commodore sat relaxed, waiting, letting the minutes pass as he watched the watcher without obviously doing so.

Finally Gerswin stood and stretched, then ambled toward the still open dining area. Coincidentally, his path would take him by the seat occupied by his hunter.

The man unhurriedly closed his case and stood, adjusting his tunic, and fiddling with the case itself. He turned as Gerswin neared, and his face screwed up as if in recognition.

"Commander Gerswin?"

Gerswin looked puzzled in turn, but said nothing, although he stopped where he stood.

"Don't you remember me? Lazonbly, from the *Valeretta*?"

"Can't say I do. But what could I do for you?"

Gerswin wondered how far he could push before the operative panicked.

Lazonbly stepped closer and shook his head, as if he could not really believe it was Gerswin. "You haven't changed at all."

Gerswin smiled. "Who's paying the Guild for this?"

Lazonbly blinked, but only once. "I don't believe I understand."

"Lazonbly died in Feralta ten years ago. The Guild has accepted a contract on me. I'd like to know who your client is, not that you'd know."

"I'm afraid I don't understand, Commander."

"Very good. Very good. You realize I know you can't use long range energy weapons here. Standard knife or laser cutter?"

Lazonbly moved his arm, showing a glint of blue. "Laser cutter, Commodore. Shall we go?"

"At least you've dropped the pretenses." Gerswin stepped back so quickly that Lazonbly could not react without appearing obvious. "As you wish. Toward which dark corridor?"

"The public fresher serving beta three. You first."

"How about side by side?"

"You first." Lazonbly's voice remained jovial.

"Rather not." Gerswin eased back slightly as he disagreed.

"Commodore, don't force the issue."

"And what do I have to lose? You don't want your kill recorded on the public monitors. You've obviously taken care of the monitors on that corridor. So why should I go with you?"

"Because you think you might have some chance of getting away." Lazonbly shifted his weight in an attempt to move closer to Gerswin.

"And you're willing to gamble on that?" asked Gerswin.

"No gamble."

"No, it's not." Gerswin frowned. "Lazonbly, where did you get your orders?"

"Haven't the faintest idea what you're talking about, Commodore. Not the faintest. But you talk well, especially for a man of your ad-

vanced age. Rejuvs may give you back muscle and appearance, but
they don't improve old reflexes. So . . . shall we go?"

"I see you are rather hard to reason with." Gerswin smiled. He
half turned and walked away from Lazonbly in even steps, toward the
corridor the operative had indicated.

The heavyset man followed easily, trying to close the gap between
the two without making it too obvious.

Gerswin let the other approach, glancing over his shoulder and
listening for a change in breathing patterns or steps. He would rather
have faced the Guild assassin down in the lounge except for one
thing—the Imperial inquest, which would doubtless have delayed his
departure long enough for another Guild assassin to strike.

As he walked, Gerswin slipped the leather thongs and rounded
stones from his belt.

The corridor narrowed as the two men neared the three beta
concourse, then made a gentle left turn.

Gerswin decided Lazonbly would move as soon as they were
screened from the other monitors. He readied the thongs of the
sling.

Click. Click.

Gerswin threw himself to the left, rolled, and came up with the
thongs whirling.

Thunk!

Thud!

Lazonbly's body pitched forward onto the tiles, his face as impassive in death as it had been in life. The laser cutter lay centimeters
from his hand.

Gerswin walked away after pocketing the round stone, not looking back. There was nothing to connect him to Lazonbly, and nothing on Lazonbly to connect him either to Gerswin or to the Guild.
And there was no record anywhere of one Commodore Gerswin's
proficiency with the sling weapons of Old Earth, let alone anyone on
New Augusta who would deduce with certainty the exact cause of
death of the Guild agent. Gerswin had no doubt "Lazonbly" was at
least noted as a potential Guild agent in Imperial files.

He turned the last corner. Several other shuttle passengers now
waited near the portal, obviously ready to board the same shuttle on
which Gerswin was booked.

Gerswin and the *Caroljoy* were now headed for Scandia, which
represented a sudden change in destination. He wondered if he
would be in time, or if it were a false alarm. If so, so much the better.

If not, there was not much else he could do. No one else could get there sooner, not even a message torp.

Would he lose another son he scarcely had known? He shook his head at the thought.

With less than ten minutes before the shuttle lifted, Gerswin doubted that even the Imperial authorities would be able to react in time to block off the entire shuttle port to resolve the strange incident with Lazonbly. Particularly when the tools which were doubtless in Lazonbly's case were found to have been those that disabled the corridor monitors. Either that or the entire case had melted itself down, which would certainly intrigue Imperial intelligence.

Fifteen minutes later he sat on the shuttle as it hummed toward the accelerator. His thoughts were already in orbit, already plotting the jump points for Scandia.

XXXIX

It is an article of faith for the Believers that their captain destroyed the first and only Empire without legions, without loss. A number of scholars, Elender among them, have made the case for such a sweeping generalization.

Certainly, what records were salvaged from the rape of New Augusta do contain limited references to a foundation promoting biologics, and the fragmentary information which outsiders have been allowed to examine in detail would seem to show a definite series of links between the foundation's research grants and the systems where the biologic innovations which brought down the Empire were first introduced and commercialized.

That biologics hastened the fall of the Empire is not the question, though some have questioned the importance of that hastening, nor is the fact that the biologic revolution foreshadowed the development of the Commonality in question. Neither, for that matter, will this commentary question whether the captain actually developed or merely spread such biologic techniques.

This, of course, lays aside the central question of whether there was a captain in the sense that those on Old Earth or the Believers have consistently claimed. That is a question for another time, since *someone,* or some series of individuals, did in fact promote biologics, and that promotion was the cause of a great and widespread unrest among the majority of systems then associated with the Empire.

What must be questioned most strongly, however, is the naivete that unhesitatingly assumes that such tremendous social and political changes were accomplished "without legions, without loss." It is conceivable that the initial introduction of such techniques may have been accomplished with minimal unrest, but the subsequent history has been, if one wills, illustrated in the blood of the casualties.

One can only wonder, at times, assuming there was a captain, at either the callousness or the obsessions which could have motivated him, not to mention the personal burden . . .

> From *COMMENTS*
> Frien G'Driet Herlieu
> New Avalon
> 5536 N.E.C.

SINCE CORSON HAD not left Scandia yet, if the Guild were after him, that was where the Guild operatives would be, reflected the pilot with the impassive face.

He had debated not using the orbit station and grounding directly on Scandia, but could find no advantage to doing so. He had not yet been forced to reveal that capability of the revamped scout, and did not want to any sooner than he had to, especially with the Guild involved.

So now he sat in a rear seat in a Scandian shuttle as it dropped toward the port below.

He wished he had been able to reach Allison, but the orbit comm center indicated that her receiver had been blanked. Corson had no separate outlet. He had been forced to leave a message that he was arriving, and hoped that he was either in time or unnecessary. He was afraid he was simply too late.

His fingers drummed on the armrest, and he looked at the pale metal overhead. Scandians did not believe in passenger ports or screens in their shuttles, and he always worried about the piloting of others.

He sensed the nose lifting into a slight flare as the shuttle came out of the port turn, and he imagined the view as the pilot centered in on the landing grids, stark black against the winter white of the Scandian hills.

"Please recheck your harnesses. Three minutes until touch-down."

The shuttle pilot's voice was repeated by the overhead speaker with the metallic overtones of equipment typically Scandian—durable, long-lasting, and not designed to do a single bit more than necessary for the complete job at hand. No stereo or full fidelity capabilities for mere voice repeating speakers.

Clump.

Gerswin's grip on the armrests relaxed as the shuttle touched the grids, and one hand reached for the harness release as the other rechecked the belt knives and sling leathers. He wore no stunner for the simple reason that all energy projection weapons were forbidden on Scandia. While he had no doubts that the Guild had circumvented that prohibition, he saw no sense in wearing one only to have the Scandians secure it for the length of his stay. If he used it, then more explanations would be required.

Gerswin stood at the lock before the others had even begun to unstrap, forcing himself to remain relaxed as he waited for the ground crew to open the double portals.

A senior commander, I.S.S., his brown hair shot with gray, joined him, while the couple who had been sitting in front of him waited in their seats.

"You spent time in the Service?"

Gerswin nodded with a faint smile, then added, "Some."

"I thought so. You had that look on your face before touchdown."

"Look?"

"You had to be a pilot or nav type. You people all seem uncomfortable when someone else is doing the piloting."

Gerswin permitted himself a half-sheepish grin.

"Guess you can't hide it."

Clank.

"You being stationed here?" Gerswin asked, though his attention was more on the unsealing locks.

"No. I'm retiring. My wife's from here, and I decided to join her."

"Scandians do stick together," observed Gerswin before turning back to fact the pleasant-faced young functionary who was standing in the lock.

"That they do," agreed the retiring commander.

"Your entry forms, ser?"

Gerswin proferred the folder.

The woman checked the name, and her face took a distinctly sympathetic look, not even a professionally concerned one, but an expression showing real emotion.

"Commodore Gerswin . . . uhhh . . . your . . . they're waiting for you . . ."

"Gerswin?" asked the commander behind him. "The Commodore Gerswin?"

The Scandian official's look darted from Gerswin to the older-looking and uniformed officer.

"Is there a problem, Commander?"

"No. Not at all. I just didn't realize . . . to have been on the same shuttle . . ."

"I'm afraid I don't understand, Commander . . ."

"Snyther . . . Commander Snyther."

"Commodore Gerswin is not here on pleasure, unfortunately, and unless there's a problem, I would like to clear him immediately."

"No, miss. Not at all. Please clear him. Please."

The woman shook her head, returning her attention to Gerswin's documents and scanning them quickly. She ran his pass from the orbit station through the hand scanner, and then nodded.

"You're clear, Commodore Gerswin. The Ingmarrs are waiting right outside the debarking gate."

Gerswin felt the emptiness inside him grow. The signs were clear enough. Too clear. The "Ingmarrs" had to be Allison and her brother Mark.

The Guild had gotten to Scandia before New Augusta.

"Thank you," he said quietly, aware that his face had become more impassive and grim, but unwilling to make the effort to change it.

His steps echoed through the narrow tubeway as he marched toward the small concourse. As he stepped from the tubeway, he glanced around the space in which he stood. Ahead was the portal into the central concourse area, where doubtless Allison and Mark waited. The floor tiles were the same light ceramic as they had been on his only other visit, and the walls were the same yellowed cream, decorated with wood-framed scenes of Scandia.

"Reacting, that's all you're doing," he muttered as he stopped and stared at the pictures, stopping before proceeding through the next portal.

"If Corson . . ." He let the words trail off, and a grim smile creased his lips.

The woman functionary wouldn't have been a Guild agent, because escape routes would have been closed off. That was no longer true once he was inside the main concourse. And the Guild didn't forbid energy weapons on Scandia, even if the Scandians did.

His hands checked his belt again.

He took a deep breath, sighed, and walked through the portal.

On the other side he scanned the entire visible concourse, before focusing on Allison and Mark, who stepped forward from where they had been talking less than ten meters away, at the foot of one of the two-meter-square structural columns that supported the soaring ceiling of the terminal.

Mark Ingmarr had put on weight. While he had not been slight or slender, he was now more than merely solid, though short of outright obesity, and the clean-shaven look had been replaced with a square cut, full beard. His blue eyes were bloodshot.

So were Allison's, but her face was thin, nearly to haggardness, and her face was pale beneath the light tan, the incipient wrinkles, and the lines of strain and grief.

"How . . . how . . . did you know?" began Allison even before he was close enough for comfortable conversation, as if the question had been waiting for his appearance and could restrain itself no longer.

Gerswin's eyes flickered to Mark Ingmarr's face. The look behind the apparent concern was enough for him.

"I . . . just . . . knew . . . ," Gerswin answered, letting the words space themselves as he moved more toward Mark.

Gerswin looked past them, to see who or what remarked his arrival, and took another step, at an angle, to Allison's puzzlement, to place himself directly before Mark Ingmarr. He glanced over his left shoulder as he did.

The movement was slight, imperceptible to anyone else, but clear enough to a devilkid on the hunt.

Gerswin threw himself forward, brushing by Mark, rolling left before meeting the tiles, and turning as he came to a crouch next to the wide structural column.

Wssstttt!

"*Unnnnhhhhh.*"

The commodore ignored the falling figure of Mark Ingmarr and picked out the man in the quiet business tunic who dropped his faxtab as if in surprise with the rest of the open-mouthed bystanders. As the others began to scatter, he moved with them.

In less than three steps Gerswin was crossing the terminal at full speed toward the Guild assassin.

The man glanced back, as if to protest, yanking his case around so that the long edge pointed toward Gerswin.

Thunk! Thunk!

Both knives buried themselves in the assassin's chest virtually simultaneously, and his case spilled to the floor, where it rested momentarily, before smoke began to drool from the corners, as it began to consume itself.

Gerswin retrieved his belt knives, wiped them on the dead man's tunic, and replaced them in his belt.

He walked back to the center of the concourse where Allison, dry-eyed because she could cry no more, stroked her brother's forehead.

Screeee!

Gerswin looked away from Allison to see the emergency medical cart whining down the center of the open section of the terminal toward them. He did not shake his head, but had Allison not been looking at him, he might have.

"Why . . . ? Why?"

"Because he and you were close to me," lied Gerswin.

"That many enemies, Greg? That many?" Her voice broke.

Gerswin nodded. He saw no reason to tell her the whole truth now. Except for the Guild, his enemies lay in the future. Now that Mark was out of the picture, they would continue to chase him, to destroy him merely from professional pride.

He stared down at the clinically dead man that the medical team had connected to three separate life-support systems.

The body called Mark Ingmarr might live, but the warped personality that had paid for Gerswin's and Corson's deaths would not survive the treatment, one way or another.

Gerswin sighed slowly. Once again, it had been his fault. If he had not tried to provide for Corson, if he had not treated Mark so cavalierly . . .

He shook his head.

Allison's eyes followed the medical team as they moved the tubed and connected figure into the mobile treatment center, and as the whole apparatus began to move toward the far end of the terminal.

A uniformed figure motioned to them.

Gerswin ignored the officer and remained standing beside Allison, not that he could say anything.

Allison ignored the officer as well, turning to Gerswin, looking down on him once more.

"This means that Corson's—accident—it wasn't really an accident?"

Gerswin nodded.

"But why?"

Gerswin glanced down at the hexagonal floor tiles, knowing that he could not tell her the exact truth, but knowing she would detect an outright lie.

Finally he lifted his eyes, aware that additional law enforcement officers had surrounded the area of the concourse where the Guild assassin had died and where his case had melted itself down into metal and plastic. Had the assassin panicked and fired hurriedly? Or had it been planned? Gerswin would never be certain whether the man had fired to protect Mark from Gerswin, or to silence Mark because he thought Gerswin's appearance meant that the Guild had been crossed, or because Gerswin was to be killed at all costs.

In the long run, the reason was lost, and irrelevant.

Now, a pair of enforcement types stood behind him, and another pair waited beside Allison.

"Because death seems to strike those I love, Allison. I did not avoid Scandia because you asked me, you know."

He waited.

"I thought so. Now I know."

The silence stretched out.

"Wasn't there anything you could do?"

"I did my best. If I had tried to guard you two, that would have been like posting a sign, and it would have put you in a cage. Did you want that? Ever?"

This time Allison looked at the six-sided floor tiles.

"No. I guess it was better this way. Especially for Corson. Happy . . . never knew what happened . . ."

Despite his own resolve to be impassive, Gerswin could feel the wetness in his own eyes. He said nothing, although he could feel Allison's eyes on him, and kept his gaze fixed on the far end of the concourse, on the portal through which the emergency medical team had taken one dead man, and then another.

"But you care . . . you loved him . . . you loved me . . . and you never insisted. I don't understand. Why didn't you?"

Gerswin took a deep breath, refusing to wipe his cheeks, but his voice was like cold lead as he gave her his answer.

"Because you were right. Because Corson deserved his own life,

not mine. Because you deserved your own life in the sunshine of
Scandia. Because I have . . . miles . . . miles to go."

Allison touched the back of his hand, then withdrew her fingers.
She looked away from him.

The silence stretched like the distance between the stars that had
separated them and still did.

"Commodore?" asked a softer, apologetic voice. "Could we have a
moment?"

Gerswin looked up to the tall officer who stood next to him with
a sad expression.

"A moment?" he answered. "Yes. Time is what I am rich in."

At the sound of his voice, Allison took a step away from him and
toward the officer who waited for her.

Gerswin doubted he would ever see her again, but he followed
the enforcement officer.

He had left Allison what he could, little as it was.

He shivered and swallowed, and the taste was bitter. But he took
another deep breath, and another step. And another.

XLI

"THE GERSWIN AFFAIR . . . not exactly a shining example of our
prowess, was it?"

"We did not have all the facts."

"The late client assured you that the commodore was formida-
ble."

"A client recommendation only."

"A *Scandian* client recommendation. Can you recall when a Scandian was prone to admit personal deficiencies or to exaggerate?"

"There are always exceptions."

"Was this an exception?"

The silence gave the answer.

"Now, with the client gone, our professional reputation remains.
We took a contract, and we did not fulfill it. What do you suggest, regional chief?"

"We have two choices—either a crash search, which would be
prohibitive and pointless, or making Gerswin a designated target of

opportunity with a triple bonus for the successful agent. I would recommend the latter."

"I concur, but reluctantly. Given the commodore's independent and erratic travel schedules, it is the only realistic approach."

"What if he attempts to attack us?"

"You think that is a serious possibility? One man against the entire Guild?"

"A moment ago you were cautioning me against underestimating the man. He has turned the tables on two armed agents."

"I do not doubt his considerable capabilities, as well as his resources, but in the end even the commodore will slow down as he ages. The Guild will not, and Gerswin is not the type to hibernate, not for long. Besides, no one has ever escaped the destination as a target of opportunity. Ever."

"That is true enough." The words expressed doubt rather than affirmation. "Is that all?"

"That is all."

CLING.

The screen flickered twice, and the priority code appeared in the upper right-hand corner.

Lyr bit her lip, relegated the information on the screen to memory, and accepted the call from the commodore she thought of as a commander, and probably always would.

"Why a local beam?" she asked as his face appeared on the screen. "You usually prefer guaranteed privacy."

"Prefer safety as well," responded the golden-haired and hawk-eyed man.

"You care to explain?"

"My name has become too well-known to some for me to travel as freely and anonymously as I once did."

She frowned at the unexpected verbosity, then realized that on a public link he would be somewhat less specific than normal. She studied the background, which she did not recognize, but which looked technical, almost like the bridge of an Imperial ship.

"Where are you?"

"In orbit station. That was so I could hook into the local Imperial comm network. Once this is done, I'll be leaving.

"The lack of mobility could be troubling in the future, and so my far limited experience indicates it might pose problems for others as well."

"How would it affect the foundation?"

She was surprised to find him grinning at her through the screen. "Always business, I see." He frowned as quickly as he had grinned. "Limited degree. Would like some recommendations from you. Research. If they fall outside normal business, please bill my account. . . ."

Lyr nodded.

"Remember the grant we reviewed about a standard year ago . . . one involving modified bodlerian algae? Looking for information specialists in that system, people who could accumulate and codify background information on most Imperial systems, as well as the ability to provide perfectly legal incognitos for business travelers."

"Legal aliases?"

"Correct. As I understand Imperial law, one may use a name not his own if no illegal intent is involved. No illegal intent would be involved. For example, if a jewel merchant has to use a courier on a regular basis, unscrupulous interests could scan the passenger lists for that name. . . . But if accepted aliases were available, a merchant or dealer could use his own courier with greater security.

"If a commercial baron's agent wanted to check out a new enterprise, he could do so without alerting the system he was out to check. Such an enterprise might be profitable. Combine that with the information background of the type that commercial types need and have to develop themselves . . . anyway. My local counsel suggests it is legal, but with your contacts in that system . . ."

New Avalon was the system, if Lyr remembered correctly, and with the university there, it was certainly a good location for such an information processing concern.

"Doesn't anyone provide services like this?"

"Not to all comers on a cash or commercial basis."

Lyr smiled faintly. The pattern to the commodore's operations was becoming clearer.

She bit at her lower lip. Whether or not his ventures applied directly to the foundation, there was no question that somehow the foundation always seemed to benefit. With each of his activities, unsolicited contributions seemed to appear. Despite his prohibition on any form of solicitation, outside funds continually appeared to swell the capital and the income from investments of that capital.

Already she was receiving more than routine information requests from the Imperial government on the foundation's finances and tax reports, the sort of attention that was reserved, in her experience, for the more important of the charitable and academic foundations.

She caught herself and cut off her reverie.

"What do you want me to do with the information?"

"Send it by torp to the information drop I use most often."

"That would be—"

"NO!"

She shook her head ruefully. "I'm sorry. I forgot we could be on an open wave. How soon do you want it? Yesterday?"

The commodore nodded.

"I'll get to work on it, and, commander, I think you'll be billed for research services."

"That's fine. Understand."

The screen blanked.

Lyr left her own screen blank, making no move to retrieve the material she had been studying before he had faxed. She had seen the man in action. For him to worry about his personal safety—even to mention it—meant that he was more than just casually worried. Much more.

If he had enemies that powerful, what did it mean for the foundation?

She began to pull what her banks had on security systems. After she finished with getting the commander's—the commodore's, she corrected herself mentally, knowing she would continue to slip—project under way, she would undertake a few improvements for the foundation headquarters. Just in case.

And she needed to reinforce some of her ties with Alord and his friends at the Imperial Humanities Foundation, as well as those with Dimitra at the I.A.F.

The commander hadn't given her any instructions, but he hadn't forbidden it, either, and it looked like they both might need the allies, information, and protection in the years ahead.

Her fingers moved across the console board, and her forehead cleared as she began to plan.

XLIII

THE MAN SMILED and swung his case up for inspection. His teeth were white and even, and stood out against the darkness of his skin, which was sun-darkened olive.

"Destination, ser?"

"Markhigh."

"Your pass?"

The traveler proffered the folder, and the port official nodded, his clearance nothing more than an affirmation of the more detailed clearance already given by the security section of the orbit station.

The olive-skinned man stepped through the portal and walked toward the monorail station platform, toward the spot where he would wait for the train that would carry him back to his small art dealership.

As he waited on the platform a man with shoulder length silver hair with a matching handlebar mustache edged up to him.

The art dealer studied the other, comparing height, coloration, and build against a mental file he carried, finally discarding all of the comparisons and relaxing slightly.

The older man had the relaxed but alert bearing of a former officer or security agent, but not the harried look of a target or the indefinable tension of a hunter. Nonetheless, the art dealer's elbow activated the slide sheath, just in case his spot assessment had been incorrect.

"Ser Giriello, I believe."

"I do not believe we have met."

"We have not. I recognized you because I have visited your low gallery in Markhigh. Your collection of Raiz' his rather remarkable."

"Thank you."

The art dealer scanned the platform. No one else was anywhere near them, not that it made that much difference with directional pickups and focused lasers, although the coating of his cloaks and tunics were designed to give him the fractions of seconds necessary to escape that sort of attack.

"Particularly remarkable for someone whose real business is elsewhere."

Giriello did not answer, but readied himself and stepped backward, as if affronted and puzzled.

"Ser . . . ?"

The ploy failed because the silver-haired man moved with him, and Giriello found himself held in a grasp that was steellike in intensity.

"Giriello, this time—this time—nothing will happen. You are to deliver a message. The message is simple. Merhlin will destroy the Guild. That's all."

There was a sharpness at the back of his neck, and the art dealer could feel his knees buckling as the hard pavement came up to meet him, could hear the stranger yelling for medical help. He wanted to laugh at the hypocrisy of it all, except that the darkness washed over him.

LYR PULLED AT her chin as she slipped through the portals to the foundation office.

She knew the commander—the commodore, she corrected herself yet another time—would be waiting. His voice had been ice-cold.

Automatically she closed the portal behind her and touched the lock stud as she surveyed the reception area and found it lit, but vacant.

The faint sound that was a cross between a whine and a hum told her that the analyzers in the tech space were operating, and in a linked fashion.

"Come on back, Lyr."

She sighed and stepped into the tech room.

His privacy cloak lay draped over one of the console chairs. He stood and pushed back the swivel where he had been working.

"I didn't expect to see you so soon again," she said.

"Didn't expect to be back so quickly. Have a problem. Not strictly foundation, but it does impact us. Need to trust someone, and you're elected."

She opened her mouth, and he held up a hand. "I know. You have to account for everything. Perfectly legal for you to provide analytical services, provided you charge for them. Charge me the going rate, or MacGregor Corson. Charges aren't the problem."

"What is? Why did you insist on my being down here in the middle of the night?"

"Been a few other nights when you were," he observed laconically. "Running on a tight schedule. Ship time doesn't always agree with Imperial mean time." He grinned, and the lack of warmth in the hawk-yellow eyes sent shivers down her spine and chills through her body. She was not certain she wanted to know anything more.

"What do you want analyzed?"

"Lists and destinations."

"Lists and destinations? For that you got me up—" She broke off in midsentence as for the first time she saw a fire in his eyes that represented anger, or a view of hell.

"What do you want from the analysis?" she temporized.

"Patterns." He sighed. "Let me explain. A group of individuals is engaged in a highly profitable and exceedingly illegal business. They use aliases, false destinations. Almost no possibility of determining which alias is a commercial traveler on honest business, which a philanderer, and which the deadly anonymity of this group."

"That's not merely impossible. It would require a miracle—"

"I've contracted for a travel research contract for a shipping firm, and will be obtaining the monthly listings of selected passenger destinations. Not the names, just the arrival and departure ports. I will be adding to that major commercial meetings, conferences, fairly reliable estimates of military personnel and dependents traveling on commercial ships, and other data."

"But what do you want?" she asked tiredly.

"I told you. Patterns. Probably take years, but there should be continuing patterns. Clear ones. You develop the possibilities and send them to me. I'll test them and let you know."

"I still don't understand what you want."

His eyes flared. Then he looked away, almost as if he was afraid of hurting her, it seemed.

"Let me give you a hypothetical example. If on the second week of the second and tenth months of the Imperial year, there are always two passengers booked from New Augusta through New Glascow to Ydris, it means something—from whether that represents a regularly scheduled conference, a recurrent meeting, a regular fund transfer. It means *something*."

His voice softened. "The organization I am trying to locate has roughly nine hundred members on twenty planets, but ten planets are considered the key. New Augusta is the only major system not included, but remains a widely used transfer point. Therefore, anyone booked from New Augusta who belongs to this group must have come from somewhere else.

"Now, that doesn't mean I want you to exclude all others. If you can determine that the Brotherhood of Universal Peace has set patterns, let me know, and I can verify and modify. Eventually, by eliminating the obvious groups, by using the tourism stats, we should be able to eliminate everyone but the target."

Lyr shook her head. "That's *at least* a ten-to-fifteen-year project."

"Could be less. Maybe able to get you more and better information. Your console has the specifics, along with the beginning data base, as well as the entity to bill for the services, and the travel service for whom you will prepare the monthly report. In turn, that service will send its payment to MacGregor Corson, care of OER Foundation, and you will bill me for the balance of time and costs owed."

"What . . . that I think I finally understand, Commander. Why . . . that is another question."

"One you're probably better off not knowing." He circled around behind the swivel and picked up his privacy cloak. As he donned it, with the full-fade uniform, he transformed into a shadow, despite the clear lighting in the tech section.

"Good night."

Lyr did not shake her head. Instead she moved to the console he had vacated earlier.

"You know what he wants, don't you?" she said quietly to no one. "You'd think that even he would know better than to take on the Guild. Unless they already have taken him on."

She shivered, but her hands remained steady on the console controls.

XLV

"*WHUFF . . . WHUFF . . . WHUFF . . .*"

The man's breath came in jerky gasps, one dragged out after the next, as he struggled to put one foot in front of the other. His head wobbled from side to side in the darkness, although he did not look over his aching shoulders.

He could hear easily enough the *pad, pad, pad* of his pursuer's even footsteps. He could hear, but not believe.

None of it was believable.

"*Whuff . . . whuff . . . whufff . . .*"

His feet and lungs labored as he staggered along the empty riding trail. He looked toward the heavier undergrowth beside the trail, but decided against that tactic. The searing pain that shot from his left arm every time he moved too suddenly reinforced that decision.

"*Whuff . . . whuff . . . whuff . . .*"

Whoever . . . whatever . . . chased him not only could see in the darkness of Haldane, but could move silently when it wanted. Whatever it was, it toyed with him.

His more rational side told him to stop, that attack had proven fruitless, and that flight was even less fruitful, but he kept putting one leg in front of the other.

"*Whuff . . . whuff . . . whuff . . .*"

How much longer he could move, let alone breathe, he did not know, only that each leg felt like lead, that flashes of hot light pricked behind his eyes, and that his mouth hung limply open.

Whhrrr!

Crack!

The sound of the unknown weapon jolted his momentarily still legs into a shamble onward down the slight incline before him.

His pursuer was invisible, silent except for the sometime padding of feet, silent except for the occasional missile like the one that had shattered his left arm.

"*Whuff . . . whuff . . . whuffff . . .*"

Each breath was harder to draw, but he kept putting one foot in front of the other. In the back of his mind, the thought flared—you're being hunted, like a fox, a garbou, like a dog.

But his unseen hunter refused to let him turn, driving him with the shadowy presence, with the silent *whrrr* of pain.

Right after he had seen the dark figure, he had charged the unknown, had actually touched the alien, if that was what it was, for the steel muscles of the shadow figure had paralyzed his remaining good arm and tossed him aside like a doll.

"Run . . . assassin . . ." Those had been the words hissed at him.

He had not run, not him. Not then. Instead he had turned and attacked with all the skill taught by the Guild. And had been tossed aside again. Like trying to catch a shadow at night. And it had been barely night then. Now dawn was approaching.

Each of those early rushes toward the alien blackness had found him sprawled into the dirt, into the grass of the park.

"*Whuff . . . whuff . . . whuffff . . .*"

When assault had failed, he had stood his ground. Until the terrible projectiles had whirred past his head, the second shattering his left arm.

"Run . . . assassin . . ." And the alien had hissed his terrible message again.

He had stood—until the shadow rose from nowhere next to him and had twisted his pain-wracked arm.

"Run . . . assassin . . ."

Whhrrr!

He had run—not wisely, but well, for who had ever outrun him? Who had ever outrun the Hound of the Guild?

"*Whuff . . . whuff . . . whufff . . .*"

His legs were shaking. The flares behind his eyes left him nearly blind to the path ahead. Staggering, he managed to catch his balance, lurching leftward, then right, until he came to the gentle slope upward, a slope that became more steep with each meter.

"*Whuff . . . whuff . . . whuffff . . . whufffff . . .*"

How could you fight something that struck in darkness, stronger than any man, that treated you with such contempt, that ran you down more easily than you had ever run any quarry to ground, and with seemingly less effort?

He dragged himself another step forward.

"*Whuff . . . whuff . . .*"

Whhrrr!

His legs balked at the uphill effort. He stood there, gasping, swaying like a tree about to crash into oblivion.

Whhrrr!

Crack!

He did not feel the stone that killed him, nor see the dawn that spilled from the eastern sky of Haldane a handful of minutes after his body had slumped into an untidy heap on the viceroy's private riding trail.

XLVI

THE HOODED MAN at the head of the table cleared his throat.

"And now, for the unsubstantiated information . . ."

"It's gossip time," whispered a uniformed admiral in the corner to his nearest colleague.

The whisper was not low enough. The hooded man, the figure known as Eye, turned and looked. While Eye's expression was hidden, the admiral wilted as if he had received a withering glare.

"Gossip, perhaps, but it has its uses. First, the Ursans are working on their own version of a jumpshift. We have a team looking into that.

"Second, an unknown group has moved against the Guild. While our sources have not been able to verify that, we have verified that there have been a number of deaths associated with individuals suspected of Guild activity. We have been able to investigate three deaths of this type and found reason to believe that the victims were also associated with the Guild."

"A question?"

"Yes."

"Why no faxnews stories?"

"The deaths have been spread over ten systems and roughly a standard year, but there is a pattern."

"Do we know who or what is involved?"

"We have a name, believed to be a code name. That name is Merhlin. Who or what it represents is unknown at this time."

"Do we want to get involved?"

"I doubt that is to our interests," answered the hooded man.

His response brought a series of low chuckles from the Imperial officers around the table. One woman shook her head slowly.

"You disagree, Admiral Storz?"

"I would only point out that if an unknown has the resources to take on the Guild, not only without being discovered, but without being stopped, what would prevent such an organization from then applying itself to our agents?"

"Good point. Discovery, however, is not the same as involvement. I should have made myself clear. We are working to discover this group or agency. We do not intend to aid either party."

Admiral Storz nodded.

"Any other questions on this one?" Eye surveyed the shielded figures around the table in the shielded room. "If not, the next item is the unreleased Forsenian communique which would require the registration of all Imperial agents with the local Forsenian government. . . ."

XLVII

THE MAN IN the full-fade blacks sighed.

War was hell, it had been said from the beginning of man's recorded history, and he did not look forward to the next phase of his war against the Guild. But the Guild was becoming more and more a tool of the unscrupulously wealthy, and the Empire did nothing.

Until he had the final product from the information the Infonet and Lyr's integrators were piecing together month after standard month, he had to continue to keep the Guild off-balance.

So far his efforts had been isolated enough to give second thoughts to individual agents, but the faxers and the other media had tumbled to the identity of the dead in less than a handful of the cases.

He shrugged.

The Infonet he had set up on New Avalon had proven a commercial success, but the mass of information he needed was still not complete. His personal wealth was accumulating faster than either ecological knowledge or knowledge about the Guild.

The Guild continued to monitor all the communications on the open bands in and out of New Augusta, and while he wondered to what degree they could pick up on his short torp messages, he found his own concerns were making even normal foundation business harder to carry out. While Lyr could still make credits hand over fist, and while existing grants could be extended, not as much in the way of new and innovative research was getting started as he would have liked, not when he had to watch his own step every meter of the way.

This time, this time his action should give the Guild some pause.

He checked his equipment and slipped into the lift, headed for his first target in the Tower. The regional Guild councils were not quite as careful about their security precautions as the Overcouncil.

While none had arrived at precisely the same time, and while their reservations did not share common lengths, for two nights the top eight members of the arm council would be in the same Tower, at least theoretically.

Saverin appeared to be the one listed as Kerlieu, on the eighth level—the same Saverin once known for his proficiency in needle-point laser work.

Gerswin stepped from the lift and walked down the brightly lit but deserted hallway, his shiny bright privacy cloak with the crimson slash covering the shadows of the full-fade blacks beneath.

Saverin's portal was locked from inside, but the Tower's locks were standard. Gerswin pulsed the circuits twice, then opened the portal. He stood well back as the doorway irised open.

Whsssttt!

A needle flare of energy slashed across the space where he had been operating the portal controls an instant before and completed a quick arc search pattern.

Gerswin waited until the flare died before edging a black film decoy into the laser-wielder's line of sight.

Whhsstt!

Another needle of blue light burned through the black film and into the corridor.

As the laser flare winked out, Gerswin flashed inside the closing portal.

Whsst!

This time the blue needle came from Gerswin's laser, straight through the head of the white-haired man with the laser, dropping from his limp hand.

Whsst!

Gerswin sent another beam through the chest of the still-falling body.

Thud . . . clank.

The laser rang dully as it impacted the hard synthwood of the suite floor.

Gerswin had rushed past the body, but his haste had been un-necessary. Saverin, as always, had been alone.

Gerswin used his elbow to tap the exit stud and slipped out through the portal without having touched anything in the suite.

The weakness with lasers, reflected the hunter, was that they took a few fractions of a second between bursts, and those fractions were all he needed. But then, surprise should have been in his favor. Saverin had reacted well, considering he should not have known he was being tracked and that he had not been an active assassin in several years.

Gerswin swirled the privacy cloak fully back around himself, checking to insure that the mask was still completely in place. Although he had disabled the remote telltale circuitry of the Tower before he had started, he would inevitably run into guests and other recording devices. Even if his tampering with the Tower circuits had been discovered right after he had completed it, it would take a good technician more than a standard hour to undo what he had done, and Gerswin planned to be out of the Tower long before that.

Nonetheless, the mask remained a necessity.

Gerswin frowned as he moved down the corridor. While he had not had trouble with Saverin, the former assassin had been quick, either lucky or forewarned.

The next target, on the eleventh level, was not renowned for her reflexes. Margritta DiRenzo plotted out assassinations through carefully arranged accidents.

A pudgy man, belly boiling out over a too-wide golden waist sash, stepped on the lift as Gerswin stepped off. A lecherous smile crossed the heavy man's lips as he took in the privacy mask and cloak, and he inclined his head in mock salute as he passed Gerswin.

The thinner man nodded in return as he turned to the left, away from the target suite, toward the service access. The corridor was clear as he used his equipment to enter the small closet and stepped inside. Once there, he cut aside the access panels with a cutter, then used two quick movements to sever the power leads. The corridor outside the closet turned pitch black before the emergency lamps returned a dim glow.

Gerswin retraced his steps past the lift and toward the proper portal. He tapped twice as he cut his way into the service box and used the manual controls to open the portal.

"Maintenance!" he called.

"What is the difficulty?"

The woman spoke, although accompanied by a slender man. Both held stunners pointed toward the portal. A small portable light in the room outlined their forms in a faint glow, leaving their faces dim smudges.

Gerswin remained in the shadow of the portal.

"Lost all power on this level—"

Thrumm! Thrumm!

Both man and woman dropped to the bolts from Gerswin's stunner without triggering their own.

Gerswin closed the portal behind him and turned over the unconscious pair one by one. The man fit the description of a lover of Margritta's, a sometime Guild agent.

He looked around the room for something to complete the job in the proper format. The scowl beneath the mask turned to a grim smile as he saw the ancient projectile gun on the bedside table.

Three shots later, the job was complete.

It would be reported, at least initially, as a murder-suicide, as an accident/tragedy.

The Guild would know better, but they were supposed to.

Gerswin closed the portal behind him as he left. No one along the corridor had even peered out. He suspected that those occupants who were in their suites intended to stay behind locked portals, at least until power was restored.

He took the stairs to the twelfth level, where the lights were on, unaffected by his actions below since the Tower was designed with power controls set on two level increments. Still swirling his cloak about him, he sauntered down to the technical access closet, where he casually cut his way in, then through three plate covers, and burned through the main conduits for both levels twelve and fourteen. There was no level thirteen.

Although it was theoretically possible to disable all power shunts for the Tower at one point, that one point was a junction center that would have required a full-sized laser and would have alerted not only the Tower security forces, but system security types as well. By disabling only the levels he needed out of the way, Gerswin avoided such alerts, and delayed even the entry of Tower security forces.

Gerswin did not intend to disable more than the two centers he had already put out.

The first suite he wanted was halfway down the hallway on the left, but Gerswin did not have to worry about opening the portal. It was wedged open.

He frowned. That meant quick action—extremely quick action— and that both Council members were probably in the Sendaris suite at the far end of the corridor.

He took the chance of darting into the empty suite and picked up a tumbler, half-filled with something, not that he intended to drink any of it. Then he ambled along the corridor, letting the glass slosh in his hand.

A light flashed from the corner suite of the Tower where he was headed, sweeping the corridor ahead of Gerswin.

So they had a guard.

The direct approach was still the best.

"Hallooo, there. You got power?"

"Who's there?"

"Just old Modred. Looking for Welson's suite, you know, on the corner." Gerswin lisped the words, and let his gait appear unsteady.

In his left hand were sling leathers, looking like a set of ribbons dangling from unsteady fingers. The tumbler sloshed in his right.

The light centered in on him, and he strained for the sound of a stunner whispering from a holster as he put his left arm up across his face, as if to block the glare.

"Easy . . . just looking for Welson."

"Hold it right there."

The voice was that of a bored professional, expecting no trouble from an obviously drunken partier, but ready to drop him at the slightest excuse.

Gerswin wobbled to a halt, several steps taken toward the light, as if in an attempt to catch his balance and stop.

"You're not Welson," he accused the guard behind the light.

"Wrong suite, buddy. Better check downlift."

Gerswin could see that there were two of them, both in dark brown uniforms, the second holding not a stunner but a powergun filled with explosive pellets, although it was not aimed directly at him.

"Sorry, sorry . . ." Gerswin made his voice whine with apologies as he turned and took one step, then another, back toward the direction from which he had come.

The light wavered as the guard flicked it to one side, then the other. While the aim was to see if Gerswin had been trying to misdirect them, to see if he had any accomplices, it was the wrong aim.

.Gerswin dropped and turned.

Whhhrrr! Whhhrrr!

Crack! Crack!

Brrrrp-Crump!

Crack!

Gerswin came out of his dive with knives ready, ignoring the shrapnel cuts from the single burst of the powergun.

They were not necessary, and he resheathed them as he moved past the bodies.

The next step was anticlimactic.

Gerswin triggered the door overrides and tossed two circular objects through the portals, reversing the polarity and closing them before they had barely admitted the two grenades.

One was gas, the other antipersonnel.

Crump!

Crump!

The twin explosions reverberated satisfactorily, though muffled by the closed portal.

Gerswin jammed the filters into his nostrils, but forced himself to wait two full minutes before opening the door, surveying the corridor the entire time.

Then he used the regular controls to open the portal, standing well aside.

From the entrance he could see three bodies, but he waited, listening, as the gas filtered past him into the corridor.

Finally he moved into the suite, but his speed was unnecessary. There were four figures sprawled across the furniture, and all were dead—quite dead. Three he recognized as Council members, including Sendaris himself.

He left more quickly than he had entered, spurred, as he headed down the corridor to the emergency exit stairs, by the sound of a portal being forced open by someone who had obviously not read the emergency instructions. He slipped through the manual doors, designed for power and other failures, and began the descent.

He checked the time. Less than forty standard minutes since he had begun, but too long. Much longer than he had hoped. The time, combined with the obvious awareness of the Council that someone was after them, made up his mind, and he continued downward and away from the last target on the fourteenth level.

He who runs away lives to fight another day, reflected Gerswin as he reversed his cloak to the flip side, with the forest green shimmering outward. At the landing between the third and fourth levels, he buried his face under his arm. When he looked up and continued downward, he wore a green face shield matching the cloak.

Above him, he could hear footsteps, voices, then a scream as other Tower guests began to abandon their suites for the emergency exits. The lifts would still be operating, but those on the affected levels were not apparently stopping to try them.

A Tower employee, apparently alerted by a monitoring system, stepped through the first floor entrance as Gerswin came down the last section of stairs.

"I beg your parden, ser, but these are for emergency use—"

"No power on my level! Istvenn take it! Last time I stay here! And you say that's not an emergency? Just listen to all the others!"

Gerswin brushed past the man.

"No power?" stammered the young man.

"That's right. Listen. Just listen. Think I'd take *stairs* for joy?"

Gerswin finished stepping around the man and around the security officer behind him and into the main lobby, strutting across it with every gram of outrage he could counterfeit. He reached the electro-cab concourse without incident, and stepped inside the second one.

"Inverr House!" he snapped, loud enough for the Tower employee holding the door to step back, and for the surprised Tower patrons whom he had stepped in front of to back off.

His effrontery paid off. The shrieking and clanging of alarms began only as the electrocougar dropped away from the Tower concourse.

He changed the destination, but not the color of the privacy mask.

XLVIII

IN THE END, a decision either begins or concludes with two people. Either two men, two women, or a man and a woman.

In this case, the meeting happened to be between a man and a woman, but it could have been between two men. The head of the Guild could have been either a man or a woman, since throughout its history the senior assassins had picked both men and women as their chief. The modus operandi had varied little under either sex.

The man wore black, as he always did on such occasions, including a black face shield. The woman regarded his choice of apparel as an affront of sorts, particularly in view of his disregard for her profession.

Was the meeting in person?

Not for this pair.

Each sat before a screen, neither's true countenance known to the other.

The man was who he said he was, although he called himself Merhlin, and his true name remained hidden.

The woman was of the occupation she professed, but not exactly the person she said she was. That deception the man suspected, but found immaterial, an attitude neither she nor the woman whose place she took would have appreciated had either known.

"You are the one calling himself Merhlin? The one with some slight ongoing interest in the Guild?"

"That is one way to put it, Honored Lady."

"Assassin will do as well as any false honorific, Merhlin."

"Very well, Assassin."

"You wished the conversation, Merhlin, and paid for the privilege."

"I did. Thought it only fair to give you advance notice of my intentions."

"That you have already done. This was scarcely necessary, though we appreciate the additional income."

"Should have been more clear. Wished to deliver a specific message."

"Then do so."

"In a few moments, I will. First, a few observations." He held up a gloved hand to forestall any objections. "Observations more than relevant to the message."

"Then state them." The lady's tone had gone from bored to sharp.

"First, the Guild prides itself on professionalism. Second, the Guild will not undertake any assassination for a fee, whether or not the victim is a total innocent or not. Third, the Guild has gone from being a tool that occasionally protected the oppressed to a tool for protecting the Imperial establishment in addition to and outside the law of the Empire."

He paused.

"The Guild does not concern itself with popular opinion.

"It should. Because it does not, and has not, and will not acknowledge either restraint or morality, it is doomed. Should those who survive, and there may be a few, continue the tradition of serving the highest bidder and slaughtering men, women, and children whose sole fault is that their existence stands in the way of the powerful and the unscrupulous, the Guild will not survive."

"Are you serious?"

"Yes, Assassin. That you should already know. I am Merhlin. Call me Merhlin of Avalon, and tremble when you call upon my name. You have been warned, and your days are numbered."

The screen blanked.

The chief assassin who was not the head assassin stared at the screen. Then she tapped a code.

"Did you get that?"

"Outspace transmission. Either has his own ship or went to trouble of routing indirect through the geosynch station. No way to trace him. No way even to figure out who he is."

"We know that. He's the one who's been picking off top assassins, using their own weapons."

"Is he?"

"Why else would he go to the trouble, and the expense? This has been going on for more than five years, if I recall right."

"What about his threat? Why did he even bother?"

"That's the troubling part. That implies an even bigger effort against the Guild."

"What else can he do? We're recruiting as fast as he strikes."

"Are our recruits learning as fast as those they replace?"

"Now . . . you sound like *her*." The man paused. "But what really can he do?"

"I don't know. The annual conference is coming up. That strikes me as more than coincidence."

"So . . . ? Maybe he wanted the word spread."

"That means he knows it's taking place."

"What could he do? Destroy the entire quarter?"

"RECOMPUTE WITHOUT SUBSET two."

The small control room was silent except for the breathing of the man at the control couch and the muted hiss of the ship's ventilation system.

"Probability approaches unity. The accuracy of the data cannot be verified."

"Stet. Recompute *with* subset two and without subset three."

The man gazed at the exterior screens while he waited, studying the view of Iredesium in the distance. The moon, less than a thousand kays in diameter, housed some of the largest resort and pleasure centers outside of the home Imperial systems, each a domed oasis on airless stone, built at enormous costs for the wealthy and those who played at being wealthy. Of either, there seemed to be no shortage.

The view he watched showed the moon clearly, half white, half dark.

"Probability in excess of point nine. Exact figures cannot be determined within standard parameters of error without the information contained in subset three."

The pilot shook his head. No matter how the information was juggled, the answer came out the same.

How good was the information?

Some of it had come from Infonet. Despite the fact that he had founded Infonet and trusted the management, Infonet Class A information had a proven accuracy pattern of greater than ninety-five percent. Given the volume of the corroborating information, and the independent analyses from the foundation, which confirmed the conclusion, the chance for the final recommendation to be wrong was infinitesimal.

That the AI supported the conclusion with whole sets missing was another supporting, though certainly not conclusive, test.

Still . . . he didn't like it. When everything agreed, there was a chance that everything was wrong.

Or was it that he didn't want to pay the price to finish off what he had started? Or that he hated to solve problems impersonally?

He looked up at the screen, touching the distance control and letting the view enlarge as Iredesium seemed to swim closer in the large screen before him.

He checked the time again, for perhaps the tenth time in the last standard hour.

Less than a standard hour before the meeting below came to order, and that meant less than two stans before it was over, one way or another. Time to act, or to fail to act.

"The same old question, isn't it?"

"Inquiry imprecise. Please reformulate."

He ignored the AI's precise statement as he pondered the implications stretching out before him. Certainly his opponents had shown no mercy, nor would they even understand his mercy should he grant it. No . . . business as usual, and Istvenn protect the innocent. He sighed, and stood.

"Passive detection. Report if any targets within screen range."

"Understood. Will report standard targets."

Though there was no carpet on the deck of the small ship, his steps did not click or echo as he made his way to the locker that held the space armor.

He said nothing as he donned it, nor did the AI break the silence. Finally he stepped through the small inner lock, leaving it open as he began his checks.

"Comm check."

"Circuits clear."

After the inner lock sealed, he touched the plate that would open the exterior lock, and waited. Hand over hand, he exited, clipping his safety line to the recessed anchor beside the lock plate. He moved with a minimum of excess motion to the exterior lock to the aft hold.

From a distance, any distance, an observer using optical methods would have seen nothing, for the full-fade black of the hull and matching finish of his armor created an effect of invisibility.

Once the lock opened, he maneuvered the long shape through the narrow aperture. Next came the checks of the drive ring unit he had added below the missile's normal drives.

Slowly, he edged the massive but slender shape around the hull until it pointed at the midpoint of the terminator line of the moon that the ship, the man, and the missile all orbited.

The man took a long breath, then another.

In time, he eased back the access panel and twisted the blue dial to the number "II." Next, he broke the red seal and flipped the switch beneath to the "armed" position. He closed the panel and took another deep breath.

Moving hand over hand down the narrow shape, he came to the ring drive units, where he opened a second access panel and closed one switch.

"Done," he said quietly as he edged back to the ship's lock.

When the exterior lock had closed behind him, he stated, "Course feed to Hunter."

"Beginning course feed. Course feed complete."

The inner lock opened, and he stepped back into the ship, waiting until it closed before checking the ship's pressure.

Normal.

He began taking off the armor and stowing it back in the locker. "Commence Nihil."

"Commencing Nihil. Ignition in one minute."

He completed stowing the armor and walked back to the control station, his booted feet still silent as he crossed the hard floor.

"Ignition. Preliminary extrapolation shows Hunter on optimum course."

"Interrogative defense screens." While he knew the answer, he wanted to hear it again.

"No screens in place except normal class three precautions."

The pilot nodded. Class three screens were the standard screens against nonenergized objects, designed to divert small meteors and other space junk.

The drive units on Hunter would punch through anything but class one screens, and those were only used by ships, Imperial ships.

No dome or station could afford the energy or equipment expenditure to cover that wide an area with class one screens.

"Course lines on screen two," he ordered.

"Course lines on screen two," the AI responded.

He swallowed the taste of bile in his mouth. If he could have built a wider organization, trusted more people . . .

"Then you wouldn't have to do things like this?" he asked the empty air. "Be serious. You don't fight fanatics. You destroy them totally or you leave them alone. You didn't have a choice. Corson—what choice did he have?"

"Invalid inquiry. Please reformulate."

"Hades! Re—" He had almost told the AI to reformulate itself, but stopped as he realized he had no idea what such a drastic command might do to the artificial intelligence.

"Istvenn!"

He bit his lower lip, not quite hard enough to draw blood, as he watched the red line of the Hunter arcing down toward Iredesium. He forced himself to continue watching.

"Dampers on screens. Shield all sensitives," he added quietly.

"Shields and dampers in place."

The command had been early, many minutes before it would be necessary to protect the ship's equipment.

He could feel the nausea climbing back into his throat, and he swallowed again, still watching the screens. The red dashed line continued to drop toward the moon.

A pale blue line flashed into place above the screen representation of Iredesium.

"Class three screens triggered."

The pilot watched as the dashed red line penetrated the meteor shield without deflection and continued to dive for the target dome.

"Estimate one minute until detonation."

Ignoring the AI's statement, delivered in its impersonal feminine tone, ignoring his own urge to turn away from the information displayed on the screens, he forced himself to keep watching, glancing from the visual on the main screen to the smaller representational screen, then back to the visual.

"Detonation."

For several seconds both screens seemed unchanged. Then, on the representational screen, the dashed red line intersected the moon's surface. On the visual screen, Iredesium hung there, still showing half white, half black.

A pinflare of white flashed from the middle of the moon, spreading . . . and the visual screen blanked.

"Dampers on. Impact on target verified. Detonation height at two hundred meters, plus or minus fifty."

The man did not answer.

He had left the control couch for the fresher, where the slim contents of his stomach were emptying themselves into a small basin.

"Probability of damage within design envelope approaches unity."

"Plan beta," choked the man from the former crew section. "Plan beta."

He wiped his mouth and slowly straightened after splashing his face with a handful of cool water.

"For better or worse . . ."

His legs felt rubbery, but he walked back to the waiting control couch, still as silently as ever.

"Plot all in-system contacts on screen three."

He swallowed the bitter aftertaste and concentrated on the full screen array.

THE SPECIALLY GUARDED and prepared convention hall was nearly full.

"We have a problem."

"We have more than a problem."

"You mean the Merhlin thing?"

"Count's close to a hundred now."

"A hundred? You sure about that?"

"Two arm councils nearly wiped out . . ."

"Nobody knows who they are . . . not even Imperial Intelligence . . . say Eye himself is worried."

The hooded figure at the end of the table let the talk continue.

"Said he threatened the Council itself . . ."

The other hooded figure, sitting taller and to the right of the chief assassin, leaned forward.

"Is the threat that serious?" His voice was low.

"You know the answer," came back the cool tones of the woman. "It is the same answer as always. If the group called Merhlin is totally fanatic and highly skilled and disciplined, the threat has to be taken seriously. Fanatics can destroy anything. But the chances of the kind of knowledge and discipline necessary mixed with fanaticism? Not to mention the human element. We've always had warnings of any large scale movements against us, and how could anyone take on the entire Guild without an enormous commitment of personnel and equipment?

"Besides, would anyone today stoop to destroy an entire resort of five thousand people, most of them not involved with us? Even if they would, it would take nuclear weapons or a fleet-sized laser, and those are weapons the Empire has destroyed systems to keep to itself."

"Order!" The command was simultaneous with the tap of the ancient handgun on the metal plate.

The conversations around the meeting hall died into a series of murmurs, and the murmurs into silence.

"The first order of business is the five year report."

The Guild delegates shifted restlessly in their seats, waiting for the routine business to pass and to hear what the Council had to say about the threat to the Guild itself.

"Delegate Beta . . ."

Like most participants, Delegate Beta did not wear a privacy cloak, opting instead for a simple synthflesh false face and wig, combined with a voice distorter.

"The summaries are presented on the screen for your review. As you may recall, the screen is rear-projection and nonimaging, which means that your portable equipment will not retain the images . . ." Delegate Beta launched into his summary of five years of Guild activities and financial accomplishments.

At the conclusion he received a mild round of applause, mainly for the brevity with which the summary had been presented.

"Second order of business . . . Delegate Gamma."

Delegate Gamma stood and moved toward the podium.

She never got there.

Sun-white light seared through the roofing of the meeting hall, as well as through the rest of the Iredesium Resort Complex Red, reducing all but the heaviest metals to their basic atomic forms, turning ten square kays into a shimmering and cooling lake of molten stone and metal standing on an airless plain.

LI

"WE'VE IDENTIFIED THE cause."

Eye inclined his hooded head, but said nothing.

"Class two hellburner. Surface burst."

"Where did they get it?"

"Who got it?"

"Got what?"

At the commotion, Eye raised one hand. The noise died down.

"Please summarize from the beginning, Commodore."

"We're not entirely certain, but it appears as though the Iredesium Red Pleasure Dome was the site of the Guild's Five Year Conference. We usually find out several months afterward, although they try to keep it hushed.

"The so-called Merhlin group had apparently threatened the Guild with virtual extinction. We don't know what the Guild position was, but they didn't take the threat seriously enough. Class two hellburner went up ten minutes after the conference started, the part that everyone was required to attend. Casualties over six thousand. Probably only five hundred official Guild delegates; another two, three hundred might have been lower grade assassins. . . ."

The commodore waited for a moment, but there were no questions or interruptions.

"Definitely an I.S.S. weapon. Media faxers are already saying that it was. Delivery method unknown, but the tracked velocity was compatible with warship launch. It could have come from a private yacht, but the Iredesium complex has been choked with them this season—more than a hundred registered, and that's half of all the Imperial private ships.

"There were also three Service ships present in system—*Bismarck*, *Saladin*, and *Martel*. All their weaponry is fully accounted for."

The Admiral of the Fleet, to Eye's right, coughed.

"Are any of the media suggesting that it was an Imperial effort to destroy the Guild?"

"No. The *Free Fax* is implying that the destruction of Guild leadership with I.S.S. weapons implies either tacit Service agreement or extremely loose controls on nuclear equipment by the Service. In either case, a full-fledged investigation is necessary."

"Just what we need." The sotto voce comment came from the corner of the room farthest from Eye, but neither the Intelligence Chief nor the Admiral of the Fleet acknowledged the truth of the remark or the speaker.

"Any favorable commentary?"

"The *RadRight* had an ed-blip. They said they wished the Imperial Government had acted with such dispatch years ago."

"Wonderful."

"What is the real probability that this was accomplished by the Merhlin group?"

"One, we don't know if Merhlin represents a group or an individual with vast resources. Two, while Merhlin threatened to destroy the Guild and is reputed to have carried out close to a hundred assassinations of Guild agents in past years, we have no proof, even indirect or heresay, that the attack was in fact carried out by Merhlin. Three, if it was, I doubt that we will hear of Merhlin again. Nor will we if it was not. Four, now that the Guild has been reduced to several hundred scattered agents, the Imperial Government will face extraordinary criticism if we fail to finish the job. Five, this will result in greater economic stability within the Empire and probably short-term expansion of Imperial spheres of influence."

"In short," finished Eye, "we have no choice but to turn this terrible tragedy into an Imperial benefit. That solves one problem and leaves two. While we may never hear the name Merhlin again, whoever Merhlin is has the capability to find out information we don't. He or she also has no compunctions about acting when necessary. And no conscience. What do we intend to do about it?

"Second, we need someone to blame, and it can't be Merhlin. How could we admit that some unknown power can do what we can't, that they knew what we couldn't guess? So whom do we blame to get on with the job?"

"No one, ser. We will blame the anarchists and claim that the Guild and the anarchists collided. We have taken steps to round up the necessary accessories, and we will. And, in the future, enemies of the government can be tagged as anarchists, like those who murdered six thousand people at Iredesium."

"It might work," reflected Eye. "It might at that. But don't collect too many dissidents. We can't have this seen as a pretext to tighter social control."

"What about Merhlin?" asked the Admiral of the Fleet.

"We keep looking, quietly. I don't think we'll find him or her. Merhlin got what he or she or they wanted. But people forget. Especially, they forget faceless tragedies. Who got seared at Iredesium? Assassins, cold-blooded killers, and playboys and joy-girls. Who's going to feel sorry for them for long? How can you create outrage about them?"

LII

CLICK. CLICK. CLICK.

The single set of footsteps echoed in the sub-zero chill of what would have been dawn, had the sun not been lost behind clouds that filtered fine snow over the hills and frozen lakes.

Click. Click.

The footsteps halted on the smooth stone before a marble wall. On the wall were rows of gray metal plaques, each the color of gun metal glinting in the dim light.

The man's eyes centered on the last three plaques, picking out the names.

> "Corson MacGregor Ingmarr."
> "Mark Heimdall Ingmarr."
> "Allison Illsa Ingmarr."

He repeated the names to himself silently, then continued to stand, looking at the three names, ignoring the long rows of plaques above them, ignoring the blank space of the stone below them.

An occasional flake of snow drifted in from his left, under the flat marble roof and between the square and smooth columns that upheld the stone edifice, but he paid the weather no attention.

The wind whispered, ruffling and shuffling the snow that covered the grass and walks around the lone structure.

The gray of his jacket and the gray of his trousers gave the impression of a ghost visiting other ghosts, a spirit paying his respects to other spirits.

Outside, the fine snow falling from the dawn began to thicken, until the hills surrounding the family memorial were less than white shadows, though they lurked but a kilometer from the mount on which the mausoleum stood.

The visitor glanced toward the brighter light of the east and surveyed the falling snow and the shrouded hills, his eyes seeming to burn through the white veil to see the slopes beyond the trees, and the lakes beyond the rocks. Then, as if dismissing the winter, he returned his attention to the wall, and to the three last plaques upon it.

Finally he turned, and his shoulders dropped momentarily, and he faced west, staring out over the line of footprints nearly filled in by the drifting and dropping snow, footprints that would lead him back to another shadow of the past, a ship that belonged to a time predating even the construction of the centuries-old monument and mausoleum within which he stood.

Click. Click. Click.

Without a word, without a gesture, the visitor walked back across the stone slabs of the floor, down two wide marble steps, and into the snow, into the snow that cloaked him, that hid him and the hills toward which he walked.

THE ADMIRAL SHIFTED his weight in the chair, waiting for his ultimate superior to appear behind the antique desk. His eyes took in the single Corpus Corps guard, as well as the sparkle to the air between him and the desk that indicated an energy barrier.

He wiped his forehead with the back of his hand.

Click, click, click.

The man whose steps preceded him eased his tall and lanky but stooped frame through the portal and into the recliner behind the ancient artifact that had no screen.

"You requested this meeting, Admiral."

"Yes, sire, I did."

"Begin."

The admiral cleared his throat as quietly as possible. "I requested a private meeting because I cannot support my concerns with hard evidence, and because I cannot trust those who would normally provide such hard evidence."

"You do not seem to trust our Eye Corps."

"No, ser."

His Imperial Majesty Keil N"Troya Ryrce Bartoleme IV waited for the Admiral of the Fleet to continue.

"You know that a Service hellburner was employed on Iredesium. What you may not know was that a single weapons pack of nuclear torps was diverted from New Glascow nearly twenty years ago. That represents the only loss of nuclear weaponry in the entire history of the Service. I have no choice but to believe that the hellburner used on Iredesium had to come from New Glascow. I also find it rather difficult to believe that a private group, or even a planetary system, would keep such weaponry either unused or unadvertised for nearly twenty years.

"Further, sire, I have to ask what group is the single group that has challenged successfully the Eye Corps over the past century." The admiral shrugged. "I have no answers, sire, and my surmises cannot be verified, or probably even asked as questions, but I thought you should know."

"We appreciate your concern, and your candor. That is an issue in which the Prince has expressed some interest. I would appreciate it, Admiral, if you would contact Ryrce directly in the future, should you have further inspirations or any factual support for your theory."

The admiral wanted to wipe his steaming forehead, but did not. Instead he waited.

The Emperor stood.

"We are not displeased. We also appreciate your sense of tact. Therefore, your effrontery will not be punished, and we urge you to continue your direction of the Service with the same sense of dedication you have so far shown."

With an obvious effort, the elderly ruler turned and departed, his feet clicking as he made his way across the tiles toward the exit portal.

The admiral let his breath out slowly, as evenly as he could.

GERSWIN LEANED FORWARD on the control couch and checked the results displayed on the data screen again. According to every conceivable test, the plant produced a thread stronger and finer than any synthetic, needed no special fertilizers, and thrived in a wide range of climate and soil conditions.

The field tests, limited as they were, supported Professor Fyrio's research and contentions, as did the limited evaluations Gerswin had commissioned from the University at New Avalon.

Gerswin shook his head. The problem wasn't the biology, nor the data, but that none of the commercial enterprises or agricultural interests contacted quietly had shown any interest in what was principally an agricultural product suitable only for nonfoodstuff uses.

The damned plant would make someone a fortune, and no one was interested because there was "no real money" in agriculture.

The man in black stared at the data screen of the small ship, ignoring the larger pilot displays above and before him.

"What else can you do?"

"Inquiry imprecise. Please reformulate," answered the AI in its clinically impersonal but feminine tones.

Gerswin ignored the standard request, then tapped the keyboard, his fingers flying across the arrayed studs.

"Set for blind torp. Route beta three. Code Delta with databloc trailer. Lyr D'Meryon."

"Blind torp in position to receive. Ready to bloc feed."

The pilot squared his shoulders and faced the scanner.

"Lyr. Need some basic information. Details are in the databloc attached. Need recommended corporate type business structure with voting control removed from the system where the business operates. Also need a list of systems permitting absentee ownership. Suspect it would include systems like Byzantia, El Lido, and Dorlian. Send a copy of the systems you come up with to Infonet, my code, and request full background on them. I'll pick up the final from my drop there."

He paused, pursing his lips.

"Doesn't make much sense, I know, but looks like we need demonstration ventures to prove profitability of biological products and solutions. The commercial types accept biotech for medicine and raw materials, but not for finished or semifinished products.

"Enough said for now."

He tapped the closure, and hoped that she would read between the words.

With a sigh, he called up the information in the Fyrio files and began to reformat what he needed for the compressed databloc to accompany his transmission.

When he was finished, he coded it to the torp message.

"Torp pack complete. Send at max two."

"Readying torp for max two path."

Nodding, Gerswin indexed the research files for the information

on protein. Somewhere, somewhere, he recalled a project on replicating animal protein structure with a common plant, a weed nearly,
that had used Amardian/T-type genetic fusion.

"Torp released on max two path."

"Amardian genetics," he tapped into the keyboard.

Three cross-references appeared on screen five, the data screen.

"In-system contact. Two eight five at one point five, plus three ra-
dians. CPA two hundred kays, plus or minus twenty."

"Interrogative classification."

"Tentative identification in-system ore tug, class three. Low power
orbit recovery."

"Stet. File and report deviations."

He returned his attention to the screen, and to the background
on Amardian genetics research.

Wondering whether he could have been more efficient with a
fixed headquarters, Gerswin paused, then shook his head. He'd have
long since drowned in the reports, and who else could have tracked
down what was important in the long run? This way, he could make
decisions, request information, and move enough to avoid terminal
boredom while, he hoped, the research grants began to generate the
biological techniques needed so desperately by Old Earth.

In the interim, poor Lyr drowned in the reports.

Once he finished tracking down what he needed on the meat
substitute possibility, it would be time to head for Aswan to reenergize
and to take a break before returning to the tedious tracing and veri-
fying that seemed to follow inevitably from each possible lead that his
own research in the grant files showed up. For each hundred approved grants, perhaps ten held some promise, and of those with
promise, one or two showed either commercial or technical possibilities.

On the other hand, after nearly forty years since he had insisted
on innovative grants, the research product totals had become impressive. The foundation already had an impressive and growing income from some of those developments, nothing that yet matched
the income generated by Lyr's skillful manipulations of income and
assets, but he could see when that had to come, perhaps sooner than
Lyr expected.

His own thread venture, if it worked out, could conceivably add a
great deal, since the potential was enormous, and since the license
fees belonged to the foundation.

"Energy reserves below ten stans."

He shook his head again. Might as well head for Aswan before fin-

ishing up. While the times were currently peaceful, he hated to let the
ship drop into a low energy state, or to purchase power commercially.
The fewer the records about unknown yachts or the *Caroljoy* that
showed for Imperial Intelligence or other interested parties to pick
up, the better. And the cheaper as well.

"Plot course line for jump points," he ordered as he returned the
genetics research to the files and centered himself in the control
couch.

LV

JORGE FUGAZEY LIKED fax screens, a fact clear from the massive
console and the more than thirty screens that angled gently upward
around him from his control position.

His fingers played the control studs in lightning flashes, almost as
quickly as his deep-set black eyes flickered from display to display.

He did not look up as the younger man approached.

"Father . . . ," ventured the thinner man, who also had angular
features and dark eyes. The son did not vibrate with the focused intensity of his sire, though most men and women would have paled beside either.

"Screen six alpha—the flashing one, Duran. Your source was correct, long past correct. He has retired from the Service, but still collects an annuity. Signifies that he is still alive. You can act—if you
choose."

"Choose? What choice do I have? You have expressed interest in
the Daeris connection, and Helene has made it clear. Quite clear.
That leaves a choice?"

The performance behind the consoles came to an abrupt halt as
the older Fugazey tapped two control plates in succession.

"Never said you had to contract with Helene. Only that you
choose a social and economic equal with a strong family. You chose
her, without my advice."

The son shrugged. "Given the alternatives . . ."

"Study the dossier on this man, Duran. Reconsider what you must
do. Do not decide before that. More there than meets the eye. Data
missing that should not be missing."

Baron Fugazey watched as a red light flashed next to one screen, then another, and a third.

"Who can stand up to me, especially with your support?"

"About half the barons in the Empire," noted the elder with a sour turn to his mouth.

"But he is not a baron, not even a magnate."

"Titles are not everything, Duran."

The baron shifted his weight uneasily as the number of red lights on the screens beside and behind him continued to increase.

"I have met the Honorable Alhenda Strackna Daeris, Duran," added the older Fugazey. "She crossed paths with the man once before, and neither the Strackna nor the Daeris connections were adequate. I said you had my backing and, right now, I will not back down if you wish to continue, but I do ask that you review the files and reconsider . . . reconsider whether you must have Helene."

"I will. It won't change things, but I will."

Duran snapped his jaw shut with a quick motion and turned away too quickly to see the frown that crossed his father's face. Then, too, he had never looked to see the shadows under the eyes nor the tightness with which the angular Fugazey features were bound.

The baron watched his son's back as the man who was scarcely beyond his student years marched out through the portal coded only to admit immediate family.

The warnings on more than a dozen screens were flashing red and amber by the time the baron returned to his manipulations.

LVI

GERSWIN WAS SURPRISED to find a message torp waiting for him at the Ydris drop. Not astounded, for occasionally Lyr had used it for information that she thought pressing or of particular interest. But for the torp to be waiting at Ydris meant that she had sent more than a few.

He wanted to cut short the formalities with the port captain to retrieve the torp, since it belonged to the foundation, though sent by the Imperial Service, and find out why Lyr was searching him out.

The captain, a correct lady by the name of Isbel Relyea Herris, shared the tendency toward formality that the senior tech of the *Fleur-dilis* had always exhibited, although Isbel insisted she had no relations to whoever had served in the Imperial Forces.

"Wouldn't have it! No self-respecting Ydrisian would ever serve for that conglomeration of bullies and apologists for the commercial thugs that comprise the Empire. Yourself excepted, Commander."

"No need to except me, Isbel. That assumes I was one of the bullies in Imperial Service."

"No assumption. Fact. Your name's no more Shaik Corso than that scout's the private yacht she's registered, apparently registered, as."

Gerswin had raised his eyebrows, but said nothing.

"Scout's too old and too well rebuilt for the Impies to have done it. And they wouldn't think of using an *old* design. New is always better for them. You're too young to have been senior and retired. That leaves few options. You're independently wealthy, or you freelance, or both.

"You're successful, and that means experience. Wealth doesn't buy experience. Leaves age or Impie service.

"Since you're not that old, you have to have Impie service. Besides"—and her eyes twinkled—"you wear everything so properly, even shipsuits. Like uniforms."

Gerswin shrugged. "What can I say? Certainly sounds so much more impressive than my own poor background, and who am I to instruct the always correct port captain?"

He inclined his head. "But I do have a few matters . . ."

"I know. Anytime someone sends a private torp, it's urgent or Hades-fired close. You're excused. Shaik, and cleared into Ydris again. But I'd feel more comfortable calling you 'Commander.'"

"You, Isbel, can call me anything you wish, even if it is not totally accurate."

"Break orbit, Commander." She smiled nonetheless as Gerswin collected the torp pack and arranged for the torp itself to be carted to the *Caroljoy.*

He retreated to the ship as quickly as possible.

Once back inside the scout, he dropped the torp pack into the console.

Lyr's face, straight features, and carefully combed sandy hair filled the screen.

"I still can't get used to talking to a blank screen, Commander, but I thought you ought to know what's going on. I hope you have a chance to pick up one of the torps I've sent before Baron Fugazey surprises you."

She squared her shoulders and brushed back a strand of hair.

Gerswin realized that it was gray, not silver, nor dyed, and shook his head. He thought of her as always there, and unchanging. While she might be there for a long time to come, given Imperial medical technology, she was not unchanging nor immune from the aging process. He wondered if she were the type whom a complete rejuvenation would benefit as he refocused on what she was saying.

". . . first sign was a nuisance suit charging that the foundation was employing its special status to subsidize competition to Fugar House . . . then a rather sophisticated attempt to penetrate the databanks . . . continuing shadows on me . . . taken the liberty of hiring Kirnows as antishadows . . ."

Gerswin continued to listen as Lyr rattled off the lengthy list of attempts, all of which she seemed to have brushed off with style and without calling much public attention to the foundation.

". . . That's a brief update on the situation. A more detailed chronology is speedcoded into the trailer at the end.

"For all the furor about the foundation, Fugazey could care less about OERF. Prove that I could not. But he could have tied us up in legal battle after legal battle, which would have been tremendously expensive. He didn't. Once it was clear he could not get the information he wanted with a given strategy, he immediately changed tactics. My own sources, and you suggested I cultivate a few, as I recall, indicate that Fugazey is employing a small fraction of his not inconsiderable assets to obtain the information from the only other possible source."

Gerswin knew what was coming, even before she said it.

"The baron has a number of contacts within the I.S.S., and it is a matter of time before he obtains the information necessary to prove that Commander MacGregor Corson Gerswin is the same MacGregor Corson Gerswin who is employed by the OER Foundation. After that, he will use what he can to narrow your location. Why this is so important to him I do not know, but his interest may be linked to an attachment his son, Duran, would like to form with a young lady named Helene Strackna Daeris . . ."

Gerswin shook his head. Of all the damned-fool reasons to have someone looking for him.

". . . and from what I can determine, her mother was a Major Alhenda Strackna, who was court-martialed and dismissed in disgrace from her position as Executive Officer of the cruiser *Fleurdilis*, then under the command of a senior commander named Gerswin."

Gerswin wondered how she had tracked down all the information as he listened to the remainder of the message.

". . . and that's it. If you wonder how I found this out, it was not that hard for the standard Kirnow ops to track the rumors from the Fugazey household. Apparently dear Helene, while attractive in visage, has not endeared herself to anyone." Lyr frowned and cleared her throat. "Someday, Commander . . . Commodore, more than one of the loose ends from your past is going to catch up with you, and since you won't give in, and neither will some of the people you've doubtlessly offended, the Empire will end up paying for it.

"Good luck on your latest. By the way, at last there's some Imperial interest in the growing commercial power represented by biologic technology. Barons Megalrie, Niniunto, Tvarik, and others are pressing for an Imperial Commission on the subject, and on firms such as Enver Limited, Corso and Associates, MCG Biologics. Thought you'd like to know. Needless to say, the foundation is opposing such a commission unless it includes an investigation of the activities of traditional firms to block biologic commercialization. I predict a stalemate, now that the Imperial Trust has endorsed the OERF position.

"In any case, now you know most of what I do."

Her image remained unspeaking, then she pursed her lips, licked them, and added, almost as an afterthought, "Attached is a databloc coded for entry and locked to your private code."

Her image vanished.

Gerswin touched the console.

"Record and store the information, visual and coded."

His fingers added the necessary codes to complete the entry, and he sat waiting before two blank screens as the AI went about its job.

The information had reached him before Baron Fugazey's agents had. If he had gone to Westmark, or Standora, or El Lido, or . . . he shook his head again.

Resourceful as she might by, Lyr was certainly not about to send torps and messages all over the Empire, and she couldn't send them outside the Empire, even though Gerswin moved there as well.

Too bad there wasn't the equivalent of a planetary communications network for intersystems communications, regardless of political jurisdictions. The jumpshift was the only way so far known to exceed light speed.

He snorted.

One day, unfortunately, with his expanding sphere of operations, as each of the operations he directed grew, he would be out of touch for too long. To be able to keep ahead of the Baron Fugazeys of the Empire, not to mention the I.S.S. and the Intelligence Service, he needed something he didn't have. Between the few cargo ships and the independents, one could reach the major systems, but it might be three days or four weeks.

He pursed his lips, then turned to the AI. He stopped and frowned.

Like it or not, he would have to have Lyr get the information . . . somehow . . . assuming he could also deal with Fugazey. But he would have to get Lyr started and hoped he could survive to finish up. He laughed, a hard barking sound. If he didn't survive, the whole point was mute.

"Message for Lyr D'Meryon. OER Foundation. Stand by."

"Awaiting message," the AI replied.

Gerswin sat up straight and squarely before the scanner.

"Thanks for the information about Baron Fugazey. Hope I can solve his problem my way rather than his.

"Brought to mind another area that might be fruitful. Need some background information first. Would you find out quietly if there are surplus I.S.S. message torps available, and at what price. If not, what would it cost to purchase or build one thousand of them from other sources? That's right. One thousand. Any support data you could dig up would be helpful.

"Let me know as soon as you can."

He touched the controls on data screens again.

"Interrogative analysis on the Fugazey data."

"Analysis incomplete."

Gerswin drummed his fingers on the edge of the control board and continued to wait, thinking about how to organize a torp-oriented message system on a commercial or public utility basis.

Finally, after he had mentally designed and discarded three schemes for a system, the AI chimed and interrupted his reflections.

"Analysis complete."

"Put on screen four."

He straightened and began to read, left index finger regulating the speed of the summary text.

When he had completed the first run-through he was frowning, pulling at his chin. He looked at the main flight controls, then at the AI panel.

He coughed and cleared his throat, then rekeyed the summary. As he ran through it again, his eyes flickered over the pages as fast as they appeared on the screen.

Then he leaned back in the control couch.

Lyr had done a good job, more than a good job, and the conclusions were clear.

Fugazey avoided confrontations whenever possible and only retaliated when his enterprises were seriously threatened or if his family appeared personally threatened. In those few cases, professionals, the closest equivalents to the now defunct Guild, were apparently employed, although no bodies ever surfaced.

The picture was that of a coldly sensible businessman who used the best tools possible and never acted primarily from emotion, except where his family was concerned.

Gerswin frowned. That meant he could not focus on the son, who had probably caused the problem, without dragging in the father. Eliminating Helene would enrage both the Fugazeys and the Daeris clan.

Theoretically, the best approach would be to convince both Jorge Fugazey and his son Duran that vengeance against one Commander Gerswin was neither wise nor desirable and that allowing Helene to dictate their course was particularly unwise. And he had to do so in a way that made the point clearly, but which left them able to save face.

LVII

THE RHINOPED SNORTED, shifting its weight from left to right side, as if flexing the muscles that could propel its three ton mass at close to forty kays.

At the far end of the elongated clearing, a man, small by comparison to the beast, in turn shifted his weight, not taking his eyes off the rhinoped, as if to ensure that the red and flowing sheetmail weighed evenly across his massive shoulders.

Well over two meters tall, the giant swung his sword in prescribed arcs, waiting for the double bell, waiting for the sonic barrier to drop, that unseen wall that both held and infuriated the beast.

The combat was third on the card, more than a crowd warm-up, but still three events before the finale, where two firelizards, a blooded rhinoped, and a jackelion were pitted against a single man.

The giant in red mail did not have to accept those odds, since he entered the arena by choice, not necessity. In turn, the crowd cheered the animals rather than him, at least until the combat was over.

Just before the twin chimes sounded, he glanced upward, over the artificial terrain, over the synthetic recreation of the Alhurzian high forest toward that part of the spectator area bordered by the golden rail.

Whether he saw any mark of favor from the line of barons' tables or not, he made no acknowledgment, as he recentered his attention on the snorting rhinoped.

Cling! Cling!

Thirty meters above the purple-veined replicas of Alhurzian morloch vines, the copper-haired woman with the flowing curls that glistened and the bright green eyes that flashed with cold fire sat alone at the box rail table of a baron.

That it was the box table of at least a baron of the Empire was clear because only barons were permitted to purchase the inner line of tables along the high rail overlooking the arena. That she was recognized and belonged there was clear from the bowing and scraping accorded her by the staff, the depth of whose genuflections tended to be proportional to the wealth and position of those before whom they bowed.

That she was not the baroness herself was clear from the intensity in watching the arena, for she had not yet acquired the refined indifferent cruelty born of experience, though her carriage and manners were perfect in every ostensible sense.

Three tables down, to the left, also against the railing, sat an angular-featured young man, accompanied by a younger woman scarcely out of girlhood, and by a silver-haired and slender baroness whose veiled eyes slowly shifted from point to point, surveying everything but the action in the large arena below.

Most of the baron's tables held one or two people, though each could accommodate eight in grand style and up to twelve in a more intimate arrangement.

In the fringe area to the left and right of the baron's tables, where the status of the holders was in the undefined limbo of those greater than commercial magnates, but not officially recognized as barons, a black-haired, black-eyed man dressed in black sat alone. His hair was short, but tight-curled, and while his manners were almost indifferent, the staff tiptoed nearly as deferentially to him as to any baron.

The table belonged to Fernand H'Llory, but the man who sat
there was not H'Llory, for H'Llory had never attended the spectacles
at the arena and had obtained the table for the convenience of his
wide range of guests and associates, all of whom were at least the
equal of commercial magnates, if not more. The placement of the
table afforded an accommodation between shades of status satisfactory to all, particularly to H'Llory.

The man in black was obviously from the fringes of the Empire,
for he wore the black with absolute authority, certainly, and flair, de-
fying the current unspoken convention that while women might wear
black, no man of worth would do so, for black had been the color of
the assassins, and they had been broken, and those who remained
and followed the profession independently were obviously inferior.

The copper-haired woman clapped politely, as did most of the
other Imperials, as the red-mailed man in the arena dispatched the
three-meter horned rhinoped. The kill had been serviceable, but
little more. He had avoided injury, but taken more than the pair
of normal kill strokes required to destroy the twin hearts of the
beast.

The single woman let her eyes drift toward the man in black, who
had not even made a gesture toward applause. As her head turned,
the angular-faced young man's eyes followed hers, although he had to
strain slightly to see her actions from the three table distance.

"Who is he?" asked the angular-faced man's sister.

"I don't know. He was here last night. Black then, too."

"Gauche," the girl observed.

"By current standards," noted the baroness.

"You approve, Mother?"

A wry smile crossed the baroness's face. "Whether I approve or
not will affect society's judgments and fads little." She turned her
head. "But the man is handsome, rather, in a dark way."

The angular-faced young man frowned, his complexion paling a
shade. His sister touched his arm. He removed her fingers gently, but
quickly.

"What can I do? Two agents missing, and that Commodore Gerswin has disappeared, almost as if he knew they were after him. Helene has refused to consider any contract or further contact until
that's resolved. She says she is sorry, but whoever her contract-mate is
will have to clear that blot."

He watched as the copper-haired woman known as Helene summoned a towering staffer in cold violet formal wear, watched as she

instructed him or requested something, and watched as the tall man stepped away.

He was still watching as the functionary appeared at the table where the man in black sat.

The man in black inclined his head, then shook it firmly.

"She can't do that!" hissed the angular-faced man.

"He didn't accept, Duran," observed the sister.

"That will just intrigue her more."

"Of course."

"You are too eager, Duran, too intense, like your father, though he has come to accept that failing in himself. Watch the next combat. It might be interesting."

Below, a man and a woman, each with a boar spear, bowed to the audience, which responded with an applause mainly perfunctory.

"Do you want to wager on the outcome, or the time?"

"Neither," snapped Duran, forcing himself to avoid meeting the cool glance of Helene, who had surveyed his table without seeing him or his sister and mother. "Neither."

"There will be a dance tonight. Are you going?"

"I haven't decided."

"Well," added his sister with a smile that did not hide the cruelty, "Jaim Daeris told Forallie that Helene was going. Alone."

She refrained from saying more as the baroness's cold gray eyes caught hers.

"I haven't decided," Duran repeated. "I haven't decided."

LVIII

LYR D'MERYON MUMBLED under her breath, touched the screen controls, and surveyed the information again.

"One thousand torps. That was bad enough."

Her finger jabbed at the console controls.

"Now he wants to know about surplus in-system relay stations—and the possibility of simplified designs for both torps and stations. What does he want? His own private message delivery system?"

She brushed a strand of hair back off her forehead, wondering why she had ever even considered that her mysterious commander—

strange how she continued to think of him as a commander—would settle into a more regular pattern after he retired from the Service.

Settle down? Regular? Not only could she never find him in a hurry, but the work load had more than tripled in the last ten years.

And the creds! Everything he touched seemed to generate money. The more he spent, the more it created. Plus the funds from strange names and friends, names and friends that were never explained.

Was Shaik Corso an acquaintance or an alias? She suspected the latter, but the documents were in order, and the foundation's records had to show the latter. MacGregor Corson was so transparent, proper records or not, that she wasn't about to risk an Imperial censure. So "Corson's" contributions and expenses were listed as a subset of Gerswin's.

The commander might complain, but the foundation was going to be run right. Period.

She sighed, and mentally added the thought—as far as she was concerned.

She switched screens again, trying to unscramble the codes on his latest voucher, shaking her head all the time.

Where it would end, she didn't know. If it would end.

The supposedly ancient commander still looked and acted like a man in his standard thirties, but the background she had found indicated he was well over a century old—at least.

She frowned at the thought that he might outlive her, then smiled a wry smile. She had a few more decades, at least, before she even had to worry about it.

"Ms. D'Meryon, can you check out item three on four beta?" asked the on-line tech.

"Hold one."

She transferred screens again, calling up the questioned item.

"That's an approved transportation item, deductible under 33(a)(1). Note that in the remarks section."

"Thank you."

She returned to screen one. Satellite relay systems? Surplus? Where should she start there?

She frowned once more, then tapped out a number.

LIX

DURAN STOOD IN the corner, half shielded by the ice sculpture of the rhinoped, and watched the dancers sweeping across the low grav of the dance floor in time to the ancient waltz.

His eyes followed a copper-haired woman in a formal coppered dress that should not have complimented her pale coloration, but did, as the dance ended and as she bowed to Carroll, the elder son of Baron Kellenher, and turned away, leaving the young man standing there with words on his lips left unsaid.

Duran grimaced.

At least she was equally cavalier with others, or some others.

A flicker of black caught his eye, and his head jerked around involuntarily.

The black-haired man skirted the dancing area, brushing the massive forearm of a giant in red, who whirled to confront the slender figure in black.

Duran smiled.

He did not know the giant personally, except that as the younger son of a minor mining baron, Trigarth had achieved a certain notoriety by surviving in the arena and a certain success with women by dropping to the level of combat in the circus and succeeding.

Duran's angular features relaxed as he watched the confrontation develop.

". . . apology . . . ?" asked Trigarth.

The man in black inclined his head politely, but quizzically, as if he could not believe what Trigarth had asked.

"I think you owe me an apology." By now the hall was quiet enough for the words to reach Duran.

"I beg your pardon, but I believe I owe you nothing."

The smaller man turned, his carriage conveying his opinion of the big man, an opinion Duran silently seconded, though he would never have been fool enough to voice it.

Trigarth stepped around in front of the other, blocking his departure.

"I would appreciate that apology."

The smaller man's eyes surveyed the massive two plus meter form of Trigarth. His lips quirked, as if to sneer, then his face cleared.

"Are you trying to insist that sheer dumb mass requires respect?"

Duran's mouth dropped, as did a number of others'. Was the man mad? The wealth of Trigarth's house could pay off any death claim.

"Never . . . have . . . I . . . been . . . so . . . insulted."

"Then you have been extraordinarily fortunate. Now, if you will excuse me . . ."

Duran caught sight of Helene among the watching dancers. Even from ten meters he could see the unnatural brightness in her eyes as she watched the pair.

"I could crush you!" rumbled Trigarth.

The man in black laughed twice. Two cruel barks conveyed a sense that Trigarth was less than the lowest of the low. Then he shook his head sadly, as if to convey pity on the big noble and gladiator, and began to turn.

Duran could see it coming, watched as Trigarth lost all control and launched hands and body toward the smaller man with a speed that caused Duran and others nearer to the pair to draw back.

Duran, his angular features tight again, waited for the stranger's dismemberment, his own reflexes keyed so that the scene seemed to play out in virtual slow motion.

Trigarth's whole body drove toward the man in black, who stood motionless for long instants. Just before hammering arms blasted through him, the smaller shifted, and his hands and body blurred as he moved.

Thuddd!

Duran gaped.

The small man appeared untouched, unmussed, and was again shaking his head sadly, this time at the unconscious figure of the giant on the floor.

Three of the staff guards arrived too late, expecting apparently to rescue the stranger's remains.

"He is unconscious, but you should find that he will be all right, except for a bruise on his jaw where he struck the floor. He must have had too much of something."

The senior guard asked something.

"Merhlin of Avalon, guest of Lord and Baron H'Llory. I will be staying as his guest for at least several days more."

Another question followed.

"I suppose I could claim I was a baron, were I so inclined. Would that make any difference?"

Duran shook his head. So fast . . . so incredibly fast. And so strong. Was the man human? Then he bit his lip.

As Merhlin of Avalon dismissed the security force, a copper-haired woman touched his black-sleeved forearm. The woman's eyes glittered in the light.

This time, instead of dismissing Helene, Merhlin surveyed her coolly, then offered his arm.

Duran gulped the last from the goblet in his hand, choking it down, and ignoring the burning in his throat. He clutched the empty goblet as if he wanted to crush it into powder.

Instead, the unbreakable crystal squirted from his fingertips and struck the ornate floor tiles, bouncing away from him.

Clink! Clink. Clink.

He could see his sister Aermee look up in surprise, and then avert her eyes as she recognized that he had been the culprit. The couple next to him drew back and looked away.

The sound of the bouncing crystal echoed in Duran's mind as he turned away, but he was not quick enough to avoid the smirk on Helene's lips as she swept up the ramp with the man called Merhlin.

Duran swallowed and slowly retracted his steps across the hall. Even people he did not know drew away in distaste as he headed for the exit not taken by Merhlin and Helene, the exit that began the long walk back to the family suite, and, in all probability, toward a quiet talk with his mother, the baroness. Either shortly, or the next morning, when Aermee would have reported her extreme embarrassment at his behavior.

Duran sighed, loudly enough to cause another set of averted faces.

LX

THE COPPER-HAIRED woman shook her head, tossing the glistening curls back over her bare shoulders, conscious of the effect as she again exposed her breasts. She straightened her back as she reached for the crystal wineglass.

Leaning back against the pillows, she brought the crystal to her lips, first to scent, then to sip.

Gerswin refrained from shaking his head. The hard line of her jaw and the ever-occurring cruel glint in her eyes were so at odds with her slenderness and the softness of her skin.

He whistled three notes, double-toned, more as a test than anything else.

Helene shivered at the sounds, but said nothing and took another sip that became a gulp.

Gerswin paused before beginning another song, forcing himself to keep his face almost impersonal as he watched her reactions.

She raised her eyebrows, arching her back again.

Gerswin began another song, not a love song, for Helene had proved strangely indifferent to the gentle songs, the wistful ones, and had been aroused by his adaptations of the military themes, the ones where he had played hope against force, honesty against betrayal.

'That's right," the woman whispered hoarsely as she set the wineglass aside. "That's right."

Her lips parted, her tongue running over her lower lip, wetting it and retreating. Her breathing deepened as his double-toned notes built toward what he would have called hope and its betrayal.

Her shoulders shifted, her hips beginning to move with the conflict of the song, as she began to lean toward him.

Gerswin could see her darkened nipples stiffening further as whatever fantasy played out behind her too-bright green eyes intensified with the last notes of the song.

Even before the tones died away, her fingers were digging into first his forearms, then his back as he in turn drove into her, directly, brutally, and without finesse or foreplay, knowing that such power was what she wanted, what she expected.

"AaaaaaAAAAHHHHH!"

Her cries filled the not inconsiderable expanse of the bedroom as her legs locked around him in a series of thrusts, and as her body arched into him and upward, upward.

Waiting until she subsided, he did not leave her, but turned his head to start another song, with a more muted conflict theme, drawing her into another series of releases, more gentle than the first, and letting himself go as well, trying to shut out other faces, other places, with a final thrust more brutal than he had intended.

"Ooohhh!"

Helene lay against him only momentarily before easing back onto the bed, propped against silken pillows, a faint smile on her face.

"You are a magician."

The coolness of her tone brought him back to his purpose.

"Never said one way or the other." He managed a cool mocking tone, which masked the contempt he felt, both for himself and for her.

"Where did you come from? I've never met anyone so strong."

"Anyone you couldn't wear out, you mean?"

Without the spell of his music, she might easily have outlasted him, and then some, but that wasn't the question. He needed certain revelations from the copper-haired harpy.

"I would scarcely confess that, even if it were true."

"What would you confess? You know, I know nothing about you, except your name and status. You could be some baron's young wife, for all I know, but he'd be a fool to let you run this free, and twice the fool not to."

"Oh?"

Gerswin matched her smile with one a shade more mocking. "But then, you'd never let yourself be bound, would you?"

"That answer takes no magic."

"But you do admit I possess some small magic?"

"I'll admit that, at least in some areas." She sat up and took the wineglass, downing the remainder of the wine in a single gulp.

"Will you admit that you're sought after?"

"Surely. But for what? Body? Or money?"

"Both. For your wealth by the older, and your body by the younger. Like that angular-faced young fellow who couldn't keep his eyes off you at the arena. A puppy dog."

"Him. He's nothing."

"Some baron's offspring, I presume, ready to propose a contract in an instant."

"He already has."

"But you're here," laughed Gerswin, "instead of in young what's-his-name's arms. Not that you couldn't be and still have accepted."

"Duran wouldn't know what to do. No strength. No magic."

"Seemed capable enough for a youngster."

"Youngster is precisely right. He'll never grow up. He'd never be more than just a tool, even if I did accept his contract."

"That indicates you have not. You're a hard lady, willing to use anyone . . . or your own magic." Gerswin forced a leer, let it be seen that it was forced.

"Why not?"

"You feel no guilt," asked Gerswin with a quirk to his lips, "about holding your body out to this Duran to get him to do whatever you want?"

"Of course not. Why should I? If you can use your magic to get my body—not that I mind—why shouldn't I use my body to get what I want?"

Gerswin laughed, a hard bark, knowing that the hidden scanners had more than enough on tape.

"Poor Duran . . . poor anyone. Whoever gets you won't know how to handle you."

"Duran won't get me. He's too weak. Besides, I'd probably find a way to avoid the contract even if he did everything I asked."

"Everything?"

Helene stretched, tossing her copper curls off her bare breasts.

"Sing me another one, a stronger one." Her eyes brightened as she slowly dropped her head, letting her hair fall back across her breasts, before tossing it over her shoulders, squaring her shoulders, emphasizing her translucent skin, her nipples again taut with anticipation.

Her tongue moistened her lips once more as Gerswin began the progression of double-toned notes, this time weaving the theme of betrayal versus betrayal.

LXI

DURAN'S LONG STEPS took him toward the portal of his father's screen center. He barely nodded at the security console as he passed through the endurasteel pillars, but his carriage stiffened and he slowed as he recognized the figure in black sitting in the chair across from his father.

His second surprise was the stillness, for all the screens had been blanked, save one, which displayed only the name "Helene" upon it.

The man in black stood, as did Jorge Fugazey.

"I believe you have at least seen Merhlin, Duran," offered the baron to his son.

"Twice." Duran's tone was as angular as his strained face.

"Merhlin has brought me some rather impeccable references, which I have checked thoroughly, as well as some rather interesting information."

"I see."

"The question was whether I let you see it before making my decision and whether I asked your opinion, or whether I did what I thought best and merely informed you."

Duran inclined his head. "It must be rather earth-shaking for you to have consulted with and gone to the difficulty of investigating a total stranger."

Both his father and the stranger ignored the unconcealed bitterness in his tone.

"Before we continue, Duran, I suggest you view the segment of the tape on the console. I can verify, and have done so, that the speaker is indeed Helene, and that the tape has not been altered. There are no stress levels in her voice."

The older man's voice contained a sadder note, one that brought Duran up short as his father continued, for he had never heard it before. "Knowing how you feel, please remember that the one thing I have never done is lie to you. That is also why I have gone to the trouble of having all aspects of this thoroughly checked."

"Why all the sudden concern?"

"Because I would prefer that you leave yourself something besides the choice of suicide through a woman and suicide through stupidity or stubbornness."

Duran swallowed. For his father even to have admitted the stranger, and then to have spoken so directly in his presence, meant that the man was either immensely powerful or in his father's trust, or both.

"There is a sound block around the screen. For your own peace of mind, I suggest you use it."

Duran glanced from the pale face of his father to the impassively hawkish visage of the black-haired stranger, then walked to the console and tapped the sound block controls. The wall of silence enfolded him.

He touched the stud to start the sequence, sinking into the swivel as he watched Helen's unclothed figure swim into view on a rather imposing bed, tossing her glittering curls off her naked breasts.

Duran wanted to shut out the words, to turn away from the scene even as his eyes drank in the cruelty and lust in her face and the slender voluptuousness of her body.

He did not turn, forcing himself to hear every last word. Mercifully, the sequence was short, the betrayal shorter.

He reran her damning words twice, then blanked the screen.

After sitting there silently for several minutes, he dropped the sound block and stood, turning to face the other two, his eyes scanning the man identified as Merhlin, wondering how old or how young he was.

Certainly older, but how much?

He was letting his thoughts drift, Duran realized. Concentrating on the moment, he eased himself into the vacant swivel next to his father.

"Do you want my opinion?" he asked. Even to himself, his voice sounded thin.

"Do you want to give it?" asked his father gently. "You don't have to give it, you know."

"It couldn't have been faked," Duran admitted. "Don't tell me how, but I know that." He paused and pulled at his chin. "Does it matter? I don't know. I knew I should be able to accept her for all her faults, knowing what I would get and what I wouldn't. Or I should be able to say good riddance."

"What is the price you pay for taking her?" asked Merhlin.

"A man has to die. But all men die."

"Would you stake your life on that?" asked Jorge Fugazey.

Duran looked from his father, the baron, to Merhlin and back again.

"I'm not sure I understand."

"For all practical purposes," added the baron, "you may regard both Baron H'Llory and Merhlin as allies and dependents of Commodore Gerswin."

Duran sat immobile. After a time, he spoke.

"Does that mean you are withdrawing your support, should I continue my efforts to have Commodore Gerswin removed?"

"No. It means that the commodore can remove or negate any protection I can offer. That would mean some risk. Considerable risk. That I cannot deny, nor could I let you proceed, should I choose to, without your knowing that. That is why I thought you should see the tape. You are my oldest son, and you will be sacrificing your life for someone who cares nothing for you. From her, you would have neither respect nor love."

Duran looked at the floor. "Do I have to decide now?"

"No. It might be better if you thought it over."

Merhlin rose to his feet. "Fear my actions have caused a great deal of trouble, but I have been as honest as possible, and I think it would be better if I withdrew."

"Do you call that honesty?" Duran's hand stabbed toward the console he had so recently sat before.

"Helene is free to make her own choices. So are you. You can live or you can die." While Merhlin's light baritone penetrated, his tone was gentle, as if instructing a child.

"You think I'll die?"

Merhlin took a step backward. "That is what you must choose, Ser Fugazey."

"Are you betraying Helene, then?"

"Scarcely."

As Merhlin's eyes caught Duran, the younger man felt as though he were pinned in his seat.

Merhlin bowed to Jorge Fugazey, the bow of an equal, Duran observed, and said, "I will depart . . . as I arrived."

He stepped out through the portal, which closed behind him.

"What did that mean?" snapped Duran.

"Duran . . . your foolishness could have cost us both dearly." The Baron Fugazey's voice was harder, in a resigned way, than Duran had ever heard it.

"I don't understand—"

"That's right. You don't understand. Console three beta. Run it before you utter another word."

As Duran stumbled toward the indicated console, the older Fugazey stood. His steps took him in a tight circle, and his eyes darted to the console where his son studied a series of scenes.

When Duran had completed his assignment and blanked the screen, he turned and eased himself toward where the baron stood.

"I sound like a locked loop, but I can't say I understand. Could you explain . . . please?"

"Duran, those last scenes. Who was there?"

"Me, Mother, Aermee, you, Donal, Frynn."

"And the vantage point?"

Duran glanced down. Never had his father asked so many questions he couldn't answer. Accounting and law—there he could hold his own. The same for marketing, tariffs. But this?

The baron swung his head from side to side slowly.

"Do you know who Merhlin is?"

"No. Does it matter?"

"Yes. While I do not know exactly who he is, I know what he is. Besides being supported by Fernand H'Llory, who by the way fears him rather thoroughly, and besides being, shall we say, an agent of Gerswin, he's a professional assassin of assassins, who, if he's who I think he is, was the one who broke the Guild, the one whom the Eye Corps refused, it's rumored, to attack."

Duran looked absently puzzled, knitted his forehead in a quizzical gesture, and looked up to see the continued disapproval in his father's face.

"It's obvious that your life has been too sheltered, Duran." The baron wiped his forehead with the back of his left hand. "I'll put it in simple sentences. That sequence showed clearly that Merhlin could have assassinated every one of us in less than a three-hour period, and done so without triggering a single security precaution within the villa.

"That sequence with Helene showed that Gerswin would rather not do so, and was directed at me, not at you."

"At you?"

"At me. Gerswin simply delivered a clear, two-pronged message. First, that Helene isn't worth a conflict over, and second, that if I disagree he understands he would have to destroy the entire family, not just you, and that he is fully capable of doing so."

Duran could feel the color draining out of his face.

"Now . . . I see you are beginning to understand. Do you also understand that Merhlin saw you did not understand and left so that you could not act before we could discuss the matter?"

"But why?"

"I don't know. Gerswin is not adverse to violence, necessarily, though he tries to avoid it." Jorge Fugazey looked at the blank screens arrayed to his right. "The second sequence had a preface, but it blanked after the first scan. He said he hoped I would understand. I remember his words clearly. He and Merhlin speak in the same tones. He said, 'Once I had a son . . .'"

The elder Fugazey shook his head. "Too sentimental, but it makes no difference. He's offered us a way out, one that doesn't ruin us, and a way to save face."

"He's insulted you!"

"If showing me that your intended is both a bitch and a tramp, as well as not up to keeping her word, if refraining from destroying me and everything I've built because of your stubbornness and inadequate research, and if doing it with enough tact to keep it quiet—if all this is an insult, then by all means think so. But I will, with great regret, inform Gerswin that your quarrel with him is strictly personal and does not involve Fugar House. While I love you, Duran, hard as that is for you to comprehend, I also love Margritte and Aermee and Donal and Frynn. And if you want Helene after all this and after all she has already put you through, what you really want is suicide."

"What will people think?"

"Nothing. They won't know, unless you tell them."

"But . . . Helene?"

"You confirm to her that you have totally withdrawn your offer for contract, with great regret, and you leave her free to follow her heart, as you cannot meet her conditions. What can she say? If she tells anyone the reason is because you refused to murder someone you do not know, then you come out looking like you have better judgment than you so far have shown. The only question in people's minds is why it took you so long to see through her."

"You leave me no other choice."

The Baron Fugazey sighed. "No. I do not. Someday, perhaps, you will understand with your heart as well as with your head."

Duran matched his father's sigh.

"I understand now. But don't expect me to like it . . . not now."

The two regarded each other across the open space between them.

"May I go now?"

"You may go, Duran."

"I will send confirmation of my withdrawal as you suggested. Then, I think, I will leave for New Avalon."

Jorge Fugazey nodded, but said nothing as his son left. An even deeper sigh escaped him as the portal closed behind the young man.

He had not told Duran that he had sent a copy of the sequence showing Helene to the Baron Daeris, with his own notation that any further action against one Commodore Gerswin would be most unwise, particularly from the viewpoint of the commodore, Fugar House, and Baron H'Llory.

Daeris would understand, even if Duran did not.

"NOW . . . IS THERE any other business?"

Eye sat in his customary position at the end of the Intelligence conference table, sat in his shadowed splendor, flanked by his two shadowed regents, and surveyed the room.

Silence prevailed as the uniformed Service officers looked back and forth at each other, finally fixing their gazes on a single and white-haired Rear Admiral.

"It would seem that your contemporaries feel you have something to say, Admiral Thurson."

The round-cheeked Admiral smiled ruefully. "Under the circumstances, I guess I have little choice." He cleared his throat with an apologetic gesture before continuing. "We received a rather disturb-ing report from New Avalon, which we managed to track back to a confirmation from a source in Fugar House. Of course, we reported the information to Eye Corps. I was wondering what the current sta-tus or classification of the follow-up might be."

Eye nodded so imperceptibly within his hood that the movement was unremarked by anyone else, particularly since all eyes were on Admiral Thurson.

"I presume that you are referring to the apparent reappearance of a man calling himself Merhlin of Avalon?"

"That is the report we received."

"As you know, there is no system or locale known strictly as 'Avalon' within the Empire or other known human systems, which in-dicated that the man using the name was doubtless an imposter. Nei-ther the man nor that identity has surfaced since the incident you uncovered. Consequently, Eye Corps has not been able to trace any-thing further on the individual in question, since we were unable to obtain any sort of firm biological identification, and since the few holos we were able to obtain revealed gross physical parameters ap-plicable to at least ten percent of the male Imperial population."

"Ten percent?" That whisper came from someone behind Thurson.

Thurson nodded. He cleared his throat again. "A literature search revealed that the only Avalons in history existed on Old Earth. I presume that Eye Corps efforts to identify this Merhlin, also a myth-ical figure from Old Earth, attempted to tie Merhlin to those with Old Earth ties."

"That was attempted, but no degree of certainty was possible, and in view of the Imperial position on Old Earth, without certainty, no action would have been possible."

Thurson nodded. "Mythical figures can be rather difficult to lay to rest."

"What are they talking about?"

"Thurson's on to something."

While the whispers should have been inaudible to Eye, they were not. Nothing within the conference room escaped his eyes or ears, enhanced as they were by his personal equipment.

"Should we be able to determine the identity of any true male-factor, of course, and should the Emperor concur, we would take the necessary steps to resolve the problem."

Again Admiral Thurson nodded, not bothering to wipe the dampness off his forehead.

"Are there any other questions? Any other matters to be brought before the Council?" Eye paused. "If not, the formal meeting is adjourned. I might also add that since Admiral Thurson's retirement will become effective before the next meeting, we all wish him well." Eye stood.

Thurson managed to keep his jaw from falling open in the quiet hissing of whispers that circled the conference room.

"Just promoted to Vice Admiral . . ."

". . . never announced it . . ."

". . . really hot, whatever it was . . . poor bastard . . . likely to be found dead of heart failure within weeks . . ."

". . . why you never ask questions . . ."

Eye strode out, flanked by his regents, and the Service officers clustered around Thurson, who had taken out a large white cloth and was wiping his forehead, despite the chill that remained in the room.

LXIII

HIS FACE WAS as always, the same blond, curly hair, hawk-yellow eyes, although the image was frozen on the screen.

The Senior Port Captain of Ydris glanced at the image, then at the contract on the console, then at her own work sheet on the third screen.

"Aboveboard and foul in the dirtiest way possible, Corso! You devil!"

She smiled in both wry admiration and humor.

The ex-Imperial officer she called Corso had her caught squarely by her own ideals, and those of Ydris.

If she failed to recommend his offer, then the communications system he had developed would become the tool of the commercial interests and eventually would sell out to the highest bidder, no matter how noble the initial purpose. That such a bidder would use the system against Ydris was also inevitable.

If she endorsed his proposal, then Ydris would inevitably become an information and commercial hub second only to New Augusta. Even there, Corso had calculated cleverly. The distance was great enough that New Augusta would gain more than it would lose—at least for decades.

His motivation—that was what bothered her. Why would anyone go to the tremendous effort and expense of acquiring the equipment, developing detailed operating plans, and obtaining the necessary permissions for the key systems ... and then turn it over to someone else?

He'd offered a clear explanation, right on the databloc.

"Isbel. You're going to ask why. Answer is simple. I need an interstellar communications system I can trust, one independent of the Empire, and one that will maintain confidentiality.

"I can afford to build it. What I can't afford is the time and dedicated people to run it. And I need someone whose ideals will prevent them from corrupting it. That's you and Ydris."

Should she trust him? Could she afford not to?

She smiled wryly and touched the stud that would forward the proposition to the Council. Her recommendation to accept was attached.

The Council would accept it. Like her. Ydris could not afford to decline, could not afford to pass up the chance to control her own destiny.

Still ... she wondered why the mysterious man known only as Corso was willing to find such an altruistic enterprise, only for a minute return on his investment and years before any repayment of the principal was due.

LXIV

"BUT I CAN'T be!" protested the woman. "I can't be."

"It is not a matter of debate, milady," answered the physician as he looked back at the console. "Contraceptive implant failure is rare, to be sure, but not unheard of."

"Have you reported this to my father?"

"Of course. You are the only Daeris of this generation. How could I not? He said he already knew."

"He knew? But how? I'm not one of his brood mares!"

"That, milady, is between you and your father." The doctor's eyes were calm and level, as gray as his dark gray hair.

She glanced from one side of the office to the other, idly wondering if she could reach the balcony that overlooked the grounds. Then she shook her head.

Not that way. If worse came to worst, her father could have the heir. At least once it was over he could have no objection to her living her own life, and outside the restricted sphere of a baron's controlled environment.

She unthinkingly tossed her glittering copper curls back off the cream of her tunic and over her shoulder. Was it already tighter than she remembered?

Despite the controls and the guards, she'd managed to get herself in trouble, and he hadn't said a word. Not a word, almost as if he'd hoped for it. But he'd known, known before she and the doctor had! How?

She bit her lip.

Her father had known.

What else did he know?

She looked again at the balcony railing, then back at the thin older doctor.

"What about decanting?"

"Your father—"

"Damn his fundamentalist beliefs! Damn him . . . yes, I know . . . Of course, I know . . . how else could it possibly be?"

She glanced again at the balcony.

"Milady . . . ?"

"Yes, Hierot?"

"Is there anything else? Before you go?"

Helene shook her head with a quick motion, a violent, short snap. There was nothing else. Not now. Not ever.

She looked toward the balcony.

LXV

WHEN THE COMMANDER'S—strange how she could never keep from calling him a commander, although he never used the title and had retired from the Service as a commodore—face filled the screen, as soon as the image cleared and went real time, the question was out of her mouth.

"You bought another biologics complex? For what? Do we need another full-scale research facility?"

He closed his mouth, as if he had been about to say something else and had decided against it. He waited.

"Why did you buy it?" she repeated her question.

"I did not buy it. Made the first payment, and obligated you to complete the contract."

Lyr's mouth dropped open. "You . . . obligated the foundation. How much?"

"Fifty million?"

"Fifty million? From the Forward Fund?"

"That's what it's for." He frowned. "An acquisition grant, not for research. Production."

"What does production have to do with promoting biologic research?"

"Read section three, clause five of the foundation goals."

Lyr worried at her lip, brushed a graying hair off her forehead. When he cited sections of the bylaws, he was invariably right.

"I don't suppose you would like to tell me why you have involved OERF with production now?"

"Lyr. Someone has to translate research into reality. Done what I can personally. But took the commercial fields, and plowed money back into research, back into the foundation."

"I know."

"Hope that some more spin-offs from what the foundation had stimulated would be appearing. They're not. Not one. Yet I'm making creds. It's almost as if—" He laughed once. "Never mind."

He looked below the screen, then back at her before continuing. "Need certain technologies developed now. No other way to do it. But don't worry. It's profitable."

He grinned. "That's another problem, I know, but that's one you can solve."

"You have such illusions about my abilities."

"No bitterness, please." His tone was gentle.

"All right." Lyr bit back the intemperate comment she had almost launched and frowned at the screen, waiting to see what else he said.

"Is your dream beyond a dream still the same?"

"My what?"

"Once we talked about dreams beyond dreams. Yours was a chalet on Vers D'Mont. Do you remember?"

"That was in another life, Commander."

"Another life? Perhaps, but is the dream still your dream?"

"There are days, Commander, when it is even more attractive than it ever was. Why do you ask? Do you really care? Or is it just to humor me?"

His expression tightened, as if her words had been even more barbed than she had meant.

"I thought you could tell when I was humoring you. Did you ask that . . ." He shook his head. "Never mind."

"You know I have never tried to undermine you—no matter how outrageously you behaved." This time there was anger in her words. "You never let anyone know how you feel. You make me guess what you really want, and once in awhile I even get a pat on the head." She paused, but not enough to let him speak. "More likely, you tell me to give myself a pat on the head."

Surprisingly, he only nodded. "You're right, Lyr. Not too much I can say that will rebut that."

"Don't you ever get angry? Don't you ever get hurt?"

"Yes. I do get angry, and I have been hurt, and I will be again, no doubt." The gentleness in his voice disarmed her own lingering anger.

"When?" There was more curiosity than steel in her tone.

He sighed. "Rather not go into details. Let's just say that I've buried two sons, three lovers. Not technically correct, but all five are dead. Some were killed to strike at me, and some were killed when my back was turned."

"And you can take it that calmly?"

She could see his face harden.

"Quietly. Not calmly. I have thrown my share of thunderbolts, and the guilty and I have both paid. Paid in full. Still paying."

Lyr shivered as the coldness seemed to rush from the screen and enfold her. She wondered, again, whether his anger was the cold of deep space, the devastating destruction of absolute zero.

"You still make them pay?"

"No. They paid. I still pay. Will with every mile left in life."

He smiled his grim smile and laughed softly. "But enough of me . . . I asked about you."

"I'm not sure we're finished. . . ."

He sighed once more, and the grim smile was replaced with a still sadness, the guarded look of a man willing to take an assault without attacking in return or raising a defense. Lyr did not recall ever having seen that expression, the weariness in his eyes, or the sudden vulnerability.

"What else would you like to know?"

"I don't know. Except that after all these years, I still feel like I don't know you. Like you feel all things more intensely than any man should, and yet you show so little. As if what you do is consuming what you are."

His shoulders gave a small shrug. "You're probably right about

the last. But I warned you about that in the beginning. Told you that
I was a fanatic."

"That doesn't excuse it."

"Not trying to excuse it, Lyr. I know what I am."

"Do you? I wonder."

He smiled, and the expression was momentarily boyish. "All
right. I know at least some of what I am."

"And what about the rest?"

"Guess I'll find out."

This time she was the one to shake her head. "Heaven help us all
when you do."

"Not that bad." He grinned. "Enough of this somber stuff. Let's
get back to what I asked."

"What did you ask?"

"If you still had a dream beyond a dream."

"Some days. Why do you keep asking?"

"Every once in a while I care about people's dreams, a little more
often than they think."

"I stand reproved. I think."

"Not reproved. You're right, but can we leave it at that for now?"

"Why?"

"Because the timing is getting critical. A number of things are
coming together, and you'll probably need more staff, and I'm not
sure I can afford much more introspection. Not now."

"What do you mean?"

"More large purchases, some more acquisitions, that sort of
thing."

"I'm not sure I understand, but you do much more than you're
doing, and I'll need more staff."

"Go ahead and add what you need."

Lyr took a deep breath, feeling as though she had somehow
missed more than the quickest glimpse into the commander's soul.

"What about you?" she asked, trying to steer the conversation
back onto a more personal level.

"Probably more traveling. Trying to coordinate. Headed for El
Lido next, the way it looks. Not sure past that on the specifics."

"But what about you?" she asked again.

"I'll survive. Somehow. Always do. Probably always will. Not much
else that I can do."

"Try to keep in touch, Commander." She paused, and her voice
softened as she finished. "And take care."

"I will, as I can. Keep doing your best, Lyr. You're the only one who can keep this end together."

The screen blanked as her mouth dropped open. She had never expected either the admission of her efforts or the abruptness of his closing, not after the disclosures she had forced from him.

She rubbed her chin. On the other hand, perhaps he had to break the connection quickly. Perhaps he could not afford to become too personal . . . perhaps.

Shaking her head, she cleared the screen.

With his attitude and more purchases like the last, her efforts might not be enough to keep the Empire from digging deep into the foundation, and while the foundation might endure, she wondered about the implications for its trustee—and for its administrator.

THE SHADOWED MAN studied the arrangement.

The single guard sat in a shielded riot box set in the wall, swivel set high enough that he could survey the sloping lawn in front of the wall without his eyes being more than a slight angle from the screen that switched from snoop to snoop.

The chair itself was an indicator. Gerswin had watched as the present guard had replaced his predecessor, watched as the seat had lifted slightly when the guard's weight was removed.

From the shadows he dropped his glasses.

While he would rather have handled it personally, on a face-to-face basis, that was certainly what Carlina was expecting. She had obviously studied his past interactions and was counting on his reputed sense of fair play and direct action with principals.

He shook his head and slipped soundlessly back along the relatively unmonitored pathway he had tracked through the surrounding grounds, back to the flitter.

He took a deep breath as his quick and light steps cleared the unmarked boundary of the estate and as he entered the undeveloped tract where his flitter waited in the small clearing.

After a short flight to a more distant location, he changed craft, from a small black one to a larger black one. Once inside his ship, and seated before the control console, Gerswin touched the communications studs. The picture remained a swirl of color.

He recognized the swirl as a scramble from the receiver, a protective pattern that blocked even his own command access codes. His lips quirked as he waited to see how soon and if the pattern would clear.

Fully two minutes passed before the abstract color patterns resolved themselves into the picture of a silver-haired woman, with a straight, firm nose and violet eyes. Gerswin knew both eye color and nose had been purchased from a high-priced cosmetic surgeon.

Before she had risen to become Administrator of CE, Limited, on El Lido, Carlina D'Aquino had displayed muddy brown hair and eyes, and a much larger and wider nose.

"Shaik Corso! I had not expected you. I thought someone was testing our security system." Her smile showed the warmth that only years of accomplished insincerity could project.

"I regret the inconvenience, Carlina, but your recent reports have displayed a rather depressing lack of profitability, and I thought I might be of some service in assisting a rather rapid recovery." Gerswin doubted that his smile was nearly as warm as Carlina's.

"Oh, dear Shaik, you shouldn't have bothered. I'm afraid there's little you can do to change that. You know, our overhead has increased so much. You remember all those fancy hidden entrances and gas systems that Delwar had installed—I assume it was Delwar— that led to his replacement? Well, I thought they were really too much of an invitation, and I thought about replacing them. But then I found a few others that even Delwar hadn't known about, and decided I would never know whether I had ever found them all. So I moved the headquarters, and I turned the old buildings into the administrative center for our latest ventures, and they're guarded by DomSec."

"That showed a great deal of initiative, Carlina, especially since you were relying on my good faith."

"Now that you're back, Shaik, you could call a meeting, but, you recall, under El Lido law the meeting would have to be held in headquarters unless you could get a two-thirds vote, and to do that you and I would have to agree."

"That is true, and I might consider that." Gerswin smiled. "How is Ferinay?"

"Poor Ferinay. He suffered a second and rather unfortunate stroke last month, and the doctors say he will never be quite the same again."

"You have your own successor?"

"I don't plan on leaving in the near future, particularly since we have just landed the armor contracts for the Ministry of Domestic Security. They helped me with the design of our new headquarters. Did you know that?"

"I can't say I'm particularly surprised. How did you get around the rule prohibiting contracts with police and armed forces?"

"What provision was that?"

"I think I understand," Gerswin responded. "And, of course, they believe that the Shaik Corso who founded CE, Limited, might be a fiction, or should remain a silent partner."

"You do indeed understand. Perhaps a slight improvement in the reported profits might encourage that?"

"Might that have something to do with the fact that you are having difficulty tracing the origin of my call?"

"Dear Shaik, you are so suspicious."

"Is there anyone else with you, Carlina?"

"Why do you ask?"

"I was hoping for a witness."

"To what?"

"Just a witness, but it would probably be immaterial. Good day, Carlina. Remember that an honest thief stays bought."

"Is that a threat, Shaik?"

"No. I make no threats. Good day."

Gerswin broke the connection, then tapped out another combination and waited as the relay finished the circuit.

"Rodire and Fergamo." The dark-haired receptionist was plain, but real, and a welcome sight after Carlina.

Gerswin smiled at her image. "Shaik Corso for Hamline Rodire."

"Will he know you?"

"Hope so. I'm his landlord, so to speak."

"You're *that* Shaik Corso? I'm so sorry, but I expected . . ."

Gerswin laughed, a single bark. "I know, you expected a dark and mysterious stranger who mangled words and sentences."

"No . . . no . . . ," she protested, apparently unsure whether he was joking or serious.

He smiled. "Don't worry."

"I'll get him."

Hamline Rodire, Senior Partner, appeared on the screen. In spite of his mental picture of Rodire's aging since he had helped the then-younger attorney found an independent practice, he found it hard not to stare at the eagle-beaked and silver-haired advocate.

"Hamline . . . it's been longer than I thought."

"With you, Shaik, I suspect it always is." The older-looking man grinned, and Gerswin was reassured by the twinkle in the green eyes and the warmth in the voice. "You never age."

"Are things going well for you?"

"Personally, quite well, although we only get the required minimum from CE, Limited, since Carlina consolidated her hold there. Most of that is boilerplate."

"Yes."

"Are you calling about Carlina?"

"Maybe time for—let's say I need to transfer some of my holdings—time to place some more local controls. A few strings, however."

"Such as?"

"You'll have to vote my proxies when you call the shareholders' meeting."

"The annual meeting was just two months ago."

"There will be another shortly."

"Carlina has made both her estate and headquarters into personal fortresses."

"I understand, but you need not worry. After I complete my business, I do not intend to return to El Lido, not for some time, and I need to leave control in local hands I can trust. I trust your honesty, and you will see why."

"You make things sound so mysterious."

"Nothing mysterious at all. Since Carlina insists that might makes right, I merely intend to point out to her why that can be a dangerous philosophy." Gerswin shook his head abruptly. "You still have that estate of yours?"

"Why . . . yes . . ."

"Still like it as much as when you first purchased it?"

"Probably more," laughed the advocate. "You aren't . . . that is . . . I didn't exactly purchase it, you know."

This time, Gerswin shook his head evenly and slowly. "Hamline, has Carlina managed to instill distrust all over this planet?"

"No . . . not exactly . . ."

"Excessive caution, I can see. Is she as well connected to the Ministry of Domestic Security as she implies?"

"Unfortunately . . . yes."

Gerswin wondered if he ought to write off El Lido completely, since CE, Limited, had been designed as a profit venture and since he did not need anything beyond the proof that the plants did work in wide scale production. But Hamline and a few others deserved a chance, if they would take it. He wondered if they understood the price, really.

"Remember the wonderful time you had with the windboards? And the place where you met a stranger who decided El Lido needed an independent advocate?"

"Yes."

"Have lunch there tomorrow. Bring some transfer orders for CE, Limited, common and preferred stock."

"What—"

Gerswin broke the connection. While his end could not be traced, he wasn't about to underestimate Carlina, or Domestic Security. Even so, they would have had a hard time, since he had tapped into the system from a reflector satellite he had deployed before leaving orbit. He doubted that the local technology existed to tap his beam without some knowledge of the *Caroljoy*'s location.

He stood up and stretched. Then he sighed before heading toward the sealed and shielded locker. Dirty work required dirty weapons.

The man who had been a commodore bit his lip, but did not hesitate. Simple graft was bad enough, but to sell out to a central government with enough control to publicly name the secret police the Ministry of Domestic Security was beyond redemption.

Removing the two canisters from their long resting place in the hold took a few minutes. Setting up the gear he needed and checking them through the equipment in the hold took nearly an hour. Gerswin left both objects clamped in place and climbed out of the cramped three-by-three-meter space that was uninhabitable except when the scout was planetside.

He settled back in front of the console.

"Interrogative screen tap status."

"Negative. No energies detected."

"Interrogative satellite scan."

"Negative. No energies detected."

"Code Jam Trap Two. Code Jam Trap Two."

His fingers touched the studs of the keyboard. Although the communications trap program was displayed, the trap code kept the AI from understanding the contents of the program.

"Interrogative open channel access. How many different commnet systems can you access simultaneously?"

"Private systems or public nets?"

"Some of each. Try an eight private to two public ratio."

"Under operating parameters, ten per standard second for a maximum of three minutes."

"Stet."

Gerswin set up the modifications he needed, then accessed the official and unofficial maps of Lidora. As he expected, the headquarters of the Ministry of Domestic Security was clearly marked.

He smiled to himself as he ran the two locator programs for the two canisters that waited below to be fitted on the launchers of the armed flitter that waited outside in the other side of the hangarbunker that temporarily housed the *Caroljoy*.

That done, he pocketed the course discs and returned to the sweltering space beneath what had once been the crew room to remove the two long canisters and to reseal the lockers and the equipment.

After closing the hatch plate, he left the *Caroljoy* and stepped into the cool air of the bunker, air that retained a trace of the mustiness of a space seldom used. The lands adjoining Rodire's estate were left unmanaged, and Rodire was responsible for insuring that the tax payments were made, that the land was posted, and that would-be settlers and squatters were quietly evicted on a periodic basis.

Wherever possible, Gerswin liked to set up such remote retreats. Usually after five or ten years even the people who had constructed them had forgotten where they were. After less than a year, most people had forgotten their existence, particularly since Gerswin used them so little and tried to arrive at night and as quietly as possible.

Two flitters waited on the far side. Gerswin directed his steps toward the armed and shielded one, not that there was any obvious external difference between the two. But with Carlina's allies, he would forsake some speed for arms and shielding.

He rolled one canister under the port stub, nearly under the intake cover, and returned for the second, which he edged under the starboard stub. Then he retrieved the tools from the adjoining bay.

His skills were rusty, and all in all it took him nearly three hours to convert the two missiles and to mount them to his satisfaction.

He completed the job, returned the tools, resealing them in their protected containers, and returned the empty canisters to the *Caroljoy*. After that, he climbed into the ship to stretch out and, he hoped, to sleep until morning.

Sleep there was, and dreams as well, dreams of dark ships dealing death, and of corvettes with orange screens failing, and of iceboats disintegrating, and of landspouts hurling flitters into purpled-clay plains.

He shook himself awake once, trying to escape from the tumbled images of the past, but when he slipped back into slumber and restlessness, the images reappeared.

Caroljoy, young in the darkness, aging into a white-haired and fragile duchess as he watched, useless words caught in his throat. Kiedra, reaching for him and throwing herself into Lerwin's arms, then aging into sadness with her daughter's death. Young Corwin, their son, turning gray and disappearing into a cloud of ashes. And the other devilkids, Lostwin, Glynnis, each walking down a long dark tunnel away from him, marching proudly toward certain death as he urged them on.

A man in black smiling as he watched a hellfire flash across an airless moon to flatten a pleasure dome, smiling a smile of contentment, his lips quirking like a dark devil's.

"NO!!!!!!"

He sat up with the sound of his own scream in his ears.

Both his thin undersuit and the sheets on his bunk were soaked.

Slowly the one-time commodore eased himself off the dampness where he had suffered, and, without a word, stripped off his own damp sleeping clothes, then ripped the sheets from the bunk. He wadded all of the damp articles together in short and savage motions, then took them across the small cabin to the clothes fresher where he unceremoniously stuffed them inside.

Then he stuffed himself into the personal fresher.

After emerging, he donned a uniform brown tunic and trousers, his normal boots and belt. Then he added a few items to the disguised equipment belt.

To settle his thoughts, he fixed a small cup of liftea and alternated sips with a ration cube, trying to refine his approach to Hamline.

He'd picked the Windrop Inn because he knew it was one of the few places where Hamline and whoever shadowed him would have to walk. Neither flitters nor groundcars were permitted in the shoreside blocks of the Bayou Rio.

He sipped the last of the tea and replaced the cup, cleaning up the small mess he had made before returning to the control cabin.

After five minutes spent on completing the exit programming for the *Caroljoy,* he was easing the unarmed flitter from the hangar bunker. He wanted to be early. Quite early, in order to be in place before the opposition.

THE MAN WITH salt-and-pepper hair studied the sheet of antique paper again, rereading the brief message.

Momentarily, he set it aside and carefully wiped his forehead, not wanting anything that could trace it back to him to touch the sheets. He wiped his gloved hands on a clean towel before picking the sheet back up and letting his eyes study the brief message again.

Sire:

Anonymity is not necessarily the refuge of the coward, but necessary if one must continue serving his Emperor. The rebirth of old myths can only spell the end of the Empire, yet Eye and the Eye Corps ignore those myths. They claim it is done in Your name. Why was Merhlin not traced? Why could the Eye Corps not discover who stole Service hellburners? Why does Eye systematically remove Service officers loyal to the Emperor? Why have flag officers with early retirements been killed by so many "accidents" so soon after retirement, particularly if they opposed Eye and supported the Emperor? Check on the background of Vice Admiral Thurson, if you can, as one example.

Folding the single sheet into an equally ancient envelope, he stood and slipped the envelope inside his tunic.

With the hour of open court approaching, he could place the missive in the Emperor's hand with no one the wiser, and should the new Emperor turn it to Eye, even that functionary would have difficulty tracing the envelope from more than half a thousand of the Empire's peers who would have had such an opportunity.

In any case, the risk was no worse than already existed, not with Eye already trying to isolate the young Emperor.

The junior peer who had once been a senior officer shrugged. Unless His Majesty Ryrce the Quiet silently removed Eye, his days and the Emperor's were probably numbered.

Cling.

He stood and released the hold on the portal.

An older man, slender and dark-haired for all that he was a decade or two older than the man he visited, stepped into the small antechamber.

"Ready to visit His Majesty, Selern?"

"As ready as I'll ever be, Calendra." He debated telling the other about his letter, then decided against it. One could never be too careful, especially since Eye had to be one of the peers normally in New Augusta.

"Let us hope he is more outgoing than on the last open court."

"Extroversion does not necessarily make an Emperor."

"What else does he have?" asked Calendra wryly.

Selern shrugged. "Too soon to tell."

"You may be right."

Selern followed Calendra through the portal, and the two walked side by side toward the Grand Throne Room.

LXDIII

HAMLINE RODIRE WIPED his forehead again.

"You all right, squire?" asked the pilot.

"For some reason, I'm warm today, Jorio. Just warm."

"You are sure you are well?"

"I am fine, just fine," lied Hamline. More than ten years ago, it had seemed to easy to take on the whole planet. Now Corso was back, looking as young as ever, those hawk-yellow eyes demanding allegiance and—harder to deny—justice, and it wasn't quite so easy.

"Anyone trailing us?" The fact that he could ask the question without raising Jorio's suspicions about the reason would have embarrassed him a decade earlier.

"Not close, if they are."

Rodire leaned back in a wide rear seat, tried to ignore the whisper of the wind past the canopy as the flitter sped toward Bayou Rio, tried to push away the glimpse of sadness he had glimpsed behind Corso's eyes, the sadness that made Rodire feel decades younger than the wealthy Shaik.

Where Corso had come from, Rodire wasn't sure, though he had strong Imperial connections of some sort. Nor was the source of his

wealth known, only that he had set up CE, Limited, with a unique biological process, one that allowed production of a cheap nonpolluting organic thread substitute for standard synthetic hydrocarbons
and silicons.

From that, CE, Limited, had branched into a number of other
products, including most recently battle and stun vests for the planetary police, since Carlina had discovered that the thread produced by
the CE proprietary hothouse "plants" could be interwoven with synth-
steel threads to produce a cheaper, lightweight, and effective body
armor.

In return, the Ministry of Domestic Security had employed some
of its agents to track down employees who had taken cuttings of the
plants to insure that the company remained the sole supplier of the
special organic thread.

Rodire frowned as he recalled the developments. He had not remembered Corso ever worrying about employees who tried to grow
their own plants. Rodire had mentioned it once, and Corso had
laughed it off by pointing out that even a garden full of the plants
would only support a family and that most people didn't want to work
that hard merely to get thread.

"We're nearly there, squire."

"Fine, Jorio. Fine. Just wait for me, please."

The pilot set the flitter down and eased it toward the left edge of
the paved square on the gentlest of ground cushions.

The rear door popped open, and Rodire let his stiff frame carry
him down the steps. He glanced around to get his bearings. It had
been years, but from what he recalled, the inn should be off to his
left.

He turned, taking a firmer grip on the case with the documents
within.

"I beg your pardon, ser."

Hamline's head shot up at the intrusion, ready to snap until he
saw the brown uniform of Domestic Security.

"Yes, officer?"

"I suggest you return to your flitter, ser. This area has been cordoned off . . . Hamline . . . And please try not to react too strongly,
old friend."

Rodire choked down a response, and shot a glance at the officer,
recognizing, with a chill, the same hawk-yellow eyes, realizing that the
uniform was not quite standard.

"Yes, Officer Corso, I'll do . . . as you say." He managed to drag
the words out.

Rodire turned back toward the flitter, which, he noted absently, Jorio had not shut down. The "security" man followed.

"What is the matter, squire?" Jorio peered from the cockpit.

"Nothing, except the officer has indicated that this area has been closed. We'll have to . . ." Rodire looked back at Corso.

"Why don't you return to your estate?"

". . . go on out to the country place. . . ."

"But, squire . . ."

Rodire reentered the cabin, and, while surprised that Corso followed, was more surprised when the Shaik lifted a stunner.

Thrumm!

Clank!

Corso yanked the unconscious pilot from his seat, kicking aside the dart pistol that had not been fired by Jorio, and set the body on the cabin floor before settling himself behind the controls.

"Let's see . . ."

Rodire watched, half-numb, as Corso's hands played over the controls, as the steps retracted, as the cabin door closed, and as the pilot's canopy snapped into place.

Click. Snap.

"There's probably another homer planted somewhere, Hamline, but we'll have to see. They can't object if you merely go home. Besides, they don't function well at low levels. Carlina's friends are out in force, although they didn't close off the pad. That was a liberty that I took. Funny . . . no one even protested, and that's not a good sign."

The attorney sank into his padded seat, not looking at his own pilot, who he had never dreamed would have been armed.

"I'm not sure I understand."

"You do. Or you will. You will. Got those forms? Fine. Make out the transfer orders to transfer thirty percent of the common stock from me to you."

"Thirty percent? Thirty percent?"

"Right. Gives you working control and no excuses. You still have twenty-one percent, I assume. How much does Carlina control?"

Rodire nodded to Corso's first question.

"Yes or no? How much? I can't look at the moment."

"Yes," rasped Rodire. "She controls around forty percent. Don't know what she owns. Worked under the rules that off-planet proxies are controlled by the administrator."

"That will end. Fill out the forms. Leave the cert numbers blank. We can fill those in later, when I give you the actual share certs."

Rodire opened the case, grasped it to keep from spilling the contents as the flitter banked.

"Just another few minutes . . ."

"Until what?" asked Rodire. His voice sounded hoarse.

"Until we're where we need to be."

The advocate listened to the higher roar of the wind and sharper pitch of the turbines. A glance outside told him that Corso had the flitter racing scarcely above the trees.

"Isn't this dangerous?"

"Not so dangerous as getting shot down, or tracking . . . some of the wilder storms I've been through."

Rodire forced himself to try to relax, but found his arms gripping the armrest on the right and the seat cushion on the left.

The whine began to drop. The wind's whistle dropped. The advocate felt his stomach rise into his throat before dropping back into place. He squinted as the summer light was replaced with dimness. The turbines quit.

"You can fly this, can't you?"

Rodire looked up to see Corso standing over him.

"Yes . . . of course . . . still do sometimes."

"Good. When I'm done, you'll have to fly yourself to your estate. Not that it's fair. I assume you know where we are."

"I can guess."

"Let's go."

Rodire stumbled out onto the bare tarmac. His eyes caught sight of an armed flitter across the bay, and another larger and blacker shape on which his eyes had trouble focusing. Rather than force his eyes to make out the black ship, since Corso was leading him there in any case, he turned to take another look at the flitter.

His eyes widened as he saw the two missiles mounted under the wing stubs.

"Corso . . . where . . . those are missiles . . . what . . . ?"

"Oh, yes . . . those. We should get to that shortly."

Rodire scratched his shoulder absently and followed the Shaik up the ramp into the shadowy ship. The space inside was smaller than he had anticipated, with only a small control room, and a crew room not much larger, where Corso sat him in a small collapsible chair.

"Will these take care of it from my point of view?" Corso thrust a file at him.

Rodire took the file. Inside were sets of the original share certs, all authenticated by the Imperial Bank and signed over. Only the transferee space was blank.

"How did you get that? They're not supposed to do that."

"It's legitimate, believe me."

"I believe you." Rodire shook his head. "That's more than enough. But what do you want me to do?"

"They're yours. Thirty percent of the common stock, plus the proxies for my remaining small interest."

The advocate wiped his forehead, once, twice. "For me?"

"Who else?" Corso caught his lower lip with his teeth, then let go. "Once Carlina ceases to be a factor, you need to be Chief Operating Officer, at least long enough to get someone honest to run CE. That's what I want, and what El Lido needs. Get away from dealing with the government unless it's impossible not to. And destroy the company, plants and all, if you have to take orders from Domestic Security."

"But the Ministry of Security . . ."

"I'll make them leave you alone."

Corso turned away toward the wall of blanked screens and indicators.

"Commence Jam Trap Two. Commence Jam Trap Two."

"Commencing Jam Trap Two."

The coldly feminine voice that answered chilled Rodire to the bone. He wondered again who Corso really was, wondered how he had gotten involved. Rodire looked down at the fortune in his hands, then up at the slender man facing the controls.

Corso swung back to Rodire.

"Hamline. You have everything. Time for you to get to your estate. Sit tight. Sit tight for at least twenty-four hours. Don't leave your estate. Your town house is on the north side of Lidora, is it not?"

The attorney nodded.

"Call your children—you didn't remarry, I assume—and have them flit out within the next two hours. Call it a personal crisis, but get them here.

"Don't ask me why. Just do it. Hope all goes well, but the future is more important than a few people, even those I like, and that also includes you and me."

Corso barked a single, hard, laughing sound that expressed neither humor nor relief.

"Now . . . go. I'll open the bay port from here. Take the folder and your case."

Rodire mechanically took the folder and put it in his case, the case he had not even realized that Corso had brought from his flitter. He stood, and his steps carried him from the crew room and through the lock, down the ramp, and back to his own flitter.

LXIX

GERSWIN SHOOK HIS head sadly as Rodire's flitter wobbled out through the open hangar bay.

"Hope he makes it."

Half the hope was for Rodire. The other half was for CE, Limited, and the people of El Lido. One way or another, one Shaik Corso would be a quiet persona non grata for a number of years, assuming his plans worked out.

He redirected his attention to the AI.

"Interrogative status of trap jam."

"Code Trap Jam sustained for four minutes forty seconds. Initial links verified at 2,645."

"With a standard repeat factor, how long before the planetary commnet freezes?"

"Probe thrusts indicate system approaching eighty percent of capacity. Estimate capacity in twelve minutes."

Gerswin nodded.

The trap program was designed to link every possible receiver and fax outlet and to keep the connection open and unbroken. As a self-replicating program, the longer the system remained operational, the farther the programs spread. The end result would be the total paralysis of all public communications systems. The odds were that the unclassified military and security systems would also be paralyzed because some of the terminals and screens in government offices would be employed for both systems. The open transmit links would also create an enormous power drain on the planetary system, enough to grind some segments of the planet to a total halt.

The last feature of the trap program was that, if any terminal was not purged of the program, the same chain could start all over again once power was restored, although without the massive input used by Gerswin, the commercial systems and the government could eventually confine the damage and regain control.

The program worked. The remaining questions were how completely and for how long.

Gerswin touched the *Caroljoy*'s controls, made some adjustments, and stood, surveying the cabin. Still wearing the pseudo-DomSec uni-

form, he left the ship, walking down the ramp without watching the
locks close behind him as he hurried toward the armed flitter.

The concealed bay doors opened as he went through the checklist, and, within minutes, he was airborne. He kept the flitter just
above treetop height, and shifted his communications monitors to
the military frequencies, since the civilian frequencies were already
dead.

"Gnasher two . . . vector to homestash . . ."

"Negative, Gnasher two. Operating emergency power. Beyond
trace range . . ."

"OPNET Emergency. OPNET Emergency! Clear this frequency!
Clear this frequency!"

Gerswin watched, scanned the board, and waited as the flitter
skimmed the trees on its way toward Lidora, roughly fifty kilometers
westward. No other transmissions sounded except for a series of high-
pitched squeaks, and he shifted frequencies again when he realized
that the one he had monitored was now being used for data transmission.

"Far Cry, negative your last . . . negative your last . . ."

"Thunder one, arrived DomSec. Thunder two, provide cover."

Gerswin nodded. So far so good. The DomSec boys weren't used
to being under siege. He checked the forward farscreens, but outside
of the background energy levels, could detect nothing specific.

"EMERGENCY!"

"SSSSKKKKRRRR . . . EMERGENCY . . . Due to failure of the communications network and widespread power difficulties, the Premier
and the Ministry of Domestic Security have declared a planetary
emergency. Repeat, a planetary emergency. All unauthorized flitters
and other aircraft have fifteen standard minutes to land. All civilian
craft are immediately prohibited in the Lidora capitol area. Any aircraft in the capitol area will be forced down or destroyed. I say
again . . ."

Gerswin edged the thrusters back from full power. He'd reach Lidora, or the point he needed to reach outside Lidora, within minutes,
and there was no need to waste the power yet.

In some respects, he wished he could have done the job from the
Caroljoy, but had she been modified to carry weapons, even he would
have been unable to obtain certification, and he needed that certification to visit New Augusta and the more developed systems that actually inspected and guarded incoming ships.

In any case, to have made sure of the targets he would have had to drop below orbital defenses, which created the same problem he faced now—namely, how to keep clear of the mess he was about to create. The other advantage of using the flitter was that both the El Lido government and the Impies would have to investigate local sources.

Gerswin checked the course line against the targets.

Taking his right hand off the thrusters momentarily, he wiped his forehead with the back of his sleeve. The DomSec uniform was hotter than he would have preferred.

Cling!

The farscreen alarm sounded, and the pilot checked both the screen and the horizon at two o'clock. A black dot of increasing size was aimed toward him.

His scan showed that the forest beneath was thinning and the terrain becoming hillier as it gradually rose toward the eroded plateau on which the center of Lidora was built. Gerswin had chosen his course inbound over the Great Parkland, hoping to minimize the chance of groundfire. At a time when the planetary communications and power networks seemed under attack, he doubted that the Ministry of Domestic Security would be deploying large numbers to cover the parks.

"Flitter over the Parkland! Flitter over the Parkland! Reverse heading. Reverse heading."

Gerswin debated whether to answer, finally touching the comm stud.

"Gnasher four, returning DomSec. I say again, Gnasher four, returning DomSec."

"That's negative, four. That is negative. Divert or return homestash. Divert or return homestash."

"Understand and will comply. Diverting. Diverting."

Before he moved the stick, Gerswin touched the release button for the first missile. Next, he triggered the combat harness, simultaneously rolling in toward the oncoming patrol and pushing the thrusters around the forward detent into full combat thrust.

The dark dot swelled into a lightly armed police flitter.

"Gnasher four . . . change course . . . FIRE ON THE SUMBITCH!!!"

Gerswin dropped the nose, then eased the stick left, then back into his lap, coming up over the police flitter. At the last instant he cut power, dropped his own nose, and triggered the heavy stunner at point blank range into the police flitter's canopy.

Thrrrummmmm!

He did not watch the DomSec flitter spin downward, pilots and electronics hopelessly dead.

"Unidentified combat flitter, bearing two seven zero. Fireflit two, he's yours. Fireflit two, I repeat. Fireflit two, range and destroy. Range and destroy."

Gerswin smiled grimly. The Ministry of Domestic Security certainly wasn't prepared for any real resistance. Not that he had expected it would be. Unfortunately for the people.

Scanning the farscreens quickly, he recentered the flitter for the last few moments to provide the steady launch platform he needed. Then he touched the second release stud.

With the faint lurch of the departing missile, he banked hard left and jammed the thrusters to full power as he turned tail eastward back across the Great Parkland, the whine of the thrusters screaming full pitch.

He checked the distance readout and the time. Roughly another two minutes before the first missile reached target. By then his separation would be more than thirty kays. Not wonderful, but enough that the flitter would be beyond the worst of the shock wave.

He dropped the flitter until it skimmed scarcely meters above the trees, then scanned the clock again.

Less than a minute.

"Two incoming released . . . interrogative defenses. INTERROGATIVE DEFENSES!"

"Lasers not up. DomSec Control . . . be roughly ten more . . ."

"That's not—"

Sssssssssssssssssssss!

The screaming hiss blocked all transmissions.

Gerswin flinched in spite of his training and experience as a second sun flared behind him. He did not dare look back, trying to coax more power from the thrusters for the CE, Limited, headquarters.

Sssssssssssssssssssss!

Before the first blast had faded, the second flared, though it had been the first launched.

Gerswin kept his eyes on the controls, mechanically checking the indicators as the armed flitter screeched toward his base, listening to what scattered transmissions he could pick up.

"Gnasher two . . . tachead . . . repeat tachead . . . DomSec HQ . . . other capitol target . . ."

"CLEAR THIS FREQUENCY! CLEAR THIS FREQUENCY FOR EMERGENCY USE!"

". . . terrorist attack on Lidora . . . nuclear weapons . . ."

"Lucifer . . . fallen . . ."

The flitter bucked as the attenuated shock wave struck.

Gerswin eased the nose back up as the flitter almost dipped into the trees, let the craft climb a few meters higher to keep from hitting the trees with the next wave.

"Can you read . . . Gnasher one? Can you read . . ."

"CLEAR THIS FREQUENCY! CLEAR THIS FREQUENCY!!"

". . . casualties . . . thousands . . . small   nuclear   device . . . air launched . . . near surface impact . . ."

". . . the evil . . . upon is . . . upon our souls . . . repent . . . repent . . ."

Crmppppp!

The nose flipped up thirty degrees with the second shock wave. Gerswin let the flitter ride and eased it down, checking the heading, and beginning a gentle bank toward the north.

". . . read this . . . homestash . . ."

". . . repent you of your sins . . . Lucifer . . ."

"CLEAR THIS FREQUENCY!! CLEAR THIS FREQUENCY!!!"

Gerswin adjusted his course as he brought the flitter level, tapping out the access codes on the transponder to open the hangar bunker.

"Another flitter from the east approaching." The cool tones of the AI chimed in on the private override.

"Interrogative ETA."

"Three plus after your arrival."

"Stet."

Instead of powering down for a conventional approach, Gerswin left full power on.

At two kays out, he dropped the thrusters to nearly idle, raised the nose, and bled the speed back to thirty kays. Just before the flitter started to fall like a headsman's ax, he added full power, nose up, and dropped though a left-hand turn, mushing to a complete stop in the hidden bay.

He snapped off the power, opened the canopy, and unstrapped himself in a single motion. As soon as the canopy was retracted enough, he vaulted clear and sprinted toward the *Caroljoy*.

He made it inside, instants to spare, as Hamline Rodire's now battered flitter wobbled inside and mushed into the armed flitter.

"Screens!"

"Screens on."

"Begin departure power up."

"Beginning departure power up."

Gerswin watched the silver-haired attorney struggle out of the safety webbing that had triggered on his landing/impact. Rodire fought his way free and stumbled toward the *Caroljoy*. In his right hand was a pistol-shaped object.

Gerswin pulled a long-barreled stunner from beside the console. "Drop screens."

"Dropping screens."

Gerswin dashed for the lock and the ramp.

"You were looking for me, Hamline?"

"I . . . am . . . looking . . . for . . . you . . . you . . . killer . . . Corso . . . ," panted the advocate, starting to bring up the weapon.

Thrummm!

The stunner bolt sizzled past the older looking man's shoulder.

"Drop it, Hamline. Now!"

". . . never listen . . ."

Thrummm!

Clank!

Rodire clutched his numb right arm with his left, then let go and knelt to scoop up the fallen laser with his left hand.

Thrumm!

Gerswin watched him drop before he moved toward the half-conscious man.

An image crossed his mind, of another man, retching out his guts at the results of a hellburner blast. Of a man going into single combat to avoid unnecessary casualties to a potential enemy.

Gerswin swallowed, once, twice, as he pushed the mental images away and moved toward the fallen attorney.

LXX

RODIRE BLINKED, SQUINTING, although the light around him was dim.

"You awake?"

The voice was familiar. Then he remembered. Corso! The demon he had thought was merely a man! The man who had launched nuclear weapons into the capitol! When Lisa had been downtown . . . He tried to lurch toward Corso but could not lift himself off the bunk.

"I see you are."

"You are a killer, Shaik. Nothing but a killer."

"Admit to being a killer. But not just a killer. Never said this would be easy." Corso laughed once, the same annoying bark that was not a laugh. "You're as much to blame as I am."

"Me! I didn't unleash Lucifer. I didn't kill ten thousand innocents! You did! Not me! You!"

Corso sighed, and his shoulders dropped. "You really don't understand, do you?"

Rodire wanted to scream. Instead, he frowned. What was there to understand?

"Farscreen shows energy concentrations," interrupted the cool voice that had chilled Rodire before. "Standard heavy search pattern."

"Interrogative time before reaching detection range."

"Estimate fifteen standard minutes, plus or minus five."

"Stet. Commence checklist. Hold at prelift. Hold at prelift for voice command for liftoff."

"Understand checklist to prelift. Commencing immediately."

"Commence checklist at full-power status."

"Full-power status. Commencing checklist."

"Stet."

Rodire felt as though the Shaik was living in a different universe, and squinted, trying to let the younger man's words penetrate, trying to understand why Corso would say that he, Rodire, didn't understand.

"Hamline. Not enough time to explain. I'll dump what I can. Fast. Hope you can understand. Then I'm throwing you out."

As he talked, Corso had approached the bunk and touched something Rodire could not see. The harness released and retracted away from the attorney.

"Don't move. You're going to be dizzy if you move your head quickly, and you can't afford to pass out. Now. Where to start? All right." Corso's words were quick, more clipped than usual, and burst out in short groups. "You live on a repressive planet. Law controlled by a few firms. Food by a few family enterprises. Bureaucracy by a few others. People don't have much freedom to change. Personal freedom adequate, until Carlina started linking with DomSec. Declining now. Probably get worse, possible police state.

"Not enough education for most people to resist. Change has to come from the top, to begin with. People like you.

"Thought you might help. Thought a new business, built on new lines might start people thinking. It did, except Carlina, her type, decided CE was another route into the standard oligarchy. You let her do it, when you could have stopped her. Could have sent a message to me.

"Could have set up another administrator strong enough to stop her. Maybe I expected too much of you. You're a product of your culture. Unable to see beyond the patterns."

"But . . . my family . . . ," protested Rodire. Didn't the man understand? Carlina had no children, no heirs, no hostages to fortune.

"The future of your family was lost the moment you put their immediate comfort above your ideals, Hamline. So were you. I didn't know. Should have. My fault. Precedent here is terrible."

"Precedent? Is that all you think about?"

"Precedent is everything in your culture. Carlina's precedent means that everything new, everything that offers hope, can be turned into another instrument of repression. How could anyone ignore that? But you did. We'll both pay."

"ETA ten minutes, plus or minus four," added the cool voice from the control room.

"Get up. Slowly," commanded the hawk-eyed man. "You have to survive. For your remaining children. If not for them, for the people you betrayed once already."

"Betrayed? Who betrayed whom?"

"Hamline, would you please use your brains?" Corso's hard voice seemed tired. "You betrayed them when you refused to stand up to Carlina. You betrayed them again when you failed to notify me. You betrayed them a third time when you let her join forces with the secret police. You put your immediate family and comfort above the needs and rights of all the people. Don't talk about betrayal to me.

"So what did I do? I destroyed—crudely, but time was short—both the top of DomSec and CE, Limited. Shows that the system can be brought down. That might makes right doesn't always triumph, or at least, that there is a greater might to fear. Gives you an opening. That's all. The rest is up to you. Now get moving."

"Where?" Rodire slid to his shaky feet.

"Home. As soon as you get out of the scout, head for the far bay. Remember? Tunnel there. Comes out about a hundred meters from your estate. Take it and move. DomSec will blast anything in the air and around here, you included. Turn this into rubble."

Rodire stumbled as he entered the lock. "But what do I do?"

"What you should have done in the first place. You run the damned company. You treat the people like people. Not serfs. If you don't, you and your descendants will suffer. I mean *suffer!* Now get down the ramp. I'm lifting. If you're around when I power out, you'll be fried. Wasted too much time talking."

Rodire fell on the hard pavement as the ramp retracted. He staggered to his feet as he heard the lock door clank shut, and lurched toward the far bay and the tunnel.

Wheeeeeeee.

The whine spurred his lurch into a shambling trot.

When he finally reached the oval portal, he rested against it momentarily before hauling himself upright to survey the mechanism.

No access plates. No levers, and only a small wheel. He tried it. It spun easily clockwise, and the portal began to open. He peered inside, where the lighting was dim, but adequate.

Whhheeeeeeeeeeee!

Staggering inside, he took a step before turning back and spinning the other wheel, the one on the tunnel wall. The portal closed smoothly, cutting off the sound.

As he remembered what Corso had said about the security forces, he trotted raggedly down the tunnel, gasping with each step.

After fifty meters he slowed to a walk, his legs cramping with the aftereffects of the stun jolts his body had taken, but he kept putting one foot in front of the other, one in front of the other. Underfoot, the flooring began to vibrate, first lightly, then enough to make his steps feel unsteady.

As quickly as it had come, the vibration halted.

Rodire kept walking, but looking back over his shoulder. He could no longer see the tunnel port where he had started. In front of him, the smooth-walled tunnel began to slope upward, and a dark splotch appeared ahead in the faint ring of light that the walls reflected into the distance before him.

Even though he was walking slowly, he was still panting.

Crump. Crump.

The muffled concussion shook the tunnel, hard enough to make him stagger, but he continued to move forward toward the exit portal.

Crump.

Reaching out with his right hand and touching the smooth plasteel of the wall, he steadied himself, then plodded upward.

Whhhirrr. Crump!

The tunnel no longer seemed to stretch forever, but only a few yards toward a round black doorway of some sort.

He stopped and took two deep breaths.

Crump!

The floor beneath vibrated, and he lurched forward.

Finally his right hand touched cold metal, and he halted, trying to catch his breath, hoping that the wrenching cramps in his calves would ease.

He waited, wondering if the explosions would continue.

Crump!

He began to spin the wheel, watching carefully through the ever-widening slit, and listening.

Stepping into a moldy cellar, he frowned as he looked up to discover that just the foundation remained of whatever structure had once stood above him. Then he glanced back at the still open portal, which was beginning to close itself, to see how the vines had been planted to conceal the relative newness of the tunnel exit. There was no exterior wheel to open the portal, and the exposed portal looked no different from the rest of the weathered foundation.

Rodire dragged himself toward the overgrown ramp that led to the ground level of the forest.

Wheeeeeee.

At the sound of the eastbound flitter, he ducked, then straightened. No one, assuming they could scan under the old and gnarled trees that covered this end of Corso's lands, was going to bother with a tired old man on foot.

Once out of the foundation, Rodire could see enough through the wide-spaced and massive trunks to get his bearings. His own lands lay less than a half a kilo ahead.

He limped forward.

Wheeeeee!

Crump!

Rodire shook his head. The security forces were late. Everyone was always late. He'd been late. Corso had been late, and now the remainder of the DomSecs were late, as if more force could undo what had already been done.

He shrugged as he plodded toward the immaculate white, stone wall that marked his estate. He could see Eduard and some of the staff standing higher on the upper lawn peering toward the column of smoke behind him where he knew the flitters were still circling.

He supposed he had some work to do. He shrugged again. Not doing it wouldn't bring back Lisa. If Corso didn't like the way he ran CE, then Corso could have it any way he wanted. Rodire wouldn't block him. Carlina had, and what was left?

He refused to think about what might happen if the terrible Shaik were thwarted a second time. "You will *suffer*..." That had been clear.

Rodire sighed. No walls and fortresses for him. He might survive, and he might not, but one experience in watching Corso had been enough. One trip through hidden tunnels had been enough. And one daughter lost because he had not done what he had promised to a stranger was quite enough. Quite enough.

Corso might be the devil himself, but he kept his word. Both ways. And few enough did that.

The trees thinned as he neared the white, stone wall.

Eduard caught sight of his father and began running down to the wall.

Rodire smiled at the sight of the long-legged teenager covering the bluish grass more in leaps than in strides.

He waved, and his son waved back.

LXXI

AS RODIRE STUMBLED down the ramp, Gerswin launched himself at the control couch, throwing the harness straps around himself even before he settled fully into position.

"Retract power connections."

"Power connections retracted."

"Retract ramp, and seal for liftoff."

"Ramp has been retracted, and locks are sealed. Ship is fully self-contained."

"Interrogative power status."

"Power status is point nine nine plus."

As he spoke to the AI, Gerswin tapped out the Omega code on the comm link to the nerve center of the facility he was about to leave. Shortly, hopefully well after he had lifted clear, the inside of the hangar bunker would self-immolate in a raging inferno, leaving no trace of its history or recent usage. With the DomSecs likely to pinpoint his base of operations ... he shook his head.

Nothing had gone exactly as planned. Now—another perfectly good retreat, another perfectly good source of revenue, both lost. Lost because ...

He could dwell on that later, assuming there was a later. His eyes scanned the data and representational screens, checking the reported positions and projected search patterns of the approaching DomSec flitters.

His fingers continued through the liftoff checks as he studied the screens and as he spoke again.

"Get the DomSecs on audio. Local tactical."

"Local tactical on audio," the AI repeated without inflection.

A hissing began as the AI tried to raise the signals to audibility without the direct link to the facility antenna array.

"Fareach two . . . negative on energy flows . . ."

". . . port, three zero. Vector two six zero . . ."

". . . Thunder three. Say again . . . three . . ."

". . . casualties estimated at three zero thousand . . . three zero thousand . . ."

The man in the counterfeit Lidoran DomSec uniform tightened his lips, wiped his damp forehead, and touched the control keys once more, watching the screens to ensure that the departure gates were fully retracted and clear of obstructions.

"Target contact, Beta class flitter, at ten kays, bearing zero eight zero," the AI's cool voice interjected, overriding the Lidoran transmissions momentarily.

"Thanks."

Gerswin's fingers touched the last key on the board prior to the liftoff sequence, and the whining that signified full power-up began to build.

"Going to be a *full* power lift," he remarked to no one in particular.

"Acknowledging full power lift," the AI answered his remark that needed no answering.

The *Caroljoy* edged from the center of the hangar into position before the tunnel.

Whhhhheeeeeeeeeeeeeee!

The scout slipped up the tunnel and burst through the carefully maintained gap in the trees, a black streak screaming like lightning back toward the heavens from which it had struck.

". . . target at two six five. Target at two six five . . . tentatively identified as deep space craft."

"Gnasher two, cleared to attack. Cleared to attack."

Gerswin had already dismissed the flitters. Most atmospherics didn't carry high acceleration missiles, nor missiles with any range. Even if the DomSec flitters had, unless they had launched those the

moment they had acquired the *Caroljoy* on their screens, it would
have been impossible for them to have caught any scout on a full
power departure.

The real problem would lie with orbit control, and whether there
were system patrollers close at hand.

His departure was programmed for atmospheric envelope exit on
the opposite side of El Lido from orbit control. While DomSecs could
speculate, they couldn't be absolutely certain until he actually broke
orbit.

"Switch to orbit control frequencies."

"Orbit control on audio."

Gerswin continued to scan the screens, checking the ever increasing gap between the *Caroljoy* and the DomSec patrols, noting
how the security flitters began to use their shorter range missiles on
the recently vacated retreat.

The *Caroljoy*'s auxiliary screen showed the energy concentrations
around the facility as the DomSecs turned their thwarted fury on the
concealed hangar-bunker already far behind and below.

"Facility self-destruct has commenced," the AI noted.

Gerswin nodded at the announcement. Shortly, between the destruct thermals and the DomSec bombardment, there would be nothing left but fused and broken metal, stone, and ceramics, over which
the DomSecs could pore to their hearts' content.

"Orbit control, this is Thunder three. Interrogative intercept on
outbound target. Interrogative intercept."

Instinctively, Gerswin checked his position. The *Caroljoy* was almost clear of the envelope, and, as he had plotted, in position with
the planet between him and orbit control.

"Thunder three, outbound target screened from orbit control.
Projected course beyond range of either orbit control or patrollers
on station."

By now the rear screen showed an El Lido whose image was
rapidly becoming a disc that would fill less than the entire rear
screen.

Monitoring the scout's power status, Gerswin shook his head.
Eighty percent, down twenty percent just for liftoff. No wonder he had
gotten clear so quickly. But power was expensive, even on Aswan, if one
considered the acquisition costs, and speed was paid in power terms.

Then, everything about El Lido had been expensive, he reflected
as he returned his attention to the representational screen, which now
displayed the entire system, including El Lido and its orbit control.

Two winking red dots along the general course line to system exit corridor one indicated the two on-station system patrollers.

Gerswin had already sent the *Caroljoy* hurtling along a different course—the one to the less favored exit point. The second corridor, because the system's irregular gas corona extended farther on one side of the system, required more travel time in-system before a ship could reach space clear enough for a jumpshift.

He calculated, hands hovering above the console. Roughly, at his present screamingly uneconomical acceleration, he could have reached the jump point along corridor one in two hours.

Worrying at his lip with his teeth, he checked the screens again. "Time to jump?"

"Three hours, plus or minus point five."

The farscreens were clear, except for the distant patrollers, not surprisingly, since jumpship travel anywhere was scarce, and to El Lido, isolated as it was, even scarcer.

The red lights of the patrollers, flashing against the darkness of the representational screen, seemed almost accusing.

"Accusing about what?"

"Inquiry imprecise. Please clarify," requested the AI.

"Disregard," snapped the once-upon-a-time commodore.

What had gone wrong? Or had anything?

The biologics would continue to be produced, and Hamline would doubtless exert some effort to improve social conditions. And thirty thousand casualties represented . . . what? An initial payment?

"Are you still asking too much of people?" he muttered, not letting his eyes leave the screens.

"Question represents a value judgment. Without further data, no answer is possible." The AI's cool feminine tone was like ice down his spine.

Whose values? Whose judgments? He had killed or injured thirty thousand people, some theoretically innocent, because he felt it necessary, because he felt his own creation had been perverted to serve an already too-repressive government. Did he have that right?

"You took that right the day you decided to restore Old Earth."

Did that make him right?

He shook his head. Right was a value judgment, as the AI had said so coldly.

Had he been too hard on Rodire? Had he expected too much of the young idealist when he and his children had grown older? Did the children make that much difference?

Corson, what would you have been like, had we shared a life? Would you have turned me, too? Turned me from fire and ice?

He pushed that thought away from the trails down which it had led him too many times before.

"Time to jump?"

"Three hours, plus or minus point two."

Why did people let themselves be ruled so easily? Why did they let others enslave them? Why didn't they fight?

"Why didn't they fight?"

"Question imprecise. Please reformulate."

The businessman who was an idealist with a vision and who had been a commodore did not rephrase his question. Instead he stood up and turned away, pacing from the cramped control room into the equally small, but less cluttered, crew room.

Finding the techniques to reclaim his home had proved difficult enough, and the refining and producing was even more difficult. Plus, refinement and production required resources and funding, and while obtaining both had been the technically easiest part, it had been by far the most time-consuming, and had created the most problems. But without the resources to bankroll the development and the field testing and the production, all the foundation's research products would be worthless.

Then, still unknown, was the question of the Empire. While it would certainly continue to passively oppose any wide-scale adoption of the techniques the foundation was developing, how soon would the forces marshaling against Gerswin be able to turn the Empire against him.

He had Lyr to thank, time and time again, for turning the inquiries and blunting the attacks, but Lyr and her allies could not hold back the tide forever.

He shook his head. One thing in his favor was that his opponents did not know where they stood. Nor would they for years to come, though Gerswin could sense it now. And his own stupidity in using tacheads! Thirty thousand innocents because he hated tyranny and personal greed. Thirty thousand innocents because he had held others to his standards. He shook his head. Better to write off an enterprise, or to wait until no one suspected he could return. Brute force wasn't the answer. Yet, knowing better, he had turned to it.

He shook his head once more.

"You'd better hope it's considered an isolated case. You'd better hope."

He walked back toward the controls, thinking about Rodire, and about the man's family.

Corson, where are you? Beyond? Never? Martin . . . ?

But Martin he had not known, even briefly, only known about when there was nothing he could have done.

He reseated himself at the control couch, tilted now into a standard seat, and tried to refocus his thoughts on his next operations.

He couldn't afford another mistake like El Lido. Not for himself, or Lyr, or Martin, or the people involved.

Not ever.

THE GOLD STARBURST in the center of the console flared.

The man known as Eye stared at the golden light, which remained burning brightly. Behind his shadow mask his mouth nearly dropped open.

The Emperor's call—but why?

He frowned, wondering whether he should answer the almost mythical summons, still sitting before the console.

Three red lights blipped into place on the screen readouts, and his eyes widened.

He shook his head. Apparently the old procedures still held. All his defense screens were down.

What was it that Thurson had said years ago? That the myths always triumphed in the end, whether a man believed in them or not?

With a sigh, he stood, not that he had much choice as a squad of Corpus Corps assassins bracketed his private portal.

"The Emperor awaits, you, ser."

While all gave him a wide berth, they seemed almost excited as they escorted him along the secret tunnels, tunnels he thought only known to the Eye and the two Eye Regents.

"How did you know this was the way?" he asked the Corps squad leader.

"The Emperor gave us the map, ser, after he dropped your screens, ser."

Eye said nothing further until the tunnel narrowed, a narrowing that reflected nearness to the palace.

Opposite the portal that exited in his own guest quarters, assigned to him in his person as the Duke of Calendra, the Corps squad leader halted and touched a databloc against the inlaid tile of the Imperial seal that stood man-tall on the right side of the corridor.

The seal swung back to reveal another tunnel, one that seemed to lead upward.

With a shrug, Eye let himself be escorted away from his own quarters and toward whatever destination the Corpus Corps killers had in mind.

Even with his age, he had no doubt that he could have dispatched at least two of the Corps troops. But there were eight, and he did not want to give them any excuse to kill him out of hand.

He had reasoned with the Emperor before and occasionally gotten his point. Reason provided a better hope than attack.

The squad halted at the liftshaft.

"Go on, ser." The squad leader gestured. "This is as far as we go."

"Alone?" Eye asked with mild sarcasm.

"Alone, ser."

Eye shrugged and stepped into the shaft, letting himself be carried upward.

The trip was but seconds long before he stepped out into a small room. A single Imperial Marine stood before another portal.

"Lord Calendra, the Emperor will see you shortly. You may sit, if you wish."

Eye shivered. That the guard knew his real name even while he wore the privacy cloak and black shadow of Eye did not look promising.

He studied the guard, debating whether he should take on the single impressive specimen who stood between him and the portal or whether he should still opt for his chances in reasoning with the Emperor.

The almost unseen haze that stood between him and the marine decided him. That it was a screen of some sort was clear, but of what intensity was not. He decided to wait.

Frowning to himself, Eye tried to determine how he might have failed the Empire, or displeased the Emperor.

Could it have been the incident on Harkla? Or the uprising in Parella? The commercial war on El Lido? That had been messy. But a commercial war?

He shook his head. Could the Ursans have sprung something new on the Fleet? Or was the Dismorph resurgence more of a threat than he had reported?

"Lord Calendra, the Emperor awaits."

Eye stood, straightened his black cloak, and stepped evenly toward the portal as the Imperial Marine moved aside.

Once through, he found himself in a small study, scarcely larger than the formal office of a small commercial magnate. Solid wooden shelves lined the sides of the room, while the Emperor sat behind an apparent antique writing desk, his back to a full window overlooking the formal Palace gardens.

"Your pleasure, sire," Eye stated evenly as he inclined his head and waited.

"Have a seat, Calendra."

In private, His Imperial Majesty Ryrce N'Gaio Bartoleme VIII did not appear any more impressive than in public. His eyes were bulbous, bright green, and set too close together. His hair resembled plains grass scattered by the wind, and his fat cheeks gave him the air of a chipmunk. Only his deep bass voice was regal—that and the dark sadness behind the bright eyes.

Eye settled himself into the small chair and waited.

"This is something I would rather not do, you understand, Calendra, but it has been too long, and there have been too many Eyes, your predecessor among them, who seemed to feel that they represented another force in government besides the Emperor."

"I am not sure I understand, sire."

"I am not sure you do either, Calendra," answered the deep voice, resonating as if separate from the almost comical figure behind the desk. "I am not sure you do either."

The Emperor pointed a surprisingly long finger at the head of the Intelligence Service. "Tell me. What is still the one weapon that the people of the Empire fear most?"

"Nuclear weapons."

"And why? There are greater forces at man's command."

Eye shivered, but forced himself to reply. "I suppose it must be because of what happened on Old Earth."

"Exactly! And during your tenure, twice have those weapons been used. And you have yet to discover how those weapons were removed from Imperial control or by whom."

Eye looked down, then raised his eyes to meet the green glitter of the Emperor's gaze. "Neither has anyone else, sire."

"No. But they are not Eye. Nor are they specifically charged with insuring that such weapons do not enter private hands." The Emperor paused. "Do you have any idea as to who might have obtained them?"

"Ideas, yes. Facts to support them, no." Eye smiled a grim smile. "At this point, would it make much difference?"

"Not really, since we're being candid."

"Then, since he has brought me down, he may as well bring you down as well, sire."

With a calmness he did not believe he possessed, Eye triggered his own internal nerve destruction, trying to look alert even as his thoughts began to blacken, as the toxins poured through his systems.

Let the devilkid's revenge be Eye's as well.

His mouth dropped open in a chuckle that he never completed as the Emperor, His Imperial Majesty Ryrce N'Gaio Bartoleme VIII, shook his head sadly and pressed the console summons for the disposal squad.

IN ENDLESS TWILIGHT

THE ONCE-UPON-a-time scoutship jumpshifted, and for a moment that was both instantaneous and endless, black light flooded the two small compartments, the one containing the pilot and the crew space that contained no one. That instant of shift seemed to last longer than normal, as it always did when the actual shift was near the limit.

"Interrogative status," asked the pilot, a man with tight-curled blond hair and hawk-yellow eyes that swept the range of displays on the screens before him.

"No EDI traces. No mass indications within point one light. Destination estimated at four plus." The impersonally feminine tone of the artificial intelligence would have chilled most listeners, but the pilot preferred the lack of warmth in the voice of the *Caroljoy.*

In his rebuilding of the discarded and theoretically obsolete scout, the former Imperial commodore could have programmed warmth into the voice when he had added the AI, just as he could have opted for more comfort in the spartan quarters, rather than for the raw power and extensive defensive screens the beefed-up ex-Federation scout now enjoyed. The pilot had avoided warmth in both the ship and the AI.

He leaned back in the control couch, trying to relax, as if he wanted to push away a particularly bad memory. He did, and as he often also did he whistled three or four notes in the odd double-toned style that was his alone.

The AI did not acknowledge the music, since the notes represented neither observation nor inquiry.

What was past was past. The two tacheads he had used on El Lido, along with the thirty thousand casualties, would certainly draw Imperial interest, but he doubted that they would call Impie attention back on him. Not yet. After all, one of the two targets had been CE, Limited, in which he, as Shaik Corso, had held the controlling interest.

Now, Hamline Rodire had control, and the former commodore hoped that Rodire would use the influence that CE, Limited, represented for the benefit of all of El Lido.

He shook his head. He had run through the arguments all too often to change his mind, or the past. What was past was past. Time to concentrate on the future, on running down the rest of the research leads that he and the foundation had neglected for too long. Time to refocus himself on the long range and eventual mission, on getting the technology he needed for the reclamation job on Old Earth, a job that was too big for the underfunded and ignored Recorps to complete.

"EDI traces at forty emkay."

"Interrogative signature pattern."

"Signature pattern tentatively identified as standard system patroller, class II."

"Course line?"

"Preliminary course line indicates target headed in-system. Probability exceeds point eight that patroller destination is planet three."

Former Commodore MacGregor Corson Gerswin nodded. That made sense, particularly since planet three was Byzania.

"Interrogative other patrollers."

"Remote EDI traces from exit corridor two. Probability exceeds point five that second system patroller is stationed within one hundred emkay of jump point."

"Interrogative other system targets."

"That is negative this time."

Gerswin's fingers played across the representational screen, checking the relative positions and travel times.

He pulled at his chin.

After the debacle on El Lido, he had plunged into trying to tie up a number of loose ends. That had been fine, but he hadn't bothered to update Lyr on those activities. Not what had happened on El Lido, but on his OER Foundation-related efforts, the ones she monitored and on which she had to keep records for the Empire's tax collectors and various departmental snoops.

First, though, he really wanted to take a rest, one of several hours while the *Caroljoy* cruised in-system.

He reached for the control couch harness release, then straightened.

Might as well do the update and send it. The energy required would be less the farther out-system he was when he dispatched the torp. And the less energy required for the message torp, the more left with the ship.

Who could ever tell what he might require?

From what he recalled, Byzania, while not unfriendly, was a rather tightly controlled society. But, first, the update to Lyr. Then he could worry about sleep and Byzania.

Once she got the update, she could be the one to take on the worries about the latest implications of what he was doing, not that she wasn't already.

He cleared his throat and tapped the data screen controls.

BUZZ!

At the sound, Lyr dropped in front of the console.

The screen showed the face of the man with the curly blond hair and hawk-yellow eyes.

"You never change," she observed safely, since Gerswin was really not on the screen, his image only the beginning of a prerecorded torp fax for her.

She first tapped the controls to store the entire message and the mass of data that always accompanied his transmissions, then tapped the acknowledgment stud to start the message.

"Lyr. Finished the Grom'tchacher lead. Your first impressions were right. Leased the lab, took the cash, and left. Nice prospectus, though. Theory's interesting, if not down our line. Might be worth a commission job for one of your friends to investigate."

Gerswin looked down, then back into the screen. In the shadows behind him, Lyr could make out the accel/decel shell/couch that dominated the control room, and the manual auxiliary control banks that Gerswin had insisted on retaining even after centralizing the direct controls in the simplified bank before him, secondarily, in the AI center.

In scanning the background, she missed the next words, not that she could not have replayed them anytime.

". . . off to Byzania next. Hylerion—the precoded accelerated tree grower—heard some interesting reports. Never collected the last installment of the grant. Suspicious enough to make me think the idea worked.

"Be back in Ydris to check their system after that. Send a report there."

He grinned at the screen.

"Since you're the cred worrier, some good news. In tracing down Grom'tchacher, ran across some business. Managed to broker a lab lease and some other property along with ours. Finder's fee arrangement. Took it personally, but felt some belonged to the foundation. Means no draw on my operating account for a while. Remainder of the OERF share is coming through the general receipts. Code blue."

Lyr frowned. That she'd have to check. Credits were often the last thing the commander worried about, the very last thing.

". . . off to Byzania. See you soon."

He always closed that way, she reflected, tapping the studs to store the message in the permanent file, but it had been more than five years since he had been anywhere near New Augusta.

She pursed her lips, knowing she should be somewhere other than before the console at 2030 on a spring evening. At less than seventy, she certainly wasn't novaed; her weight was the same as it had been years earlier; and her muscle tone, thanks to her exercise regime, was probably better. She looked far younger than she was.

"That could be the trouble . . ."

She cut off her monologue before it began and called up the general receipts account and the commander's code blue entry.

"Unsolicited donation. Fyrst V. D'berg, Aerlion. One million credits. Codes follow. . . ."

Lyr ran her tongue over her chapped lips. Gerswin and his unsolicited donations ran to as much as several million annually. Where he found them she wondered, but they always were supported.

And his ventures . . . she really wanted to ask him what else he had been doing besides tracking completed grants and projects and grantees who had failed to report or collect. Always the ventures, like the fabrication plant on Solor and whatever he was doing on Westmark with that plant protein substitute. Add to that the aliases . . . she worried at her lower lip with her upper teeth.

After forty years with the foundation, she could see an accelerating trend, even more than in the first few years after the commodore's retirement, a trend where things were building. To what, she didn't know, but once again she had the feeling that the Empire and the commodore were going to clash.

She'd really have to talk to him about it—assuming he ever came back.

III

"SELERN? THE NEPHEW of the old Earl?"

The deep bass voice disconcerted Selern, coming as it did from the chipmunk cheeks and bright green eyes of a fool. But His Majesty Ryrce N'Gaio Bartoleme VIII was no fool, reflected Selern, not if his actions in removing the previous Eye indicated anything at all.

"That is correct, Your Majesty."

"Surprised, weren't you?"

"At becoming the Earl? Quite."

"That was not the reference I meant, Selern."

"Then I do not understand the question." Selern swallowed and hoped that the gesture had not been noticed.

"That I doubt." The current ruler of the Empire of Light pointed toward the single small chair on the other side of the inlaid and old-fashioned wooden desk. The occasional shimmer of dust motes that intermittently resembled a ghostly curtain revealed the defense screen that separated the two men. "Have a seat."

The newest Earl of Selern sat cautiously, keeping his eyes fixed on the Emperor. Ryrce wore neither circlet nor crown. Wispy strands of straw-tinted hair framed his all too-round face.

"Caution carried to excess, Selern. That warning about Calendra—the old Eye—could only have come from one or two sources. None of them would have had the nerve to deliver it, even anonymously. So I checked the peerage lists for the newly elevated and for recent heirs. Had to be you. Would you care to comment?"

Selern smiled. The smile was forced, but with a bit of humor. "You apparently have me on all rights, Your Majesty." He paused, then added, "I thought I was more discreet than I was."

"You were discreet enough—assuming your Emperor was trustworthy."

"Are you?" asked Selern, trying to keep the tremor out of his voice.

"No Emperor can afford to be trustworthy, Selern, except when he benefits by it." Ryrce laughed softly, a deep chuckling sound, before speaking again. "Then, he cannot afford not to be."

Selern waited.

"As of tomorrow, you assume the position of Eye. Both Eye regents have also been terminated."

Selern swallowed hard.

"What else could I do? Either they chose not to stand up to Calendra, or they agreed. I suppose they might also have failed to see his plans."

"Your action makes sense." Selern nodded slowly. "Unfortunately."

"You noted the question of certain nuclear weapons. What do you propose?"

"Finding them, if possible."

"If you cannot?"

"Trying to avoid situations where they might be used."

"And if that fails?"

"Waiting for the ax to fall when they are used again."

Ryrce laughed once more, this time a bass and booming guffaw.

"At least you understand for whom you work!"

Selern—the new Eye who had never desired the position—waited.

"There should be some records. Calendra implied that a single man controlled them. He saw that man would be my downfall as well."

Selern repressed a shudder. One man? One single individual with that kind of power?

"If the remainder of those missing tacheads and hellburners are used in the wrong way," commented Selern slowly, "that just might undermine all the centuries of peace."

"I doubt that any one individual could have that great an impact on the Empire," observed His Imperial Majesty. "But with nuclear weapons . . ."

The implication was clear. Selern's job was to keep the Empire whole and hearty, including the prevention of any one man from undermining its authority and image. Trust was the glue that held the Empire together, and the Empire was the structure of humanity, the one remaining web binding man in a common purpose.

Selern sighed.

Ryrce N'Gaio Bartoleme VIII nodded at the sound from his new Chief of Intelligence, nodded and stood to signify that the private audience was at an end.

GERSWIN RUBBED HIS forehead, massaged his eyes, and looked away from the data screen on the right side of the *Caroljoy*'s control console.

"Two plus before Byzania orbit station." The AI voice, the voice of the ship in real terms, was pleasant, cool and clear, emotionless, unlike the warm and faintly husky voice of the woman for whom he had named the modified scout. The dichotomy did not bother him, perhaps because he avoided thinking about it.

Gerswin rubbed his temples with the thumb and forefinger of his right hand, closed his eyes, and leaned back in the upslanted shell seat.

With each totally new system, it became a little harder to assimilate the information he needed. But he couldn't blunder around strange planets without at least a fundamental idea of their government, customs, and legal structure. Not doing what he was doing.

The standard structure he'd developed with the Infonet professionals had helped, both financially and in reducing the information to the absolute minimum he needed. But it was still more than he wanted to learn, time after time. And that was a danger itself, since it pushed him toward continued dealings within systems he already knew.

He frowned, and, eyes closed, tried to sort out Byzania.

Government—quasi-military, despite the trappings of more democratic institutions. Popularly elected senators formed an upper chamber which could approve or disapprove any law or regulation, but which could not propose either. Laws were enacted by the lower chamber, composed of delegates selected from each political party's preference list in proportion to the total vote in the general election. Head of government—prime minister, appointed from the military by the Chief of Staff.

Gerswin suspected that the preference lists provided by the political parties were screened by the military, which had its hand in everything.

Population—roughly thirty million, the majority on the largest and first settled continent.

Economy—largely agricultural, with enough local light industry to provide a small middle class. Two M/M (mining/manufacturing) complexes on the largest moon of the fourth planet in the system.

Culture—Urabo-Hismexic, with emphasis on male-dominated honor.

Gerswin pursed his lips and opened his eyes.

By all rights, unless the ecology was hostile, and the population and agricultural figures belied that, the system shouldn't need a military or even a quasi-military government. Byzania produced nothing of high value and low cubage, i.e., nothing worth the energy costs of jumpship transport as an export, and wasn't strategically located vis-à-vis the Dismorphs, the Analexians, the Ursans, or the two other intelligent and technologically oriented races found by the Empire.

"Search capabilities of Byzania orbit control?" he asked the AI. He refused to personify the artificial intelligence or to program in any human traits, or to otherwise associate it with the ship or her namesake.

"Inquiry imprecise."

"Do they have the ability to pick out the *Caroljoy* from orbit if I took her down on the southern continent?"

"Probability approaches unity."

"Do they have the technology to crack the hull without fracturing the scenery if I set down at the shuttle port outside Illyam?"

"Probability is less than point one."

"What is their hard credit balance?"

"That is classified. Estimated as negative."

"The fact that it's classified tells me that. What about fax outlets? How many are independent?"

"Estimate point five of all media origination points, including fax outlets, are independent. No official censorship."

"It's a risk, but we'll go in. Evaluate the probability of acceptance—agent of Imperial family looking for a very private retreat."

"Probability of disapproval less than point two. Credibility less than point five."

"In other words, they'll let me do it, but won't buy the excuse. Well . . . let's hope so."

Gerswin wondered if he were being overdramatic. At the same time, when grantees didn't collect hard currency drafts, even at bayonet point, there was a reason, and the reason wasn't normally friendly. Still, he needed to get on the ground in one piece, and he wanted to find out if Hylerion had succeeded with those special trees.

Caution could be discarded later, if he had been overcautious. It was difficult to reclaim after the fact.

"Contact Byzania control. Arrange for landing rights and touchdown at Illyam shuttle port. Use code red three ID package."

"Contact is in progress," the console announced.

The control area went silent. Gerswin wouldn't have to say a word unless Byzania control and the AI came to some sort of impasse, which was unlikely. A private yacht meant hard currency, and Byzania needed whatever it could get.

In the interim, he went back to studying background information on the system, attempting to get a better slant on why such a largely agricultural planet had adopted such a strong military presence.

The climate on the two main continents was nearly ideal for synde bean production, and other easily-produced foodstuffs. What land areas weren't under cultivation supported wide local forests, generally softwood akin to primitive earth-descended deciduous trees.

Some scientists had theorized that the lack of a large moon and/or light comet activity during Byzania's formative period plus the larger proportion of light elements were responsible for the low mountain ranges and slow crustal action, as well as for a general lack of easily reachable heavy ore deposits. For whatever reason, it was cheaper to mine the largely nickel-steel and other metallic deposits on the fourth planet's irregular asteroidal satellites than to sink deep mines on Byzania itself.

"Clearance obtained," announced the AI, breaking into Gerswin's study. "Anticipate arriving descent orbit in one plus point four. Our name is *Breakerton*."

"Acknowledged," growled Gerswin, returning his attention to the information before him. He couldn't afford to use the deep-learn technique, to have all the information he needed poured into his brain through direct input—not if he wanted to remain sane long enough to finish his self-appointed mission for Old Earth. Deep learn systematically used up brain cells, which wasn't a problem, given the millions available, if you expected to live a century or two only. Gerswin expected he would need all of his brain cells healthy for much longer. He might be disappointed—bitterly so—but it was a risk he chose not to take.

At least, when he scanned something, he could choose what he wanted to concentrate on and what he wanted to retain. While it gave him a short-term headache, he hoped it would lengthen his productive years.

"Better than a head full of useless data," he muttered as he turned to the cultural background.

"Input imprecise," noted the AI.

Gerswin ignored the comment. He had little more than a standard hour before he should be ready for touchdown.

GERSWIN CHECKED THE public fax listing for Illyam, keying in on all names beginning with "Hy."

"Hyler, H'ten Ker . . .

"Hylert, Georges Kyl . . .

"Hylon, Adrin Yvor . . ."

There was no listing for Jaime Hylerion. Either the missing biochemist lived elsewhere on Byzania, which was possible, but unlikely, since the Illyam listings held most of the planet's professionals, or he had emigrated, which was theoretically possible, but highly unlikely.

He sighed, and put the small screen console provided by the Hotel D'Armand on hold.

Glancing around the room, from the faded heavy gray, crimson-edged draperies that bordered the rectangular window overlooking the courtyard to the dull brown finish of the four-postered formal bed that looked uncomfortable rather than antique to the replica of some ancient writing desk that was too small to sit at, Gerswin felt cramped. More cramped than before the *Caroljoy*'s controls. More cramped than in the tightest flitter cockpit.

He stood up and moved away from the desk, stretching.

From the landing at the shuttle port onward, everyone had been *so* polite.

"Yes, Ser Corson."

"This way, Ser Corson."

"Will there be anything else, Ser Corson?"

His credentials as a purchasing agent for RERTA, Limited, as well as the Imperial passport, gold-bordered, and the maximum credit line on Halsie-Vyr, showed him as one MacGregor Corson, but the locals were scarcely interested in his name, but in the credit line he represented.

The Empire might, in time, find out about the name and wonder if MacGregor Corson and Commodore Gerswin were one and the same, but the Imperial bureaucracy could have cared little enough about him as Gerswin, and doubtless cared less about him as Corson, so long as no trouble was overtly attached to either name.

The former commander wrinkled his nose, suppressed a sneeze. Despite the spotless appearance of the small suite, really a large room divided into two halves with a thin wall, it smelled musty.

"Assshooo!"

The violence of the too-long repressed sneeze sent a twinge through Gerswin's shoulders, made his eyes water momentarily. After rubbing his neck and shoulders with both hands to loosen the muscles, he stared at the list frozen on the console.

To search for all the names in the entire planetary listing which began with "Hy" would be enough of an alert to have every security agent in Illyam trailing him.

"You're assuming too much."

Gerswin realized that he had spoken aloud, and that there had been no echo whatsoever.

He frowned, ambling around the suite as if to familiarize himself with the furnishings, though he was more interested in the underlying construction.

The relative smallness of the window overlooking the courtyard had already struck him, but not the massiveness of the casement surrounding it, nor the thickness of the armaglass which did not open.

That the hotel had the latest in heavy-duty portals, rather than hinged doors, seemed out of character with the antique furnishings, unless Gerswin assumed certain things about the character of the government of Byzania. Those assumptions were solidifying as more than mere assumptions.

He returned to the console and seated himself.

"Time to get to work, Corson," he told himself and the sure-to-be listening agents as he reset the console and accessed land agents.

A dozen names appeared on the list. Gerswin picked the third and tapped out the combination.

"Cerdezo and Associates."

"MacGregor Corson. I'd like to make an appointment with Ser Cerdezo."

"Your interest, Ser Corson?"

"Must remain relatively confidential."

"Ser Corson . . . I know not how we can help you without adequate information," suggested the sandy-haired young man who had taken the call.

"I understand your problem. Perhaps my credentials would help to resolve the difficulty."

Gerswin placed his passport, credentials, and authorization for maximum credit in the scanning drawer, with a blot bar across all three. The thin strip was designed to prevent the scanning equipment from reading the magfield codes contained in each of the three flat squares.

"Ah . . . I see . . . ," said the Cerdezo employee. "I will check with Sher Cerdezo's schedule. She may have an availability this afternoon."

Gerswin waited, not volunteering more information, but retrieving his credentials from the scanning drawer.

"Would you be free at 1430?"

"Local time?"

"Yes, ser."

"That would be agreeable. I am at the Hotel D'Armand. What is the best way to reach your offices?"

After getting directions, Gerswin called two other firms and obtained appointments.

Now, if he could get access to another console, without using his identification . . . He shrugged. There were ways, even in Illyam. The important thing was not to be too impatient. While he had more time than most, he didn't have any more lives.

He spent the next hour or so retrieving background, tourist-type information from the console, and reading between the lines, before freshening up for his first appointment.

Leaving the hotel was another exercise in politeness.

"Good day, ser."

"Enjoy your stay, ser . . ."

Byzania was an interesting planet, reflected Gerswin as he strolled down the Grande Promenade toward his appointment with Raymond Simones. With the agricultural predominance and the military control, he had expected a climate warmer than the midday high of 18°C, as well as police on every corner.

Outside of the man in the standard brown tunic who had shadowed him from the hotel, and the one uniformed policeman in a small booth three blocks down from the hotel, he had seen no other obvious police representatives among the light scattering of people on the streets.

While there were some flitter-for-hire stands, the majority of citizens visible to Gerswin chose either to walk or to take the small electric trolleys that seemed to run down the center of all the major avenues.

The people in Illyam looked like people everywhere—no one extravagantly dressed, no one in rags. Some smiling, some frowning, but most with the preoccupied look of men and women with somewhere to go, something to do.

Tunic and trousers were the standard apparel for both men and women, but the men wore earrings, and the women did not. The women wore colored sashes, and the men wore dark belts.

One absence nagged Gerswin for most of his walk. Just before he entered the Place Treholme, he identified it. No street vendors of any sort. None! Nowhere had he traveled, except in systems like Nova Balkya, which was an out-and-out police state, and New Salem, with its religious fanaticism, had been without some street sales. Likewise, the streets and avenues were bare of comm stations or public comm consoles.

Gerswin nodded to himself. The pattern was becoming clearer, much clearer. Both absences fit in with the total lack of cash. Byzania was strictly a credit/debit economy. All transfers of credits went straight from your account to someone else's. All were doubtless monitored by the government. The principal formality at the entry shuttle port had been to open a Byzanian universal account for one MacGregor Corson.

Even the so-called free services of the society, such as console access to the public library facilities, required a universal account card. With such tight social control, Gerswin couldn't yet figure out why the military even needed such a high profile in government.

Raymond Simones, Land Agent Extraordinaire, had his offices on the third level of the four-level Place Treholme, which was more like an indoor garden surrounded by balconied offices than a place for transacting business.

"MacGregor Corson," he announced.

"Ser Simones is expecting you. He will be with you in a moment. Would you like a seat?"

Gerswin took the seat, only to stand abruptly with the bounding and enthusiastic approach of Simones.

"Ser Corson, I am honored. So honored."

He bowed quickly, twice, as he pronounced his honor.

"If you would care to join me in a liftea . . ."

"A small cup . . ."

The taller palms of the indoor courtyard leaned nearly into the conference room, although sonic shields kept both leaves and sounds out on the one side, while the closed and old-fashioned door presumably kept the staff excluded on the other.

"This liftea . . . straight from New Colora," offered Simones as he poured from a steaming carafe into two crystal demitasses.

"To your health and our mutually profitable business."

Simones lifted his demitasse.

"To your health," responded Gerswin, following suit, but taking only a small sip of the dark beverage.

"You are an agent of something called RERTA, Limited, you said. RERTA, Limited, has no real records. Obviously you are merely a front for someone or some group searching for a large tract of land, someone who does not want their identity known."

"Why would you say that?" asked Gerswin.

Simones shrugged his shoulders. "Is it not obvious? You have access to great credit; you are looking at a planet developed enough to have the necessary amenities, but one underdeveloped enough to have large amounts of land available for purchase. Further, you arrive in a nonmilitary ship with screens of a class available only to the Court or the very wealthy, and you arrive alone. That means you are trusted, but expendable, that you have access to money, but that there is enormous power and wealth behind you. Alone, who would care? But you are not alone, merely an advance agent."

Gerswin laughed, not quite a bark, but not quite gently.

"I never claimed to be more than an agent."

"Ah, but what one claims is not always what is. In your case, however, the props are too expensive, too real, to be anything else but the truth. The real question is not just what you want, but why you and your patron wants it.

"Do you want farmland to provide an estate for the junior branch of a wealthy family? Or do you want a more isolated and scenic retreat for other purposes? Or perhaps a tract which offers both?"

Simones took another sip of the liftea and looked at the built-in console screen at his left elbow, as if to suggest that he was ready to begin in earnest if Gerswin were.

"My mission is rather delicate . . ."

"I can certainly understand that."

". . . and my latitude is broad within certain parameters. While RERTA is more interested in as pleasant a site as possible, and one which is somewhat off the beaten track, economics, especially these days, would indicate that it is prudent for any local site to be capable of being self-supporting, should the need arise."

Gerswin frowned as if to convey that he did not want to say much more, and waited for a reaction.

"That is a rather broad description, and without some general boundaries might be hard to narrow." Simones' bright blue eyes clouded, and he brushed a stray lock of blue-black hair off his tanned forehead.

"The optimal size," offered Gerswin, "would be ten thousand squares."

"Ten thousand square kilometers?"

"Depending on location, resources, transportation, and whether the property is virgin or improved."

"I see."

What Gerswin could see was that Simones wanted to ask price ranges, but didn't know the client well enough to broach the issue.

"While price is a consideration, it is not the sole consideration. RERTA is always better served if the price is as reasonable as possible for the value involved."

"Reasonable is a term open to a wide interpretation, Ser Corson, and one about which there could be wide disagreements."

"That is true. We need a better frame of reference. While I could access the information myself, perhaps you could give me the average price per kilosquare for prime agricultural lands, for forest lands, and for wilderness."

"Ah . . . averages. So deceiving, especially when the transactions are large. Do you realize, Ser Corson, that the average synde bean estate on Conuna runs about fifty thousand squares?"

"I understand. Have any changed hands recently?"

"Last year, I believe, the Harundsa estate was sold to General Fernadsa. The registered transfer was in the neighborhood of 250 million credits."

"How many squares?"

"Sixty-three thousand."

"Assuming the registered price was the sole consideration, that means a minimum of four thousand credits per square, or given the underlying considerations of that transfer, more likely five thousand credits per square."

"That was a bargain sale."

Gerswin got the point. He didn't know whether the General Fernadsa who bought the property was the prime minister or merely related, but the sale had not been an entirely free-market transaction.

Simones was also testing Gerswin on Gerswin's client. A foundation might find Byzania not entirely to its liking, while certain Imperial families could well end up playing the local games better than the locals.

"RERTA might well be interested in obtaining property where future bargains could be had," Gerswin countered.

"One cannot predict bargains," answered Simones. "They happen, and they do not."

"True, and that is why one must be fully informed on the market and the players."

"Ah . . . yes. So many players, and some so well connected, particularly in the land business." Simones shrugged, then frowned. "I might offer you some advice, strictly an observation, you understand."

Gerswin nodded.

"You will doubtless interview other agents, and some will appeal to you, and some will not, but, should you deal with a noble lady, be most careful."

"I was not aware of an Imperial family here."

"Local noblesse, Ser Corson. Fallen nobility of a sort. The name is Cerdezo, and the lady can be most charming. Most charming. You might find her socially entertaining, and quite brilliant."

Gerswin nodded again. "I appreciate your . . . observation."

"Now . . . in regard to your search . . . let me check certain aspects of the situation, and I will get back to you." Simones rose to his feet.

Gerswin rose also, and half bowed. "A pleasure to meet you, and I hope to hear from you before too long."

"Doubtless you will, Ser Corson."

A tacit agreement had been struck. Simones had gotten some idea of what game Gerswin was playing and warned him that the locals played hard. Gerswin had accepted the information and indicated that he was still interested. Simones had concluded by saying that he would see what was really available, or might be, at what real price.

The one thing that bothered Gerswin was the out-of-character reference to Sher Cerdezo. Was Simones tied into security? Did he know that Gerswin had contacted Cerdezo and Associates? Why was Gerswin being warned off? Because the lady was sharp and dangerous, or because security wanted to keep off-worlders away?

Gerswin did not frown as he kept his face pleasant and bowed again before turning to go.

Outside the Place Treholme, the slender man in the brown tunic was waiting as Gerswin hopped an electric trolley for his 1430 meeting with Sher Cerdezo.

THE FLITTER CIRCLED the holding west of the thin and glittering green river that split the neatly and mechanically cultivated synde bean fields.

The few buildings, obviously used for storage and machine repair, stood at the top of a gentle rise, scarcely more than thirty meters higher than the gentle rolling hills covered with the rust brown of the synde beans about to be harvested.

Gerswin, in the right front seat of the four-seat flitter, could see from the indentations in the hilltop that other structures had been removed.

"This was the original estate house of the Gwavara's, but when the grandfather of the present colonel married Vylere's daughter and consolidated the holdings of both families, the estate house was moved to Vylerven. That's about one hundred kays east," added Constanza Cerdezo, who sat directly behind Gerswin, providing a running commentary.

The silver-haired land agent reminded Gerswin more of a dowager aunt than the sharp-dealing professional the other two agents had warned him to steer clear of.

"Why is this available?"

"It is considered too remote, and the production levels have fallen considerably in the last four or five years. Neglected shamefully."

"Not much scenery here," groused Gerswin.

"That is true, but as I indicated earlier, were you to indicate a firm interest in this land, and your client's desire to maintain and improve it, the Ministry of Forests and Agriculture Development would look most favorably upon your application to purchase, say, twenty thousand squares of the adjoining forest reserve. With the stipulation that your client retain all but a small fraction in forest, of course. Still, two percent of twenty thousand squares is four hundred squares, and that would be adequate for any estate house, landing field, roads, and local produce gardens."

"And the normal fee for consideration?"

"I would suggest something in the range of five thousand credits, with a deposit of one million credits on the forest reserve application."

Gerswin didn't bother to ask if the deposit were refundable. Whatever she said, in practice, no deposit for special consideration would ever be returned.

"Could we swing over and see the forest reserve lands you're talking about? I've seen maps and holos, but there is no substitute for seeing the actual parcels."

"Forest reserves are protected from overflights," the pilot stated baldly.

"How can I recommend RERTA buy something I have not seen?"

"You could rent a landcruiser," suggested the pilot.

"That would take days," complained Gerswin. "And I still would not have the sweep, the overview necessary."

"I sympathize, Ser Corson, but the regulations are regulations."

"Regulations are regulations, I know, but isn't there some exception, some variance, for special circumstances?"

"Ah, an exception permit," offered the pilot. Then his voice fell. "But you must apply in advance."

Gerswin shrugged and turned to Constanza Cerdezo. "Have you any suggestions?"

"Ser Corson, must you overfly the whole parcel, or merely see it from the air?"

"Perhaps if I could see at least part of it from the air, I could decide whether more flights were necessary, and then I could decide whether to apply for an exception permit."

Constanza addressed the pilot. "Michel, can you fly the demarche line?"

"Ah, yes, Sher Cerdezo. If I inadvertently stray . . . the fine is five hundred credits."

Gerswin picked up the hint. "Michel, I can understand your concerns about such delicate piloting. Should you inadvertently stray onto the wrong side of the line, I will be responsible for the monetary fine. If you are successful, as I know you will be, and you are not fined, the five hundred credits that would go to the government will be your bonus."

"Ser Corson and Sher Cerdezo, I will do my best."

The flitter banked left and swung toward the low hills thirty kays west of the old Gwavara holding.

As they neared the low hills, covered with a uniform dark green carpet of trees, with scattered clearings that appeared more as gray smudges, Gerswin thought he saw a faint line of smoke.

"Is that smoke?"

The pilot and Constanza both stiffened, almost imperceptibly, and the pilot swallowed.

"Ser Corson, why do you ask?"

"It seemed strange. Everywhere else the air is so clear. Even in the forests outside Illyam. First smoke I've seen."

"Perhaps it is smoke."

Michel brought the flitter around heading southward, along the gently curved line separating the rising and treed hills from the cultivated fields. Between the trees and the bean fields ran a dust-covered and narrow road. For fifty meters on each side of the road the ground was grassy, the grass a purple-tinged gold.

From his viewpoint, Gerswin studied the forest reserve. The low trees were gray-trunked, the foliage more purple–olive-green than the green of New Augusta or even of New Colora. He could see no towering monoliths, but a regularity in height, despite the obviously irregular and natural growth spacing of the individual trees.

Several distant glimmers, either lasers or light reflected from polished metal, twinkled in the distance, from what looked to be the second or third line of the hills that rose gradually as their distance from the cultivated area increased.

About the reflections Gerswin said nothing.

"The smoke . . . ?"he asked.

"Ah, yes, the smoke . . . it may be smoke."

Gerswin turned to Constanza. "Perhaps I understand. Even in the most ideal of societies, there are those who would not work for what they receive, who would rather live like savages . . ."

He could sense the relief in the pilot and the land agent, which indicated he was either off-track totally or had reassured them with his observation.

"Yes, Ser Corson," answered Constanza, "we do have a few of those. And occasionally their campfires go out of control."

"And the Ministry of Forests and Agriculture Development is spread so thin that it would welcome someone who could protect and manage a small section of the forest reserve?"

As he asked the question, the flitter passed a small clearing, and Gerswin thought he saw the charred remnants of three identical houses side by side before the view was obscured by the flitter's stub wing and the intervening trees.

"There have been other lease/purchases granted on that basis."

Gerswin nodded, thinking more about the sight of three identically burned ruins in a small clearing.

"I take it that in normal circumstances, building in the forest reserves is not allowed? That is true on most worlds, I believe."

"That is true on Byzania as well. How else could a reserve remain a reserve if any savage could . . . build a . . . dwelling . . . anywhere he wanted?"

Gerswin noted the hesitancy in word choice and filed it mentally for future reference.

"Who actually protects the forests? The Ministry of Forests and Agriculture Development?"

"Protects?"

"Keeps people out, makes sure that savages don't destroy the trees, that sort of thing."

"All protection is the responsibility of the Chief of Staff. Any guard duty, whether at the shuttle port, or in the forest reserves, is the duty of the armed forces." That was from the pilot.

"So your armed forces are concerned with both the prevention of crime and the protection of natural resources?"

"Ser Corson, we have little crime here on Byzania. Surely you have already noticed that."

Gerswin had noticed that and said so before changing the subject.

"How far would twenty thousand squares go?"

Constanza had a map on the console screen in front of Gerswin, and with her instructions and the map, he could see how the combined holding would indeed be a most attractive property. Most attractive.

Attractive as it would be, he thought he also understood Sher Cerdezo's game.

RERTA would apply for the forest reserve purchase, and the government would turn it down. The deposit would be forfeit, unless RERTA could bring pressure to bear, in which case the deposit would become the processing fee or the equivalent. Whatever the eventual result, RERTA would be out an additional 1,005,000 credits, of which a large share would probably go to Sher Cerdezo.

A further refinement would be the requirement that RERTA purchase the estate land before it could apply for the forest reserve purchase. If the forest reserve purchase failed to go through, the foundation, in RERTA's ostensible name, would have overpriced farming land, unless it resold at a loss, possibly through Sher Cerdezo.

He almost smiled.

The locals played rough, too tough to be ultimately successful, particularly if a few experienced Imperials moved in.

Gerswin could see another smoky patch in the forested distance, which he ignored, as well as a longer flash of light from the same general direction.

He could not ignore the three combat skitters, presumably carrying troops for which they were designed, which zoomed through a low ridge between two hills and spiraled up into a holding pattern above the smoldering patch in the reserve.

"Forest fire?" he asked blankly.

"I do not know," answered the pilot.

"Nor I," chimed in Constanza.

They both lied. Gerswin did not press the issue, but merely studied the skitters for a moment before turning his head to look at another area of the forest reserve.

"Most attractive land parcels, Sher Cerdezo. Most attractive."

"Do . . . do you think your client might be interested?"

"RERTA might indeed be interested. There are several other possibilities I have yet to investigate."

"I doubt that they measure up to this."

"They may not. If so, then I can honestly report that this is the most attractive." Gerswin looked at the pilot. "If there is nothing else you think I should see . . ."

"Of course. Michel, let us return Ser Corson to Illyam."

Gerswin leaned back as if to relax, then sat up and half turned in his seat.

"Sher Cerdezo . . . you are so familiar with so many of these estates. Almost as if you had . . ." Gerswin looked down and did not complete the statement.

". . . as if I had been raised on one?"

"My apologies if I have created some awkwardness."

"No." She laughed, and the laugh was the practiced easy kind that comes to those who make it their stock in trade. "My origins would be obvious to anyone raised on Byzania, even without the name Cerdezo. My uncle was once the prime minister—before he had an unfortunate accident while hunting turquils in the western reserve."

"Then you moved to Illyam, away from the memories?"

"They are good memories, but times change. I enjoy the city life, and the chance to meet off-worlders now and again. When one has a small household, one has no need for estates, and what I have is adequate, more than adequate, for my needs."

"I did not mean to pry."

"No, Ser Corson. You did not intrude. You understand a great deal more than most off-worlders, and for that understanding I am grateful."

Gerswin turned back to stare out the front of the armaglass canopy at the dim blotch on the brown horizon, the dim blotch that would become Illyam.

No matter how he turned the problem over in his mind, he couldn't see any quick solution. Not one that didn't point the finger at one MacGregor Corson long before he could track down what he needed.

That left the option of action, and of using others to force the issue before his cover was thoroughly shredded.

All he could do was wait until touchdown. Wait and hope that there wasn't a welcoming committee yet, not that he expected one until the locals had figured out how to get their hands on as much hard currency as possible.

As he expected, there was no greeting party when the flitter landed at the shuttle port, not if he excluded the small groundcar that waited for Sher Cerdezo at the edge of the tarmac where Michel had set the flitter down.

Gerswin observed the military style of the landing, which confirmed another of his suspicions.

As Michel shut down the thrusters, Gerswin stretched, began to unbuckle his belt harness.

"Uhnnnn . . ."

The pilot slumped forward over the stick, his beret sliding off his head and onto the control board.

"What . . . what happened?" asked Gerswin, swiveling away from the outside view and leaning over the pilot.

"Michel!" added Constanza Cerdezo.

Gerswin pocketed the pilot's credentials and universal credit card as he laid the man back and across the seat.

"He's breathing . . . heartbeat seems all right . . ." Gerswin looked at the land agent. "Is there . . . I mean . . . how do you call for an emergency health vehicle?"

"Perhaps we should take him to the dispensary in my groundcar," suggested the land agent. "By the time—"

"Good idea."

Gerswin fumbled around with the controls more than necessary before locating the door and steps release and activating them.

As the canopy slid back and the doorway opened and steps extended, the groundcar purred toward the flitter.

Gerswin edged the limp pilot to the doorway, climbed out, and gave the impression of staggering as he lifted the man into his arms and over his shoulder. With one hand on the single railing, he lurched down and toward the olive drab of the groundcar.

The driver wore the standard armed forces uniform and had leapt out to stand by the open front door of the car, his right hand on the butt of the holstered stunner.

"Sher Cerdezo, what happened?"

"Michel collapsed right after landing. He breathes, but he is not conscious. Can we take him to the dispensary?"

"That would be no problem." The driver raised his eyebrows as he surveyed Gerswin.

"We'll just bring Ser Corson with us, Waldron. He is a client of mine, but Michel is the important thing."

As they talked, Gerswin eased the pilot's form into the rear seat, and pulled himself in as well, shutting the door behind him. Waldron seated Sher Cerdezo before returning to the wheel to begin the trip toward the dispensary.

"Medical, medical, this is Waldron. Pilot Michel unconscious. Request emergency team upon arrival."

As the car whined toward the low building that was the dispensary, Gerswin could see a glide stretcher and two white-clad figures waiting under the emergency entrance's portico.

No sooner had the groundcar come to a halt than the armed services medical technicians were easing Michel out and onto the stretcher.

The way they handled the unconscious pilot verified another of Gerswin's suspicions.

As the medical team bundled Michel off, Waldron turned in his seat so that he half faced Constanza, in the front, and Gerswin, in the rear.

"What really happened to Michel?"

Gerswin could have taken offense and been in character, but decided against it. Waldron was more than a driver. More like Constanza's jailer.

"He just fell forward. One minute he was fine. The next minute he was slumped on the controls."

"Before or after the doorway was opened?"

"Before, I think," answered Gerswin. "I wasn't looking at him at all."

"Why not?"

"Because I was considering what I would do with the land parcels that Sher Cerdezo had shown me."

"Did you see anything, Sher Cerdezo?"

"No. I was picking my case up from the floor. When I looked up, Ser Corson was looking at the groundcar. Then Michel groaned and fell forward." She glared at Waldron. "And if you are through treating us . . . like trainees . . . would you be so kind as to take us back?"

"Of course, Sher Cerdezo. Of course. And what about Ser Corson?"

"Unless you have any great objection, he comes with me. Michel's seizure stopped us from completing our business."

Waldron said nothing as he squared himself in his seat, seemingly oblivious to the lady's biting tongue. The whine of the electrics increased, and the car pulled away from the dispensary. The front glass darkened automatically as the car turned into the late afternoon sun.

Constanza sat straight, facing forward, silent. Gerswin followed her example, hoping he had read the lady correctly.

As the electric vehicle pulled up the long circular drive to a house—which, while appearing modest by the standards of the larger estate holders, would have been the envy of many an Imperial functionary—Gerswin had to wonder in what sort of splendor had Constanza Cerdezo grown up. She had referred to her quarters as small and modest.

At the portico waited two other men, both of whom wore livery that marked them as servants, but both with the manner of military personnel.

Before the car pulled away, Gerswin turned as if to help the white-haired lady from the front seat. One of the guards had already opened the door for her.

"Sher Cerdezo, I am not familiar with this section of Illyam. Once we are completed, finished, is there some sort of transportation?"

"I am sure that Waldron would be more than happy to drive you back to your hotel."

"Most assuredly," said Waldron, smiling broadly.

At the smile, Gerswin hastily revised his plans again.

"My study would be best," said Constanza, "since I have my console and the larger maps there."

Gerswin followed her through the double doors and through the hardwood-floored foyer to another doorway on the right and a smaller hallway, with rough-finished white walls. At the end was the study, a long high-ceilinged room with rows and rows of built-in wooden bookcases, nearly all filled with old-style books, on the right, or the exterior wall. On the left was a nearly solid expanse of glass looking into the low gardens of the central courtyard.

"Might I borrow your console for a moment or two?" asked Gerswin.

"Certainly. I will get the maps out."

Gerswin used Michel's card to ask for the planetary directory and three names. General Juen Kerler and General Raoul Grieter had been mentioned in the faxnews, while Jaime Hylerion was the name he really wanted.

Hylerion was not listed. Period. The generals were, but only by name, with just a vidscreen drop number for messages.

As he sat at the console, Constanza walked over, placed her hand on his shoulder. Gerswin looked up, ready to remove her hand at the first sign of trouble. Her eyes widened at the Hylerion name.

Gerswin took a sheet of print paper from the console and printed an inquiry.

"Does the armed services keep samples of the house trees?"

He studied her face.

She looked at the question and shook her head. "Could we finish up now, Ser Corson?"

He crumpled the paper and put it in his belt pouch.

"If it does not take too long. I do have other engagements, and I would like to finish."

Translated loosely, he didn't have much time.

Gerswin pulled a datacube from his belt pouch and dropped it into the scanner, tapping out the five lines of instructions he had memorized. He hoped the information worked as advertised..

Then he stood.

"I'm not sure what else we have to discuss, unless you have some recommendations on guarantees for obtaining a forest reserve purchase. Without that, it would be difficult to recommend buying only the estate lands. It is the combination which is so desirable."

"I am afraid I misunderstood you, Ser Corson."

Gerswin took her arm in his, and guided her back toward the front of the town villa.

"No misunderstanding, Sher Cerdezo. We may not be far enough along to finalize this. I have sent off the information, and I thank you for the use of your console, for further relay. Now, if you would care to see me off. Or do you have to meet someone in town?"

He squeezed her hand gently with the question.

"Perhaps I should. I had not thought . . . ah . . . it is no matter."

The car, and the smiling face of Waldron, were waiting at the portico for them.

"Are you going somewhere, Sher Cerdezo?"

"Yes. I had forgotten that Diene had asked me to stop by. So you can drop me there, and then take Ser Corson to his hotel."

"But . . . Sher Cerdezo . . ."

"I am sure you can arrange this, Waldron."

Gerswin helped the slender woman into the backseat, then walked around and sat down behind the driver.

"Hotel D'Armand," he offered in his most helpful voice. He could see the driver shrug slightly.

"En route Boulevard Fernadsa, then to the Hotel D'Armand," Waldron mumbled into the speaker.

Constanza shifted her weight as the car whined forward and down the drive.

Gerswin watched as Waldron wheeled out onto the nearly vacant boulevard, then stretched, his hands extended near the driver. He waited.

As the driver started to slump, Gerswin slid over the seat into the front, yanking the man from his spot behind the wheel with a single-armed vengeance that left the older woman openmouthed.

The car careened toward the left curb. Gerswin twisted it back on course, while removing Waldron's beret and jamming it low on his own forehead.

Already, Gerswin could see some of the results of his handiwork as lights began to flash on and off at random throughout Illyam.

After touching his datalink to the *Caroljoy* and punching in the emergency standby code, he twisted the electric's power up full and headed down the Boulevard Eglise toward the shuttle port.

Their arrival was anticlimactic, since the *Caroljoy* was grounded on the civilian side with a single military guard, still looking bored as Gerswin whined up.

"Halt!"

Thrummm!

The sentry never even had the time to look surprised.

Gerswin continued with the groundcar right to the point where the ship's shields, now pulsing blue, touched the tarmac. He jumped out, opening the rear door.

"Coming?"

"Now . . . ?"

"One and only chance."

She looked around the port, from the civilian receiving area where amber lights alternated with white, to the flat western horizon where the golden greened sun was able to touch the flat smudged line that represented the endless squares of synde beans, to the muddied gray of the tarmac, and across the gray to the armed services compound a kay away where sirens blared and intermittent lights seared the late afternoon sky.

At last, her glance strayed to the groundcar and the slumped figure within.

Constanza Cerdezo swallowed, and squared her shoulders.

"Yes. I'll go."

"We're not done yet, you know?"

"I'm scarcely surprised at that, Ser Corson, if that is indeed even your real name."

Gerswin was half listening as he jumped the screen out over them and began to guide the former land agent/prisoner toward the *Caroljoy.*

GERSWIN TAPPED HIS fingers on the bottom edge of the control keys as his eyes darted from the main screen to the representational screen to the data screen in a continuing scan pattern.

"Private yacht *Breakerton*. Private yacht *Breakerton*. This is Byzania Control. Byzania Control. Please acknowledge. Please acknowledge."

"Request instructions," the AI asked.

"Do not acknowledge. Maintain screens."

"Maintaining screens. Unidentified object departing orbit control. Probability exceeds point seven that object is orbital patrol with tachead missiles."

"Query!" growled Gerswin. "Interrogative probability of orbit control destruction through field constriction drive swerve."

"Inquiry imprecise."

"If we force the patrol to fire at an angle that will cause the missile to skip off the atmosphere, can we use the mag band constrictions to control the missile course for a return to orbit control, with subsequent detonation?"

"Probability of damage to *Caroljoy* exceeds point four. Probability of damage to orbit control exceeds point nine."

"No good. What kind of tachead does orbit control use?"

"EDI proximity is employed by more than point nine five of all orbit defense systems."

"Can you maneuver us so that, when you blank out EDI traces, the tachead will seek out orbit control?"

"Not within current gee restriction envelope."

"What is the minimum gee load requirement for a probability of orbit station destruction exceeding point nine with a probability of damage to the *Caroljoy* of less than point one?"

"Point eight probability of successful maneuver, defined as a point probability of destruction combined with a point one probability of damage to *Caroljoy*, can be obtained with an internal gee force loading peak of six point three for up to ten standard minutes."

"Interrogative time before maneuver commencement."

"Ten standard minutes, plus or minus two."

Gerswin stood up and walked across the narrow space and into the tiny crew cabin that was normally his.

Constanza Cerdezo sat on the built-in bunk that doubled as an acceleration shell.

"Constanza?"

She turned, letting her feet hang over the side. "You have a problem?"

"I need an answer. What sort of physical condition are you in?"

"Why do you ask?"

"Because I need to know. Do you have any heart or lung problems? What's your chron age? Estimated bio age?"

"A lady . . . ," She broke off. "You are serious. I know of no heart or lung problems. My age is fifty-seven years standard, and three years ago my biological age was set at fifty."

"Query," Gerswin asked the empty air. "Interrogative probability of severe biological damage, assuming standard profile, female, biological age fifty-three, slender frame."

"Probability of severe bruising exceeds point eight. Probability of internal bleeding less than point one. Probabilities based on maximum maneuver time of less than ten standard minutes at peak gee load of six point three."

Gerswin looked down at the white-haired and tanned woman, straight into her black eyes.

"The problem is simple. We have two choices. Cut and run. That's one. Without finishing my mission. Or use some fancy shipwork to knock out orbit control."

"You cannot come back and try again?"

"No. Excluding the costs, after what I did to the communications net, and to their air defenses on the way up, they will doubtless change things to prevent any recurrence. Next time, they just might destroy any untoward private ships who visit."

"There are risks?"

"Risk to you. About a five percent chance you'll be injured. Maybe more."

"And if you succeed?"

"I will get what I came for and, in the process, probably upset the current government."

"Would the Empire step in?"

"No. Against policy. Never have, and never will. Could quarantine the system until a local government regains total control."

The silence stretched out.

"Time until arrival of orbit patrol is five minutes plus or minus one." The AI's clear tones echoed in the small cabin.

The silence dropped over the two, with only the background hissing of the ventilation system.

Constanza Cerdezo looked at Gerswin, then lowered her shoulders. "Do what you must. I can do no less."

Gerswin lifted her off the bunk and set her standing on the deck. Next he ripped the sheet and quilt off the bunk and slammed them into a locker beneath. He touched the controls to reconfigure the bunk into an acceleration shell and, as quickly as he had made the changes, just as quickly lifted Constanza and placed her in the shell. Three quick movements, and the harnesses had her webbed firmly in place.

"Now. Once the acceleration hits, don't even move your head. Leave it straight between the support rests here. Don't lift it, and don't try to shift your weight once the gee forces start.

"At times you may have no weight, or things may seem normal. Don't believe it. Don't get out of here for anything. Is that clear?"

"Time for orbit patrol arrival at estimated firing point is three plus or minus one."

Gerswin dashed from the cabin to the control, scrambling into his own shell and adjusting the overrides for fingertip control.

"Use your six point three gee maneuver to get that tachead orbiting back at the control station."

"Command imprecise."

"Commence the maneuver you computed earlier, using a six point three gee envelope, to place the *Caroljoy* in a position where any tachead fired at the *Caroljoy* can be skip-deflected or otherwise placed in a position to allow it to home back on orbit control."

"Instructions understood. Due to delays and the position of the orbital patroller, maneuver with same probability of success requires an envelope of seven point one gees."

"Do it! Commence maneuver."

A giant fist slammed Gerswin deep into his accel/decel shell.

He tightened his stomach muscles to fight off the blackness, to keep his eyes open enough to see the readouts projected in red light into the sudden darkness of the ship.

"Orbit patrol readjusting position, holding on tachead release."

The pressure on Gerswin eased, back to five plus gees, he estimated. Because of the differentials in orbits, the strategy was to change positions rapidly enough while moving toward the patroller to force the patroller to fire quickly enough not to be able to compute the probabilities. Plus, the patroller did not know the configuration of Gerswin's ship would allow him to blow all EDI traces.

Gerswin hoped it was enough.

The gee force continued to ease as the *Caroljoy* boosted her speed at a decreasing rate.

"Closing on patroller. Tachead released. Commencing evasive maneuvers."

This time, the gee force blow to Gerswin did roll him into the blackness, though only momentarily.

"Patroller has released second tachead."

"Evade it, idiot," grunted the pilot.

"Stet. Evading."

Gerswin felt like he was being stretched across the couch. Supposedly, yachts, not even former scouts, were not capable of maneuvers like atmospheric craft, but Gerswin felt the *Caroljoy* was being handled more like a flitter than a deep-space ship.

For a moment, the *Caroljoy* went weightless, almost seeming to flip on her longitudinal axis.

The pilot's stomach ventured toward his throat before being jammed back below his hips by the next gee blast.

When the acceleration eased, Gerswin rasped out another command before he was pressed farther into his shell.

"Put Byzania tactical comm on audible."

"Stet. Frequency available."

Another gee burst slammed more breath from Gerswin than he thought he had left, and just as suddenly, all weight left him.

"Full screens, and complete EDI blockage," announced the AI.

The minutes dragged by.

"ByzOps. Hammer one. Returning. Target avoided both persuaders."

"Stet, Hammer one. Understand persuaders avoided."

"That's affirmative."

"Do you have visual on target?"

"That is negative."

"Interrogative EDI."

"Negative. Lost EDI after first release. No visual."

". . . don't like this . . . ," Gerswin smiled wryly.

"Maneuvers completed," stated the AI.

"Interrogative closures? Position status?"

"One quarter orbit distance plus two relative Byzania orbit control."

"Aren't we close to an orbit relay?"

"Relay inoperative."

"I take it you rendered the relay inoperative."

"That is correct."

Gerswin shivered. That was one facet of releasing control to the AI that he did not relish. It was also the reason why neither the I.S.S. nor any commercial ships linked their AIs to the controls directly. No one yet had figured out a workable system that embodied the day-to-day ethical and human considerations required. Every direct "ethical" system ever attempted froze or took too much time to make decisions. The only workable systems were those designed without ethical parameters.

"Return to advisory status."

"In advisory status."

"Give me at least five minutes warning of *any* approaching object, anything at all."

"Five minutes warning of all objects."

"Stet."

Gerswin scrambled out of his shell, wincing at the instant stiffness his muscles seemed to have acquired, and staggered into the small crew cabin.

A quick study indicated that Constanza was breathing, but her face and tan and white tunic were streaked with blood.

The white-haired woman's chest rose and fell regularly, but the beginnings of heavy bruises were showing on her uncovered forearms.

He fumbled for the medstar cuffs, finally plugging them in and attaching them.

"Interrogative medical status of subject."

"Subject unconscious. Probability less than point zero one of internal bleeding. Gross scan indicates no fractures."

From what he could tell, the blood had come from a nosebleed. He wiped her slack face as clean as he could, but left her in the harness to wake up naturally.

No sense in taking chances.

Back before the controls, he also strapped himself in.

The audio crackled.

"ByzOps. Unidentified object approaching orbit station."

"Hammer two, scramble. Launch and destroy."

"Two scrambling. Interrogative clear to launch."

"Cleared to launch. Cleared to launch."

"Affirm. We're cradle gone. Cradle gone and clearing."

"Vector on incoming, plus one five at two zero seven. Plus one five at two zero seven."

"Understand vector plus one five at two zero seven."

"Stet. Vector and intercept. Intercept and destroy."

"Intercept impossible. Intercept impossible."

"Can you impact?"

"You want me to ram it?"

"That's affirmative."

"ByzOps, this is Hammer two. Clarify your last. Clarify your last."

"Hammer two. If intercept not possible, use full thrust to impact and deflect incoming. Identified as persuader, class two."

"That's impossible, ByzOps. That's—"

EEEEEEEEEEEE.

"Energy pulse indicates probable destruction of Byzania orbit control."

"Does that mean all incoming traffic will have to communicate planetside directly?"

"That is correct."

"And the planetary commnet is effectively out of commission," mused Gerswin, "at least until they scrub the entire link.

"So it's time to drop in on our friends, the savages, and see if they do have those tree houses of Hylerion's."

The *Caroljoy* began to drop from orbit toward the patches of forest reserve Gerswin had tentatively marked from his orbit and map scans.

VIII

THE TALLER GENERAL looked over his shoulder. Three silver triangles glittered on his shoulder boards. Otherwise, his khaki uniform tunic was unadorned.

"Are you sure it's secure?"

"Nothing is secure now. With the communications links down, we're operating on emergency power, and we don't have the energy for sonic screens. I doubt anyone else on Byzania has the energy for peepers."

"Gwarara, summarize."

Colonel Gwarara squared his shoulders and faced the three generals.

"Generals, the situation is as follows. First, Ser Corson, whoever he is, dropped a trap program into the comm-link system. It was an expanding and replicating program. Furthermore, it ordered a printout of the program itself from every hard-copy printer on Byzania that linked into the net before we shut down the power grid."

"Shut down the power grid? The entire grid?" That was General Somozes, Chief for Atmospheric Defense, blond, stocky, clean-shaven, and square-chinned.

"Every minute that the system remained operational, another two hundred to one thousand vidterms were locked in. We estimate that it will take between twelve and thirty-six hours to scrub the entire system. That's if we can use all available personnel. We will have to return power in sections. If we miss one link, it could repeat the original lock."

"What did this devilish program do?" asked the other general, the short, thin one named Taliseo who headed the marines.

"General, it was a simple program. All it did was link together terminal after terminal, and leave the connections open. That did several things." Gwarara paused, took a deep breath before continuing. He wanted to wipe his damp forehead. The bunker was getting warmer with each passing minute.

"First, no comm system actually stays on line all the time with all terminals. The actual link times are pulsed, compressed if you will. Corson removed the pulse feature and made all the contacts continuous. Enormous increase in the power requirements."

"Is that what caused the blinking lights and the power fluctuations?"

"Before we shut the grid down? Yes."

"What else?" asked the tallest general, Guiteres, the Chief of Staff.

"Second, as I mentioned earlier, this was a replicating program. Each connection transferred the program to the new terminal and left it displayed there, as well as printing it wherever possible."

"You mean, there are hundreds copies of this . . . this monstrosity printed all over Byzania?"

"More like thousands, but the distribution would be very uneven. When we shut the grid down, the penetration of Conuno was close to ninety percent. Probably only about seventy percent for Conduo, and less than twenty-five percent for Contrio. Most of the terminals don't have power-fail memories. By killing the power we automatically destroyed close to ninety percent of the vidterm duplicates."

"What about hard copy?" asked the Chief of Staff.

Colonel Gwarara frowned. "A rough estimate would be close to fifty percent of all hard-copy facilities with power-fail memories."

"But every dwelling in Illyam has a hard-copy capability. That's more than two million."

"It would be less than that, General," corrected the colonel. "The access was only to vidterms with on-line printers, not backup units."

"The point is the same," sighed General Guiteres. "There are more than enough copies available that anyone who wanted to repeat the program could."

"No, ser. We can shield against this program being used again by anyone."

Guiteres stared at the colonel. "You can shield against this particular program. Can you shield against another that has a different introduction? Or a different mechanism? Can you hide the basic concept?"

Gwarara looked at the hard and gray plastic of the bunker floor. "No, General."

"Gentlemen," Guiteres said softly, "the revolution is over. And we have lost."

"What?"

"Are you insane?"

The Chief of Staff waited until the shock silenced the other two generals. The colonel said nothing.

"I do not propose admitting this publicly. Nor have we lost the immediate control of the situation. But the society we have today is doomed, no matter what we do. We have been able to maintain control because we held all communications, because the distribution of food, information, and transportation was monitored and regulated through the communications network.

"Ser Corson, whoever he really is, has handed those who oppose us both the format and concept of shutting down those communications channels. How many blockages can we take before the entire fabric unwinds? Three . . . five . . . a dozen?

"He has also destroyed orbit control, somehow. We do not have the resources to replace it, nor can we purchase a replacement if Byzania is quarantined, which seems likely. Further, without the satellite control links, our access to the relay monitors is limited to line of sight. That will give the savages more time to act and to avoid our patrols. To keep the communications relays operating will require maintenance from the shuttle port, which is expensive and energy intensive."

"So . . . ?" asked Taliseo. "So it costs us more. So it requires a stepped-up patrol effort to keep the savages in line. So what?"

"Don't you see?" responded Guiteres. "To maintain control under our present system will require more troops, more force. More overt use of force will create more resentment and unrest, which will generate other blockages, requiring greater force."

He stopped and looked around the bunker, wiping his own forehead with the back of his left hand.

"Assuming you are correct, and I have some considerable doubts, what do you suggest?" asked Taliseo.

Somozes frowned as he watched the two senior generals debate.

"In general terms," answered the Chief of Staff, "the answer is clear. We have to build a more decentralized system and society, using the existing political framework and economic structure, and we have to begin before the savages and the other opportunists understand the real situation."

"I disagree," interjected Somozes. "Why should we give anything away? We've given them prosperity, eliminated most crimes, and a pretty honest government."

"How many dissidents have vanished? How many radical friends of students have taken 'trips' and never returned? Do you think that a prosperous people ever considers the hardships that otherwise might have been?"

"That doesn't matter. We still hold the power."

"How many personnel in the armed forces?"

"Three hundred thousand."

"How many people on Byzania?"

"Thirty million."

"How many spacecraft?"

"One cruiser, one light cruiser, ten corvettes, ten scouts, and five freighters. Plus the orbit patrollers."

"And how many savages in the outer forests? How many student dissidents we know nothing about?"

Somozes shrugged, as if to indicate that he didn't know and could have cared less.

"More than four thousand, on all three continents," answered Taliseo. "That's not counting the underground within the cities."

"Half our armed forces is required to keep the forest groups in check. Half! Do you not understand?" Guiteres glared at Somozes, who seemed to ignore the look. "With our credit account system, we could isolate individuals. Does Miguel order more food than a family of three needs? We knew. Who does he call? We knew. What electronic components are produced and shipped? To whom? For what? We knew, and we could cross-check. Now, it is only a matter of time before the dissidents discover that they can destroy that tracking and control system. Even a single blockage will allow uncounted tons of material to be diverted."

Guiteres raked the three others with brown eyes that radiated contempt.

"Because we controlled the education, we could keep track of those who had the training on comm systems. We perpetuated the myth that great education was necessary to understand and engineer and program them. In one stroke, Ser Corson has begun the destruction of that myth. How soon will we see the students trying to duplicate his efforts?

"I do not know, but I doubt it will be long. And what will you do to them? If you can find them?"

"I doubt it is that grim," answered Taliseo. "Why do you think that?"

"For one thing, the Imperial offices have already been evacuated, and their ship lifted as we met, possibly leaving to recommend quarantine."

Taliseo frowned as the implications sank in.

Somozes frowned also, muttering under his breath, asking a different question entirely. "But what did we do to Corson? What did we do to him?"

Gwarara looked from one general to the next, then to the floor, as he wiped his streaming forehead with the back of his sleeve.

Guiteres shook his head slowly as he surveyed the three other officers and the emergency communications board behind Gwarara, an expanse of unlit screens and lights, totally lifeless.

THREE QUICK TAPS on the controls, and the figures reeled onto the data screen.

Gerswin had enough power for two more liftoffs and touch-downs—that plus boost out to jump point.

Two clearings had proved fruitless, merely burned-over ashpits long since deserted by the elusive rebels or the pursuing armed forces.

The one toward which the *Caroljoy,* operating as private yacht *Breakerton,* now settled was the most isolated he had been able to find, which seemed to meet the theoretical parameters outlined years ago by Hylerion.

"Any luck?"

Despite her recent ordeal, Constanza's voice came from the cabin with remarkable lilt and cheer.

"Know shortly."

The open space in the clearing was barely enough for the short touchdown run of the scout. Once down, Gerswin swiveled the craft slowly in order to leave her in position for a quick departure. He also left the screens in place, despite the additional energy requirements.

"Anyone around?"

"Detectors show no heat radiation above background within two hundred meters."

Gerswin almost snorted. All the rebels had to do was lie in a ditch to avoid heat detection in the warmth of Byzania.

"Let's have a sweep from all the exterior scanners."

Unburned, the clearing was covered with a ground-hugging blue-and-gold-tinted grass Gerswin had never seen before. The trees were low, lower than the pilot had expected, and wide-trunked, the branches of the tallest reaching less than fifteen meters into the washed-out green-gold of the sky.

The fine dust raised by the scout's landing had already settled, giving the closer grass and trees a gray overtone.

"Freeze on the last image."

The image he had caught showed a regularity, a hint of an oblong structure, in the right lower corner.

"Expand the right lower corner."

Gerswin studied the blurred image.

"Constanza? Would you come here?"

"I am here." The closeness of her voice, right behind his shoulder, jarred him. He started, unsettled that she had managed to move so close without his noticing, then frowned briefly at the thought that his skills might be deteriorating.

"I did not mean to surprise you."

"What does that look like to you?"

"A dwelling."

"The scale is wrong. Less than half size. Unless . . ."

"Unless what, Ser Corson?"

He turned his head to look at her, his eyes moving past the dark blotches on her arms.

"Unless someone is building half-sized houses, or half-sized people," he temporized, unwilling to voice his own hopes.

"There are rumors . . ."

"Of what?" he snapped.

She drew back from the intensity in his voice and hawk-yellow eyes.

"You seemed to know already . . . of houses that grow like trees . . . of the marines burning them wherever they find them to keep the rebels . . . the savages . . . on the run."

"We'll have to see." He stood up and stepped away from the control panels.

"Keep full screens in place," he ordered the AI.

"Full screens in place," replied the AI impersonally.

"Do you want to come?"

"Certainly. If you think it is safe."

"Nothing's safe. Not totally. Stay inside the screens. They'll stop any energy weapon, or explosives, or projectile guns."

He touched the panel by the lock. The inner door opened.

"It's tight," he observed as she crowded in with him.

As the outer door opened, Gerswin's first impression was of a desert as the flood of hot and dry outside air washed over them.

He bounded down the extended ramp and held out an arm to help the former prime minister's niece.

No sound marred the stillness. No breeze moved a single stalk of the blue and gold ground cover. Only the muffled crunch of the vegetation under Gerswin's black boots could be heard as he walked toward the rear of the scout to see if he could get a better look at what he hoped was Jaime Hylerion's house tree growing behind two older trees.

Gerswin stopped a meter inside the twinkling and faint blue pulsation that marked the screen line and peered through the first line of trees.

He frowned, bit at his lower lip.

The second line of trees obscured his view, but a regularity existed behind the trees. Whether it was man-made or a house tree was another question.

Whhrrrr.

"Corson!"

He ducked and turned, but not quickly enough, he realized as he felt the sharpness bite into his right arm. He glanced down at the stubby arrow imbedded there, shaking his head at his slowness, and his stupidity at not having kept himself in fighting order.

Without hesitating, he moved, grabbing the light-boned woman in his left hand and forcing himself up the ramp and into the lock.

"An arrow, for Hades' sake . . . ," he muttered.

He blinked once, twice, as he stumbled into the control area, releasing Constanza as he felt his knees turning to jelly.

"So dark . . ."

The night struck him down with the suddenness of lightning from a landspout.

COOL, COOL . . . GERSWIN could feel the dampness across his forehead, a contrast to the heat of his body.

He tried to open his eyes, but the dampness blocked his vision. His arms felt leaden, and his throat was raspy and dry.

"Uhhhh . . . ," he croaked.

The faint pressure on his forehead eased as the cloths were removed from across his eyes.

A white-haired visage wavered in and out of focus.

"Corson? Can you hear me?"

Corson? Who was Corson? Corson was dead, dead at the hands of

the Guild? Was it Allison, asking for her son? But Allison was long
gone . . .

"Urrr . . ."

For some reason, he could not speak.

"If you hear me, blink your eyes."

Gerswin blinked.

"That's good. At least you understand. You shouldn't be alive, but
Hyveres says if you have made it this far, you should recover completely . . . in time."

Corson, Hyveres—who were they?

Frozen—that was the way his face felt, with the hint of needles
tingling under his skin.

He wanted to ask how long he had been immobilized, but could
not. Instead, the darkness, with its hot needles and forgetfulness,
crept back over him.

When he woke again, the cabin—and this time he could tell he
was lying in the crew-room bunk—was dim. The hot points of needles
burned and jabbed through most of his body, but the pain was worst
in his legs.

"Urrr . . ."

The woman—was it Constanza, Caroljoy, Allison—must have
heard him, because she appeared with damp cloths to help soothe
the drumming staccato of the needle jabs behind his blistering forehead.

"Just relax. You should be better soon."

Relax? How could he, lying paralyzed with needles driving through
him? What if the paralysis were permanent? How had anything gotten
through the screens?

The questions spun in his head until the overhead blurred into
red dimness, and then into hot blackness.

When the darkness lifted once more, the jabbing of the needles
seemed less intense, nearly gone from his face. He tried to move his
arms, but while they twitched, they did not lift from his sides.

". . . hello . . . ," he rasped.

He could hear the light pad of footsteps, and a face appeared. He
pulled the name from his recollections.

"Constanza?"

"Yes. I'm here, Corson. Can you swallow?"

"Can try."

"Please do. You're terribly dehydrated."

He could feel the coolness of the water against his lips, wetting the cotton dryness inside his mouth. Nearly gagging, he concentrated on swallowing, managing to force the water down.

"That's enough for now. In a bit, we'll try again."

The pounding in his temples eased, and the blurriness of his vision cleared, although his eyes seemed to wander at will.

"Could . . . more water?" he husked.

"A little."

She was right, he discovered, because the second sip felt like lead as it dropped into his stomach.

Closing his eyes, he waited, letting himself drift back into the not-quite-so-hot darkness.

When he woke again, the throbbing in his head was gone, and only a tinge of the needlelike pain remained, and that in his lower legs and feet. The cabin was lighter, but he did not hear Constanza.

Should he try to lift an arm?

Gerswin realized he was afraid he might not be able to. At last, he concentrated on reaching his belt.

Shaking, almost as though it did not belong to him, his arm strained up and touched the square fabric edge of his waistband. Slowly he turned his head toward the arch between the crew cabin and the control area.

No Constanza, not unless she was standing nearly on top of the control screens.

Where was she? How long had he been totally out of commission? What had happened?

At that, he remembered his right arm and turned his head. A pressure bandage from the first-aid kit covered the spot where the arrow had entered.

An arrow! He would never have thought of that.

A scraping sound caught his attention, and he gently eased his head to where he could view the inner lock door as it was manually cranked open.

Constanza came in with a basket of food on her left arm and a loop of cord in her hand.

"Hello."

"You seem much better."

"I am, I think."

"Can you restore the power?"

"Power?"

He blinked, recognizing for the first time since his collapse that the only illumination was from the emergency lighting.

"How long has it been?"

"Three days."

"Is everything down except the screens?"

"I think so. I didn't want to experiment much. I don't understand the manual controls, and the ship did not recognize me."

"Not designed that way." He licked his dry lips and tried to ease himself into a sitting position.

"Let me help. You're still weak, and I'm not sure Hyveres believes me when I keep telling him you're still alive."

"Hyveres?" The name still meant nothing to him.

"He is the rebel leader in this forest cell."

She stood behind his left shoulder and folded the quilt into another pillow, then slipped it behind him. Gerswin could feel the tightness in his muscles protesting the movement.

"More water?"

He was too tired to object to her holding the beaker for him.

Three days? He shivered. By now, even the most disrupted of governments should have been getting the power system back into service.

"Has the government resumed scouting flights."

"Not here. Hyveres says there are reports of some limited resumptions on Conuno." She perched on the end of the bunk.

"Conuno?"

"First continent. We're on Contrio. That's why I asked about power. Hyveres was hoping we could leave. He doesn't want to use the few weapons they have collected in trying to destroy your ship. They don't want the government seeing it and attacking."

"Probably couldn't destroy us. Jolt it enough so the concussion might kill us."

"Can you take off?"

"Technically, yes. Once I can get to the controls. Not sure I could last through the sequence to jump. Besides . . . not done here. Don't have what I came for."

"And what was that?"

He saw no point in dissembling further.

"I wanted seeds, spores, whatever the propagating mechanism is, for the house tree. We funded the original research."

"House tree?"

"What we saw through the trees just before your friends the rebels stuck me with their little arrow. What was on that arrow? Did they tell you? How did you get the food with the ship shut down?"

Now that he was beginning to think, the unanswered questions were piling up.

Constanza laughed. "You will recover, Ser Corson." Her face smoothed out, and she went on. "Hyveres told me that no one could cross the screens without dying. Is that true?"

"Yes. Form of field inhibitor. Stops most energy, and since thought is energy . . ."

"I pointed out that unless I could get you to recover, which takes food and water, sooner or later the armed forces would find your ship and do their best to destroy it."

Gerswin nodded for her to continue, but this time reached for the water beaker himself. He managed to take a solid sip with a trembling left hand.

"We reached an accommodation—"

"What about the house trees?" interrupted Gerswin.

"They have hopes, but none of them grow much bigger than what you saw."

"Know why," he answered. "And the arrow?"

"They have found a local nerve poison. How did the arrow get through the ship's screens?"

"Arrows . . . nonenergy . . . low velocity . . . should have thought about it." Suddenly he was drained.

His abrupt weakness must have showed because Constanza stood up from the end of the bunk where she had been sitting.

"Lean back; just relax."

Could he afford to? What about the government?

"Until you are stronger, you cannot do any more."

He let the held breath out through his teeth, trying to relax and not wanting to. There was so much to do . . .

. . . but he dozed.

When he woke once again, he discovered two things. He was soaked, and the tingling in his legs was gone.

He eased himself upright and let his legs dangle over the edge of the bunk.

The gentle sound of breathing from the control room told him that Constanza was sleeping.

He stood slowly, and began to peel off the stinking trousers and tunic. Then he leaned against the bulkhead to rest. A moment later he straightened.

"Activate—status." He followed the command with the activation codes.

"Returning to active status," the AI acknowledged for the ship, and the normal lighting, returned.

Gerswin dragged himself into the fresher, standing there while the spray cleaned him of grime, sweat, and urine. By the time the charged air had dried him, he was leaning against the inside of the stall.

After dragging himself back to the lockers, where he pulled out shorts and a black shipsuit, he struggled into the clean clothing.

All the time Constanza slept, which told him how tired she was.

Finally, he stuffed his filthy clothing into the cleaner, along with the quilt and the sheet, then collapsed onto the uncovered bunk to catch his breath. In time, he sat up and finished the last drops in the water beaker on the bunk ledge.

A few minutes later he shuffled toward the controls, where he half leaned, half sat on the bottom edge of the accel/decel shell seat where Constanza lay curled into a half circle, her tiny white-haired figure fragile against the black yield cloth.

"Interrogative power status."

The figures appeared on the data screen. He nodded. The loss wasn't as bad as it could have been. He still had enough for liftoff and through two jumps, with minimum reserves.

"Exterior views from the sensors."

The scenes in the screen had a reddish cast, indicating it was night and that infraheat was used for imaging. Outside of the footprints from the lock ramp, there was no sign of any activity. The rebels must have swept up their tracks every time they had brought food to Constanza.

The lady moaned in her sleep and turned, her foot striking his back.

He waited until she seemed settled again.

The acrid scent of air recycled too little burned his nose.

"Full interior recycle. Exterior air through filters."

All he could do now was wait. Even if he woke her, trying to find the rebels in the hours before dawn would be useless, except to find another batch of arrows aimed in his direction.

"Wake me with the alarm if anyone approaches the ship or if she leaves the control couch."

With that, he shuffled back to the bunk and stretched out, not willing to make the effort to remake it.

Cling!

Gerswin started out of his sleep at the alarm, slowed his reactions as he sat up gingerly while Constanza peered through the arch at him.

"You restored the power."

"While you were sleeping.'

Gerswin felt guilty. She still wore a now grimy tan and white tunic and tan trousers, while he was relatively clean in fresh clothing.

"Would you care to use the fresher?"

He stood and headed for the control couch, by way of the water tap, where he refilled the beaker. His legs felt steady.

"After you're through," he said, "we need to make some decisions."

"What about my clothes?"

Gerswin remembered he had never removed his own outfit and bedding from the cleaner.

"Put them in the cleaner—the brown and cream tab there. You'll have to take out my things. Put them on the bunk for now."

"Why don't you—" She broke off the sentence. "It is hard to remember how sick you are when you talk so clearly."

"Not that bad now."

"Hyveres says you are the first to survive the poison."

"Wonderful."

He turned away to devote his attention to the control readings and data displays.

"Can you pick up any commercial news?" he asked the AI.

"Negative. No satellite relay."

"What about audio?"

"Byzania has no separate commercial radio."

"Armed forces tactical freqs?"

"Imprecise command."

"Pick up the strongest armed forces tactical signal."

The only sound Gerswin could hear at first was static, which was barely audible over the hiss of the fresher. As he concentrated he began to be able to distinguish some phrases.

". . . Red command . . . blue attackers . . ."

". . . corvette down . . . Illyam . . ."

". . . flamers . . . flamers . . ."

". . . grid still down . . . Jerboam . . ."

". . . forest cell tiger . . . fire at will . . ."

Gerswin shook his head slowly as he listened to the story play out with each fragmented transmission.

"It is that bad?"

He had been aware of Constanza's return and her listening with
him, but not how much time had passed until she touched his shoulder as she asked the question.

Turning his head, he nearly whistled. The lady looked nearly as
picture-perfect as before their first tour of the countryside.

"Amazing what a ship fresher and cleaner can do," he marveled.

"Thank you. What is occurring?"

Gerswin told her.

"But why?"

"My guess is that someone wouldn't believe someone else. Once
the secret is out, they can't keep control the way it has been. Probably why the armed forces kept after the tree houses, because free shelter would have been a first step to escaping the generals."

"The house trees do not grow large enough."

"They would if they had more time and water. You can't grow
them too close to other trees. Need a lot of solar energy. But any time
someone grew them out in the open, I'd bet the armed forces fried
them."

"I still don't understand why there's fighting between segments of
the armed forces."

"Someone believes there will have to be change, and someone
else disagrees. Power shortages are going to get worse, and there's no
real backup system. The Empire will quarantine the system, as soon
as they can get a fleet here. That's another reason why I need to get
some seeds or spores and lift out."

Constanza sat down beside him.

"I don't know whether I should like you or not. You rescued me
from a prison, and then you destroyed everything I grew up with."

Gerswin shrugged. "Not much I can say to that."

He waited.

She said nothing.

He cleared his throat. "Do you want to leave Byzania with me? I'm
sure you would be welcome on . . . in a number of places."

"You are gracious . . . and very cautious. But, no. No, thank you. I
think I would be welcome with Hyveres, more welcome than in the
cities, and happier than on a strange world."

Gerswin touched the controls and the screens filled with the exterior view and the morning sunlight.

Constanza rose.

"I will tell him, and we will get you your seeds."

"You know, Constanza, the future on Byzania rests with Hyveres."

"I know. You have determined that. Like a god, you change

worlds. Yet you will never have what a man like Hyveres will, for you will never rest. You will never be content, no matter how long you live."

Gerswin stood and took her hand. He bent slightly and brushed the back of her hand with his lips. His legs remained steady, but he sat down as he released her fingers, afraid that his legs might yet betray him.

She put her hand on his shoulder, squeezed it, before stepping back.

"I think I am grateful to you. I can now look forward to the un-expected."

She reached forward to touch his shoulder again, gently, before moving toward the lock door.

"We will bring you the seeds you need. And you will go. You will fight your fate, and we will fight ours. What else is there to say?"

Gerswin lifted the screens and watched from inside the ship as the slender woman went out to touch hands with the rebel captain for the first time. A rebel captain nearly as slender as she, nearly as white-haired, and who sported a bristling white handlebar mustache.

Although she had looked not at all like Caroljoy, neither when his lost Duchess had been young or old, Constanza reminded him of Caroljoy, though he could not say why.

Then, again, perhaps he did not want to know why. The young woman who had been his single-time lover and Martin's mother had become a dream, and no man wants to examine his dreams too closely. Not when the dreams must constantly battle the realities of the present.

Besides, in her own way, Caroljoy had made it all possible.

Yet Constanza had some of the same iron strength.

He shook his head slowly as he watched the screen.

He watched. Watched and waited for the seeds of the house tree. Watched and listened to the beginnings of a society and an Empire crashing into anarchy.

THE PILOT TAPPED the last control stud of the sequence and dropped his hand, which was beginning to tremble.

He wanted to shake his head, but, instead, laid back on the black yield cloth of the control couch while the modified scout shivered . . . and jumped.

At the instant of jump, as always, the blackness inundated the scout, blinding the pilot with the darkness no light could penetrate, then disappearing as the ship reappeared tens of systems from where it had jumped.

Gerswin reached out tiredly and touched the control stud that would recompute the *Caroljoy*'s position. He could have asked the AI to do it, but even as exhausted as he was he still hated to ask the AI to do what he felt the pilot should.

He could feel his hand shake, and he compromised.

"Position. Interrogative possible jump parameters."

His voice even shook, and he wanted to scream at the weakness. His eyes flickered down at his right arm, where the slight thickness under the long sleeved tunic indicated a pressure-tight medpad. The ship's medical system had assured him there was no infection. He was just tired—totally exhausted from fighting off the effects of the nerve poison.

Constanza had questioned whether he was up to leaving, especially to handling a long flight, but he had insisted, not wanting to wait until there might be an Imperial quarantine force in place or until some faction of the Byzanian Armed Forces happened onto his ship, particularly given the shortness of his power reserves.

Now there was nothing he could do but finish the trip.

"Position at two seven five relative, distance two point five, inclination point seven. Ship is in opposition," the AI announced in its professional and impersonally feminine voice.

"Interrogative short jump. Power parameters."

"Short jump possible. Depletion of reserves to point five. Interface probability is less than point zero zero nine. Power consumption will leave ship with three point five plus stans at norm, plus half reserves."

"Jump."

"Commencing jump."

This time he let the AI handle the jump, with the milliseconds of apparent jump time so short he scarcely noticed them.

"Time to Aswan?"

"Two plus at norm."

"Normal acceleration. Notify, full alarm, if *anything* approaches the ship or if any anomalies appear."

The odds were that he'd hear the alarm at least three times before they hit orbit distance, but he obviously wasn't up to watching himself.

Four alarms later, the *Caroljoy* was in orbit, ready for planetdrop over the planet he called Aswan.

None of the alarms had amounted to anything besides debris, not that Gerswin had expected them to, since the system was out of the way, to say the least.

Aswan was the fourth planet, and the one of two that orbited the G-2 sun in the "life zone." The third planet of the relatively young system might develop intelligent life someday, unless it already had, but without overt signs of such development. Gerswin doubted it, but since no one had intensively scouted the surface, who could say?

The fourth planet, Aswan itself, offered a different dilemma. Certainly some intelligent life had built the wall of white stone across the flat plain of the perhaps once-upon-a-time ocean. Bridge? Dam? Who could say?

With no moons other than tiny and captured asteroids, and a thin atmosphere mainly of nitrogen, Aswan was not on anyone's list of places to visit. But someone or something had indeed built a bridgelike structure nearly two thousand kays long, straight as an arrow, running from northwest to southeast, or, if one preferred, from southeast to northwest. The bridge was clearly visible from orbit against the maroon dirt/dust/crystal that covered most of the planet, the two-thirds that was not out-and-out rock.

While the dam, as Gerswin mentally identified it, rose out of the maroon crystalline to a height of nearly one kay, the high point was not at either end, nor in the center, but two-thirds of the way from the southeast toward the northwest end. As if to balance, in a strange way, one-third of the way from that southeast end, connected to the dam, rose a four-sided diamond-shaped tower—provided a set of unroofed walls rising more than three hundred meters skyward above the level of the dam itself could be called a tower.

The tower itself was roughly two kays on a side, while the dam was only four hundred meters wide.

The stones which composed both dam and tower seemed identical for their entire length. Identical and huge—each as large as the *Caroljoy* and each a glistening white shot through with streaks of black.

When he had first scouted Aswan, he had taken scans and samples for analysis. Granite, that had been what the geologists at Palmyra had said, but a variety they had never seen, with an internal structure that suggested tremendous building properties.

Gerswin had refrained from laughing.

The samples he had obtained by trimming the interior of the tower. He had found no stone unattached to the dam or tower. None.

The flush-fitted top layer of stones made touchdowns and take-offs easy, with nearly as much ground effect as on Old Earth.

The pilot shook himself out of his reverie and began the descent that would take him to the base he had built within the tower, the core of which was the atmospheric power tap system, which had cost enough, but which produced power in abundance, in more than abundance.

"Descent beyond limits," advised the AI.

Gerswin shook himself and made the corrections, forcing alertness until the *Caroljoy* was settled next to the power tap connection.

Slowly, slowly, he unstrapped, and pulled on the respirator pack and helmet, dragging himself to the lock.

Once the ship was connected to the power system, he could and would gratefully collapse.

The cable system was bulky, obsolete, but relatively foolproof, and did not require constant monitoring, unlike the direct laser transfer systems used by most ports, and particularly by deep-space installations.

"Still," he muttered, under his breath and behind his respirator, as he touched the transfer stud to begin the repowering operation, "what isn't obsolete? You? The ship? Your self-appointed mission?"

He licked his upper lip.

"Who cares about Old Earth? Do all the Recorps types really want the reclamation effort to end? Will anyone really remember the devilkids and the blood they spent on a forgotten planet?"

He snorted. The thought occurred to him that, if by some remote chance, his biologics actually worked, that he would be the one in the legends and the devilkids who had made it possible would be the forgotten ones.

As if that would ever happen!

He glanced at the white stone rising overhead into the maroon twilight, stone that seemed to retain the light long past twilight, though that retained light never registered on the ship's screens.

He sighed, shook his head again, and trudged back to the ramp up to the *Caroljoy*, up to swallow ship's concentrates and water, up to sleep, and to heal.

XII

LIKE THE PIECES of a puzzle snapping together, the fragmented ideas that had been swirling around in the commodore's head clicked into place as a clear picture.

He shook his head wearily.

So simple, so obvious. So obvious that he and everyone else except, perhaps, the Eye Service had overlooked it. No wonder the Intelligence Service had not acted against him. No wonder the majority of the biologic innovations developed by the foundation had gone nowhere except when he had pushed and developed them. And he had thought the ideas had been accepted on their own merit!

It might work to his own benefit, and to the benefit of the foundation and Old Earth. It might—provided he could lay the groundwork before the Empire understood what he was doing. Once they understood . . .

He paced around the circular table on the enclosed balcony, stopping to look across the valley, over the black of the lake toward the chalet under construction on the high hill opposite his own retreat. That other chalet would be needed soon, he expected, sooner than he had anticipated.

He smiled in spite of himself, before resuming his pacing, as he considered what to do next.

"Profit isn't enough. It never has been. Profit only motivates those who lead."

That wasn't the whole problem. How could you motivate people toward self-sufficiency when the technology was regarded as magic by most, when few understood the oncoming collapse when the power limit was reached? Not that there had to be a power limit, but the current technologic and government systems made it almost inevitable.

He halted and looked down at the small console he had not used, a console built into the simple wooden lines of the table, a console with a blank screen still waiting for input.

Smiling briefly, he tapped the stud to shut down the system.

"Since the political leaders follow the people, and the people follow the true believers, that means they need some new true believers to follow."

The commodore in the gray silk-sheen tunic and trousers that looked so simple yet could be afforded by only the richest pursed his lips as he began to plot the revolution.

XIII

THE GANGLY MAN with the alternate braids of blond and silver hair squirmed in the hard chair, shifting his weight as he reread the oblong card once more.

He studied the cryptic note attached to it yet again, trying to puzzle out what lay behind it.

What would you do with the grant you requested? Be specific. Be at my office on the 20th of Octe to explain. Call for appointment.

S

The card was stiff, formal, and nearly antique stationery, with a single name embossed in the upper left-hand corner. The name? Patron L. Sergio Enver.

The man with the blond and silver braids frowned. He'd assumed that Enver was related to the commercial baron Enver who had founded Enver Enterprises. Certainly the local Enver office had been accommodating when he had faxed for confirmation.

"Yes, Ser Willgel. You are on the patron's calendar. At 1000." That was all they had said, as if that had explained everything. Either that, or they did not know any more than he did, which made the matter more mysterious than ever, particularly since he had never expected a response from the routine inquiry he had made of a number of newer enterprises.

Because the Appropriate Technology Institute was five small rooms in the back of a rented warehouse, Willes Willgel had arrived early and sat waiting for the mysterious Patron Enver.

He checked the time. One standard minute until his appointment, not that promptness meant anything to the commercial barons. Willgel knew he could be waiting hours after his scheduled time, and he dared not complain. He was the one asking for funding.

The former professor sighed, aware as he exhaled of how thin he had gotten, of how baggy his tunic felt.

"Ser Willgel? Would you come this way?" A stocky woman stood by a closed portal.

Willgel leapt to his feet, then swallowed a curse at his own eagerness, and forced himself to walk slowly the four meters to the portal. He frowned, and tried to wipe it away, but failed. He worried more about the promptness of the patron than if he had been summoned later.

"Unless the patron asks you to remain, you have ten standard minutes. Do you understand?"

Willgel nodded. "I will do my best."

"Go ahead. He's waiting." The dark-haired greeter did not return the nervous smile that finally came to Willgel's lips, but gestured toward the opening portal.

Willgel crossed through the gateway and into the office in three strides, head bobbing from side to side on a too-long neck as he tried to take in everything.

The office was large, but not imposing. The wall to his left was covered with a blue-black fabric on which was reproduced a night sky which Willgel had never seen before, from a system farther out in the galaxy, apparently, where the stars were more widely scattered. The ceiling was a faintly glowing gold, while the sheer gold curtains covered the full-wall windows to his right and directly before him. Standing straight in front of him was a smallish man, with tight-curled silver-gray hair and yellow eyes.

Beside him stood two modernistic armchairs, and behind the patron was a combination desk and console, where all surfaces were covered with a tight-grained ebony wood.

"Sergio Enver," offered the patron. "Have a seat, Ser Willgel."

His voice, while a light baritone, filled the office.

Willgel sat.

Enver did not. He stepped back until he was leaning against the wooden desk, a functional piece with no apparent projections besides the console itself.

"Your proposition did not explain what you meant by 'appropriate' technology. How would you define it?"

"That is probably the most difficult challenge the Institute faces, Patron—"

"Harder than fund-raising?" asked the baron, lips quirking.

"Others raise funds easily. I, obviously, do not. But no one has really defined what technologies are appropriate to man, or to society, or whether differing societies should seek differing levels of technology, and what those levels should be.

"Put that way, what are the parameters of an appropriate technology?"

Willgel swallowed. "I'll try to be as succinct as possible. As you know, Patron, man's drive for more and better technology lies far back in history. Underneath that drive is the unspoken assumption that more technology is better and that improved technology will result in a better life for mankind. The problem with applying technology broadscale is that the benefits are uneven. Mass production of communications consoles may improve people's lives by allowing them more freedom in how and where they work and live. Use of technology in agriculture to concentrate control of production in the hands of a few at a cost which prevents competition allows economic control by a small elite. A standardized communications network allows a richer cultural life, but reinforces the possibility of social control by a few."

"Wait." The patron held up his hand. "Generalizations address no real problems. You have also not defined what you mean as 'better.' Is 'more appropriate' better? Why do you think that certain types or applications of technology are better or more appropriate than others?"

Willgel licked his lips, then licked them again. Outside of the fact that Enver was generally linked into biologic technologies and was a major agricultural supplier, he really hadn't been able to determine what the patron's economic interests were.

"I take it that your need for funding is warring with your ethics," observed the commercial magnate dryly. "If you don't wish to offend me, you might consider that intellectual dishonesty offends me more than attacks on my income or products."

Willgel swallowed again. "I see, Patron."

"Do you? I wonder. Go ahead, Professor, and try to get to the point."

Willgel coughed.

"As you suggested, I was leading to the question of appropriateness. 'Better' and 'appropriate' are tied together, because both are value judgments. Personally, I find that a technology or a use of technology that increases individual freedom is better than one that restricts it. A technology that radically decreases liberty, even if it reduces costs of products, is not."

"Aren't those definitions arbitrary?" asked the patron. "You are stating that decentralization and greater freedom are 'better' than centralization and a possibly higher standard of living. What about interstellar travel? What about the need for defense against outsiders?

What about the great cramped artistic communities of the past? What about the still unsurpassed technology of crowded Old Earth?"

"Perhaps I am arbitrary," answered Willgel with a shrug that ignored the perspiration beading on his forehead. "The problem with larger and more concentrated societies, Patron, is that they require increasingly more complicated social codes or laws, or both, and more social restrictions, to maintain order and to avoid violence. Human beings are distressingly prone to violence and disorder. Further, increasingly concentrated societies create concentrated wastes. Higher technology can support more humans in a smaller area, which spawns a greater and more toxic waste problem, which requires, in turn, a higher level of technology to handle. And for what purpose?"

The scholar plunged on. "While you can argue that the creation of jumpships requires high technology, and that interstellar society requires the communications they supply, it is harder to argue that low population societies like Barcelon really require the centralized control of agriculture and communications for either order or food. History has shown that a moderate number of privately owned agricultural enterprises is normally more successful than large and highly concentrated ones. History has also shown that centralized, but nongovernment communications systems are more successful—both in terms of maintaining freedom and lower costs—than are government monopolies or the anarchy of small competitors. If you will, there is a level and a type of technology ideally appropriate to each human culture or subculture. Our mission is to define what those types and levels might be, along with the ramifications."

Willgel paused to catch his breath, then waited as he watched Sergio Enver nod.

"What happens if your Institute declares that the current use of technology on Barcelon amounts to totalitarian slavery and the Barcelon government protests to the Empire? Or if you declare that the Imperial policy of using synthetics is creating a totally inappropriate toxic waste problem that is diverting unnecessary energy resources for ongoing cleanup? What if the Empire decides to ban your publications?"

Willgel smiled. "We are a long ways from either. First, we must study the energy and personnel parameters for critical technologies, balance the input and output against the wastes and other diseconomies, and then pinpoint areas of diminishing returns, where the use of more high technology may not produce commensurate benefits."

"Diminishing returns? A jumpship is certainly an example of diminishing returns for a small system. But I wouldn't advocate doing away with them."

"No. But you would not advocate building millions, either, I suspect."

Abruptly, Enver straightened and stood away from the desk/console combination.

"There are a considerable number of fallacies in your reasoning, Ser Willgel, as well as monumental naivete in the implications of what you propose. I have neither the time nor energy to disabuse you of the fallacies, nor to better inform you on some hard realities."

Willgel could feel his face fall.

"But the core of your reasoning is sound. So is the Institute, although I would suggest that you need some solid crusaders and true believers to spread the word. Pick up your draft authorization on the way out. And, Ser Willgel," added Enver as he walked around the console.

"Yes?"

"Make sure you not only do those studies, but that you publish them. Circulate them, and—I shouldn't have to tell a former professor—get as much of the academic community involved as possible. A good idea circulated and discussed in the schools is worth a million brilliant ones buried in the archives. Good day."

Willgel shook his head and turned. Such a brief discussion, if he could call it that. Enver had given him the impression that the patron had already considered much of what was only speculation on Willgel's part. Willgel shivered.

The portal closed behind him as he stood in the dimmer green confines of the outer office once more.

"Ser Willgel?"

"Yes?"

"Your authorization."

Willgel walked to the console where the stocky woman sat. She handed him a single sheet.

He took it and read it. Then he read it a second time, and a third before he lowered it.

One hundred thousand creds! For one year. One year. Renewable at two hundred thousand for a second if published standards and educational efforts met the technical standards of the patron.

Willgel didn't pretend to understand. For whatever obscure reasons he might have, Patron L. Sergio Enver had decided that there should be a strong Appropriate Technology Institute, one with technical excellence and a strong outreach program.

Willgel let himself smile as he held the authorization. Technical excellence and outreach—backed by sound reasoning. Enver had made it all too clear that he wouldn't stand for studies or reports that said nothing, or for fuzzy definitions.

The former professor wondered whether the baron fully understood what such an Institute was capable of, given time and some financial support.

His stride lengthened as he marched down the corridor to the public tube train that would take him back to the warehouse and his budding Institute.

THE HEAVYSET PROFESSOR trudged from the entry portal into the small sitting room that opened onto the high balcony overlooking the University Lake.

"Who . . . who . . ." Her mouth grasped at the words as she saw the curly-haired man sitting in the recliner, sipping from one of her antique wine glasses.

"Professor Dorso, I believe."

"Uh . . . who . . . what are you doing in my home?"

"I apologize for the intrusion." His voice was light, but compelling, and his hawk-yellow eyes glimmered in the twilight dimness. "I've come to collect."

"Collect? What in Hades are you referring to?"

"Roughly twenty years ago, you accepted a modest grant from the OER Foundation. In return, you promised to develop a certain line of biologics based on your published works, and to hold that material until called for, up to fifty standard years, if necessary. I have come to collect."

The professor collapsed into the other chair with a plumping sound, the synthetic leather squeaking under her bulk.

"My god! My god!"

"Did you develop what you promised?" The man's tone was neutral.

"I . . . worked . . . just took the drafts . . . never questioned . . . but no one ever came . . . wondered if anyone ever cared."

He had stood so quickly she had missed the motion, so quickly she had to repress a shudder and failed. Taking a deep breath, then another, she could smell an acrid odor, a bitter smell, a scent of fear. Her fear.

"Did you ever attempt the work?"

She began to laugh, and the high-pitched tone echoed from one side of the room to the other.

Crack!

The side of her face felt numb from the impact of his hand.

She stared up at the slender man. For some reason, her eyes tried to slide away from his body, and she had to concentrate on his face. Hawk-yellow eyes, short and curly blond hair, sharp nose, a chin neither pointed nor square, but somewhere in between—he could have been either an avenging angel or a demon prince. Or both at once.

"I did what I promised." Her voice was dull. "You don't know what it cost. You couldn't possibly understand. Don't you see? If I had failed . . . if I had died . . . but I didn't. I was right . . . and I couldn't tell anyone."

His face softened without losing its alertness. "You will be able to. Before too long. Wish I could have come sooner. All of us pay certain prices. All of us."

"How soon? When?" wheezed the professor as she struggled to sit upright.

He handed her a thin folder. "Study these specifications. I would like to have your spores packaged that way."

He held up his hand to forestall her objections before she could voice them.

"The fabrication group you are to use is listed on one of the sheets. I have already set up a line of credit for your use. Your authorization is included, and I will confirm that tomorrow.

"I want it done right. That's why you're in charge. That was also in your contract."

The woman sank back into her recliner, her eyes half-glassy.

The stranger turned and gazed out at the now-black waters of the University Lake, beyond the dim lights of the balcony, where the twilight submerged into the clouded start of night itself.

After a moment, he touched the panel. The armaglass door slid open, and a hint of a breeze wafted in, nearly scentless, except for the trace of water hyacinths underlying the cool air.

"Shocks . . . we all get them," he mused. "Things are not what they seem. Memories from the past appear as real people. People who were real disappear as if they never existed. Work overlooked becomes critical after it seems forgotten . . ."

Abruptly he turned and stepped back before her.

"Look at the last sheet."

"I can't see it."

He laughed, a harsh bark, and touched the light panel, watching as the illumination flooded the room, as she fumbled with the sheets from the folder.

"Oh . . . oh . . . that much! Why?"

"Look at the date."

"Five weeks from now? After twenty years?"

"That's for payment for your work, for your supervision in building the equipment. Turn it over."

The professor slowly turned over the uncounterfeitable credit voucher drawn on Halsie-Vyr. The amount represented ten years' salary. On the reverse was a short inscription.

She read it once, then again.

"I can? I really could?"

He smiled, faintly, understanding that the recognition would be worth more than the massive credit balance she would receive.

"The actual release form is also in the packet. If you complete the work on schedule, you will be able to publish your work immediately, including all the earlier research results, and the ATI Foundation will undertake its wide-scale distribution."

Her hands trembled as she methodically went through the sheaves of sheets, looking for the single release form, finally pulling it out, checking the authentications. Her dark brown eyes flickered from the certificate to the stranger and back to the certificate. Back and forth.

He turned again to the lake and beheld the darkness surrounded by the lights of the University Towers. Where the waters were clear of the hyacinths, reflections of the lights twinkled like the stars hidden above the clouds.

"Who are you?" Now her high voice was steady.

"I am who I am, Professor. No more and no less." He did not turn away from his view of the darkness and the reflected lights in the black waters beneath the balcony.

"You won't tell me."

"No. Except that I represent the foundation. That's what counts. That and the fact that your work will be spread throughout the galaxy. It will be. My purposes are more immediate and selfish."

She pursed her lips, and her brow wrinkled, as if she were trying to remember something.

"Even so, it can't be that quick."

"I know. And we should have recognized the value of what you did earlier. At least we have now."

He turned back and faced her, looking down as if from an immeasurable height.

"The packet tells you where the packaged materials should be delivered." He frowned, as if debating with himself. "Would you be interested in other biologically related research? Completing some unfinished projects from notes, fragmentary materials?"

"That would depend."

"The conditions would be the same. Not that way," he interrupted himself. "All results could be released within a year of completion, whether or not it was picked up or used. Each project would be separately compensated, and well."

"Provided that I could start my own organization, with independent facilities, I would be very interested."

"How much?"

"I don't know."

"If you're interested, work up a proposal. Send it to the foundation. Probably be accepted. Plenty of work."

"Who are you?" she asked again.

"I'd rather not say. Just a man with a job to do, and one running out of time." His lips quirked before he resumed. "Once the applicators are finished, this job is done. If you really are interested in doing more work, send that proposal. If you do, I may see you again."

"May?"

As she opened her mouth to ask the last question, the slender man had already turned and slipped toward the portal.

"Good night, Professor," he called as the portal closed behind him.

Slowly, slowly, the woman stood, placing the folder on the table by the recliner, and looking down at the maroon-bordered patterns of the threadbare, but irreplaceable, ancient carpet.

Leaving the folder on the table, she took four long steps to the open door onto her railed balcony. She stood there, the light wind pushing her short brown hair back away from her ears, watching the muddled lights reflected from the blackness of the lake.

After a time, she sighed and turned back to pick up the material laid upon the table. She left the door gaping wide, remembering the feel of the wind in her hair, remembering the stranger beholding the lake as if it were a treasure.

"SER WADRUP?"

Hein Wadrup raised his slightly glazed eyes to the brown uniform of the guard, not bothering to offer a response.

"Ser Wadrup, your counsel has posted the necessary bond." The guard's magnetic keypass buzzed as he touched it to the lock. The door swung open.

Wadrup frowned.

"I don't have a counsel. Don't have the funds for one. What kind of joke is this? Another one of your 'build-his-hopes-up specials'?"

"No joke, Ser Wadrup. You make the jokes, it seems. Ser Villinnil himself posted the bond, and that one—he never works on good faith."

Wadrup struggled off the flat pallet, his legs still rubbery from the going-over he had received from the guards the day before.

The sharp-nosed guard, a man Wadrup had never seen before, turned and led the way down the block.

None of the other prisoners, one each to the uniform cells, two meters by three meters, even looked up.

From what the former graduate student could tell, the guard was retracing the same route along which he had been dragged two weeks earlier.

By the time Wadrup had traversed the less than seventy-five meters to the orderly room, he was breathing heavily.

"That Wadrup?" asked the woman sentry stationed in the riot box outside the armored portal to the orderly room.

"That's him."

"Ser Wadrup, please enter the portal."

Wadrup paused. Either it was a subterfuge to get him to walk to his own execution, or he was being freed. He looked at the guard who had fetched him, standing ready with a stunner, and the sentry with a blastcone. Finally, he shrugged and stepped through.

The portal hissed shut behind him, and for the first time in two weeks, he was away from the cold black of the plasteel bars and flat floor pallets.

In the orderly room stood two men—a booking corporal of the

Planetary Police accompanied by a heavyset local wearing a gold-banded travel cloak and a privacy mask.

"Ser Wadrup?" asked the anonymous civilian.

"The same."

"Could you trouble yourself to tell me the title of your unpublished article on the role of agriculture and government?"

Shaky as his legs felt, Wadrup almost grinned, but as quickly as the hope rose, he pushed it aside.

"I beg your pardon, but do you mean the last one submitted for publication, or the one rejected by the Aljarrad Press, to which I may owe my present residence?"

"Whichever one you sent to one Professor Stilchio."

Wadrup wanted to scratch his scraggly beard and squint under the unaccustomed brightness of the lights.

"Oh, that one. That didn't have a title, because it was submitted for the 'Outspeak' column, but the subheading was 'Prosperity Without Force.' The other one was titled—"

"That will do." The civilian turned to the police corporal. "I'll accept. Direct all further communications from the Court to my office. The bond is standard, nonrefundable if the charges are dropped."

"Your print, honored counselor?"

"Certainly. Here is my card, and the verification of the credited bond deposit."

Wadrup squinted again, fighting dizziness, trying to hold his vision in focus.

The civilian counselor turned.

"Ser Wadrup, if you can manage another fifty meters, my electrocar is waiting for us . . ."

"I'll manage."

Wadrup followed the heavier man through another portal and down another corridor, passing Planetary Police as they went. A third portal opened into the main lobby of the University Police Station, from where the police insured order for the complex that included five colleges and three universities. There were no others on Barcelon, and the reasons for such centralization had become clear to Hein Wadrup only after he had been picked up after trying to obtain forged working papers necessary to get a job to raise the funds necessary to leave Barcelon.

Outside the station stood a squarish, high-status electrocar, shining black. The rear door was being held open by a narrow-faced and well-muscled woman in a tight-fitting olive uniform.

Wadrup collapsed through the opening and onto the soft seat.

Almost immediately, the door shut, and the car began to move, smoothly, but with increasing speed.

Wadrup relaxed, too exhausted to hold on to consciousness.

"Wadrup!"

"Just carry him. Get him to the flitter."

The former student could feel himself being half carried, half lifted out of the car and through the dampness he had come to associate with Barcelon.

Hands strapped him to some sort of seat, and beneath him, he could hear the whine of turbines.

Again he lost consciousness.

When he woke, he could feel the stillness around him, broken only by the faint hiss of a ventilation system.

"Passenger is awake."

"Thanks."

"Passenger?" he blurted, even as he tried to sit up in the narrow bunk into which he was strapped.

"Just lie there. Nothing wrong with you that rest, food, and a good physical conditioning course won't solve."

Wadrup turned toward the voice, but his eyes refused to focus on the blackness that seemed to speak.

"Don't worry about your vision. You can't see me. Partly for your protection, but mostly for mine."

"I am obviously in your debt, whoever you are, but would you care to offer any explanation?"

"Let us say that there are few enough people around with the capability to think, and it would be a pity if the iron-fisted government of Barcelon or any other water-empire system wasted that ability."

"You want something."

"Yes, but not anything with which you would disagree."

"Are you going to explain?"

"Shortly, but take a sip of this first."

"Drugs?"

"No. High sustenance broth. Want you thinking more clearly."

Wadrup watched as what seemed an arm of darkness touched the underside of the bunk, and the harness released. He sat up and took the cup of broth, half-amused that he could not see his benefactor, even while the man stood nearly beside him. From the light baritone timbre of the voice, he assumed that the speaker was male, but who could be sure? Who could be sure of anything these days?

He sipped the broth slowly.

"Be back in a moment. Please stay where you are."

The graduate student found he could drink less than half the liquid, so shrunken was his stomach. Holding the cup, he surveyed his quarters.

The bunk where he sat propped up was set into metal walls. Across the room to his left was another metal wall, punctuated with a closed and narrow doorway, four lockers, and two sets of four drawers built into the wall. The actual floor space measured less than three by four meters, perhaps as little as two and a half by three. The metallic ceiling was slightly more than two meters overhead.

In the middle of the bulkhead which ran from the foot of the bunk to the wall with the lockers was a squared archway into another compartment, but from the bunk all that Wadrup could see was another indistinct metallic wall, lost in the dimmer light of the adjoining room.

Wadrup puffed out his cheeks in puzzlement. He was missing something obvious. He squinted and lifted the broth to his lips, taking another sip and slow swallow.

"Feeling better?"

"What can I call you? Ser Blackness? I don't like not being able to see people."

"Well . . . you could use Blackness, or Hermer. That's not my name, but it means something to me without meaning anything to you."

"All right, Ser . . . Hermer. You posted a fifty-thousand-credit bond. You didn't do it for nothing. What do you want?"

"It was a hundred thousand, all told. Fifty for you. Forty for Villinnil, and ten to bribe the police. That's the beginning."

"Beginning?"

"Beginning. You need a new name, identity, prints, and enough financial backing to continue your work."

"But what do you want?"

"For you to do what you've been doing. But with more understanding and a little more common sense. You've been acting like most student radicals, assuming you were half playacting, half gadfly."

Wadrup sighed.

"I'm lost. Really lost. Could you start at the beginning?"

"Suppose so. We've got another five hours."

"Until when?" The question was out of Wadrup's mouth before he understood what had been nagging him. The room where he was recovering looked like the crew room of an antique scout, the sort of thing that might have come from the early days of the Empire, or even from the federation.

"Where are you taking me?" Wadrup demanded.

"For some rest and, after that, wherever we decide."

"Who's we?"

"You and I."

Wadrup sighed. "Questions aren't getting me anywhere. Why don't you start at the beginning?"

The unfocused black figure pulled up a ship chair and sat down across from Wadrup, who could see now that the man wore a black privacy mask over his face, and that the mask was the only feature that seemed to stay in focus.

"Too complicated. Let me start another way. With a series of questions. Let me ask them all. Don't try to answer.

"First, are there any truly powerful systems which do not produce an agricultural surplus? Second, could any system operate a centralized control of the economy and a large armed forces without control of the communications network and the food supply? Third, why is the Empire discouraging the biological and technical development of what might be called appropriate technology? Fourth, doesn't the use of centralized resources for local agriculture and communications actually reduce the energy and resources available for interstellar communications and travel? Fifth, hasn't history proven that State control is the least effective in maximizing resources for the overall benefit of the people?"

Wadrup took another sip of the broth before clearing his throat.

"I agree with you . . . I think, but aren't you assuming a great deal?"

"You will have a chance to make that evaluation firsthand. Assume for purposes of discussion that the Empire has resisted biological innovations. Assume that at least one system has attempted to destroy a tree genetically programmed to grow itself into an inexpensive house. Assume that someone has rediscovered the earth-forming techniques of Old Earth that created the biospheres of many Imperial systems, and that the Empire will shortly be hunting those techniques down."

"Ser Hermer, assuming that such farfetched things have or will happen is asking a great deal, even in view of my deep gratitude for your actions."

"Ser Wadrup. Think. You were imprisoned because you wrote a rather mild series of papers suggesting that war was not possible without the control of agriculture, that social control is linked to central control of the food supply, and that throughout history the people have been better fed when government refrained from meddling with agriculture and other forms of food production.

"Correct me if my reasoning is faulty, Ser Wadrup, but if you were wildly incorrect, why would anyone have bothered with you? Why would the government of Barcelon decide to spend hundreds of personnel hours chasing you long after you had stopped speaking publicly or writing? For no reason at all?"

"They jail people for no reason at all."

"How many students do you know who disappeared?"

"Plenty."

"How many? Name more than ten. You can't. Consistently, about ten students a year are jailed . . . or disappear. You were one of the ten. On a mere whim?"

"But no one paid any attention to my papers or speeches."

"That's right. And as soon as it looked like someone might, you were jailed."

Wadrup finished the broth and placed the cup on the ledge behind the bunk.

"So, Ser Hermer, what do you want?"

"I want you to found the 'Free Hein Wadrup Society.'"

"What?"

"You disappeared on Barcelon. Your body has never been found. There is no record of your leaving the system. The Barcelon government will deny it, but cannot prove you were not disposed of. The last record of your existence that was open to public verification was your time in jail. If the Barcelon government denies your death, it will seem as though they lie. If they say nothing, they can be charged with ignoring their own unpleasant actions."

"But it's suicide to go back to Barcelon, even with a new identity."

"Who said you were going back? You'll tour the systems that permit free speech, ostensibly agitating for the release of Hein Wadrup, telling why the Barcelon government has secretly imprisoned poor Hein Wadrup. Because they're totalitarian despots who control their planet through their control of the food supply. You will praise, faintly, more enlightened planets, while saying that it's still too bad that there isn't a better way to produce quality food for people."

"That's all you want?"

"Ser Wadrup, it seems a great deal to me. You give up your name, your family. You give up any fixed home for years to come. In return,

I supply the necessary funding and the factual information to supplement what you already know."

"Hardly a great loss for me. My family is still working in the pump
works on New Glascow, and I haven't been home in nearly ten years.
I never had enough money to concentrate on what I believe in."
Wadrup paused. "I'm not sure I like the charade of freeing myself."

"If you have a better way of getting the message across without
ending up in prison again, I'm willing to listen." The man in black
stood. "I'll be back in a moment."

Wadrup listened. He could hear another voice, impersonally feminine, cool, clear, nearly icy. He shivered. Compared to that tone, the
man in black seemed to radiate heat.

"Interception course. Probability approaches point seven."

"Lift one radian. See what they do."

"Lifting one."

Wadrup wondered who the pilot was, if she were the narrow-
faced cold woman who had acted as the guard for the counsel who
had secured his release.

"Ser Wadrup. Some evasive action is necessary." The black-clad
man returned, reached across Wadrup, and took the empty cup,
placing it in one of the wall receptacles. He returned to the graduate
student.

"Please straighten yourself. Like this."

Wadrup found the harness around himself again.

"For your own safety, no matter what happens, do not try to release the harness. Your success in doing so could guarantee your own
death."

The unknown man disappeared again.

Wadrup listened, not moving, but straining to make out the conversation between the pilot and his captor/rescuer.

"Interrogative time to jump."

"One point one."

"Margin for jump in five minutes."

"Less than point eight."

"Not worth it. Intercept probability?"

"Point nine without evasion."

"Intercept probability with evasion within standard stress envelope?"

"Point five."

"Probability within personal envelope?"

"Imprecise inquiry."

"Intercept probability with evasion maneuvers within pilot's personal stress envelope."

"Less than point zero five."

Wadrup heard a clicking, realized that someone was strapping into a harness.

"Commence evasion."

An invisible piston crushed Wadrup into the bunk, squeezing, squeezing, until he felt the darkness rush over him.

Time passed. How much he did not know as he drifted between sleep, unconsciousness, pressures, and a half daze.

Then, once more, he could hear the inhumanly clear voice of the pilot before he was fully alert.

"Passenger is awake."

"Monitor. Interrogative time to jump."

"Three point five minutes."

"Screens?"

"Negative on screens. Patroller is at one point three."

"That's beyond range."

"Affirmative. Tentatively identified as class two."

"Probability of identification is climbing, isn't it?"

"Please clarify."

"Fewer patrollers, but more seem to be looking for us. Can you verify or offer statistics?"

"Statistically unverifiable. Variables too extensive. Gross number of patroller contacts up ten percent in last five standard years."

"Must be my imagination. Here we go."

The room turned simultaneously black and white around Wadrup, and he felt as though an electric shock had passed through his body. The moment of jump lasted no time at all, even while that instant of timelessness stretched and stretched.

Another shock, another white and black flash, and the crew room returned to its familiar metallic coloration.

"How far out are we?"

"Estimate three plus hours to orbit. Screens clear."

"Call me if anything shows, or if any abnormality reaches point zero five on the anomaly index."

"Stet. Will alert at point zero five on the anomaly index."

Wadrup turned his head toward the whispering sound of light-footed boots and watched as the shadowy black figure swept into the crew room.

"Sorry for the delay, Ser Wadrup."

Snick.

Wadrup stretched as he shrugged himself loose from the webbing of the restraint harness.

"Who are you?" Wadrup asked.

The other shook his masked head. Despite the fuzziness of the image the man in black presented, by looking from the corners of his eyes, the graduate student could get a better idea of the general motions of the man.

"All right. What are you?" Wadrup rephrased the question.

"You could call me a man with a mission. Won't tell you the mission except to say that the present attitude of the Empire, its systems, and those across the Arm threatens that mission. That's where you come in. You and a few others have been recruited to speak out, to give the people some ideas and some hope. If you will, to get the next generation's opinion leaders to think. To be receptive to change. That's what I hope."

"Nothing small, I see. Merely to change the thought patterns of millions in tens or hundreds of systems."

"No. Nothing small. But we have some time. Time and the fact that we are right."

This time Wadrup shook his head. He still knew next to nothing. Or did he?

Ignoring the black-clad figure across from him, Hein Wadrup added up what he knew.

The man was wealthy, wealthy enough to own and equip a high-speed scout as a personal yacht. He was not interested in personal luxury. He was able to find people like Hein Wadrup for his own purposes, which meant some sort of organization. He was opposed by at least some system governments, and he did not want Hein to see his face, which meant he was not totally unknown.

He couldn't be too old, because he wouldn't be able to accept high-acceleration evasive maneuvers, and his tolerances were higher than Hein's. He was also totally at home in the small ship, which meant a great deal of experience.

Wadrup frowned, shifted his weight, and dived at the man, hands reaching for the privacy mask.

Thud!

Wadrup sprawled on the deck. Before he could shake his head to clear it, he could feel the man's hands lifting him back onto the bunk, hands that conveyed the feeling of immense strength. Yet the man was obviously shorter and more slender than Wadrup.

"Ser Wadrup, even in your best condition, you would find your moves inadequate." He laughed, a single harsh bark. "Are you inter-

ested in my proposition? Or would you rather that I drop you off at
the next port?"

"Next port?"

"New Avalon. I will supply the transportation free, but, of course,
I could not bring your passport and universal ID, for reasons we both
understand."

"That's blackmail!"

"No. On New Avalon you would be perfectly free to stay. The
Monarchy does not allow extradition. You would be safe, also, since
they do not permit foreign agents."

"But I'd be stuck!"

"Ser Wadrup, I rescued you at great cost, with some risk, trans-
ported you to a place of safety, and am willing to let you go without
any strings. I offered you a simple business proposition. You may accept or refuse. In any case, you are alive and free, and you would be
neither by now had you stayed under the care of the authorities of
Barcelon."

Wadrup bit his lip. He couldn't deny any of it.

"I'll have to think about it."

"I want a totally free decision. I will be here on New Avalon for
several days. In the meantime, I will give you, say, one hundred credits. If you are interested in the proposition I made, contact me
through the port. I will be registered under the name of DeCorso. If
not, consider yourself a fortunate young man."

Wadrup frowned.

"In the meantime, I have some things to do. Please remain here.
The narrow doorway across from you contains a small but adequate
fresher, which you may use.

"The second locker contains those belongings of yours Ser
Villinnil's staff were able to locate, including some clean clothes."

Wadrup looked up to see him passing through the archway and
stopping to touch something. A flat metal wall extended from the
archway, turning the crew room into a well-equipped cell.

"Strange . . . strange . . ."

The thought of getting clean again overruled more intellectual
considerations, and he headed for the fresher. He'd have to give the
stranger's proposition a fair evaluation, but not for a while, maybe not
until he had the chance to see the situation on New Avalon.

"TELL ME AGAIN." Baron Megalrie's voice dropped to the soft silkiness that was a telltale warning to those who knew him.

The Vice President of Marketing knew the tone also.

"Yes, Baron. We cannot meet the competition. Bestmeat—that is the firm—is selling to the restaurant distributors and the food centers for twenty percent less than we are."

"Our markup is more than twenty percent," observed the Baron in the same silky tone, looking pointedly at the real wood of the conference table, then brushing an imaginary speck from the left forearm of his long-sleeved crimson silk-sheen tunic.

"That was my first reaction, Baron." The red-haired man swallowed hard. "Statistics pointed out, however, that the twenty percent level was the maximum profit-maximizing level for Bestmeat. That is, low enough to take the roughly forty percent of the Westmark trade we don't have absolutely controlled, but high enough—"

"Spare me the basic economics, Reillee. To what obscure point are you leading?"

"Through happenstance, sheer happenstance, you understand, it came to my attention that Bestmeat was banking more than five million credits a standard month in their investment account alone."

"What firm?"

"Halsie-Vyr, Baron."

The baron's voice dropped even lower. "And how much did this happenstance information cost you?"

"It was happenstance—"

"Reillee . . ."

"Five thousand."

The baron stared levelly at Reillee.

"We have several problems, Reillee. You didn't pay enough for that information. That means everyone will know shortly that you were concerned. We will return to that problem later."

He glanced behind Reillee at the closed portal, then stared at the red-headed man.

"Can I draw the conclusion that since Bestmeat is not out directly to ruin us, which seems unlikely with their heavy profit margin, that they have some new meat source or process that means they actually can undercut our ranches and mutated beefaloes? Can I draw that conclusion?"

"Yes, Baron."

"Do you know what that source is?"

"I have reports, Baron."

"And you do not trust them?"

"No, Baron."

"Why not?"

"Because they all say that Bestmeat has developed a special kind of plant that produces protein better than the best meat steaks."

"Yes, that would be hard to believe."

Reillee tugged at his tunic, looked at the conference table, then at the baron. He was unable to keep his eyes focused on the commercial entrepreneur's dark orbs and dropped his glance.

"And what success have you had in solving this problem?"

Reillee did not answer.

"Where are your successes?"

By now, the baron's voice had dropped so low that it had lost its silkiness, so low that it was a rasping knife cutting through the conference room.

"There . . . are . . . none."

"Can you explain why not?"

Reillee gave a shrug, as if to indicate the matter had passed well beyond his control.

"Because, Baron, it seemed clear that price cuts would not work. We still are banking a profit. We cut prices and run in the red, while Bestmeat cuts their prices and runs in the black."

"Reillee, your ingenuity seems limited."

"Yes, Baron, I know. I tried to block their suppliers by invoking the sole source clause with all of ours, but they don't deal with anyone who deals with us. I invoked the emergency power clause, and they jumpshipped their own generators in.

"I used the brotherhoods to deny local labor, and they brought in outsiders under the free work laws, and paid them higher wages. That left the brotherhoods most unhappy, and we had to match the Bestmeat wage levels. I pulled off the construction workers for their new employee housing, and they used some new technique to grow houses—"

"Grow houses?"

"I don't believe it either, but all four Infonet agencies came up with the same reports. And they did get the housing built, and to standards as well. It's virtually solid wood."

"Solid wood? Real wood?"

"That's right.".

The baron looked away from the trembling Reillee, then touched the wide band on his wrist.

The portal behind the Vice President of Marketing, Westmark System Division, opened. A thin and dark man with hooded and heavy eyelids, in a dark blue tunic and trousers, stepped inside the conference room.

"Ahmed, Mr. Reillee. Mr. Reillee has outlined a problem to me. He will outline it to you. If he has done everything he has said he has done, then he has done all that I could expect. Please check on it.

"If Mr. Reillee has done all these things, or even most of them, he deserves a ten percent bonus for calling this to our attention, and you need to take the necessary further steps. If not, Mr. Reillee needs a new occupation, and you will do what is necessary. In either case, I expect your ingenuity will be required. Please do take care of it."

Reillee looked down. Ahmed nodded, and the baron stood.

"There is a problem on Haldane. After tomorrow, I will leave. Problems, problems. Such is the life of a Baron of the Empire. I will expect a report from each of you to be torped to headquarters within two standard weeks."

Reillee turned, realized that Ahmed was waiting to follow him, and departed. The special assistant followed as closely as a shadow, and as darkly.

The baron frowned at the closed portal.

GERSWIN SCANNED THROUGH the report.

Should he follow his instincts and strike directly at the heart of the problem? Or should he let nature take its course?

Megalrie would certainly attempt a strong-arm operation—that was his style. And it would be one with maximum force. Finesse was not the baron's trademark, nor was personal involvement. One of the baron's special assistants would take care of it.

Gerswin tapped out the codes for access to the financial status and projections. Then he studied the figures.

If Bestmeat of Westmark were folded, left beached and belly-up, he could pull out roughly 100 million credits, but Megalrie would destroy the hytanks and the land under cultivation. On the other hand, if he could turn over the operation to someone, he could still come out with about fifty million credits and the chance for the operation to survive.

To fight Megalrie directly would take too many resources and, more important, too much time and visibility at a time when the Empire was becoming too interested in biologics. To remove the latest special assistant would only postpone the baron's final actions.

Gerswin shrugged. The answers were obvious, not that he had much choice. He could not fight Megalrie, nor could he allow the baron to win.

According to the report, Megalrie was about ready to leave for Haldane on his yacht, the *Terminia*.

He tapped out another code on the console screen.

"Ser Jasnow's office—oh, yes, Shaik Corso."

The screen blanked, and Jasnow's face appeared.

"Yes, Shaik?"

"Like to talk to you. In person. Now."

"Ah . . ." Jasnow's thin and pale cheeks became thinner and paler as he sucked them in.

"Now," repeated Gerswin.

"I will be there."

Jasnow blanked the screen before Gerswin did.

Gerswin laughed mirthlessly.

Within minutes, Jasnow was marching through the portal with an air of offended dignity that only an academic convinced of his own importance could have matched.

"Ser Corso—"

"Quiet."

Gerswin motioned to the chair across the console from him. "Sit down."

Jasnow sat.

"I would not have asked you if it were not important. Also aware that you have snoops in my office. Hope you are the only one with access to the cubes, for your sake.

"Now, Baron Megalrie is about to try another strong-arm operation on us, and this time it will be something impressive, like a power satellite misfocusing on one of our plants, or on this building."

Jasnow's white face paled even further.

"He wouldn't."

"He will. Therefore, in the interests of *your* survival, here is what you will do. You offer Chancellor Gorin control of Bestmeat, West-mark, to the government. It will be run as the same sort of public cor-poration as the linear rail system and the water system. With you as president. That will give him the popular support he has lost with the collared crew. His wife is a nutritionist. She will be offered the posi-tion, paid as well as you are, as consulting nutritionist for the State."

"As much as—"

"Right. If you want to keep your neck and your job."

"What if she weren't a nutritionist?"

"You'd offer her something equally exalted and highly paid." Ger-swin paused. "Everyone will know it's a package deal, and everyone will know why you did it, and some will even be amazed that you had the common sense to do it. This way, though, you get to retain your considerable salary for a while, at least, and an operating corporation and fancy title."

"What if I don't?"

"Then you will be either dead or out of business and luck." Ger-swin's flat tone conveyed absolute certainty.

"How will that stop Megalrie?"

"He's not about to take on a system government, especially if he's still making a profit. Besides, he'll figure that eventually the ineffi-ciency in a government operation will drive prices up, and his profits will follow."

"You seem sure that Megalrie will see it that way."

"Megalrie will see it that way." Gerswin smiled, and he could tell it was not a friendly expression because Jasnow shrank back in his captain's chair. "He will."

Gerswin stood.

"Get through to Chancellor Gorin. I know you can. Be as candid as necessary. Gorin will buy the idea. Right now, he'll buy anything, and even if this doesn't give him the election next year, it will give him and his wife more than a year's high salary from her position."

"But—"

"But what? You've got less than a day to make the deal and make sure it goes public. Make sure that Megalrie's man Reillee gets the in-formation as well. If you don't put this together, you'll have nothing."

"What about you?"

"Me? I'm selling out to you. That gives you absolute control. If you want to gamble, be my guest. It's your life."

Jasnow shivered. "You think so?"

"Have I been wrong before?"

"No."

"Then I'd suggest you follow through. In the meantime, I'll be completing the transactions to transfer my interest to you and setting up the form for you to follow in turning Bestmeat over to the government."

Jasnow pursed his lips, finally shrugging as he turned.

As soon as Jasnow left, Gerswin began to program the transactions necessary and to arrange the fund transfers to the shielded account in the local Halsie-Vyr office.

Shortly, he would use the private exit for his flitter and the trip back to the producing wastelands he had bought for next to nothing years earlier, back to the small strip and bunker where the *Caroljoy* waited while being repowered.

Too bad he wouldn't have a chance to check out all the plantings on all the scattered lands, the ones that neither Jasnow nor the staff knew about.

Once the secret was out, there would probably be a government effort to destroy all the meatplants not under government control. The thousands of plantings would probably thwart that, and if not on Westmark, then on the half-dozen other planets where Bestmeat operated.

X ▽ I I I

AS EYE, HE could almost convince himself that his duty was clear. The gray-haired and rail-thin man flicked the console to standby and rubbed his forehead before leaning forward to rest his head in his hands.

The more he studied the fragmentary background, the surprisingly sketchy Service records, the more convinced he was that Calendra had been right—assuming the mysterious individual he had mentioned to the Emperor had indeed been Gerswin. There was more to MacGregor Corson Gerswin than met the eye, far more. And yet . . .

". . . who could disagree with his goals, at least in the abstract . . . ," muttered the man charged with the ultimate control of Imperial security.

If it *had* been Gerswin who destroyed the Assassin's Guild, could he, especially as Eye, fault that destruction? Hardly. If it had been Gerswin who used the tacheads to smash the tie between the oligarchs and the secret police on El Lido, had not the results been in both the interests of the Empire and the average El Lidan?

Without Gerswin's support and work for the OER Foundation, would all the foodstuffs and medical advances from biologics have occurred so soon?

Eye sighed. Even worse, except for Gerswin's connection with the damned biologics foundation, there was no proof. Endless probabilities poured from the Eye Service stat-system, but no hard proof. Not that proof was a limit to Eye.

As Earl of Selern, he was reluctant to employ the full power of his Intelligence office without some shred of hard evidence. Calendra had acted without proof and without rationale too often, and look where that had led.

To complicate matters more, the majority of the probabilities, except for the propaganda negatives associated with the use of nuclear warheads, indicated that the actions attributed to Gerswin and his range of aliases supported, or apparently did not harm, the Empire. Virtually all were politically popular.

Eye frowned without moving his head. His instincts told him a different story. Gerswin was not out to harm the Empire, at least not in the short tun, but the man jumpshifted under different stars. If you could call him a man. He also appeared to be one of the handful of known biological immortals. How long Gerswin could retain function or sanity was another question.

Selern took a slow and deep breath, touched the screen, and scripted a compromise.

Should Gerswin himself, under his own identity, dock in Imperial facilities or main systems territory, he would be detained and restrained for a full investigation.

Eye smiled wryly. Gerswin might well escape, but that would provide proof of sorts, and no one had ever escaped the full might of the Empire, even with the equivalent of a small warship.

Besides, he needed to report some action to the Emperor.

GERSWIN STUDIED THE readouts on the data screen. The snooper he had left in orbit just beyond the *Terminia* had relayed the latest.

The EDI twitches indicated that the *Terminia* was being readied for orbit-out, probably as soon as a shuttle from Haldane arrived.

"Relay indicated approach to target." The AI's voice was as impersonally feminine as ever.

"Characteristics of object approaching target?"

"Object indicated as armed shuttle, class three. Characteristics and energy signature match within point nine probability."

"Stet. As soon as object departs target proximity, deploy full shields."

"Stet."

Gerswin took a sip from the open-topped glass of water, then swallowed the remainder of the water before standing up and heading into the fresher section to relieve himself.

The next few hours were going to be interesting, more than interesting, to say the least.

Gerswin had strapped into the accel/decel shell couch and was wondering if the *Terminia* would ever depart.

"*Terminia*, clearing orbit." The transmission was on the orbit control band.

"Happy jumps, *Terminia*."

"Shields up," announced the AI. "Target vector tentatively set at zero seven zero Haldane relative, plus three point nine."

"Close to within one hundred kays, same heading."

"Closing to one hundred kays. Estimate reaching closure point in five standard minutes."

The two-gee surge in acceleration pressed Gerswin back into the shell.

He touched the console and reviewed the numbers again, pursing his lips. The maneuver should work.

At times such as these, he wondered if it wouldn't have been easier to have added offensive weapons to the *Caroljoy*. Probably no one would have discovered them, not the way he had operated, but the penalty risks were too high for the benefits.

Privately owned and armed jumpships were one thing the Empire was deadly serious about. So serious that entire Service squadrons had been deployed for years to track a single pirate. Since ship and jump costs were so high to begin with, and since the energy costs of avoiding the Service made any commercial piracy infeasible, and since the I.S.S. hadn't had that much to do since the mistake known as the Dismorph Conflict, there weren't any pirates. Not that lasted long.

Gerswin sighed as he waited.

While he had once "borrowed" the Duke of Triandna's yacht, with the help of the Duchess, that woman who he had known only as Caroljoy on a single warm night until long afterward, he had not considered himself a pirate. After all, he had only been carrying out the Emperor's promises. Even if the Emperor hadn't really wanted to supply those arcdozers for the reclamation on Old Earth. Even if the dozers had only been to buy time for the devilkids as they struggled to reestablish a foothold on Old Earth. Even if they were all dead or dying by now. Even if . . .

He shook his head violently. He needed to finish the business at hand. The sooner he could get it over with the better.

"Change heading to parallel target at distance of one thousand kays."

"Changing heading."

Gerswin waited until the readouts indicated the return to a parallel course.

His fingers began the rough computations that he could have left to the ship's AI.

"In one standard minute, commence maximum acceleration with internal gee force not to exceed five point five gees. Maintain for point five standard hour."

"Stet. Maximum acceleration possible with internal gee force not to exceed five point five gees. Will maintain for point five standard hour."

Gerswin waited for the force to press him back into the control shell, almost welcoming the physical pressure as a test with set and understandable limits.

"Commencing acceleration."

"Stet."

Test or no test, by the time the half hour ended, Gerswin felt sore all over.

"Stop acceleration. Maintain internal gee field at one standard gravity. Maneuver the ship back at full acceleration along target course line. Suggest forty-five-degree heading change for two minutes, followed by a reverse two-hundred-twenty-five-degree sweep turn."

"Recommend Kirnard turn."

"Proceed Kirnard turn," Gerswin affirmed. Damned AI! That was what he had wanted to begin with.

He wanted to come back in on the reciprocal course with as much velocity as possible. His generators would take at least twice the strain as those of the *Terminia*, perhaps more, since the other yacht was reputed to be filled with luxuries, and luxuries meant energy diversions.

"Interrogative closure time."

"Time to CPA estimated at point two five standard hour."

"EDI lock?"

"Negative on EDI lock. EDI trace available."

"Time to intercept?"

"Inquiry imprecise."

Gerswin frowned. Damned AI! He wondered if the AI had a sense of self-preservation.

"Interrogative. Are we confirmed on head-on-head reciprocal courses?"

"That is negative."

Gerswin sighed.

"Change course to maintain reciprocal courses. I want a head-on-head intercept."

"Probability of physical contact exceeds point zero zero five."

"I suspect so. Interrogative time to intercept."

"Point one five stans."

Gerswin waited, confirmed the AI verbal reports with the actual data on his own screen.

"Probability of physical contact exceeds point zero one."

"You may make any course changes necessary to maximize survival and minimize contact *after* screen contact."

"Stet. You are relinquishing control to AI?"

"That is negative. Negative. Allowing emergency override after screen contact to avoid physical impact."

"Stet. Override only after screen contact."

"Only after *defense* screen impact," Gerswin corrected.

"After defense screen impact," parroted the AI.

Gerswin could feel the sweat seeping out of his palms as he tightened his harness and leaned back in the shell couch.

He checked the fingertip controls, checked and waited.

"Time to contact?"

"Point zero five."

Gerswin wanted to wipe his forehead.

"Divert all power to defense screens. Minimal gee force."

"Diverting all power."

The control-room lights dropped to emergency levels, and the whisper of the recirculators dropped to nothing. Gerswin felt light in the shell as the internal gees dropped to roughly point one as the power from the gravfield generators was poured into the defense screens.

"Target commencing course change."

"Match it. Continue head-on-head intercept."

"Probability of physical impact approaching point one without course change."

"Understood. Maintain intercept course until full defense screen impact."

A drop of sweat lingered in Gerswin's left eyebrow, tickling, but refusing to drop. He wrinkled his brows, but did not move.

"Screen impact."

Whhhrrrrrr!

Gerswin was thrown sideways in his harness for an instant.

The lights flickered, then came back up to normal levels.

"Course alteration in progress."

"Turn it into another Kirnard turn."

"Stet. Converting to Kirnard turn."

"Status report."

"Number two main screen generator is down. All other systems functioning within normal parameters."

"Interrogative target status."

"Target has stopped acceleration. Negative screens. Negative EDI track."

"Interrogative turn status."

"Completing Kirnard turn."

"Fly by target. Drop torp probe for confirmation of target status."

"Stet. Full instrumentation check with torp probe. Note. Torp probe is last probe."

"Understand last probe. Reload on Aswan."

Gerswin finally wiped his soaking forehead.

The impact of the *Caroljoy's* heavy screens should have blown every screen generator in the *Terminia*. Milliseconds later, the *Car-*

oljoy's screens would have impacted the *Terminia* itself, with enough of a concussive impact to fragment everyone and everything within the hull.

That had been the theory. The torp probe would either confirm or deny the results. Too bad the *Caroljoy's* only operating launch tubes were limited to message torps or their smaller equivalents. But he'd been through that debate with himself before. Probably better that he had no easy way to launch the remaining tacheads and hellburners. Then again, the thirteen remaining nuclear devices would probably outlast both Gerswin and the *Caroljoy*. After El Lido, and the expression on Rodire's face, he had no desire to launch mass death again, even in support of the greater life his biologic efforts represented.

As he was coming to appreciate, the best use of force was on a wide and diffuse scale. The Empire found it easy enough to recognize direct threats, but not those without an overt focus, such as the changes in society that his biologic innovations were beginning to bring.

No . . . the tacheads and hellburners represented the past, and best they remain in the past and unused in the future.

He pulled at his chin as he straightened in the control couch and returned his full attention to the display screens before him.

"Probe away."

"Stet."

Gerswin remained flat in the shell, just in case something went wrong.

He could see the end of the road ahead. Before too long, even the slow-moving Empire would begin to put the pieces together, to understand what he was attempting. Soon, all too soon, it would be time to fold his tent before they understood the implications or traced his real purposes back to Old Earth.

"Just what are your real purposes?" he asked himself in a low voice.

"Query not understood."

"That makes two of us."

He waited for the report from the torp readouts.

"Probe results. Negative screens. Negative EDI traces. Free atmosphere dispersing from target hull. Heat radiation unchecked and dropping."

Gerswin took a deep breath. End of Baron Megalrie. End of *Terminia*. Beginning of end for Gerswin's Imperial activities.

"Stet. Can you recover probe?"

"Negative."

"Set course to nearest early jump point. Full screens available. One gee."

"Understand fullest possible screens. One gee course to early jump point. Estimate arrival in one point one."

"Understood."

Gerswin unstrapped himself and swung out of the shell. While the system energy monitors would doubtless pick up the energy burst created by the screen collision, no one was going to find the dead hulk of the *Terminia*, not at the tangent created by the collision. Gerswin shook his head, not wanting to dwell on the yacht's crew, not wanting to think about the ever-mounting implications, not wanting to think about the decisions lying in wait ahead.

The peaceful years were over, assuming they had ever been. Assuming that such peace had not been a recently acquired personal illusion.

The disappearance of the baron would be linked to Gerswin, as would all the other probabilities for which there was little or no proof.

He sighed.

Commodore MacGregor Corson Gerswin could never appear again in Imperial territory, at least not under his own name. And it wasn't likely to be long before all of his other identities would also be targeted, assuming that the baron's efforts had not meant that he was already under indirect Imperial attack.

No, the peaceful years were over, for a long time to come, if not forever.

DESPITE THE SILENCE in the kitchen, Professor Stilchio looked from side to side, cleared his throat, finally touched the light plate and brought the illumination up to full.

He coughed.

In the corner next to the preservator was a shadow, an odd shadow. He tried to look at it, but his eyes did not want to focus.

A certain dizziness settled upon him, and he put his right hand out to the counter to steady himself.

"Professor." The address came from the shadow he saw and could not see.

The academic cleared his throat again, but said nothing.

"Professor, you might look at the folder on the counter."

Stilchio refused to look down, hoping the shadow might disappear. Slightly intoxicated on good old wine he might be, but shadows did not talk.

His right hand groped for more support and brushed something that slid on the smooth tiles.

In spite of his resolve, he looked down. By his right hand was an oblong folder.

"That folder contains an excellent short paper on the social implications of mass agriculture and its use in controlling populations and supporting centralized governments."

"So . . . what . . . ," stuttered the professor, still trying to steady himself.

"It strikes us that it would be an excellent piece for the eccentricities section of the *Forum*."

"I'm not . . . not exactly . . . approached . . . this way."

"You have never published a single paper or article that suggested anything wrong with centralized agriculture or of government control of the food supply."

"Who would help the poor?"

"The government. If they are so interested in the poor, let them buy food for the poor. Better yet, let the governments stop blocking new biologic techniques that would let the poor feed themselves."

"But—"

"Professor, time is short for you."

Thunk!

Stilchio turned his head to gape at the heavy knife buried in the cabinet door by his head. His hand reached, then drew back as he saw the double-bladed edge, the mark, he feared, of the professional.

"You have been asked to do nothing which is not in keeping with your publicly professed ethics, nor which would in any way personally endanger you. The credentials of the writer are adequate, to say the least, and certified in blood. If this article is not published in the edition being released next week, the following edition will carry your obituary.

"You have a choice. Live up to your publicly quoted beliefs in free expression of ideas or die because you were a hypocrite at heart."

"The police . . ."

"Can do nothing, nor will they. Would you care to explain that while you were drinking, you were threatened for hypocrisy? Would anyone really ever believe you?

"Read the paper in the folder. You will discover no incendiary rhetoric, just facts, figures, and a few mild speculations. Tell anyone you were threatened over such a scholarly paper, particularly by this author, and they might lock you away or relieve you of your duties for senility or mental deterioration.

"Good night, Professor. We look forward to the next edition of the *Forum.*"

Stilchio stood absolutely still as a black shadow walked up to him and withdrew the knife, effortlessly, from the wood of the cabinet. Then, just as soundlessly, the shadow was gone through the archway and toward the front portal.

Finally, the kitchen was silent, the loudest sound the beating of the graying professor's heart.

His hands explored the wedge cut in the wood. His eyes glanced at the folder, then back at the cut, then toward the closed portal.

He walked, slow step by slow step, toward the dispenser, where he filled a goblet with ice water, where he stood, sipping at the chill water whose temperature matched the chill in his heart.

With a sigh, he edged back toward the folder on the counter, from which he extracted the short article. Studying the title page for a long moment, he sighed again. Then he turned to the first page of text.

He had hoped that the proposed article would have proved poorly written, propagandistic, or threatening. He doubted it was. He recognized the author, who was, unfortunately, deceased. Deceased, it was rumored, at the hands of the Barcelon government.

Another sigh escaped him as he turned to the second page.

His eyes darted back to the wedge-shaped cut in the cabinet, as if to wish the mark would disappear. It did not.

He looked back at the brown tiles of the floor.

Too old, he was too old to refuse to publish such an article. It was well written. While he disagreed with the conclusions, to publish it would only bring praise from his critics and allow him to claim impartiality. Not to publish it . . . he shivered, recalling the pleasant tone of the professional who had visited so recently.

Too old—he was too old to be a martyr, not when it would serve no purpose, not when no one would understand why.

He shook his head as he shuffled toward the console in his study.

XXI

THE SUMMER PARK at Londra, New Avalon, had its Speakers' Corner, as did all the public parks on New Avalon.

Constable Graham twirled his truncheon, smiling under the morning mist that was beginning to lift. Overhead, a few patches of blue appeared between the ragged gray clouds.

The constable slowed as he approached the paved area and the three public podiums. He studied the small crowd—less than fifty, and mostly university students on their midmorning class breaks.

Graham frowned as he saw that a number of the students were poring over identical leaflets. That was unusual, since most of the speakers were either expatriate politicians trying to recapture their glory days or political science students practicing for later campaigns. The reputation of the university was such that even a few of the younger sons of the first families of the Empire studied there. Few others could have afforded the jumpship passage costs.

Consequently, seldom was literature passed out. Even less often was it read.

The constable edged closer to the single speaker, seeing only a dark-haired young man, wearing the traditional and formal black university tunic.

"Power? I ask you—what is it? What is its basis? Power is the ability to control people's lives. Ah, yes, a truism. So simple. But look beyond the simplicity. Look beyond the mere words, beyond the obvious phrases. Ask what composes control.

"You need food. Whoever controls your food supply controls you. You need shelter. Whoever controls the providing of shelter controls you.

"Take that a step forward. Let us say a man gives you a handful of seeds. He says, 'One of these will grow into a house that will provide shelter, and the rest will become plants to provide all the good food you will ever need.'

"I ask you, is this in the interest of any government?

"No! A thousand times, no!

"Just take the food. If each man or woman could grow his own with little effort, what need would there be for millions of hectares of land for farms, for government agriculture pricing policies. And if each family grew their own food, how could the government ever produce enough of a surplus to maintain an army? Or a secret police force?"

Graham frowned again, letting his truncheon drop to his side.

"Rubbish," he muttered under his breath, looking up at the student on the podium, who seemed too old to be anything but a senior graduate fellow. The policeman studied the man. He did not recall seeing the speaker in the park before.

"You!" demanded the speaker, and Graham stopped, held momentarily by eyes that flashed yellow. "You! Constable! Do you believe a government's purpose is to serve its people? Or should the people serve it by feeding its soldiers?"

Graham retreated without speaking, grabbing a leaflet from the first bench he passed.

"Come, Constable! If the government has no massive farmlands and no great agricultural surplus with which to support a nonproductive bureaucracy and an unnecessary army, how could it remain oppressive?"

"What about feudalism?" snapped another student.

Graham ducked away, leaflet in hand, glad of the reprieve and to escape from the yellow-eyed speaker.

". . . feudalism was based on scarcity . . . on the fact that self-sufficiency was limited . . . outdated by modern communications and modern biologics . . . advances hidden away from you by the Empire . . ."

"Isn't that the same old conspiracy theory?"

"No conspiracy. People need organized society . . . need protection . . . but the lack of independence in obtaining the basics has left them at the mercy of government. It is no accident that repressive governments cannot exist on new frontiers, where individuals can support themselves or can readily leave. Repression exists where there are no alternatives . . ."

The constable continued away from the speaker, folding the leaflet and tucking it away to read later. It might actually be interesting. He resumed twirling his truncheon and checking the benches, absently noting the regulars and the newcomers, tipping his antique helmet to the few mothers and their small children as he neared the playground.

Idly, he wondered about the leaflet, about the quality feel of the paper. The whole business seemed strange.

He shrugged.

All the speakers had something strange about them, but the commonwealth believed in free speech, always had, and always would, no matter how strange the students that flocked to the university. Even if they had yellow eyes and strange ideas.

XXII

LYR CHECKED THE invoices again. She frowned, then tapped in an inquiry and analysis program.

"What is he up to now?" she muttered as she waited for the results. While she should have returned to reviewing the budget flow, she decided against it, arbitrarily, and let her thoughts wander as the analyzer sorted through the invoices and purchases made by the commander over the past year.

It could be her imagination. Then again, it might not be imagination at all.

From what she could tell, lately his efforts had moved from the research and new grants area far more into field testing and production, in some cases even into granting licenses.

All had generated substantial revenues and strange amounts of new contributions to the foundation; many of which were from entities she suspected were no more than aliases or ciphers from the commander himself.

He seemed uneasy with the growing attention he received, and particularly when he learned that his own name had appeared in the listing of commercial magnates of the Empire (unrecognized section).

Lyr smiled wryly. She had no doubts that the total holdings of the commodore she still thought of as a commander were more than sufficient to place him well up among the barons of the Empire.

She had mentioned that, once.

"You had better hope that no one puts that together, then, for both your sake and mine."

"Why?" she had asked, but he had not answered the question, as he often did not when the inquiry revolved around his personal activities.

Cling.

She looked down at the screen as the results from the analyzer program began to print out.

As each statistic appeared, she nodded, smiling faintly as the figures confirmed her suspicions.

"Conclusion?" she tapped out.

"Probability of terraforming operation being developed with biologic technology exceeds point seven. No evidence of delivery vehicles included."

She frowned at the last. What would be needed for such a delivery system?

Her mouth dropped open as she recalled an obscure fact—one that Gerswin had mentioned more than once. The Empire had originally forbidden terraforming because it had been thought that the development of the techniques had been what had devastated Old Earth. While the prohibition had technically lapsed, the attitude had probably not.

She scripted another inquiry, hovering over the screen for the analyzer's response.

Cling.

Tapping the keyboard studs, she watched as the conclusion scripted out.

"Without foundation data, probability of successful analysis of terraforming project is less than point two within five standard years. Exact calculation of future probabilities impossible, but trends analysis would indicate that successful analysis by outside sources possible within ten standard years and approaches unity in less than thirty years."

No wonder the man seemed driven, almost as if he knew his projects would be discovered.

But what were they? What planet or planets did he want to terraform? What planet would appeal to a hawk-eyed immortal?

Lyr shivered, not certain she wanted to know the answer to the question she posed. She did not frame another inquiry for the analyzer.

Instead, her hands framed the sequence to delete the entire file she had created.

XXIII

BLACK THE SHIP was, and streamlined in the ancient tradition that predated the Federation that had predated the Empire that would precede the Commonality of Worlds. Black the ship was, and with a nonjump speed that indicated a scout. Black with the full-fade dark finish that no eye could grasp in the dimness of space.

The pilot ignored the lunar relays and their inquiries, flashed well clear of the geosynch station for the High Plains port, and dropped the scout into a high-temp entry that would have vaporized most ships that attempted it, and one which required a deceleration beyond the physical limits of most ships and pilots. Such a deceleration was impossible for contemporary ships, with their automatically linked shields and gravfields.

The scout's full power was tied to the shields during entry. Using the gravfield would have diverted too much energy from the deceleration, particularly since the streamlined configuration of the scout was far from optimal for a gravfield inside an atmosphere.

The lunar detectors lost the scout in less than half a descent orbit, and the geosynch station picked it up later and lost it sooner.

"Scout, characteristics . . . high-speed entry . . ."

The entire data package was light-stuttered to the entry port operations at High Plains, filed in the lunar relay banks, and ignored in both locales.

The scout pilot, pressed into the accel/decel couch, looked to be perhaps thirty standard years, blond, curly-haired, and wore a dark olive uniform without insignia.

His fingers alone reacted to the data screen and the data inputs flashing before him.

A dull roar and rumble marked his passing through the clouds, that, and the puzzled look on the face of a duty operations technician.

"Captain's luck! Unauthorized entry, and they both lost it. Not even a hint of descent area. How are we supposed to find it?

"Old war scout, from the profile. Refugee, smuggler, or . . ." He paused because he could not think of a realistic alternative with which to complete the sentence.

Finally, he posted up the entry for the operations officer, who would have the final responsibility for action, not that Major Lostler could do much with neither locale nor down time. Then he punched the entry into the log, and completed his duties by relaying the bulletin to the other Recorps subposts.

He smiled briefly. Smuggler or refugee, what could the one or two people in a small ship do, particularly with no energy sources left anywhere but in Recorps territory?

By the time the scout had settled into the twisted ecological nightmare that had once been called Northern Europe, the tech had dismissed the reported unauthorized entry as insignificant.

"INTERROGATIVE SHIELDS."

"Shields in the green."

"Interrogative outside energy levels."

"No outside energy levels."

The man at the control couch leaned back, sighed. Outside of the momentary scan from the lunar detectors, his return had apparently gone unnoticed. Either that, or no one really cared.

"Current number of dispersal torps?"

"There are twenty full message-sized torps, one hundred ten-percent torps, and ten thousand shells."

"Commence pattern Beta."

"Commencing pattern Beta."

The obsolete scoutship began the drop run over the planet's most desolated continent, scheduled to receive five of the full-spectrum torps and thirty of the ten percenters. Because he was limited to the small message torps by both the ship's limited capacity and the size of the permitted launchers, the seeding would take time, perhaps too much. But he was limited to what he had. Even if but a few of his torps were successful, eventually the spread would complete itself.

With luck, as much as twenty percent of the reclamation seeds and spores would survive.

Even if only one percent made it, over time, the ecology would recover. It would not be quite the same ecology as before the collapse, not with some of the additions and built-in stabilizers, but what else could he have done? The dozers were still at it, and they had been far from enough. No pure mechanical technology would ever have been enough.

"Energy concentration at two seven five, five zero kays. Probability of long-range monitor approaches unity."

The pilot nodded at the mechanically feminine tone of the AI, but said nothing as his hands played over the screens before him.

"How long until the first turn?"

"Ten plus."

"That will bring us back toward the monitor?"

"That is affirmative."

"Probability of crew."

"No crew. Monitor is Epsilon three, stored burst, link transmitting type."

"Can you detect transmissions?"

"No transmissions detected."

Gerswin nodded. The monitor had not yet detected the *Caroljoy*, or an immediate transmission would have gone out.

He shrugged.

"Break Beta pattern. Commence Delta in two minutes."

Gerswin strapped himself in place for the high-speed drop series that was about to follow.

While a monitor could not harm the *Caroljoy*, the scout had no exterior weapons with which to silence the monitor, and as soon as the monitor discovered a scoutship where one did not belong, it would relay that information, and satellite control or some other authority might well decide to send something which did have the power to disable or damage the scout.

Why Recorps or the Impies were wasting energy on surveillance monitors was a mystery that could wait, one that he did not need to investigate at the moment.

"Monitor is ground scanning."

"Cancel Delta."

"Canceling Delta."

"Interrogative ground scanning. No other scans?"

"Monitor is ground scanning only. Scan pattern indicates that no other surveillance patterns are in use."

"Resume Beta pattern as planned. Notify me if monitor shifts from ground scan."

"Will notify if monitor scan patterns change."

Thump.

His ears picked up the sound of the first full message-sized torp launch. He waited to see if the Epsilon monitor reacted, but neither the AI nor his scan screens detected any change in the pattern of the Recorps monitor, nor any transmissions from it.

Thwip.

The softer sound of a ten percenter barely edged into his hearing. The AI was releasing the shells at a much faster rate, but they were so small he could not detect the individual releases.

Gerswin shifted his weight, waiting as the scout/yacht called *Caroljoy* continued to deliver the cargo he had promised so long before.

Thwip.

"Beta, section one, complete. Commencing pattern section two."

"Stet."

Gerswin split the far left screen and tapped a code. The homer signal, tight and far off-band, was clear. He should not have been surprised, but he was. The north coast refuge he had built so many years before was still there, still functioning, still apparently undiscovered.

Thwip.

"Get me a broad band sample."

He listened, trying to pick out intelligible phrases from the transmissions, most of them made a quarter of a planet away.

". . . Dragon two . . . tracs . . . home plate . . ."

". . . negative . . . is negative this time . . ."

"Outrider three . . . vector on . . . scout bearing . . ."

". . . have Amstar hold . . ."

". . . ScotiaOps . . . Dragon two . . . return . . . say again . . . return . . ."

For a time, static alone filled the speakers.

Thwip.

Thump!

"Completing Beta, section two. Commencing pattern section three."

"Stet."

Gerswin shook his head.

So anticlimactic. No guards, no armed flitters, no fanfares. Just blanketing wastelands with spores and seeds.

"What did you expect?"

"Query imprecise," answered the AI.

He ignored the artificial intelligence.

"Query imprecise."

"Withdrawn," he snapped.

Thwip. Another ten-percent torp launched.

The pilot massaged his forehead, rubbing his temples with the fingers and thumb of his right hand.

"What next, great reclaimer?"

"Pattern section four is the next section of the Beta pattern," chimed the cool and impersonal tones of the AI.

Gerswin wanted to shake his head, but just kept rubbing his temples. Usually, he tried to avoid asking himself questions when the AI was operational. He was slipping.

Slipping in more ways than one. Each year, it was harder to separate the memories, harder to keep them all in order, to remember the differences between Caroljoy and Constanza, between Faith and Allison, between Lerwin and Lostwin, between beta- and delta-class flitters.

And it was harder to think things through, harder to separate the dreams from hard plans for the future.

He let his hand drop and looked up at the screen, the blackness showing the plot, the *Caroljoy*'s position and the distant blip that represented the ground-scanning monitor.

What next?

Shaking his head slowly, he let his eyes drop.

He had stepped up his physical training, in hopes that it would help his mental sharpness. The physical reflexes were still as good as ever, perhaps better, automatic and maintained with practice. But the mental abilities . . .

Soon he would have to face that question. That and the future. Would a single-focused project help? Give him time to sort things out while not juggling a thousand variables?

He couldn't think that through yet. Not yet. Not until the last shell, the last torps, until all had spread their cargo across the desolated spaces of Old Earth. But that would only be a few dozen hours away.

Thwip.

"Completing Beta, section three. Commencing pattern section four."

"Stet."

Thump!

XXV

THE PILOT SAT back in the control couch, staring at the blank main screen.

"Now what?"

"Query imprecise."

"The query is not for you."

"Stet," responded the AI.

The refuges, north European coast and western continental mountain, were both waiting, apparently undiscovered. And he had done what he had promised them all, promised young Corwin, assuming the boy had survived and returned to Old Earth, and Kiedra and Lerwin and Caroljoy. He had carried out his trust, hadn't he?

Even now, the ecological torps were beginning their work, beginning the biological processes that would do what all the dozers he had stolen and begged and pleaded for so long ago could not.

Even now, people were reclaiming the planet of their birth, having children, slowly spreading from the reclaimed high plains and from the Scotia highlands. And soon, soon, they would have help from the biological agents he had seeded.

That aid would take longer on Noram because he had only been able to seed the outlying areas without too high a risk of detection. But he was done. Finished. Completed.

He had carried out his trust, hadn't he? Hadn't he?

"Haven't you?"

"Query imprecise."

"Withdrawn."

He tried to ignore the AI, still staring at the blank screen before him. The Imperial Intelligence Service, not to mention more than a few barons of the Empire, would soon be looking for retired Commodore Gerswin, Shaik Corso, and all the other names and identities he had used. They would turn up the *Caroljoy*, if the search were as diligent as he foresaw, as diligent as it was bound to be silent.

And what about the foundation?

What about Lyr, sitting dutifully and quietly within minutes of the Intelligence headquarters?

He slowly shook his head. Caroljoy had been right. He had more miles to go, many more, than he had thought.

"Interrogative power requirements and parameters for Aswan."

"Double jump from thirty plus ecliptic possible with point five power reserves remaining. Power to jump will require point one of reserves. Power from reentry jump will require estimated point three from reserves."

Not much leeway, either for the jumps or himself. But there wouldn't be, not in the days and years, hopefully, ahead.

"Break orbit for jump point."

"Breaking for jump point."

No doubt the energy flows would be picked up by the lunar relays, but not analyzed until the questions were academic. Besides, there were no Impie ships in range to do anything.

The pilot leaned back, wishing he could rub his aching forehead.

Rationalization or not, he had a few things more to do. A few things more that might make the galaxy a bit safer for Old Earth, and a debt to one last other gracious lady.

The refuges could wait. They'd waited more than a century already, and could wait another two if necessary, if he had that much time.

He smiled mirthlessly.

The Empire was slow, but scarcely that slow. His wait, the time until his last return home, one way or another, would not be that long.

XXVI

THE CONSUL AND Second Secretary of the Embassy of Barcelon touched the screen.

"FREE HEIN WADRUP! FREE HEIN WADRUP! FREE HEIN WADRUP!"

He grimaced and lowered the volume before turning to the political attaché.

"What started this?"

The attaché shrugged. "It started on the university grounds. You saw the briefing tape. Wadrup jumped bail. He was never seen again. There is no record of him leaving Barcelon. His body was never found."

"What really happened?"

The taller man shrugged again. "The police say he jumped bail. Who really knows?"

"FREE JAIME BEN! FREE JAIME BEN! FREE JAIME BEN!"

The Consul winced at the new chant from the screen, showing the scene in the park across from the commercial complex.

"This isn't doing our talks much good. The Sunni government believes in civil rights."

"What can we do? Even if we wanted to, there's nothing we could do. They've picked people who can't be found or freed."

"Smart of them."

"Too smart for a bunch of students."

"Can you find out who's behind them?"

"No. We traced one of the leaders, the one who started the Hein Wadrup movement. Graduate student from New Glascow studying on New Avalon. He's definitely from New Glascow. Even his voice patterns check out. He's a real student, and someone else is funding him—liberally. Who? How can you trace double blind drops and fund transfers over three systems and through that Ydrisian commnet?"

"That tells you one thing."

"Right. Whoever it is has money. Lots of it. Like several thousand commercial magnates in the Empire, and none of them are terribly fond of Barcelon."

The consul frowned and turned back to the screen, half listening to the words of the speakers.

". . . of Barcelon . . . designed to keep control of agriculture from the people . . . without food, no police state . . . no accident . . . Hein Wadrup knew agriculture policies . . . what did he know? What did they fear from Hein Wadrup? . . . nothing to fear, then free him . . . tell Barcelon . . . prove us wrong . . . PROVE US WRONG! PROVE US WRONG!! . . ."

"Just a short media incident," observed the political attaché.

"It's not the single incidents that bothers me. It's the pattern, the continuing growth of such incidents. Always around the best universities. Almost as if targeted at the students, and the teachers. And those students will become teachers."

"Not on Barcelon!" protested the attaché.

"No," answered the consul, "on Barcelon, they'll either be jailed or become revolutionaries." He sighed. "I'd rather have the teachers, thank you."

He touched the screen, which blanked.

XXVII

THE GARDENER WHISTLED a low series of notes as he finished weeding the next-to-last row of his plot in the public garden. Already, the row of dark green plants had shed the first set of blossoms, and the nodules were darkening nearly to purple and beginning to take on the tubular shape of the fruit, if an organic product that tasted like the best hand-fed steak could be truly called a fruit.

The second set of blossoms was another week from bursting into full flower, but the silver-haired gardener nodded as he checked each of the fifteen plants in the first row.

The outside row was a hybrid bean common to Forsenia, with nearly the same dark leaves as the bestmeat plant. The bean plants composed the third and fifth rows as well, while the second and fourth rows were filled with bestmeat plants.

"How they coming, Martin?" questioned a lanky, pointed-chinned, and white-haired woman from the next plot, cordoned off from his by a meter-high snow fence pressed into alternative use as a plot-divider for the short summer growing season.

"Growing. Growing fine."

"Next year, like to try whatever you got there with the beans. Looks interesting. Lots of buds already."

"Give you some seeds if it works."

"See then," grunted the woman. "Got to finish before noon. Get my granddaughter. Long tube ride." She straightened. "You're always here mornings. Got creds. How'd you qual for public garden?"

"Small pension. Impie service. Work nights at Simeons. No family. Make ends meet."

The older woman shivered. "Say lots of DomSecs at Simeons. Watch yourself."

The man with the short-curled silver hair blinked his dark eyes, trying to flick the gnat clear before the bug got under the tinted contact lenses. Finally, he waved the insect away and returned to his gardening, working his way on hands and knees down the fifth and last row.

"See you, Martin. Off for Tricia."

"See you," he answered without looking up.

Seeing he was alone, he resumed his whistling, the doubled notes softly following his progress.

After a time, he stood up and brushed the soil from the old flight suit he wore, a suit stripped of all insignia, although still with an equipment belt. Some of the original tools were obviously missing, and he had placed the hand hoe in the empty sidearm holster.

His eyes surveyed the small plot registered in the name of Martin deCorso, Interstellar Survey Service, technician third class, retired, and he nodded. Within weeks, the bestmeat plants would be producing, and within days of production he would be sharing his bounty with the other gardeners. Each of the long pods to come would also contain a central seed pod that would allow them to grow their own.

He hoped the Forsenian DomSecs were as indifferent to the retired and elderly as first appearances indicated. If they weren't, then he'd have to try something else.

Fingering the seed packet within his belt, he started back down the plastreet pathway toward the checkout gate, where an older DomSec waited to ensure that no one but approved gardeners entered, and where, when the plants bore fruit, the amount produced was also entered, theoretically, he had been told, for record-keeping purposes.

Since the bestmeats resembled giant cucumbers, Old Earth variety, he did not anticipate any problems to begin with. Forsenia was far enough from Shaik Corso's enterprises and Westmark that the bestmeat furor was unknown to the Forsenian authorities, as were the house tree and a few other biological innovations.

The man shook his head. He was not at all certain about the wisdom or the success of his venture, but he needed time to concentrate on one project at a time, to let things settle inside his own head. He'd told Lyr that he would be out of touch for some time, perhaps more than a standard year. Wise? Probably not. Necessary? No doubt of that.

He glanced around. More than half the plots were being actively tended, even though the temperature was rapidly approaching its midday peak, close to 30°C. The temperature would stay near the high until midafternoon, when the thunderstorms would roll down from the highlands and drop both torrential rains and the temperature, leaving a steamy twilight and evening that would turn progressively drier as the night progressed.

The slender gardener took his hands from his belt and slowed his steps as he neared the guard post.

"ID?" growled the overjowled and near-retirement age DomSec. He peered over the gate at the silver-haired man.

The gardener proferred an oblong card, covered with tamper-proof plastic and bearing appropriate seals and a hologram picture.

Creaakk. The gate swung open.

"On your way, oldster."

"Thank you, officer." He did not smile, but neither was his statement obsequious, merely a simple courtesy.

"No thanks. Everything you grow means more for someone else."

The gardener refrained from a nearly automatic headshake and kept moving down the narrow steps toward the almost-deserted boulevard.

The tight control of both urban land and of transportation had made one phase of his project more difficult than he had anticipated.

Nowhere near the city was there any overgrown land. Any abandoned plots were cut regularly by the Forsenian equivalent of the chain gang—citizens required to spend nonworking hours in community service for their overuse of transportation, energy, or food.

Halmia was, as a result, a clean city, a well-tended city. But there were no overgrown corners on which to plant bestmeats or house trees. And the nearest forests and farm areas were beyond easy reach of local public transit. The longer-range public transportation was monitored even more closely by ID scans through a centralized computer system. Private transportation, except for DomSec and military officers, was nonexistent.

Not that such shortcomings had stopped him entirely, but he had experienced more blocks and delays than he had anticipated, and the bestmeats had not been spread nearly wide enough to ensure the success he needed.

The public gardens were another avenue, and he'd passed out seeds quietly to gardeners to other areas, telling them that the seeds were a squash derivative whose fruits were best sliced and then boiled or fried. Once they tried them, he suspected, there would be a substantial increase in the growth of the "squash" derivatives.

He'd also made stealthy forays to garden areas in several other cities, planting his seeds in other plots.

He smiled briefly, before frowning as he remembered that a smile was an automatic invitation for a wandering DomSec to inquire as to one's health and destination. He shivered, despite the heat, wondering why he was going to such lengths for a system like Forsenia.

"Are you trying to establish places where you can't create a revolution?" he whispered to himself under his breath, before pursing his lips as he recalled the use of directional pickups. Rapidly, rapidly, was he beginning to understand the paranoia generated in tightly controlled societies.

He would probably need all three complete identities, if not more, by the time he was through, assuming he didn't have to bail out before then.

A DomSec guard stepped from a wall booth.

"Your card, citizen?"

The retired spacer handed over the oblong that entitled him to exist on the People's Republic of Forsenia.

"Where are you going, Citizen deCorso?"

"Home from the gardens, to rest before I go to work this afternoon."

"You work?" the guard asked as he dropped the card into the reader console.

"At Simeons."

The guard looked at the screen, then at the silver-haired man, and handed the card back. He nodded for the man called deCorso to continue on his way, but said nothing.

The slender man turned the corner with slow steps and even pace until he reached the three-story dwelling where he rented an attic room—a room too warm in this summer season, and probably too cold in the winter. With any luck, he would not be spending the winter in Halmia.

He shook his head as he slipped through the heavy front doorway. Most private homes did not have portals, but old-fashioned hinged doors that the DomSecs rapped on far too frequently.

"Long morning at the gardens, Martin?"

His eyes flickered to the thin and pinched face of Madame Dalmian. She coughed twice, waiting for his response.

He shrugged. "Warm. Two security checks. Always the security checks."

"We don't have crime here anymore, not the way it was in my grandfather's time."

You don't have freedom, either, he added silently.

"That is true, Madame. All the same, it has changed somewhat since I joined the Service. I do not recall so many guards, so many restrictions. But I suppose that is the price we pay for order and security, and it may become more valuable as I get older."

"Martin, the DomSecs would not think that was exactly the proper perspective."

He shrugged. "Have I said anything against either the Domestic

Security forces or the government? No. All I said was that I did not re-call so many guards. Perhaps there were. A child would not recall that, and I was scarcely more than that when I enlisted."

She coughed again.

"You should watch that cough, you know," he offered. "I remem-ber when we landed on one planet, a place so far out it didn't even have a proper name. It just had a catalogue number. Still does, for all I know. The air was so hot it seemed to steam.

"Half the crew began to cough, just like your cough, that's what reminded me, and they coughed. Oh, how they coughed . . . airborne bacterials, they said . . . terrible . . . and the shakes . . . even the Impe-rial drugs . . ."

He slipped into the long-winded persona of the retired techni-cian recalling his glory days, and, as he talked, watched the woman's eyes glaze over, and her efforts to edge away without seeming rude to her boarder.

With her, boredom was his best defense.

XXVIII

LIEUTENANT CATALIN SET the mug of spikebeer on the table with a thud. The mug's impact shook the heavy table, and the remnants of the beer sprayed onto the arm of the passing barmaid.

"Another spiker, lass." Catalin's fingers grasped the woman's arm above the elbow, ready to bite into the nerves should she attempt to leave.

"Right away, Lieutenant." Her husky voice was level, but pitched to carry the five meters from the table to the bartender. Her eyes fol-lowed her voice.

The bartender received her unspoken plea, and filled another iced mug. The steam rising from the combination of cool liquid and subzero synthetic crystal circled his face, adding an element of unre-ality to his sharp features and silvered and curling hair. For a mo-ment, the bartender could have been a ghost.

"It's coming, Lieutenant." The woman tried to disengage the se-curity officer's grip without overtly struggling.

"That's not enough, Lyssa."

This time the woman did not repress the shudder when she heard her name and as Catalin's grip forced her around.

His eyes were perfectly normal brown eyes, but the set of his jaw, and the upward twitch at the corners of his mouth, along with the dull dark brown uniform, revealed the sadistic streak he made no move to conceal or disavow.

Lyssa sat down heavily in the chair next to him, forced there by his unrelenting grip. Her breathing was heavier than moments before, her eyes darting back toward the silver-haired and slender bartender as he slowly placed the spikebeer on a small tray.

"Lyssa, your customer's spiker is ready." Despite the man's light baritone and the background noise from more than fifty other patrons, his voice carried easily.

Lyssa started to rise, but sat back with a thump as Catalin jerked her arm.

"Have him bring it here."

"Martin. Please bring it here."

Although her voice was lost in the hubbub, the bartender nodded and slipped out the back side of the bar, carrying the tray in both hands, obviously not in the habit of serving customers from the tray itself.

"Your spiker, ser."

"Lieutenant to you, oldster." Catalin turned to the woman. "Where'd Si pick this one up? From a graveyard?"

The lieutenant picked up the empty mug with is free hand.

"Take this back, pops—if you can!" With all the power he could muster from a near two-hundred-centimeter frame, Catalin backhanded the mug toward the frail-looking bartender's midsection.

Had the mug connected, the impact would have been considerable. Since the bartender ducked backward impossibly quickly, the force of Catalin's blow, aided by the bartender's quick footwork, overbalanced the security officer, and his chair began to teeter. Then it fell and broke under the DomSec's weight. The officer was on his feet before the plastic shards stopped clattering on the tiles.

The bartender retreated several steps, toward an open space, and waited for the towering security officer.

Catalin lurched to a halt as he saw the older man's stance, took a deep breath before he whirled to catch Lyssa as she tried to ease around the table toward the kitchen entrance.

"Come here. Need to talk, woman."

No one except the bartender even looked as the massive security officer led the dark-haired woman back to his table.

The bartender retreated behind the bar and motioned to another barmaid.

"Take Lyssa's section."

"But—"

"He's Security."

"Poor kid. Her little boy's just five."

"No contract?"

"Dead. Impie spacer. Unofficial. No comp. No status."

The bartender shook his head, but continued to watch the table where the young woman sat, head down, and listened to whatever proposition the security officer was making.

In response to a question, she shook her head. Once, then twice.

Crack!

The sound of the slap penetrated the entire saloon, stilling it for the instant it took for the patrons to see the perpetrator was a security officer. Then the conversations resumed, more quietly, with everyone avoiding the pair at the rear corner table. Everyone except the bartender, who eased out from behind the bar toward the table.

The other bartender watched with a frown.

"Lieutenant? You here on official business? Yes or no?"

"Yes."

"Fine. Could I see your warrant?"

"Don't need one."

"Constitution says you do. I say you do."

"No, Martin!" pleaded the woman. "You don't know what he can do."

Catalin smiled and stood suddenly.

"See you later. Both of you. You'll wish you'd treated me better, Lyssa. Much better."

Both the older-looking man and the woman watched the security officer's broad back disappear through the front entry.

"He'll be back with a full crew as soon as he can round them up."

"And?"

"He'll take us away. Martin, don't you understand what you got me into?"

"Assumed you didn't want to be his property to get used and abused and generally beaten."

"I don't. But I'd submit to it for Bron's sake."

He touched her arm, watched her suppress the wince. "Does he know where you live, or your full name?"

"No . . . I don't think so. Never saw him before tonight."

"Where could he find out?"

"Central payroll, or from Si."

"Will he tell anyone else about you? Or will he come for me as a subversive to prove he can hurt anyone?"

"Uh . . . probably . . . for you."

"Good." He paused. "Go home. Now. Don't argue. You're sick as a dog."

"But—"

"I need to get ready, and Si won't push you. You draw too many customers."

"Martin, you don't understand. Subversion means the Security Farms, and no one comes back from there. Never!"

"I didn't say I was going. Now get home, and, by the way, Lyssa, the name isn't Martin. It's Gerswin. Only tell your friends that. Don't worry about Catalin. He won't bother you again. Or anyone else.

"Now, go."

She gathered herself together, then flounced toward the kitchen, as if offended.

The bartender smiled behind his blank face, and he, in turn, swung around and walked down the side corridor to the back rooms. Once inside the room he wanted, he retrieved a battered and cheap-looking case that nothing short of a field-grade laser could open.

"Leaving, Martin?"

Gerswin caught sight of the stunner in Simon Lazlo's right hand.

"Temporarily. You have some objection? Or are you interested in having me neatly trussed up for the Security Forces?" Gerswin was relieved to find Simon concentrating on him. That probably meant that Lyssa could leave. Gerswin did not set down the case he was holding, but let go with his left hand, leaving it behind the case.

"Let's say I object in practice to my employees alienating Security Forces."

"Then you approved of the way that lieutenant used his rank to force himself on a defenseless woman?" Gerswin edged his hand toward his belt.

Lazlo shrugged. "I don't have to like it, but there's not a great deal I can do about it. Unlike you, I have no illusions and no pretensions. And I have to live with the DomSecs. I just can't run away, Martin."

"Name's not Martin. Call me Gerswin, and I'm not running."

Without raising his voice, Gerswin made three moves simultaneously, hurling the case at the stunner with his right hand, throwing the belt knife with his left, and flinging himself forward and to the right.

Thrumm!

Crunch!

Clank.

The stunner lay on the floor, and Lazlo squirmed to pull himself from the wall where the heavy knife held him pinned.

"Bastard Impie! HELP!"

Thrumm! Gerswin retrieved the stunner and turned it on the saloon operator.

Lazlo slumped.

Gerswin checked outside the door, surveying the narrow hallway. No one appeared, and the noise from the patrons continued unabated. He reclosed the door and retrieved the knife. With the thin door locked, he laid Lazlo out on the floor. The owner's shoulder wound still bled, but not heavily.

After opening the case, he slipped into the black full-fades and strapped on the equipment belt, transferring the knives from his bartending clothes.

He closed the case with a snap and opened the door, slipping down the last few steps to the rear exit. The serviceway outside was dimly lit in the early evening, dimly lit, and empty, with enough shadows for him to leave and take his position without visual detection.

The security squad would doubtless arrive at the front with a flourish after several less obvious troops first appeared to cover the rear.

Gerswin waited in the shadows.

Shortly, he heard the clicking of boots on the synthetic pavement. Three security types stationed themselves at points equidistant from the rear entrance of Simeons.

Gerswin continued to listen, but could hear but a single other set of boots, a single other set of breathing. He checked the stunner.

Thrumm! Thrumm! Thrumm!

The three went down like the sitting ducks they were.

Gerswin did not move, knowing that the fourth guard had been caught unawares and had no real idea from where the fire had come.

Finally, the other guard moved, and Gerswin caught sight of him in the shadows of the nearest parallel serviceway.

Thrumm!

As he dropped, Gerswin hoped that the obvious instructions to maintain comm silence had held. Certainly he had heard no voices, even whispers, from the four. He waited, remaining motionless and silent, listening to see if there were others.

At last, he took out his knives, and did what had to be done.

He left a fair amount of blood with the four bodies.

Fear . . . the only thing those who create it fear is fear.

Surprisingly he felt no remorse for the dead DomSecs, not after what he had seen in the streets and at Simeons.

He moved to the shadows near the front of the building, carrying three stolen stunners and the laser rifle that the last guard had borne.

Lieutenant Catalin had yet to make the grand entrance he had promised Lyssa.

Again, Gerswin waited, straining for the sound of the approaching electrocars, wondering if his judgment of Catalin had been correct, that the man would ignore the silence of his rear guards and plunge ahead.

He was half-right.

Two electrocars purred up. From the first poured five men, who lined up in a rough order, glancing at the facade of the saloon and back at the lightly armored vehicle. One was the lieutenant.

Gerswin shrugged and hefted the heavy laser.

Hisssss.

Thrumm! Thrumm! Thrumm! Thrumm!

Catalin had been the first to fall, with a laser burn through his skull.

Gerswin had missed the fourth guard with the stunner, and the man, with quicker reflexes than his compatriots, had dropped behind the electrocar.

Thrumm!

The return bolt missed Gerswin by more than three meters, but, unfortunately, showed the guard had the general idea of where Gerswin was.

The man in the shadow clothes eased back down the serviceway to the emergency escape and slowly edged upward on it, trying to keep from making any sounds that would carry. Once on the roof, he crossed to the front of the building and surveyed the street below from the facade.

The guard had not bothered to look up, a sign of either poor training or no real opposition.

Hisss.

The exposed guard crumpled, unaware he was dead until the fact was academic.

Still, no one had emerged from the second electrocar, nor was there any action from the slab-sided wagon.

Finally, Gerswin eased away from the facade and to the opposite escape ladder, slipping down it as quickly as possible and edging along the narrow space between the buildings until he was back at the front shadows, on the other side from his first attack. Flattening himself next to the wall, he checked the sights on the laser, then levered the power up to full, enough for two full shots.

Hisss.

The first severed enough of the rear plastaxle for the left rear wheel to buckle.

With such provocation, the side door slid open, and two hulking figures emerged.

Gerswin grinned. The idiots! Both were clothed in riot suits, guaranteed to reflect any laser or stun weapon short of Imperial artillery.

Both carried hand lasers and stunners. Each headed for a different side of the building, the side from which he had first fired, and the side where he now waited.

Gerswin retreated five meters, inching up onto a ledge in a meter-deep recess well above eye level, which, given the darkness and the shadows, should have concealed him until the riot-suited guard was close enough.

Gerswin was wrong. The guard did not even look up or check the sides of the narrow serviceway, but walked through, almost as quickly as possible, firing both laser and stunner at random.

Once the guard was past, Gerswin threw both knives in quick succession.

Thunk! Thunk!

The riot fabric, while proof against energy weapons, was more than vulnerable to old-fashioned throwing knives. The guard collapsed into a sack of muscles and fabric.

Once more, Gerswin clambered up the fire escape after retrieving his knives and taking the guard's most highly charged laser.

It took both knives to stop the second riot guard as the man panicked his way back toward the front street after, Gerswin surmised, finding four bloody bodies. Gerswin swung down and wrenched both knives from the body.

While he would have preferred to have finished off the entire troop, he could hear the distant, but oncoming, whine of more than just a pair of electrovans, and decided to do the prudent thing.

He ran, silently, picking up the case and cloak from where he had hidden them. But he ran, stretching out his strides into the effortless and ground-covering lope of a devilkid ahead of the she-coyotes, racing the landspouts and the terrors of Old Earth.

But he ran, real and imagined terrors pursuing.

XXIX

THE COPY EDITOR scanned the screen, frowning as he read the headline.

"No Need For Protein Restrictions."

"Where did that come from?" he muttered, calling up the full text, speeding through it as he did. Then he reread the first paragraph.

"(INS) New Augusta. 'No system government should need to impose protein restrictions on its people,' claimed D. Daffyd Werlyn, Proctor of Agronomy at the Emperor's College, in his farewell address.

"Werlyn stated that the 'bestmeat' plant, once banned in the Fursine system, could bring about the end of hunger and protein restrictions in any system. 'It's tasty, nutritious, and grows under the most adverse conditions, from poisoned sewage to sand, but produces untainted slices of protein undetectable from the finest organic steaks.'

"Werlyn noted that several systems have banned the growing of the plant because it causes 'agricultural disruption.' The Fursine provisional government just recently revoked such a prohibition and stated that 'bestmeat' was a national treasure, since a small garden could provide enough protein for an entire family of four year round.

"The Novayakin system government recently banned the home cultivation of the plant . . . claiming it provided support for outlawed Atey rebels . . ."

The editor read the squib again, then checked the routing codes, which indicated an Imperial message torp, as opposed to a Ydrisian commercial torp.

He frowned, then tapped his fingers across the board, waiting for the response to his inquiry. The story had already run on two successive netwide faxnews prints.

At that, he smiled briefly before touching the red stud on the console, the special red stud that only a few of the news service personnel had.

The comm screen centered on a man in the dark brown uniform of Domestic Security.

"DomSec, Andruz."

"Pellestri, FPNS. Thought you should see something that crossed the net, Andruz."

"What now, Pellestri? Another subversive headed this way? Another Atey deploring the inappropriate and restrictive technology of Forsenia? Or perhaps another intellectual critiquing the regime from behind the protection of New Avalon's Ivory Towers?"

"I'm sending the squib direct, if you want to receive."

"Send it."

Pellestri touched the transmit stud and listened to the high-pitched bleep. Then he waited, confident that Andruz would not cut him off and that there would be a reaction.

He was disappointed.

"So there's a new food plant? So what?"

"Just doing my duty, Andruz. The regulations say I have to report anything which has a potential of upsetting planetary order."

"So . . . you did what you thought was best. Break."

Pellestri broke. Then he touched the keyboard again, quickly.

"Pelle! And during the day, too."

"Do you have a hard-copy terminal there?"

"Yes. But . . ."

"Take this and see what you can do. All right?"

"Do?"

"Just see if you can track down the subject. Call it personal interest. Might be more than a good story. Might even make life . . . give it a better flavor, if you will."

"Aren't you mysterious. All right." The dark-haired woman nodded slowly, without betraying her understanding of how important the matter was to him. "Send it, and we'll get on it."

Pellestri sent another bleep through the terminal and broke the connection.

Then he went back to editing, although his thoughts did not.

Marta had the old homestead back in the hills, beyond the military perimeter, out beyond where the regime had confiscated private property, and if half of what the squib had hinted were true, it all might be possible, in the months ahead, or at least by next year. But they'd have to be careful. Most careful.

His hands continued to edit the material on the screen as it crossed before his eyes.

THE MAN IN the full-fade camouflage suit waited in the shadows for the scheduled DomSec patrol.

Despite the high-intensity pole lights, when the evening fog was thick, as it usually was right after sunset, gloom dominated most of the interval between the circles of light.

A set of footsteps, light and quick, pattered toward the man who lay stretched under the ornamental hedge bordering the public gardens. His eyes followed the thin, middle-aged woman who nervously hurried from pool of light to pool of light toward the tube station three hundred meters farther down the boulevard.

The sound of her steps rang down the nearly silent boulevard long after her image and shadow were swallowed by the yellow-gray of the fog.

The man who waited could feel the vibration coming from the tube buried ten meters beneath him. He quirked his lips and hoped the woman had made it to the station. If not, she had a long wait for the next train this late.

Whhhrrrr.

The purring of an electrovan sounded from the cross street a hundred meters downhill to his right, then faded as the van continued eastward.

Click. Click, click. Click.

The measured tread of military boots on the pavement continued to increase in volume, although the fog concealed the DomSecs who wore those boots. The man in the depression behind the hedge remained there, flattening himself still farther.

Two sets of steps meant increased concerns. At that, he permitted himself another brief smile. Then he waited. With two guards, there was a good chance one was carrying and using a heat sensor, but sensors were line of sight, and his position was not. He remained hugging the grass behind the hedge as the steps neared.

Click, click. Click, click.

"Scope?" asked a deep voice.

"Negative."

"Waste of time."

"Maybe. You want to be an Atey casualty?"

"Stow it."

Click, click. Click, click.

"Somebody in front of us. See?"

"Small prints. Almost gone. Scope pattern says a woman."

"Who says it's a man after DomSecs?"

"Who says it's one person?"

Click. Click, click. Click.

The steps passed.

The man edged into a crouch, edging along behind the DomSec pair, but well to the side and trailing them, shadowing them, while fitting a small rounded object into a leather sling.

Whirrrrr!

Crack!

Clank!

Hisssss! HISSSS!

The remaining security officer used his laser like a hose, spraying every shadow in sight.

The man in the full-fade blacks had melted back into the ground, behind the hedge and below the line of sight of the laser.

"Fyrdo! Square six, halfway to five. Gerlys down. Ambush! Say again. Ambush. Gerlys is down."

Whirrrrr!

Crack!

Clank.

The man in black, more shadow than the shadows that concealed him, did not wait for confirmation of the second sling, but began the ground-eating strides that would take him through the public gardens. As he ran, he replaced the weapon behind his equipment belt.

What the DomSecs had yet to learn was that in a city, a well-conditioned man who could run quickly, right after the attack, was quicker than their reaction, particularly if his attacks were always aimed at outlying areas and patrols away from the dispatch points. He had made sure they were.

He smiled.

The point was to force retrenchment or repression, or both. Either would do, as would the destruction of the myth of DomSec invulnerability.

XXXI

AFTER STRAIGHTENING HIS tunic, the man with the brown and gray curly hair and full beard eased out his doorway toward the stairs leading down to the second floor.

He stopped after one step, listening, his acute hearing picking up fragments of the vidfax conversation from the room below, where Carra Herklonn, the woman from whom he had rented the upstairs room, spoke in a voice barely above a whisper.

"... I'm sure he's the one you want ..."

"... said his name was Emile De L'Enver. We are definitely looking for a man named Martin deCorso, who is a Forsenian national formerly in Imperial Service."

"... same build, and he didn't rent the room until after deCorso, whatever you called him, disappeared. So he has brown and gray hair and a beard. Anyone can color their hair and grow a beard ..."

"What is the name, Madame ... Madame ...?"

"My name is Herklonn, Carra Herklonn, and his name is Emile De L'Enver. D-E-space-L-apostrophe-E-N-V-E-R. De L'Enver."

"Just a moment, Madame Herklonn."

"... don't understand why they let people like that run around ..."

The man on the top step of the stairs began to edge down the steps silently, still listening as he moved.

"Madame, there is also an Emile De L'Enver, with perfectly good credentials and credit, who also recently returned to Forsenia. He has been interviewed several times, as is our practice with returnees, the last being several weeks ago, before Ser deCorso disappeared, in connection for his travel permit. It would seem somewhat unlikely that Ser deCorso would be in Halmia at the same time that Ser De L'Enver was in Varenna ..."

"... but he doesn't talk like a Forsenian, not even one who spent years away in the Empire. There's an odd lilt there. You know. You just know. And he doesn't have the right attitudes ... about Domsec ... about anything ... and he's scary ..."

"What do you mean, Madame?"

"Sometimes I get the feeling he's heard everything I've said. He moves so quietly you can never hear him. He doesn't act like an old man, even if he does limp a little."

"He limps?"

"Just a bit, when no one is looking, almost as if he were trying to hide it, and that seems strange. And then there's the suitcase. It has Imperial locks on it, the kind Alfred would have called security locks. Not your normal locks, but the kind that look like you could never break them . . ."

"Perhaps we should have another talk with Ser De L'Enver. Is he there now?"

"He's upstairs . . . resting, he said."

"A patrol should be there in the next few minutes, perhaps as long as ten minutes, Madame."

"All right."

"If he is the man we're looking for, he has avoided hurting anyone except security officers. But I would stay out of his way. And I would not mention you faxed us, of course."

"I was not planning on announcing it."

"Good day."

"Good day."

The man known as De L'Enver waited until she had stepped away from the console before walking into the second-floor room.

"Might I ask why you are so intent upon turning me over to the DomSecs, Madame?"

Carra Herklonn started to jab her hand toward the console, but De L'Enver was quicker, and caught her arm before her fingers reached the keyboard.

Despite her greater height and weight, she found she could not break his grip.

"Help!"

"No one else here," he observed with a twist to his lips.

"It was worth a try." She smiled wryly.

"You a former DomSec agent?"

"No. InSec, part-time, before—" She attempted to twist and drive her elbow into his midsection.

"Ooooo." The expression oozed out as his fingers tightened on the nerves above her elbow.

"Before?"

"Before I met Alfred."

"You don't mind all the social control? The government trying to tell you what to do and when?"

Her reply was another attempt to break away, followed by an effort to smash the bones in the top of his foot with her boot heel.

"I take it you approve of all the repression."

"I don't see it that way. You mind your own business, and neither InSec nor DomSec bother you. They don't torture people, like on Barcelon or Gondurre. There's enough food, and the government doesn't tolerate parasites . . ."

De L'Enver shook his head almost sadly.

"You prize order so highly that you have forgotten freedom."

He cocked his head to the side, as if to listen, then gripped her arm more tightly and moved her away from the console, nearly lifting her off the floor with his right hand.

His eyes caught hers, and despite their muddy brown color, they seemed to flash.

"Do most people share your feelings?" he snapped.

She tried to move away, away from the stare and the force of a personality she had not seen before behind the nondescript facade.

". . . I . . . think so. Very little crime . . . or unrest . . . not that many people in prison . . . not that many emigrants . . ."

He frowned.

"Who would have thought—"

"Thought what?" she parried.

"That so many people would like such a repressive society."

He turned toward her, his left hand coming up like a blur. She twisted and tried to scream, but the pressure across her neck tightened, and finally she slumped.

De L'Enver laid her out on the carpet and dashed for the third floor.

Within seconds he was up the stairs and back down by the front door, carrying only an attaché case, leaving clothes and what appeared to be personal possessions in the third-floor room.

As he stepped out onto the narrow stoop, he did not hesitate, but adopted the brisk walk of a businessman in a hurry, of a man late for an appointment, but a bit too dignified to rush.

Three blocks from the Herklonn house, he picked up the whine of an overstrained electrovan behind him. Forcing himself not to pick up his pace, he continued toward the tube train station, presenting an alternative credit card, not in the same of De L'Enver, to the gate.

Once inside and down the ramp, he ducked into a private stall in the public fresher and made several quick changes. The beard was replaced, though he left longer sideburns than he had used as Martin deCorso, and the enzyme solution he combed through his hair changed the brown to black, leaving the streaks of gray intact. The brown contact lenses were replaced with a darker shade that left his irises black, and lifts inside his boots added another three centimeters to his height. He reversed the business tunic from brown to a crisper charcoal, and attached a pencil-thin mustache above his upper lip with a skin adhesive that would resist anything but a special disolver. He added a reddish blotch on his cheek below his left eye.

Last, he replaced his identification card as Emile De L'Enver with that of his third prepared identity, that of one Lak Volunza.

After joining half a dozen others on the platform, he watched to see if any DomSecs appeared, but even five minutes later, when he stepped aboard the four-car train to western Varenna, no security types had appeared.

He resisted shaking his head.

Forsenia represented a closed and controlled society, more tightly run than either Barcelon or Byzania, and yet there were few signs of unrest, and the DomSecs were strangely inept as a planetary police force. While the government imprisoned dissidents, the accommodations, according to all accounts, while spartan, were adequate, as were food and medical treatment. Hardcore opponents were sent to the state farms, but there too was the treatment not terribly repressive.

Yet few escaped or tried to, nor were there any underground movements visible. Istvenn knew, he'd looked.

De L'Enver, now Volunza, sat in a two-person seat one seat back from the sliding doors and observed the handful of other riders.

The train slid to its first stop. The doors opened, and another fifteen people trooped into the car, almost silently, as if each individual were wrapped in a blanket of his or her own thoughts.

The man calling himself Volunza studied the car itself.

No litter on the floor. No graffiti on the walls. No tears or rips in the faded upholstery, which appeared to have been recently scrubbed.

The tube trains were scarcely new, occasionally squeaked or swayed, but were well maintained. While some passengers talked quietly, Volunza could see that they were individuals who already knew one another.

His eyes checked the map on the car wall. Three more stops before his destination.

The train squealed as it braked for the next underground station, but only five or six passengers rose.

Once the car halted and the doors opened, the small crowd outside on the platform waited until the departing passengers left before entering. With a hiss, the doors closed, and the train lurched gently as it began to pick up speed.

Lak Volunza continued to study the passengers, the stranger accepting citizens of Forsenia, while the train hummed and hissed along.

When the train slowed in its approach to the next to the last station on the western line, called Red Brook, Volunza stood, along with a handful of others. The majority of passengers remained seated, obviously headed for the end of the line, as he stepped out onto the platform.

While the DomSecs appeared slow, they might be one step ahead, and waiting for him to exit the train at the end of the line—any line. Even if they could track which cards he had used, they would have to wait until he left the station, unless they wanted to stop every passenger on every platform, whether incoming, outgoing, or transferring. He doubted that the DomSecs were worried enough yet to blanket some sixty stations; many of which had much higher traffic volumes and more than one exit.

If their data system were good enough, they could track anyone from the two tube stations that were equidistant from the Herklonn home and compare the names against addresses. That would take a few minutes, but not many, and would certainly narrow the focus of the search.

That possibility was the reason why the credit card he had used did not bear the name or credit codes of Lak Volunza, but those of a newshawk association, the kind of card given to people who traveled on business too frequently to be justified as personal use. Such cards were registered in both individual names and in the names of the organization. His card represented the state news organization, FPNS.

Brisk steps took him up the inclined ramp to street level, where he turned southward along the boulevard lined by squat and oversize dwellings of gray stone, presumably the homes of well-paid functionaries of some sort.

Volunza checked the time. Only midafternoon, far earlier than he would have wished to be less conspicuous.

At the next corner he turned westward, keeping an eye open for uniformed DomSecs and anyone else. He passed a young woman wheeling a buggy, in which a sleeping infant lay, covered with a light, but bright red blanket.

He nodded, somberly, without smiling, as he passed.

Surprisingly he received a tentative smile in return.

He reached the green expanse of the Novaya Park without passing another soul on the broad streets, and with just two or three electrocars humming past.

The park had no gates and presented a series of grassy areas interspersed with dark conifers and the heavy trunks of the ancient and imported oaks. The size of the trees, if nothing else, confirmed the age and stability of Varenna.

As he headed toward the permanent summer pavilions, he wished he had made his hair even grayer. Then he could have joined the group of older men at their endless games of chess.

While the cool breeze felt warm enough for him, he suspected most Imperials would have found Forsenia far too chilly, especially in any season besides the too-short summers.

A whining sound tickled his hearing, coming from the road to his left where it wound toward the common area a hundred meters in front of him. Volunza set his case down by an oak and wiped his forehead, leaning against the tree as if to rest for a moment. Then he sat down.

From the base of the old oak, he had a clear view of the men at their stone tables, as well as of the women playing cards at a second row of tables. His position also kept him shielded from direct observation from the perimeter roads around the park.

The electrovan continued to the common area and the summer pavilions, where it stopped. A uniformed man and woman climbed out and walked over to the men playing chess, stopping by an older man who was watching, standing in the kiosk that sold drinks and dressed in a gray tunic. The seller nodded as the three talked for several minutes.

The two security officers walked into the section of tables shaded by the pavilion roof. The female DomSec pointed to a white-haired man, then looked back at the man in gray, who nodded.

The white-haired man, the object of her attention, bolted upright. Despite his obvious paunch, he charged the male DomSec, bowling him into another table, and scattering chess pieces in the process.

Both DomSecs turned, but did not draw weapons, as the paunchy man careened off the immobile stone table, pounded past the kiosk, and threw himself through the still-open driver's door of the electrovan. The door slammed closed.

The van began to whine, picking up speed and volume as it whipped back down the road toward the far side of the park.

Wsssh!

The man who temporarily called himself Volunza blinked.

A searing flash of light flared across the grass, so quickly it cast no shadows.

Volunza blinked, rubbing his eyes to regain his vision.

The first thing he saw, when he could see again, was the seething lump of metal that had been the DomSec electrovan. He turned his head slowly to survey the park, but could see nothing else.

"Booby-trapped," he observed to no one in particular.

He watched the group in the center of the park. All but a few of the older men and women returned to their cards and chess. Those that did not merely sat and stared blankly.

The gray-haired kiosk attendant and the two DomSecs strolled casually up the winding road toward the hot metal that had once been a paunchy man and an electrovan.

Volunza quietly eased himself farther down at the base of the oak, nearly invisible to anyone more than a few meters away, and took out a tattered book. Better to wait for the time when everyone was going home before trying to move anywhere farther.

He reminded himself not to borrow any government vehicles. Their rental rate was more than he wished to pay.

He wished the night would come, and with it the shadows that would offer some concealment.

XXXII

THE PURPLE-SHADED squares on the map represented the territory controlled by the government, territory being enlarged by the DomSecs day by day. The light green represented the shrinking area of rebel control.

Gerswin frowned, shook his head, and folded the latest version of the thin plastic into a small oblong which he stored in the thigh pocket of the shipsuit he wore under the winter furs.

"Forsenia rebel file. Interrogative projections."

"Insufficient data."

Gerswin nodded again. He couldn't expect the AI of a scout, even his overendowed scout, to have the capability of a tactical AI, but he had hoped.

Despite the advantage of terrain, despite the advantage of surprise, and despite the tactics and stupidity of the DomSec commanders, the rebels were losing, bit by bit, kilometer by kilometer.

Even without the tanks and drones of the security forces, the rebels had more than adequate weapons, and the DomSecs were so careless about theirs and their supplies that neither weapons nor ammunition were a problem. The rebels had, thanks to the bestmeat plant, local flora, and the carelessness of the government troops, more than adequate food. And no one liked the DomSecs.

Gerswin paused in his mental summary.

At the same time, few of the Forsenians actually hated the security forces or the government. They were minor evils to be endured, like the winter, the snows, the continual freezing temperatures.

Did freedom require an inborn hatred of control and government?

He shook his head tiredly.

What in Hades was he really doing? And why? What would a revolution on Forsenia do for either ecological development or Old Earth?

He had had a reason when he started. Hadn't he?

He shook his head again, and stood, gathering the winter furs around him as he walked toward the lock. Regardless of the questions, he could not leave unfinished what he had started, not yet, at least.

Thumbing the lock stud, he waited for the lock to open fully, before slipping out into the darkness, out onto the thin skis, and into a ground-covering pace toward the town ten kilos to the west.

He expected to arrive there before the small DomSec garrison began the day, perhaps in time to liberate quietly a disrupter or two, or something equally effective.

XXXIII

ANATOL SHEFSIN PURSED his lips as his brown eyes passed over the two men who stood on the opposite side of the bank of data screens from him.

"Yes?"

"You asked about the Imperial reaction, First Citizen."

"I did. It seemed likely that no quarantine would result so long as the unrest involved neither ships nor heavy weapons. Is that the Imperial position?"

Shefsin's brown eyes were as hard and shiny as the polished

brown fabric of his tunic and trousers. He waited without apparent impatience.

"Basically," answered the blocky man in the dark black tunic used in place of a uniform by all senior DomSec officers on Forsenia. "There were words about evaluations and status of the government, but the Imperial office did not seem enthusiastic about recommending a quarantine."

"Refreshing change," observed Shefsin dryly. "Of course, it couldn't have anything to do with the shortfalls an Imperial revenues, could it?"

Neither subordinate ventured an answer. Both stood as if they would stand in the same position until dismissed or forever.

"Of course not," Shefsin answered himself. "The Empire is as it has always been, insisting on our pro-rata share, holding itself as our sole protection against the alien horrors of the galaxy. In the meantime, population pressures around . . ." The First Citizen waved an arm toward the exit portal. "You may go. You have done your duty, and well, and the Republic appreciates it. More importantly, I appreciate it."

Both DomSecs inclined their heads slightly.

"Thank you, First Citizen."

"Thank you, First Citizen."

Shefsin watched and waited until both men had departed before smiling.

He recalled the plans he had studied earlier, the ones for the Republic's first armed jumpships. Before long, before long, the Empire would have to pull back from the Forsenian sector.

The Atey rebellion was fortunate in many ways, he reflected, particularly if he could prolong the conflict until the new heavy weapons complex was in full operation.

While the Empire might need Forsenia and its contributions, the Republic hardly needed the Empire.

Smiling more broadly, the First Citizen looked at the crest displayed on the wall opposite him.

The jagged lightning sword across the olive branch—right now the lightning glittered with promise.

XXXIV

GERSWIN SHIFTED THE heavy-duty disrupter to distribute the weight differently and continued trudging toward the center of the rebel camp, wishing he could shed the bulky and heavy furs for his thin and insulated winter whites or grays.

"You there."

Gerswin ignored the voice.

"You with the 'ruptor!"

Turning slowly, Gerswin faced the caller, a bear of a man who wore the double bands of a force leader.

"Yes, Force Leader," he answered noncommittally.

"Where are you going with that 'ruptor?"

"Back off patrol. To turn it into the armory."

"Not through camp center. Around the perimeter."

"Yes, Force Leader."

Gerswin turned and let his seemingly tired steps carry him back toward the perimeter, waiting until the big but junior officer had lost sight of him in the gathering gloom and increasing snow.

He pursed his lips. Worrying about whether troops carried disruptors through camp center was scarcely the priority setting one would expect of a rebel command facing an approaching DomSec force with the worst of the winter chill yet to strike.

Whether rebel or DomSec, military or civilian, all Forsenians seemed to share a concern with procedures and routine, sometimes to the apparent exclusion of reality.

The man who wore the white furs of a scout sighed. He knew he had learned a great deal from his experiences on the chill planet, but at the moment he was not exactly certain why he had bothered. Not that it would be long before he left, but that bothered him as well.

The armory was a crude bunker whose entrance was shielded from the snow with a small sport tent.

Gerswin stepped inside. A thin and graying man in fraying Imperial winter whites stood inside, glaring at a weapon on a flat bench.

"Log it in, soldier." He did not look up.

"New weapon," offered Gerswin.

The rebel armorer looked up. His eyes widened a touch.

"Where did you get that?"

"The DomSecs were a bit careless."

"Energy level?"

"About ninety percent."

"I don't think I'll ask. Wish we had more like you. Your name?"

"Volunza."

"Oh, you're that one. The scout."

Gerswin nodded.

The older man returned his attention to the disassembled laser, as if Gerswin were not even in the bunker. Gerswin racked up the disrupter, added it to the listing, and used the small stencil gun to etch a number on the butt plate.

He slipped back out into the snowy evening, drifting toward the center of the encampment, listening, occasionally stopping, picking up fragments of conversations.

"When I was with the Twelfth on Herrara . . ."

"Not at all like the Service . . . not at all . . ."

". . . always think the Impies do it best . . ."

He paused, then turned toward the mess tents.

As the smell of burned corbu wafted toward him, he changed direction again and moved toward the command center, easing up toward the guards outside Torbushni's tent.

"Volunza! What did you bring in today, old man?"

"'Ruptor. Guess the DomSecs are getting even more careless. Don't seem to care." Gerswin nodded toward the commander's tent. "What goes with the commander?"

The guard looked down at the packed snow, then around the pathways before answering, his voice low. "Now, old Torbi thinks that the DomSecs won't attack, just circle and wait. Circle and wait for us to try to get out. Try to starve us out."

"Might be right."

"Sure he's right. What did they cook tonight?"

Gerswin smiled. "Burned corbu."

"Same as yesterday. And the day before." Salnki spat into the snow to his right. "Except for you scouts, nothing happens. The DomSecs march closer. A blind man could pick off half of them. Torbi says no. Don't get them mad. All the officers agree. Thought this was a revolution."

"Me too."

"Not now. See how many empty tents? Torbi's right, all right. Push comes to shove, and winter really sets down . . . no rebels left, except a handful. Too few to fight." Salnki stiffened.

So did Gerswin.

"Salnki? Who's your friend?"

"Volunza, ser. The scout."

"The one who brought in the case of stunners?" asked the two-meter-high towering figure of Commander-Colonel Torbushni.

"Yes, ser," answered Gerswin.

"Wanted a messenger, but you'll do fine, Volunza. Can you get Senior Force Leader Gruber from communications up here?"

"Yes, ser. If he's in camp."

"If not, get whoever is the senior comm man."

Gerswin nodded as Torbushni retreated back into the heated comfort of his insulated bubble tent, retreated without waiting for an acknowledgement.

Salnki shook his head.

Gerswin quirked his lips and turned back downhill. Gruber had already disappeared into the hills, but Torbert, remaining comm force leader, would be happy to confer with Torbushni—even if it were an attempt to negotiate a surrender.

Gerswin shook his own head as he trudged through the snow—a snow that represented fall and not winter—the cold beginning to bite into his cheeks as the wind picked up and the temperature dropped further.

XXXV

NO SOONER HAD he slipped inside the lock than he began to prepare for liftoff.

"Prelift sequence."

"Beginning sequence."

"Full passive spectrum scan. Put the sequence on screen beta."

"Scan results appearing on screen beta," replied the AI.

By this time, he had the furs and the soiled shipsuit off, and was pulling on a fresh singlesuit, stuffing the used clothing into the cleaner. A full cleanup could wait until the *Caroljoy* was clear of Forsenia.

He strapped into the control couch.

"Interrogative time until liftoff status is green."

"Plus five."

Gerswin scanned the board and screens in front of him.

"Display on main screen the estimated positions of the rebels and the DomSecs. Change to screen delta when liftoff status is green."

The force display showed no marked change from the way things had stood when he had slipped clear of the rebel headquarters the evening before. The DomSecs had the rebels effectively surrounded, but were not using heavy weapons, although they had brought enough to level the rebel encampment, had they chosen to do so.

How could he have so misread the Forsenian character? They might have a tightly controlled society. They might have a few abusive security officers, and they might not like the Domestic Security Forces, and there might be a few malcontents. But few indeed really wanted an alternative, or could have formulated one they would have preferred.

"Nothing to fight for . . . ," he mumbled to himself, low enough for the ship's AI not to interpret it as a command or a question.

So? For what had he disrupted three cities, half a planet, and personally killed several dozen DomSecs?

Some, like Lieutenant whatever-his-name-had-been at Simeons, had certainly deserved what they had gotten. Quite a few had not, Gerswin suspected.

"Live and learn . . ." But what had he learned?

What he'd known in theory long before. That people have to have dreams. That they have to believe in those dreams, and that they have to prefer the uncertainty and the risk of seeking those dreams to the security of the present. Without those, nothing could change.

Nothing would change.

"One minute until liftoff status is green."

Gerswin broke away from his questions and reverie to check the screens.

"As soon as possible, begin switchover to orbit monitoring, including all Imperial bands."

"Standing by for liftoff."

"Lift," ordered the former commodore, his voice cold.

A dull rumble washed out from the lifting and screened scout, a rumble that rained sound into the snow that dropped on the DomSec and rebel encampments, drowning out momentarily the whispering and comm-linked conversation between Commander-Colonel Torbushni of the rebels and Colonel Ruihaytyen of the Forsenian Domestic Security Forces, as a night-black scout older than the Empire raced into the clouded skies toward the deeper night of space.

XXXVI

THE MAN KNOWN as Eye drummed his fingers on the table, as if he were impatient. The two others, also wearing privacy cloaks, may have smiled behind their own hoods, for the timing of the gesture was off slightly, enough to indicate that the mannerism was contrived.

Contrived or not, it fulfilled its purpose, as the whispers died away and the participants sat up, waiting for the business at hand.

"Do these names break orbit?" He paused, then read from the list projected on the screen flush on the table before him. "Patron L. Sergio Enver, MacGregor Corson, C. J. Grace, Ser Delwood Ler Win, N'gio D'Merton, Commander or Commodore MacGregor Corson Gerswin, Captain M. C. Gerswin, Shaik Corso . . ."

"Eye section has had a watch on retired Commodore Gerswin," answered the figure to his right. "Tracks research projects for some foundation—OER Foundation, I believe. He has a retirement place on New Colora and quarters in the Atlantean Towers here."

"That is what he would like you to believe," answered Eye.

"The other names are not linked to his in the records."

"They are not officially linked to his in any case, and the probabilities are less than point two in some cases. Probabilities aside, Commodore Gerswin is the reason for this meeting." Eye looked around the room, away from the projected list, and silently cleared his throat.

"One of my predecessors twice refused an admiralty request to have the Corpus Corps target the commodore. That was after his successful 'transfer' of close to two cohorts of landdozers to Old Earth. Those actions led to the creation of Recorps, but Gerswin refused Recorps status and chose exile, although he would have been commandant."

"Why?"

"That is why we are here."

"I don't think I am going to like this." That was from the third figure, the one who had said nothing thus far.

Eye ignored the comments. "The names I listed, plus a number of others without any probabilistic basis, are used by Gerswin in a large number of enterprises spread throughout the Empire. The majority of these enterprises are based in the field of biologics, and in all

Gerswin has what amounts to the controlling interests. His *verified* holdings place him above all the commercial magnates in the Empire and above many of the barons. Yet, he has never sought or accepted such recognition."

Eye swept the shielded room with eyes hidden in the depths of the cloak's hood.

"Most important, nothing he has done is in the slightest bit illegal, not that can be traced, not of which there is the slightest bit of proof. But there is a strong suggestion that he is the one who brought down the government of Byzania, and the use of nuclear weapons against one of his suspected holdings on El Lido raises other questions. Unfortunately, we can prove nothing. In the nuclear weapons case, he was ostensibly the victim."

"Why our concern? Gerswin has to die sometime. He's certainly no longer a young man, and rejuves have a limited extending power."

"First, Gerswin has never had a rejuve. He has retained a biological age of roughly thirty standard years for well over a century. His last medical exam by the Service showed superior reflexes and reactions, a neural superiority over the average Corpus Corps member. That was when he was well over a hundred years old chronologically.

"Second, and more important, he seems to have a long-range mission to bring down the Empire."

"Ridiculous!"

"It might be, except he seems to have time on his side. In addition, he understands technology. He was the commandant of the Standora Base, the one who turned it from an obsolete scrapheap into the best refit yard in the Empire."

"That Gerswin?"

"But his interest seems to have turned to biologics after his retirement. The majority of his holdings and interests lie with ways to replace high technology with simplified biological processes."

"I'm not sure I follow that rationale."

"I am trying to make it simple. But think! The power in Imperial society is based on the allocation of resources, the use and control of knowledge, and the ability to communicate. If Gerswin is successful in his biologics, the need to allocate resources is decreased, the need for high-level technical knowledge is reduced, and thus, communications control becomes less vital."

"That is rather theoretical, to say the least."

"One example. One of the products reputed to be his is a so-called house tree. All it needs is some simple wiring and power installation, and really not even that in some climates. What does that do to the construction industry, the heavy durables, the furniture manufacturers? What about the raw material suppliers?

"Another product is a biological spore sponge that cleans up anything. Another line of products features high-protein plants that can't be distinguished from meat in content and taste. They also grow anywhere. Who knows what else he may be getting ready to produce?"

"Wait a moment," protested the hooded figure to Eye's right. "That's all well and good, but you don't seriously think that the people of New Augusta are going back to growing their own food, no matter how tasty, and living in a tree house?"

"Of course not. That's not the point. If the outlying planets, or even a large number, take up societies based on biologics, what does the Empire have to offer? Why would anyone want to threaten them? Why would they need protection? Why would they need a large military establishment?"

"Ohhhh . . ."

"You see? Our resource basis is already so fragile that any large erosion of support would be difficult to deal with. But the Emperor and the admiralty believe in due process, and Gerswin has stayed well within the law. Besides, an all-out effort is likely to make him a martyr, assuming that we could even succeed with a direct application of force.

"His profile indicates that he will revert to total survival, including homicide, if faced with a physical threat. This pattern is likely to dominate more as he gets older. There are some indications that this has already happened in one or two instances, but not that we could prove. Were someone to continue such pressure on him, however . . ."

"I see . . ."

The other deputy to Eye nodded. Once.

PING!

Engrossed as he was, the pilot of the Imperial scout jerked his head up from his Strat-Six battle with the scout's computer at the warning.

"Who could that be?"

"Identity unknown," answered the board.

The pilot glared at the system, which took no notice of the glare, and tapped several plates, then entered additional queries into the system.

"Whew!"

He checked the closure rates again. Then he put them on the display on the main screen, as if he could not believe them.

"Gwarrie," he addressed the computer, "are those figures correct?"

"Assuming the inputs are correct, the readouts are correct."

"Are the inputs correct?"

"The reliability of the inputs exceeds point nine."

The pilot jabbed the transmit stud.

"Hawkwatch, this if Farflung two. Contact. Quad four, radian zero seven zero. Closing at five plus. I say again. Closing at five plus. Data follows."

He shook his head. "That won't do it."

With the incoming alien, and it had to be an alien at that velocity—either that or something the I.S.S. had just invented—the stranger would be past him before he received the return transmission from Marduk Hawkwatch.

The Imperial pilot checked the stranger's indices once more.

The incoming ship, if it were truly a ship, had shifted course, directly toward Marduk. By now, the scout pilot doubted he could have caught the stranger.

He relayed the shift in heading with another data burst transmission, not bothering with a verbal tag.

"How close will she pass, Gwarrie?"

"More than two zero emkay."

"Can we get an enhanced visual?"

"Not within standard parameters."

The pilot frowned for a moment. "Let me know if there's another course shift. Your move."

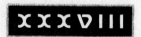

HAD IT BEEN visible to the naked eye without its lightless full-fade finish, the scout would have looked like an obsolete Federation scout.

The energy concentrations within the dark hull resembled those of a miniature battle cruiser, while the screens could have taken anything that a full-sized light cruiser could have delivered.

Speed and power cost, and the trade-offs were crew size (one); offensive weapons (none); gravfield generators (crossbled to screens); and habitability (minimal by Imperial standards).

The pilot checked the signals from the modified message torps he waited to launch. There were three, each adapted to discharge two dozen reentry packets on its atmospheric descent spiral. Each packet contained the same spores and seeds, though the proportions varied.

"Unidentified craft, this is Marduk Control. Please identify yourself. Please identify yourself."

Gerswin smiled, but did not respond to the transmission, instead checked the distance readouts and his own EDI measurements of the Imperials who circled the planet ahead.

"Unidentified craft, this is Marduk control. Please be advised that Marduk is a prohibited planet. I say again. Marduk is a prohibited planet.

"Desct Mardu firet ortley . . ."

The Imperial patrol craft repeated its warning in a dozen different languages, human and nonhuman.

All of them Gerswin ignored as the *Caroljoy* knifed toward Marduk, his hands coordinating the kind of approach he wanted, with enough evasiveness to make it unpredictable.

Gerswin also listened to the I.S.S. tactical bands as they were filtered through the AI and played out through the console speakers.

"Hawkwatch, Torchlove one, one to launch."

"Torchlove one, cleared to launch. Target course zero nine three, E plus three. One point two emkay."

"Hawkwatch, Torchlove two, one to launch."

"Torchlove two, cleared to launch. Target course, zero nine two, E plus three."

"Hawkwatch, Torchlove three, one to launch."

"Torchlove three, cleared to launch. Target course, zero nine zero, E plus three."

The man who had once been a commodore smiled and touched the screens' generator status plate.

Satisfied with the readout, he nodded, then tightened the harness about him, and eased himself into the full accel/decel position, the controls at his fingertips, and the critical screen readouts projected before his eyes.

"Hawkwatch, this is Torchlove one. Target locked on EDI, no visual. Say again. Locked on EDI, no visual. Range point nine emkay."

"Hawkwatch, Torchlove two. No EDI lock. No visual."

"Torchlove one, two, three. Opswatch calculates target class one alpha. Class one alpha."

The *Caroljoy's* pilot grinned sardonically. Class one alpha—high speed, armed, and dangerous. Two out of three wasn't bad for the Impies without even a visual.

"Torchlove one, two, and three. Recommend spread seven, spread seven, with jawbones. I said again, spread seven with jawbones."

Gerswin studied his own readouts.

The Hawkwatch Commander wasn't exactly rolling out the welcome mat, not when he was ordering a tachead spread for the *Caroljoy* to meet.

He also wasn't terribly bright, doing so in the clear. But then, it had been a long time since anyone challenged the Impies, and perhaps they were too slow on scrambles and codes to react. Or, more likely, who cared?

Gerswin touched the full-screen activation button, slumping into his seat under the acceleration as the screens took power diverted from the gravfield generators.

"Hawkwatch, Torchlove one. Lost EDI lock. Lost EDI lock. Still no visual."

"Hawkwatch, Torchlove two. Lost EDI."

"Torch three. No EDI. No visual."

"Torchlove one, two, and three. Launch spread seven based on DRI, Spread seven based on DRI . . ."

Gerswin eased the controls, tensing his stomach as the *Caroljoy* veered slightly—enough to confuse the DRI at his speed and with the screens the modified scout carried.

A sliver of blinding light appeared in the forward exterior screen—momentarily—before all exterior signals were damped to blackness.

The detonation of twenty-one tactical nuclear devices created a glare that would have been observable from the day side of Marduk itself, had there been anyone there to watch the fireworks.

Gerswin edged up his scout's speed, using his own screens and fields to bend the additional energy from the detonations into further boosting his own velocity.

"Torchlove one, two, three, EMP bleedoff indicates target fully operational and extremely dangerous. Probably position two eight five, E minus two."

"Hawkwatch, this is Torchlove one. Interrogative target position."

"Two eight five, E minus two. That's from you, Torch one, at point two emkay."

"Nothing's that fast!"

"Torchloves, interrogative last transmission."

" . . . ssss . . ."

Gerswin would have laughed at the obvious silence had he not been pinned down in his shell, but smiling was difficult under the four plus gees.

"Hawkwatch, this is Torchlove two. Probability of contact of non-Imperial origin."

"Probability point eight. Calculated characteristics impute either higher gee tolerance or non-Imperial technology."

"Blithing alien . . ."

"Torchloves, interrogative last transmission."

A faint signal returned. "Interrogative yours."

"Torchloves, mission abort. Mission abort. Estimated target beyond spread range. Return to base. Return to base."

"Hawkwatch, Torchlove one. Stet. Returning to base."

Gerswin scanned the indicators, altered course again fractionally. The *Caroljoy* would skim by Marduk before lifting above the ecliptic for the long trip back to Aswan.

"Three until drop," the console informed him.

The pilot left his ostensibly obsolete scout on course until the three lights winked red in quick succession, then green.

"Torps away. Launch path is clear and green through reentry."

"Hawkwatch, Torch two. Target discharged missiles on reentry course for Basepath."

"Torchlove two, interrogative interception."

"Hawkwatch, that is negative."

"Understand negative."

"That's affirmative. Negative on intercept. Missile reentry curve will commence prior to intercept."

"Torchlove two, hold data. Say again. Hold data for analysis."

"Hawkwatch, stet. Holding data for analysis. Returning base this time."

Gerswin debated releasing full screens to return normal gravity to the *Caroljoy,* but decided to hang on for another few minutes. It would be just like the Impies to have a few jokers planted around the system.

He altered course again, well within the general departure corridor, but enough to confuse a DRI tracker using the launch curves for the torps as its data base.

His screens blanked again.

"Distance and weapon?" he asked the AI.

"Three triple em cluster at point one emkay."

Nothing like proving yourself correct on the spot. He checked the screens, but they seemed to have held under what had been an extremely close miss.

"Impact near previous course line?"

"Impact less than point zero one from previous track."

Gerswin decided to leave the screens up longer than he had decided a few moments earlier.

"Hawkwatch, this is Turtlestrike. Target evaded DRI line, on high exit course Hawk system."

"Stet, Turtlestrike. Interrogative status."

"Status is red five from EMP backblast."

Gerswin translated. Turtlestrike, whatever craft that represented, had also been too close to the detonation and would be down for at least five stans, long after the *Caroljoy* had made the first of the return jumps toward Aswan.

Gerswin left the screens up, though he dropped acceleration to allow a gee drop to three gees, until he was within minutes of the jump point. Then, and only then, did he return to normal operations for the jump. The switch from three-gee acceleration to near weightlessness nearly cost him the pearapple he had eaten before he had entered the system.

He swallowed hard, gulping back the bitter taste of regurgitated fruit, and plowed through the prejump checks.

While the modified message torps carried enough of the spores and seeds to transform Marduk back into a livable planet, given several thousand, or more, years, the Imperial Interstellar Survey Service would still have Marduk as a source of supply for its toxic warheads for several dozen centuries, hopefully longer than the Empire would be around to use them.

He shook his head and touched the jump stud.

The stars winked out; the blackness swam through the *Caroljoy*; and, after a short infinity, another set of stars dropped into place as the scout resettled in real spacetime twenty systems from Marduk.

XXXIX

The Overlords of Time have called upon the Underlords of Order under the Edict of the West Wing of Chronology.

Listen . . .

Can you hear the whispers of the old papers rustling in the stacks where they were placed by the servators to ensure that the records would be complete?

Can you understand the mumbled words of the languages so old that their alphabets have been lost, so antique that outside of the library no record exists of them or of those who spoke such soft sibilants?

Do you wonder who filled the library, for it was neither repository nor refuge by design, but Hall of Destruction, built for the Ancients by the Gods of Nihil?

Do you stand in awe of the Black Gates that no tool can scratch, that not even the Empire could understand, and that the Commonality quietly refuses to see?

Hush . . .

In the silence that falls with the west mountain shadows, you may hear a set of footsteps, if you are in the right corridor, catch a glimpse of the captain.

The captain, you ask? That figment of imagination? That illusory paragon of legend? That satyric sire of our long afternoon? That man whom sages deny?

Hush . . .

Three steps, each lighter than the last, a silvered black tunic, and hawk-burned eyes—did you see? Did you dare to see?

Ahhh . . .

You turned your head, away from the sole chance you had to see the captain as he was. For he was, and is, and will be, as we were, are, and will be.

The Shrine? That time-clouded prison? For now, it holds his body, his thoughts, but not his soul. Not his soul.

His soul is here, along the corridors designed to resist the fires of Hades, where you may see him if you are lucky, when twilight falls from the mountains across the Black Gates. His soul belongs not just to the gentle, nor to the green, nor to the ladies, but to the past, to the storms, and the spouts.

One soul, one man, one barrier that separated the Gods of Nihil from the green of the new Old Earth, and you have missed the chance to see.

There never was a captain, you say?

Are there none so blind as will not see? None so deaf as will not hear? None so alive as will not live?

Speak not of Faith! Faith is but a belief in what cannot be known, and the captain was, is, and will be. Knowing and known—the captain, keeper of the Black Gates . . .

> *Mystery of the Archives*
> Kyedra L. deKerwin
> New Denv, Old Earth
> 5231 N.E.C.

XL

THE CONTROLS MOVED easily under his fingers, even though Gerswin had not used the flitter in more than a year. All indicators were green, and the preflight check had been clear.

Perhaps he was being overcautious. Even after setting down the *Caroljoy* on his own secluded property on Mara, theoretically a hunting preserve not directly traceable to Gerswin or the foundation or to his identity as Patron L. Sergio Enver and the local subsidiary, Enver Limited, which had taken over the commercial culturing and production of the biological sponges that could remove and decompose nearly any organic toxic, he was skeptical. Skeptical about the workings of a sealed flitter in a hidden bunker.

On top of the skepticism, he had doubts about the wisdom of continuing to build biotech enterprises and continuing to collect ever-increasing income, income he was having more and more difficulty investing and handling.

"So why do you keep at it?"

He wasn't sure he knew the answers to his own questions, outside of the fact that Old Earth wasn't ready for his return, outside of the fact that stopping would require some serious thoughts and self-evaluation. He pushed that away.

The contracts with New Glascow had represented a nice boost to his personal holdings, besides leading to the first steps in turning that smelter/manufacturing planet into someplace livable—not that the New Glascow Company knew that would be the end result of using Enver products. All they knew was that if they dumped the spores into waste piles they got total organic breakdowns and heavy metals on the bottom of a settling pond. In short, some water, some oxygen, carbon paste, free hydrogen, and a gooey mess worth its weight in metal for easy refining and recycling.

Someday, Gerswin suspected, when the air began to clear and fish began to appear in all the streams, they'd discover the overall picture. In the meantime, with a modest take from the enterprises created from the application of grant research, all properly licensed, of course, Gerswin, under close to a dozen names, was able to finance his own operations with but a token tap on the foundation budget, while pouring additional contributions into OERF.

He hoped that his efforts to keep separate from the foundation would limit the Imperial scrutiny, or delay it somewhat.

As far as Enver, Limited, went, he was Patron L. Sergio Enver, who preferred play to work, but who occasionally visited the facilities and didn't complain too much if his senior executives voted themselves expensive bonuses—provided production and sales continued to increase and provided they kept their eyes open for new biological technology opportunities.

Already, on Mara and other nearby systems, half a dozen other competitors were using information stolen from Enver.

Gerswin smiled as he thought of it. If they knew how easy he had tried to make such theft! You could offer knowledge on a silver platter, and no one would take it. Once you made money with it, suddenly people would cut throats for it.

He cocked his head as he listened to the whine of the turbines. Despite its inactivity, the flitter handled well, and the engine indicators were normal.

Sooner or later, he knew, the Empire would come calling, and he would have to leave precipitously. Perhaps that was why he avoided worrying about continuing, preferring to leave that decision up to the Empire. The coward's way out . . .

He tapped the signal for the homer as the flitter neared the local Enver headquarters. While he did not announce his visits in detail, he did not want to catch his loyal employees totally by surprise. Usually he sent a message torp indicating the general time of his next inspection.

Here, on the main continent, the sun had dropped behind the western hills, and the twilight had fled for solid night.

Gerswin dropped the flitter into a sloping descent toward the rooftop pad reserved for the patron on Enver, Limited. The homer signal remained green on the screen.

As the flitter slowed, he closed his eyes and triggered the flash strobes, searing the roof with a blaze of light. In the following instant, he cut all exterior lights, and the flitter settled onto the hard-surfaced building.

Releasing the canopy of the old-fashioned combat model flitter, Gerswin dropped to the roof on the right side, the side of the fuselage that had no handholds or extended footbars.

With his own unhampered night vision, he could see the watchman rubbing his eyes. But beyond the control bubble . . . was there another figure?

The pilot flattened behind the right stub skid, bringing his stunner to bear.

Two figures with long rods that suspiciously resembled projectile rifles were sighting on the flitter. Their quick reaction to the blinding glare he had flooded the landing pad with meant that they wore night glasses to protect their vision. Night glasses on the roof meant some level of government. Competitors would have used poison, long-range sniping, or some other less violent or more stealthy method.

Government involvement also meant that the pair wore conductive stun armor and helmets.

Gerswin estimated the distance from the flitter skid to the low wall from behind which the two agents waited. Slightly more than thirty meters.

He had to act, and quickly!

In seconds, they would start looking for the pilot, one Gerswin, and, on finding him, calmly riddle his position with whatever projectiles they were carrying—fragmentation, straight shells, or gas.

Thirty meters was too far for the stunner, even without their armor to consider, and certainly too far for the throwing knives.

Gerswin settled on the watchman, who had to be an accomplice, tacitly or otherwise.

A weak distraction, but better than none.

The watch bubble was fifteen meters away, on an indirect line between him and the agents.

Thrumm!

The first stunner bolt flared on the bubble, the second through the open door. It staggered the watchman.

Gerswin sprinted.

He made it halfway to the pair before the taller of the two agents, catching the motion from the corner of his eye, whirled.

Gerswin pumped his mad rush an instant longer, then dived low and rolled to the left, zigging forward, and coming up with the knife.

Scrttt.

Clunk.

The other agent brought her weapon around, hampered by its length, even as the taller one went down, his weapon echoing on the roof.

Whuppp.

Before she could get the barrel toward Gerswin, he knocked it from her hands and swept her feet from underneath her.

The woman tried to bring her legs into play, but he twisted and dropped his full weight onto his right knee, which slammed into the side of her neck. The dull crack and instant limpness of her body signaled her death.

Gerswin followed her down, dropping behind the ledge that had not been sufficient shelter for the agents, and reached for the projectile rifle.

Strummm!

The frequency of the stun bolt—heavy-duty military model—confirmed his earlier impression of the watchman.

Still flat, he glanced at the first agent, wearing a full marauder-issue camouflage armor and matching helmet, twitching with the knife through his chest, though each shudder was slower and the time between each longer.

Gerswin edged along the walkway, head below the coping level, until he could retrieve the knife. Before he could pull the knife out, the man shuddered a last time and was still.

As the man in business gray checked the long weapon, he discovered it was configured for frag rounds. He squirmed another meter toward the watch bubble, keeping his body well below the wall.

A quick look, and he squeezed off one round.

Crummppp.

He squirmed farther, and tried another.

Crummppp.

There was no answering fire.

Several meters farther, nearly at the corner, he darted another look, then slowly peered once more.

The watchman was sprawled halfway through the open bubble port, and the darkness spread across his shoulders was not sweat.

Now what?

He could leave, if he left immediately, before the reinforcing troops discovered that the wrong man had survived. But then he wouldn't know what was behind it all.

Besides, if the Impies had really known what was happening, they would not have pulled such a weak operation. So it hadn't been organized by the Imperial government.

A good Imperial records check would have resulted in a direct assault or investigation of the foundation itself, either with more finesse or with overwhelming force.

He would have shrugged as he moved toward the watch bubble and the lift house behind it, but he saw the glimmer of light.

"Once again."

He took a deep breath and charged the portal, managing to cross the ten meters and drop into the darkness behind the side of the portal as the two replacement guards walked out. The portal closed before they were even fully aware that something might be wrong.

The right-hand guard turned toward Gerswin, something in his hand.

Crummpp!

The shot turned the marauder uniform into scraps of flesh and cloth.

Before the second guard could turn, Gerswin reversed the weapon and brought the stock into his diaphragm even as he knocked aside the guard's weapon hand.

Leaving both the dead guard and the unconscious one where they lay, Gerswin scrabbled around to the back side of the lift shaft, looking for the concealed access port he knew was hidden there.

His fingers traced the outline, and he backed away. A snap kick, and the plate fragmented, as designed.

He reached down and punched the three studs in one of the preset combinations and, without waiting, scrambled back to the front of the lift where the remaining living guard was dragging himself toward his weapon.

Gerswin kicked it away, pulled the stunner from his pouch, and fired.

Thrummpppp!

At that range, even the guard's armor offered little protection. His knees and legs buckled him into an untidy heap.

Keeping one eye on the lift portal, Gerswin picked up the body of the unconscious guard and carried it to the flitter, quickly locking the now disarmed man into the cargo bay.

His return flight was likely to be very quick, followed by an even quicker departure on the *Caroljoy*.

Before he made that flight, he needed to claim whatever he could from the latest of the ongoing work and see if he could determine what exactly had occurred.

Returning to the lift shaft access portal, he pulled a respirator pack from the recesses and pulled it over his nose and mouth, then, stunner in one hand and frag gun in the other, he returned to the lift port and touched the stud.

While the light poured out, no one stood on the lift landing. He crossed the landing and peered down the shaft. Empty.

First things first.

He dropped to the private loading dock where his shipments were assembled, not that they were addressed as such, nor did even the Enver company employees know the real addressee. The official labels announced a destination as Research Center, c/o Drop Five, New Aberdeen.

There were three packages, total weight roughly ten kilos. Gerswin debated, finally dropped the stunner. Anyone who was awake after the dosage of sleep gas that had flooded the building and the others in the complex would be hunting and shooting to kill.

With the frag gun in his left hand and the three packages tucked under his left arm, he eased up the three flights of emergency stairs to his office, officially the office of the Patron, Enver, Limited.

Instead of using the main portal, he walked to the storage closet at the end of the corridor, avoiding the three sprawled bodies in Planetary Guard marauder suits, and opened it, twisting the end of a shelf like a lever, then tapping a code on the plate that appeared.

Inside the spacious office were five more unconscious forms, one in a marauder uniform, two in dress Guard uniforms, and two in civilian dress.

Gerswin studied the office, since he wouldn't see it again, ran his eyes over the Enver seal on the wall behind the wood-paneled executive console, and surveyed the twin leather and chrome couches, the conference table with the underslung recliners, and the Saincleer replica on the inside wall above the low old-fashioned bookcase.

The original Saincleer was for Lyr; she'd mentioned once how she admired the artist. It looked as though she would receive it a bit sooner than he had thought, provided he finished up and stopped meandering.

Gerswin turned his attention to the older of the two civilians—the one with the short blond hair and square chin, with the incipient potbelly.

The planetary premier—the same man who had taken the credit for landing Enver, Limited, as a major new employer—had apparently regretted his action.

Why?

Gerswin frowned. He would love to know why Alerio had decided on or accepted such strong-arm tactics.

He shook his head, glanced back at the Saincleer replica, then at the premier. The only possibility was the Empire—the only possibility.

He gathered a few small items from the console as he considered the implications.

Item—if the Empire had actually decided to move against Gerswin and the OER Foundation, then there would have been some rumors on New Augusta.

Item—if the Empire were to move, then the I.S.S. or the Corpus Corps would have been involved, not the Maran Planetary Guard.

Item—Alerio could not have had access to the Privy Council or the Emperor.

Conclusion?

Gerswin laughed once, silently, behind his respirator pack.

Eye Corps had set up Alerio to set up Gerswin, to give Eye the excuse to declare him an enemy of the Empire.

The decisions were already made. All he had to do was to move faster than the Empire.

He stood by the executive console and tapped in a series of numbers, waiting for the acknowledgment. When the confirmation came, he tapped in another set of numbers on a tight beam to the *Caroljoy.* Those would begin the evacuation options for Lyr. Once he returned to the ship and broke orbit, the message torps would take care of the rest. At least in that area, he had anticipated the need.

He waited, then tried to access Enver data. The screen remained blank. He tried the most urgent priority codes, but the result was the same. No data.

Finally, he entered the last code.

The data in the files was gone—entirely gone. Within twenty-four hours, the buildings of Enver, Limited, on Mara would cease to exist. That might even buy his competitors, and their stolen techniques, some time before the Empire realized their enemy was not Gerswin, but the changes in society bound to occur as his biologics became more widely accepted.

Gerswin took a final glance around the office he used perhaps fifty times and left through the storage closet.

The corridor was still deserted, but he used the emergency steps to the roof—three more flights.

Once in the open air, he could hear the distant sirens converging. After sprinting to the flitter, he dumped the guard from the cargo bay onto the roof, then scrambled into the flitter, beginning the take-off sequences even as he strapped in.

The fading scream of thrusters on full power, four dead and one unconscious guard, and dust swirling over them were all that the Maran backup force found on the roof.

The Maran Planetary Guard's atmospheric strike force—thirty assorted flitters and skitters—arrived at a dusty field in a distant corner of the remote hunting preserve of the Count de Mermont just in time to feel the concussions created by the hasty departure of a high-powered and unseen spacecraft.

Orbit control tracked, but failed to intercept, the streaking ship that ignored all departure procedures and conventions.

THE SCREEN CHIMED, and she acknowledged.

At the blond hair and yellow eyes, she smiled, but her smile was wiped away by his first words.

"Are you all right? Is there anyone with you?"

Normally, he launched into whatever he had in mind.

"Yes, I'm fine. And there's no one here except the normal staff. Why?"

"You have reservations on the luxury transport *Empress of Isabel* from the Imperial shuttle port tomorrow morning. Take only what you would take on a short vacation. Everything else has been arranged. The necessary documents and itinerary are in your name at the normal Halsie-Vyr drop."

"In my name?"

He ignored her question and continued onward.

"The *Empress* is an Analexian ship operated for profit, and the human quarters are quite opulent, I assure you. I thought the change would be beneficial."

"Why? I just can't drop everything and run off on a vacation." She brushed a gray hair off her forehead.

"You'll understand once you're aboard. I can't explain further. Take too much time, and time is short."

"Can't it wait?"

"No. Get your itinerary from Halsie-Vyr and get on the *Empress*." Although he did not raise his voice, his eyes seemed to leap through the screen at her, and in all the years she did not recall such intensity directed at her.

Perhaps she was tired, for she found herself saying, "Of course. Will I see you there?"

Instead of answering directly, the image softened.

"Take care, Lyr. Take care."

And the screen, with the background of the scout, blanked as suddenly as he had called.

As she stared at the vacant console, she began to worry. After the first conflicts, the commander had almost never ordered her to do anything. While going on an expensive vacation was not an onerous order, there had to be more to it than met the eye. With him, there always was.

Then, too, he had seemed rushed, almost as if he were trying to complete a long list of tasks without enough time.

Finally, unlike him, about whom she knew more than he realized, or at least more than he let on she knew, Lyr was not the adventurous type once the subject got beyond financial management.

And he was promising an adventure.

"CAN YOU EXPLAIN it?"

"No, ser. I can measure the changes, but that's about all."

The Commandant of Recorps, Old Earth, cleared his throat. "Environmental improvements suddenly occurring, and we haven't any explanation?"

He glared around the conference room, ignoring the blotches on the walls that indicated all too clearly the age of the building. "So what are we doing? Why are we holding together antique dozers with Imperial castoffs? Why are we risking lives day after day on the off-shore purification pumps? Why are we working nights to educate shamblers?"

"Commander." The voice came from the woman, but it was cold and deep enough to chill the conversation.

"Commander," she began again, "whatever biological processes are involved are localized cases, at least so far. We cannot track the cause, only the results, and so far they have shown up in the Rhyn River effluent. There may be others, of course. While there are changes in the forest patterns near the river, with increased under-growth, these are so far inconclusive.

"In the meantime, Recorps has reclaimed nearly thirty percent of the most arable land left in Noram, plus nearly all the High Plains area. We have similar successes, albeit on a later time line, in Norcan and the Brits. No one else has even tried so much."

"Except the captain . . ." That unspoken thought loomed. Or had someone voiced it?

"You're right, Mercelle," observed the commander with a tired shrug. "Hard to keep things in perspective. We'll keep at it, keep track, and see if nature will at last give us a hand. Istvenn knows we deserve it."

"We forget," added Mercelle, "that biological cleaning is a grad-ual process. Sometimes, you can't tell it's even taking place. Besides, until an entire region is clean, it really isn't complete. In the mean-time, we finally have an increasing population that needs the new ground we reclaim every year.

"For the first time, we're actually making an export surplus from the luxury items. Not much, but it's positive."

"And," added the executive officer, "we need to keep that progress up to justify the budget from the Privy Council."

"Right. The budget, always the budget," concluded the comman-der sardonically. The logic was clear. With all the increasing pressures on the Imperial Treasury, and the decreasing revenues from the as-sociated systems, unless Recorps could show continued numbers of hectares reclaimed annually, as well as an increased amount of re-supply goods for visiting fleets, Recorps would be cut to what it could subsist on from foreign exchange from its minuscule exports, and that was nothing by comparison.

What else could they trade on but tradition—tradition, reclama-tion, and sentiment?

He pushed aside the thought that someday, someday, sentiment would not be enough. Nor would the tradition of Old Earth be sufficient.

That was when they would need the mythical captain!

XLIII

THREE MARINES, CLAD in full battle armor, wheeled the laser cutter up to the portal.

A combat squad deployed behind the three technicians in the corridor of the building which had been sealed off. All the other offices had already been evacuated, silently, and one by one.

The senior marine technician gestured. The deployed troops dropped their visors, and the two other techs began to bring the laser on line.

The bright and thin purple lance of the cutter was nearly invisible as it knifed through the endurasteel casement of the portal, a reinforced structure designed to resist anything less.

Thud!

The tiles of the corridor carried the vibration as the entire portal assembly fell inward into the office it had served and guarded.

More than a dozen marines sprinted into the office—a space totally empty of people—sweeping the area with stunners to ensure that the smoke caused by the abrupt rise in temperature created by the use of the laser did not hide anyone.

Their duty completed, the assault squad returned to their deployed positions as the I.S.S. technical specialists who had been waiting behind the barricades trooped forward into the office.

The most senior technician, white-haired, thin-faced, sat down at the main console, the one with the finish below the keyboard dulled with age.

He frowned at the unfamiliar layout of the symbols.

"Logart, this is an old Ferrin model, updated with Usart couples."

"Ferrin? Never heard of it."

"Ferrin Symbs hasn't turned out anything since the twenties, maybe earlier."

"What was this place?"

"Some foundation. According to the offreq scans, used as a cover for some of the Atey rebs. OER Foundation, I think the name was."

The third tech, a dark brunette who was inventorying records, decorations, and other loose items not actually in the data banks, looked up with a puzzled expression.

"Jocham, this is original equipment."

"So?"

"So," answered the white-haired tech, "that means this place has been around a lot longer than the Atey movement."

"How do you figure that?"

"Simple—"

"Techs," interrupted a fourth voice, one belonging to a figure wearing a privacy cloak over full-space armor, "all speculations are better confined to your official report, and backed by specifics."

The senior tech saw the woman about to complain, not realizing the organization the armored man represented, and cut her off.

"Geradyn, official reports, as the Eye Service has requested. Official reports, with all relevant data."

Geradyn blanched. "I didn't . . ."

She broke off her statement and returned to her inventory under the shadowed eyes of the Intelligence Service officer who paced from one side of the OER Foundation offices to the other.

The white-haired technician almost smiled, but replaced the expression with a more appropriate frown as he began to attempt the indexing job, based on the fragmentary codes provided by the Intelligence Service.

The screen remained blank, but the energy levels indicated it was functioning.

Somehow, he did not know how, though he could have devised an equivalent method, the use of force had resulted in the entire data set being destroyed.

Outside of hard-copy reports, the Eye Service wasn't about to find out much new about whatever the OER Foundation had done, or what it had been.

He did not voice his opinion, but, instead, continued to try all possible methods for discovering or recovering the dumped information, but, suspected, based on the codes already provided, that neither he nor the best from Eye Service would have much luck.

These conclusions, of course, he would reserve for the official reports, submitted after all efforts had failed.

The Intelligence officer continued to pace as the marines waited outside.

XLIV

"LORD ADMIRAL, WE do not have the resources to keep this up much longer."

The silver-haired admiral silently studied the figures on the inset screen before him, his lips quirking.

"You realize that, ser?"

The silence resumed as the Service chief refused to comment.

Teeth chewing at his lower lip, the commodore glanced back at his own screen, wondering if the admiral was studying the same simple projections his own screen held, wondering why it took so long for the man to respond.

"What is interesting, Ambester, is what is not on the screen."

"Ser?"

The admiral glared at the commodore, momentarily ignoring the other two more junior flag officers.

"We can provide the more detailed backup information, if you would like."

"More data never solved any problem, Commodore. Hades few, anyway." He paused, then inquired, "Has anyone investigated *why* there are more quarantines? With the relaxations on local armed monitors and greater local autonomy, one would expect fewer quarantines, not more. None of your information addresses that."

"Political problems are followed by the Ministry of Internal Affairs."

"Have you contacted them?"

"No, ser."

"Then I suggest you do. Your data is clear on one point. We cannot continue to enforce quarantines at this rate. It's also clear on another. The conditions creating unrest and local political breakdowns are increasing. Any of you could see that."

His hard gray eyes raked the three other officers.

"So why didn't anyone ask the reasons? You all know the resource pressures on the Service."

There was no answer.

"Last question. Does anyone else have this synthesis?"

All three heads nodded in the negative.

"I doubt that either, but maybe not very many people know yet.

Now get me that information. We'll probably need to get together with Internal Affairs."

The admiral pushed back his swivel and stood. Nodding abruptly, he turned and left the small conference room.

XLV

AS SOON AS the flitter touched down at the landing pad above the chalet, she jumped out, feeling twenty years younger, or more, in the cool, light mountain air.

The chalet was just as she had imagined, from the wide balconies that jutted from three sides, from the view overlooking Deep Loch to the crags both behind the chalet and across the loch on the far side of the valley.

Her steps felt lighter than they had in years, not surprisingly, considering the treatments she had received, and she smiled as her feet touched the wide wooden planks of the balcony.

After a long look down at the crystalline green of the loch, she took slow steps down to the rear portal of the chalet, which the land agent had opened for her.

Inside, the spaciousness was more than she had anticipated. The off-white rough finish of the walls, the light wood beams, and the expanse of lightly tinted armaglass all added to the openness while retaining a feeling of warmth.

In the main living area stood a stone hearth and fireplace with real wood to burn, and off from the fireplace was the study she had always coveted.

She stepped inside the study, and her mouth dropped in an amazement she was not sure she could have felt. Above the simple desk, which she admired in passing, was an original oil by Saincleer, one she had never seen, and one which probably cost more than the chalet itself.

Whoever had furnished the chalet, and she could guess but did not want to speculate, yet, had known her tastes.

Some of the pieces she might move slightly, and perhaps one or two she might not have chosen, but the overall effect was spectacular; exactly the sort of home she had wanted, but one which she had never spent the time to discover or to have built, had she been able to afford such a place, let alone in such a location.

"You approve?" The agent was a young local woman who had met her at the Vers D'Mont shuttle port and who had presented a card that had matched the directions included with her itinerary.

"Approve . . . approve? It's magnificent!"

"There is a message."

Lyr saw the envelope, sitting alone on the desk under the Saincleer

Lyr.

That was all that was on the outside, and she wondered if the script were his. She shook her head. To think after all the years that she had never seen his writing.

She did not open it immediately, but held the envelope in both hands.

There was so much she had not known, had not anticipated— from the impossibly expensive rejuve treatments reserved for her aboard the *Empress* to the star-class accommodations, to the flowers every night, and the personally tailored wardrobe.

She wondered if she dared to open it, or if she dared not to.

After her years of priding herself on being the type not to be overwhelmed, she asked herself whether the commander had set out to overwhelm her. First, the star-class passage on the *Empress,* then the identity as Baroness Meryon Von Lyr, with all the supporting documents, and the sizable credit balance with Vinnifin-Yill, and now a chalet retreat on Vers D'Mont that might be the envy of most commercial magnates of the Empire.

So why did she feel something was missing?

She took one deep breath, then another, and brought the envelope up to her eyes, not that she needed to now. Her eyesight had been restored to what it had been more than fifty years earlier, along with her figure, muscle tone, and hair.

After a time, she opened the envelope.

The single, plain cream-colored sheet was folded in half, and she unfolded it. His message was half-printed, half-scripted, looking more childish than she would have thought.

Again, she looked away, lowering the message without reading it, and stared without seeing at the loch glistening in the white gold of the early afternoon sunlight.

The faint cry of a circling soareagle roused her, and she looked back down at the black words.

Lyr—

As you may have guessed, Lyr D'Meryon no longer exists. She died in a tragic fire in her Murian Tower dwelling. Only the Baroness Von Lyr remains.

She brushed back a stray hair, a lock which, with all the others, had been restored to its original sandy blonde shade, and which, she had been told, would retain the natural color for at least another half century. Still holding the envelope in her right hand, she glanced out through the armaglass at the crags across the loch and then back inside, not wanting to examine the contents of the envelope.

She settled on the vidcube library, filled with cubes, and the antique built-in bookshelves, overflowing with neatly arranged volumes.

She blinked back a single tear, and looked down at the envelope, then at the land agent.

The other woman apparently understood.

"If there is anything you need, let me know. Your own flitter is hangared underneath. There is some food, as well."

Lyr swallowed hard before speaking.

"Has anyone . . . lived . . ."

"No. It has been kept for you. No one, not even the man in gray, has ever spent the night here. About that, he was quite adamant."

Lyr could feel her eyes beginning to fill, turned away from the other, and sank into the corner of the long white couch that had been placed exactly where she would have placed it.

She still clutched the envelope.

Through the swirl of her feelings, she could hear the rear portal close as the other left, hear the whine as the flitter lifted, and the silence that dropped around her like a cushion.

After a time, she looked back down at the envelope. The top of the *L* was blurred where a tear had fallen on the black ink.

First, cold details. In addition to the Vinnifin-Yill account, you have an account with the local trust, Gerherd, Limited, and another account on Ydris with Flournoy Associates. Sundry other assets to match your background are listed in the console memory under your personal key.

The chalet is yours, fee simple outright in perpetuity, and there is a townhouse in New Mont'plier if you yearn for a more urban existence at times.

The Empire will fall, perhaps in your lifetime, which should be long, perhaps not. It is one reason for the diversity of your holdings. But stand clear of New Augusta.

By now, the Empire has seized the foundation and the remaining assets, although there is no data left to track, and has an alert out for me, both for crimes against the Emperor and other offenses. I intend to avoid the Empire for a time, until it will not matter.

I wish I could have told you more, or that I dared now. You trusted me, made my future dreams possible. I have given what I can, poor repayment. Knowing you, it is poor indeed.

Knowing me, it is for the best.

G

Lyr finally rose from the perfectly placed white couch, though she could not see through the cascade of tears, and walked toward the armaglass door that opened as she neared the balcony. Her shoulder brushed the casement as she stepped onto the wooden planks.

Though she shuddered with the weight of more tears than she could ever shed, her eyes cleared, and she clutched the letter in one hand and the smoothed wood of the rail with the other, and stood on the shaded balcony, with the breeze through her hair.

In the afternoon quiet, in the light and in the cool of the gentle wind, the shudders subsided, and so did Administrator Lyr.

As the breeze died, the Baroness Von Lyr wiped the last tear, the very last tear ever, from her eyes and turned back toward her perfect chalet.

She did not notice that the darkness behind her eyes matched what she had seen behind her commander's eyes.

XLVI

Each man expects his day in the sun. Each god raised by a culture may expect not days, but centuries in the brilliance of adoration and worship.

On men and gods alike, in the end, night falls. For men, that darkness comes with merciful swiftness, but for gods and heroes, the idols of a race, the darkness may never come, as they hang suspended in the glow of an endless twilight, their believers dwindling, but unable to turn away, their accomplishments distorted or romanticized, and their characters slowly bleached into mere caricature.

Under some supreme irony, the greater the hero, the greater the power attributed to the god, the longer and more agonizing the twilight of belief, as if each moment of power and each great deed requires more than mere atonement . . .

> *Of Gods and Men*
> Carnall Grant
> New Avalon
> 5173 N.E.C.

XLVII

" . . . RELEASE ALL FURTHER interest in Ydrisian United Communications for other good and valuable considerations, as outlined in the addendum."

The pilot paused and reread the lines on the data screen. Possibly not as legalistic as it should be, but the Empire would hesitate to take on the Ydrisians, and the release of his interests would deprive them of their strongest pretext. That was the best he could do. Had he been wise enough to divest himself of the residual ten percent interest in the network, the question would have been moot a century earlier.

His eyes blurred. The text was the last in the series, and the AI had already programmed the torp. He had earlier loaded the necessary physical documents.

Isbel's granddaughter would be surprised to receive actual documents from the torp, but there was no helping it. The Empire was not about to try to intercept even a single incoming torp to the Ydrisian hub station, not with the outlying systems wanting their own pretexts.

"What is the girl's name?" he mumbled, aware that his words were slurring from the mental effort of trying to wind up all the financial angles of his businesses.

"Inquiry imprecise."

"Well aware my inquiry is imprecise . . . not directed at you. Directed at my own confused memories."

Isbel—that was the old port captain, and her daughter was Fienn. But Fienn's daughter?

That was the trouble with all his enterprises and all his contacts. After nearly three frantic centuries, the faces, the scents, and the names became harder and harder to separate. Not when he saw people face-to-face—that wasn't the problem, because the reality sorted out the recollections—but when he was by himself trying to sort them out.

Fienn's daughter?

Murra? Had that been it?

"Interrogative destination code, Ydrisian Hub, for Port Captain Murra Herris Relyea."

"That is affirmative. Code on screen delta."

The pilot sighed. "Stet. Torp two to destination code for Port Captain Murra Herris Relyea."

He tapped the complete block for the material on his data screen, the message to Murra that would explain her obligation.

Simply put, in return for the ten percent interest she was receiving from him, she had to transmit the transactions and instructions packed into the message torp to their addresses—all various Gerswin enterprises. He had done his best to divest himself of such interests, if only to keep the Empire at bay. Some of those concerns would survive. Some would not, but most of the techniques they had brought into commercial acceptance would survive, along with the increased levels of biologic technology.

He wished he had left himself the time to conduct the last steps of divestiture himself, but he wasn't about to try, not with three Imperial squadrons reputed as committed to find him.

Far safer to leave the remainder to the Ydrisians. They owed him, and they knew they owed him. And Ydrisians paid their debts. No matter what the cost. Always.

That brought up another question.

Debts.

"And have you paid yours?"

He did not bother to shake his head, knowing the answer. Like an insolvent institution, he had not rendered full repayment on each credit. Like a chronic gambler, he had bet more than he had, using other people when he could not cover his bets. Other people, like Lerwin, and Kiedra, like the poor altruistic Ydrisians, like Lyr. Especially like Lyr.

Her whole life had gone to the foundation, nothing more than a charade and a cover for his determination to reclaim Old Earth. She might guess, but would never know, could never know, how successful that real mission had been.

While he had given her back some of those lost years through the extensive medical therapy and rejuves he had arranged for her, he had led her on with promise after promise . . . and had never delivered.

"Will I see you there?" Those had been her last words, and he had not even answered them.

For a time, his eyes looked beyond the views on the screens before him, beyond the exterior view of the uninhabited system where he orbited while he completed his last Imperial-related business. He saw neither sun nor stars, recalling, instead, a sandy-haired woman, earnest and intense, and the warm wood of an exclusive private club.

How many trusting souls had he led on? How many had there been, particularly women, each thinking he had given them something, when he had no more than given them a glimpse?

Caroljoy . . . Faith . . . Kiedra . . . Allison . . . Lyr . . .

Those were the ones it had hurt for him to hurt. But had it stopped him?

And what of the others, the ones he had blazed past in hours or days, never turning back, his eyes on a future that might never come to pass?

"Interrogative dispatch instructions," asked the AI, the cool tones of the disembodied intelligence cutting through his memories.

"Dispatch torp two."

"Dispatching torp two."

With another sigh, the pilot turned his attention to the controls, and to the jump-point plots.

"Time to jump point?"

"Two point five."

He touched the controls and began to plot the coordinates and course line manually, rather than letting the AI do it, understanding that he did so not only to prove his abilities, but to avoid the memories that seemed ever more ready to spill out and to draw him into endless self-debate.

He frowned, pursing his lips, as he watched the plot, wondering how quickly the Empire would act, or whether it would bother, for all the rumors, for all the speculations reported so far.

There were arguments for every possibility.

He shrugged. One way or another, he was going home. Although it was no longer the home he had known, there was no other place that could or would claim him.

He sealed the course, leaning back in the couch.

After a time of keeping his thoughts blank, he dozed, trying to push too many shadowy figures back into his subconscious, half waiting for the time when the AI would sound the chime that signified that the jump point was approaching.

Cling!

"Jump point approaching."

"Stet."

He scanned the board, twice, then ran through the parameters . . . feeding in three possible post-jump courses, probably unnecessary, since the odds of an Imperial patrol being within an emkay of his reentry were minuscule. If the odds, however long, were wrong, he needed to be ready.

"Ready for jump."

The pilot scanned the screens and the data board one more time, his survey still conforming to the military patterns he had learned so well and so long ago.

"Jump."

The familiar black-white flash that seemed instantaneous and endless enfolded the ship and its pilot, then deposited them on the outlying edge of the arrival/departure corridor for a G-type sun, one no different than any other from the distance at which the scout emerged.

"EDI traces toward system center."

"Interrogative distance."

"Beyond one standard hour at standard reentry velocity."

"Interrogative closure."

"That is negative."

The pilot frowned at himself. He should have realized after all the years that there would be no closure—not yet. His instruments were picking up EDI traces that could have been hours old. It would be several minutes more, at least, before the Impie patrol, if that was what the traces represented, picked up his reentry.

"Full screens. Commence acceleration at one gee toward contact."

"Commencing acceleration. Full screens in place."

As the *Caroljoy* began the inward trip, the pilot began to study the information as it built upon the screens before him. Given the angles and the placement, and his own energy reserves, there was no way to avoid some confrontation, and the straight-line approach he had picked would minimize his exposure.

He continued to study the data, sometimes nodding, sometimes frowning, but mostly waiting. Waiting until the pattern and the distances became clear enough for his actions.

As the ancient scout slipped in-system, the silence in the control cabin remained unbroken except for the hissing of the ventilators and the occasional click of the pilot's fingers on the control board.

The numbers on the data screens changed, as did the locations of the contacts on the representational screens, but the pilot said nothing as he watched those changes, as he watched his ship as it neared the Imperial patrols.

Finally, he touched the control panel, and the speakers hissed into life.

"Double eye, this is Longshot one. Jump entry wave at one eight five, plus point five."

"Interrogative characteristics."

"Negative this time. Negative EDI trace. Could be midjump. Sending data track."

The pilot of the incoming scout smiled, relaxed as his course curved him above the normal reentry plane path. Transecliptic courses used more energy, but he wasn't planning a return.

"Longshot one, this is Double eye. Data track indicates incoming is target. Probability exceeds point eight. Suggest optical distortion scan. Track against standing wave. Target screens capable of EDI block."

"What in Hades else does he have?"

"Target capable of higher acceleration than standard scout."

"Ist—" The rest of the transmission was cut off.

Gerswin smiled. The fact that the Intelligence-ordered intercept group did not have all the information on the *Caroljoy* made it possible—just possible—that he could get almost on top of the outlying pickets before they realized his speed.

What he would do when he got close to Old Earth was another question, since he could not attempt atmospheric entry without deceleration. Not if he wanted to arrive planetside in fragments larger than dust particles.

His hands continued to flash across the controls, more from habit than from necessity.

Cling!

"Contact, zero zero five relative, thirty emkay, minus one," observed the AI.

"Stet. Continuing present course," returned the pilot.

The *Caroljoy* would pass nearly one emkay above the corvette.

"Interrogative probability of detection at ten emkay. Assume contact has optical distortion scanners."

"Probability of detection by contact is point two at ten emkay."

Gerswin checked his harness, then rechecked the scout's energy status and the projected reaction times.

At the moment of detection, he would have twenty-two seconds before the Imperial ships' optical distorters would register a change in his speed or acceleration. The lag time was critical. For Service torps to travel faster than ships, they had to make mini-jumps, and such jumps did not allow course adjustments in flight. When both combatants were moving slowly, around orbital speeds, the torp drives were most effective. At higher speeds in deep space, the torps lacked maneuverability and required good predetermined target positions.

Gerswin shook his head. He couldn't remember the maximum gee acceleration for Service ships. After so many years in Service, he couldn't remember?

Rather than voice his inquiry, he put it through the data console. Number in hand, he set the *Caroljoy*'s first acceleration burst for thirty seconds at ten percent above the Service maximum. Then he programmed in a series of course changes, applied at differing intervals than the acceleration changes, that would lead his scout back toward the normal reentry channel, but behind the picket line.

"Interrogative range to contact."

"Nine minus emkay."

Gerswin's gut tightened, and he tapped the preprogrammed acceleration/course sequence into action, grunting as the gentle pressure pushed him back into the shell. While he had hoped to wait until he had been closer, his instincts had insisted he not delay.

As if to confirm his feelings, the screens flared and blanked, and the speakers relayed the tactical Imperial frequencies.

"Contact. One eight zero, system orient, at *plus five relative.* Spread one away."

Gerswin shivered. Even with his experience, it was unnerving to have the detonation arrive before the announcement of its dispatch.

No sooner had the *Caroljoy*'s screens cleared than they blanked again, despite his course changes.

"Longshot two, this is Double eye. Interrogative target acquisition."

"Double eye, Longshot two. Negative this time."

"Double eye, Longshot one. Negative on spread. Target undamaged. Second spread away."

Gerswin pursed his lips, waiting for the AI's report.

"Detonation patterns ranging from one five zero to two one zero relative. Point zero five emkay."

Gerswin changed heading, nearly at right angles, and triggered another acceleration burst.

Once more, the screens cleared, only to blank with the flash of another detonation.

"Double eye, Longshot one. Spread three away. Interrogative instructions on spread four."

"One, Double eye. Fire on best track data."

Gerswin grinned. With luck, all he had to worry about was whatever the Eye Service had managed to deploy around Old Earth itself. His grin faded as he reflected that what he had just evaded would be a short and easy exercise compared to what awaited him.

The ship's screens cleared and blanked briefly a fourth time.

Gerswin made another small course change and boosted the acceleration, but negated the rest of the programmed changes.

"Double eye, this is Longshot one. Scanner information indicates target is continuing Old Home."

"Stet, one. Understand. Regroup Double eye. Regroup Double eye."

Gerswin set the alarm and leaned back in the control couch, finally dropping the acceleration to normal gee force to conserve the most possible of his remaining energy. Further acceleration would not help, and could only require more power to kill at destination.

More than a standard hour passed before the alarm chimed softly.

Cling.

"EDI traces in destination area."

"Display on main screen. Note deviation from system plane."

From what the sensors could pick up, there were three corvettes and a light cruiser orbiting Old Earth.

"All for poor old me?"

"Inquiry imprecise."

"Stet. It's very imprecise."

"Please reformulate."

"Disregard."

"Disregarding imprecise inquiry."

He wiped his forehead with the back of his right hand. Would the same general strategy work twice?

He smiled. If it did, it would certainly play Hades with Imperial tactics manuals. And the reentry path he had planned would leave communications a bit ragged. Ships weren't supposed to split the planetary polar force lines.

He touched the command keyboard to put the Imperial frequencies back on the ship's speakers.

"... negative on incoming this time ... verify reported velocity ..."

"... can't be human at that ..."

"Please restrict transmissions to tactical objectives, Hotshots one and two."

"Stet, restricting."

Gerswin boosted the ship's angle to the system plane. In-system, paradoxically, it was easier, with less dust. Too bad you couldn't jump-shift that close to a sun.

Given the ship dispersion around the planet, and the position of the lunar relays, the three corvettes, but not the cruiser, might have a shot at him. But not as much as they anticipated, not unless they wanted to have tacheads detonating in Old Earth's upper atmosphere. Gerswin doubted that the Emperor, even the current Emperor, would approve of the uproar that could cause.

"Eye Cee, this is Hotshot three. Tentative target acquisition through optical distortion scanners. Bearing two seven five relative. Mean radian seven zero."

Gerswin swung the scout another ten degrees and began deceleration.

"Hotshot three, cleared to fire."

"Range to contact." Gerswin swallowed.

"Seven emkay."

His fingers ran over the console. For all practical purposes, he was going to have to decelerate from his present velocity to damned near nothing if he wanted to get down in one piece. With the corvettes on station, the simple business of establishing orbit, then determining descent, was shot to Hades.

That meant the distances he was now covering in minutes would take more like a half an hour, giving the Eye group more chances, and requiring more evasion than he would have liked.

He keyed in a near-random deceleration schedule and waited, listening, as the scout began to slow.

Abruptly, the forward screens flared and blanked.

"Range and distance?" inquired Gerswin, feeling the sweat on his forehead, and waiting for the transmissions that would tell him, because of the transmission lag, after the fact.

"Spread pattern, three detonations. Nearest approximately point zero four emkay at one seven zero."

The pilot wiped his forehead, still waiting for the Imperial transmissions.

"Eye Cee, Hotshot three. Target acquisition remains tentative. Deceleration pattern not within analyzer parameters."

"Hotshot three, fire when possible. Use best approximations."

In the static between transmissions, Gerswin adjusted his course "downward" and away from a direct intercept with the corvette, increasing the deceleration more steeply than on his original plan. He shifted his weight to get more comfortable in the two gees riding on him.

The screens cleared, only to blank with another flare.

"Eye Cee, spread one missed. Estimate error of point zero three emkay. Reassessing track."

"Hotshot three, fire when able."

"Hotshot two, this is Eye Cee, interrogative arrival point delta."

"Eye Cee, two here. Estimate arrival delta in ten plus."

"Four estimates arrival in one five."

Gerswin calculated. If point delta were where he estimated, then neither of the other corvettes would be that much of a problem. Hotshot four might not be a factor at all.

"Eye Cee, spread two away."

Gerswin grimaced. The captain of three was delaying his reports to throw Gerswin off by more than the transmission delay lag.

"Range and distance?" he asked the AI.

"Point zero three emkay. Zero one zero relative."

For the third time, the screens blanked. This time the scout shivered.

Gerswin wiped his forehead and frowned, ignoring the extra effort it cost him under the gee load. The captain of Hotshot three was better, far better, than he would have liked. He turned the ship farther from the corvette than he really wanted to, and increased the deceleration further, squinting at the increased flow of sweat from his forehead.

Gerswin gambled and eased the *Caroljoy* all the way back to a head-to-head course with the corvette, but left the deceleration untouched.

"Eye Cee, spread three impacted near target, but prior scanner data indicated target still on possible reentry course."

"Stet, three."

"Hotshot two, Eye Cee. Interrogative target acquisition."

"Eye Cee, negative this time."

Gerswin squared himself in the shell and keyed in three minutes of maximum deceleration, trying to keep his mind clear and picturing mentally the changing relative positions.

"Eye Cee, this is Hotshot three. Reported lost optical distorter scan. We may have reacquired. Say again. May have reacquired. Target managed to obtain decel below tracking parameters."

". . . what in Hades is that scout? . . ."

"Please restrict transmissions to mission!"

Gerswin stopped the deceleration totally, breathing deeply in normal gravity, and hoping that the corvette had managed to lock in at maximum deceleration. He watched the seconds unroll on the tactical clock.

The exterior screens blanked. The interior lights flickered and dimmed, before resuming their normal intensity. A series of red point lights flared on the systems status display, then faded. All but two.

"Damage report!"

"Screen shock impact at two. Auxiliary power buffer inoperative. Secondary screen generator status delta."

Gerswin scanned the systems board, rechecked the *Caroljoy*'s relative and absolute velocities, then squared himself for another two minutes of maximum deceleration. If he had calculated correctly, *if,* then he would need only another two-minute maximum decel just before the near right angle polar reentry path he had plotted.

"Eye Cee, this is three. Report final spread impacted target screens. Target screens held to plus five."

"Plus five? Interrogative plus five."

"Affirmative, Eye Cee. That is affirmative."

". . . what that thing riding . . ."

"Please restrict transmissions to target net."

"Hotshot two, this is Eye Cee. Interrogative target acquisition. Interrogative target acquisition."

"Acquisition negative. No EDI tracks. Optical distortion scanners down. Down as reported two days previous."

Gerswin smiled as the deceleration load lifted. The bitterness in Hotshot two's transmission told more than the words used in the transmission.

He recalculated. From his plot, Hotshot four would not be in intercept position, except for less than a ten-second window, and two had no way to track him, provided he did not remain on a steady course.

With that self-reminder, Gerswin tapped in a series of random length zigzag course changes to position the *Caroljoy* erratically over the next several minutes.

Finally, he fed it into the AI.

"Suggest changes as noted on the data screen," the AI commented.

Gerswin studied the changes and nodded, then incorporated them into the reentry codes. While he would have liked to make the final descent personally, the timing was too tight. So the AI would have to handle it, until the *Caroljoy* was well within the atmospheric envelope.

"Hotshot two, this is three. Data indicates target will be zero one zero relative to you at point three emkay in one minute from mark. Fire spread delta . . . MARK!"

"Damn him . . . too damned good," muttered Gerswin as he changed course again and keyed in twenty seconds of acceleration at half max.

Wheeeeeee . . .

Before the acceleration ended, the ship staggered, and the cockpit dropped into the red gloom of the emergency lighting system.

Thud . . . thud . . .

The two jerks of an EMP shock wave slammed Gerswin against his harness.

The status board was half-red. As Gerswin focused his attention on the systems, ignoring the ringing in his ears and the throbbing in his head, some of the lights turned green. A good ten shifted to amber, and five remained in the red.

"Damage and status!"

"Secondary screen generator omega. Primary and secondary power buffer systems omega. Grav systems delta. EDI omega . . ."

Gerswin ignored the rest of the damages. The *Caroljoy* was sound enough to make it down, provided nothing else was thrown at him.

He shook his head slowly, afraid to move suddenly.

"Eye Cee, this is two. Fired on mark from Hotshot three. Detonation, but no instrumentation."

"Eye Cee, three here. Impact at less than point zero zero five emkay. Target screens held to plus seven."

". . . holy Istvenn . . ."

Gerswin ignored the Imperial byplay, since neither corvette could fire again without risking planetside damage, and strapped himself more tightly than before.

"Eye Cee, this is Hotshot four. Have target acquisition, but unable to deploy without possible damage orbit control."

"Stet, four. Hold until able to fire."

"Three here. Four cannot hold. By the time orbit control is clear, target will be in reentry."

Gerswin smiled reluctantly under the gee force at the captain of Hotshot three. He never seemed to give up.

"Four, continue to hold until you can deploy without damage to Old Home or orbit control."

"Four, holding."

Gerswin looked at the controls as the gee force went from half maximum to more than seven gees, jamming him back into the couch.

"Commencing reentry program."

"Eye Cee, this is Hotshot three. Target commencing reentry on max-gee curve through main magfield taps."

". . . said scout wasn't human . . ."

". . . one squadron not enough . . ."

eeeeeeeEEEEEEEEEEEEEEEEEEEEE!!!!!!

Gerswin winced at the high-frequency static pouring from the speakers, the noise created by his own unique reentry path.

For the following five to ten minutes, most atmospheric communications in the northern hemisphere of Old Earth were going to be difficult, if not impossible.

Instead of fighting the sound, he shifted his attention to the readouts, ready to override the AI if necessary.

The pressure across his chest began to ease, as did the screeching on the comm bands, replaced with a deeper and less intense growling that began to fade as he caught scattered fragments of the Imperials' communications.

". . . unique reentry . . ."

". . . alert Eye Cee . . . possible planetside follow-up . . ."

". . . nothing like . . ."

". . . orbit control . . . track . . . interrogative track . . ."

". . . negative . . . this time . . ."

". . . lunar relay . . . position inaccurate . . ."

The transmissions became fainter and fainter.

"Reentry complete," announced the AI.

Gerswin sat forward and checked the coordinates against those for the Euron retreat, nodding at the relatively short distance remaining. His head ached, and his ears still rang.

Then he tapped in the last courses, monitoring both the course line and the far screens as the scout edged toward the hidden bunker that had waited so long. The bunker from which the *Caroljoy* could never rise.

"Time to touchdown?"

"Estimate five plus."

He watched the waves beneath on the screen, and then the blotched land that alternated between golden grass, scattered trees, and purple clay and its matching scraggly purple grass.

"Homer is on."

"Descent path clear."

Gerswin mumbled the landing points to himself, slowly easing the black scout through the concealed bunker door and down the tunnel and into the hangar. Scarcely a fitting grave for the scout.

"Gates closed."

He sighed, letting his muscles relax for a moment before releasing the harness.

"What now?"

"Inquiry imprecise. Please clarify."

"What do I do now?"

The AI said nothing, as if it had not heard his clarification.

"About the ship, about you . . . doubt I'm coming back. May use the flitters . . . no energy left . . . not to speak of . . . nowhere to go . . ."

He wondered why he was talking as he did, but it seemed almost as if he were trying to justify what he said, what he was going to do.

"Terminate."

Terminate? The single coolly feminine word hung in the control room. Had the AI actually said terminate?

"Please clarify." This time, the pilot asked for the clarification.

"Energy reserves insufficient for continued full-status operation. Pilot has expressed no further need for ship and AI. Therefore, suggest full shutdown and AI termination."

"Why?"

"No further purpose for ship. Ship cannot be lifted. Cannot be repaired."

He swallowed hard. How could he feel sentimental about a chunk of metal and electronics? Even if he had built it? Even if it had been home, on and off, for a century?

"Request AI recommendation for optimal outcome for AI."

"Termination optimal outcome for AI. Pilot has expressed no further need for AI. Ship cannot use AI. No remaining function for AI."

How could he do otherwise, practically and in fairness?

"You left everyone else, didn't you?"

Neither he nor the AI answered the question, as, hands trembling, he began the series of codes that would fulfill the only request the AI and ship had ever made. The only request.

XLVIII

TOUCHING HIS TONGUE to the side of the special tooth, the gaunt man, the rail-thin man who had carried the title of Eye for too long, sighed. Sighed again, and touching the side of the tooth with his tongue again, read the cryptic message a second time.

"Devilkid home. Exact location unknown. Energy consumption indicates probability of lift less than five percent."

Eye frowned. No probability involving Gerswin could be that low, not with the resources and ingenuity involved.

He tried to relax the muscles in his face, but failed.

Despite the power squandered in the deployment of three squadrons, despite the continuing use of energy such deployment required, and despite the sacrifices and efforts of the overstrained Service as a whole, Gerswin had gone home. Just as the man had done whatever else he wanted. Gone home and left a devil's brew behind. Gone home, brushing aside the Service as an inconvenience.

Although he had left the foundation behind, the administrator was dead in a strange fire, and the records were blank, except for scraps that confirmed Eye's worst fears. The bank records, those few that Eye could reach, only confirmed the confirmation.

The gaunt man touched the golden call button.

Unlike his predecessor, he would not wait to be called by the Emperor. He had already waited too long.

Then again, it had been too late before he had taken the reins. Calendra had known, but neither he nor the Emperor had believed Calendra.

The Earl of Selern touched the call button and began to wait.

XLIX

ONULL CROUCHED AT the base of the largest boulder between her and the demon. She shivered in the fog that had swept in off the northern sea, the fog that the doc had said would come because of the black demon that twisted eyes.

She had not seen the demon when it had flown over the huts and into the hills the day before. Devra had, and now she would not speak of what she had seen. Devra had seen and refused to come back to tend the southern flock.

That was why Onull was there, crouched into as small a ball as she could make herself, hoping that the demon would not notice.

Like the other youngsters from Wallim's village who had been in the forest, gathering, she had smirked behind her hand at Devra's tale, and at the visions seen by the old women who sat in the square by the well. She had even volunteered to watch the flock the next day, until Wallim decided who the new shepherd would be. Watching sheep was far easier than grubbing and gathering in the muck of the woods.

Then, just moments before, the ground had trembled beneath her feet, and she had run for the rocks, her mouth agape as the flat cliff had split in two and revealed a dark cave down to whatever depths the demon had come from.

She shivered again, waiting for the demon to come and take her, afraid to move, for fear any motion would call her to the attention of the monster.

The fog continued to swirl in from the not-too-distant sea, wrapping itself around the hillocks and dropping from the higher hills as it flowed inland.

Onull hoped its grayness, and the tattered gray garment that was her cloak, would shield her.

Click, click, click, click.

She shuddered at the metallic sounds, drawing herself closer to the boulder, wanting to look, and afraid to look.

Rurrrrr . . . clunk.

The ground vibrated under her feet, and she glanced upward.

Through the mist, she could see that the gray cliff face was smooth, totally smooth, as it had been through all her life.

She shuddered.

Who else but demons could make caves appear and disappear in solid rock?

Click.

She finally peered around the boulder.

At the base of the sheer cliff stood a figure, seemingly in black, looking out toward the sea, though it could not be seen, Onull knew, except from the very top of the hill above the cliff, and then only on a clear day.

She darted another look, ready to duck her head behind the stone that sheltered her should that black-clad figure turn her way.

It looked like a man, a slender man with golden hair, but with demons, doc said, you could never tell.

The demon man turned toward her, and she flashed behind the stone before he could see her.

Click . . . click.

Her heart began to pound as the terrible steps moved toward her, and she wanted to run. But her feet would not move, and she curled into a ball at the base of the stone that had not sheltered her enough.

Click, click, click. Click, click.

She could hear it coming around the boulder, as if it knew she were there, searching her out.

Click. Click.

The footsteps paused, and she could feel the burning gaze of the demon as it penetrated her thin and ragged cloak. But she did not move.

"So much fear. So much. Best not . . ."

Then its voice deepened.

"If you wish to live beyond the instant, promise yourself you will not speak of this moment and this meeting."

Though the words sounded strange, she understood. She shuddered, but said nothing. Knowing she would never, could never mention what she had seen, even if the demon had not bound her.

Click, click. Click. Click.

The awful steps died into the fog, echoing ever more faintly through the stony hillside, until at last the demon was gone.

Onull scraped herself into a sitting position, shivering, wondering if she would ever feel warm again, and wrapped her cloak more tightly about her as she stumbled back to the village.

L

THE MAN WHISTLED as he walked south along the dusty trail above the river, pausing at times to stop and to listen, but always resuming his steps toward the southern mountains.

The patches of lifeless ground were fewer in the higher reaches, as were the twisted trees and stunted bushes. Occasionally, as he viewed an area where house trees flourished or where the ecological recovery seemed well along, he nodded.

Before him, the trail veered left abruptly, away from the river. He stopped.

The reason for the path's change of direction was clear enough from the purpled ground, the scraggly growths, and the tumbled bricks and stone. He peered over the low rock and rail barricade at the desolation.

After completing his cursory study, he paused again, letting his ears and senses take in the environment around him, alert for any sounds or indications of movement. The waist-high undergrowth that surrounded the path was silent, and from the forest that began a good hundred meters up the hill, he could hear only the distant sounds of a single jay. Farther away, there was the intermittent caw of a croven.

The dust of the path showed day-old scuffs of a wide-tired wagon, the kind pulled by the traveling peddlers who brought Imperial and Noram goods into the back reaches of the continent.

His right hand on one rock post, he vaulted the rail barrier and landed lightly on the purpled moss. In a dozen quick steps he was down the hillside and in the shadowed hollows of what he assumed had been some sort of factory or commercial establishment. Farther downslope he could see the cracked pavement of the old highway, the sterile strip that hugged the eastern bank of the river, without even the traces of that scruffy purple grass that struggled up in all but the worst polluted areas.

Off came the backpack, and from it two thin canisters.

Picking spots with shelter and soil, no matter how contaminated, he planted two minute seedlings. Next came the pouch with the capsules.

He lifted his head and estimated the area. Three capsules, one of the spores and two of the virus. He pricked the first, the catalytic virus, and scattered the contents with a practiced motion. Within weeks the improvement would be dramatic.

After repacking and reshouldering the black backpack, he took another dozen long steps and scattered the contents of the second capsule, the spores. On the far end of the sundered complex, he released the contents of the third and last capsule.

Although his journey was more survey, more for personal satisfaction and knowledge, while his supplies lasted, he would try to provide an additional boost to the most blighted spots.

As he had suspected, once he crossed the factory site, the path returned to its previous course paralleling the river. Again, he vaulted the makeshift rock and rail barrier to continue his southward trek.

"Just a regular jonseeder," he murmured as he stepped up his pace.

In time, the slender man in the dark olive singlesuit reached a junction where a larger trail, nearly a road, emerged from the forest and met the river path to form what appeared to be a major route southward.

He wondered if he should have donned his black cloak as he caught sight of another traveler. A heavyset man, who had appeared from a shadowed section of the wider trail shadowed by the overarching trees, waddled down the gentle slope toward the river and the man in olive.

"Yo!"

The waddling man, who resembled the extinct walrus in his brown leathers and flowing mustache, hailed the man with the pack.

The slender traveler waited.

"Yo!" hailed the bigger man again.

The slender man who waited returned the greeting with a wave vaguely akin to a salute, but said nothing until the other was within a few meters.

"Beg your pardon, but I speak the local tongue poorly."

"No problem," exclaimed the overflowing man. "No problem. Panglais, then?"

"That would be better," returned the other in Panglais, "if you do not mind."

"Fine! Fine! All the same to me. Language is language, I say." He shivered and looked at the faint sun, strong enough to cast shadows, but struggling nonetheless to disperse the high gray haze.

"Would that words could warm as well as the sun should. And you, a peddler of some sort, I bet. That or a pilgrim, heading south and over the deadly mountains to the fabled southern shrines."

"No. Just a traveler, seeing what I can see." His ears had picked up the rustles in the underbrush. He gestured generally as he spoke and placed his hands so that his thumbs rested on the wide equipment belt.

The walrus man gestured in turn. "Werner D'Vlere, at your service. Minor magician, basso profundo, and bon vivant." He carried but a small satchel of scuffed brown leather that, in general terms, matched his jacket and trousers.

The traveler inclined his head. "Magician?"

"A bit of sleight of hand, a few jokes. Enough to guarantee a meal or two from the small clumps of cots that call themselves towns."

The traveler said nothing, but nodded, as if to ask the magician to continue.

"And you, my friend the traveler, how do you pay your way through these backward reaches?"

"Somehow, I find a way. Usually I perform services." He shifted his weight and stepped to the left a pace. The rustlings continued, though more quietly and slowly.

"Services? Well, I would suppose that a traveler such as you would have some skills that they would not have."

"I manage. Better some places than others."

While the sounds from the underbrush had stopped, the traveler was aware that the individuals who had created them were alert, quite alert. Either the pair in hiding had no energy weapons, or deigned to use them on a lone traveler.

He stepped toward the heavy man, stopping less than a meter away.

"Will you introduce me to your friends?" He gestured toward the underbrush.

"Alas, you have seen through my sleight of hand." A small projectile pistol appeared in the left hand of the leather-clad man. He gestured with his right hand, and from the shoulder-high brush rose two youngsters, both in leathers stain-darkened in blotches to create a camouflage effect.

"May I see your pack, if you please? And gently, please. If you would put it—"

Like a spring wound nearly to the breaking point, the traveler uncoiled, his hands blurring from his waist, and his body moving sideways at the same speed.

Thunk! Thunk! Thunk!

Three silver flashes creased the heavy riverside air, and the traveler crouched beside the body of the walrus man, the projectile pistol in his own hand.

He stood.

The two youngsters looked down, openmouthed, at the heavyweight knives buried in their shoulders, knives that had struck with enough impact to force them to drop the long knives they had carried.

The traveler nodded at the two.

"Come here. Leave the knives on the ground."

As they edged toward him, he studied the pair, still listening for the telltale sounds that would indicate reinforcements.

He realized that the one on the left, as they converged from their spread positions, was a young woman, and that they were related, probably brother and sister. Their eyes differed from earth-norm, not like the hawk-searching of the devilkids, but more catlike, with a reflected luminescence that suggested night vision.

"Sit down."

He pointed to a spot for each. Then he tucked the gun into his waistband, and eased the pack off, ready to drop it and disable either or both if necessary.

He pulled out what he needed and set the pack on the ground, out of the way.

"Speak Panglais?"

"Yes." That from the woman, scarcely more than a girl.

He nodded at the other youth.

"Yes."

"I'll take the knife out and treat the wound. If either of you moves, I'll kill the other."

He smiled at the confusion his remark caused, knowing instinctively that each would want to protect the other.

He started with the young man, not out of reverse chivalry, but because he couldn't count on the brother's good sense if he began with the woman.

The knife came out simply enough, since it wasn't barbed. The weight and design were for initial shock value and reusability, not for cruelty.

Next, he sprinkled some bioagent into the wound and covered it with gel.

"That's it. Muscle tear is pretty bad. Should start healing immediately. Won't have any infection if you don't mess with the gel. Don't touch it."

The youth twitched when he pulled the knife from the sister, but said nothing as he treated her wound as well.

Then he retrieved the third knife from the body of the dead man, cleaning all three quickly and replacing them in the sheaths hidden in his belt.

Standing and stepping back, he surveyed both siblings.

Dressed identically, with black hair, cut roughly at shoulder length, pointed jaws, cat-green eyes, smooth chins, and virtually no body hair, he guessed. The man's features were marginally heavier than the woman's, and his legs, under the loose leather trousers, indicated thicker muscles.

"What should I do with you?"

"Don't turn your back," suggested the man.

"Do you really think you could move faster than I can? Heard you all the way down the hill. Remember, you had your knives in hand. I did not. Also, I chose not to kill you. Could have."

"You sleep," observed the girl, ignoring the implications of his statement.

"Bad assumption." He paused. "What about your defunct friend?"

"No friend."

"Pardon. Former employer."

"We had no choice."

"Oh? And you talk about surprising *me*?" The traveler raked them with his eyes. "What do they call you here? Devilkids? Nightspawn? Devilspawn? Fire-eyes?"

The two looked at each other from their cross-legged positions on the dusty flat where the three paths joined, then back to the slender blond and curly-haired man, seeing for the first time his own hawk-yellow eyes.

Their glances dropped away from the intensity of his gaze as he pinned first the man, then the woman.

"Here?" she asked. "There are others?"

"There are always others."

"Will you take us to them?"

"Not now. My path does not lie in that direction. Might call me a pilgrim. The heights." He pointed up the river toward the unseen mountains that lay over the hills and beyond the horizon, beyond the seemingly endless young forest through which the deadly river flowed.

Both shivered.

Finally, the woman spoke. "The trees disappear in the distant hills. No one lives there now. Not with the cold and the poisons."

"I know. But that is where I travel. There and beyond."

Silence stretched between the three.

The traveler pointed. "Stay here until you cannot see me. Then do what you will. But do not try to surprise me again. I know your step."

Both dropped their heads, though they still watched him. The traveler knew they would wait until his steps had taken him clear and out of sight.

While he had time, perhaps forever, he did not like delays on his road to nowhere.

With that, he shouldered his pack. With quick strides he was close to fifty meters up the river path before the pair looked at each other.

Shortly, the two were lost over the hill and behind the gray haze that had dropped onto the region.

He wondered what their names were, or if they had any, and whether they would follow.

He began to whistle another of the newer double-toned songs he had composed as he crossed the continent. The older ones he tried not to remember too often.

After a time and a number of songs, he looked back over his shoulder, down the winding stretch of trail, for it now had narrowed so greatly it could scarcely be called a path, toward the two figures who marched as effortlessly as he himself.

He shook his head.

"Damned fools."

But he stopped and waited, and as the light began to dim, they approached the scrawny tree under which he sat. Both walked slowly now, showing open hands, palms up as they neared him.

Finally they stopped.

He stood.

"Yes?"

"I am Tomaz. My sister is Charletta."

"You may call me Gregor. Close as anything these days. Now that the pleasantries are over, what do you want?"

"We would like to travel with you. Or until you find others. Others like us." The woman's voice was light, with an odd huskiness he found appealing.

Careful there, he told himself.

"How do you know I'm not an evil magician?"

"You are not."

"If you say so."

He spread his hands, palms up.

"Onward, then. For a place to sleep."

"There are caves farther up," offered Tomaz.

"Best offer so far. Lay on, McTomaz."

"McTomaz?"

"Let's go."

He shook his head.

Always trying the singles game, and always someone seemed to come along and join up. Not that it didn't work out, but never quite as he had imagined.

No, never quite as he had imagined.

"FROM THE VIEWPOINT of those of us in Stenden, Commander, under the Imperial presence, things have been all downhill since the days of the Commodores Gerswin and H'Lieu."

Nodding solemnly in response to the Stenden official, the overweight man in the dress uniform cleared his throat.

The skies were clear, but with the thirty-kay winds from the east, the commander had tucked his dress visor under his left arm. Regulations forbade it, but regulations were not what they had been. His balding forehead gleamed in the afternoon light. He cleared his throat again before speaking.

"The Empire understands your concerns, Ser Mayor. In turn, I am sure you understand the fiscal pressures, especially with the increasing commitments facing the Service, and the reduced maintenance requirements of the current Fleet . . ."

"We understand, Commander. Believe me, we understand. Fewer ships need fewer repairs, and Standora is far out on the Arm. That is why we made our proposal." The Stenden official's voice was even, his crisp dress shirt as formal as his diction.

"Ah, yes . . . about the proposal . . . the proposal . . . you understand that the Empire has always attempted to live up to its commitments . . ."

"That was certainly true of Commodore Gerswin."

"Ah, yes, Commodore Gerswin. Quite a . . . really larger than life . . . that is . . . I understand he was rather impressive . . . according to . . ." replied the I.S.S. Commander.

"I am not always certain that Stenden Panglais is the same language as Imperial Panglais," observed the Stenden mayor. "Commodore Gerswin observed all the protocols. He made Standora Base a most highly regarded repair and refit facility, and he won the respect of his peers in the Imperial Service and the admiration and respect of the people of Stenden. His example has become, for better or worse, a local legend."

"Quite. Much larger than life, but times change, Ser Mayor, and with these changes we all must change."

"Regrettably," answered the mayor. "And what about the proposal?"

"The Empire has considered your generous offer to maintain the facility and to offer services and preferred treatment to Imperial vessels. Quite a generous offer, I might add. Unfortunately, the base now represents quite an investment in resources . . ."

"The base or the refurbished ships in the museum? Those that have not been recalled to duty?"

"As I indicated, Ser Mayor, the times do change."

"You may certainly have the ships, all of them, since they were Imperial ships before the Empire declared them scrap and sold them to the museum. And the museum has always operated under Imperial charter.

"While Stenden would have preferred to retain the ships here, we would still like to maintain the base itself, and we would still provide preferred maintenance for Imperial vessels."

"The majority of the basic facilities could not be moved, we all know, Ser Mayor, and the Empire would certainly be remiss in not opting for the best possible use of the facilities. Stenden has certainly made an offer which should be considered, although, as I indicated earlier, the times have changed."

"I take it that means you want the ships and the few remaining fusactors."

The commander's eyes darted toward the aging plastarmac under his polished shoes, then to a point beyond the mayor's shoulder. Finally, after clearing his throat, he spoke. "You have a solid grasp of the situation, Ser Mayor."

"Fine. We'll take the base over, and you take the remaining museum ships and fusactors. You have such an agreement, I trust?"

The commander nodded without meeting the mayor's eyes.

LII

TIRED, THE MAN limped along the ancient pavement toward the wall surrounding the settlement. Behind him a pair of youngsters trudged. All three moved so slowly that their feet raised scarcely any of the fine and dry dust that kept drifting back across the pavement.

To the west, to the right of the trio, the sun peered through the haze and dust with an orange light strong enough only to cast eastward-leaning shadows barely darker than the dust itself.

On both sides of the dirt road stretched fields filled with stunted plants and weeds, sprinkled occasionally with patches of purpled grass.

The man shook his head and stopped, rubbing his forehead.

The wall was nearly a hundred meters away, but the pair of guards at the gate had shouldered their shields and stood, waiting.

"Shields," he muttered, tossing the black cloak back over his shoulders and straightening.

"These the people the forest people fear, you think?" he asked the girl.

She shrugged.

The boy said nothing.

The man glanced over his shoulder at the distant mountains behind them before confronting the sentries. Then he, in turn, shrugged, and walked toward the wall and its sentries, the tiredness seemingly gone from his step.

As he approached, he could see that the wall was constructed more like a stone fence than a true wall. While the stones were fitted together roughly and rose to nearly three meters, the construction included chunks of crumbling and ancient concrete, smooth blocks of odd-sized ferrocrete, bricks, and assorted stones cut ages before for differing purposes.

"Halt!"

"Of course."

"Your business in Gondolan?"

"Travelers passing through. To have a good meal and some rest."

"How do you propose to pay?"

The young man and woman exchanged glances, their expressions puzzled. So far, everywhere the man had stopped, he had been welcome. Greeted and fed for the knowledge and information he brought. And he had often repaired devices or offered suggestions to solve problems.

Travelers were few indeed, and to be welcomed in a marginally hospitable land.

"What do you suggest?"

The guards now exchanged glances, as if unsure how to answer. Finally, the taller one, dark-haired and dark-skinned, with a full beard, looked back at the traveler, staring at the slender man in a black cloak who traveled with two who seemed scarcely out of childhood.

"Weapons. Service to the king."

The traveler laid down his wooden staff and spread his hands.

"Weapons? You have weapons, not a poor traveler such as myself. All I can offer is knowledge. Some information the king might find of value."

"He knows what he needs to know," offered the shorter and stockier sentry, spitting into the dust.

The traveler reclaimed his staff.

"Then I can offer little, and we must travel around your wall."

Once more the youth and girl exchanged glances, as did the two guards.

"Then you may not pass."

The traveler shrugged. "What would you have us do?"

"You're young enough. Serve in the guard; so could the boy. As for her"—leered the tall dark guard—"there's always a place for young women." He reached toward the girl, awkwardly, spear in his hand.

The staff in the traveler's hands blurred.

Crack!

Crack!

Both soldiers lay on the fringe of cobbled-together pavement that reached but a few meters outside the closed gate. The blond man dragged one body, then the other, into the guard shack.

He pounded on the gate.

"Gerlio?"

The traveler pounded again.

"All right!" the gruff voice exclaimed, and the gate swung ajar, pushed by a single wide-bellied man, wearing the same leather uniform as the two dead guards. His shield and spear leaned against the town wall, and a sheathed sword hung from his soiled leather belt.

His unruly brown hair was streaked with gray, and his mouth

gaped soundlessly as the traveler slipped inside the gate before he could remove his hands from the rachet wheel.

Crump!

This time the traveler's hands struck, and the third guard dropped, merely unconscious.

The blond man motioned to the two outside the gate, and as they entered, he used the wheel to close the gate behind them.

Then he walked toward the central square, hood back over his head and cloak down around him like a robe, staff in hand, trailed by the two youngsters.

The girl glanced down at the uneven pavement, then behind herself, but the boy jerked her arm, as if to remind her not to look back.

As the blond-haired man passed one, then two rough-sod inns, the boy's face screwed up in puzzlement.

While several women peered from glassless and half-shuttered windows at the trio, the few men and children in the dusty streets looked away.

At the central square, little more than an open space with a handful of peddlers' tents surrounding a statue dragged from some forgotten city, another functionary in dirty leather confronted the three.

"Your passes, travelers. Your passes!"

"Passes?"

"Who let you in? You're supposed to have passes."

"No one let us in. The town gate was open."

"Open?"

"Yes, open. How else would we have gotten in?"

"Open? Open, you say?"

"That's what I said. Open. How else would a poor traveler and two children enter a walled town?"

"This is not a walled town. This is Gondolan, home of King Kernute."

"Which way to the palace?"

"That way," answered the constable. "But you don't have passes."

"You'll be able to find us, I am sure, should you need to."

With that, the traveler swept past the man and headed down the slightly wider alley that passed for a street toward the only three-story building in the town, and one of the few not built of either dried sod or crumbling local brick.

A wall two and a half meters high surrounded the royal residence, and four guards stood at the open gates.

"A traveler to see the king!" announced the black-cloaked man.

"King Kernute said he'd see no one."

The traveler shook his head sadly.

"And to think he would miss the weapons he has searched the entire continent for . . ."

He turned, as if to go.

"Hey, let's see those weapons!"

The traveler looked back.

"The king asked. The king should see."

"So you say."

The traveler shook his head, holding his staff one-handed. "If I were to reach for them, you would misunderstand."

"You got weapons, beggar man, and I'm Kernute's sister," announced the senior guard, whose position seemed verified by the metal arm gauntlets he wore. "Ought to send you to the barracks, you and the boy. Send *her* to Kernute. He'd like that."

The three other guards laughed, roaring as if the comment were the best joke in days.

As they did, the traveler took the leather straps from his sleeves and the smooth stones from his belt.

"Behold!" he declaimed. "A miracle."

Whhhrrrr. Whhrrrr.

Crack!

Crack!

The whiplash sounds echoed through the gate and back.

"You! You . . ."

Crack!

"Piggut!"

Crump!

Fast as the guards had moved, the sling and staff had been faster. Before the last body hit the ground and rolled, the leathers had disappeared into his sleeves.

"Guards! Guards! To the gate! To the gate!"

The boy turned as if to run, but the hawk glare of the traveler held him, and the three waited.

The traveler stepped over and around the bodies and moved inside the gate into the courtyard, where he stopped. Stopped and again waited. Waited as another four guards charged from the northern palace gate toward the eastern gate where he stood, where two youngsters stood behind him.

He watched as the guards came around the base of the palace thirty meters away. One was waggling a spear, and two had already drawn their short swords.

The leathers reappeared and began to twirl.

Whhrrr . . . whhrrr

"Behold the fist of God!"

Crack!

"The fist of God!"

Crack!

The traveler blurred sideways to avoid the thrown spear, and the two behind him moved with nearly equal speed. He returned with another sling cast.

Crack!

Two guards were down, but the last two were within meters.

Crack!

Thunk!

A brief silence descended upon the courtyard as the traveler slipped the heavy knife from the body of the last guard, wiping it clean on the dead man's none-too-spotless uniform before replacing it in its sheath.

"Might as well go find his royal and majestic majesty," he suggested to the open air as he began to walk toward the palace.

The boy behind him moved the forefinger of his right hand in a circular motion as it pointed at his own head, then leveled it at the head of the traveler.

"Crazy, that one."

The sister looked from the youth to the man and back again.

"No."

They followed him as he marched briskly around the corner of the first floor of the palace, giving it a wide enough berth to avoid thrown objects of any sort. The presumed royal residence was nothing more than an overgrown villa without any openings on the first floor. The second floor had narrow balconies, although each balcony was walled, as if to provide a platform for soldiers or guards, though none appeared.

The northern face of the building presented a staircase, on which soldiers/guards congregated, milling into a rough formation even as the traveler approached.

"Close up!"

"Swords!"

A muscular and scarred man in blackened leathers stood at the foot of the staircase, bellowing up the wide stone stairs.

Three younger men, dressed in smooth and better-cut leathers with ornamental chains around their necks, half stood, half lounged around the pillars at the top of the stone steps.

The traveler nodded, sighed, and pulled the slender gun from his pouch.

Thrumm!

The burly man dropped like a stone, crumpling into a sack of sinew and bone on the clay below the first step.

"Kill him!" screamed one of the younger men at the stairs top.

Thrumm!

He too dropped, rolling down the steps and scattering some of the now more-disorganized guards.

Thrumm!

Clank!

Although a second attacker had thought himself hidden as he raised a spear for a cast, both his body and the spear followed the first man down the steps.

"Hold it!"

The traveler stepped out of the shapeless black cloak, standing back from the foot of the stairs in an Imperial-style singlesuit without insignia. Insignia or not, it looked like a uniform.

Radiating authority, both with his eyes and the black weapon in his left hand, his eyes swept the score of ill-armed soldier guards.

"You tired of this dung? Tired of marching through dust? Tired of other men's women? Tired of no fire of your own?"

"Kill him!" The screamed command was shrill, from one of the two remaining "officers" on the landing under the pillars at the top of the stairs.

"You come down here and kill me, if you can." The total contempt in the traveler's voice silenced all the guards. The men on the steps shuffled and turned to look behind them.

"Come on . . ."

". . . see you do it . . ."

". . . always orders . . . no piggut . . ."

The traveler let the grumbles mount, then casually aimed the weapon.

Thrumm!

"You? You!" His voice cracked up the steps toward the remaining officer. "You challenge me?"

There was no answer. The man looked one way, down at the troops turning upward toward him, then back the other way, moving toward the nearest pillar. Too late.

Thrumm!

Clank!

"All right! You want a change?" charged the slender man. "Fine. Go in there and bring me King Kernute. I'll fight him hand to hand, or sword to knife. Whatever he wants."

The guards did not move, but shuffled their feet.

"You're scared of Kernute?"

Thrumm!

Another soldier dropped.

"Better be more scared of me."

Several figures looked up the stairs, but did not move.

Thrumm!

"Get me Kernute!"

One guard looked down at the last casualty and started to run for the gate.

Whhhrrr.

Crack!

His body pitched forward onto the clay.

"Get me Kernute."

The thirteen remaining guards began to shamble up the stairs, slowly at first, then more quickly as they disappeared into the palace.

The traveler smiled, but moved up the steps to the top, selecting a pillar near the far left end of the row of mismatched and discolored columns. He leaned against the stone, out of view of anyone within the palace's upper stories.

The sounds from within were mixed.

Several feminine shrieks, male shouts, were followed by the clashing of swords, clanging, and bellowing. Then a few muffled voices.

Finally, the traveler heard footsteps, and swords clanking.

"Who comes to challenge the great King Kernute?"

By this time, an entourage had spilled out onto the stairs. A handful of more highly armed guards, dressed in blackened leathers and mismatched breastplates, surrounded a single man, a man who stood a full head taller than the tallest of the guards.

Beside the guards and the king stood three women, one older, her hair streaked with gray, but her face and figure still that of a young woman, and two younger women but a few years out of girlhood.

Separated from the official entourage were the soldiers prodded into the palace by the traveler. One clutched a bloody arm, and there were nine others holding swords awkwardly, as if unsure of what to do next.

The traveler counted. Less than twenty armed men—about what he had expected. He stepped around the column and down the steps toward Kernute, avoiding the bodies still sprawled where he had dropped them.

"I challenge, Kernute."

As he neared the king, he could see some of the personal guards shake their heads. The ruler was clearly of greater stature, strength, and girth. The traveler appeared slim, dusty, and comparatively unarmed.

"You?" bellowed the monarch. "I wouldn't soil my sword . . ."

As if his outrage were a signal, the tallest of the personal guards charged from beside the king, spear in one hand, sword in the other, shield dropped on the clay.

This time the traveler did not use the slender black weapon which remained hidden, but waited, motionless, until the guard was nearly upon him.

Then he moved, and like a bolt of lightning blurred in the vision of those who watched.

Clank!

The guard lay on the clay, unbreathing, his neck at the odd angle that indicated it had been broken.

"I challenge," answered the slim stranger. "And if you keep putting it off, you won't have enough guards left to protect you, let alone your miserable little town." He gestured toward the bodies lying across the stairs and courtyard.

"What weapons?"

"You? Whatever you want."

"None of your magic."

"Only my hands, a rock or two, perhaps my knives."

"Your hands and knives against my sword and shield?"

"Why not?"

The traveler motioned to the personal guards. "Stand back." He looked at the soldiers. "You! There!" He gestured them toward the base of the steps.

The boy and girl who had accompanied the traveler watched from beneath the exterior wall of the grounds, twenty meters distant, as if they could still not believe that the traveler would topple King Kernute.

Kernute advanced slowly, letting his shield cover as much as possible.

The stranger watched, hands on his belt, his eyes taking in not only the king, but the four remaining personal bodyguards and the ruler's apparent wife/consort.

His hands flicked once, and a silvery knife appeared in his left hand. Twice and another appeared in his right.

Kernute was more than two meters away from the man in the dark olive singlesuit when he jumped and his sword licked out quickly.

The traveler did not seem to move, but he was not where the sword was.

"... magic ..."

"... quick ..."

Another sword probe followed, and another. Both missed.

"Stand still, you ..."

"Sorry, Kernute," said the traveler as the knife streaked from his left hand.

The four members of the personal guard stiffened as they watched the king tumble face forward over his shield.

"Ohhhh!" One of the girls buried her head in the arms of the older woman with the gray-streaked hair.

"Stop!" snapped the traveler as one of the black-leathered men lurched a step toward him.

The guard stopped.

"You four, get moving. Out of Gondolan. Not long before the townspeople will start to take you apart."

One looked at the traveler, then at the guards on the steps, before dropping his shield and scuttling toward the gate. A second shook his head as he dropped shield and followed, but more warily, as if he expected the town to be waiting outside the gate for him.

"You're the new king, I suppose?" asked the older woman as she cradled her daughter.

"No. Could care less." The traveler's hawk-yellow eyes raked the mismatched group. "This happened because the king did not welcome travelers. Strong-arm tactics don't work, not for long.

"But me ... I have a long way to go ... miles to go."

He had walked over to the heap which was composed of the black cloak and his pack, picked up both with a quick motion, still watching the remaining soldiers, and noting that the guard with the bloody arm had also slipped away.

"What you decide to do with your town is up to you. Suggest a bit more friendliness. Might stop terrorizing the neighbors. The Empire doesn't like that sort of thing. More important, I don't, either."

He shook the thin black cloak and folded it into the pack before hoisting it back onto his shoulders. Last, he walked over to the deceased ruler and retrieved his knife, wiping it quickly on the dead man's tunic and replacing it in its sheath. He stood, surveying the small crowd.

"Up to you. Try to do better next time."

He began to walk toward the gate, his pace so quick that he had passed through the northern barriers to the palace and into the small town before there was any reaction at all from the stunned group.

Belatedly, the boy and girl who had watched from next to the wall, squatting, scurried to their feet and after him.

"Devilspawn follow him . . ."

"Devilkiller . . ."

". . . watch for the traveler . . ."

The soldiers looked at each other in the chaos that dropped on them in the stranger's absence, then at the bodies strewn across the palace grounds as if by a lethal wind.

The king's widow sought to console one daughter, while an amused smile played around the lips of the older girl as she watched the remaining bodyguard strip off his black leathers and edge toward the widow.

Several hundred meters to the south, a shopkeeper parted with a few items, and thereafter, a few minutes later, a town gate opened, but did not close.

LIII

"WE ARE NOT pleased with your response to Our inquiry," stated the thin man behind the antique wooden desk and the double energy screens.

"I understand that, Your Majesty." The speaker sat quietly in the narrow and straight-backed chair. His tunic and matching trousers were a somber blue, darker than his piercing blue eyes, and almost as black as his boots.

"Then why do you not act?"

"If Your Majesty wishes, I will send a full squad of Corpus Corps troops to Old Earth. That will leave two full squads to handle what has historically taken four or five squads. Training for replacements will proceed at half schedule, and once it becomes known that we have lost a squad on Old Earth, you will have double the unrest on the outer rim systems. But, if you wish, I will dispatch a squad."

"Morren, are you telling Us that this . . . this antique relic . . . this broken down ex-commodore . . . can destroy a full squad of the best Corpus Corps troops?"

"No. But no one on Old Earth is likely to turn on a local legend, from what I know. Since no one knows where on Old Earth he might happen to be, a squad would be necessary just to locate him."

"Why not locate him with regular Service personnel?"

"The last effort to find and stop him took three squadrons filled with regular personnel. I might remind Your Majesty that the efficiency ratings of those squadrons were considerably higher than the current averages. We could locate Gerswin with regular personnel, if Your Majesty wishes to pull at least one squadron from the rim patrols. But to pin down Gerswin would still take half a squad, and the probability of success would be less than sixty percent."

"If that is the best you can do, then perhaps We should find a new Eye."

"That is Your Majesty's choice. The failure to stop Gerswin has brought down the three previous Eyes, who, frankly, had a great deal more to work with, and considerably fewer internal problems to resolve for their Emperor."

"Are you telling Us that you cannot find and terminate this relic who has caused the Empire so much unrest and loss?"

"No, Your Majesty. I am frank in telling You the cost of such an operation. The choice is Yours. I can only serve."

The thin man who wore the title of Emperor and who sat behind the antique desk of his predecessors frowned. Finally, he looked back up at his chief of Intelligence.

"Did you know this when you accepted your position?"

"Not for certain, Your Majesty, but I did suspect it might prove to be the case."

"Why?"

"Gerswin couldn't destroy the results of his first physical examination, the one before he became cautious. He also built the biggest commercial barony ever put together in a single lifetime—without anyone understanding its extent until he walked away and let its collapse ruin the economies of more than a dozen systems."

"So what is the man, an immortal genius with the talents of a dozen Corpus Corps types and the soul of the devil?"

"That might overstate the case, Your Majesty. Then again, it might not."

His Imperial Majesty continued to frown.

"Might I have your leave to depart, Your Majesty? You can always request my termination."

"Go . . . go, Morren. Let him rot on Old Earth, and preserve what you can for Your Emperor."

"As Your Majesty wishes."

LIV

THE WIND COMING off the Inland Sea streamed the once-black cloak from his shoulders like wings, and the red sun perched on the western horizon outlined him like a black marble statue above the angled stones and marble columns that remained.

The oldest of the old cities, that was all the cat-eyed people had called it, but ruins were ruins, whether they were buried beneath the purpled clay of the high plains, or but half-buried and standing on a hillside above the Inland Sea.

The lower edge of the crimson sun touched the water, and the gray and wispy high clouds melted pink. The dark water took on a maroon tinge. Once it had been called a wine-dark sea, and now it was again, though it was neither sailed nor crossed by the scattered peoples along its shore. That, too, was as it had been in the first beginning.

He had stayed too long, too long after he had helped them found and defend their settlement, too long indeed, for even the children, incredibly quick, bright, bowed as he passed.

He turned until the sun was at his back, not that the fading light carried much warmth, and began to walk upward toward the row of fallen columns for another look at the statue.

His boots clicked on the stone underfoot, the steps fractured and cracked, but still in place.

He nodded a greeting to her, her face already in shadow.

Without further gestures, he sat on the column to her right, squinting as the last rays of the sun cast a glow at the base of the fallen goddess. Her face was beautiful, in the old style, the style of a Caroljoy, but remained expressionless. Her arms were long since gone, but neither she nor he looked to hold or to be held.

He studied the white lines, the unblinking eyes, while the light dimmed.

Soon, the fog would creep in, climbing the hill toward the fallen pillars and tilted white stone blocks.

Glancing down at his cloak, no longer crisp black, but worn, faded almost into olive, with the use of the past years, worn and patched, the last patches those provided by Charletta, who had patched it while complaining that Berin would let her do nothing strenuous until their child was born, until her time had come.

He snorted as he looked at the stone goddess.

"Your time has long gone, and mine also."

If you say so.

"Already, this continent is reawakening. Was the worst of all. I belonged to the dead times."

You cannot die.

"Nor can you."

I lived only while people remembered.

"Remember? Soon I will remember little."

You do not want to remember.

"Don't want to forget either. Where does that leave me?"

She did not answer, and he looked away from the perfect white face of the recumbent woman and watched the upper tip, the last crimson slivers, of the sun drop below the watery horizon, watched the long shadows lengthen, dancing from slow wave to slow wave.

"Well, my lady, we had our times."

It is early for self-pity.

"I forget. You have watched more centuries than I have."

I have seen nothing.

"Have I? Tell me I have seen. Watched while others lived, loved, and died. Watched and killed, killed and watched. Pulled strings, played god, and for what? For what?"

You have lived, if not how you wanted. You have lived.

He could not refute her last statement, and did not try, as he sat on a ruined column, keeping company with a statue, as the twilight became night. Knowing that the next day—the next day, for he had waited too long—he must begin the trip to the place of his beginning.

LV

ABOVE THE FADED olive singlesuit, patched and dusty, hawk-yellow eyes glittered beneath tight-curled blond hair. The jaw remained elfin, and the skin smooth, but there was a tiredness behind the youthful features reflected only in the lagging steps, where each stride stopped short of briskness, each step mirrored more than mere fatigue.

The afternoon sun glared down at the solitary figure on the empty road as he trudged westward, staff in hand, pack on back.

The gently rolling hills to his right sported an uneven growth of assorted bushes and trees, none more than twice the traveler's height, and all less than a pair of decades old.

Nodding without pausing, he contemplated what would one day be a forest, recalling when the area had boasted little beyond purpled clay, landpoisons, and a few clumps of the purple grass that had been all that could grow.

Glancing to his left, he observed the recently tilled soil, and the dark green tips of the sponge grains beginning to peer through the soil that retained a tinge of purple.

A faint rumble whispered from the west.

With a sigh, the traveler turned from the packed clay road less than five meters wide and marched northward into the underbrush, finally halting underneath a small oak and seating himself to wait for the road roller to pass on eastward to the newly developed coastal settlements.

Not that anyone expected him, nor wanted him, but meeting even a roller crew in the middle of the piedmont would raise questions, and there would be enough of those when he reached the high plains. Time enough for the questions then.

He stretched out his legs and waited, listening for the faint sounds he hoped were there—the twitter of the insects, the chirp and rustle of remaining or returning birds, as well as the reintroduced species, those few that had been preserved on New Augusta, New Colora, or in reserves throughout the Empire.

The insects resumed their twitters immediately, even before he stopped moving, but the heavy and moist air brought no sounds of birds or other larger species.

As the rumbling of the roller grew from a whisper into a grumbling, the cargo vehicle topped a hill and gathered momentum to plunge down its slope on its eastward route.

Within minutes, the grumbling roar had dwindled back into a whisper.

The traveler stood, flexing his shoulders as if to remove the tightness, reshouldered his backpack, and picked up his heavy, but well-worked staff.

Soon, he would need to refill his water bottle, and to see what he could find to supplement the food he carried. Soon—but not for another five or ten kays, at least.

His steps were even as he returned to the road, where the heavy red dust had already settled back to blur the wide traces of the cargo rollers where they had flattened the right of way even more smoothly than before.

The respite had refreshed him, and his steps were brisker. He began to whistle one of the newer tunes he had composed in the last few years. Although he recalled the older ones, and whistled them now and again in his blacker moments, he usually avoided them and the memories they brought back.

At the top of the next hill, he paused to survey the gentle hills that rose into the eastern Noram mountains. He could see the darker green of their forested slopes, where the ecological recovery had been quicker than on the slower draining and clay-based hilly plains where he stood.

How long had it been since he had overflown this area?

He pushed the thought away and started down the western slope of the hill, his booted feet leaving barely a trace on the shoulder of the packed clay road.

Three kays westward, he paused again upon a hilltop, when he saw a single man standing beside a machine—a locally built tractor type pulling a tilling rig.

He shrugged and continued downward, until at last he stood beside the machine, observing the man who struggled with an assembly that controlled the tilling bars dragged by the tractor. The tractor, obviously of local design and manufacture, bore more patches than the traveler's singlesuit, but appeared clean and in good repair.

"Hades . . . ," muttered the operator, refusing to pay any attention to the traveler.

In turn, the traveler seated himself in the midafternoon shade of the large wheels and waited, taking a sip from his nearly empty water bottle.

"Hades . . . double Hades . . . grubbin' Impie design . . ."

The blond man finished the water and replaced the bottle in the harness attached to his pack, stretching his legs out to wait for the other to complete the repair or surrender to the need for assistance.

Clank!

Plop!

A large hammer dropped beside the traveler, who looked up without curiosity.

"Perfectly good machine . . . useless because some idiot tech decided it was easier to copy from a stupid Imperial design . . ."

"That bad?" asked the blond-haired man as he watched the operator clamber down from the tractor.

"Wouldn't be hard at all if I had Imperial tools, three hands, and a graving dock to immobilize the whole stupid assembly!"

The operator had the long-armed and narrow-faced look of shambletown ancestry, but wore a relatively new jumpsuit, which carried only recent dirt and grease. His black hair was short, and he wiped his forehead with a brown cloth, which he replaced in a thigh pocket of the jumpsuit.

"Mind if I take a look?" asked the traveler.

"Be my guest. Not scheduled for a pickup for hours yet. Don't seem to have the tools to fix it."

After nodding sympathetically, the traveler climbed up to the assembly with an ease that spoke of familiarity with both equipment in general and repairs in awkward locales.

The man in the olive jumpsuit frowned as he surveyed the jammed assembly. In one respect, the operator was correct. The Imperial design, obviously adapted from a flitter-door system, was far too complicated.

Still—Imperial designs usually had more than one solution.

He bent over the assembly, looking at the far side upside down. A wry smile creased his face as he straightened and checked the small tool kit which the operator had left.

Not ideal, but he thought what he had in mind would work. Even permanent connections could be removed, if you knew their structure.

Click. Click.

With the right angle, the hidden releases, and an extreme amount of pressure, he managed to get the "permanent" coupling released.

The loss of pressure on the line allowed the assembly to drop into place. With the pressure off the line, he was able to release the other end of the connector.

As the operator had probably known, the check valve was jammed with debris and hardened fluid. Within a few minutes he had it clean again, and ready to reconnect. Doing the best he could, he cleaned out the tubing and the fittings before he reassembled them.

Finally, he closed the tool kit and climbed back down to the puzzled operator.

"Think it should work now. Want to try it?"

The operator shook his head, wiping his forehead once more with the brown cloth.

"How did you do that?"

"Had some familiarity, once, with that sort of design. A few tricks I happened to remember."

"That Hades-fired assembly gives us more problems than the rest of the equipment put together. I've never seen anyone fix one that quickly."

"Luck, I suppose."

"Where are you headed?"

"West."

The operator surveyed the traveler, looked from the patched and faded singlesuit to the western mountains, taking in the backpack and staff resting against the tractor wheels.

"On foot?"

"Simpler that way. No hurry. Feet don't break down if you rest them now and again."

The operator shook his head. "Still a few wild Mazers loose. I wouldn't recommend going much beyond the next check station. Better to catch a ride with one of the road rollers. They'd be happy to take you. They like the company."

The traveler nodded. "Appreciate the suggestion."

"You sure look familiar. Swear I saw you someplace."

"Not likely. Been a long time since I passed this way."

"Well . . . whatever. I appreciate the help. Appreciate it a lot. Anything I can do for you? Like to give you a lift, but . . ." The Recorps operator surveyed the half-tilled field.

"Understand. You've got a job."

The operator nodded. "Stet. Beats running the hills. Even if I don't see the lady more than once a week. Kids always have enough to eat. Not like the old days, bless the captain."

"Pardon?"

"Not like the old days, I said."

The traveler smiled faintly, nodded, and bent to pick up the pack and staff. Straightening, he twirled the staff one-handed and inclined his head momentarily toward the Recorps tech.

"Good luck," he called to the operator as he set out toward the road and the mountains toward which it led.

"Sure not like the old days . . . captain and all . . ." He could hear the operator murmuring as the tech began to check out the equipment before returning to his tilling.

The traveler waited until he had crossed the next hilltop before resuming his whistling.

LVI

THE COMMANDER RAN his eyes over the screen, trying to focus on the words, finally letting them settle midway down the text.

". . . mysterious traveler on the Euron continent has been blamed for the overthrow of two local rulers, at least, for the death of a score of bandits, and for the establishment of a 'devilspawn' settlement on the Inland Sea . . .

". . . settlement verified, location on grid three, named Stander, allegedly founded in memory of the traveler who departed in a wagon of fire . . .

". . . not all events reported can be verified, but all verified references fall within a three-century period . . . some evidence to indicate traveler was real Imperial, perhaps a wandering scholar of some sort . . . but . . . would not explain ability with weapons . . . particularly with native arms . . ."

The commander bit his lip. No sooner had he managed to purge the superstitious gobbledygook from the main base records than it was turning up elsewhere on Old Earth.

Reclamation was a serious business, dependent far too much on worn-out equipment—equipment modified so much the original specs were useless—too few supplies, and too few trained personnel. As the Empire continued to shrink, with each subsequent cutback, there were fewer replacement parts, fewer visiting ships of any sort with which to trade for the needed technical equipment the Empire failed to supply.

With all the drawbacks, there was less and less incentive to push back the landpoisons.

His hand touched the screen and sent the report to the system files.

Bad enough that the early captain, whoever he had been, had been turned into a godlike legend. Now he had to contend with other magical forces and legends.

How could he explain the improved environmental monitoring reports from places where Recorps had never been? It had been hard enough to justify the limited Imperial support with the bad reports from the out-continents.

Despite his efforts, and the efforts of the commandants before him, Recorps was shrinking, and the rate of progress slowly but surely declining.

The records showed that four centuries earlier, Recorps had been operating the now-closed Scotia station, and that two centuries before that the Noram effort had crossed the Momiss River. Yet they still had not completed the eastern sections of Noram, despite the efforts in the Brits and on the fringes of Euron.

There never were enough techs, let alone enough officer-grade types, to fill the positions necessary. The Admin complex was filled with empty offices, empty quarters, empty labs.

Still, the spouts were less severe, and far less frequent, and there hadn't been a stone rain in Noram in over a century, and summer ice rains were a rarity, rather than the norm they had once been.

"Hard work . . . ," he muttered. Hard work, that was what had caused the improvement, not the magic of some traveler in mysterious Euron, or some long-dead captain.

Even that captain, he rationalized, had worked hard. *He* hadn't used magic, no matter what the old locals insisted, no matter what the Corwin tapes had said, no matter what the old songs said.

It would be so easy to give up, to assume things would still get better without Recorps. But until the Imperial and Recorps effort had begun, what had there been? Savages and shambletowns, a declining local population, and despair. Who wanted to go back to that?

He ran his fingers through his thinning hair, then touched the centuries-old console, the once-gray plastic sheathing now nearly black, not with dirt, but from the continued exposure to the radiation of the interior lights, designed so long ago to supplement the sunlight that had been virtually nonexistent.

Would there be a time when Recorps would not be needed?

He hoped so, but was glad it would not be soon, would not be in his time.

He flicked off the console, and stood, stretching, before he straightened his uniform and headed for his empty quarters. Unlike his predecessor, he lived in quarters, not in New Denv.

He frowned and shook his head as he went out through the open portal.

LⅤII

THE SLENDER BLOND man halted his work on the painstakingly squared golden log and stood up as he watched the agent vault from the flitter with the grace of the trained hunter.

The uniformed man moved with an easy stride from the flats where he had landed the flitter, a narrow space requiring more than mere skill, more even than recklessness or nerve.

The blond man nodded. He recognized the step of the other. He did not bother to touch the knives hidden in his wide belt, knowing that the other could not have immediate violence on his mind or hands.

He continued to wait until the agent, wearing a sky-blue uniform he did not recognize, with the Imperial crest that he did, halted several meters from him.

The woodworker smiled and set down the tool with which he had been smoothing the log.

"Commodore Gerswin?"

"Answered to that once." He nodded at the uniform. "Corpus Corps?"

"Yes. But not on official business—not the kind you mean."

"No uniform on those missions."

The agent smiled faintly and half nodded in acknowledgment.

"Nice location here."

"For me . . . under the circumstances."

The agent looked around the partly built structure, noting the perfect joint where each golden log had been fitted into place, the dark stones that seemed to fit precisely without mortar, and the way the home-to-be nestled against the cliff behind it.

"You do good work, Commodore, not that you always haven't."

The blond man smiled wryly, dismissing the compliment.

"One way of looking at it."

The agent looked down at the stone underfoot, then back at the man who looked no older than he did.

"Why did you put in the change of address for your retirement pay with the Recorps base here? And why did you use coded entries?"

"Why not? No sense in the Empire having to keep searching. Waste of resources. You either get me, or decide it's not worth it. Too tired to play god much longer."

"You? Too tired? Why didn't you use those tacheads? There were nine left . . . somewhere . . . wherever they are. Not to mention the hellburners."

"Assuming I had any," sighed the thinner man. "Just wanted to get home, not that it is, you understand."

"It isn't? Thought you were from here."

"Was. But you know better. You can't really go home. So long no one really remembers. Why I used codes. Be worse if they knew for sure I was the captain. Won't matter someday. Doesn't matter to the Empire already, I suspect."

The agent frowned, started to shake his head, then stopped, fingering the wide blue leather belt, centimeters from the stunner in the throw-holster.

"You win, Commodore, just like you always did." The words carried a tinge of bitterness.

"Didn't win. Lost. You lost. We both lost. Lerwin, Kiedra, Corwin, Corson—they won. So did the children, those lucky enough to have them . . . and keep them."

"That may be," answered the agent, "but you won. The Empire is coming apart, and the Ydrisians, the Ateys, the Aghomers—you name it, you're their patron saint."

The slender man pursed his lips, waiting.

The Corpus Corps agent studied the wiry man in the thin and worn singlesuit, but kept his lips tightly together.

"You drew the duty of having to tell me?"

"No. I asked. I wanted to see a living legend. I wanted to see the man who single-handedly brought down the Empire."

"I didn't. May have hurried things. But not me." He smiled wryly once more. "Disappointed?"

"No." The agent's tone said the opposite.

The slender man's hands blurred.

Thunk! Thunk!

Twin knives vibrated in the temporary brace by the agent's elbow, both buried to half their length.

"Does that help?"

"A little . . ." The agent took a deep breath. He could not have even touched his stunner in the time the commodore had found, aimed, and thrown the heavy knives. ". . . but how—it couldn't have just been the weapons skills."

"No. Helped me stay alive. Any man who cared about Old Earth, about life . . . any man could have done the rest . . . if he sacrificed as many as I did . . ."

The man in the blue uniform nodded.

"Now. A favor."

"What?" asked the agent cautiously.

"Better that the locals know I'm just a retiree. Don't know more, and they don't need to. Your records will go when the Empire falls."

"Should I? Why? Let you suffer in notoriety . . ."

The hawk-yellow eyes of the commodore-who-was caught the agent, and in spite of himself, he stepped back.

"Why?" he repeated, more softly.

"Because, like the Empire . . . out of time . . . out of place . . ."

The agent watched as the commodore's eyes hazed over, looking somewhere, somewhen, for a minute, then another. He waited . . . and waited.

A jay screamed from a pine downhill from the pair, and a croven landed on the rock above the flitter, but the commodore noticed neither the birds nor the man in blue.

Finally, the Corpus Corps agent stepped forward.

Thunk!

A third knife appeared in the brace, and the former I.S.S. officer shook himself.

"Sorry . . . reflex. Hard to keep a thought. Too many memories," apologized the commodore, who still looked to be a man in his middle thirties.

The agent, despite his training, shivered.

"I understand, I think, Commodore." He paused, then saluted, awkwardly. "Good day, ser. Good luck with your house."

He turned and slowly descended the even-set and smooth stone steps, then walked along the precisely laid stone walkway, still shaking his head slowly as his strides carried him back to the flitter.

"We all lost. Him, too."

He was yet shaking his head as the flitter canopy closed and the turbines began to whine.

Behind him, the blond man picked up his tools and returned to smoothing the golden log, smoothing it for a perfect fit, a perfect fit that would last centuries.

LVIII

WEARY. OLD. EITHER adjective could have applied to the still-buried building that served as the landing clearing area for the few travelers to visit Old Earth.

The historian/anthropologist took another step away from the shuttle-port entry before stopping. Her recorder and datacase banged against her left hip as she halted to survey the hall. Compared to Imperial architecture, the ceiling was low, and despite the cleanliness of the structure, a feeling of dinginess permeated the surrounding. That and emptiness. There had been two passengers on the annual Imperial transport—most of the space was for technical support equipment for Recorps.

She debated taking a holo shot of the receiving area, then decided against it. She squared her uniformed shoulders and stepped up to the console.

A bored clerk in a uniform vaguely resembling hers waited for the lieutenant to present her orders.

He took the square green plastord and eased it into the console.

"Your access code, please, sher."

"I beg your pardon."

"You have special orders, Lieutenant. Service doesn't trust us poor cousins. For me to verify your arrival, you have to punch in your own access code." He pointed to the small keyboard built into the counter. "Right there."

The lieutenant shrugged. Her precise features, thick, short, and lustrous black hair, and an air of command gave her more of an "official" presence than the Interstellar Survey Service uniform.

Stepping over to the keyboard, she tapped in the access code and waited.

Several seconds later, another console beside the clerk beeped. He retrieved the plastord square and handed it back.

"Welcome to Old Earth, Lieutenant Kerwin."

"Thank you. What's the best way to reach the old Recorps Base?"

"Old Recorps Base? Didn't they tell you? You're in it. There's never been more than one main base. Outside of the work ports in Afrique and Hiasi, this is it. Oh . . . we have a few detached officers in Euron and around the globe, but here's the center."

Lieutenant Kerwin looked around the open gray hall, again, even more slowly.

"You want base quarters . . . go to the end of the hall. Take the left fork. That leads to the tunnel to Admin. Plenty of room these days."

"These days . . . ," she murmured.

"Days of the captain are gone, Lieutenant. Lot of nostalgia, especially with the big Atey report," added the suddenly loquacious rating. "Their Institute sent a team last year, but haven't seen a report. May not have one, Captain Lerson says. Lots of nostalgia. Sensicubes all romance it. Don't believe it. Never was a captain, not like that, anyway . . . if you ask me. You'll have to make your own decision."

"Who told you that was my job?" asked the officer softly, with a touch of ice in her tone which pinned the man back against his console.

"Told you what?"

She smiled, and the smile was a cross between sudden dawn and the pleased look of the reintroduced hills cougar sizing up a lost beefalo calf.

"Surely you're joking?" she asked with a laugh, and the laugh had a trace of silvered bells in it, with steel behind.

In spite of himself, the rating failed to repress a shiver.

"Just around, Lieutenant. Someone from the Empire coming in to study the myth of the captain. To check our records. Two passengers, and the other was a hydrologist recruited from Mara. Had to be you."

"Around? That's interesting." She pursed her lips before continuing. "Don't put down myths, Reitiro," she concluded, picking his name off the tag on his tunic pocket, "they all started with reality. You might think about the reality of the captain."

Reitiro frowned as the Survey Service officer turned and left, moving with an easy stride down the hallway toward the tunnel to the Administration building, the tunnel a relic from the days when the environment had been totally out of control.

From before the days of the captain, if the myths were indeed correct.

LIX

THE FACE IN the screen was gray. Whether grayed by the age of the tape or whether the gray reflected the actual physiological age of the man could not be answered.

The tape itself came from a databloc out of the sealed section of the Recorps archives, from a tape that should have been blank, and was not. The exterior had contained neither date nor other identifiable information. Why it had been left remained as much of a mystery as what it contained.

"Commander Lerwin said I ought to scan this and leave it in the back of the archives. Someone should have it."

The silver-haired man had an unlined skin, and neither beard nor mustache. His voice was so soft, even with maximum gain, that the I.S.S. officer and the base archivist/librarian had to strain to catch his words.

"Already, people are doubting what the captain did, or what we all did. As the land improves and there are fewer spouts, they forget the days of the stone rains and the ice that could strip a flitter bare in minutes. The old crews are scattering, dying, having children, and the captain's not here to hold it together. Soon, no one will remember that there was a captain. They'll doubt the records, or change them."

The narrator looked down, blinked, and lifted his head to face the viewers.

"But there was a captain. And he brought the earth back to life when it was dying.

"Am I mad? I suppose I am. But a madman has nothing to tell but the truth. Who designed the river plants? The captain. Who commandeered the dozers when the Empire wrote Old Earth out of the Emperor's budget? The captain. Who forced the creation of Recorps?

"I could go on, but already none of this shows in the histories. How could it? Only a devilkid could have carried it off, and none of them knew he was a devilkid, or what a devilkid was. *We* knew—"

The man's face was replaced with a swirl of color, and then by an even gray.

"Is the rest of the tape like that?" asked the lieutenant.

"I've run it through twice. That's the only fragment left intact. It was deliberately scrambled, and probably in a hurry."

"Why did they leave the beginning?"

"They didn't know they had. The man who made the recording didn't understand the recording limits. On these older blocs, you were supposed to run twenty to thirty centimeters before beginning the recording. This starts with the first millimeter. Everything beyond thirty is blank."

"But wouldn't a scrambler catch it all anyway?"

"No. The outer layer of the tape expands against the casing. The reason for the procedure is that you can't blank the first lead of a bloc without actually running it."

"Why would anyone want to erase something like that?" Why indeed, wondered the historian.

"It's a pity," observed the librarian. "Now that the days of the captain have become a myth, it would be helpful to have firsthand reference material. Amazing how quickly the process took place. Less than four centuries, and no one knows what really happened back then. Would be nice to know."

"Someone didn't think so."

The rating shrugged. "What can I say, Lieutenant? I finished training less than a year ago, and it's pretty dull. Most of the reclamation here on Noram is done, and they say the natural processes are taking care of the rest.

"No minerals, and with the Empire almost gone—excuse me—with the Empire taking a less aggressive position, we don't get much interest in the archives these days.

"Everyone else just wants to know if we've gotten any of the Imperial sensitapes. Probably have to close Recorps before too long. Not much Imperial funding, and the export trade is down. Two-thirds of the old quarters are already empty."

"Can you tell when the erasure was done?" asked the lieutenant, bringing the issue back.

"Could have been done a hundred stans ago, or two. That swirl pattern doesn't happen when you use what we have now, and our stuff's at least fifty years old. Besides, you saw the dust on that rack."

The officer rose. "You mind if I just browse through the rest of the old blocs?"

"Regs—but who cares. Just don't blow it around."

She smiled at the young rating.

"Thank you. I won't."

The librarian scratched his head as he watched the lieutenant head for the master indices for the archives.

He rewound the old cube and closed down the viewing console before he picked it up to carry it back into the storage area. After that, he'd have to go back to the main console, not that there would be much business.

The word was already out that the Imperial ship hadn't brought any sensitapes.

STARK—THAT WOULD have been the politest word she could have used to describe the interior of the dwelling.

Neat it was, and light enough, though age had darkened the golden wood that comprised the walls and matching roof beams. But there were no hangings on the walls and no coverings on the floors. The air was cool and clean, but the starkness made it seem almost chill.

The hawk-eyed man turned in the antique swivel, but did not stand as his eyes ran over her. The directness, the blaze, of his gaze sent a chill down her spine.

He added to that chill with an odd two-toned whistle so low that she could barely hear it even as she felt its impact.

"First time someone like you has come looking for me."

His eyes flickered as he took in the uniform.

"Service. Don't recognize the specialty insignia."

"Research. I understand you might be able to answer some of my questions."

"Doubt it."

"Would you try?"

"So what does the wonderful and crumbling Empire want with me?" He looked away from her and out through the circular bubbled window that she recognized as having come from an alpha-class flitter, despite the painstaking custom framing that made it seem an integral part of the structure.

She frowned, letting the fingers of her left hand wrap around the styloboard more tightly than she intended. Shaking her right hand loosely to relax it, she hoped she would be ready to use the stunner if she had to, but that it would not be necessary. The whole idea was not to upset someone as unbalanced as he was reputed to be.

His head snapped back toward her.

"Forget about the stunner. You couldn't reach it in time. Too close."

Automatically her eyes gauged the distance from her feet to his relaxed posture in the antique recliner/swivel. More than three meters.

She lifted her eyebrows.

"Could prove it. Will. Maybe. Later."

He glanced back out the bubble window, the only outside view from the dwelling.

The Imperial officer took the time to study the structure, noting the fit of the native logs, squared so evenly that there seemed to be no space at all between them. The wide plank flooring showed the same care, despite the hollows worn by years of use. There was more than enough light, thanks to the four skylights. The more she studied the structure, the more she began to realize the effort and design that had gone into it, an effort and design that seemed strangely out of place on Old Earth.

She shook her head. There were so many strange examples, as she was learning all too quickly.

This hideaway south of the Recorps Base was yet another, a seemingly rustic cabin whose design, orientation, and construction demonstrated more expertise and knowledge than she had expected, far more.

Her attention drifted back to the man, now regarding her with an amused smile, as if he had read her thoughts. He was clean-shaven, and the faded gray tunic and trousers, once probably of Imperial issue, were spotless, though worn.

"It's said you're native to Old Earth," she began.

The amused smile remained, and she did not realize she had stepped backward until her shoulders brushed the wood behind her.

"It's also said that you were an Imperial officer for a long time. One rumor is that you once commanded the Recorps Base."

"Who would say anything that fantastic? Never commanded the Recorps Base."

"The Maze people . . . some of the older New Denv families . . ." She tried to match his light tone.

He sat upright, leaning forward. "Every place has its stories. When it doesn't, it's dead. Nearly that way here once. Now they tell stories."

In a silent flash, he stood upright, next to the swivel, which slowly returned itself to a position not quite upright. His feet, wearing Imperial-issue boots, had not made a sound as they hit the wooden floor.

"What do you really want?"

What did she want? To track down a rumor? To chronicle the debunking of a myth to put the Service at ease? She shook her head again. Her mission seemed less and less clear.

"Your thoughts, your recollections about how things really were," she said, trying to recapture the sense of purpose that had driven her to Old Earth, back to a forgotten corner of a world the Empire would just as soon forget.

She took a step sideways, as much to remind herself that she would not be backed into a corner as to get closer to the former officer, and waited for his response.

His eyes raked over her again, as if he could see beneath the undress tunic and trousers. She could see his nostrils widen, as if he were drawing in some scent.

Hawk or wolf . . . or both?

"You smell familiar."

"Familiar?" Istvenn! He's got you off-balance and keeping you there. "I don't see how. I've never been here or on Old Earth before."

His lips tightened, and his eyes narrowed.

"Could be. But somewhere . . ."

"Is it true you were an Imperial officer?"

"True as anything else you'd hear." The intensity with which he had regarded her subsided, and he turned so that he faced neither her nor the bubble window, but a narrow tier of inset wooden shelves that reached from ankle height to the base of the roof beams.

Her eyes followed his. She could see that a number of the antiques on the shelves were actual printed publications, which indicated their age. Printed pubs were used only on frontier worlds or in remote locations where the use of energy for a tapefax or console was not feasible, and there had been sufficient energy on Old Earth since the rediscovery.

Without being able to read the faded letters on the spines of the volumes, she knew that most were Imperial manuals.

"Why did you leave the Service and settle here?"

He gestured toward the wall behind her, then laughed a short laugh.

"Nowhere to sit."

"It's not really necessary—"

He brushed past her and did something to the wooden panel behind her.

The lieutenant stepped aside as the blond man lowered a double width bed from the wall and pulled a quilted coverlet, red and gray, from a recess over the bed, and spread it over the Imperial-issue colonist's pallet.

She could see his nostrils quiver as he straightened and motioned toward the couch/bed.

"Still familiar." His low statement was made more to himself than to her.

He frowned, but with three quick strides returned to the swivel and dropped into it, turning toward her as he did.

"Two questions. One asked. One unasked. Last first. The Imperial supplies? Maintain some credit balance at the base. Lets me buy what I need. First last. Why here? Nowhere else to go."

His words answered one question, but not the other. Only a retired or disabled member from Recorps or one of the Imperial Services had base-purchasing privileges. But he had not answered why he had settled on Old Earth.

"Why did you settle here?"

"Why not? Didn't settle. Born here. Not that anyone would remember. No place for me in the Empire. No place for me in Recorps, either. Not when all the barriers are crumbling."

"Barriers?" The single-word question tumbled from her lips. Why did she sound like such a simpleton? Why? Why? Why?

"You can take the stress so long. Had to be civilized. That meant barriers . . . if I wanted to survive. I built them, but not strong enough. Time wears down all walls. Remember. Grew up when the shambletowners hunted the devilkids."

"Shambletowners?"

"Old Mazers . . . what they called them then."

She could see that the hardness was gone from his eyes, the terrible intensity muted, misted over.

The lieutenant waited for him to go on, wondering why he was so obsessed with age. He had to be a mental case, or disabled. He didn't look much older than she was, and she certainly wasn't ready for retirement, not just five years out of the Academy. But the dwelling was undeniably his, and the locals called him old. Why?

"Watch out for the old devil," at least three of the reclam farmers had told her. "He knows everything, but he moves like the lash of the storm, like the *old* storms."

She studied his face, the so-short and tight-curled blond hair, the

tanned and smooth skin of his face, trying not to stare, waiting for
him to go on.

The afternoon wind whined, but the cabin did not shake, unlike
some of the town buildings. While their native wood bent, it never
broke, not with the local design.

"When the Empire rediscovered, they were lucky. Between storms
of summer and howlers of winter. No landspouts that day.

"Could be we were lucky. Time should tell. Couldn't see the sky
then, just the gray and gray of the clouds, and purple funnels of the
landspouts. Screaming and ripping through the hills and plains. Rock
rains all the time. Sheerwinds could cut rivers in half.

"Silver lander. Went hunting and found a devilkid."

He laughed, a short hard bark of a laugh that contrasted with the
soft penetrating intensity of his light voice.

"That was six centuries ago. You act like you were there."

He ignored her interruption. "Great Empire decided they had
some obligation to poor home planet. Guilty conscience. Decided to
fix us up. Till the local budget got tight, and they decided to recruit
locals. Couldn't find anyone, except a devilkid. Other couldn't hack
it. Devilkid ended up in charge. Called him captain. Still a devilkid in
soul. Scared the Impies until the day he walked out. End of story."

"You haven't told me anything."

"Who are you?"

"Me?"

"No matter. Told you everything. Now listen. My turn."

She frowned, then leaned back as he began to whistle in the
strange double-toned sound she had heard him let out momentarily
when she had arrived.

The song had a melody, a haunting one, that spoke of loss and
loss, and yet somehow each loss was an accomplishment, or each accomplishment was a loss. The melody was beautiful, and it was nothing.

Nothing compared to the off-toned counterpoint, which twisted
and turned her.

The tears billowed from her eyes until she thought they would
never stop, and his song went on, and on, and on.

When the last note died, she sat there. Sat and waited until he sat
beside her and stroked her cheek.

As he unfastened her tunic, she shivered once before relaxing in
the spice of his scent, before letting her arms go around him, drawing him down onto her.

The song was with her, and with him. Nor did it leave until he did, and she laid back on the coverlet, shuddering in the rhythms of music and of him, her movements drawing her into a sleep that was awake, and a clarity that was sleep.

She woke suddenly.

Her clothes were where they had dropped, next to the bottom edge of the bed, and her stunner and equipment belt had been moved to the highest shelf, the one without the old books on it.

She rolled away from his silent, and, she hoped, sleeping form gently, until their bodies were separated. She waited, half holding her breath, to see if he moved.

Next, she eased into a sitting position, a position she hoped would not wake him. Again, she waited.

An eternity passed before she edged to her feet, and silently padded across the smooth and cold wooden floor.

First, to get the stunner.

By climbing onto the bottom shelf, she reached the belt and eased it down. Her fingers curled around the butt of the weapon, and she drew it from the holster.

"Wouldn't."

She brought the firing tube up and toward him, but before her fingers could reach the firing stud, his naked form of tanned skin, hair-line scars, and blond hair had struck across the room like the flash of coiled lightning he resembled. His open hand slashed the weapon from her fingers.

Ramming her knee toward his groin, she drove to bring her right elbow toward his throat.

Before she could finish either maneuver, she found herself being lifted toward the bed, her right arm numb from the grip of his left hand.

"NOOOO!"

"Yes."

She could feel her legs being forced apart, his strength so much greater that her total conditioning and military training were brushed aside as if she were a child, and she could feel the hot tears scalding down her face, even as he heat drove through her like hot iron.

You were warned, a corner of her mind reminded her. *You were warned.*

But they didn't know. They didn't know!

When he was done, this time, again, he kissed her cheek, ran his hands over her breasts. But he did not relax.

Standing quickly, he went to the hidden closet and pulled out a

loose, woven gray robe and pulled it on before sitting at the end of
the bed, his hawk-yellow eyes exploring her.

She wanted to curl into a ball, to pull into herself and never come
up. Instead, she took a deep breath and slowly sat up, cross-legged,
and faced him.

"Was it necessary to hurt me?"

"After a while, need the thrills. Beauty isn't enough. Neither is
scent. With you, it's almost enough." He frowned. "Shouldn't have
tried for the stunner. High-minded lady. Sexy bitch. Changed her
mind and tried to zap old Greg. Hard to resist the instincts. Don't have
many barriers left, and fewer all the time. Happens over the ages."

He straightened, leaning back with his eyes level with hers, for an instant before he stood. She could see the blackness behind the yellow-
flecked eyes, a blackness that seemed to stretch back through time.

She shook her head to break away from the image.

After crossing the room with a slight limp she had not noticed before, he turned and walked back, picking up her clothes, and sorted
and folded them, putting them on the foot of the bed. Next he put
the equipment belt down, without the stunner.

He shook his head, hard.

"You had better leave. Not exactly sane, not all the time, anymore.
Never sure which memories are real, which are dreams."

She dressed deliberately, afraid that undue haste would be construed as fear, which seemed to be a turn-on, or that slowness would
be a tease.

By the time she was together, boots and belt in place, she realized
that he had also dressed, though she did not remember him changing from the robe back to the gray tunic and trousers.

The late afternoon light was flooding the cabin with the dull red
that preceded twilight when she stepped outside the door.

In another quick move, he was at her side.

She looked down. The stunner was back in her holster. Neither
acknowledging the weapon's return nor flinching at his speed, she
took a deep breath and opened the door.

His right arm held her back, went around her shoulders, and she
found herself against him again, face-to-face, the strange spice scent
of his skin and breath still fresh.

His fingers relaxed as he kissed her neck and brushed her cheek
with his lips.

"Good-bye, Caroljoy. Thought you'd never come. Good-bye."

He released her, standing there, face impassive, as she slipped out and onto the wide stone slab that comprised the top step on the long stone staircase down to the old highway and her electroscooter.

The tears she could not explain cascaded down her cheeks, a few splashing the dust from her boots, a single one staining the last step of the stairway.

Her carriage perfect, she did not look back, but felt the door close, felt that as it closed it sealed away a forgotten chink in the past as surely as though she had destroyed the sole copy of a priceless history text.

Eyes still blurring, she started the scooter back toward the base.

LXI

"INCOMING. EDI TRACKS. Corridors two and three."

The senior lieutenant relayed the report from his screen to the Ops Boss, both on the audio and through the datalink. He did not altogether trust the ancient and patched-together equipment, but there was no new equipment and nothing left to cannibalize.

"Understand EDI track. Incoming Cee one and Cee three."

"That is affirmative."

"Interrogative arrival at torp one range."

"Unable to compute," the lieutenant responded. "Synthesizer is down. Data fragmentary."

The lieutenant wiped his forehead.

"Interrogative arrival estimate," repeated the disembodied voice of the Ops Boss.

The lieutenant ran his thick hand through his thinning hair, wishing he could undo the brevet that had jumped him from senior tech to full lieutenant, wishing he were back in the old days when the Service had really been the Service.

"Data is fragmentary," he repeated. "I say again. Data is incomplete."

"Understand data limitations. Interrogative *estimate* of incoming at torp one range."

The lieutenant sighed to himself. "*Personal* estimate, based on trace strength and standard incoming combat closure. Personal estimate of incoming ETA at torp one range in less than point five stans."

"Understand arrival in less than point five stans. Interrogative incoming classification. Interrogative incoming classification."

"Data incomplete. *Personal* estimate of incoming is uniform three delta."

". . . damned Ursan cruiser . . . ," muttered the rating at his elbow, ". . . coming in for the kill. . . "

"Understand Ursan heavy cruiser."

"That is current estimate." The lieutenant wiped away at his damp forehead, unable to keep the sweat from the corners of his eyes, with the building heat in the orbit control defense center. The station's internal climatizers were just as old and patched as the non-functioning synthesizer and the unreliable defense screens behind which they all waited for the inevitable.

Two red stars flashed on the display panel. The lieutenant swallowed. Both corridor control centers destroyed—more than an hour ago, with the data only arriving at light speed, not all that much ahead of the incoming Ursans.

"Control Alpha and Control Delta. Status red omega. Status red omega this time."

"Interrogative . . ."

The audio request and the display panel before the lieutenant blanked. The lieutenant sat gaping as the lights overhead dimmed, then went out. The hiss of the ventilators whispered into nothingness. Only the dim red glow of the emergency light strips remained.

The orbit control center had been the last functioning base between the Ursan raiders and New Augusta itself. The last, and it no longer functioned.

". . . raiders . . . just damned raiders . . . not even a fleet . . . ," muttered the sour-faced rating.

"Begin evacuation plan delta. Evacuation plan delta . . ."

The lieutenant, out of habit, touched all the shutdowns before easing himself from behind the screen, shaking his head in the gloom as his fingers slipped across the age-faded plastic surfaces.

LXII

THE TEN MONTH winds came. Came with the black clouds that whistled death, as those clouds had whistled death through all the centuries they had struck the easternmost hills of the continent-dividing mountains. Came and whistled death for those who ventured out into the violent gusts, bitter cold, and ice arrows that attacked with the force of a club.

None of the hill people, nor the high plains farmers who lived downside of the hills, left their dwellings while the ten month winds blew, but huddled inside their well-braced homes. The hardy might dart forth in the lulls between storms, but always kept an eye toward the west and an ear cocked for the low moaning that preceded the devilstorms.

Cigne, from neither high plains nor hill stock, had waited, and waited. This time she had played coy, forcing down her nausea, then, as her chance came, she had bolted from Aldoff into the low wailing that foreshadowed the winds. Praying that the killer gusts would arrive in time, she had scrabbled from the tiny cottage Aldoff had acquired for them. Clawing, stumbling, falling, and staggering up, stumbling again, she had scrambled into the hillside trees before he had managed to get his other leg back into his trousers and his heavy boots back on.

Cigne hated those heavy brown boots. To think she had once thought him rugged and handsome!

Less than two hundred meters into the trees she fell headlong.

"Oooohhh." A stone gouged into the purpled bruise on her left thigh.

"Cigne! You bitch! I find you . . ." Aldoff's voice carried above the low wail of the dark winds sweeping in from the west.

She jerked herself back to her feet, ignoring the shock that ran from her hip to her calf, and tottered uphill, willing herself toward the taller spruces and the darkness beneath them. Moving uphill, her breath leaving sharp white puffs, Cigne staggered on, winced at the sharp small stones that had invaded her shoes and had sliced even her callused feet. Blood welled out of a dozen cuts, leaving the thin town shoes she wore slippery from within, and making each step less and less certain.

Whhhppp!

The first ice missile crashed through the spruce overhead.

The cold air chilled further, as if winter had arrived instantly with the ice. The afternoon gloom deepened, as though twilight had descended. The wind's low whistle lowered into a deeper moan, rattling the branches above and around her on the hillside.

"Bitch! Bitch! Cigne! Get self down here!"

She had put more distance between them, for his voice, even at full bellow, was fainter.

Just because she had not been able to conceive—was that any reason to turn against her? With every other woman having the same problem? It was not as though she were some freak. And Aldoff refused to believe it might be his problem—not big, bull-strong Aldoff.

. Stumbling again, she reached out instinctively. Her hand touched a boulder nearly waist-high. With a sharp breath of cold air, she halted and looked around. She looked up. Looked up and took another, fuller breath, in an effort to repress a shiver.

The overhead sky boiled black, black as night, as it erupted gouts of ice and flung them at the earth and forests below.

Cigne steadied her grip on the rocky outcrop and glanced around her, searching to see if she could find a better shelter than the pair of upthrust boulders no higher than her waist. The two slanted toward each other and would provide some protection.

Whhhpppp! Whhhppp!

With the sound of the ice missiles, she scrabbled under the outcroppings, burrowing as far under the larger as possible, huddling with her left leg, the still one, as covered as far as she could stretch the leather skirt.

Aldoff had sold her leather trousers, the ones provided by her family. Then, she had not known why, she had not protested the cavalier actions of her rugged husband.

Whhhpp! Whhhppp! Whhhppp!

The ten month winds struck the trees, struck from the black clouds with ice and gusts that splintered branches and ripped bushes from exposed hillsides. Struck from the black clouds that represented destruction, that condemned all those unsheltered to near-certain death.

Whhhp! Whhhppp! Whhpp!

With and through the winds flew the ice spears, whistling death from the blackness above, as they had for all the centuries since the Great Collapse.

Cigne flattened herself still farther into the depression under the outcropping. Already the spruces were bending in the shuddering gusts of the winds. In the distance she could hear the wailing moan of a devilmouth spout as it raced through the heavens toward the high plains east of the hillside where she lay.

The spouts never touched the hills. But the killer winds did, pulling spruces and golden trees out by their roots, smashing entire stands of trees flat, hillside by hillside.

After the winds lifted, before the snows drifted across the desolation, the woods crafters would come, picking the best of the downed timber for furniture and for the vans and simple machines that could be fabricated without metal, or with minimal use of metals. Then would come the builders, to take their timbers and planks from the second cull. Then, finally would come the fuelmakers, to salvage what remained for alcohol and stoves. Even the chips would be put to use, for paper and kindling blocks.

At last, in the spring, when the snows melted, months after the annual devastation, would come the planters, armed with seedlings and the spores and knowledge to rebuild the hillside.

Cigne huddled under the rocks, shivering with each ice chunk that rebounded from the trees against the thin jacket that had been all she could grasp as she had fled. Each impact would leave a bruise, she knew. More bruises. As if a few more would matter now.

"Cigne! Bitch-woman! Down come! . . . Freeze until spring, bitch!"

In the lull between gusts, she could hear Aldoff's bellow, as he stood at the base of the hillside.

Whhppp! Whhppp! Whhppp!

Another wave of ice missiles clipped smaller branches from the upper limbs of the spruce. The wind shrieks peaked momentarily, then dropped off.

"Hope you die! . . ."

Cigne shuddered between the rocks as she listened to Aldoff's parting words.

She likely would die, lying on a hillside she scarcely had seen from her confinement in the hut Aldoff had called a cottage, lying in the chill of the ten month winds. But go back to Aldoff and his rages?

Snap! Craaaaacckkkk!

A spruce uphill from her broke at the base, and she winced, waiting for the tree to fall into the narrow space between the boulders and crush her.

Crack! Crack! Crack!

Trees were now falling like lightning around her, one after the other as the winds scythed the hillside with nearly the precision of the ancient lumberjacks.

Whhhppp! Whhp! Whhhppp! Whhhppp!

Without the taller trees to intercept the ice chunks, more of the smaller missiles and ricocheting fragments began to strike Cigne's exposed back and left leg, the one Aldoff had kicked so hard she could not bend it to get under her.

She shivered continuously as the ice pelted her, as the wind whipped around her, and as the darkness swallowed her. Dragged her into the night she knew would be endless, the night she fought even as she wondered why. The chill seemed warmer, but as she drifted toward the darkness, she tried to move immobile muscles, tried to push away the seductive warmth of that darkness.

When she woke, half-surprised, Cigne could not feel her hands, nor her feet, but she was moving, being carried.

"NO!!!!" she croaked.

She jerked, trying to get out of his arms, for it had to be Aldoff, carrying her, carrying her back to . . .

"Gentle . . ."

At the sound of the voice, a light baritone, and because she could not move against the steellike arms that held her, she collapsed, half in shock and half in relief that her rescuer or captor was not her husband. She let the darkness reclaim her.

An unaccustomed warmth woke her the second time, that and the pain of having the bruises on her legs being touched.

She could smell a bitter, but faint, odor, the one she associated with the visiting medical teams from her childhood.

"Oooohh."

"Tried not to hurt, but could be some infection here."

Although she tried to sit up, Cigne found a firm but gentle hand on her shoulder, holding her down.

"Don't move. Concussion."

"Concussion?" The word meant nothing, and the subtle lilt in his voice told her that he was from somewhere else, certainly from no district she knew.

"Head bruise."

After forcing herself to relax, Cigne waited until his hand left her shoulder. Then she shivered.

Without lifting her head, she shifted her eyes around to see where she might be. The eye movement alone left her head throbbing.

The muted roar of the wind and the warmth told her she was sheltered. The first savage onslaught of the ten month winds had passed. A steady yellow illumination meant a glow lamp, and a glow lamp meant her rescuer was no ordinary farmer or woodsman.

She hoped the man was her rescuer, and not something worse. With that thought, she shivered again.

She appreciated the warmth of the coverlet that he drew up to her chin, although she did not try to look at him, not with the pain behind her eyes.

"Relax . . . quiet . . . you need to sleep . . ."

"No. Aldoff. He will find me." Her voice was no more than a raspy whisper.

"No one will find you. No one will take you."

The chill certainty in his tone made her shiver, even as she slipped back into sleep, as she realized she had yet to see his face.

When she woke, for the third time since she had bolted from Aldoff, Cigne did not move, but slowly opened her eyes, waiting to see if the throbbing resumed within her skull.

The place where she lay was no longer lit by a glow lamp, but by the diffuse, grayish light of afternoon, of a ten month afternoon. She could still hear the background hum of the wind, as low as it ever got during the tenth month.

Slowly . . . slowly, she inched her head sideways, toward the strongest light. Overhead, she saw the vaulted ceiling, one composed of beams supporting fitted planks, all of golden wood. While she was not a crafter, she recognized the workmanship as the sort that only skilled crafters or the merchants who sold and traded their works could afford.

Her eyes focused on the strange oval window, framed carefully within golden wood as well.

Through the clear off-planet glass, she could see trees, not the brittle bud spruces, but firs with heavier and darker trunks and, between the dark spruces, heavy bare-limbed trees. She had heard of the trees that had leaves that shed like the scrub bushes, but had never seen any so large before.

Click.

Her head jerked toward the sound. She winced as a muted throbbing began behind her eyes.

The man who stood inside the heavy door he had just eased shut could not have been much taller than she was. Slender, wiry, with golden hair curled tightly against his skull, he studied her without stepping toward her, without moving a muscle.

"How do you feel?"

"Not good." Her voice rasped over the two words.

"Thirsty?"

"Yes."

He turned toward a narrow alcove.

Cigne heard the sound of running water. Running water—she thought she had left that luxury when Aldoff had insisted they leave the Plains Commune for the woods beneath the mountain hills.

"Here."

She had not heard him, nor seen him move, but he was kneeling next to her, offering a smooth cup.

Cold—that the water was. The chill eased the soreness in her throat, a soreness she had not felt before.

As close as he was, she could smell him. A scent of spice, a clean scent, so unlike Aldoff, and so different from the odor of sweat and dirt that had cloaked her farmer father and brothers.

Rather than dwell on his scent, she fixed her thoughts on the smoothness of the cup, with its simple yet elegant curves, and comfortable handle. A handle heavy without seeming so.

The glazed finish of the pottery held within it a web of fine lines, indicating it was hardly new.

Cigne had not realized how tightly she had gripped the cup until her fingers began to tremble.

"You can have more later . . ."

She surrendered the cup reluctantly and tried to keep from tensing her muscles as he eased her head onto a single thin pillow.

"Shouldn't lift your head at all, but your eyes are clear." He spoke softly, as though he were talking to himself, rather than to her.

With the pillow under her head, she took in the room more fully.

She lay on an elevated double width pallet, under a soft gray and red coverlet. On the far side of the large central room were two of the strange oval windows, wider than any she had seen—one opposite her. Before the other stood a desk. From the simple lines and the flow of the wood, Cigne saw it was the work of a master crafter, just like the rest of the woodwork she could see.

Even the grains of each plank in the wall between the twin off-planet windows seemed identical. Her mental efforts to compare the planks intensified the throbbing in her head. Cigne closed her eyes, still listening.

She could feel the man moving away from her, although she could not hear footsteps. When she eased her eyes back open, he was setting the old cup upon the desk.

She shivered, despite the warmth of the coverlet. But she could feel her eyes getting heavier.

The dwelling remained silent except for the moaning of the ten month winds.

LXIII

THE WOMAN SAT on one side of the narrow drop table and picked up the empty cup one more time, studying the webwork of lines underneath the porcelain-smooth glaze. A simple cup, heavy, with a handle ample for a man, finished in a uniform off-gray. On one half was a golden diamond, faded. On the other was a stylized spruce tree, green and brown.

When she studied the two designs closely, she could see precise brush strokes, finely done under the heavy and clear glaze. Both the cup and the two designs were unique in small ways, almost in the feel of the cup and the sense of the designs. Both the object and its decoration had been produced by a skilled hand.

Cigne shook her head. The man who had rescued her from the ten month wind and storms, winds and storms which still were striking the surrounding hills periodically, had produced both house and cup. Or so he had said.

If he had, he was extraordinarily skilled. If he had not, he was rich, or a thief, or both.

Greg—that was the name he had offered. But she had refused to use it. So far she had avoided any form of address.

Click.

Cigne kept her eyes on the cup as he walked to the other side of the table.

"Feeling better?"

She nodded, but did not meet his eyes. The old legends had been dismissed by most, but she remembered to be wary about "the old man of the hills" with the demon-yellow eyes. Still, he had been nothing but gentle when easily he could have taken advantage of her.

He had not pressed when she had refused to discuss why she had been out in the storm or from whom or what she had fled.

In turn, she had not pressed him on how he could so easily dare the gusts that felled bigger men.

"Still don't want to go back?" He waited for her answer.

This time, this time, she shook her head.

"What about Denv?"

"I have no money. No goods. No trade. Besides . . . a woman who cannot . . . without . . ." She stopped and looked up to see his reaction, but the smooth face with the near-elfin face remained impassive.

Finally, he spoke slowly.

"Forget money. Never a real barrier. Nor goods. You know enough."

Her chin moved as if to nod, but she halted the movement almost before it started.

"Real problem elsewhere."

She did not have to nod.

"No children?"

She looked down at the smooth inlays of the table, taking refuge in the abstract design of the dark and the light wood. Wondering how he had been able to set such intricate and curving strips of hardwood within the boundaries, and to match the repeating patterns so identically time after time.

"He blames you."

Cigne could not trust her voice and continued to study the inlaid pattern of the table.

"Wondered about the bruises. Figures. Need population. Fewer children, but no recognition yet. Macho types. So far."

His laugh, while gentle, was mirthless, and chilling, as if he understood something that no one else could possibly see.

Both his words and laugh had not been addressed to her, and she did not answer. Not that she had understood all that he had said, but the tone had been clear. He had not sounded pleased.

Cigne shivered.

Although "Greg" had not raised his voice around her, she could not forget how he had carried her through the winds that had staggered and stopped Aldoff, those winds that the strongest of the hill runners feared. She recalled the unyielding strength of his arms, a strength that made Aldoff seem childlike, and she reflected on his speed and the silent way he moved, so quickly he seemed not to cast a shadow.

"Money and a child—what a good widow needs . . . ," he mused.

Cigne frowned, but looked up at the amused sound in his voice. He stood between the table and the nearer portal window.

As she glanced toward him, his eyes caught hers, and she was afraid to look away.

"Do you really want your heart's desire, lady?"

Cigne looked down at the table, afraid to answer, afraid not to.

"Be careful with wishes, lady. Certain you will never return?"

"I am sure. I will never go back."

"Suppose not. Not if you were willing to try the spout winds." He turned halfway toward the oval transparency before his desk. "And the other makes sense. Especially if you could get to Denv. Not that it would be a problem."

"Denv? Not a problem? It is kays and kays away."

"No problem."

He sat down in the strange leaning chair by his desk and pulled off the light black boots.

"Listen for a time, lady. Just listen."

The lilt in his voice seemed more pronounced, and she looked toward him, but he was gazing into the window.

"Listen?" she asked.

"Just listen." He turned back toward her, but she would not meet his eyes and stared at the dark spruces in the afternoon light.

"A long time ago, in a place like this, the people were dying, for each year they had less food, and each year there were fewer of them. The winter lasted into the summer and the summer was cold and short and filled with storms. And the summer storms were like the ten month storms, while the winter storms hurled boulders the size of houses and ripped gashes the size of canyons into the high plains.

"In this old time, a young man escaped from the cold and storms in a silver ship sent by the Great Old Empire That Was. And he went to the stars to learn what he could learn. He wished a great wish, and it was granted. And he came back to his place, and it was called Old Earth. And he broke the winter storms of the high plains. And he taught the people how to grow the grains and make the land bear fruit they could eat. But the storms elsewhere still raged, and the people in those places away from the high plains sickened and died, and the ten month storms raged through all the year but the short summer. And still the trees would not grow.

"The young man wished another great wish, and it was granted. But the price for the second wish was that he must leave his people forever. He climbed back to the stars, and in time he sent them the Rain of Life.

"The trees grew once more, and the people no longer sickened, and the summers returned. And the people were glad. In their gladness, they rejoiced, and as they rejoiced they forgot the young man and the two great wishes.

"As the great years of the centuries passed, the young man climbed back from the stars and returned to the place he had left. But it was not the same place. He was still young in body, but old in spirit. And his people were gone, and those who now tilled the soil and cut the trees turned away when they saw him. For they saw the stars in his eyes and were afraid.

"The women he had once loved had died and were dust, and those who saw him feared him and would have nothing to do with him

"But his wishes were granted."

Cigne shivered at the gentle voice telling the fable that she knew was not a fable. She said nothing, but looked back down at the inlaid pattern on the table, endlessly repeating itself.

"There is a danger in wishing great wishes."

She lifted her head, though she did not look at him, and spoke. "There is danger in not wishing."

This time he nodded. "True. All wishes have their prices, and the price we agree to pay is the lesser of the prices we pay. Are you certain you wish to pay such a price? For you will pay more dearly than the spoken word can tell."

Holding back a shiver, she nodded.

"Then listen again."

He stood and turned toward the window. A single note issued from his lips, lingering in the late afternoon gloom like a summer sunbeam trapped out of season.

A second note joined the first, both singing simultaneously, before being replaced by a second pair, then a third.

Though she had never heard of the songs of an old man who looked young, she listened. Though she feared the demon who might kill with gentleness, though she had never heard of the double melody, and its double price, she listened. And she heard, taking in each note and storing it in her heart, though she knew each would someday wound as deeply as a knife.

A tear welled up in one eye, then the other, as she began to cry. And still she listened, and heard the sadness, and the loneliness, and the loves left long since behind, but not forgotten.

His arms reached around her shoulders, warm around her, and the song continued, along with her tears. The tears become sobs, and the sobs subsided.

As the last note died away, his lips fell upon hers, and her lips rose to his. She let her body respond to his heat and his song, knowing that the child would be a daughter, her daughter, for whom she would pay any price. For whom she would have to pay any price.

And one tear, and one kiss—they were for the old man who looked young and never had been.

One tear and one kiss, and a single great wish.

LXIV

THE MAN GLANCED out the window, letting his eyes slide by the oval window that had once been the viewport of a ship even more ancient than he was.

His peripheral vision caught a movement, a dash of red, and his attention recentered on the scene outside. Outside, where the warmth of late spring slowly removed the last of the long winter snows. Outside, where only a scattered handful of snowdrifts remained, and where the golden oaks were putting forth the first leaves of the new season.

The figure in red was a woman, wearing a clinging pair of leather pants and a thinnish leather jacket. The jacket was doubtless imported, reflected the blond-haired man with a quirk to his lips. No local dyes or fabrics glittered that brightly, and the emerging local ethic opposed the use of synthetics except where no alternatives existed.

Looking around the central and golden wood-paneled room, he stepped back from the window. His smile was part amusement, part anticipation.

The winter, with the exception of a few pleasant interludes with those who needed what little he had to offer, had been long, as were all winters on Old Earth. While he could not refuse those in need, most were ignorant of the life beyond the High Plains. As he had once been. Only one had been farther than Denv. Denv, while a model of the environmentally oriented and integrated community, remained laudably practical.

The woman whose shiny leather boots now clicked on the stone walkway he had built years ago seemed haughtier than his earlier visitors, as if she might attempt to control him.

Control him?

He chuckled at the thought. Some had, but not by attempting to do so.

"Will you stoop that low?" he asked the empty air.

He grinned a cold grin in response to his own question.

Clack, clack.

The heavy wooden knocker sounded smartly, twice.

He opened the door without a word, surveying the woman who

stood on the stones before him, waiting for her to speak. Her face was pale, and her shoulder-length hair was black. So were her eyes.

"You don't look like the old devil of the hills." Her voice was hard, like the shiny finish of her black leather pants and glittering red jacket. The accent was Old Earth, unlike the clothing.

"If I were a devil, would you expect me to look like one?" He did not smile, for the imported fragrance with which she had doused herself was overpowering, far more effusive to him than it would have been to most men. The perfume and her attitude both repelled him, while freeing him to toy with her.

"Not very big, either," observed the black-haired woman.

"Am what I am." He paused. "Would you care to come in?"

"What's the price?"

"For what?"

He had almost stopped questioning those who came, stopped denying since denials did no good. Perhaps his acceptance was a sign of age, age that had not showed in his face or body, or perhaps he had repressed the anger because he feared its release.

But this woman, with her hard and demanding attitude, her expensive imported clothes, who used her body for her own ends, deserved questioning, deserved contempt.

"For what you are rumored to provide." Her painted lips tightened.

"Rumored to provide?"

"Off with the innocence, old devil. Those little girls, that boy. They all look like you. Never seen anyone else around here who looks so much like you."

He stepped back and half bowed, satirically gesturing toward the main room.

"Please enter, lady. What little I have is yours for the moment."

"Thanks." Her heels clicked as she walked past him into his home.

Her eyes widened as she took in the paneling, the few carvings, the inlay work in the small table by the wall, and the antique books in the shelves.

"You must collect at double mastercraft."

He almost chuckled at her overtly mercenary nature.

"Not a credit. No need to."

"Not a credit," she mimicked. "Then how did you get all this?"

"Magic."

For the first time, the hard and self-assured expression on her face faded.

"Do you know who I am?"

"Should I?"

"I am Gramm Lostwin Horsten's daughter."

"And he is?" the former devilkid answered in a bored tone.

"Head Councilman of Denv."

"I am suitably impressed." So Lostwin had descendants around, descendants who had done well. Well indeed by their forebearer.

He smiled at the recollection of those times, and noticed that the brassy woman backed away.

She was not as young as her outfit proclaimed, well past first youth, and probably past thirty, perhaps even older if the devilkid genes ran strongly in the blood.

"Take it you have no offspring, and your husband may look to greener forests?"

"My reasons should not concern you."

"Your reasons are your reasons." He turned and closed the door, slipping the heavy bolt into place and shielding the action with his body.

For whatever obscure reason, she reminded him of another woman from the past, a copper-haired woman who had also used her body beyond her wisdom, and paid dearly. Even though there was little physical similarity, beyond a slender waist and full breasts, the woman before him, thrusting herself at him while demanding recognition, reminded him of the earlier lady. Reminded him of her, without the subtlety, without the refinement.

"You never answered my question."

"About the price?" He smiled again as he moved back toward her. The smile was both hard and amused. "No price, nor will I accept one. You pay the price from your own body and soul."

"Philosophy is cheap."

He did not contradict her, knowing this woman would not understand. How few there were who understood. How many women had there been, and how few like Caroljoy, or Faith, or Allison, or Lyr? Or even Constanza?

His eyes looked past the woman in red, who stood, a full pout on her lips, before the built-in shelves on which rested the ancient volumes he still collected and read.

He did not look at her, even as she shrugged her way out of the red jacket.

Swissshhh.

The jacket, tossed carelessly, landed on the desk, with one sleeve dangling halfway to the polished golden wood floor planks.

Under the imported red jacket, she wore a filmy formfitting blouse, under which she wore nothing.

The devilkid could see her nipples, nonerect, and a creamy and pampered skin beneath the gauzelike blouse. His nostrils widened as he drank in the mixed odor of excessive fragrance, woman, fear, and imported powder.

"Sit down."

She turned her head toward him as he stepped into the center of the room, but did not move.

"Sit down!"

At his seldom-used tone of command, she sat, dropping into an old swivel in spite of herself.

"Now listen."

Explaining would do no good. Neither would a gentle approach, not that he was in the mood for gentleness. Not after her attitude. Not now.

He began the song with a near military stridency, a march-driving beat, keeping his eyes on the woman as he did. The power of the double-toned music caught her. She began to lean forward, her body moving toward him against her judgment.

Slowly, slowly, he began to weave in the theme of betrayal, adding the notes that sounded power. He could see her breathing deepen, as the music began to reach inside her.

She said nothing as he finished the first tune. Then, he walked over to the wall and extended the double-width pallet, spread the crimson and gray comforter.

He walked back to her and offered his hand.

She took it and followed his lead back to the pallet.

"Sit here."

When she sat, he knelt and pulled off, first, her right boot, then her left. He turned away from her, beginning the second song.

The second song screamed lust and power, power and lust.

As he reached the end, trailing off the last notes, he edged back toward her, noting the raggedness of her breathing, noting how she had opened the front of the thin blouse.

Her arms reached toward him.

"Not yet."

He could feel the cruelty of his smile, and nearly laughed, ignoring the desperation in her eyes.

He began a third tune, more demanding in its own way than the first two.

Before he finished, her hands were on his arms, tugging him toward the pallet.

"Please . . ."

"Not yet," he whispered between notes as he worked toward the finish of the third melody, dragging it from the depths where it had rested undisturbed for so long. His eyes glinted as he saw her remove the blouse and began to slide her nakedness from the tight trousers, her hips moving with his music.

He barely hesitated before beginning the fourth song, the hardest one, the one that mixed power, lust, teasing, and betrayal.

When the last note died, the woman who had worn red, who had thrust her hips and bared nipples at him, lay huddled on the corner of the raised pallet, curled into herself, even as her body shuddered to unaccustomed rhythms.

The devilkid ran his tongue over his lips, slowly removed his tunic and trousers.

The woman did not notice until his hand touched her shoulder.

"Bastard . . . devil . . ." Her voice held desire, hatred, fear, and desperation.

But she pulled him down and into her.

His right hand pinned both hers over her head, holding her helpless, for all that she did not struggle against him, but with him.

Finally, after long combat, her shudders lapsed. Then did he release her hands.

The one-time devilkid watched her breathing ease as the two lay in the indirect light of the late morning, watched as her nipples relaxed, and as the hardness crept back into her face. Watched as she shook herself and sat up.

Half-sitting on the fold-down pallet, she reached for her trousers.

His hand disengaged hers from the clothing.

"Once is enough, devil man. You do well. Well as I've had."

She reached again for the trousers.

This time his hand was firmer, less gentle.

"Business is business." she said, with the hardness completely restored to her voice. "Now. What do I really owe you? None of this offage about no payment. Everything has its price."

He swung off the pallet, setting his feet lightly on the smoothed plank flooring, then reached down and tossed her trousers across the room.

"True."

"Then what do I owe you?"

He laughed, a hard, barking, mocking laugh.

The woman shivered, although the air in the room was not at all cool.

"Humility . . . if anything."

"Humility?"

"Think everything is yours to take. Or buy."

Her eyes met his, then recoiled.

"It's been an interesting conversation, but I should be going."

She stood, but barely had her feet reached the floor before he stood next to her.

"Not yet."

She inched sideways, unable to back away from him because of the pallet behind her knees.

"This has gone far enough, little man."

Smiling, he did not move.

She inched toward her blouse, then leaned down to lift it.

His hand caught hers, so swiftly and with such power that her fingers opened and the gauzy garment floated back downward.

She moved her body toward him, sliding her skin against him, seemingly relaxing, letting her hands reach as if to go around his neck.

Her knee knifed toward his groin.

Thud.

She lay on the floor, momentarily, then began scrambling toward the desk and her jacket.

The devilkid did not move. Not until her fingers touched the dangling sleeve of the jacket. Then he seemed to flash across the space between them, his left hand slashing down and knocking the dart pistol from her fingers.

"Very interesting, lady," he said sardonically. "So you were going to use the old devil, then assassinate him to retain the family honor?"

The whiteness in her face confirmed his statement.

"So what shall we do—"

Another quick kick toward his groin, but he blurred, and his hands shifted position. Abruptly he lifted her overhead, with his hands holding her tighter than iron bands. Then he carried her toward the pallet, releasing her suddenly.

Thump.

He watched as the impact left her breathless. Watched as she scrambled to get her feet under her. Watched as she dashed for the front door.

He pounced again, picking her away from the still-bolted exit and carting her back to the pallet. Her breathing was ragged.

Again, he stood there, naked, watching her, also naked, as her eyes darted around the room, as her eyes glanced from one door to the other, from front to rear. Waited as she looked at the wide and closed side windows.

"Sick! You're sick."

He said nothing, letting his eyes run over her skin, inhaling the mixed scents of previous arousal and current fear.

Once more, he did nothing immediate as she feinted toward the front door, then dived for the less obvious rear door.

He caught her, holding her overhead again, dropping her on the pallet a second time. Waiting, letting his eyes take in her fear and nakedness.

"What do you want? You want something different? Tell me. Tell me. I'll do it. Just let me go."

He shook his head.

She gathered her feet under her, but, shoulders slumping, settled into a sitting position on the edge of the pallet, looking at the floor.

He took one step toward her, deliberately, then stopped.

She looked up, eyes wide.

Then he took another. Stopped, letting his eyes rip across her nudity.

Her mouth opened, soundlessly.

He took another step. Now he was close enough to touch her.

She looked away, then back up, her mouth opening wider, tears forming in the corners of her eyes.

"... no ... no ... no ..."

He stepped back. Waited.

She seemed unable to close her mouth, panted raggedly.

Letting the heat build within him, he held back, knowing he was treading the thin edge of sanity. He raked her pale body again with his eyes.

As he stepped back toward her, she scuttled backward toward the top of the pallet.

Like a laser, he was on her. Pinned her hands over her head, forced her legs apart in a single rough body movement. Drove deep into her, ignoring the single scream that was a sob, shriek, and cry.

Ignored the small voices in his mind, and let himself be devilkid, again, if only for a few fleeting moments. Let himself forget the iron discipline of the commodore and the wisher of great wishes. Let himself pay her back for all those who had used him, for all those he had let use him.

His own payment would only last forever . . . and he drove into her to forget the long past and longer future.

LXV

THE JAYS BROKE off their chattering.

Gerswin stood in the target yard and balanced the heavy knife in his hand, listening for the sounds he half expected, half feared.

He paused, ears alert for the slightest indication of the hunters, trying to hold back the memories, to concentrate on the moment at hand, to let the old training and instincts take over.

Abruptly he slid the knife back into its hidden sheath. After checking the sling leathers and his pouch of smooth slingstones, he let his trained feet carry him from the shaded and walled target yard into the trees, off the few paths and toward the possible routes his attackers would take from the town.

He doubted if any knew the way, or that Lostwin's many times removed granddaughter would have been fool enough to give exact directions.

Click.

Faint . . . the sound came from his distant right.

Gerswin eased from tree to tree, taking advantage of the few winter bushes and patches of sparse undergrowth that were scattered beneath the old spruces.

Old spruces they seemed, yet none was as old as he.

As he moved cross-hill to position himself behind the group of towners, he counted as he went. Eight. Just eight, and none were crafters or woodsmen.

Gerswin smiled faintly. Some were still his tacit allies, or feared the old devil of the hills more than they feared the growing strength of the towners.

Gerswin's expression turned bleaker as he began to stalk the rear guard of the party. His fingers brushed over the butt of the ancient, but quite serviceable, stunner he had brought.

The last man looked back, too late to utter a word. Gerswin's hands flashed—one choking off any outcry, the other leaving the man momentarily disabled.

Thrumm.

The rear guard had lagged far enough behind and to the right of his nearest companions that the single stunner bolt would not be heard.

Besides, reflected the hunter, not a one of his attackers had ever heard an Imperial weapon. Not in this time, not with the Empire gone from Old Earth.

Gerswin's second target was less than twenty meters from a heavier man Gerswin recognized as Verlint, the husband of the once-haughty lady.

The devilkid twirled the sling.

Swissshhh.

The slingstone whispered through the spruce bough to the right of Verlint's companion.

Swissshhh.

Verlint crashed onward in spite of his efforts to step softly. The second man scratched his head and turned toward the soft sound. Gerswin moved.

Thrumm.

Within minutes, the second man was trussed and laid aside.

Verlint was next—a simple stalk and stun shot, since the five others were on the far side of the shallow ravine.

Thrumm!

Leaving Verlint trussed as well, Gerswin resumed his stalk, forcing himself to move carefully, despite the lack of caution on the part of those ostensibly tracking him.

The next man was a straggler, stunned quickly, and trussed almost as swiftly.

The remaining four moved together, whether from lack of response from their companions, or from nervousness. Less than four meters separated them. Two carried laser rifles, antiques that might work. Or might not, releasing all the energy in their power packs in a single unwanted detonation.

As if a laser were a good forest weapon to begin with.

Sighing silently, Gerswin decided to rely on herd instinct.

Craccckk!

The first slingstone slammed into the tree on the right side of the man farthest from Gerswin. He dived leftward, and began to scuttle toward the others.

"What's that?"

"Rouen? Where are you?"

"Where's Verlint?"

"Quiet!"

Gerswin grinned, melting back toward the other side of the group.

Cracckk!

"Devilkid!"

Cracck, cracckk!

"Down! Get down!"

"Where?"

Craacckk!

All four were huddled within meters of each other, crouching behind two boulders.

Craacckk!

The four edged even closer together, as if under siege.

The once and always devilkid checked the stunner. The power reserve would be more than adequate.

Slipping from spruce to spruce, like a shadow in the late afternoon, he moved to within meters of the quarry.

Thrumm!

"Dynlin!"

Thrumm!

"Get him!"

"How?"

Thrummm!

"Devil . . ."

Thrummm!

After wiping his forehead, Gerswin waited, listening to see if the forest sounds would resume, if he had missed someone, or if someone else were coming.

In time, a jay chattered once, then again. A squirrel scrabbled down a nearby tree. The hum of the scattered insects began to build.

At last, Gerswin began the tiresome process of lugging the unconscious men to a single clearing, trussing those he had not bound and disarming them all. The weapons he placed behind a stone-topped low hill, out of their line of sight.

Arranging the eight in a double line of four in the middle of the clearing, he sat down on the large stone to wait, letting his thoughts drift where they always seemed to drift. Into the past, into the darkness where he had met Caroljoy, into the Service where he had met

Faith, and Allison, and where he had lost Martin and Corson. Into the shadows.

In time, he glanced up into the spruces overhead, noting the growing shadows, seeing the straight trunks, half hearing the jays, the buzzing of the flies, an occasional scurry of the still-rare chipmunk, and the chitterings of the ubiquitous squirrels.

If his memories were correct, when he had returned to Old Earth the first time as a junior lieutenant, the lands where he now sat had been nothing but wasted red-purple clay, where the cold winds blew summer and winter.

Nodding at the improvement, he glanced back at the figures on the needle-covered ground, then toward the hidden location uphill where his dwelling nestled into its own past.

Not that he could blame the eight men, who had been out to protect what they thought was theirs to protect. All were too young, adults though they were, to understand that no one person could ever own another. Perhaps they were too wrapped in the fragility of their own masculinity to recognize that.

He laughed harshly, suddenly.

"You . . . of all people . . ."

He returned his thoughts to the squirrels, comparing the sleek animals that scampered along the branches to the scraggly refugees he recalled from centuries past. Shaking his head, he waited for his restless captives to wake.

"Who . . ."

Gerswin dropped his introspection, but said nothing. Just watched as the awareness, and the confusion, before him grew with each awakening man.

"Verlint! You here?"

". . . old man . . . you said . . ."

"How did we . . . what happened . . ."

". . . get here . . ."

". . . told you . . . not to get him angry . . . but you . . ."

Almost as quickly as the babble of voices had risen, the noise dropped away as each man strained at his bonds to see Gerswin sitting on the low boulder, waiting and saying nothing.

The silence drew out.

"Dirty ambusher!"

"Sneak! Used Imperial weapons!" The outburst came from Verlint.

"Like your laser rifle?" asked Gerswin. "Rather I used my knife?"

There was no answer.

"What should I do?" Gerswin's eyes raked the trussed figures. "If I let you go, just come back. Execute you, and the Council will have to order something. Means I'll have to disappear. Too old for that."

". . . doesn't look that old . . . ," muttered the man lying next to Verlint.

"You don't fight fair," stated Verlint.

"Lost that ideal long ago. Fought to survive. Still do."

"That was then. This is now."

Gerswin smiled, and his expression chilled the afternoon like sudden night.

"You want a fair fight? Fine. One on one. Any one of you against me. You pick the weapons."

"No weapons," rumbled Verlint.

Gerswin shook his head sadly. "If that's the way you want it."

"You fight him, Verlint. Your problem," mumbled another trussed figure.

"I'll fight. Not just my problem."

Gerswin nodded in agreement with Verlint's assessment. A knife appeared in his hand, as if by magic. He was beside Verlint, and the knife flashed. Flashed again, and Gerswin stood back by the boulder as the dark-haired and bearded, heavy-shouldered Verlint freed himself from the just-severed leather thongs that had bound him.

"Wait."

Although Verlint had already started to move toward Gerswin, he stopped at the light, but penetrating, voice of command.

"You're too stiff. Might take a drink of your water. I'll wait."

Gerswin sat easily on the stone while the bigger man rubbed his arms, stretched, and shrugged his shoulders.

"Terms?" asked the man with the curly blond hair. "Falls, first blood, broken bones, or death?"

"Blood or bones, whichever comes first. Scratches are not blood."

"Death!" screeched the thin man at the end of the seven bound figures.

"You're not fighting. Besides, he could have killed us all. He didn't."

Gerswin stripped off his tunic, folded it, and laid his belt on top of the pile.

He moved toward the level end of the clearing, his back half to Verlint, listening in case the man might lunge for the weapons Gerswin had stacked behind the rock.

Verlint did not, but trailed Gerswin.

"Ready?" asked the heavyset man.

Gerswin nodded, his face impassive, concentrating on what he would have to do.

Verlint did not move, but centered his weight on the balls of his feet, ready to react to Gerswin.

Gerswin sighed, took a deep breath, and edged closer to the dark-haired big man, to whom he had easily spotted twenty centimeters and more than twenty kilos.

"Kill him!" screamed the thin man.

Verlint ignored the scream, as did Gerswin.

The devilkid blurred toward Verlint, who tried to dance aside. With a duck, a swirl, Gerswin slipped inside Verlint's too-slow arms, lifting the man overhead, then hurling him toward the needle-covered ground.

Crack.

Gerswin had held the bigger man's right arm until the last moment, when the strain snapped the bone.

Verlint did not move for long moments, then, ashen-faced, struggled into a sitting position, cradling the broken right arm with his left.

Gerswin trotted back to the rock, where he pulled his tunic back on and replaced his equipment belt and knives.

Verlint staggered to his feet, but did not leave the clearing where he had been thrown.

"What . . . are . . . you . . . ?"

"Am what I am. Born here a long time ago. Die here, I hope, a long time from now."

The throwing knife appeared in Gerswin's hand, and he knelt by the first trussed figure.

Moving so quickly that there was little reaction, Gerswin severed the thongs holding all seven men before the first had finished stripping the leathers from his hands and feet.

"What do you really want, devil?" demanded the loud, thin man.

"To be left alone. To let anyone visit me who will. That is all I have asked since I returned."

Verlint nodded, then spoke. "And what if others do not listen?"

"Then I will do what I must."

All eight men shivered.

"Your weapons are here." Gerswin gestured toward the rock. "Suggest one man carry them all. Do not expect to see you again."

He stepped into the trees, sliding sidehill and out of sight before they could react.

He hoped that fear and reason would prevail—that and the hope of the women, the women who would come to be the leaders.

He smiled, wondering if the daughters could escape the sins of the father, fearing they might.

Fearing they might.

LXVI

[CV] "Are the Lostler hypotheses correct?"

[W] "That is a difficult question to answer directly. The children appear to have a life span around two hundred, roughly twice the Imperial/Commonality averages, but the aging factor is negligible. Muscular and neural development are better by a factor of two to three. Raw intelligence, as well as you can measure, averages thirty to fifty percent above the standard first quintile—"

[CV] "You mean thirty to fifty percent brighter than the twenty percent who are normally the brightest?"

[W] "That is correct."

[CB] "What about leadership?"

[W] "That is an intangible. How can one measure leadership? If you mean accomplishments, there is no doubt. His direct first generation offspring all manifest—"

[CB] "We know that, but can you predict or measure the difference?"

[W] "Only by the characteristics. For example, the traits marking the distinctions—eye coloration, reflex speed, musculature, curly hair—don't pass to the second generation except when both parents actually manifest them. But any child who is his has them all."

[CV] "What happens if a third- or a second-generation descendant without the traits has children with a direct child of his?"

[W] "It's recessive. No . . . that's not accurate. It is as though the traits wash out if they don't carry on as dominant."

[CZ] "Artificial insemination? Is that—"

[CV] "We couldn't do that! What about—"

[CB] "That wasn't the question. We have to investigate all possibilities."

[W] "Assuming you could do so, by deception, I would assume—"

[CZ] "A willing woman, so to speak?"

[W] "—the probability is surprisingly low, according to the samples already obtained. While we could work on it, without understanding more of his body chemistry, I could not in good conscience advise that as a practical alternative. The high . . . viability . . . is offset by a low capacity for preservation."

[CV] "So we're back where we started from? One source of genius, one source of inspiration, and one source of leadership? After all your research . . . that's where we're left? Kerwin and Lostler were right?"

[W] "Substantially . . . yes."

Excerpt—*Council Records*
[Sealed Section]
Remembrance Debate
4035 N.E.C.

THE BIDDING CONFERENCE was coming to a close.

The woman at the podium surveyed the group around the two long tables in the open courtyard. She wore a simple rust tunic and matching trousers, and her short blonde hair showed tight natural curls. Green hawk-eyes and a sharp nose dominated her lightly tanned face.

Her presentation of the Council's requirements was long done, and now she was presiding over the comments and questions that had ensued from the presentation.

"The power requirements are substantial, particularly for a planetbound system," observed the representative of Galactatech.

"For this project alone, we will accept the necessity of fusactors or any other appropriate self-contained system. We understand the technical limitations which preclude our normal methods." The Council representative's tone was matter-of-fact.

"All underground?" questioned the woman engineer from Altiris.

"An absolute necessity. You could create an artificial hill if it fits the overall plan."

No one else spoke for several seconds.

The Old Earth Council representative stood, her hawk-green eyes cataloguing the mixture of off-planet entities bidding on the project.

Her hand on the stack of datacubes, she asked, "Any other questions about the proposal?"

The Hunterian representative nodded, and the councilwoman almost recognized him before belatedly realizing that the nod meant "no" from him.

"If not, all the technical specifications are in the cubes, as well as the bidding requirements themselves. I will stress again the absolute necessity for retaining the present locale and structure without disruption and without change. Any landscape changes must be out of the line of sight of the existing structure for the first phase of the project, until the distortion generators are fully operational."

She stood back as the interested parties came forward to authenticate their interest and to receive a datacube.

A half smile on her face, she listened as the comments drifted around her in the crisp fall-smoke air of the courtyard.

"Istvenn-expensive project."

"Barbaric . . . waste of resources . . . never stand for it at home . . ."

". . . sentimental gesture . . ."

". . . look for the technological challenge . . ."

". . . of course we'd take it . . . make us famous . . ."

". . . else could you expect? He did it, if you believe the myths, single-handedly. Have you seen the old hist-tapes . . ."

For all the remarks and commentary only three of the more than twenty invited to the conference declined to bid and to accept the datacubes.

The councilwoman stayed in the courtyard long after it had emptied, looking at the screen on the portascreen, centered as it was on a hand-built dwelling nestled into the trees and against the hillside. The scene did not show the planned park, the hidden field generators that would be installed, the progressive sonic barriers to protect unwary intruders, or the years of debate that had made the conference possible.

She sighed, wondering if the project would solve the problems facing Old Earth, or at least the associated problems facing the Council. Those in the bidding group who had caught the expectation aspect had certainly been right.

What else could they do, needing what they needed? What else could they do, owing what they owed?

And what else could she do, daughter to father, owing what she owed?

LXVIII

"YOU ARE THE high priestess?" asked the angular man in red. His accent was thick, with the rounded tones that signified that he came from beyond the Ydrisian Hub, from the far side of the Commonality.

"No. I am the Custodian." With calm and penetrating voice and hawk-piercing yellow-flecked eyes, she answered him.

"But you are . . . in charge . . . of the . . . shrine?" The angular man persisted.

"It is not a shrine. Merely a dwelling within a stasis field. I am responsible for its maintenance and security."

The man in rust-red glanced at his companions, a man dressed in grayed green; a man not quite so angular, but darker of complexion and with a tight black mustache to match his short-cropped black hair; and a woman with silver hair, young despite the hair color, who wore also the grayed green tunic and trousers.

"Perhaps we do not understand. We understood this was a shrine to the One Immortal, the one who brought down the old ways. . . . So it is told even in the far placed . . ." His voice trailed off.

"You have come from quite a distance on slender hope," observed the Custodian, not relaxing her scrutiny of the three.

"We are scholars, of sorts, uh . . . Custodian . . . scholars of our world's past. Byzania, it was once called, but now Constanza, it is said, in recognition . . . but that is not important now, and too long to tell, for the ships come infrequently, and we have little time. You must understand . . ." He looked at the woman in grayed green, then back at the Custodian, dropping his eyes from the sharpness of her study. "You must understand that the climb back for us has been less than easy, harder than for most, and still we have no ships of our own."

"Yet you travel far."

"We have our culture, and in some things are considered advanced. We have mastered the house tree and its uses, as well as other secrets of the forests and the great rolling plains.

"The past, some say, is the key to the future, and some of those keys are missing. Others are only myth. Most puzzling is the mystery of the great Ser Corson, who shattered armies, it is said, with his words alone, and who brought us Constanza to set us free. But I digress. My words wander.

"A traveler mentioned to us your shrine, and we came to study but found nothing to observe, save a great park, and a shrine, a mysterious dwelling of the past, locked behind the great stasis fields. We were directed here."

"Why do you think our park, or anything we have here on Old Earth, would have any bearing on your past?" For the first time, the Custodian's words held more than her normal warm courtesy.

"That we cannot confirm, but it has been reported that Ser Corson was ageless, and in the entire Commonality and without, there is only one shrine to an immortal, only one legend." He paused, clearing his throat.

"Your pardon, but it is reported that he looked like you, with the eyes of a hawk, and the curled hair of the sun, and the strength of ten. That he stopped on Constanza for a brief time as a part of a greater mission that would take him to the end of time. And Constanza herself said that he would be found living yet when the suns died."

The Custodian's eyes softened. She sighed, then smiled. "Be seated, gentle folk. There may be some that I can add to your knowledge, but there may be more that you can add to ours."

LXIX

UNDER THE DUSKY violet tent of the evening, lit by the flickering stellar candles called stars, stood a circle of smaller tents, each circular, walled but halfway, and comprised of alternating panels of black and white.

Those who gathered for the Festival of Remembrance, as they did on the last evening of summer every tenth year, set out the delicate foods, and wondered if the captain would appear, not that he had ever failed them.

For this one evening, and only for that one evening in each decade is the Park of Remembrance closed to everyone but a select few.

And who are those few who might enter? Lay that question aside for a time and look upslope, to the cottage as it emerges from the mist of time.

View the man.

He wears a uniform of black and silver, freshly tailored, but no uniform like it now exists in the Commonality of Worlds, or in the outlaw systems. His hair is curled gold, and his eyes are clear, yellow-bright like a hawk's, and pierce with the force of a quarrel, equally antique.

As he strides down the curving walk from the small cottage under the tall oaks toward the tents of black and white, his step is quick, firm, as if he were headed for his first command.

The sky shades toward black velvet, and the first candles of night overhead are joined by their dimmer sisters. The breeze from the south brings the tinkling sound of a crystal goblet striking another object, perhaps a decanter of Springfire.

Glowlights are strewn in the close grass which appears close-clipped, but which is not, for it has been grown that way. Under the nearer tents are tables upon which rest crystal, silver, delicacies such as arlin nuts and sun cheese, and the spotless linen that is used so sparingly elsewhere in the Commonality.

The captain steps from the fine gray gravel of the flower-lined walk. His heels click faintly on the four stone steps that will bring him down to the tents and those who await him.

Nineteen faces turn toward him, and even the breeze halts for a moment.

Slowly, aware of the unspoken rules, each of the nineteen averts her gaze. One picks up a goblet of Springfire she does not want.

Another, red hair flowing, tosses her head to fling her cascade of fire back over her bare shoulders.

A third looks at the grass underfoot, points one toe like the dancer she is not before shivering once in the light night air.

The captain slows, edges toward the second tent, the one where the two decanters of Springfire sit on the middle of the single white-linened table.

To his right is a blonde woman, scarcely more than a girl, in a shift so thin it would seem poor were it not that the material catches every flicker of the candlelight and recasts it in green shimmers to match her eyes.

His eyes catch those green eyes, and pass them, and she looks downward.

From the table he picks a goblet, looks toward the decanter.

"May I, Captain?" a husky voice asks.

"If you wish." He inclines his head, the goblet held for her to fill, and his glance rakes her with the withering fire of the corvettes he has not flown in more than twenty centuries.

"Thank you."

His glass full, he bows to her. "Thank you."

She steps back, black-ringleted hair falling like tears as he turns and leaves the tent.

He takes a dozen steps across the grass between the black and white of the tent.

The slender, brown-haired woman who had been squinting to make out the silhouette of the cottage on the hill above catches her breath as his fingers touch her shoulder.

"No . . . ," he says, as those fingers, gentle, unyielding, turn her to bring her face around. "Not . . . yet . . ."

His voice trails off, and his fingers slide down her arm from her shoulder to take her hand. He does not release his hold on her as he begins to speak again.

"You seem familiar. These days, everyone seems familiar. Once . . . wrote of the 'belle dame sans merci' . . . of enchanted hills. If you disappeared, you were gone for a century."

He chuckles, and the golden sound is that of the young man he appears. His face smoothes, and he leans down and places the goblet he has not touched upright upon the turf. He straightens.

"These days . . . you have the enchanted prince who cannot remember. What else can I claim?"

She takes another deeper breath, finally attempts an answer.

"No one . . . they . . ."

"Because my mind wanders, shattered with the weight of memory . . . assume I cannot reason . . . do not appreciate my position."

Momentarily his eyes glaze, as if he has looked down the long tunnel to the past and cannot see the object for which he has searched.

Her hand squeezes his fingertips, though she does not understand why, and she waits.

Again . . . he laughs, and the sound is harsh, barking.

"Sweet lady, not my princess, nor can I seal your eyes with kisses four. But walk with me."

From the corners of their eyes, the other sixteen, those not already dismissed, stand, wondering, waiting . . . unsure.

The captain points, and his arm is an arrow that flies toward the stars.

"See—that faint one? Near the evening star. Beyond that, the tiny

point, Helios, sun of New Augusta." He lowers his free hand, and his
eyes, and resumes his walk.

"You are not . . . let me put it another way. Would you mind if I
called you Caroljoy?"

"Tonight, as long as you want, I will be Caroljoy to you."

"Longer for me than you, sweet lady." He releases her hand and
stands silently for a moment that is longer than a moment.

"Sweet lady, not my princess, nor can I seal your eyes with kisses
four. But walk with me yet." As he speaks he bends toward her and offers his right arm. She takes it as they walk slowly down away from the
circle of tents.

"That star I showed you, Caroljoy. Wasn't really Helios. Cannot
see it from here. But it was where I pointed. Life. You point at something and . . . not what you thought.

"Martin never lived long enough to understand that. Caroljoy . . .
my first Caroljoy . . . she understood . . . told me that. Didn't believe
her."

The two stop at the top of the grassy slope that eases down to the
lake where the black swans sleep on the water.

He stops, releases her hand and arm.

"Do you know? No. You would not, but you might. I can think.
But I cannot try to remember. All I am is what I remember, and I must
not."

His face creases into a smile that is not.

"Better this way. The longer sleeps through time give me some
strength to be myself—'le beau capitaine sans merci'—for a time."

"Without mercy?"

"Without quarter."

He whistles a single note that is two-toned, then another. The
melody builds until the stars twinkle their tears into the black lake,
until the eighteen who have waited behind them slip away into the
velvet night beyond the park, each one wondering what she has lost,
and what her sister of this single night will gain.

At the precise moment the song has ended, without a word, the
captain and his lady touch lips.

Without another word, they carefully seat themselves, side by
side, holding hands, and facing the lake where the black swans sleep
and where the dreams rise from the depths like the mist of the centuries past.

"My lady . . . ?"

"Yes."

"Do you mind . . . knowing what you must know . . ."

Though she says not a word, her answer is clear as they turn to each other, as their arms reach around each other, and as the summer becomes fall, and they fall into and upon each other.

The swans sleep in the almost silence, in the music that must substitute for both love and worship, for the loves that he has lost and will always lose, and for the worship all who walk the grass of Old Earth have for their captain.

Anachronistic? Barbaric?

Perhaps, but unlike other ancient rituals, there is no bloodshed. There are no sacrifices, nor is anyone compelled against her will. Nor has any woman ever been required to spend a summer/fall evening in the Park of Remembrance. At least, not in all the centuries since it was first designed, not since the days before the temporal fields enclosed the hill and the cottage upon it. Not since the days of the captain.